BELLA MAFIA

LYNDA LA PLANTE was born in Liverpool. She trained for the stage at RADA, and work with the National Theatre and RSC led to a career as a television actress. She then turned to writing – and made her breakthrough with the phenomenally successful TV series *Widows*.

She has written a great many novels, and her original script for the much-acclaimed *Prime Suspect* won BAFTA, British Broadcasting and the Royal Television Society awards, as well as the 1993 Edgar Allan Poe Writer's award.

Lynda La Plante also received the Contribution to the Media award by Women in Film, a BAFTA award and an Emmy for the drama serial *Prime Suspect 3*, a CBE for services to literature, drama and charity in the 2008 Birthday Honours, and has been made an honorary fellow of the British Film Institute.

LYNDA LA PLANTE

BELLA MAFIA

PAN BOOKS

First published 1990 by Sidgwick & Jackson

This edition published 1991 by Pan Books
an imprint of Pan Macmillan, a division of Macmillan Publishers Limited
Pan Macmillan, 20 New Wharf Road, London N1 9RR
Basingstoke and Oxford
Associated companies throughout the world
www.panmacmillan.com

ISBN: 978-0-330-53311-9

1 3 5 7 9 8 6 4 2

A CIP catalogue record for this book is available from
the British Library.

Typeset by SetSystems Ltd, Saffron Walden, Essex
Printed and bound in the UK by
CPI Mackays, Chatham ME5 8TD

Visit **www.panmacmillan.com** to read more about all our books and to buy
them. You will also find features, author interviews and news of any author
events, and you can sign up for e-newsletters so that you're always first to hear
about our new releases.

'*A nation is not conquered until the hearts of its women are on the ground. Then it is done, no matter how brave its warriors nor how strong its weapons.*'

Cheyenne Indian saying

Bella Mafia
is dedicated to
my fearless editor
Susan Hill

Prologue

THE ARREST of Tommaso Buscetta, one of the most knowledgeable members of the Mafia to turn informer, not only began the round-up of the heads of three New York families, but led eventually to their roots, to Palermo and the Mafia's biggest trial in history.

About to be arrested on charges of extortion, the suspected head of the Gambino family, Paul Castellano, was murdered as he entered a Manhattan steakhouse.

Sentences of a hundred years each were given to Anthony 'Ducks' Corallo, Carmine Persico and Anthony 'Fat Tony' Salerno. The prosecutors felt that only sentences of this length could ensure the end of the powerful dons' ability to continue their rule even from behind bars. If there were a chance that the headmen, the dons, would be released within their lifetimes, they could still dominate, still threaten, and their orders would be carried out. But with hundred-year sentences no one would be afraid of them.

In the long run, it was hoped, the invincibility of the Mafia would disappear. There was no longer any valid point to being a member. If the leaders could be convicted of their real crimes rather than just tax evasion, more and more people would risk turning against Mob rule.

Buscetta had opened a dam, and others prepared to breach *omerta*, the Mafia's strict rule of silence, began to come forward. In the United States many of the Mafia's so called new recruits, well-educated second- and third-generation Americans, were arrested. The high-ranking bosses began to complain about the validity of these recruits and the cracks in their powerful organization caused rifts between them.

The US Government estimated that the Organization made over $5 billion profit in 1987 from gambling and $700 million from loan sharking, but the profit on narcotics was much greater. This side of the Mafia business is still based in Italy and Sicily, the true home of the Mafia. Palermo has always controlled the heroin trade to the USA.

As Buscetta gave his statements in New York, Sicily received a major break with the arrest of Leonardo (Lenny) Cavataio. Although only a small-time narcotics dealer, he had first-hand information and detailed knowledge of the drug barons.

Whilst the United States tried to break the Mafia's stranglehold there, the Italians and Sicilians, acting on Buscetta's and Cavataio's information, made a gargantuan swoop. One thousand extra police were shipped to Palermo. Four hundred and sixty-eight alleged Mafia members were arrested, accused of a total of a hundred and ten murders, plus robberies, narcotics trading, extortion, fraud, tax evasion and organized prostitution. Hundreds more wanted men went on the run. The investigators were assisted by new legislation which

4

allowed them to break the professional confidentiality of the banks in their search for Mafia funds.

Palermo became a shifting mass of tension. On the walls of the reinforced, bomb-proof, concrete jailhouse where the suspects were held during the trials, the words '*mafiosi finito*' were scrawled.

There was dancing in the streets; the atmosphere was reminiscent of the end of the Second World War. The excitement built; it truly appeared to be the end of a despotic rule that had held Sicily in its grip for centuries.

Then it began: a terrifying, insidious retaliation. The celebrations, it appeared, were premature, and jubilation turned to fear. Hit men gunned down two of Palermo's top crime-squad officers. Five magistrates were systematically wiped out, and the courts were becoming increasingly desperate to fill more than fifty vacant positions. Witnesses began to disappear or withdraw their statements and the much-heralded trial, the final end of the Mafia, began to look less than secure.

Spirits rose once more when Paul Carolla, who called himself *Il Papa*, the Mafia 'Pope', wanted on both sides of the Atlantic on narcotics charges, was trapped in his Sicilian mountain hideout. Carolla's personal fortune and his methods, including torture, of evading arrest had ensured his freedom during the months of the American trials. Carolla's arrest was indirectly assisted by the statements of Lenny Cavataio; he knew the hideouts, the refineries, and now added further information against Carolla when accusing him of a murder committed more than twenty years ago.

Carolla's arrest led to witness after witness disappearing. His power continued to reach out from the prison cell. The danger was obvious and the trial proceedings ground to a halt while the barristers and lawyers conferred. The prosecutors were afraid not only for their own lives but for those of their families. They were in great difficulties trying to prepare their cases without witnesses. The opening handed to them by Buscetta was closing fast as terrified men withdrew their statements. Then the prosecution received the worst news possible: their main witness against Paul Carolla had been shot. Lenny Cavataio had been brutally murdered. As the gory details of his horrific death leaked out, more witnesses disappeared.

The trial was halted at the request of counsel. At ten o'clock in the evening on the second day of the adjournment, one of the chief prosecutors, Giuliano Emmanuel, received a telephone call at his apartment. He was tired, and nearly refused the call, but he took it when he was told that it was Mario Domino, an old legal adversary from his early court days. Although retired, Domino was well respected, and Emmanuel valued his opinion greatly.

Domino wasted no time on pleasantries. He said simply that he would appreciate a private meeting with Emmanuel, and if it could take place immediately he was sure Emmanuel would find it to his advantage.

The security surrounding the Emmanuel household was strong. Domino was searched when he arrived at the main entrance and again at the front door. When he was finally allowed to enter, the two old friends clasped each other in greeting. He refused a drink and sat down, opened his briefcase and asked quietly if it was certain the room was not bugged, even by the police. It was of utmost importance that no one should overhear their conversation. Puzzled, Emmanuel assured his guest that he could talk freely.

Domino handed Emmanuel a photograph. 'If you recognize this man, just nod your head. I do not want his name mentioned, one cannot be too sure.'

When Emmanuel looked at the black-and-white photograph the hairs on the back of his neck began to prickle. Of course he recognized the face; the man was well known in Palermo. It was Don Roberto Luciano, the man to whom the people had given the title *Il Papa* – unlike Carolla, who had simply adopted it. He was the real 'Boss of Bosses', a man very different from Carolla: a war hero, an elegant man whose principles echoed the past, when the Mafia was a mighty force. Some said it was a force that was needed for the good of the poor people unable to fight for their rights. He had been a part of the Organization for more than fifty years, but no one knew if he was still active. Now over seventy, he was honoured, even revered, in Palermo.

Emmanuel handed the photo back to Domino, quietly acknowledging that he did indeed recognize Don Luciano.

'Then you will also know that for many years he has been a close friend of mine. I have acted on his behalf on numerous occasions. He wishes to meet with you, but is well aware of the danger – not only to himself, but to his family, should it become known.'

Emmanuel hesitated. His mouth felt dry and he swallowed. 'Does this client of yours have a reason to meet with me?' he asked.

Domino nodded. 'As I said when I called, I think you will find it beneficial. There is to be no financial gain for my client – the deal will be on condition that you can arrange top security for his family and himself. It is also imperative that his identity should not become known until it is absolutely necessary.'

As the two men shook hands, Emmanuel could hardly contain his excitement. Domino would contact him with a time and place; as he left he once again impressed upon Emmanuel the importance of protecting his client's identity.

The call came two nights later. The meeting took place in a small restaurant, the San Lorenzo. As instructed, Emmanuel had changed cars three times to be sure he was not being followed. At one moment he had felt he was being watched, but by the last changeover he was certain he was alone. His stomach churned with nerves; he was placing himself in grave danger without his security men.

A waiter placed on the table a bottle of good local wine wrapped in a starched napkin. Inside the napkin was a handwritten note. His nerves were in shreds as he rose from the table. He walked through a small archway and up a linoleum-covered staircase.

From a doorway stepped a grey-haired man in his sixties. With a cursory nod of his head, he asked Emmanuel to raise his hands and proceeded with a thorough body search. Finding nothing, the man gestured for Emmanuel to follow him up to the next landing and into a small, elegant dining room hung with red curtains.

To Emmanuel's consternation, there was no one else in the room, although the single table was set for three.

The grey-haired man seated him at the table and poured him a glass of wine, then left.

Emmanuel waited fifteen minutes, then he heard quiet, unhurried footsteps on the stairs. He turned expectantly as the door opened. Domino removed his coat and bowed to Emmanuel, shook his hand and sat down. He picked up the wine bottle, examined the label and poured himself a glass.

The moment the glass was full, the curtains moved aside and a waiter entered with an elaborate tray covered in silver dishes. This man was also elderly; his movements were deliberate and unhurried. He bowed to both men and placed the tray on a serving table. Emmanuel looked at his watch, then at Domino. He was growing impatient, and was about to speak when the curtains were drawn aside again.

Don Roberto Luciano entered the room. The photograph had not conveyed the man's aura; even at seventy he was impressive. More than six feet tall, his frame was straight with wide shoulders. His thick white hair was well cut, framing a face with dark, heavy-lidded eyes and a slightly hooked nose.

The waiter moved forward to remove the camel-coloured cashmere coat which was draped casually about Luciano's shoulders. Underneath it he was wearing a pale fawn linen suit, cream silk shirt and dark blue silk tie in which sparkled a diamond pin. Emmanuel caught the glint of gold from heavy cuff links. Luciano had not spoken a single word, and yet the room was filled with his presence. Emmanuel felt a little awed.

Luciano went first to Domino, placing both hands on his friend's shoulders and kissing his cheek. Then he turned to Emmanuel, his right hand outstretched. His grip was strong, and any last thought that Emmanuel might have had about Luciano being in his dotage was dispelled. The man exuded energy and made Emmanuel feel immediately and unexpectedly at his ease.

Luciano seemed to be concerned only with the food, talking to the waiter and appearing to wait for Emmanuel's approval of the menu. Then he tucked his napkin into his collar and they proceeded to eat the delicate dish of seafood rolled in fresh pasta. It was delicious, and Luciano murmured his pleasure, eating well, breaking his rolls and dipping the soft, fresh white bread into the sauce. Throughout the meal the three men made polite conversation. Luciano complimented Emmanuel on his handling of a number of cases, then discussed a mutual friend with Domino, which gave Emmanuel the opportunity to study *Il Papa* more closely.

The large, strong hands made fluid, almost hypnotic, gestures. On the little finger of his left hand he wore a ring, and Emmanuel could make out a circle and a moon picked out in gold on the blue stone. The nails were square-cut and polished. These were not the hands of an old man – far from it.

Brandy was served in balloon glasses, and cigars were lit. Luciano sighed with pleasure as the smoke billowed above his head. The waiter disappeared behind the curtains with the dishes and Emmanuel heard a door closing and a lock click into place. He straightened in alarm, but Luciano, smiling, placed a comforting hand on his arm. 'I am prepared to stand as your main witness for the prosecution, on condition that you protect my family. I must have your word on this before I give you one shred of the evidence that will, I assure you, mean

10

the death sentence for Paul Carolla. Of course, my evidence will have repercussions and no doubt incriminate many of the others who are being held, but Carolla is the man I want. I am doing this for that reason only – you may call it revenge, call it the end of a twenty-year vendetta, whatever you choose, just be assured that the information I have may prove the premature writing on the jailhouse walls a fact . . . *Mafiosi finito* . . .'

The pause was electrifying in the small, enclosed room. Domino tapped the ash from his cigar. 'Would it be possible for you to arrange such security without divulging my client's name? We do not believe that the government or the police are free of corruption, so it is imperative that no one knows his identity until the time comes for him to take the stand. This is not just for his protection, but for his family's, and for your own. Can you, in your position, organize such protection?'

Emmanuel hesitated. He could not give his word either way and he knew it. Desperate not to let the opportunity slip through his fingers, he mentioned that he would need some proof that Luciano was indeed as valuable as he said he was.

Luciano smiled, then laughed a deep, guttural laugh and shook his head. He tapped his temple with his finger, then leaned towards Emmanuel. 'Come, my friend, do you really think I would put anything on paper to substantiate my offer? What do you take me for? You are looking at a seventy-year-old man who would not be alive if he was the sort of man who made notes.'

Detecting the Don's growing impatience, Domino told Emmanuel that if added proof were required he could simply check out everything that would be told him. But Emmanuel persisted that he would still need something to verify the Don's claims. This caused Luciano to stiffen, the warmth gone, his eyes flashing angrily. Domino began to sweat; Emmanuel was treading on dangerous ground. He had the offer of a fish so big he would need no other, and the fool was questioning its authenticity.

Emmanuel continued, 'You must understand it from my point of view. I go to the government and ask for surveillance, round-the-clock guards, safe houses, for a man whose name I can't divulge. The only way you can be assured of the protection you will need to keep you and your family alive, to keep me alive, is if, and only if, you give me something that will prove without doubt that the prosecution will have a witness worth protecting.'

Luciano looked up at him, then at Domino. After a moment, he rose to his feet and placed his hand on Emmanuel's shoulder. The big hand felt like a dead weight.

The room was eerily quiet. Luciano seemed to be scrutinizing Giuliano's face. A deep, haunting darkness was in the expressive eyes but the hand never moved, did not tighten, just remained motionless on the young prosecutor's shoulder. He tried to show no fear but it was a moment that would remain with him for the rest of his life. He was afraid of this man and the relief, the lightness as the hand slowly lifted, made him gasp.

'Lenny Cavataio gave you a statement regarding the death of a young Sicilian boy. Cavataio was prepared to take the stand and name Paul Carolla as the instigator of the murder.' The eyes didn't flicker. They held Giuliano's attention as he whispered, 'The dead boy was my eldest son.'

Not even in the soft, cultured voice was there a hint

of what Don Luciano was feeling. Giuliano swallowed but could not say a word. Luciano continued in the same, calm way, 'Now, my friend, I am not prepared to talk with you further. I have said I have the evidence, now it is up to you. You have one week. I will wait to hear via Domino. My granddaughter is to be married, and it will be the first time the whole family has been gathered together for many years – my sons, my grand-children. If you are able to give me the protection I need, then that is the moment I will tell them of my decision. They will be in danger, and I feel that they are safer together. They will not approve, but my mind is made up and I will not retract my offer. One week – and I thank you for coming to meet me. It has been a pleasant evening.'

The door opened without any obvious command, and he was gone, leaving behind him a sweet smell of fresh limes. But for that cologne it was as if he had never been there.

Domino drained his glass and gave a long sigh. 'Don't underestimate what he is offering you, not for one moment. You will make your career on his back. You will become a very famous man, or a dead one.'

Emmanuel snapped, 'Do you think I don't know that? He wants protection for his family – dear God, what about mine? As it is they balked at giving me two round-the-clock guards. You'd think I'd asked for a personal army, and that is what Luciano will need – a bloody army.'

'That is what you would need if it were ever to leak out that Luciano was your witness. And if you even think about whispering his name to anyone, *anyone*, before the trial, he will not live to take the stand.'

13

Emmanuel's mind was reeling. 'Why? Just give me the reason why he's doing it, why he's prepared to do it.'

Domino, eager to be on his way, paused at the door, which had been left slightly ajar. He pushed it shut with the toe of his polished English brogue, and leaned his back against it, hands in his coat pockets. 'You heard him say it was revenge, the end to a vendetta? In a way maybe it is. He idolized Michael, his first-born, an extraordinary boy. They tortured him, beat him, until even the mortician could not repair his features. His father carries that in his heart, the blame for that broken body, the disfigured face. He has never forgotten, he never forgets for a single day, and you should think about that. He forgets nothing. You ask why he has waited? A man with three young sons is vulnerable. Now they are men and only now is he free to take, as you say, revenge. But what he believes in is justice. He has turned not to cold-blooded murder but to the law, prepared to jeopardize his life for his long-awaited justice. Now, if you will excuse me, it's been a long night and I'm tired. It will be wise if we are not seen leaving together. You have a car? Good, then I bid you goodnight.'

Emmanuel arrived back at his apartment to find one of his guards washing down, yet again, the main entrance. Red stains could be seen on the cloth as the man wiped the door. Emmanuel sighed. 'Another cat? They carry on like this and there won't be one left in the neighbourhood.'

The guard shrugged. He didn't know how they managed to do it. Once or twice a week a dead cat was pinned to the door, its guts hanging out, pitiful legs pinned as if crucified. 'This one's a bit different,' he said.

Emmanuel looked, not even sickened any more. 'Oh, yes?'

'Yes, it's yours.'

Part One

CHAPTER 1

GRAZIELLA LUCIANO was awaiting her husband's return. She watched from her window as he alighted from the Mercedes and ducked his head to straighten his coat casually on his shoulders. He was smoking a cigar, and seemed relaxed, sharing a joke with his driver.

It was a while before he entered the cool, shuttered bedroom. She smiled at him through the mirror and he smiled back. In the low light from the bedside lamps her hair took on a golden glow, the strands of grey and white scarcely detectable. In the soft light she might have been the young beauty with the hair of gold that he had fallen in love with at first sight. The white cotton nightgown disguised her rounded body, once so slender. As he bent to kiss her neck, she smiled, but her once-brilliant blue eyes, faded now, showed that she was tired, and there was a hint of fear as she said, 'Well?'

'Yes, on my terms, my conditions. We will tell the family nothing, not until after the wedding. The extra guards will be a precaution for the wedding, they will accept that . . .'

There was a slight tremor in her hands as she continued to brush her hair. She said nothing more, offered no reproaches, no arguments, and his heart burst with love for this woman who had stood at his side for over forty years. He kissed her lightly and murmured that he would not sleep yet, he had things to do in his study.

But at the door he paused, feeling it necessary to say something more, give her more reasons for his decision. 'I could not die with my son's death still . . . clinging to me. I feel that this will absolve me, cleanse me.'

She whispered very low, 'But it cannot bring him back, nothing ever could. I know that now, and if I were to lose you . . .'

He had already gone. As she brushed her hair, she glanced at the silver-framed photograph of her son Michael. She did not pick it up and kiss it, bless it, as she usually did; instead she stared hard into the dead boy's face for a moment, then wrapped her shawl around her plump shoulders and went downstairs.

Before, she had always knocked on his study door. No matter that he was her husband, this was his private room where he held his meetings and it was not her domain. But tonight she walked straight in and closed the door firmly behind her.

She folded her arms and looked at him, her chin well up. 'This must be discussed between us. I want to be a part of it, I want to know everything, your every intention. I have never asked this before, but this is your life, my life, and the lives of your sons and your grandchildren at stake.'

His initial anger at her intrusion was immediately dissipated by her bravado. Her round face was childlike in her concern to be firm and controlled. He wanted to put a protective arm around her, but she sat down and placed both hands on the desk. They were rounded hands, and her wedding ring cut into the flesh.

He sighed, and spoke softly. 'They will have complete protection, there will be total security during the trial for me and for my family. No one will know I am a witness until the day I go into court. By that time it will be too late for retaliation. We have been allocated fifteen men, who will guard the villa in shifts. Every day the cars will be checked by my own men. Only trusted friends will be allowed into the church and here at the villa for the wedding.'

'You'll tell the family at the wedding?'

Luciano gave her a shrug and a small, glum smile. 'Maybe not at the actual wedding, but that is a good time to tell my sons – when we are together, united, at our strongest. Dispersed, we are too easy . . .'

He did not have to continue. She laid her hands over his to stop him embroidering the risks any more than was necessary. She knew there was nothing she could say to dissuade him, not now.

Through the weeks leading up to this moment she had felt him become distant, and wanted desperately to draw him closer. Every morning she watched him as he read the newspapers; more and more witnesses were being murdered or withdrawing their statements. She had seen his anger building, an anger that had previously almost gone, like himself, into retirement. There were flashes of the way he had been as a young man, and those moments had frightened her because she knew something would happen. What she had not bargained for was his decision to stand as a witness. It was too late now to go against him – not that she would, his decision was final.

She bowed her head, her hands still resting on her husband's. 'In case anything should happen to you, you must educate me in your affairs. Pray God, nothing will happen, but if it should, I will be prepared . . .'

He smiled down at her and raised one eyebrow. 'And when have you not been educated in my affairs? You with your university education, your three languages – tell me when?'

His teasing about her education had gone on ever since they had met. The daughter of a well-to-do shop-keeper, with a university degree and a chance to go into a law firm, she had been far removed from Roberto Luciano, a boy from the slums of Naples whose only hope of bettering himself was to join a gang of thieves.

Graziella looked sidelong at her husband as he thought over what she had said. His hawk-nosed profile, the shock of thick, wavy hair – how different he was to the wild boy she had met all those years ago. His hair had been coal-black then, his cheap suits loud, as loud as his manner and his roaring laugh. They had met in a restaurant – or, rather, they had been in the same restaurant at the same time. Graziella, dining with her family, had paid little attention to the table at the far end where six men were eating. Roberto, then a driver, had come in to speak to one of them.

As he passed Graziella's chair he inadvertently knocked against it, which resulted in her spilling her wine. Apologizing, he ordered them another bottle, but Graziella's father refused it, and insisted the family leave the restaurant immediately. He had seen the way the boy stared at his daughter and knew he was connected with the group sitting at the back – men he wished to have nothing to do with. And he did not want his daughter ever to have cause to thank the young man with the hooded dark eyes. He had seen Roberto follow them out of the restaurant and stand on the pavement, shading his eyes against the midday sun as their car drove off.

Roberto's friends had laughed at him when he returned and asked them about the family, but they had not bargained for the young driver's determination.

A blonde Sicilian, Graziella had eyes of a brilliant, icy blue, but it was her hair that attracted him most. It was like spun gold. He was obsessed with her, and shadowed her whenever he had time to spare. She was completely unaware of his growing infatuation; if she had known she would perhaps have been afraid, but she went about her life as if Roberto Luciano did not exist. Graziella often walked with her parents in the countryside after church on Sundays, and he followed her whenever he was not required to drive his boss. He polished Joseph Carolla's Buick until it shone, and frequently persuaded him that it needed the services of a mechanic. Don Joseph smiled tolerantly. He knew what Roberto was up to; every Sunday for months his car had required 'maintenance', and he joked with his cronies that the Buick was in the best condition of any American car in Sicily.

At last, on a blazing June day in 1933, Roberto struck lucky. She was alone. Graziella was carrying a parasol to protect her fair skin from the heat of the sun. Eventually, he drew abreast and jumped out, his arms full of flowers.

His carefully prepared speech was forgotten when Graziella burst out laughing. He grew red in the face with embarrassment, and in his panic he stuttered a few words and thrust the flowers into the astonished Graziella's arms. Then he turned and ran back to the Buick, slamming the door and pounding the steering wheel in impotent rage. Finally he roared past, leaving a trail of blue smoke behind him.

For three weeks he did not even attempt to see her, then Carolla offered him an opportunity to go to Chicago. It was a chance he could not refuse, and he was almost relieved to be going away. Just before he was due to leave, he was hurrying past the Hotel Excelsior on the Plaza when he saw her.

He introduced himself, blushing to the roots when she quietly murmured that she had hoped to see him to thank him for the flowers. She accepted his offer to carry her books, and together they walked towards her college.

On the steps of the college, he blurted out that if she had time, perhaps he could buy her coffee that afternoon. He looked crestfallen by her polite refusal, and she explained that she was taking exams and all her time was taken up with her studies. She was very aware of the interested glances from her fellow students hurrying past them into the building. Roberto was quite a sight in his flashy suit and dreadful two-tone shoes. She thanked him again and turned to walk up the steps, but he caught her elbow. The familiarity evoked a look from her that made him let go immediately, and she continued up the steps.

'Another time, perhaps? I'm going to America for a while. Maybe when I return . . .?'

It was her turn to be flustered. She really had no intention of seeing the boy again, but there was another surprise in store.

'I'll write to you, OK?' Then he smiled, his white, even teeth making his rather wolfish face suddenly look boyish. All she did was return his smile and run into the building.

The letters with the flamboyant American stamps began to arrive – always to the college, never her home.

Childish, misspelt, they were not love letters. They were short, cryptic notes of what Roberto had seen, of the American way of life he had quickly come to love.

Just twenty years old, Roberto was proving himself a valuable 'soldier' of the family. Joseph Carolla, his boss, was fighting for territory in Chicago. Roberto earned good dollars and spent them freely. Often in his letters he would tell Graziella if there were anything she wanted him to bring home for her, she only had to write to him. But she never did, and yet the letters kept coming, once a month for a year. Then, abruptly, they stopped. He never said why, but a postscript in his last letter said he was doing well and might never return to Sicily.

Roberto was moving up in the family, partly due to his total dedication to Carolla. He was soon promoted to Carolla's personal bodyguard and travelled everywhere with him. He adored the old man and cared for him, although he had reservations about young Paul, the Don's son. But he kept his feelings to himself.

Prohibition was almost at an end, and the mobsters needed to find other means of making money. The family were branching out into slot machines, or 'one-armed bandits', as they came to be called. At that time there was no federal law against them, and truck-loads would cross the state line into Illinois. Carolla became the major distributor, and it was Roberto's job to travel around the districts and 'persuade' the small shopkeepers, bars and clubs to install the machines. The owners would receive 30 per cent of the takings. Many did not want to co-operate, did not want or approve of crowds of kids with their nickels and dimes, stealing and causing mayhem in the restricted space of their business premises. But they had no choice.

The racketeers fought each other, hijacking each other's cargoes, their methods just as violent as they had been in the liquor trade. Carolla became a target; the quick-thinking Roberto saved his life three times. He worked overtime, taking his job seriously, guarding the man he thought of as a father with his own life. He was duly rewarded, and yet there was still friction building between himself and Paul Carolla, who had become very jealous of Roberto's obvious closeness to his father. The Don, however, dismissed his son's carping attitude; he was only sixteen, not yet old enough to take responsi-bility. He flatly refused to hear a word against Roberto, trusting him with more and more duties.

Time and again Roberto proved himself. He was a fast learner, and a good grasp of the language was one of his priorities. It became obvious to everyone that Roberto had a great future. Above all, he was fearless, and remained calm in every situation. It was chilling in a man so young, but already Luciano had tasted life behind bars, had known abject poverty. Now he had an apart-ment of his own, he dated numerous girls, and was having the time of his life. He was making something of himself, and no one would take it away from him.

Mob rule was reaching its pinnacle in America. As the racketeers became more and more powerful, men like Roberto Luciano became more necessary. Carolla wanted to expand from Chicago to New York, and would have to blast his way in. Always protective of Paul, his son, Carolla chose Luciano to make the move. If Paul had felt slighted before, he felt positively belittled now. He did not accept his youth as a reason for being excluded from the war that was about to take place. He ranted and raved at his father; it was always Roberto, Roberto who had the power, who was trusted, and his father was insulting his own flesh and blood. The old man listened, and eventually quietened his son's rage by telling him that when the takeover was complete he would send Luciano back to Sicily for his own safety. When Luciano was gone, Paul would stand at his father's side. He did not mention that, on his return to Sicily, Roberto would take over his operations there. He would be promoted to *capo*.

Roberto carried out his orders to the letter. It was whispered that he had single-handedly taken out more than seven men. Whatever the rumours, Luciano was highly regarded, a man to be reckoned with, a man to watch. He had become wealthy, and five years of good living in America had changed him. He still had a taste for loud suits and perfumed oils on his hair, but now he smoked good cigars and wore expensive jewellery.

The time came for him to leave America. The Feds had marked him; his apartment was bugged, he was followed, and he knew he had to move to take the heat off. Carolla asked for a private meeting a few hours before he was due to depart.

The old man was sitting up in bed, complaining of chest pains and difficulty in breathing, but he still smoked his usual Havana. He patted the silk coverlet for Roberto to sit close.

Luciano could see the familiar heavy gold ring with

27

the dark blue stone which Carolla now wore on his forefinger, due to his loss of weight.

Carolla touched the younger man's strong, broad hand and then gripped it tightly. 'You have been like a son to me, always at my side, trustworthy, honourable. In all the years you have never said no to me. For that I will show you my appreciation.' His English was heavily accented, although he rarely used his native tongue now.

Roberto bent his head to kiss Carolla's hand. 'I have enough appreciation, Papa. You have always been generous to me.'

Carolla wheezed and shook in a coughing fit that stopped only when he puffed heavily on his cigar. 'You go home, until the heat is off. Then you will return, but not until I ask you. You have much work to do at home, Roberto. There are properties I want you to buy, and some little businesses you should look into. I have bought you a villa, with good orange and olive groves, which I give you as my gift.'

Roberto kissed the ring and repeated his thanks. Carolla lay back on his pillow and closed his eyes. 'God forgive me, but I must also warn you against my own blood, my own son. He is still young, but there is something inside him that I cannot control. He is hungry, Roberto, and he prowls around my bed waiting for me to die. All this he will grab if I should die too soon. But you will have your orange groves, and by that time, pray God, you will be strong enough. But you must protect yourself. I will make him understand your value, make him see that although you are not my blood, you have been to me like a son. May God bless you and keep you safe.'

They kissed, and Roberto left Carolla only when he

28

had fallen asleep. Even then his chesty cough did not abate.

In early November, 1937, Graziella was working as a legal assistant affiliated to the Palermo Courts of Justice. She was twenty years old, and engaged to marry a young lawyer, Mario Domino. They had arranged to meet for lunch.

She had to wait a few minutes as Domino had a client with him, and when his door opened she rose from her chair. The client was Roberto Luciano.

He recognized her immediately, but when they were introduced she gave no indication that she remembered him. She held out her hand to shake, but he raised it to his lips and kissed it.

Domino said, 'If it's all right, darling, Mr Luciano will be joining us for lunch.'

She smiled sweetly and walked ahead of the two men, out into the brilliant sunshine.

Luciano seemed familiar, and she slowly realized that he was the young boy who had written her such strange, semi-literate letters more than five years ago. He had changed, acquired a wolfish quality that would never leave him, and a new air of confidence and ruthlessness. She found it terribly embarrassing and wished her fiancé had not suggested that they all dine together the following evening.

Without mentioning that she knew him, she voiced her mistrust of Domino's new client, but Mario would hear nothing against him. There was a lot of work involved, mostly property development schemes and conveyancing work on warehouses he was purchasing.

Times in Sicily were hard, war loomed, and such clients were not easy to find. Domino did at first query where such vast amounts of money were coming from, but his own financial situation was so stretched that he avoided delving too deeply into Luciano's background. He wanted to be a criminal lawyer, and he needed time and money for studying. Luciano's business could help him achieve his ambition.

Domino was thrilled to be dining at the expensive Hotel Excelsior, at a table overlooking the Plaza. Luciano proved to be a wonderful host, keeping them amused with stories of life in America but without giving so much as a hint of what his real work had been. He even laughed at Graziella's questions, knowing she was prying into how he had done so well. He told her simply that he was in the import-export business and his boss was an exceptionally brilliant man who had taught him everything he knew.

The orchestra was playing American show tunes, which tempted Domino. He excused himself and led Graziella to the small dance floor. She danced stiffly, without speaking, and he asked if she was all right.

'I would like to leave, I have a dreadful headache.'

'Why didn't you say? Of course, if you don't feel well, we'll go immediately.'

Abandoning the dance they returned to the table, and Domino reached over to pick up Graziella's wrap from behind her chair. Luciano smiled, quizzically. 'You're not leaving?' He insisted that they use his car instead of taking a taxi. At his suggestion they dropped Domino first, as his apartment was close by and Graziella lived on the other side of town. She had no chance to disagree, as Luciano had already instructed his chauffeur.

On the short journey Luciano joked that Domino would probably end up working exclusively for him. Graziella interjected, her voice quiet and cold, 'I doubt it, Signor Luciano. You see, my fiancé will soon be a criminal lawyer, and I am sure your business activities will not require his services in that capacity.'

He laughed, throwing back his head, and when he turned to look at her his eyes were frightening. 'Yes, let us hope I will never have to call on him. Ah, we're here . . . Goodnight, Mario – I hope you don't mind me calling you Mario? Good. It has been a pleasant evening, and I will call you tomorrow.'

The two men shook hands, and Domino waved as the car drew away. Graziella smiled from the back seat of the highly polished black Mercedes.

Luciano remained in the front seat and didn't turn to her once. She sat in the darkness, resting her head on the leather upholstery, and wondering how he knew where she lived. But she said nothing, and they rode on in silence until, aware that they had been travelling for some time, she glanced out of the window.

'We are going the wrong way, Signor Luciano. We are going in the wrong direction.'

'I want to show you something, I want to see if you like it.'

'Please stop the car, I'll get a taxi. Please just stop the car.'

He turned and stared at her, then tapped the driver on the shoulder. They screeched to a halt, then did a sudden U-turn and picked up speed on the way back into town.

'Stop this! Please *stop*!'

Again the car stopped, tyres squealing, and Luciano

braced himself on the dashboard. He looked at the driver and shook his head, then turned to Graziella. 'I'm sorry, I think he is over-eager to please. Would you like to get out and walk for a while – it might help your headache?'

'I don't have a headache. I would just like to go home.'

Luciano told the driver to get out of the car until he was called. He hesitated when Graziella asked him to remain, but Luciano shoved him out. Then he opened the glove compartment and took out a small ring box. 'This is for you, I bought it for you.'

'I don't want it! Please just take me home.'

'When you have opened the box.'

She sighed in anger and leaned forward, snatching the box from his hand. In it was a solitaire ring, the diamond at least ten carats. She just stared at it.

'Do you like it?'

She snapped the lid closed and held the box out to him. 'It's very nice.'

'It's for you.'

She let the box fall into his lap and looked nervously around for the waiting driver, who was standing with his back to the car. 'I am afraid I cannot accept your ring, Signor Luciano. I should be most grateful if you would please take me home. You gave me your word, if I opened the box you would take me home. Please . . .'

He moved over to the driving seat and the car roared into life. Graziella pressed herself back in the seat and covered her face as the countryside flashed past.

Suddenly, Luciano braked sharply to a stop and rested his hands on the wheel, looking straight ahead. 'I'm sorry, I'm sorry . . . I just wanted you to see my new house.'

He climbed out of the car, walked a few paces and lit a cigarette. As the match flared she could see his face, then it was swallowed in darkness again. He tossed the match aside and heard the car door open, then she was standing slightly behind him.

He whispered, 'I don't know where you get the ability to make me behave like a five-year-old boy. I apologize for the way I have treated you tonight, but you have always had this effect on me. Ever since I spilt the wine at your table. You make me feel small, you make me feel foolish – nobody else can do that. I think you're laughing at me because I wrote you those letters.'

There was a long pause before she spoke, her voice controlled, emotionless. 'Why did you write them? They never said very much.'

'So you'd know I was still alive. Know that I'd be back.'

'I didn't even know you.'

'No, I guess you didn't.'

'I still don't know you.'

She was so close, he knew he could touch her if he reached out, but he didn't dare. If she tried to avoid his touch, he might kill her. He had never wanted anything so much in his life, and she was within his reach, yet he did not know what to do. He could not even turn to meet her eyes. He shifted his weight from one foot to the other, then took a breath as though to speak but let it out, unused. His hands clenched in spasms of mounting tension.

She could feel the violence, the frustration mounting, yet she felt no fear. She had to talk him down, quieten him. It was the animal in the man she could sense, and at this moment a dangerous animal.

'Is your new house very far?'

He shook his head as if his neck were constricted in some way and made a guttural sound.

She continued, 'Well, as it's still early and it's not too far we could go and see it? We could go back and collect your driver?'

He nodded, seeming to relax, but his hands still gave him away. He walked round to the driving seat, hesitated, and returned to open the passenger door for her. She stepped in, careful not to touch him, and thanked him politely. She watched in apprehension as he walked back round to the driving seat, bracing herself in readiness for the car to hurtle forward. But he drove carefully, slowly, gripping the steering wheel so tightly his knuckles were white. She realized he had no intention of returning for the driver.

'How long have you had the house?'

'It's a villa, not a house. It's a villa.'

'Is anyone there? I mean, have you moved in?'

'No, it's empty.'

He turned his head slightly and she saw it was over. He smiled. 'I won't harm you, you have no need to be afraid. But you know that, don't you?'

Before she could answer, he pulled up at a set of old wrought-iron gates. He got out of the car and, bathed in the light from the headlamps, dragged them open. Then he smiled at her. It made him look boyish, and he told her excitedly that they were not seeing the villa at its best. In the day, the sun steeped it in warm gold. It was hard to believe that this was the same man, the one who had stood like a stone at the side of the road. He was talking fast, pointing out his favourite bushes in the garden as the car bounced over potholes in the long driveway. He chuckled and said they would be filled in – everything would be as perfect as he could make it in time, it only needed time.

He fumbled for his keys and swung the old glass doors wide open, trying to remember where the light switches were located, then gave up and struck a match, holding it above his head.

'See? Look at the ceiling, the carving on the doors . . . You know, they say this belonged to a prince, how about that? And me, Roberto Luciano, I am going to move in. You know what I am going to do? Make this a palace . . . yes, this is going to be a palace,' he exclaimed as he found the light switch.

She had no fear of him now. In fact, she had started to enjoy him. His enthusiasm was contagious as he ran from room to room, throwing open the doors. He couldn't remember which room was which, and he made many mistakes, saying to her at one point, 'OK, now wait . . . this room, this is the room you've *got* to see.'

With a theatrical gesture he threw open the door to a broom cupboard. His expression was so funny that she convulsed with laughter.

'Aw, shit . . . OK, it's this way. Come on.'

He stood at the entrance to a wonderful drawing room, with heavy, leaded windows reaching from floor to ceiling and opening onto a long wooden verandah. It was a truly lovely room, apart from the cobwebs and bits of broken furniture left by the last occupant.

'Now come upstairs, come on . . . There's a bathroom that's not been changed since 1896, doesn't work, but the tiles came from Vienna. Every one hand-painted.

That light, by the way, is from Venice, Venetian glass, you like the colours? Hand blown in Murano. A lot of this glass is Venetian.'

She laughed again at his excitement, unable to get a word in.

He looked down into her face. 'You know, you got a nice laugh . . . OK, now this is the bedroom, the master suite. 'Course, it's not a suite yet, but it will be . . .'

He strode in, then turned back, he'd got the wrong room again. Without thinking, he caught her hand, a natural move, to pull her to the correct door. She was so aware of his touch that she almost missed it when he said softly, 'This is our bedroom.'

She pretended not to have heard him, looking with feigned interest around the room and nodding her head. 'It's very nice, Roberto, and very large.'

He released her hand, looking at her seriously. 'Tonight is the first time you said my name. The first time.' He made a small gesture, lifting his hands as if asking her to come to him. There was nothing she could do but move into his arms. It was as if he were always meant to hold her. He wrapped her in his arms, so close that she could feel his heart beating.

He sighed, and buried his face in her soft, golden hair. 'I love you, Graziella di Carlo, I always have.'

He broke away from her and held the door open for her, then guided her down the stairs, holding her elbow lightly. His touch confused her; it was as if he were caressing her whole body.

At the gates he stopped the car and pointed to a stone plaque set in the wall: 'Villa Rivera'. Then they drove slowly back to town, in silence. When they reached her home he switched off the engine and lights, and sat looking out of the window. 'I would like to call on your parents.'

'My father died two years ago and my mother is very frail, bedridden.'

'I'm sorry.'

'What of your family?'

He stared ahead without replying, and she reached for the door handle. He said suddenly, 'What of Mario?'

'We are to marry in the spring. Now, I must go in, Mama will be worried. She always waits up, never sleeps until she knows I am home. Goodbye. I don't think we should see each other again, ever. Please don't try – if you do care for me, you will honour my wishes.'

She realized the ring box was still on the seat behind her. She retrieved it and tried to hand it to him, but he ignored it and hurried round to open the door for her.

He walked her to the entrance of her apartment block. Again she proffered the box, but he still took no notice, leaving her standing there as he returned to the car and drove off.

Somehow she expected to see him in the next few days, but there was no word. She was afraid to go to Domino's office, not because she might see Roberto, but because she might not.

Five days later, Domino was waiting for her when she finished work. He was so excited he couldn't wait to tell her that he was going to Rome to study. Luciano had made him an incredible offer – to finance his studies and set him up in his own office as a criminal lawyer when he passed his exams. Luciano had told him to look on it as a wedding gift, he would need the very best for his bride.

He gathered Graziella in his arms, thrilled at the prospect of getting out of his dingy office, away from the endless round of contracts and housing projects, and renewing his studies. When she eased herself away from him, his expression turned to concern; he had expected her to be as pleased as he was, happy that he had the opportunity he had always wanted.

She sighed impatiently and her voice was cold. 'And what has he asked in return? Why does a man give all this to someone he hardly knows? Mario, don't you realize that if you accept this "gift" you'll be in his debt for the rest of your life? His kind don't ever do anything without a reason . . . can't you see what he is, can't you tell?'

Mario had his suspicions about Luciano, and he flushed slightly. 'Is that so bad? What have you got against him? It's not as if he's giving it for free. I will still work for him, but out of the office, with time to study. And then walk straight into a practice.'

He blushed, turning away from her, and his face tightened. 'So I'll be indebted to him, so what? Have you any idea how many years it would take for me to pass my exams if I remain in this office? And even when I'm qualified, how long do you think it would take to get into a decent firm?'

Her voice rose in anger. 'You don't know him, Mario! You don't know anything about him except that he walked into your office one day with a fistful of contracts! Where did they come from? What business is he in that he has so much money? Do you want me to spell it out to you? You know what he is, you know, and you're *still* prepared to take it from him?'

She was right, he knew it, he had known all along that Luciano's money came from the American-based racketeers, but he didn't want to lose the opportunity of a lifetime.

'Is it so bad, Grazzie? To want to succeed?'

She slipped her arm through his and they walked together. She was sorry for him and felt she had been unnecessarily cruel. 'It isn't wrong, of course it isn't, but it is wrong to get involved at this level – because you will never be free.'

'But I like him, you know, and in some way I really trust him. Maybe he is what you say, I don't know . . . Now I don't know what to do.'

It was her perfect opportunity to tell him what she knew, but she didn't. She should have said something about knowing Roberto before, but she didn't because she hadn't really known him. She could have told Domino about that night at the villa, about the diamond ring, but she didn't. They walked, arm-in-arm, and she told him quietly that it was over between them. He tried to make her change her mind, even asked if it was because of Luciano's offer, but she shook her head. It was because she had realized she did not love him.

He promised to have nothing more to do with Luciano if it meant so much to her, but instead of changing her mind it reconfirmed her decision. She became adamant, and at last he knew there was no point in arguing. A week later he left for Rome.

Graziella thought about Roberto every single day, until she could neither eat nor sleep. At night the ring drew her like a magnet. She would open the box and see the diamond glinting, sparkling, and even when she threw it in the back of a drawer she knew it was there. Eventually she took it out and put it on her bedside table.

Graziella's mother knew something was terribly wrong with her daughter, and believed at first that it was because of the broken engagement, but as time went by and Graziella remained closeted in her room, she began to think the girl was really ill.

Graziella turned her key in the lock and let herself into the apartment. It was shuttered and dark, and she thought she could smell flowers . . . She sighed and put her briefcase on the table. Then she removed her coat, but when she went to hang it up she noticed a camel-hair overcoat on the hall-stand. Her hands shook as she touched it, telling herself that it couldn't be, couldn't possibly be his.

Her heart thudding, the blood rushing to her cheeks, she made the tremendous effort it required to move her leaden feet the few steps to her mother's room. The door was slightly ajar and now she could smell Havana cigar smoke. As she eased the door open she could see nothing but roses, dozens and dozens of roses, and her mother sitting in bed surrounded by a sea of them. But there, sitting in a chair with his back to the door, was Roberto Luciano.

Unable to move another step, she stood in the doorway as Roberto rose slowly to his feet and turned to her. His face was ravaged, gaunt, and he could not meet her eyes. Finally he broke the silence by taking her mother's hand and kissing it softly, murmuring his thanks for being allowed to visit her. He was so tall he seemed to fill the room – and he was trapped, he would have to pass by Graziella in order to leave. Hesitating, he ran his fingers through his thick, black hair, and as he dropped his arm his elbow caught one of the many vases of flowers. It toppled; roses, vase, water and all fell to the floor, and he stood there looking helpless.

Graziella stepped forward immediately, and they both bent down at the same time to pick up the mess. He made a nervous remark about his clumsiness and the tension was broken. They turned like startled children when Graziella's mother suggested that her room was too small and they might be more comfortable in the sitting room.

Luciano gave her a small bow. 'Thank you, Signora di Carlo, but I have to leave. My apologies, and my thanks again for letting me visit you.'

Graziella followed him into the narrow hallway. She reached for his coat and held it out, but he shook his head, so eager to be gone that he draped it over his arm. As she unlatched the door, he was standing directly behind her, and suddenly he dropped his coat and trapped her against the door with his arms. She turned to look up at him, then cupped his face in both hands.

Her voice was choked with tears as she said, 'I love you . . .'

They were married quietly, with only a handful of guests.

Roberto had been to Rome and returned with Domino to act as best man. Domino offered not a single word of reproach to Graziella; he couldn't, she was so radiant with happiness. She kissed him warmly, thanking him for his understanding, his friendship. He told her that he was about to take his finals, and within a couple

41

of years he would be practising criminal law in Palermo. His friend and mentor, Luciano, had been as good as his word.

They honeymooned in Capri. Until their arrival there they had not been alone together since the visit to his villa. In the meantime Roberto had overlooked nothing, even selecting the best nursing home where Graziella's mother could be properly looked after.

The hotel manager met them and showed them to their suite of light, airy rooms.

Graziella noticed the way her husband paid close attention to the security of the building. A large balcony covered with a striped awning gave them a view of the harbour, and he made sure that no one could enter their rooms that way.

Graziella began to ache to be alone with Roberto, but first champagne was delivered with the manager's compliments, then a basket of fruit, then flowers, followed by the bellboy bringing their monogrammed leather cases. Hers were filled with clothes Roberto had insisted she buy; everything she had was new, from underwear to furs.

At last they were alone. Roberto threw his jacket off, kicked off his shoes and loosened his tie, then began unpacking. Graziella went to his side and whispered, 'Doesn't the hotel provide a maid to do that?'

He immediately reached for the phone and she laughed, taking it away from him. 'I was joking.'

He was embarrassed, as though he had been caught out. Then he smiled and pulled off his tie and undid his shirt buttons. 'You think everything's OK? I mean, if anything's not right you will tell me, won't you? I want this to be perfect, everything's got to be perfect.'

She was puzzled. Everything was perfect, now that they were alone at long last, and yet he was pacing up and down, pausing to fiddle with the bedcover – he kept taking a few paces towards her and then veering off to start fussing around again. She had wondered if she would be nervous, if she would feel uneasy with him, it had been so long since that night at the villa, and yet now she felt more relaxed than he was. Any moment now, she thought, he'll go and count the towels in the bathroom. She giggled. 'What are you doing?'

'I . . . er, well, just making sure everything's all right. You want to eat? Are you hungry? If you want, I can order food?'

'Do you want to eat?'

'Me? No, no, I'm not hungry.'

He opened the sliding windows to the balcony, stepped out and leaned on the railings, his back to the room. Graziella took off her dress and wrapped herself in a silk dressing gown. She stared at his back for a moment, then stepped out to join him.

They looked out over the harbour, at the rows of yachts, the shimmering blue sea, the cloudless sky. Their hands on the rail were only inches apart, yet it was such a distance that neither could make the first move. Their emotions were so chained, so battened down. Roberto even found it difficult to speak, as if something was gripping his throat. He coughed . . . and then, to her consternation, he moved away yet again. She tried to follow, but he raised his hand as a signal to her to stay where she was.

He cleared his throat again. 'I want to tell you

43

something. I never believed I could . . . I never thought I would come this far in life, you know? But wherever I get to, wherever I'm going, it won't mean a thing without you. When . . . That night in the villa I thought you could be mine, and I don't think I'd ever experienced such a feeling. And when I thought I'd lost you, it was like I had died. Everything I'd worked for, hoped for, meant nothing to me. I love you, and I love you with my whole life.'

She stood looking at him, but said nothing. He continued, 'I wanted you to know that, I want you to know what you mean to me. I've had many other women, I won't lie to you, but I love you.'

Graziella turned away from him, shading her eyes against the sun. The diamond solitaire glittered on her finger. She took time to assimilate exactly what she wanted to say to him, because they were very different. He spoke the dialect of the poorer areas; hers were high-class, aristocratic tones.

Choosing her words carefully, she said, quietly, 'After the night at the villa . . . I have never known such a sense of loss, even when my father died. I want you to know that even before you offered Mario his chance in Rome, even before then I had decided to end our engagement. So don't place me on a pedestal, don't put me somewhere that is above you, because I am not. I'm yours, and my life is your life. I love you.'

She turned to him and smiled, and he was overcome, like a helpless child. She smiled again. 'I just wanted you to know that, because we must be honest with each other. And also, I have never been with a man.'

His tall form blocked out the sun as he came to her, took her hand and led her inside. He pulled all the blinds down until the room was in semi-darkness, then switched on the bedside lamps as he made his way to the bathroom. He turned the bath taps on and spilled oil and smelling salts into the foaming water.

Graziella sat at the dressing table and picked up her hairbrush, uncertain what to do. It was she who was nervous now, not of Roberto but that she might not please him. He came to stand behind her and took the brush from her hand, then gently brushed her hair until it gleamed as gold as the sunlight. Then he bent and kissed her neck and sat behind her on the long stool. Slowly, he undid the sash of her gown and inched it from her shoulders, kissing her softly as the silk slipped to the floor. She was wearing a satin and lace slip with fine, thin straps, and she lifted her hand to move one, but he stopped her by gripping her wrist. He shook his head; he wanted to undress her, slowly . . . He lifted her to stand before him and eased the silk over her head. It crackled with electricity from her hair, and strands of it shimmered around her face and shoulders. He cupped her chin gently between his hands and kissed her lips, his tongue flicking into her mouth, so fast, then he kissed her ears, the nape of her neck.

She wanted to hold him, but he lifted her in his arms and carried her to the bathroom, placing her gently down on the thick carpet. In the mirrored room they could see each other touching and caressing. He loosened his shirt and she ran her hands over his chest, fascinated. She had hardly been aware of how he was built until now, and she compared his dark tautness with her pale, almost translucent skin.

He looked into her eyes in the mirror and smiled. 'The princess and the groom,' he said.

The steam from the bath began to fill the room, and he bent to turn the taps off. She noticed the scars on his lean body; one long one under his arm, another just above his shoulder blade. She traced them with her fingers, inquisitive, wanting to know every inch of him.

He stepped out of his trousers and bent to pull off his socks one by one. Sitting where she was on the floor she found herself facing his underpants, and she blushed. She looked up into his face, and he read her hesitation and pulled her to her feet. He pressed himself to her so she could feel his growing hardness against her belly, then he drew her hand down to where she could feel him . . .

She gasped and tried to pull her hand away, but he gripped her firmly, making her touch him, and she relaxed, inching her hand inside his pants, stroking the silky skin of his penis. Again she looked to him for reassurance, but his eyes were closed and he moaned. His obvious arousal affected her own feelings, and she used both hands to probe and stroke. He arched his back, pulled her head down, making her kneel again before him, pressed his erection into her face until she could feel the wiry pubic hair. Not knowing what to do she turned her face from side to side, afraid again as he gripped her neck harder and pushed and pushed . . .

Suddenly he seemed to realize what he was doing and he once again raised her to her feet. He wrapped his arms around her, held her against his chest. 'My baby, my baby . . . don't be frightened, don't be frightened.'

He kissed her neck, her shoulders, down to her breasts, and her breath heaved as she clung to him, not wanting it to stop, wanting him to keep his lips on her nipples. But he fell to his knees, licking and kissing her belly. He gripped her buttocks, pressing her closer and closer, and she was squirming and moaning without even knowing what it was she wanted. His big hands moved lower until his fingers found her vagina from behind, easing her open while his tongue probed, pressing into her. She responded, spreading herself open until his tongue was deep inside her, thrilling her . . . and then she couldn't catch her breath, she couldn't breathe, and her gasp was part moan, part scream . . . Her chest heaved and she shuddered; suddenly her body began to move of its own free will, opening wider and wider, and her mind splintered into a single long scream of pleasure.

She felt damp and limp as he lifted her into the foaming, soapy water, and she clung to his neck, kissing his face, his chest. She thought it was the most beautiful emotion she had ever known, and she sighed as she settled into the water.

Roberto climbed in with her and began soaping her, bringing her back almost to the point of exhilaration, but then he took her hands and guided them to his body, showing her what to do. To her astonishment she saw him grope for the sides of the bath and grip them as she massaged him . . . He moaned, and suddenly he was roaring, and her hands were covered in his sperm. He lay back in the bath with a long, deep sigh. She reached for his hand, asking if he was all right, and he opened his eyes and laughed. He had never felt better in his whole life.

Graziella towelled him dry and he wrapped her in the sheet-sized white towel. Then he swept her off her feet and carried her to the bed. As he laid her down, he told her he was going to make love to her now. Astonished, she looked at him with innocent eyes and wondered what they had just been doing if it wasn't making love.

Whatever it was she had enjoyed it more than anything in her life.

Signor and Signora Roberto Luciano stayed in the suite for the entire honeymoon, never out of each other's sight for more than a moment. Neither wanted it to end, but it had to; Roberto was needed back in Palermo. They travelled back feeling happier and more complete than they had ever thought possible.

Only one moment, one afternoon, she tried never to think about, but it would always be with her. Lying next to him in the bed, she had propped herself on her elbows, looked into his handsome face and asked him about his family. He tried to change the subject as he always had whenever she brought it up, but this time she wouldn't let it drop. She asked if he was ashamed of his family, as they had not attended the wedding and he had never mentioned what they did or where they lived. He had eased back the covers and swung his legs over the side of the bed as if to get up, but he remained sitting with his back to her. He reached out and poured a glass of champagne, sipped it, then offered her the glass. She shook her head and stared hard at him, wanting him to talk.

'I have little contact with my family. There is nothing to tell.'

'But they are alive? Have you brothers? Sisters?'

His face tightened and he sipped the champagne, then put the glass down carefully. 'My father is a carpenter – well, when he can get work. He was injured in a factory when he was a boy, and is in pain all the time with his back. He was born in Palermo, but he went to work in

Naples when he was married. My father is a stubborn fool. My mother takes in washing, cleans for a couple of families, and I have one brother. He is eighteen, and joined the army a few months ago. I had two sisters, but they both died of consumption. And that, my love, is all I have to tell you.'

'Can I ask you something?'

He shrugged, stood up and started to pace the room.

'All this money you have, is it yours, or do you work for someone?'

'Yes, I work for someone.'

'He is in America?'

'Yes, he is in America, but he returns to Sicily now and then.'

'Will I get to meet him?'

'He's a very busy man. Maybe, maybe not.'

'Is he a racketeer?'

'No, he's a businessman, as I am.'

'What is this business?'

'I export certain things.'

'What things?'

His eyes were dark, unfathomable. 'Orange juice, olive oil . . .'

'To America?'

'Yes, and to England, wherever it is needed.'

'What work did you do in America?'

'I worked for a businessman.'

'Who?'

She knew he was holding back his temper, but he answered, 'His name is Joseph Carolla.' He looked at her, hard, his hands on his hips.

'Is he a *mafioso*?'

He pulled open the balcony doors and then slammed

49

them shut. His mouth was a thin, tight line. He looked cruel, like a stranger.

'You don't ask any more questions, OK?'

'What will you do to me if I continue? I have a right to know, I am your wife.'

'You have no rights, understand me?'

'What did you say?'

'You heard me.'

She leapt up and screamed at him, 'I have no rights? What the hell do you think I am? No rights? Do you think I am stupid? Do you think I can accept all this . . .' she threw the diamond ring at him, 'this and this . . .' as she ripped off her silk robe that had cost more than a week's salary, 'without ever questioning where it all came from? Do you?'

She began pulling clothes from the drawers and hurling them across the room. He grabbed her by the neck and slapped her, slapped her so hard her ears rang, and she slumped to the floor. But in a second she was back at him, kicking, trying to scratch his face and screaming blue murder. He couldn't control her, and the more she fought him the more he had to hold himself back from hurting her. Eventually he pushed her away from him so that she fell against the bed, then rolled off and lay curled in a ball at its foot.

He went out onto the balcony, slamming the doors behind him, and paced up and down. Through the windows he could see her throwing things into a suitcase. Eventually she sat down on the bed and began to weep. He let her cry, let her sob herself into a state of exhaustion, then at last he came back into the room. He stood some distance from her as he said, 'I will never,

never, strike you again, but you must not . . . you must promise me not to . . .'

'Go away! I won't promise you anything, nothing . . .' She wiped her tear-stained face with the back of her hand. 'So much for my love! You must think me a very naïve woman. It is because I love you that I should know everything about you, everything you are . . . That is why I asked so many questions. If I know, no one can come between us, no one. Whatever you are I am now part of, must be a part of . . .'

He began quietly, without emotion, telling her of his life in the slums of Naples as a child. He drew a sad, pitiful picture for Graziella, leaving nothing to her imagination. He described his days of thieving, the street gangs, the reform institutions, his mother's weeping, his father's beatings.

'Then . . . Then I met Ettore Simosa, and through him I was introduced to people who knew Joseph Carolla. First I was cleaning the cars, then I was allowed to do a little work on the engines, until I was upgraded to driver. I was bringing home good money, money my family needed desperately, but my father threw it back in my face. He almost got me arrested, but Carolla's men bought off the police. So I left home. I was sixteen years old and still not Carolla's driver, that was to come . . .'

He gave her a strange, guarded look and picked up a pack of cigarettes.

'One of Carolla's friends, a man in America known as "Lucky" Luciano, asked about my family. When I told him I had walked out on them, he asked if I was prepared to join another family, one that would take care of me – his family. "A most honoured society," he said, as I remember. So I took the oath of *omerta*. It is not a simple thing; it is binding, it involves great humility and manliness, and I gave my promise never to co-operate with the legal authorities. I began collecting money, driving the cars for the pick-ups. I was very good, and soon Carolla asked me to drive for one of his close friends, then for him. When he went to Chicago, I went with him and acted as his driver and bodyguard over there. He is my father now, and my work is for him and his family. He gave me the villa and the orange groves as payment for being loyal to him. That's it.'

Graziella looked at his bowed head. She reached out and took his hand, made him look at her, meet her eyes. 'I see. And now you work for him here, whilst he is in America? Have you ever killed for this man? Would he ever make you commit murder?'

He cupped her face in his hands. 'No, I swear to you, Carolla would never ask that of me. He is a good man, a man I would give my life for.'

Graziella sighed with relief and rested her head against his chest. 'If I ever so much as lift a hand against you, I will cut it off.' She laughed softly, whispering that maybe she would make him angry enough some day, but she would hold him to his promise.

Later that night she lay awake beside him and realized how far she had removed herself from her own family. If her dead father had only known that she had married one of the men he had always warned her against. And she had known right from the beginning that the man she loved was part of that feared Organization. It gave her a certain feeling of excitement as if she too had been initiated, had her forefinger slit and her blood mingled with that of others, as if she too had taken the oath of

52

omerta. She cuddled closer, and in his sleep he reached for her and drew her to him. She would protect this secret with her own life, a life she knew would be radically different from now on.

Poverty grew to desperate proportions in Palermo, and war threatened ominously. Mussolini's voice rang out over radios and loudspeakers were erected in the streets. It began slowly, at first just undercurrents, Nazi slogans daubed on the walls, but it was festering and about to erupt. The word '*Judas*' began to represent fear for many.

The death of Graziella's mother blighted her happiness for a while. It meant the last link to her old life was severed, and now the only family she had was her husband. She was overjoyed when, six months after the honeymoon, she discovered she was pregnant. They were living in the Villa Rivera, which had been refurbished and decorated to Graziella's taste, and they began to prepare a nursery for the baby.

The security and comfort of the villa protected Graziella from the outside world, and she felt as safe as the child in her womb with her servants and an armed bodyguard patrolling outside the wrought-iron gates.

Michael Luciano was born at the villa. He weighed nine pounds two ounces. He was a perfect child, having inherited the blonde hair and blue eyes of Luciano's 'princess'. He was the pride and joy of his father, who idolized him. Some said his beauty was wasted on a boy, he would have been better off as a girl.

Cocooned in safety, Graziella made infrequent trips into town. What she saw there frightened her. There was open Jew-baiting and Fascist slogans everywhere. Soon, there was violence. Graziella expected Roberto to join up at any time. When he laughed and said it was a simple matter of paying off the right people, her reaction was the cause of their second argument.

Mario Domino arrived at the villa one day in army uniform. He had remained a friend, and had fulfilled the role of godfather to Michael. Graziella felt ashamed of her husband. Domino, too, found it difficult to accept that Roberto could so easily escape conscription. It soured what had begun as a delightful evening, and even after he departed, the atmosphere in the villa remained frosty.

Most of the village boys and the men who had worked for them had enlisted, but Luciano was contacted by Carolla in New York, who told him to pack his bags and get over there fast to escape enlistment. If Luciano insisted on staying where he was, Carolla could give him names of people from whom he could get medical certificates. Luciano, however, asked for reinforcements to take over the running of the business – he was going to war.

A week later he was measured for his uniform. His fine silk shirts and tailored suits were put aside, and he stood in front of Graziella, saluting. When she saw him she wept; she was glad, in a way, that he had given in to her pressure and joined up, but it didn't make it any easier.

Carolla sent two *capi* to take over, and promised Luciano that, if he survived the war, everything would be as he had left it, would all be waiting for him.

CHAPTER 2

SOMEHOW THE Villa Rivera withstood the bombs, the devastation of the orange groves and the burning of the crop land surrounding the property. The driveway leading to the villa was a mass of craters, and a direct hit to some outhouses had started a fire that destroyed one wing of the villa.

Roberto came home on leave. He was no longer concerned about the business, and gave not a moment's thought to how it had survived the war. He was relieved that his wife and family were alive and healthy, but they were surrounded by abject poverty. Sicily was starving.

His leave was all too short. It seemed that no sooner had he arrived than he had to depart again. Graziella's eyes shone with pride; he was now a man she could have introduced to her father. He was an officer, decorated twice for bravery, and a man his sons could be proud of – she had given birth to Constantino a few months after he had gone to the front.

Food was scarce, and ration cards were issued, but this did not affect Graziella particularly. 'Friends' of her husband often brought supplies. She was very frugal, and did what she could to help others, but her boys were the most important people in her life. They were trapped in the villa now, to move out would be dangerous, and with the new baby she could not give Michael the attention he had been used to. These were Michael's formative years, and she gave in too easily to his demands because she knew he was missing out on so much. He was an extraordinarily bright child, always asking questions, and full of life and devilment. She had noticed that when Roberto came home on leave, father and son were inseparable, but that Roberto did not have the same bond with Constantino. She put this down to him not being at home for his second son's birth.

Roberto also missed the birth of his third son, Alfredo, which coincided with the telegram telling Graziella that her husband had been taken prisoner.

The end of the war, American troops streaming into Sicily, brought relief and desperately needed supplies for the starving population, but it was another five months before Roberto was released. He was gaunt and quiet, his experiences of the prisoner-of-war camps a nightmare, but he returned a hero.

Graziella knew the war had changed her husband, as it had everyone. There was much that needed doing at the villa, but he could not find the energy even to begin. His deep depressions hung on, clinging to him while all around them people tried to rebuild their lives. Mario Domino had survived and had even begun to practise law again. She asked him to visit in the hope that it would at least kindle some spark in her husband.

Domino knew what Roberto had been through and was sad to see the change in him. He tried to get through to his old friend but all he received was a dull-eyed shrug. It seemed nothing would alleviate the misery.

Michael had been warned not to annoy his father, not to disturb him in the bedroom where he was resting. But at seven years old he was irrepressible, and rarely obeyed his mother. He sneaked in and crawled up onto the bed.

Roberto was asleep, and the little boy laid his hand across his father's mouth, meaning to stop him calling out if he should wake, but Roberto threw the boy from him.

Michael backed into a corner, terrified, but suddenly righteous anger overcame his fear and his little face went red with rage. 'You never play with me any more! I was going to kiss you awake, because you are like a dead person.'

Shaking, Roberto gathered his son into his arms and buried his head against him. As he wept, Michael stroked his father's head and made the cooing sounds he had heard his mother use to comfort Constantino and Alfredo. Somehow the child had touched a chord inside Roberto and brought his father back into the land of the living.

It took time, but gradually he began to take an interest in his surroundings and, at last, his wife, who had stood by him and waited so patiently. But Roberto still gave no thought to his business. He found the idea of one-armed bandits somehow distasteful now.

As Graziella cleared the dishes after dinner one day, she shooed the children away to play in the hall and asked Roberto to stay; they had to talk. 'The larder is empty, the ration books don't give us enough food for the children, let alone me.'

He stared at her, then dropped his eyes and fiddled with his napkin ring, letting it roll from hand to hand.

She continued, 'Your friends have been very good throughout the war, seeing that I had eggs, a little butter, even some meat occasionally, but they have not sent anything since you returned. I was wondering if you could contact them, if maybe you could . . . I am with child again.'

Still the napkin ring rolled back and forth, back and forth. 'They brought you food?'

'Yes, almost every week to begin with, then maybe once a month.'

'Who? Did they give you a name?'

'No . . . it would be on the doorstep, and once a boy brought it in.'

He stood up and went to the window, his hands thrust deep in his pockets. 'I'm not going back. Maybe they won't let me out, but we shall see. My old commander said I might get work with the American troops, as an interpreter. That would be good as I'd be able to get stores from their barracks . . .'

'Papa! Papa, come and see what I've found!' Michael rushed in and grabbed his father's hand, pulling him towards the door. Graziella watched from the window as Roberto walked out into the garden, Constantino at his heels. The younger boy, now almost four years old, raised his little arms up to his father, but if Roberto saw him he paid no attention, wrapped in his game with Michael. Once again she realized how little interest

Roberto took in his other children – it was always Michael.

Three months later, Graziella was baking bread in the overheated kitchen. The sounds of hammering and sawing floated in at the open windows from where Roberto was refencing the orange groves.

The wrought-iron gates of the villa had been taken away to be melted down during the war, so the gleaming black Mercedes drove straight up to the front porch. Graziella washed her hands and involuntarily patted her hair, then realized what a mess she must look. Eight months pregnant, her skirt was pinned over her bulging belly and her blouse was stained. She called Roberto, then watched as an elderly man with a walking cane was helped out of the Mercedes by the burly driver. The old man leaned heavily on his stick and looked around from beneath the brim of a hat that seemed too large for him, then took a pair of gold-rimmed sunglasses from his pocket and put them on. Graziella, still at the window, knew instinctively that this was Joseph Carolla.

Roberto came around the side of the house, dressed in old corduroy trousers and a shirt open to the waist, exposing his deep tan. He took Carolla's right hand and kissed it, then they clasped each other and kissed cheeks.

Roberto led his guest into his study and closed the door firmly. He did not call Graziella to meet him, and she took the opportunity to wash and change, combing her hair and coiling it into a neat bun at the nape of her neck. Then she went in search of the children and made them presentable.

Sitting in the most comfortable chair, Carolla clipped the end of his cigar and took his time to light it. He leaned back, smiling at Roberto as a father would to a favourite son, then reached for Roberto's hand.

He spoke in English. 'It is good to see you, good.' He paused a moment, and continued, 'I have been in Palermo a week. I expected to hear from you, but in the end, as you see, I came to you.'

'Thank you. I must ask you to forgive me, I did not know you were in Sicily.'

'From what I hear you don't know very much. You have not made contact with Ettore Calleah, or Simosa. They have not seen you since you came back. Is there some reason?'

'I have not been well.'

'And now you are?'

'Yes, yes . . . better . . .'

'So what is your problem?'

Roberto made his way slowly around the desk to his chair and sat looking at Carolla. 'Does there have to be one?'

'Yes. As I said to you, when the war was over, if you came through, then all you helped to build up would be waiting for you. I have many men hungry for work, hungry for anything I choose, yet you . . . You don't even go and see what has been happening since the war ended. Lemme tell you what hunger is.'

'You don't have to tell me. I have been hungry, Papa.'

'Maybe your hunger and mine are different. Out there

60

they are clawin' over each other for food. People will pay well for it, and I know how to get supplies. Remember, always think supply and demand, supply and demand . . . Right now there's not enough money for the slots, not enough for anything they cannot eat . . .'

'You think I don't know that? I'm having a hard time feeding my own family.'

'What? I gave orders you were to be given anything you needed. What are you sayin' to me, tellin' me you don't have food? You? What, are you crazy?'

'As I said, I have been ill, I have not . . .'

'Roberto, don't play games with me. I can see you, even with my bad eyesight. I can see you are fit and healthy. Maybe here . . .' he tapped his head, 'here, in your mind, you are sick.' He blinked his eyes rapidly, always a sign of anger. 'You must be crazy to let things go.'

'I am trying to rebuild my home . . . This is still my home, yes?'

'Yes, yes. Now you are being childish. I'm not angry with you, I'm angry because I gave orders that you were to be taken care of. I knew you were ill, my son, but I presumed as soon as you felt better you would have gone into town. But now I see you have remained here . . . Give me your hands, lemme see your hands . . . Look, look at the callouses, the hands of a worker, eh? You work here, cut wood, hammer nails. What are you, a labourer? You?'

'Maybe that is exactly what I am.'

'Bullshit you are. You have a fine mind, a quick mind, and an intuitively clever mind. A mind that right now I need with me, not hammerin' goddam wood. Get a man to do it, get as many as you like. You can pick and choose. There's no work, it won't cost you much.' He laughed, showing teeth that had grown yellow with age. He looked like a mangy old dog. His claw-like hands clutched at the arms of his chair and he broke into a hacking cough.

After a moment, he spat into his handkerchief, then stuffed it back into his pocket. 'I hear you may be workin' for the Americans, as an interpreter, right?'

'Yes, I have to go and see the commander. How did you know?'

'Hey, don't ask stupid questions. When did anything happen in this city I don't know about? So you go to work for the Americans . . . Now tell me, and tell me straight – you workin' for yourself? Huh? You thinkin' of getting into the black market without me? Without your Papa?'

Roberto sighed and shook his head. It had not even occurred to him. Carolla smiled and raised his eyebrows. 'I see you lost some of your quick thinkin'. Army life didn't suit you, eh? OK, this is what I want you to start doin'. First, get into the barracks, then give Simosa a rundown on what you can move. That shouldn't be too difficult for you. Always remember, supply and demand. I'm tellin' you, it's like the good old days here, you know, the days of bootleggin', when we supplied what every sonofabitch demanded. It's the same here right now, only Italy don't just want whisky. They want medicines, food, cigarettes, blankets. You name it and the black market can supply it. Everybody is tryin' to get in on it; the legit guys, ex-fucking Fascists, the Commie bastards, every sonofabitch is tryin' to make money here, an' they don't give a fuck how they do it. I'm tellin' you, the church is on to it, too, those padres know how to look the other way when you offer 'em what they need.'

Roberto sighed and rose to his feet. If he wanted to wriggle out, now was the time, and he knew it. Maybe Carolla even knew what was in his mind and that was the reason for his personal visit.

'I am leavin' for New York in one week. Maybe we should meet and discuss this again, when you have been to the Americans. Find out what you can move to us – a dozen pairs of nylons can buy you a half-share in a fuckin' bank these days, you can get a hooker for a month for a carton of cigarettes, and you, you're sawin' wood . . .'

Another coughing fit stopped him, and once again his stained, crumpled handkerchief came out. Roberto asked after Carolla's son, Paul, and the old man's face lit up.

'He come out good, he's a good guy. He's bringin' in cash, dollars, buyin' lire cheap. It's worth practically nothin' now, so we're buyin' as fast as we can get the cash movin'. He's goin' back an' forth to Tangier – changes the lire back into dollars, like a goddam merry-go-round. Gets a better price there. That boy's creamin' it in. In three months he's trebled his bank roll, gonna open his own goddam bank here. He's a good kid, stays at the Excelsior – fuckin' Germans an' Nazi officials used it like a holiday camp during the war. Now they've got it back an' they're givin' good service. You wanna take yourself there while this place gets fixed up.'

Just then Graziella walked in with the children. She took Carolla by surprise and he looked angrily at Roberto. Then he eased himself out of the chair. 'I gotta go.'

Roberto hurriedly introduced Carolla, who gave Graziella a brief nod. The children received a little more attention; the old man took a fistful of dollars from his pocket and tucked them into Michael's small, out-stretched hand.

After watching the car drive away, Roberto walked slowly back into the house. The children were running wild up and down the hall. Graziella was still in the study. He walked in and slammed the door behind him, glaring at her.

She looked up, startled, 'So that was Carolla. I must say, I expected him to be . . . Well, he looked faintly ridiculous. I don't know who his tailor is, but why does he dress like something out of a gangster movie? Anyone looking at him would know who he was . . .' Before she could say another word, Roberto had grabbed her and pulled her to the door.

'You knock, understand me? Whenever I have some-one in here with me. You never walk in, never, is that clear?'

Shocked by his anger, she stepped back and jerked her arm free. 'All right, there's no need to shout. I just thought he would like to meet your family.'

She glared at him, telling him all he had to do was ask her. Then she slammed out.

He could hear her calling the boys, but a moment later Michael slipped in, disobeying her as usual. He put his arms around his father and clung to his waist, until Roberto picked him up and hugged him. As always, the presence of his son calmed him. He nuzzled the boy's soft, white skin and stroked his hair, bleached to silver by the sun.

'Papa, look! I have money, I can feed us now, you don't have to worry.'

The brilliant blue eyes sparkled. Roberto put him down.

'It's OK, Michael, Papa's going to make some money now. And the first thing he'll buy you is a toy train, you want a train?'

Whooping with glee, Michael ran out, shouting at the top of his voice that he was going to get a train, a red one.

That night, Roberto lay in bed reading while Graziella brushed her hair. Her library of books had become a constant source of enjoyment to him, and she guided him through them, quietly continuing his education. They would often discuss what he had read, and he paid great attention to what she said. He loved these hours with her in their bedroom, sitting side by side against the big, soft pillows.

But after Carolla's visit he began to think over what Graziella had said about the way the old man dressed. She was right, he looked a movie gangster with his flashy suits and shoes, his brilliant ties. The next morning he asked her opinion of his own wardrobe, and she started sorting out his clothes. She made a pile of the things she considered fit only for film extra work, leaving Roberto with only two suits, a few shirts and one pair of shoes, but he was not offended. They laughed as she gradually weeded them out, insisting that they be given to the villagers, who would put them to good use.

Having made the decision to return to work, Roberto employed builders and gardeners to repair the villa and replant the gardens. With hardly a moment's pause since his meeting with Don Carolla, he took over the flourishing black-market network. The military warehouses were stacked with goods the Italians would give their eyeteeth for, and the Americans could buy them for less than wholesale price from the PX or commissary. A bottle of whisky cost them as little as two dollars, but on the black market it would sell for twenty times that amount. Practically the entire American population in Naples was involved, everyone ready to make themselves extra bucks, but they were hampered because they could not risk being caught selling the goods.

What was lacking was a well-organized middleman, and Roberto Luciano fitted the bill. Picking up contacts at the naval bases and among the colony of expatriate American civilians, he began opening the pipelines. His network of salesmen grew, dealing in fresh and canned food, luxuries like Virginia hams and electrical appliances such as toasters, irons, refrigerators.

Graziella benefited from her husband's return to work. The villa regained some of its old splendour, with the addition of a fitted American kitchen containing every conceivable modern appliance. The children were healthy, and the new baby, another boy, was born. He was christened Frederico.

Always a deeply religious woman, Graziella would attend three masses every Sunday before taking the children to morning service. The Lucianos had the entire front pew to themselves and were respected as leading members of the community. Roberto only joined her on special feast days, when she insisted, but he gave the church a great deal of financial support.

One Sunday, the padre accompanied Graziella home

after church. Roberto's study door was firmly closed, and rather than disturb him they waited patiently in the big drawing room with the blazing fire. When Roberto finally showed his visitors out and joined them, he gave Graziella a quizzical look, wondering what on earth had possessed her to bring the priest to the house. But Graziella simply introduced them, served them coffee and excused herself, leaving them alone.

The padre was slightly embarrassed and not sure how to approach his subject. Eventually he stammered that many of the people in his parish were suffering more hardship than was necessary, and explained that essentials, such as clothes, which the church collected and distributed amongst the poor, were being hijacked by thugs and sold on the black market.

'Why do you come to me?'

Blushing, the priest tried to explain without insulting his host. He stared into the fire, unable to meet Roberto's eyes. He was aware that Roberto had many American contacts, but the people who were hijacking the trucks were Italian racketeers, street boys. 'They are taking the lives of their own people. In this freezing weather, with so little food and no warm clothes, the children are dying of exposure. I need your help, Don Luciano, I need it desperately to help my people. I beg you to assist me.'

It was the first time Roberto had been given the title of don, and he corrected the priest, insisting on being called by his first name. He promised that he would personally see what could be done.

The following Sunday was Frederico's christening. As the family entered the church a murmur went round, and all eyes were on Roberto as he made his way to the pew. After the service, he was blessed time and again by grateful people, some simply eager to touch his hand.

The supplies had got through for the first time in six months. To Roberto's embarrassment the padre, his face flushed with joy, kissed his hand and hugged him. There was hardly a soul in the parish who did not offer up a prayer of thanks to Roberto Luciano.

'I thank you, my son. This may be a great lesson for you, too; fight fire with fire, a fire that is in all of us, but the hardest lesson to learn is how to control it.'

The words remained with Roberto, and that night he repeated them over and over. He realized that he was a strong force in the village, one that could, if he desired, be put to good use. Already tired of the black market, he began to wonder if he could actually make his land, his factories, productive enough to get him out of Carolla's rackets – if he was allowed out.

By the summer, Roberto had acquired two farms close to the villa. With the produce from the extra land he was able, despite strong competition, to obtain two new export contracts. His canning factories had increased their workforces, and the whole business was becoming viable. He knew he would not be allowed to simply say 'thank you and goodnight' to Carolla; much of the Organization's money had gone into the rebuilding. So he decided that the best way to relieve himself of his duties was to offer Carolla a good percentage on condition that he would be allowed to build his own family. If they gave him permission then he would be, as the padre had once called him, a don.

It was while he was sitting in his study, pondering how to go about it, that he received a call from Ettore Calleah. Calleah would not explain why, but Roberto was to keep himself free for a meeting, the time and place yet to be announced. As one of Carolla's top *capi* he was required to attend.

A week later, he was instructed to fly to Havana. A room had been booked for him at the Hotel Falcona, the whole of which had been taken over by the Organization. The penthouse suites were reserved for the bosses of the underworld. Not one room was available to any other guest, and the large committee room was out of bounds to all but those invited.

The first person he spotted in the hotel bar was Paul, Joseph Carolla's son. Almost ten years had passed since they had last met, and Roberto was able to size him up for a few moments before greeting him. It amused Roberto to see that the much younger Paul's height had not increased, but his girth was overflowing his trousers, and the crumpled suit that he was wearing looked as if it had been slept in.

Carolla spread his arms wide as he greeted Roberto like a long-lost brother, folding him into a bear-hug and saying in a loud voice how much he had missed Roberto. His voice retained hardly a trace of his Italian accent and was as coarse and vulgar as some of the old mobsters he had learned his English from, with every other word an obscenity.

His eyes scanned the bar, constantly checking the lobby as if afraid to miss anything. 'Fuckin' place is crawlin', see how many guys are here? I seen 'em from

69

New York, New Jersey, fuckin' Atlantic City, Chicago, New Orleans . . . Hey, you hear what the fuck's goin' on down in Florida? Fuckin' floatin' money on the sand, and Siegel is in shit up to his armpits.'

After shaking hands with a couple of new arrivals, Carolla gestured for Roberto to sit at a table. He was sweating profusely, and took out a handkerchief to mop his brow, slurping his drink at the same time. He belched, then slapped his knees, struck his chest with his fist and laughed. 'I needed that . . . So, how ya doin', all right? Couldn't be anythin' *but* all right, eh? You know I set the whole thing up for you?'

Roberto stared at him blankly, not understanding. Carolla was confident to the point of putting Luciano down, making sure he knew who was responsible for the black-market boom back home. He continued, 'I'm talkin' about the black-market scams, you know it was me? It was me arranged the truck routes in Germany. I fuckin' hadda work hand-in-glove with the fuckin' Krauts, but you got it in your lap, like the old man said. You done well . . . you hear about him?'

Roberto was very much on his guard. He asked about Joseph Carolla and Paul, unconcerned, sat picking his nose as he said that his father had been unconscious for three days, following a massive stroke. It was on the cards that the old man wouldn't pull through.

'I'm sorry, I didn't know. Is he in New York?'

'Yeah. Wanna ship him home – in a box, by the look of things.'

'Is that why this meeting's been called?'

Carolla laughed, his fat face wobbling and showering drips of sweat on to the back of the plastic-covered booth. 'Hey, where you been? You think these guys care?

70

He's small fry; they got big things on the menu to call everyone together like this. I'm here because I'm representing that tight-fisted old bastard.'

When he returned to his room at four-thirty that afternoon, Roberto found a small card by the telephone, requesting his presence in the conference room at seven o'clock sharp. He bathed and dressed very carefully, selecting a suit that Graziella had chosen for him and a tie she had bought in Rome during one of their infrequent family shopping trips. Then, satisfied with his appearance, he ordered coffee and sandwiches in his room.

At six forty-five he made his way down through the lobby to the conference room. The doors were guarded by two men. He presented his invitation to one of them and was ushered into the room. It was already set up for the meeting with a table over thirty feet long, surrounded by chairs. More rows of chairs lined the walls. At the far end was a buffet table. Several men were already crowded around it, and they all turned to see who had entered, then talked amongst themselves in hushed voices.

By five minutes to seven the room was nearly full. Men greeted each other with kisses and handshakes. The atmosphere was more like a social gathering than a very special and unprecedented meeting. It included the heads of every American family, members from Sicily and Italy, even some of the honorary Jewish members who, because of their race, had no votes.

The most famous of the latter was just arriving. Meyer Lansky was in deep conversation with a tall, hawk-nosed man whose broad shoulders swamped his diminutive companion, none other than the famous Charlie 'Lucky' Luciano, suntanned and smiling at everyone. Roberto knew he now resided in Sicily, having been extradited from the USA before the war, but he hadn't bargained for the fact that he still appeared to be the main man. The room fell quiet as he progressed among the clusters of people towards the head of the table.

The next moment, without any signal being given, everyone took their seats at the table. A thickset man gestured Roberto to a place at the very end. From half-way along, Paul Carolla lifted an eyebrow as if he was surprised to see Roberto even at the bottom of the table. The rows of seats against the walls were filling up with bodyguards and *capi* not considered important enough to sit with the bosses.

At last they were settled, and those who wanted drinks were served. Some men took files and pens from their briefcases and laid them on the tabletop. Lucky Luciano sat in the big chair at the head of the table with Meyer Lansky to his right and Don Corleone to his left. He held up a hand for silence, thanked the delegates for coming and announced that he would now be resident in Cuba and would run everything from there. He asked everyone to use his correct name, Salvatore Lucania, in future, as he did not want the American authorities to know he was in Cuba. He then read out apologies from members who had been unable to attend due to illness, imprison-ment or death, and asked everyone to pray for Joseph Carolla to recover from his stroke. He thanked Paul for standing in for his father and Roberto saw Paul playing the dutiful son, wiping his eyes with his handkerchief. Then he handed the meeting over to Meyer Lansky, the chairman, and sat back to listen. But his eyes still roamed the table, the alert faces, as Lansky rose to his feet and announced the first item on the agenda.

'The Siegel situation.' Siegel had not been informed of this meeting, and now everyone understood why. Lansky leaned forward. 'There is only one thing to do with a thief who steals from his own people – only one thing. He, gentlemen, has got to go. I ask you to put it to the vote.' The vote was unanimous, and Siegel was as good as dead.

The meeting broke for supper, and started again at ten-fifteen. By this time most of the major topics had been dealt with, or so it appeared. Roberto drank only coffee, keeping slightly apart from the others; not because he wished to, but because he felt very much an outsider with many of the American families. It wasn't until eleven o'clock that Roberto had any indication of why he had been asked to the meeting. After a small nod from the end of the table, Paul Carolla rose to his feet.

'I wanna first outline what I set up in Sicily. I was over there just when the Italians surrendered to the Allies, and the US forces set up a military government. I offered myself, being bilingual, to their headquarters, and was hired as a civilian interpreter. I was then able to manoeuvre myself into the black-market operations throughout occupied Italy. I had more American soldiers on my payroll than most of you had hot dinners. A lot of the guys were in the military and a lot were civilians, officials in various capacities. They opened the flood-gates, the doors to the warehouses. I had guys who drove the trucks and guys who had the keys, and because of my position with the government I had the freedom to move around. I gotta say I hadda move carefully to avoid suspicion. I gave my services free, I could afford to, an' you can see from my documented accounts I was raking in over one million dollars in untraceable cash. I flogged penicillin, cigarettes, sugar, olive oil, flour – you name it an' I sold it. I even used US Army trucks to shift the stuff all over Italy, right behind the army.'

Lansky began to tap his pencil on the table, tired of Carolla's self-praise and, interrupting him, asked him to get to the point as it was growing late and there was still a lot on the agenda.

Carolla lifted his pudgy hands and apologized, then looked confidently around the table. 'I'm giving you these details because I want you to understand not only how much my family have generously given as their percentage. I reckon I have something else that will make the Organization more dough than they ever dreamed of. The reason I have gone into so much detail is to show that I am more than capable of taking over my father's business, and I want the syndicate's approval.'

Again Meyer gestured for him to get on with it and tapped his watch. Carolla turned to Roberto Luciano. 'My friend here took over the running of the black-market operations after I left Sicily, and he did very well. Subsequently, he has bought up land and canning factories and is exporting orange juice, oranges, and olive oil.'

It threw Carolla slightly when Lansky held up a file which Joseph Carolla had delivered to him. He knew all about the projects, and again tried to hurry young Carolla to the point. Roberto sat forward in his chair, his attention on Carolla as he continued.

'During my time in Sicily I hadda do a few trips to Tangier, exchangin' lire for dollars and doin' a real turnaround, but it also opened up a new line. I wanna start importin' junk in a big way. I know I can do it via

Sicily, straight to New York, usin' factories like Roberto Luciano's as a cover. I guarantee it'll make millions, maybe billions, and it's right within my grasp.'

Everyone turned to the head of the table and waited. Salvatore Lucania tapped his pencil on the table, then leaned back in his chair. Carolla licked his lips, his rat-like eyes darting around, picking up on hungry eyes that knew he was speaking the truth, on men who were already dealing in narcotics and were now alerted to the possibility of him moving in on their territory. The atmosphere was electric.

After what seemed an age, Salvatore rose slowly to his feet. He had no need to raise his voice; everyone gave him their full attention.

'I always made it clear that I don't like junk. I have said this right from the word go, and I want you now to just look at the figures we've been discussin' here tonight. Look at them, look at the profits, look at your own figures, look at the takes you're all bein' handed on a plate. When have your profits been better? And you still want more, still behave like greedy fuckin' pigs. Narcotics stink . . . and you all know my feelings on junk, you have always known it. Maybe the young Mr Carolla should have talked with his papa before he gave us the rundown on his career to date. He should have talked with Joseph Carolla because he would have agreed with me. There's enough dough to be made out of everythin' else we got goin', why risk the dangers of playin' around with junk? Narcotics bring down the Feds, heavy, then Interpol come snooping . . . Understand right now, the war is over, we are businessmen runnin' businesses and givin' people what they want – and what they want is to gamble, so we give it to them, they want booze, so we give it to them. We got money in circulation makin' more money. We got politicians in our hands, we got cops, but we deal in heavy narcotics and I'm tellin' you they will stand against us, and in the end we lose out. I ask every man here to vote against importation of narcotics on the level our friend Paul Carolla suggests.'

Total silence. He looked around the table and could see that they did not agree. Their faces like carved stone, they were too hungry for more.

Salvatore shrugged. He knew he was losing. 'If it goes to the vote and you vote against me, then you know I have to back down. But I will not have anythin' to do with junk; I say it now, and I don't want any of my family involved. Maybe Mr Carolla should bide his time, learn our ways, before he makes a decision I know his father would stand against.'

The meeting adjourned until the following morning. Roberto made his way back to his room and had only just closed the door when his phone rang. It was an invitation to a nightcap with Meyer Lansky and Salvatore Lucania, an honour indeed.

Roberto was impressed with the elegant penthouse suite. He accepted the brandy and Havana cigar. When they were all settled he was informed that Joseph Carolla was dying, and before his stroke he had named him as the heir to his family.

It was never a foregone conclusion that a son would inherit his father's position. Every don had to be voted in by the members, and often it was the most trusted man, the man with the most experience in the family's business, who was the next in line. At first, Joseph Carolla had wanted his son to take over, but they had fallen out in the past year.

It appeared that, for all the old man's bravado when he had last seen Roberto, he had, somewhere deep inside him, a certain distaste for a son who had no honour for his own country. Roberto learned that Paul was already dealing in drugs; in fact he had been throughout the war, even flying to Istanbul to set up connections there. Already shipments were coming into Milan for refining. Carolla junior had been more than busy, even paying Italian pilots to ferry the junk over to Africa during the time that Rommel was in control. He had been crazy with rage when the Americans moved into North Africa because it fouled up his route. It appeared that Paul cared nothing for anyone, not even his father.

The Organization had therefore unanimously agreed that, on the death of Joseph Carolla, Roberto Luciano would take over. They were impressed by his dedication, with the way he had run the black market and rebuilt his companies from scratch. His war record also counted strongly in his favour. But this now put an end to his hopes of going out on his own. It was a great honour to be made a don, one of the youngest ever ordained, but he couldn't suppress a terrible feeling of foreboding. He knew that Paul Carolla would be crazed with jealousy.

Joseph Carolla lay in an oxygen tent, breathing in shuddering rasps, his frail hands lying limply on the starched white sheet. He seemed aware that Roberto was by his side; his hand fluttered, lifted about an inch, and Roberto bent to kiss it. When he whispered his thanks the old man could only grunt, then he was convulsed in a coughing fit. The hiss of oxygen grew louder, and the mask steamed up.

Carolla's hand was clenched around his heavy gold ring. His eyes searched Roberto's face for a long moment as he uncurled his fingers, then they clouded over and the only sound in the room was the fading beep of the life-support machine. He didn't live to see the ring on his heir's finger or to kiss his ordained son, the young boy he had taken from the streets of Naples.

Roberto slid the ring on to his finger and walked out. He went immediately to Carolla's apartment, where he was met by two *capi* who kissed his hand and unlocked the doors. From the study he removed all the private papers, then went downtown to the old man's office and did likewise. Everywhere he went he was greeted unquestioningly as the new leader, with the respect Joseph Carolla would have wanted.

Roberto remained in New York for six months. In that time he saw Paul Carolla only once, at the funeral.

The ring was clearly visible on Roberto's hand, and Paul reached out to grasp his wrist. 'You will wear his ring until I am ready to take it, and I will, one day. You remember that: it belongs to me.'

CHAPTER 3

ONLY TWO years after Joseph Carolla's death, Luciano had proved that the old man had made the right decision, but the promise made to him to take care of his son Paul had reached breaking point. Ettore Calleah had warned him persistently that Paul Carolla must be kept in line, or made to toe it, and on the discovery that he had acquired a network of men, his own small family and was continuing to deal in narcotics Luciano at last had to make his presence felt.

Paul Carolla was ordered to be at the New York Luciano headquarters as Don Roberto was arriving from Italy specifically to speak with him.

Two hours before the meeting, a messenger delivered a handwritten note. Carolla apologized, but he would be unable to attend the meeting as his wife was expecting a child. As a true Sicilian and the father of four sons, Don Roberto would understand the importance of his first child being born in Sicily.

Paul Carolla, knowing Luciano would be in New York, realized it would be a perfect time for him to do his own business in Sicily.

Eva Carolla was a diminutive woman with a fiery temper and, although no one would say it to Carolla's face, she was the only person ever able to dominate him. He worshipped the ground she walked on. She had no inclination to accompany Carolla anywhere, preferring to remain in their Manhattan apartment, cooking and cleaning. She was insanely jealous of him, however, and it was a standing joke that, wherever he was in the world, he frequently rushed to the phone to call his 'Sweets', as he nicknamed her. Anyone privy to the cooing baby-talk and loud, smacking kissing noises found it hard not to laugh, but it was obvious to everyone that Carolla really loved his wife.

Eva 'Sweets' Carolla had argued against going to Sicily because of her pregnancy. She had been very sick during the early months and now she was suffering from hypertension. The flight to Rome was hell for Carolla, and the non-stop barrage of complaints during the journey made him fly into a rage at the airport arrival terminal, but as they crossed to the flight bound for Sicily, Eva Carolla collapsed and was rushed to the nearest hospital.

Carolla was near-hysterical at the thought of losing his child, and alternated between shouting abuse at the doctors and weeping as he paced up and down outside the delivery room. He could hear Eva screaming for him in torment, but he was refused entry, and shouted to her at the top of his voice that he was there, he was there . . .

Nearly four hours later Eva was still in the delivery room. Carolla sat in a sea of cigar butts and empty coffee cups, worn to exhaustion as though he himself was in labour. Sometimes he actually felt pains in his belly, terrible pains which doubled him up. Eventually he persuaded a passing doctor to take a look at him because he thought he was seriously ill. The young intern suggested that it might be indigestion, so Carolla sent his driver out for sandwiches.

Every time the delivery-room door opened he sprang to his feet, but eventually he was so numb from exhaustion that he could only sit with a hangdog look at the nurses, who shook their heads and smiled. Two other expectant fathers joined him, and when one of them was quickly presented with a son, Carolla gave him a $50 bill. Seeing the baby in the nurse's arms made him want to weep, and once again he began pacing and hovering at the double swing doors.

The second father was led away to the wards, beside himself at the birth of twins – worse still, twin girls. Carolla had shaken his hand and once again delved into his pockets to give him some money, but it dropped from his fingers when a masked surgeon appeared at the door. He removed his mask to speak.

The surgeon's voice was strained and quiet, his face concerned. 'Your wife is very sick. We have given her a transfusion, but she is still very poorly.'

Carolla searched the man's face, swallowing hard to enable himself to speak.

'What about the baby?'

Forgetting he was still wearing his theatre cap, the surgeon ran his hands through his hair, knocking the cap to the floor. As he bent to retrieve it, Carolla gripped his arm, twisting it up the man's back as if out of habit.

'What's the matter? For Chrissakes, tell me.'

The doctor jerked his arm free, rubbing it hard. 'You

have a boy. He has been taken to Intensive Care. I'm sorry, but I doubt very much if he will survive.'

Carolla held Eva's hand and tried to keep his voice steady. It was midnight. She had been a long time recovering from the anaesthetic, and now her eyes were heavy and she was so drowsy that she seemed not to know where she was. She was looking at him in a strange manner, as if she didn't know him, then her eyes focused.

'Paulie? Is that you, Paulie?'

'Yes, Sweets, it's me. I'm here. How ya feelin'?'

She licked her lips, and he took a damp facecloth and pressed it gently to her forehead. She closed her eyes and sighed. 'I told you I shouldn't have left New York, what did I tell you? But you wouldn't listen to me. I said, didn't I? I didn't wanna leave New York.'

'Yeah, yeah, but I wanted you with me.'

She turned vacant eyes to him. 'I'll be better when we get home, I want to have the baby at home. They tell you when we can leave? I tell you, you wouldn't get this treatment in New York. Why did I let you bring me, tell me why?'

He was crying as he rinsed the cloth and replaced it on her head. 'Baby's born, Sweets, he's born.'

Her face puckered. 'I don't understand . . . He? You say *he*? I got a *boy*?'

'It's a boy, but he's not doin' too good. They got him in the Intensive Care Unit.'

Her face suddenly creased into smiles as if she hadn't heard what he said, and she clasped his hand. 'A boy? I wanna see him, Paulie, I wanna see him.'

Carolla looked helplessly at a nurse who had been

standing by throughout their conversation, and she came to the bedside. She took Eva's pulse, then tucked her hand back under the tight sheet, and spoke to her as if she were a small child. 'You can't see him just yet, we want to be fit and strong before we see our baby, don't we? Now then, you get some sleep, try to sleep and you'll feel much better.'

Obediently, Eva closed her eyes, already half-asleep. Drowsily, she said to her husband, 'Giorgio, we're gonna call him Giorgio . . . Night-night, honeybun, night-night.'

At three in the morning, the squat figure of Carolla was still sitting in the waiting room. A different duty surgeon came to the doorway and asked if he was Paul Carolla.

'I have some good news. Your little boy is still fighting, and he's got a strong will. I've come to take you to see him if you like.'

Carolla's face lit up and he followed the doctor along the corridor and up in the large service lift to the Intensive Care Unit on the second floor. The young doctor was humming Frank Sinatra's latest hit, drumming his fingers on the wall of the lift. They were met by the ward sister, who introduced herself and shook Carolla's hand, then led him along yet another corridor to her small office. She offered him coffee, but he shook his head impatiently.

'I just wanna see my son.'

Sitting down, she gestured for him to sit opposite her. Then, quietly, she told him what to expect. She felt it best that he be prepared. The child had been born with hydrocephalus, and his spine was twisted. Carolla stared, his mouth opening and shutting like a goldfish. He couldn't take it in, didn't really comprehend what she was saying.

'But he's all right? I mean, he's OK, isn't he?'

'He's alive, and he's a great fighter. We thought we'd lost him twice, but he has great spirit. So if you would like to put on this mask and gown, I shall be waiting outside for you.'

The white-clad figure looked even more comical as he stood in the corridor looking this way and that. His baggy trousers and two-tone shoes protruded from beneath a gown that was far too large even for him. The sister rushed from the ward, apologizing for keeping him waiting, and together they walked to where the warning lights of the unit flashed above the door.

They passed figures encased in glass and shrouded in oxygen tents. Heart monitors bleeped, medical gases hissed, and patients near death moaned softly. Then he heard a baby cry and stopped, looking at the sister. The cry was strong and he knew it was his son's.

She guided him to an observation window behind which lay the tiny, newborn Giorgio Carolla, whispering that he could not enter the booth or hold the child, but could see him. A nurse was in there with him all the time. Carolla pressed his hands to the partition and peered into the small cubicle. He said nothing, but his plump fingers spread wide and flattened against the glass. His body shook and he sniffed, his mask catching the tears as they rolled down his cheeks.

The child lay in the small incubator, his stick-like arms and legs splayed out. Tubes attached to his skull made soft, sucking sounds. A nappy swamped his miniature frame, and his tiny lungs were being pumped for him, the ribs heaving in and out. The angle at which he lay made it difficult to spot the curvature of his spine, but what could not be hidden was the grotesque size of his head. He was like a gargoyle, the wide eyes and flat nose dominated by the huge forehead.

Carolla gasped as though the breath had been punched out of him. He could say nothing, could not even meet the eyes of the nurse who smiled and gave him a thumbs-up sign, happy that this malformed creature was fighting to stay alive. Carolla had to get out, had to walk away from the sight. He pushed the sister aside as he half-stumbled in his haste.

The hospital chaplain was coming towards him, his face full of concern and sorrow. Carolla almost knocked him off his feet as he rushed past.

'My son, you should not . . .'

'That's my son, that . . . that *thing* in there! Don't you look at me like I was in need of fuckin' spiritual aid – what kinda god produces that? Fuck off!'

The chaplain looked at the shocked sister and gave a smile of understanding, then straightened his cassock and walked sedately to the cubicle. He looked in at the child, then closed his eyes and began to pray.

Carolla wanted to scream, to shout, howl at the injustice of life. His son, the child he and his little wife had prayed for to the Holy Virgin every night, was a nightmare. He did not wait to ask after his wife or speak to anyone. He couldn't get the sight of the face, the bloated, obscene face, out of his mind. Throwing his white gown aside he ran from the hospital, the mask still dangling from his neck by its ribbons.

He tried to get drunk, to forget his son's face, but the more he drank the more the misery flooded through him. He couldn't see how he could face Eva – how could he tell her what their union had produced? His heartache turned to fury the more he drank, fury towards anyone he could blame for what had happened. His men stood by, helplessly watching his torment.

The next morning he was told that his wife had died peacefully in her sleep. At least she had been spared the sight of the child she had wanted so desperately. He went through the funeral in a haze, allowing his closest men to see to everything, including choosing the casket.

The families of Sicily came out in force. The floral tributes numbered hundreds and, to add insult to injury, Roberto Luciano had sent one. He had received the news in New York, and had sent the wreath in good faith, but it was singled out by Carolla and tossed aside. Carolla's hatred of Luciano actually led him to insinuate that his enemy had somehow been responsible for Eva's death, a craziness which his men felt embarrassed about, but to keep the peace they said nothing to dissuade him.

They tried to make him at least see the child before he left, but he was adamant. The chaplain, who had already had one brush with Carolla, was a trifle fearful to press him further, agreeing to christen the child in the hospital chapel. Tentatively, he asked if Carolla had chosen a name.

'Call it Giorgio, no other name, just Giorgio.'

Still refusing to see the child, Carolla rented an apartment, under an assumed name, and hired two nurses to give Giorgio round-the-clock care. He also hired a housekeeper whose only point of contact with him was a post office box number in New York. The sick child was installed, having never even been held in his father's arms. When the arrangements were complete, his son hidden from sight, Carolla prepared to leave for New York.

He arrived at the airport drunk, and looking more dishevelled than ever. His suit was so creased that it hung in folds around his ankles, his belly protruded over his leather belt, and two buttons had burst from his shirt, displaying a grubby vest beneath.

He stood by the windows of the departure lounge with a glass of beer in his hand and watched the planes coming in and going out, waiting for his own flight to be called. His bodyguards stood to one side, very wary of interrupting his moody silences.

Carolla watched with dead eyes as the steps were rolled to the door of a plane below him on the tarmac. A stewardess hurried up the steps and the big door was eased back. He sipped his beer, not really interested, and stared at the disembarking passengers. Just as he was about to turn away, he saw the tall figure of Roberto Luciano emerging from the plane, looking immaculate in a charcoal-grey overcoat, his black hair glossy, and even from this distance his shirt looking whiter than white. His only hand luggage was an expensive leather briefcase. Everything about the man was vital, Carolla could actually feel his energy way up in the departure lounge. Luciano's confidence made the crumpled, over-weight Carolla feel so second-rate he wanted to vomit.

Carolla's men jumped to attention as he walked out of the lounge, wondering if they had missed the call for their plane. He snapped that he was just going to take a leak and they should wait for him.

He examined himself in the washroom mirror,

splashed cold water on his face and tried unsuccessfully to wipe the food stains from his tie. He looked like a bum, a bum with no one and nothing.

Returning to the door of the departure lounge he gestured for his men to join him. 'Let's go.'

'There ain't been nothin' called out yet, Paulie. I been listenin' in case I hadda come to the john for ya.'

Carolla jabbed him in the ribs. '*One*, you don't call me Paulie, it's *Mister* Carolla. *Two*, screw the plane, we're not leaving yet.'

'But everything's arranged at the other end.'

'So fuckin' un-arrange it! I'm not leavin', not until I paid my respects, so get your arses outta here.'

They booked into a hotel and Carolla immediately demanded to be taken to the best men's outfitters. His men trekked from one shop to another after him. He was like a man possessed; he bought a pale grey suit off the peg, a charcoal-grey overcoat, ten shirts, all white, and four pairs of shoes. He even bought new socks and handkerchiefs. None of his men could fathom what had straightened him out so fast. He gave instructions for all his old clothes to be tossed out, then ordered his men to clean themselves up, get a decent car, a Mercedes, and have it standing by. They were going out.

Roberto Luciano was looking forward to supper when his youngest son called that there was a car coming. Frederico loved to play with the intercom by the front door, although he had been told many times not to pick it up.

As Roberto looked over the banisters, Constantino ran into the hall. Roberto called, 'Have the gates been opened?'

Puzzled, because he was not expecting anyone, he told the boys to make themselves scarce and rang through to the gate. The guard told him that a Signor Carolla was waiting. Roberto hesitated a moment, then told him to let him through.

Graziella came to tell him that supper was ready. She knew immediately that someone was expected; a guard was in position ready to open the front door.

Carolla was impressed with the Villa Rivera. The grounds and gardens were beautifully laid out. He was also impressed with the security arrangements and the polite way the guards asked if they might search the visitors. It was a rule of the house; no one entered without being checked for weapons. Carolla chuckled, 'No one?' But he allowed himself to be searched.

They drove slowly up the winding gravel drive to the front of the villa. He spotted two more guards and smiled; the place was like a fortress.

He was relieved of his new hat, coat and gloves as he entered the house, and then Luciano greeted him, hand outstretched in welcome. Carolla smiled, pulling Luciano to him and giving him a bear-hug, then kissed both his cheeks.

Luciano indicated a chair for Carolla and offered brandy. Carolla accepted both, and eased his bulk into the big winged chair.

'Welcome to my home. I wish it had been under better circumstances; I was saddened by the news of your wife's death. It must have been very difficult for you.' Luciano was outwardly calm and genial, a good host.

He was conscious of the effort Carolla was making to ingratiate himself; he wanted something and Luciano knew it, but he remained charming, giving no hint of his private thoughts.

'If there is anything I or my family can do to lessen your grief, you only have to ask. I am sure your son will be a great comfort to you.'

Carolla's eyes betrayed nothing as he quietly thanked Luciano and replied that everything was taken care of, his son was in good hands. 'I will always be your friend, Roberto, but I ask of you a favour, one you cannot deny me. I am asking you to release me. I do not want to go against you, and I feel that, as man to man, we can come to some arrangement. My father treated you as his son so, as my brother, give me my freedom.'

Luciano remained silent.

Carolla continued, persuasively, 'I have been offered a position with the Gambino family, and I would very much like your approval. You must understand, Roberto, that to continue as we are would be impossible for me.'

Luciano hesitated, then he gave a brief nod. Carolla rose immediately, hand outstretched to thank him, but Luciano waved him back to his chair.

'I know you are still trading in narcotics, in junk, and I am totally against it. At the next general meeting I will again refuse my assistance to you or any of the families involved in these shipments. You know my feelings and I assure you they will not change, I shall continue to fight against it. I hope you and I shall never become enemies, that we can be friends even though we are still opposed to each other.'

He put out his hand and once again Carolla clasped him in the familiar bear-hug. The atmosphere lightened and Luciano smiled his approval, remarking on Carolla's new image. Unamused, Carolla snapped that Luciano was not the only one who dressed with style, that he realized the importance of being, and looking, respectable. 'You see, I have taken your advice, I owe you that at least.'

As they walked to the door, Luciano asked if Carolla would care to join him and his family for supper. Carolla declined, saying that he had to catch a flight the following day to New York and was thus to drive to Rome that evening, but he would hate to leave Palermo without having the pleasure of meeting Roberto's wife. Like everyone else, he had heard a lot about her and would like to pay her his respects.

He was taken aback by the warmth and the relaxed atmosphere in the large dining room. Although elegant, it had a great family feel to it. He paused, caught off-guard, in the doorway.

Graziella rose, smiling, from the table. She gave her hand to Carolla and he kissed it. Then she turned to the children; one by one, the boys rose from the table.

Frederico gave Carolla a cheeky grin. Alfredo, a little older, shook the outstretched hand, and Constantino walked around from the other side of the table to do the same. Michael, the eldest, was the last to be introduced. He was already, at ten, almost as tall as Carolla. He gave a small bow and shook hands, then asked his father for permission to go shooting rabbits the following morning. Luciano ruffled Michael's hair and said he would think about it, then left his arm draped casually around his son's shoulders.

Carolla's belly churned at the sight of the handsome, smiling boys. Four sons, and all he had was that *thing* in the apartment. He backed towards the door and bumped into the frame. Michael rushed to assist him, holding open the doors, and the whole family then walked with him to the front door.

The last thing Carolla saw as his car drew away was Luciano, surrounded by his four healthy sons. He slumped back against the seat, brooding, silent. His driver adjusted the mirror to see him staring into space, chewing his fat lip and muttering to himself.

Luciano, who had taken everything from him, also had a family, a loving wife and a beautiful home. His farms, his groves, his factories, flashed past the window as the car gathered speed, and Carolla's self-pity turned to bitter, twisted anger at the injustice. He clenched his fist. No one was going to find out about Giorgio. While he waited for the boy to die he would tell everyone he was perfect, that he was being brought up by relatives.

Carolla's sick, devious mind was working overtime. Luciano had shown his vulnerability, and when the time came for Carolla to reclaim his inheritance he would attack where it hurt most, through Luciano's beloved sons.

CHAPTER 4

AT THE Villa Rivera they were celebrating.
Michael, now eighteen years old, had won a
coveted place at Harvard, and this was his farewell party. When Graziella gave the signal the lights were
turned down and a cake, with eighteen candles, was
borne triumphantly into the drawing room.

Michael had surpassed all expectations of him. At
nearly six feet tall, he was a charming, delightful young
man, lithe and muscular with the fresh skin and vitality
of an athlete. He was going to study law, and his
godfather, Mario Domino, was the first to congratulate
him, and gave him a solid gold fountain pen.

The year was 1958. The villa was full of young people;
lights had been put up on the verandah and a small band
played popular songs. Michael was the life and soul of
the party, excited by the news of his own success, and
determined to go far. Graziella stood watching the
youngster 'bopping', as they called it, to the music, and
smiled up at her husband. His adoration for Michael was
obvious; he was bursting with pride. His son, Roberto
Luciano's son, was going to be a high-powered lawyer;
already he could see him in his New York offices. Given
a little encouragement Roberto would tell you he could

even see his son as president of the United States of America. Michael had always been in the limelight, not just at home but at school in Sicily, in Rome and even in New York, where he had studied at a military academy on Long Island. He did not stand out so much there as he did in his home town; with his blond hair and blue eyes he was taken for American born and bred.

If he had any fault it was his generosity. His openness made him exceptionally well liked and a sought-after companion, and he had an eye for the girls. He teased and flirted, but he knew enough not to get too involved with the local girls. His sexual adventures were confined to America, where he came into contact with the free and easy students. He more than enjoyed that freedom.

Roberto watched mother and son dancing together, their faces so alike, although Michael towered above his mother. When the dance was over, Michael cupped Graziella's face in his hands and bent to kiss her lovingly on the lips.

Graziella had tried hard not to favour Michael but, like her husband, the boy could lift her soul. She always called him her 'angel', though in fact he was no angel and never had been. He was a wild one, showing no fear of anything.

The house was quiet on Michael's last night. All the family were in their various rooms thinking about his departure the next day.

He could not sleep. Eventually he got up and sat by the window, thinking about the one girl he wished he could have invited to his party: Sophia Visconti.

He had first seen her in the local coffee shop while he

was with a group of friends. She had been clearing the tables and stacking the dirty crockery onto a tray. She was very young, her thin frame too big for her cheap black dress, the cotton worn so thin that the seams could be seen, giving her body a dark outline. She wore rubber 'flip-flops' on her feet and her heels were dirty with dust. Her big hands were already showing the results of being constantly in hot water, washing dishes. Her manner was different, as if she kept herself apart; it was actually shyness. There was nothing really special about her, and Michael might well not have noticed her except for a minor incident.

She was carrying the loaded tray towards the back of the café when one of a group of local boys by the jukebox stuck out his foot to trip her up. Off balance, desperately trying to save the tray, she had fallen sideways on to another table. The crockery smashed everywhere, and the couple seated at the table were covered in food scraps and cold coffee. The boy made a half-hearted attempt at an apology, saying it was an accident, but they were all sniggering.

The culprits sauntered out of the shop and gathered around their Lambrettas which were parked outside, then rode off with much shouting and laughter. Still Michael would not have paid much attention, but as he stood by the till to pay, the kitchen door swung open and the girl came to the counter. Without raising her eyes she calculated his bill on her fingers, then opened the cash register. When she finally looked up into his face, her hand held out for his money, he was so struck by her direct gaze, her almost haughty, childish manner, that he smiled. For a moment she looked puzzled, glancing around as if she wondered who he was smiling at, then gave him a shy, fleeting smile. It altered her whole heart-shaped face, and a dimple appeared in her cheeks like a painter's smudge.

A few minutes later, Michael was talking with his friends outside the coffee shop when he saw the girl leave the shop by the back door. She wore no shawl or jacket, and carried only a cheap pink plastic purse. She was crying, making no attempt to wipe away the tears that streamed down her face. He watched her hurry down the street and then pause, hiding her face against a brick wall, her shoulders shaking. When he placed his hand on her shoulder she cringed and turned away.

'Are you all right? Eh? Are you OK?'

She wouldn't look at him. Her thin hands flapped as if to say, 'Go away.'

'What's so bad that you have to cry into a brick wall, huh? Do you want to tell me? That guy in there, did he hurt you?'

She bit her lip hard, shaking her head, then turned to face him. She spoke without raising her head. 'I have to pay for the breakages. It was not my fault, but he will make me pay.'

He was surprised at her voice. It was husky, low, and very deep for so slight a girl. He replied, 'My name is Michael. Shall I walk with you?'

She looked at him then, and gave him that smile again. The dimple came and went, and she turned away. 'My name is Sophia, I am Sophia Visconti.' She said the name proudly, pronouncing the Sophia as if it was two words – Soph-ia.

They walked for a short while and then she stopped, saying it was not right for them to be seen walking alone. She held out her hand as if to shake. He bowed and kissed it, and when she withdrew it quickly he laughed, but her face was serious.

He saw her again when he settled up with the café manager for the damages. When she washed down his table, she whispered her thanks. Afterwards, he waited for her and this time they walked a little further together before she asked him to go. He learned that she lived with her widowed mother who suffered from emphysema, and had left school two years ago to try to support her. She was just fifteen years old.

When they parted, Michael walked a few steps and then turned back, calling after her, 'You know the big orchard? Near the garage? Maybe Sunday you'd like to meet me, about three o'clock?'

She looked back at him briefly and he didn't know if she meant yes or no, but he kept the date anyway.

He was sitting up on the orchard wall when he saw her, still about a quarter of a mile away, riding a bicycle. He stood up on the wall and shaded his eyes, waving delightedly, and when she took one hand off the handle-bars to wave back the bike wobbled and she crashed to the ground. He ran along the wall and jumped down near where she was lying, the bicycle on top of her. At first he thought she had injured herself, but she put her hands over her face and giggled. The giggle erupted into a throaty laugh.

'I always fall off, always . . .'

She had grazed her knee, and he dipped his handkerchief in a nearby well and gently cleaned it for her. She was wearing a print dress, its pale pink flowers faded, and a pink ribbon threaded through her freshly washed hair. It gleamed, thick, black and wavy, as it hung about her shoulders. Suddenly Michael thought his little waitress was the most beautiful girl in the world.

The orchard became their secret meeting place. Often he took small bunches of wild flowers for her, and once some chocolates. He had loved the way she hungrily devoured them, hugging the box to her and refusing to let him have a single one, laughing her now familiar, husky laugh as he chased her through the trees. He caught her in his arms and held her tightly, demanding a kiss, a single kiss, his treat as she would not let him have a chocolate.

He pressed her against the bark of a tree, holding her hands behind her back, teasing her, and she gave in. Closing her eyes she lifted her lips to him. They kissed sweetly, a young, innocent sweethearts' first kiss. When he opened his eyes he found her looking at him, deep into his eyes, and she slipped her arms around his shoulders and embraced him. The smell of her hair and the feel of her body against his made him shake all over, his heart beat fast.

'You have jewels for eyes, Michael. They are so blue, so clear, like precious stones.'

Her hand traced a path over his face, making his heart beat faster and faster . . . Overwhelmed, he spoke her name. 'Sophia . . . Sophiaaaaa . . .'

She darted away from him, running out of the orchard on bare feet, her long, thin, brown legs carrying her fast and easily. She sprang up on to the wall and looked down at him, hands on hips. 'I must go, Mama will be worried.'

She tipped her head to one side and asked if he would like to take tea with her and Mama one Sunday. He hesitated; he knew what it meant. If he accepted, her mother would automatically presume he was courting her daughter, and courting, of course, leads to marriage. She saw the doubt in his face and jumped down on the other side of the wall to pick up her bike. By the time he had climbed the wall she was scooting away down the road. He sat and watched until she was a small dot in the distance, flying along on the high, old-fashioned machine.

He stayed away from the coffee shop for two weeks. He wanted to see her, but at the same time he had no intention of marrying her. She was in his thoughts constantly, and on both Sundays he waited at the orchard hoping she would come, but she didn't.

He waited by her 'crying wall' for her to finish work. She had known for some time exactly who Michael was, and when she told her mother he might come for tea she had been so flustered that it brought on an asthma attack. They couldn't possibly entertain the Don's son in their single rented room! When Sophia had quietened her down she suggested that maybe they could meet him in the coffee shop. She was as ashamed of their 'home' as her mother was, and dreamed of getting a better place. She also dreamed of marrying a Luciano; there would be no more washing down tables.

As she tried to walk past Michael, he grabbed her hand. She wriggled free and turned to him, her face flushed. 'I am not good enough for you, Michael Luciano?

You are ashamed of me? So leave me alone, huh? I am a decent girl, don't play your games with me. You don't treat me with respect.'

'Sophia, I respect you, believe me I do. But I can't offer you marriage, not yet.'

Her eyes narrowed, then she tossed her head back. 'Then you don't follow me, you don't see me.'

'I'm going away, maybe for more than two years. How can I say what I will feel, what you will feel, on my return?'

Her heart felt like lead. 'You're going away?'

'Yes. I've been meaning to tell you. I want to meet your mother, I want to do the honourable thing, I do, but you must see that I can't . . . But I love you, and . . . look, this is for you.'

He held out a small box. She moved closer and took it from him, fingering the leather and examining it before she opened it to find a small, gold, heart-shaped locket on a chain.

'Will you take me for a drive in your car?'

'Sure. It's just up the road.'

It was the first time she had been in his car, and her face lit up. He drove the Ferrari fast through the country lanes, finally parking near their orchard. They kissed passionately, but she would not let him open her dress or let him move his hand further than her knee. She responded to his kisses and wept when, in anger, he struck the steering wheel with his fist and demanded to know why she would not let him touch her.

Her husky voice went shrill. 'Because I don't belong to you. I am not yours and if you think that buying me this, this chain, this heart, you can have your way with me, then you are wrong.'

He wrenched the chain from her hand and threw it out of the window, then started the car and roared off.

As they came near the coffee shop, he pulled over and leaned across her, flinging the passenger door open. She jumped out, slammed the door, and strode off down the road. He turned the car and was gone.

She knew now that he would never marry her, never had any intention of marrying her. Later that night she took her bicycle and searched the orchard until she found the gold heart. Then she returned home to the small, squalid room which was filled with the sound of her mother's chesty breathing.

And now, on his last night before leaving for America, he could not stop thinking about how cruel he had been. He found pen and paper, intending to write to her, but changed his mind. Instead he climbed out of his window and walked round to the back of the house.

One of the guards waved to him, and Michael put a finger to his lips. 'I'm going to slip out for a while. Have you got a bike I could use? I don't want to take the car and wake the family.'

He pedalled into Sophia's district of the town and parked the bike in an alley leading to the tenement building. He crept up the stone stairs and along the corridor, then retraced his steps until he was sure he had the right place. He tapped softly on the window.

Sophia opened the window and raised her hand for silence, then wrapped him in her arms. A moment later she slipped out, fastening her dressing gown over her cotton shift.

'Come for a last bike ride with me?' he asked.

They sneaked downstairs to the shed where she kept her old bike, and together they cycled to the orchard. She was deliriously happy, laughing as they wobbled hand-in-hand along the road. They propped their bikes against the wall. She shivered; her nightclothes were thin and she was barefoot.

They crept into the orchard and he spread his jacket on the ground for her to sit on. She knew what would happen, knew it was madness, but she couldn't stop herself. She loved him so much, he was her dream.

'I'll keep you warm, I'll make you warm,' he said as he wrapped her in his arms. As they lay together he whispered over and over how much he loved her, how much he had missed her, and she smiled. Then she pulled the golden heart from the neck of her nightdress by its fine gold chain.

'See? I came back for it . . .'

He was so touched that he hugged her until she felt she couldn't breathe, but it felt so lovely that she didn't mind. 'You can touch me . . .'

He propped himself on his elbow and looked down into her face, tracing her dimple. 'You sure?'

'Yes, I want you to.'

He untied the sash of her dressing gown and inched it away from her, slid the sleeves from her arms, then pulled the cotton shift upwards. Her body was like a young boy's, firm, but not as thin as he had thought. The smock was tight, and as he eased it up her small, pubescent breasts appeared like dark plums, the nipples dark brown, big, and rounded. He lowered his head and slowly kissed each one.

She moaned, wanting to feel his skin against her nakedness. He pulled his shirt off quickly, dragged his jeans down and got his shoes stuck in the legs . . . As he struggled, flinging his sneakers off, she covered his back with impatient, soft kisses. When he eventually rolled over her the warmth of his body made her sigh.

Their lovemaking was gentle. They explored each other, experienced each other, and finally lay close, arms and legs entwined, and promised undying love. He would write to her, send her gifts from America, and she promised to stay faithful. There would never be anyone else but him.

Next morning the chapel was filled with villagers who had turned out to say goodbye to the Don's eldest son, and as he came out into the brilliant sunshine they garlanded him with flowers.

Roberto had become a regular worshipper, enjoying the services and the warm feeling of his family standing beside him. He had done much for the parish and the village had benefited from his success because he remained among them, building his businesses with them. The farmers and factory workers alike looked upon him as *Il Papa*, and no one was ever turned away from his door. Unemployment and poverty in the area were things of the past. The Don employed more than four hundred workers in his canning factories. His dairies, fruit and vegetable outlets and slaughterhouses employed many more. There was a new school and an orphanage, and every single inhabitant had reason to thank him for his kindness. They had work, they had money, and they had a man they could turn to with all the problems of a small community. It formed them into a tight, loyal clan. The mere fact that Don Roberto had risen from amongst them and had become a multi-millionaire on their backs was to his credit; it was his right to make millions from his groves and his factories.

He had ordained many new *capi*, preferring to use men who had their own families and were therefore steadier and less inclined to violence. Indeed, the need for violence was abating, and the men appreciated it, warming to Luciano's more businesslike methods. Apartment buildings were purchased in America to house the men he imported from Palermo, so they were no longer herded into 'Little Italy'. They would not bite the hand that fed them. He was now the biggest exporter from Palermo and needed a lot of goodwill not only from customs but from the government itself. He did not have the Feds on his back or Interpol breathing down his neck.

A formidable man, Luciano had grown with his wealth. He was sophisticated, stylish, always immaculately dressed in suits and shirts tailored for him in London. His shoes were handmade in a small shop in Rome, which he subsequently bought out. In two years he had another thriving business, exporting Italian shoes to both the USA and Great Britain. Anything he touched seemed to turn to gold. In that year of 1958 he was a man who could say, without any doubt, that he was a happy man.

Paul Carolla had kept well out of Luciano's way, although their paths had crossed socially. There was no direct contact, but Luciano was well aware of Carolla's rise in the Organization. There were rumours that he was making headway on his own, and Luciano knew he had fallen out with the Gambino family, but as long as he kept himself on the other side of the Atlantic he saw no reason to antagonize what appeared to be a truce.

Carolla, on the other hand, was like a predatory animal, a lone hyena watching the pack devour the best meat – meat he was getting ready to pounce on.

On New Year's Day, 1959, Luciano received a courier from New York with a message to bring forward the quarterly meeting of the local delegates.

It came from none other than Paul Carolla. It was ominous in its brief, cryptic tone, and, to his fury, read more like an order than a request.

On the day of the meeting, Graziella was reading a letter from Michael with obvious delight. He wrote that he loved the college and had made many friends. Roberto smiled, but he seemed distant, and did not ask to see the letter before he left for Palermo.

The drive into town was uneventful, but he could not dispel the small, nagging cloud that seemed to hang over him.

A swarthy man was waiting at the reception desk to show him up to a suite on the fourth floor. Humiliatingly, he was searched, and his face was taut with anger as he was at last shown into the meeting room.

Eleven heads of local families were already seated around the table, leaving one place vacant for Luciano. At the head of the table, in a large, velvet-covered chair with heavily carved arms, sat Paul Carolla. As always, he shouted his greeting, levered his bulk from the chair and caught Roberto in his arms.

Extricating himself from the huge arms, Luciano surveyed Carolla. The man weighed at least twenty stone now. His bald head shone, his polished nails gleamed, and the shantung suit he was wearing, although it must have cost a fortune, was speckled with cigar ash and could not disguise the excess flesh. He had changed, but Luciano could not determine whether it was for the better. He doubted it. He decided it was too petty to complain immediately about the method of setting up the meeting or the body search. He would bring it up at a suitable time; right now he was interested to know why the gross Carolla had called them together.

With his cigar clamped in his teeth, Carolla bent to retrieve a battered suitcase from the floor. He unstrapped it and took out a wad of papers, which he then thrust dramatically to the centre of the table.

The men passed the papers around. The contents were, simply, a long list of figures – astronomical figures. Carolla leaned back, wiped the sweat from his top lip and sniffed. 'Those figures, gentlemen, are my earnings for one year.'

One of the delegates responded that anyone could type out a list and asked if Carolla had anything to substantiate the figures? Carolla laughed and delved into his case again, bringing out bank statements for accounts in Geneva, Cuba, the Channel Islands, and Brazil.

When they had been passed around, he replaced them in the case and tossed it aside. 'My friends, those figures represent my yearly take. I am now the single biggest heroin dealer in the world. I employ around five hundred guys to handle the stuff; shippin', refinin', organizin', then another two thousand or so that just work the streets. But I control the main supply, and now I am

106

nudging the cocaine dealers out. In time I'm gonna be the biggest dealer in everythin' worldwide. This money buys me protection, buys me runners, buys me delivery services and pays off the law. When you're dealin' in these sorta loads the fuckin' customs stick their big hands out, and even though I'm shellin' out left, right and centre, I'm still makin' more dough than you guys put together. *Capiche, amici*? Eh?'

Luciano said nothing, allowing the others to speak, to ask the questions uppermost in his own mind: 'So you're makin' big dough – what's that to us? What do you want from us?'

Carolla laughed, his jowls trembling. 'I don't want nothin', I'm givin'. I'm here to give you a cut.'

'Oh, yeah? An' what do you want from us for that cut?'

'Freedom in the ports, good, safe refineries, new methods of importing. Palermo's a perfect place for my main operations; you got ships comin' in an' out like a freeway, an' I want access. I already got men openin' up routes in London, England; I'm not just talkin' about the States – like I said, this is a worldwide project, an' I know some of you here have got very nice rackets goin'. Some of you have got big contracts in orange juice, olive oil . . .'

Luciano stubbed his cigar out carefully, attentive and eager to hear the other men's impressions. Were they all going to be hooked by greed, by the billions of dollars he dangled in front of them? They bit, leapt at it like salmon swimming upstream. They agreed too readily, offering trucks, cargo boats, shipping contracts. He was sickened; they would offer their daughters if need be. But of all the men there, Luciano was the big fish.

Even with their varied interests, he was the only one among them with established, thriving, legitimate export companies.

When they had all had their say, they turned to him, waiting expectantly for his reaction. He spoke quietly. 'Firstly, you had no right to call this meeting without my approval. In future I would appreciate being shown the respect I have earned.'

From the opposite end of the table, Carolla claimed to have the approval of every family in the United States. They had given him the go-ahead, and if Luciano wanted, he could call them all now. He pushed the telephone along the table.

Luciano was shocked at Carolla's unethical behaviour and gave him a long, cold stare, then continued in the same calm voice, 'If what you say is true I will find out for myself tonight. Secondly, you can take these figures and shove them up your arse; it's big enough and wide enough to take the whole table. You have always known my feelings on narcotics and they haven't changed. If you vote, gentlemen, to go in with Carolla, then you do so without me and without my companies. I will not be forced into any agreement. I warn you, the Feds, the customs, will turn against us so hard that none of you will survive, and Interpol will move in on every business we have. Right now you are all earning good money, making big profits – I have sons of my own, you all have children, good, strong, healthy children. Don't join, don't encourage this sickening trade, I beg you.'

Some of the men seemed to hesitate, but they had made their decision. It was all very fine for Luciano to say they were making great profits, but for some of them it hadn't been that easy. So they voted against him, and Luciano walked out, the only man not to join Carolla.

Luciano was prepared for repercussions, so that night he called New York and Los Angeles, then Chicago, but in the end he gave up. It seemed everyone had been caught by Carolla's greed; they were all going into the narcotics trade. At least Carolla had been honest about that. Luciano was badly shaken, seeing how fast the other families had sided with Carolla, leaving him out on his own. He knew Carolla would make an attempt to oust him, though the question was how he would go about it. Which of his men would Carolla lure away? Could everything he had built up be so easily smashed? Luciano would not believe that his men would betray him, and in refuting the idea he gained confidence.

But Ettore Calleah, his right-hand man, who had always warned him to watch out for Carolla, confirmed Luciano's fears. This situation with Carolla was explosive and if Luciano was to stand against him, he would stand against all the main families, in both America and Sicily.

An old soldier, Calleah could smell the danger. 'I don't think any of the families wants a public war, but he's cornered you, leaving you no alternative. You've got what they want.'

Luciano murmured, 'There is always an alternative. I have no intention of letting Carolla move in on my territory, he does not speak for the entire Organization. I have built this company from nothing, for my sons, and I have paid my dues to the Organization. If they cannot protect one of their own, then there is no honour, no justice. If I take on Carolla without their permission, I become no better than he is. I am what he wants, everything I have is what he wants, and it would not stop by simply giving in to his present demands. If I give him an inch he will take everything I possess.'

Calleah did not argue. He knew Carolla was an outsider, he obeyed no one's rules. For now all he could do was protect Don Roberto to the best of his ability.

One month later, the Commission met and Paul Carolla was overruled. Luciano was jubilant; justice had been done without bloodshed. But Calleah knew it was only a stay of execution, not a reprieve.

He was right; Carolla had already made plans. But it was Michael Luciano, not his father, who would pay the penalty.

CHAPTER 5

GIORGIO CAROLLA was washed and dressed hours before his father was due. He knew it was a waste of time as he would need to be changed again, but the nurse had insisted, as she had many other chores to do before Carolla arrived. The housekeeper had laid out all the household accounts for Carolla to examine and given the apartment a thorough clean, spraying air freshener everywhere to counteract the pervasive stench of urine from the child's room.

He had spent months in hospital after his birth. As they had predicted, the tiny boy was a fighter; he fought simply to stay alive. They had drained the fluid from his brain and eventually he was able to leave the incubator. He could never lead a normal life; even with operations on his spine his condition would gradually deteriorate. The doctors had given him a lifespan of maybe ten to twelve years.

And now he was nine years old, his head so enlarged that he could not lift it from his pillows without help. He was a very bright little fellow and had developed a strange sense of humour, bitter rather than sarcastic, to combat his terrible disabilities. His room was filled to the ceiling with toys and games, most of them hardly touched. All he was interested in was books. He read avidly; it was the only pastime he enjoyed. In books he could lose himself, use his fertile imagination.

He dreaded his father's visits. He never knew what to say, and found his father's inability to even look at him a trifle idiotic.

The more he recognized his father's horror of his deformity, the more ridiculous Giorgio found him. In fact, little Giorgio Carolla had little affection for his father in any way. He had been brought up, or 'hand-reared', to quote him, by a succession of nurses and housekeepers. He had stopped caring about them, stopped himself caring, because it was so painful when they left, although he had made up many excuses for what were often simple situations. No nurse liked to dedicate herself solely to one patient, no housekeeper wanted always to care for someone else's home, and when the domestic staff came and went with increasing regularity, little Giorgio found it safer not to have any feelings whatsoever.

He rarely went out, finding it too much of a strain and too uncomfortable. He hated to be stared or laughed at so as he grew older the apartment in the exclusive block became little more than a prison.

During one of his many stays in hospital, it was discovered that he had a small hole in his heart. When he was told about it, he looked into the concerned face of the young house surgeon and, deadpan, asked if he should curtail his training for the Olympic marathon. The doctor had roared with laughter, and this encouraged Giorgio's gift for repartee as he laughed along with the doctor. How could anyone possibly expect someone as messed up as he was to have a perfect heart? It stood to reason that he would be as screwed up inside as he was outside.

Intellectually, the child was far advanced for his age and was as hungry for conversation as he was for his books. But he had had to content himself with books until Father Orlandi, the elderly local priest, came to visit. The boy was thirsting for education, and the books his housekeeper brought him were never enough. Father Orlandi had taken the unprecedented action of writing to Giorgio's father for permission to teach him.

As well as Father Orlandi, Carolla provided Giorgio with two other tutors, also priests who taught at the local school. At last the boy's thirst for knowledge was being quenched, and he was content. The priests found their pupil very rewarding and did not consider their duties a chore, far from it. The boy's mind was so active that at nine years of age he was catching up on the able-bodied twelve-year-olds at the school, and would soon outstrip them.

Oblivious of the pain in his shoulders and the constant ache and buzzing in his head, like a sleepy bee trapped in his skull, Giorgio read with an avid persistence. He delighted in rolling new words around his vast cranium, and sought opportunities to put them to use. He often flummoxed the staff with his new-found expressions.

'Nurse, I have a severe problem with my perineum.'

'What?'

'My perineum – good God, you're a nurse! It's the area between my anus and my shrivelled genitalia – it's itching.'

'Yes, I'm sure it is. Well, get your talc puffer and see to it yourself.'

Periodically, he would have severe fits of depression

when even reading was too much for him, although his tutors never saw these bouts. His joy when they arrived for his lessons lifted their hearts. They knew that knowledge was Giorgio's entire life and that books represented parents, brothers and sisters for him. But Father Orlandi saw the other side of Giorgio when he tried to give him religious instruction. He threw the prayer book he'd been given across the room and screamed, 'Don't give me fucking psalms when I want revolution, you idiot! Don't feed me with Christ, the Holy Bloody Virgin! I hate Jesus, I hate the Virgin – she made me like this so fucking screw her and her fucking virginity!'

Shocked, Orlandi got down on his knees to pray. Giorgio sighed, informing the man that he was even more foolish than he had given him credit for. There was no heaven, no hell. Glaring, still on his knees, the priest asked what Giorgio felt there was.

The small boy closed his eyes and spoke softly. 'There is nothing, Father, nothing beyond darkness, emptiness. That's all there is. Don't you think I, of all people, would need to believe otherwise? Yet I don't, and I will be enveloped in that darkness long before you.'

At times he spoke not like a child but a bitter adult. It made Father Orlandi uneasy – how could he argue with such a young mind, a mind that knew nothing but what he had read, a boy who had never left the apartment? All he could do was bring more books of religious teachings and punish the child by withdrawing his treasured lessons.

When Giorgio was told he would get no lessons for a week he stared with that strange look in his eyes and said, 'You see, you take away from me the only thing I live for and you call yourself a man of God.'

So Giorgio's self-hatred began to cut him off from his lessons, the one thing he adored. His decline was slow, but steady. When his father arrived in Palermo for his meeting with the delegates and, most importantly, Roberto Luciano, Giorgio was rushed to hospital. Carolla was unable to see him immediately because of the meeting, and after Roberto walked out he was so enraged that his son's illness took second place.

When he did finally arrive, the doctors could not tell Carolla how long Giorgio had to live. They had not seriously considered that he would last as long as he had, but the boy was a . . .

Carolla interrupted. 'You bastards tell me one more time, just one more time, that he's a fighter, and I swear to God I'll break your fuckin' necks. You show me a fighter that looks like that poor sonofabitch, you show me, make me understand why you didn't let him die the day he was born. I don't wanna hear about him being a fighter, *I don't wanna hear*!' He pounded the wall with his fist, then stormed out to sit fuming in his car. How come it had happened to him? Why him? And why, why was the boy still alive, with so much against him?

'Your kid all right, Mr Carolla?' asked the driver.

Pursing his lips, Carolla pulled himself together. 'Yeah, yeah . . . just appendix, nothin' to worry about.' He bit a piece off his thumbnail and spat it out. 'Drop me off at the Ornella.'

At the whorehouse he asked for the blonde he had used a year ago, but couldn't remember her name. As he turned, however, sweeping the cheap nylon velvet curtains aside, she walked in.

Lydia Damienco sidestepped Carolla, not remembering him. She was a little afraid when he grabbed her arm, peering up into her face. When she made to pull away from him the madame gave her a fluttering hand signal.

'Lydia, this gentleman has asked specially for you.'

Feeling foolish, Carolla released her arm and eased his tie back up to his collar. 'Maybe you don't remember me. It was about a year ago . . . Mr Brunella?'

Lydia smiled as if in recognition, but for all she knew he could have said he was Jack Kennedy. She ran her eyes over him quickly; the expensive suit, the cashmere coat. The cash register in her brain pinged. This one had dough, she could smell it.

The doorman at the hotel gave Lydia the once-over, knowing immediately she was a hooker. She was impressed by the suite of rooms, and hung up her coat in the wardrobe, noticing the array of expensive suits and shirts.

Carolla came out of the bathroom, tying his silk dressing-gown cord. He looked even shorter than before, and she wondered if he wore lifts in his shoes. Lydia went to the bathroom and found his clothes strewn across the floor. She listened a moment at the door before going through his pockets. When she discovered his wallet, she could not believe the amount of cash that was stuffed inside. There was no identification, no cards, just a thick wad of dollars and an even bigger fold of lire. It took all her self-control not to remove a single bill. There was no doubt of her client's financial situation; she knew she had struck lucky, and had every intention of making him pay through the nose.

She combed her hair, washed her armpits and crotch, then found some cologne and splashed it all over. She still had a good body, curvaceous, even if her tits had begun to sag slightly. When she had finished admiring herself in the mirrored walls, she put on a hotel dressing gown and went back to Carolla.

She perched on the edge of the bed. 'Nice hotel . . . Like you said, it's my lucky night.'

He reached up and pinched her chin between his fingers. 'You don't remember, do you, slag?'

'What?'

'Last year, I took you to see my son. You met my son, and you know something? You are the only person I ever allowed to meet him – you, a whore. Now why did I do that, huh?'

'What? I don't speak English.'

He flopped back and covered his face with his arm. Speaking in Sicilian, he repeated that he had taken her to see his son, he was a cripple.

She remembered then, the strange chimp of a child cringing in a bed, and felt uneasy. 'Yes, yes, I met him. How's he doing?'

'He's in hospital. Had an operation for a hernia, poor little bastard.'

Apart from his wife, Carolla had only ever been with whores. Up until now, his lovemaking had consisted of a quick in-and-out job, then count out the bills and have a wash. Intercourse with his wife had been little different, except that she rarely removed her nightdress, believing sex was a duty rather than a pleasure. They had both been brought up Catholic and, although he hardly ever went to church, he accepted the values he had been taught. As his sex drive had never been particularly strong

117

he was satisfied, and no one had ever given him reason to change. Now he routinely unfastened his dressing gown to reveal his erect penis, and Lydia nearly shocked the life out of him by going down on him. He gasped, about to give her a backhander, but the sudden surge of pleasure stayed his hand. He relaxed and let her continue.

Lydia was determined to give him the works. She knew he had the money and would pay well. While she sucked and moaned, she calculated that if she played her cards right, she might even get him to set her up in her own little place.

The excitement of thinking about it was actually beginning to turn her on. She grabbed his hand and pushed it down to her crotch, pressing his fingers into the damp cleavage, moaning all the while. Mentally, she was decorating her new bedroom when she finally eased him into her. It would be draped and frilled . . .

She came with a howl of pleasure as she pictured the marble bathroom. 'Oh, baby,' she gasped. 'You are the best, the best . . .'

Stunned, Carolla lay back, thinking, *Shit, what've I been fuckin' missin'*?

Lydia stayed all night. Carolla was insatiable, he couldn't keep his hands off her, and she kept up her cooing encouragement. By morning he was so exhausted he could hardly move, but at the same time he felt such a sense of achievement, got such a kick out of his own sexuality, that he was in a wonderful mood.

She dressed, feeling a trifle edgy. Carolla was still in his dressing gown, not wanting her to leave but unsure what to do with her. She had given his life a new dimension and he was afraid to lose it, and her. In the harsh light of morning she didn't look quite so young,

118

but just looking at her as she outlined her mouth in plum-red lipstick turned him on again.

'Well, I'd better be on my way.'

Carolla sprang to his feet, looking around the room for his wallet. Remembering it was in the bathroom he went to collect it, and realized she had not touched a note. When he came out, she was buttoning up her cheap coat with the fake fur cuffs and collar. He smiled at her and handed over a wad of money without even counting it. Her eyes flickered and she tucked it securely in her cheap plastic purse.

'You wanna stay around? Maybe go shopping?'

Lydia hesitated. She was tired, and would need a good sleep before she could think of going back to work. But maybe she really had struck lucky. If she worked on him she could make enough to lay off for a whole week. Forcing a smile she said, 'OK.'

He took her to shops where she had only ever been able to gaze longingly through the windows. Lydia was close to tears, hardly able to believe it was really happening when he placed a mink around her shoulders and she wept openly, flinging her arms around his neck and kissing him. To the astonishment of the sales assistant, Carolla paid for the coat in cash.

Followed by two bellhops carrying the boxes of clothes he bought for her, they visited the shoe department and finally the lingerie section. Carolla was behaving like a kid, picking up the delicate black bras and panties, feeling the see-through nightgowns. Insisting that Lydia try them on in the little changing room, he followed her in and drew the curtain. He kissed her breasts and pressed her up against the wall, as she curled her legs around his back. The entire lingerie department

119

could hear the rhythmic pounding through the thin partition.

With their purchases piled around them, they made their way back to the hotel. Carolla's driver watched them in the mirror, smooching and petting, and couldn't believe what he saw. The old tart looked real beat, but Carolla was in the highest of spirits.

Carolla walked into the bedroom and looked at Lydia. She was deeply asleep, her mouth slightly open, hands curled at her cheek. He felt an immense protectiveness towards her, suddenly he did not want to lose this woman. He sat on the edge of the bed and stroked her hair. She moaned and turned over in her sleep, and he kissed her forehead.

Carolla believed she was special, he needed someone to share his heartache, someone who knew, and he made up his mind to open his heart to her. Once the decision was made he felt somehow relieved.

He glared down at her. 'I don't want you fuckin' any other guys, understand me?'

She shrank back against the pillow, afraid of what he might do to her. She was completely taken aback when he asked, 'Have you gotta go back to that whore-house?'

'No, it's on commission. We do as we please.'

'Right, it's settled. You stay with me, stay here until I get you a place.'

He was offering her what she had dreamed of, but never believed would happen. Somewhere she did have a husband, and two kids, but they were in the past, so far past that she had blanked out that part of her life. There was nothing to go back to, no one to care if she lived or died.

'I'm going to trust you, Lydia, trust you like I don't trust no one else. My name is Paul Carolla, but the kid is listed under another name at the apartments. I never want anyone to know his real name. Now you know. Like I said, you are the only person I've ever told, and if you were ever to break that trust I would kill you.'

It was chilling, the way he said it so matter-of-factly. It frightened her, and she knew that he meant it.

Giorgio was carried from the ambulance into his apartment, where the nurse was waiting. He was tired from the short journey, and she made him comfortable in his bed, but as soon as she closed his door Paul Carolla and Lydia arrived, laden with suitcases.

The nurse took one look at Lydia and her face set, but she did not dare say anything. Paul told her that Lydia would be staying until the new housekeeper arrived, or until she had found herself an apartment close by. Hearing his father's voice brought Giorgio back from his light sleep, and he was about to call out when he heard Lydia laugh. He listened, ears cocked.

The door opened and to the boy's amazement his father ushered Lydia in, his arm around her shoulders. He was obviously in good spirits, smiling broadly. Giorgio gave a small smile, impressed that Lydia was able to look at him as though he were normal.

'Lydia's gonna stay a while until she's found a place, and . . . wait, wait until you see what I got out there.'

Giorgio's face lit up and, ignoring Lydia's presence, he asked if Carolla had brought the books he wanted.

'No, no books! I got you a TV set, a big TV set, one of the biggest they make. Tell you what I'll do, I'll get it all rigged up for you before I go.'

The boy's face registered disappointment, and Lydia asked him, 'Don't you like TV?' as if he were a three-year-old.

'I prefer books. Did you order them, Father? The ones I asked for?'

'Hey, one thing at a time, all right? Lemme get the TV fixed up.'

He bustled out of the room while Lydia pulled up a chair and sat near the end of the bed. She looked around the room, unable to understand how he could want even more books when the room was already spilling over with them. They were stacked on every available surface, and the bookcases contained as many paperbacks as a shop.

'Can you see it OK from there, Giorgio?'

The TV set loomed at the end of his bed when he opened his eyes, and he nodded. He could see it, but to turn it on and off would mean calling the nurse; it was too difficult for him even to wriggle down the bed to get at the controls. He was now surrounded by people, a record player and a TV set, and he began to laugh.

'He's laughing, Paulie! See, I told you he would like it. Wait until he sees what else we've brought him.'

The nurse raised an eyebrow at Giorgio then stood, arms folded, watching Carolla as he struggled with the plug. Giorgio tried to show enthusiasm, but he was desperate to pee. He looked helplessly at the nurse, who did her best. 'I think perhaps Giorgio's tired. He's only

122

just arrived back from the hospital, you know, and he should rest.'

'He can rest all he wants when I've gone. I've only got an hour or so, and I want him to see his TV. Why don't you go an' make up the spare bed for our guest . . . You hungry, honey?'

Lydia shrugged and said she would like a coffee, and the sour-faced nurse left the room. Sighing, Giorgio gave in and wet himself as the television burst into life. Carolla applauded the set as if he had invented the whole thing rather than just attaching a plug. He pulled Lydia's chair over and sat in front of it to adjust the sound and the vertical hold.

Lydia stood resting her hands on Carolla's shoulders and turned, smiling, to Giorgio. 'You like it?'

The child nodded as the urine seeped into the sheets, soaking his nightshirt and stinging his chapped legs. He could do nothing but remain lying in it; the bedsores that had just healed in the hospital would no doubt open up again. He had to lie in discomfort for another three-quarters of an hour while coffee and biscuits were brought and consumed, and the three made polite, if strained, conversation, interrupted by the intrusive, flickering screen.

Giorgio again asked his father if he could have the books he had asked for as soon as possible. He was very grateful for the television, but if he couldn't sleep at night when the TV station had closed down, he liked to read. A little irritated, Carolla checked his watch and mumbled that he didn't have time to go and order any books. Lydia suggested quickly that it would be easier if they opened an account at the best bookstore in town and then all Giorgio had to do was pick up the phone and order what he wanted.

Giorgio's face shone with delight and, for the first time, he showed some vitality. His small hand reached out for his father's. 'Yes? Would you arrange that? I would love it.'

Carolla smiled and nodded, then kissed Lydia, telling her she was a clever girl. They smiled meaningfully at each other, and then she left the room. Carolla winked at his son and told him he was just going to have a wash and brush-up.

Giorgio, obviously, had no knowledge of the sex act beyond what he had read in books. His fantasies centred innocently around a fictional self, a boy who had many adventures and many friends; a handsome boy who could play football. When he heard moaning from the room next door he had no idea what it was.

The nurse entered the room to take the tea tray. 'I wasn't employed to cook and wash up, you know, and if she thinks I'm going to wait on her hand and foot, then she's in for a shock.'

The sound of Carolla's orgasmic moan made the crockery on the tray rattle, and she stood rooted to the spot. Her thin lips pursed tightly in disgust as Lydia's gasping crescendo was heard through the thin walls, accompanied by the knocking of the headboard against the partition.

'Oh, my God! I knew it as soon as I saw her! You know what she is, don't you?' She turned to the wide-eyed boy. 'She's a whore, he's brought his whore here! Well, I won't stand for it, I won't.'

'Could you change my linen, please? I'm afraid I've had a slight accident.'

'Why didn't you call me? They were clean sheets. And if you think I am going to come in and out of here to turn this TV on and off when you want, then you can think otherwise.'

Giorgio lifted his thin arms while his girl's nightdress was pulled over his head. Stark naked, his pitifully shrunken and twisted trunk looked so vulnerable and marble-white he resembled an alien creature more than a human being. Just as the nurse was about to slip a clean shift over his huge head, Carolla walked in, followed by the giggling Lydia.

They stopped in the doorway, then had the decency to back out and close the door. The sight of the child quietened them both, and she reached out her hand as if to comfort him, but he pushed her away, so roughly she banged into the wall.

'I'll be back.' He slammed the front door behind him, and hurried into the street. He kept on walking until he found a phone booth.

Juan Borsalino, along with his brother Philippe, had started work on opening a new refinery and had been expecting his call. Juan fully understood the coded message he was passing on: the package was on the plane and scheduled to arrive later that day from New York. Borsalino gave Carolla the flight details, but knowing the Organization had warned Carolla to stay out of Palermo so as not to aggravate the situation with Luciano, he suggested that Carolla keep well away from the airport. Carolla snapped that when he wanted an opinion he would ask for it. His voice sounded choked. 'My son is sick, he's just got out of hospital; now put Lenny Cavataio on and shut the fuck up.'

Carolla arranged to meet Lenny at a club he owned called the Armadillo. The seedy nightclub was in a rundown part of the city centre, and was one of Carolla's headquarters. The dive was run for Carolla by Enrico Dante, and used to launder drug money.

Dante listened as Carolla ordered him to open accounts in various stores for Lydia, in her name, as well as accounts in the book departments and all known book stores. He enquired if his new girlfriend was an intellectual, and Carolla growled that the accounts were for his son. As he said the word, he remembered the child's twisted, malformed body and banged his fist down on the bar. 'His name is Giorgio, make them out in his name and make sure he gets what he wants delivered.'

'OK, what's the address?'

'Just his name, Lydia will sort out the rest.'

Dante could make no further enquiries because Lenny Cavataio had arrived, and Carolla had waved his fat hand for him to get lost. Lenny was furtive and very ill at ease. He repeated that the package was on the plane, and would expect to be met, but he didn't like it and he didn't want to be the one at the airport. He jabbed Carolla with his finger, to warn him that he shouldn't be there either. Carolla nearly snapped his finger off, forcing it backwards, and making Lenny howl with pain.

'I spent a lot of dough, a lot of time arrangin' this and nobody is gonna fuck it up, understand me? You hand over what he wants, that's all you will be doin'.'

Carolla released Lenny's finger, and he shook his hand, the pain excruciating. 'Yeah, but you an' I know the stuff'll kill him.'

'That's the intention, Lenny, an' you make sure he gets it, now get the fuck out of here.'

*

126

Carolla decided not to return to the apartment. Somehow he couldn't face his son, and so he called from the club to say he had to leave earlier than expected. Lydia cooed and whispered that she would pine if he was away for too long, and was not amused when Carolla said she would find herself in a pine box if she cheated on him. Then he softened and told her that he had arranged the accounts for her and Giogio. She was to say goodbye to Giorgio for him and tell him he was sorry but he had to be at the airport. Even as he said it he couldn't stop himself smiling, just as no one could stop him from being there, from seeing Michael Luciano alight from the plane.

Sophia returned to work the day after Michael left, and her life was much as usual. Every day she checked the postbox to see if a letter had arrived from him, and when she found nothing she made the excuse that letters were bound to take a long time to come from America.

Her mother's health had deteriorated, and the doctor said she must go to the seaside if possible. Sophia had no option but to arrange for them to stay at the small village of Cefalu, with relatives. She left her forwarding address both at the post office and the coffee shop.

Her mother was now too ill even to pack her own belongings, and the upheaval of the move prevented Sophia from paying any attention to her own health. No sooner had they arrived at the seaside than she began to feel sick and dizzy, often having to sit down for a while to recover. She had been unable to find work for the first few weeks, but eventually obtained a position as a maid at a small hotel in the village. It meant getting up in time to be at work at five-thirty in the morning to make up the beds and wash the linen. She began to be sick regularly.

She put off consulting the doctor, although he made regular calls to her mother, who had not benefited as they had hoped from the move. The conditions they were living in did not help; they had been given a room, on the first floor of the already overcrowded house, which was far from satisfactory. The arrangement was meant to be a temporary one, and although the family tried not to show that their guests were outstaying their welcome, it was obvious they were putting a strain on the household. Money was short and rents expensive, but at last she found a suitable room above a bakery. Her spirits lifted and she hurried home.

An ambulance stood outside the house. Sophia ran the last few yards, arriving as they carried her mother out on a stretcher. She wore an oxygen mask to help her breathing, and her frightened, tired eyes showed gratitude as Sophia, gasping for breath herself, climbed into the ambulance with her.

'It's all right, Mama, I'm here, I'm here.'

Fighting for breath, Signora Visconti smiled behind her oxygen mask. 'He'll write to you, he'll come back for you. You are a good girl . . .'

Her hand tightened on her daughter's and then she sighed. Her grip relaxed. Sophia turned to a nurse who was standing by the oxygen cylinder.

'I think my mother is dead.'

The funeral expenses took what little savings they had. The family were kind and caring, but not too upset when

128

Sophia said she would still move to the room she had found. She had not received one letter from Michael, but she still had the small gold heart.

She lay on the double bed that would have served her mother and herself and moved her hands slowly over her body, her belly. She could feel it growing, she could pretend no longer, but she would not face up to it until the doctor confirmed that she was indeed pregnant.

Having heard of the situation, her aunt paid a visit. When asked if there were any chance that the father could be made to marry her, Sophia shook her head. Perhaps if it had been any other boy, an ordinary boy, but not a Luciano.

'You know whoever it is should be made to take the responsibility? Does he know?'

Again Sophia shook her head. She refused to say his name, or a single word against him. At the local convent, which had a maternity ward, the Mother Superior was kindly and understanding. She listened to Sophia without interruption, and agreed to let her stay until the birth. Sophia could help with the laundry and cleaning in return for her keep. Then she suggested that the baby be taken, immediately after birth, for adoption. Sophia's aunt had too many children already and could not take another. He or she would have a better chance in life after adoption than Sophia, a poor and unmarried mother, would be able to give it.

Sophia worked hard in the laundry, washing the sheets from the small clinic and starching the nuns' white collars. There were several other girls in the same situation as herself, plus some married women whose husbands were away or in jail. She made only one friend, a skinny girl called Raina, whose father had sexually abused her. The police had brought her to the convent for shelter.

Raina was nine months pregnant. The other girls teased her, and Sophia often discovered her crying at the back of the drying room, huddled against the boiler. She promised that she would visit Raina in the maternity ward when her baby was born and when, a few days later, the girl went into labour, she screamed for Sophia.

The ward was understaffed, with only one doctor, one midwife and two nurses. They allowed Sophia to stay with the terrified, wailing girl until she was wheeled into the delivery room. Heavily pregnant herself, Sophia waited, and was the first person the girl saw when she was taken back to the ward.

Later that night, unable to sleep, Sophia sat at her small window overlooking the courtyard. She noticed a couple being admitted by the gatekeeper and led into the main building. She returned to her bed and dozed, but was woken soon after by the sound of a baby crying in the courtyard. When she looked out of the window, she saw the young couple leaving, but now the woman carried a bundle in her arms. Sophia wondered if it was Raina's child, and if this would be how her own child would leave the convent. For the rest of the night she paced her room, sleepless, and by morning she had decided she would keep her baby.

That morning, Sophia collapsed and was taken to the doctor. The baby was not due for another week or so, but she was physically exhausted. The doctor prescribed rest and no more work in the laundry. He was a kind, elderly man who felt compassion for the many girls in his care.

When Sophia asked after Raina, he assured her the girl was well and would no doubt see her soon. She would be remaining at the convent and working in the kitchens.

'What about her baby?'

'I don't think that, dear, is any concern of yours.'

'Was it taken from her? Did she see it?'

He sighed, and told her that Raina's daughter had been adopted by a good, hard-working couple. 'Perhaps in time our little Raina will find a husband. In the meantime we can watch over her, give her an education, a chance of a life of her own.'

'But that life she gave away, what about her child?'

'Raina is no more than a child herself. Her circumstances are very different from yours. Do you want to keep your baby, is that what all these questions are for? Please don't think anyone here wants you to do something you'll regret, it is entirely your own decision. But you must make up your mind soon, because we will have to make arrangements. What about the father? Is there some reason he can't marry you, cannot take responsibility?'

'Is there any way I could stay on here with the baby, until I can speak to him?'

'Sadly, that is impossible. You must look at it from our point of view. We do not have the money to keep every unmarried mother with us. As it is we are dependent on charity to even exist . . . There is one alternative, another orphanage that might take your baby if you could provide the means to support it. They would keep it until you made up your mind, and then perhaps you

131

could get work in the vicinity so you could keep in touch with the child. I don't advise this arrangement in the long term, but I think I could organize it for you.'

She clasped his hand and kissed it. It was a chance, like a stay of execution, and she would at least try to speak to Michael, or a member of his family.

Her spirits lifted, Sophia began to plan how she could save enough money for her train fare to Palermo after the birth. She calculated in months because Michael had said he would be away for at least two years. She wanted to see him face to face and her pride would not let her go to him like a waif with a babe in arms. She would not beg, if he did not love her, would not make her his wife, she would ask for what she felt was rightly hers. It was only fair that he should provide for the child. But her faith in his love remained unwavering and she continued to dismiss the fact that he had not written, sure that when she saw him again he would honour her – he was a Luciano.

The following week she went into labour. Her relief at knowing her child would not be taken away and her fantasies of lovemaking with Michael made the last few uncomfortable days pass in a haze. But nothing, not even being with little Raina, prepared Sophia for the agony of the birth.

The plunging, dragging pains consumed and exhausted her tired body. The brief respites only heralded new waves of stabbing fire, screaming through her . . . She clung to the oxygen mask, taking desperate gulps, until the midwife wrested it from her, knowing she was taking too much. In the end, Sophia lifted Michael's small gold heart to her lips and bit hard, feeling her teeth sink into the centre, forming a ridge.

'Come on, Sophia, push . . . push!' Teeth clenched, breath snorting, she pushed down and felt her body finally open and release the child. She could hear the howling baby and tried to haul herself up to see, but they would not give him to her until he was bathed and weighed.

Gently, the doctor placed a cool cloth on her brow. He sighed, 'You have a son, Sophia.' He could not disguise the sadness in his voice. So many times he saw his frightened young patients through this ordeal on their own, so different from the couples whose joy invariably filled his heart. He was therefore taken aback when Sophia laughed, seemingly unaware of the nurses tending to the afterbirth. She repeated over and over, 'I have a son . . .'

The doctor remained in the delivery room, watching her as her newborn son was placed in her arms. He weighed eight-and-a-half pounds, a perfect child with blue eyes that, even at birth, were like jewels. He was so obviously Michael Luciano's son. Sophia looked up and smiled a sweet, childish smile, the dimple appearing in her cheek. It touched everyone in the room; she was, after all, little more than a child herself.

Sophia took her baby to the orphanage. She would be allowed to leave him there while she worked during the day. True to his word, the doctor had not only arranged a place for the baby but had found work for her at a bakery only a few yards from the orphanage.

Her fantasy flourished, and she worked every hour God gave her, saving what little she could in preparation for her trip to Palermo. She would sit by his cradle for hours, sewing her new dress and jacket. A good pair of shoes, given to her when she left the convent, would complete the outfit.

It was almost a year to the day since she had last seen Michael. Her son was now three months old, and she had called him Nicodemo. She had not put Michael's name on the birth certificate, wanting him to sign it himself. It was another part of her fantasy, that they would be together when their son was christened . . .

She calculated that it would be another three months before she had enough saved to leave for Palermo and to pay the orphanage fees for them to keep him. She would no longer need to breast-feed the baby by then. Her dress was ready, the shoes, rarely worn so they remained in good condition, were polished. She refused to allow any doubts to surface in her mind, and told the orphanage that when she returned she would take her son away for good.

There were more than fifteen babies in the orphanage, plus a kindergarten for five- to six-year-olds, all cared for by a local charity set up by the church. Adoptions were more frequent with the small babies and often, as the doctor had predicted, girls like Sophia who believed they could cope, eventually signed their children away for adoption. If money passed hands, no one ever mentioned it, but it was known to occur. The money found its way back into the charity. Some girls simply disappeared and never returned to reclaim their children, so the church had made a regulation that if the mother decided to leave the vicinity for any reason, she had to give consent for the child to be put on the adoption register after three months if she did not return. Confidently, Sophia signed the papers.

CHAPTER 6

GRAZIELLA WAS worried; it was, after all, the middle of term, and all she could think about was that her son was so ill he had been unable to speak about it on the telephone. Roberto knew there was something wrong as soon as he saw her face.

'Michael just called. He says he's coming home on Monday. He sounded ill, and I couldn't make out half of what he was saying, but he needs money.'

'What? But I topped up his account, last . . . er . . .'

'Are you sure it went through?'

'I'll find out, don't worry. I'll sort it out.'

He telephoned his bank manager, who came on the line promptly. Michael Luciano's account was $5,000 overdrawn.

The money didn't worry Roberto unduly; there had to be a reason for the amount Michael had spent. He was more concerned that Michael was coming home in the middle of term, and was tempted to contact Harvard, but decided to wait and talk to his son first.

On the Monday Roberto had a business commitment, so he sent Constantino to the airport.

Paul Carolla's breath made circles of condensation on the tall window. When the steps were wheeled up to the plane he wiped the window to get a clear view of the passengers coming down the steps in ones and twos. He began to convince himself that the boy was not on the flight. He clenched his hands, ready to punch the steamy, wet window. Then he saw him.

Michael's weight had dropped drastically. His face was gaunt and his hair looked as if it had not been cut or combed in weeks. He looked dishevelled in jeans and sneakers, and he carried a guitar case. As he started down the steps, he stumbled and clutched the rail, then straightened up.

Carolla remembered very clearly his envy of Luciano as he walked across the tarmac.

Gloatingly, he watched the sad wreck of a boy shamble from the plane. He was going to have everything that Luciano had and more, because he was about to tear apart the Don's safe, secure world and no Commission, no one, would know that he had anything to do with it.

Sweating heavily, Michael Luciano arrived at customs. The customs official opened the guitar case and asked for the receipt, as it had been bought in America. There was duty to be paid on it. Michael took out his wallet, his hands shaking so badly that the inspector asked if he was unwell. Michael replied that he had the flu. His brain began to scream, the ache slowly permeating his whole body, and pains shot from his mind to his limbs, making his legs jerk. With enormous effort he managed to control himself and pay the duty, then moved on to the arrivals lounge.

136

He looked around frantically. He was in agony, just putting one foot in front of the other was a slow and painful procedure. He muttered constantly, swearing when he couldn't see the 'john'. The relief when he spotted the sign on the door brought tears to his eyes.

There was no one in the lavatory. He clung to the washbasin, weeping, splashing cold water on his face. His legs were giving way beneath him, he couldn't hold himself upright. He had begun to slide on to the cold, tiled, urine-covered floor when he felt strong arms holding him up, a soothing voice telling him everything would be all right. He clung to the stranger, begging for help, clutching at him as the room spun around and he began to blank out . . .

Lenny Cavataio's persistent, soothing voice was asking for money. He fumbled in his pockets, knocking the guitar case to the floor, his fingers refusing to work for him, but eventually he found the wallet. Cavataio counted out the cash while Michael sat hunched against the wall. Then, afraid someone might come in, he lifted Michael bodily into one of the cubicles and closed the door.

He held several small white packets level with the weeping boy's face and, as Michael reached up for them, dropped them into the toilet bowl. The last pitiful sight he had of Michael Luciano, Don Roberto Luciano's son, was as he groped for the heroin in the toilet. He left, wondering if the boy would be able to prepare the stuff and inject himself, he looked so far gone. But it wasn't his problem, he had followed his orders. He looked about ready for death, anyway.

*

Outside the terminal, Constantino Luciano was arguing with two airport officials. They were shouting at him that he couldn't park there. While he argued, Michael called to him and came towards the car, bumping into two women travellers but seeming not to notice. He had attempted to clean himself up and had put on his Rayban sunglasses, but to Constantino's eyes he looked like a bum.

Putting Michael's leather suitcase and guitar in the back of the car, Constantino helped his brother in. The smell of body odour took him aback, and he opened the window, asking what in God's name he had been doing.

Michael rested his head on the back of the seat and laughed. Constantino could get no sense out of him, and his pleasure at seeing him again turned to anger.

'Are you drunk? Been drinking on the plane? Michael? Michael, what's the matter with you?'

Sighing, Michael stared out of the window and told his brother that he had been really ill with a strange virus which left him unable to do anything. He had talked it over with his tutors, who had suggested that he come home for a rest and get himself fit and well before returning to college. He took off his dark glasses and looked directly at Constantino for the first time. His clear, bright blue eyes were like those of a stranger.

Constantino reached over and gripped his hand. 'We'll get you well. I'm sorry, but I don't think Ma should see you like this. What do you say we drive to a hotel, get you washed and cleaned up? You know, you'll be in for a grilling.'

'Anything you say, anything you say.'

*

138

They booked into a small hotel and Constantino started the bath running, then opened Michael's suitcase. Everything in the case was filthy, so he volunteered to go out and buy some clothes while Michael took his bath.

While Constantino went shopping, Michael stripped off and eased his body into the warm, soapy bath. He was still in reasonably good shape but he had lost a lot of weight, and the tracks down his arms showed blue. Scabs had formed in the creases of his elbows.

He lay back and closed his eyes, so stoned that he began to slip beneath the water, only coming to when his head submerged. He hauled himself up, knowing that he'd better straighten himself out to be in good shape for the homecoming.

He gave himself another fix and tucked the little rubber tube back into his guitar case beside the white packets.

By the time Constantino returned, Michael was sitting on the bed wearing a monogrammed hotel dressing gown and strumming his guitar. His hair, though clean, was in need of a cut and did not have its usual sheen, but he had shaved, and to Constantino's relief he looked more like his old self.

The drive passed without incident. Michael enjoyed the warmth of the sun and seemed, as they drew nearer to home, to be stronger. At his first sight of the villa he laughed, mimicking his father, 'Just look at that place, will you look at it? Isn't it bathed in gold? It's as gold as your mother's hair . . .'

Before the car had stopped, Graziella came running from the porch, waving and smiling. The fat Frederico emerged from the shadows and the fifteen-year-old Alfredo rode towards them on a motor-scooter, standing up and tooting the horn. Graziella shrieked for him to sit down, and Constantino backed her up from the porch.

The dust created by the scooter and the Mercedes formed clouds in the hot air. Alfredo watched as Michael leapt from the car and ran to his mother, picked her up and swung her round. She could see that he was ill. He was very thin, but his energy and laughter had not changed.

'We've been waiting for hours,' said Graziella.

Constantino heard Michael give, with total sincerity, a sweeping apology to them all. 'The plane was delayed, poor Con had to wait ages for me. We came straight here, as fast as that old bus would go.'

The simplicity of the lie, without a flicker, and the way they all believed it without question, made Constantino feel uneasy.

He started up the stairs to put Michael's bags in his room just as the Don's car was heard screeching up the drive. Constantino paused by the window to watch his father run from the car like a teenager, throwing his coat aside and standing with his arms wide open for his eldest son.

Constantino knew his father loved him, loved them all, but only Michael received that look of adoration. It was so obvious when the boy with the hair of gold like his mother's went into the outstretched arms of his father. They kissed, and Michael buried his head in his father's neck and whispered, 'I love you, Pa, I love you.'

Roberto kissed the top of Michael's head, caressed his hair and then held him at arm's length, gripping his shoulders. 'You lost weight! How are you going to win the Davis Cup when your muscles are all wasted, eh? And what's this, what's this?' He reached up and parted Michael's lips with his finger. He shook his head. 'You've not been cleaning your teeth, you who had the whitest teeth in this country. Is this what living in America does, huh? Sends back my boy thin as a rake with his teeth needing a brush?'

At dinner they talked over old times and laughed at Michael's stories, but no one brought up the subject of why he was there, why he had come home. It was in all their minds but they did not ask. That would be their father's prerogative and he obviously wanted them all to have an enjoyable meal together before he took Michael aside.

It was noticeable, too, that Michael drank more than he used to. They were always liberal with wine, but Michael's thirst seemed unquenchable. He began to slur his words and appeared to forget where he was, taking out a packet of cigarettes and lighting one before his father had finished eating. Again no one said a word, but Constantino saw his father's eyes narrow and knew he was missing nothing.

The conversation stopped when Michael started smoking and leaned his elbows on the table. Finally, Roberto broke the silence, asking Michael if the flight had been good. His reply was mumbled, incoherent, and they all looked at him until Constantino answered, repeating the lie about the delay. Michael seemed incapable of keeping his eyes open. He rested his head in his hands, occasionally drooping as though falling asleep.

Roberto said quietly that he had called the airport

and been told that, far from being late, his flight had in fact arrived early. Constantino flushed, and said nothing while the tension grew around the table.

His mother put out a protective hand to Michael and gave her husband a warning look to let it drop. 'You must be tired, it's a long flight. You want to go straight to bed, Michael?'

He shook his head and lit another cigarette, then smiled around the table in a strange, dazed way. 'I guess I'm tired, you know, it's a fucking long flight and I was really sick . . .'

He half-rose from the table and his chair fell backwards. He swore again, still unaware of the effect his language was having on the family. He had sworn in front of his mother and father, something of which they thoroughly disapproved.

Graziella again reached out a hand towards her son, but her husband's voice kept her still. 'Go and rest, Michael. We'll talk in the morning.'

Michael shambled out and they stared after him, not understanding how he could change so quickly before their eyes. Graziella smiled nervously. 'I think maybe he drank too much on the plane, and then not eating . . . And with all the excitement, and the wine . . .'

Constantino excused himself from the table without saying anything about the state Michael had been in when he found him. Frederico asked permission to leave the table and Alfredo, always the quiet moody one, carefully folded his napkin and pushed his chair under the table. Like Constantino, he had seen the way his father doted on Michael and, as much as he loved his brother and would never wish him harm, he couldn't

142

help but feel a hint of pleasure that the golden one's crown had slipped a fraction.

Michael stared, dull-eyed, from his bedroom window. His brothers were walking together in the garden, talking easily and freely with one another. Michael longed to go down and walk with them, yet they seemed so far away, as though they were in a movie, not in real life at all.

Just as his mind was clearing and he had begun to think straight, it started; the deep ache in his body, the sweating and the craving . . .

Everything paled beside his need, slipped into nothingness, and all that mattered in the world was in that guitar case. The release from the sensation of drowning, the sickness, would be immediate. He crossed the room and jammed the back of a chair beneath the doorhandle, then opened the case. From beneath the guitar he took out a piece of tinfoil, folded it, and tipped a small quantity of his precious white powder into the fold.

Below, in the study, the telephone rang, and the operator asked Roberto to stand by for his long-distance call. He listened to the weird echoing and clicking until Michael's professor at Harvard came on the line.

Roberto heard the professor out without interruption. Michael had been dismissed from college half-way through his second year. His results at the end of the first term had been very poor, and his participation in the life of the college virtually nonexistent. During the first break

143

the professor had arranged special tutorials to enable Michael to catch up, but he had failed to attend. The professor implied that Michael had emotional problems which had escalated out of all proportion during his second year. His inability to settle down or show any interest in his studies had had a bad influence on the other students. He had been given a second chance but had not taken it, and there was no possibility as things stood that he would be accepted back.

There was a short pause, then the professor suggested rather abruptly that perhaps Michael had got in with the wrong set, and implied that other dismissals were connected. But he would not be more specific, feeling he was not at liberty to discuss matters over the telephone.

Finally, Roberto thanked the professor for being so direct and honest, and suggested that any refund of fees be given to charity. His hands shook and the phone felt as heavy as lead as he carefully placed it back on the rest. He sat at his desk immobile, for hours, trying to understand the web of lies his son had written in his letters.

Graziella was still awake. She smiled and put her finger to her lips, whispering, 'Listen to him sing, and he plays so well. He's been playing for over an hour. Isn't it lovely?'

They heard the discordant sound of the guitar falling to the floor and they both turned, listening. No further noise could be heard. Luciano moved stealthily to the door and opened it quietly. He heard a soft moan, barely audible, but it was enough. He was across the landing and had forced the door open in seconds.

Unable to control his greed, Michael had given himself another fix. To do so he had opened another small white packet. His face was chalk-white and he was frothing at the mouth. His eyes were wide with terror as his body jerked in terrible spasms. The needle still lay by his side.

By acting swiftly, Roberto Luciano saved his son's life. Without stopping even to tell Graziella what was happening, he picked Michael up in his arms, carried him down to the car and drove directly to the hospital. By the time they arrived, Michael was in a deep coma.

The hospital took over and Luciano could do nothing but wait. He phoned Ettore Calleah and told him to bring as much cash as he could lay his hands on to the hospital, then called Mario Domino and asked him to go and sit with Graziella. He was to tell her that Michael had collapsed, but everything was under control. Domino asked no questions, gave no hint of annoyance at being woken in the middle of the night.

It was six o'clock in the morning before Luciano knew his son was going to make it. Fears of brain damage proved unfounded; he was out of the coma and sleeping.

Calleah sat with Luciano. He was as worried as his Don; it could have been his own son in the intensive-care unit, he was so frantic.

A doctor beckoned Luciano to accompany him into the small office. He was tired, having worked most of the night on the boy. Closing the door purposefully, he indicated a chair for Luciano.

'Is it heroin?' Roberto asked, but he already knew the answer.

'I'm afraid so. He's taken a massive overdose, but he

145

was lucky you were on hand. Any longer and you would have lost him. You can see him now if you like, though I doubt he'll wake up for a few hours. The veins in his right arm have collapsed totally, and the tracks on the left are badly infected. He has also been injecting into his legs, but his body is still pretty strong, probably because he has been such a sportsman.'

Luciano wondered if it would be best to ship Michael back to the States, where centres for addicts were more common. He questioned Dr Lissoni closely about heroin addiction and what could be done to cure his son.

'There's more than one way of doing it. We can begin weaning him off with a heroin substitute, which will take a long time, probably months.'

He was slightly fazed when Luciano asked him quietly, not wishing to be overheard even in the privacy of the office, 'If it was your son, your brother, in that state, what would you do?'

'Well, if the patient is strong enough and wants to come off the junk, then cold turkey. It's a living hell for them for maybe a week or two – you simply give them nothing at all until the drug is out of their system. It's a nightmare for the people caring for them, because they'll crave the stuff and be so desperate that they'll do or say *anything* to get a fix. But it works, they do get clear. You still have the psychological problems to contend with, of course . . . they are very vulnerable, the ordeal obviously weakens them, but you asked for my opinion . . .'

Luciano thanked the young doctor and patted his arm. 'If I decided to do that for my son, could I depend on you to give him medical supervision? You would be paid handsomely for your time and for confidentiality.

No one outside this room must know about my son's condition, and you will be given every assistance.'

Luciano handed over an envelope, continuing, 'Please accept this as a small token of my appreciation for saving my son's life. Now, perhaps, if you could arrange it, I would like to see him.'

Lissoni tried to refuse the envelope, but in the end he tucked it into the pocket of his white coat. Then he took Luciano up the staff staircase to the small private room at the very end of a corridor.

Above the stiff, white hospital sheet his face was that of an innocent angel.

'Michael.' Luciano moved closer to the bed, but his son could not look at him. He turned his face away. 'Michael, can you hear me? Michael? Look at me.'

The boy's eyes brimmed with tears. He took his hand from under the sheet and searched blindly until he found his father's strong one. He gripped it tightly as if afraid to let go, afraid to lose him. With great difficulty, he stuttered, 'Help me, please help me.'

Ettore Calleah sat in the car, shaking his head. He couldn't believe it, he couldn't take it in. He blew his bulbous nose loudly. 'He was young, vulnerable, maybe had too much dough. He must have been easy pickings for some bastard . . .'

'Yeah, that's what I thought. But look at it this way – what better way to get back at me? What better way to cut me down than destroy my son?'

'We should look out for the other boys – unless this was just a warning. I'll get the guys on to it, see what they can come up with.'

'No, I'll arrange what's necessary. In the meantime, you find a safe house for him, up in the mountains. The doctor will keep a check on him. You take two good guys with you and don't come back until he's clean.'

Graziella wept when she was told that the doctors wanted Michael to have no visitors for the moment. Luciano was firm, telling her the virus had worsened to pneumonia and he needed total rest.

Knowing her husband was exhausted, Graziella dropped the subject and ordered a light breakfast for him, although it was two o'clock in the afternoon. He went upstairs to bathe.

After his bath he slipped into Michael's room and searched it, finding the packets of heroin in the guitar case. He put them in his pocket as Graziella called to him that his food was ready.

While he ate, Graziella sat at the table to keep him company. 'So now, will you tell me the truth? Will you tell me what is going on?'

'What makes you think something is going on?'

'Because he's my son. I know him, and I know you. I want the truth, don't play games with me.'

'He's sick, sweetheart, he's very sick, but he will get well. I give you my word. The boy who was here last night wasn't our Michael, understand?'

'Yes he was. He was thinner, a little drunk, a little crazy maybe, but he was still Michael . . .'

He rose from the table, leaving his breakfast unfinished, and gave her the look she always hated, that told her not to ask questions. She felt angry at the way he always took charge, even of her emotions. The anger built until she could no longer contain herself.

She went up to the bedroom and found Roberto looking at a photograph taken at Michael's farewell party.

He spoke hesitantly. 'I knew something was wrong the moment I saw him. I could almost smell the change, you know, like an animal when a strange creature strays into its lair. I kept looking at him at the other end of the table, the way he was eating like a pig, spilling wine down himself . . . and I couldn't do anything but watch. That boy, from the day he was born, has touched a part of me that no one else ever has . . .'

Graziella felt her anger evaporating. 'He touches something special in both of us, that's why it was cruel of you not to let me be with him.'

He gripped her hand until it hurt. His voice was choked with emotion as he said, 'You must trust me. You will have him back, I give you my word. When you next see him he will be well, he will be Michael.'

The gates of the villa, often left open, were now closed and guarded by two men day and night. Suddenly the boys' freedom was curtailed, and each was accompanied by a bodyguard wherever they went. They knew only that it had something to do with their brother.

Two days later, Dr Lissoni began a month's leave of absence from the hospital. That night, he carried Michael, wrapped in blankets, to a waiting car. To avoid notice, they travelled in a small Citroën with only one man to drive them. Another car containing two men escorted them at a good distance, but kept the Citroën always in sight.

After two hours they reached a point where two narrow country lanes crossed. A motorbike took up position ahead of them to lead the convoy, again keeping a good way ahead.

Dr Lissoni had told Luciano that he could not be held responsible – he would do all he could, but there was always the possibility that the boy would not be able to cope, that deep down he didn't really want the cure. Luciano had reassured him on that point, and gave his word that if he did not survive he would not blame the doctor. Unable to shake off his slight feeling of trepidation, Lissoni had accepted the deal, and Luciano thanked him with moving sincerity.

They drove on for another hour, Michael's tremors getting so strong that they were making Lissoni's own body shake. He leaned forward and tapped the driver on the shoulder. 'Is it much further? He's going to go into a seizure soon, and I won't be able to do much for him.'

The driver did not reply. Michael's whole body began twitching and shaking, his arms jerking uncontrollably. Lissoni tucked the blanket around him as tightly as possible and held him.

The small shepherd's cottage contained only three rooms. It was built of stone, with flagged floors and a wide fireplace in the big kitchen. The only source of water was a tap in the back yard. The primitive lavatory was in a hut a few yards from the back door.

The motorbike rider entered the cottage first and lit

candles, checking every room before giving the signal for the others to enter. Lissoni helped Michael out of the car and asked if he could walk. Michael could only grunt in reply, but he did manage to shuffle the few steps from the car to the cottage, leaning heavily on the doctor.

Michael and the doctor had been allocated the centre room, which contained a cot bed with sturdy wooden posts at the ends and a more comfortable one against the wall for Lissoni. A couple of chairs and a bookcase full of paperbacks completed the furnishings. The third room was for the men to sleep in. There would be people on each side of him at all times, taking turns to guard him.

By the time he was half-carried into the room, Michael was exhausted. He was shivering with cold, his teeth chattering, yet his face and body glistened with sweat. He flopped on to the bed, moaning and swearing, as the pains crept slowly up his arms and legs, then shot up his spine. Even his fingers seemed locked, each joint throbbing.

Ettore Calleah came to the door and looked sadly at the pitiful figure on the bed. 'We'll do whatever you tell us, Doc. You need any help?'

Lissoni nodded and asked Calleah to start cutting a sheet into long strips while he undressed Michael. Calleah asked if they were for bandages, and Lissoni shook his head. They were going to have to tie Michael down; soon he would begin thrashing about to such an extent that he could hurt himself, so his bonds were a necessary precaution.

Together they spread-eagled him and tied his ankles to the bedposts.

'Jesus Christ, I hope you know what you're doing, Doc. This looks medieval to me.' As Ettore spoke,

Michael reached out suddenly and grabbed him by his collar, pulling him with such force he was lifted off his feet.

'What the fuck is going on, Ettore? What are you doing to me? It's me, Ettore, it's Michael . . . Get this guy off me! What are you doing?'

Michael's strength was surprising. He grappled with the big man, punching him, and in the end they had to get one of the guards to assist. It was half an hour before they had him securely tied, the strips of fabric padded so they would not cut into his flesh. Lissoni checked his pulse and made him as comfortable as possible, bathing his face with cold water. Then he heaped four blankets on top of him and went into the kitchen to speak to the men, who were sitting around the table in sullen silence, having obviously heard Calleah's account of what had been going on in Michael's room.

Lissoni pulled up a chair and, at his request, was given a tin mug of thick black coffee. 'OK, now, he will have to remain tied up until the worst of it is over. It's for his own good, and ours. You have to understand that the boy in there is not the boy you know – he is possessed with craving for the junk, and will be for some time. I warn you he can be devious – he will cajole you and charm you, and you must not believe a word he says. Until I say differently, he remains as he is.'

'What happens if he wants to take a leak?'

'Right now he does it where he is. I can change the sheets, wash the blankets. But you saw for yourselves how strong he can be, and the last thing we want is for him to get free and do a runner. Believe me, he will try, because he will want a fix more than his life. He will kill for it – it's the sole preoccupation of his addled mind. So

152

– I will do my job, I will watch over him and do what I can to ease the pain, but no one must release him until he is more in control of himself.'

He returned to the bedroom to sit with Michael, leaving the men at the table.

Calleah heard the shouting start up again, and he sighed. 'I hope that guy knows what the hell he is doing. That kid dies and we all do, and the Doc will be the first to go.'

No one got any sleep that night. They couldn't believe how anyone could keep up such a barrage of screaming and shouting, howling and sobbing. Occasionally the doctor came out for hot or cold water, but otherwise the door remained closed until daybreak, when Lissoni asked Calleah to take over while he slept.

Calleah replied, 'None of us got any sleep. I never heard anything like it, you'd wonder where the kid learnt some of the words . . .'

Lissoni collapsed onto his own bed and went to sleep while Calleah sat on a small wooden chair at the foot of Michael's bed, looking closely at the boy. There were red weals on his wrists where he had fought to release his bonds, and the needle tracks on his arms showed clearly. The blue veins stood out as though someone had tat- tooed them on his arms. Calleah had watched this boy grow up, had sat him on his knee and played tic-tac with him, and here he was trussed like an animal. The room stank of vomit and urine, and the pillow was stained with flecks of blood. It saddened Calleah, and he was glad Luciano could not see his son right now.

The wooden shutters were closed, but gaps between

the slats allowed sunlight to enter the small stone room. Slowly, Michael opened his eyes and blinked against the beams of light. His slanting blue eyes looked like amethysts, their colour was so strong.

'The light bothering you, Mike? I'll see what I can do.' Calleah took off his jacket and hung it on a nail to cut out the light, then looked back at Michael. 'How you feeling?'

'Cold, I'm cold . . . Where am I?'

'You're safe, Micky, safe . . .'

He took another blanket and laid it across the boy, then touched him gently on the cheek. 'You're gonna be all right. I hate to see you like this.'

Michael's eyes were pleading, and he began to cry softly, begging the faithful Calleah to untie him. He promised he wouldn't try anything, but he was in pain and couldn't get comfortable.

'I can't do that, Micky. You're gonna have to take the punishment.'

The spasms began again and Calleah, unable to cope, woke the doctor. Michael had begun to vomit and the bed was soaked with his sweat, stinking sweat which permeated the whole room. Together they washed him, without releasing his bonds, then Lissoni ordered a bowl of porridge and spoon-fed him like a child. He spat it out, butted the bowl with his head, then broke down and begged Lissoni to give him something, just one hit. Just one to help him through, and he wouldn't ask again. He promised that would be all he needed.

In the next room the men wanted to cover their ears against the voice, rising and falling, the pitiful, grovelling pleas. One of the guards had to go outside, unable to stand it any longer. He sat on the low wall surrounding

154

the cottage and saw in the distance a black Mercedes rounding a curve on the hillside. Dr Lissoni sedated Michael, and sat with him until at last he slept.

Luciano gave the guard a cursory nod and entered the cottage, calling for Calleah. He snapped that he had driven straight up to the place, and if he could do it anyone could. Luciano did not ask after Michael, did not even look at the closed bedroom door.

When he was alone with Calleah, he laid a small white packet of heroin on the table. 'The junk was intended to kill him. God knows how he got it, but it's almost pure, lethal. But because it's in such a raw state it's easy to trace. Carolla's been having a lot of trouble with his refineries. Apparently it's easy to convert raw opium into morphine base, but the hard part comes when they want to turn that into heroin. The final stage is drying and crushing the junk, using hydrochloric acid to turn it into a salt. That's how they make it soluble in water, you can't inject it any other way. Carolla's been using a big refinery up north where they've got some bad chemists. If you get the temperature just a few degrees out when you're heating it, you can not only get a fucking great explosion, but you end up with bad junk. He's been producing this stuff and getting into trouble for it, so he's shifted his main lab to Marseilles. I've even traced the paper from the packet to one of Carolla's manufacturing companies. Knowing Carolla, he'll still be selling it – not to his big dealers, but on the street. He couldn't ship this stuff to the States, so it's from Palermo, and what I need to know . . .' He paused, looking at the closed door, then lowered his voice still further. 'They must have been waiting for him at the airport, and I've got to find out who his contact was. It's too much of a coincidence that a few minutes after Michael arrived from New York, Carolla flew out. I am sure now that sonofabitch deliberately set out to do this to my son.'

Calleah knew it was bound to be war if they got the evidence against Carolla. He rose to his feet and opened the shutters. The clear day, the view from the window, calmed him. Then, like an omen, the village church bell began to toll, the slow, booming ring echoing around the hills and fading into the sides of the mountains.

He turned to Luciano. 'The Corleones have killed over a hundred and fifty men in their own village, wiped them out in less than two years. To them, death is a way of life. They are a new breed, thugs hungry for drug money, and they kill each other like mad dogs for it. We hit Carolla and we hit the Corleones, are you prepared for that? It'll be a bloodbath.'

Luciano had taken out a Havana cigar and seemed intent on clipping it perfectly with his gold cutter. Then he clamped it between his teeth and struck a match, puffing it slowly into life. 'Now is not the time to make foolish accusations. It is imperative that we have absolute evidence of Carolla's involvement in the passing of heroin to my son. Then, as before, we take it to the Commission and ask for satisfaction. If that is refused, then—'

Calleah interrupted, 'I'll do it, you know that. All you have to do is ask and Carolla is dead.'

Luciano put his arm around his loyal friend, the man who had stood by him since the death of Joseph Carolla. His face and eyes were unreadable. 'Just trace the man we know met Michael at the airport, and we'll make him talk. If we prove without doubt that Carolla set out to destroy Michael, no one will deny me the right to kill him, and I will do it with my bare hands.'

Paul Carolla waited for news from Palermo regarding Michael Luciano, but no one could tell him if he were alive or dead. There had been no announcement in the newspapers about the boy's death, instead headlines blazed with the news that a refinery, masquerading as a sweet factory, had been burned down, 'Sugar and Spice Cover for Drug Route Smashed'.

It was one of Carolla's most lucrative refineries, and he had lost millions, having to close it down overnight and ship his chemists out fast. No sooner had that happened than Palermo customs began to hit him hard. They seized his small fleet of fishing boats as it set out to rendezvous with a Middle Eastern freighter anchored in international waters off Sicily, and carrying a vast shipment bound for New York. The boats were to have smuggled the raw material back to Palermo for refining, then, via Carolla's contacts, it would have been shipped on to Milan, Hamburg, Marseilles and Paris, the bulk heading for the USA via Cuba and Carolla's network of Canadian and North American dealers. The heroin was to have been hidden in cargoes of olive oil and fruit. He lost not only the heroin but all the cargoes were impounded, too, again worth millions.

Carolla was desperate, resorting to using his network of Italian emigrants as couriers, but even this was being thwarted by the US customs, who were ready and waiting for them on their arrival. Carolla was tapping every possible route, but as soon as he created one, another would be closed down.

He was also being pressured into giving large cuts to all the families he had brought into his business, cuts far larger than the value he received in return, particularly with the Corleone family. They were not interested in his problems, they demanded their percentage whether he was getting his cargoes through or not. Carolla was in deep trouble, unable to make his payoffs, and knowing someone was tipping off the authorities. He automatically blamed Luciano. He made frantic calls to Palermo, trying to find out what was going on. If he had needed the cover of Luciano's facilities before, now he was desperate. He had the product, but no way of shipping it. His hopes of bending Don Luciano through Michael's drug addiction had failed. Frightened dealers, being hounded by the *carabinieri*, pestered him with calls, while Luciano's right-hand man, Ettore Calleah, was moving closer to unearthing Lenny Cavataio. Terrified that Lenny would talk, Carolla made arrangements quickly to get him out of Palermo and to take over one of his Canadian refineries. He admonished himself for being so foolish as to have made contact with him personally.

No sooner had he organized Lenny's escape than he was tipped off that Roberto Luciano was in New York, talking to his street dealers. Carolla was certain that he was behind the drug busts, and his paranoia increased with the belief that Luciano had somehow discovered his part in Michael's addiction. He became even more paranoid when he arrived at his favourite Manhattan restaurant to find Luciano just leaving.

Luciano smiled and held out a hand. Carolla began to sweat, terrified that he was about to be hit, but all Luciano did was to take his hand in a vice-like grip. His eyes were cold and hard, and he said not a single word, which was more frightening to Carolla than if he had threatened retaliation. Carolla's heart nearly burst as a limousine drew up at the kerb behind him. He could easily have been shot from the car, and Luciano would have been away before anyone realized what had happened. But instead Luciano, releasing him, wiped his hand down his coat as if he had touched a piece of shit.

Carolla swore at his bodyguard, and from then on he didn't move unless hemmed in by at least three men. Stories spread about how he had gasped like a fish out of water, standing there in the restaurant doorway. The humiliation sat hard on Carolla and started to fester, until he was unable to say Luciano's name without wanting to vomit.

He began seriously to cover his tracks, starting with the two dealers who specialized in working over college kids.

Luciano had spent two hours with Michael's professor but the man had refused to divulge any names. As he left the college, Luciano smiled and told his driver that Harvard reminded him of the Mafia, they too closed ranks when necessary. The next night, the university's offices were broken into and Luciano had the list of all students who had been in his son's year, plus details on the boys who, like his son, had been kicked out.

There were six students in all. It was easy enough for the elegant, sophisticated man to make the acquaintance of the family in each case, as they all had one thing in common. Three of the boys were crossed off as being nothing more than rich kids who had misused their

chances, who, by the level of their academic achieve-
ments, had obviously had strings pulled for them to get
into Harvard in the first place. The other three were
different; or two, as it turned out. One boy had already
died of a drug overdose. His family were still shocked by
the bereavement and were not inclined to discuss his
tragic death. The other two, William Sedgwick Junior
and Andrew Gelhorn, were not so easy to trace, but
when Luciano found them they were worth the effort.

William Sedgwick was in a rehabilitation clinic on
Long Island. A big-boned, fresh-faced boy, he had an
open manner and was eager to hear how his friend
Michael was. He found the tall man a little austere at
first, but soon opened up to him and responded to his
questions, unlike his parents and the college staff.

William gave him the names of the clubs they had
frequented and told him of the great times they had all
had, sailing and surfing. He tried hard to recollect who
had been the first one to offer him heroin, but couldn't.
But the best place to score had been a club not far from
the college. Luciano listened closely to all the boy had to
tell him, and showed not a flicker of disapproval over the
stories of the topless waitresses . . . Then William remembered. It had been a waiter, an Italian waiter, who had
first introduced him to heroin.

Andy Gelhorn, now a registered addict, lived in Green-
wich Village. He had a job, running a seedy art gallery
and even seedier coffee bar, and was on methadone, a
heroin substitute. He couldn't wait to tell Luciano that
his family had disowned him, but neglected to mention
that they had done so after he had repeatedly stolen his

mother's chequebook and credit cards, and even sold some family jewellery. He said simply that he was kicked out of college and kicked out by his family.

Andy was shifty, and had a nervous habit of rubbing his nose, but he talked freely, especially when money was offered. And he remembered that he had first been offered heroin by a guy in a restaurant, an Italian restaurant as far as he could remember.

'I have nothing against you, Andy, and whatever you say to me will not have any repercussions for you, I give you my word on that. I am intent only on finding my son, Michael. You were close friends?'

Lighting his umpteenth cigarette, Andy puffed and flicked the ash with his finger. He crossed and uncrossed his legs. 'Well, I wasn't, you know, one of his set. He was with the sports crowd, always playing tennis or squash. His pal was Sedgwick. You know about Matthew Hardwick? He overdosed about six weeks ago. Nothing to do with me, man, I mean I hadn't seen him for months, but well, he was my roomie. He and I went around together, you know, man . . .'

Luciano let him waffle on, every now and then guiding him back to the reason for the meeting. The coffee shop closed and Luciano asked for some bottles of wine. When the staff had left and they were eventually alone, Andy at last gave him the information he wanted. He had been a regular visitor to the cheap Italian joint, but he had also been offered a considerable amount of money if he could bring Michael Luciano there one evening.

'You see, man, they said like, they were Italian, and he was Italian, you know, and maybe they knew him from home . . . I dunno. Anyway, they wanted to speak with him. And it kinda went on from there . . .'

'What went on?'

'Well, the chicks, man. I mean, I dunno where the chicks came from, but they were beautiful and they were coming across . . . We didn't have to pay them, they weren't hookers – least, I don't think they were.'

'So they supplied you with girls and drugs, right?'

'Hey, look, I don't want any trouble.'

Luciano laid a hundred-dollar bill on the table and walked out. He had heard enough.

The next stop was the club, and he took four men with him. His heart sank as they drew up outside; the place had been closed down, the front boarded over. But he didn't give up easily. He went to the local police and made donations in the right places. He was told the place had been closed down after a drug bust, and his inform- ant was able to supply the names of the employees. Luciano called Sedgwick and together they went through the list, but Sedgwick couldn't quite remember the name of the waiter.

It had taken him three weeks to get this far. During that time he had kept in constant contact with Calleah, and knew that one man they wanted to question had been given the tip-off and had disappeared from Palermo. The man, Lenny Cavataio, was just one of the many names listed and under suspicion. Neither Luciano nor his man Calleah realized the importance of Lenny Cava- taio's connection, and it was yet another fatal mistake to believe that in time they would find him. As it was, Luciano was running out of time, and knew he was neglecting his business in Sicily. Sadly, he returned to Palermo without the evidence he wanted. But he still had his son to question, and the list of men who had worked at the Italian restaurant.

Calleah was at the airport to meet him, smiling broadly. 'Wait till you see him, he's put on weight, he's in great shape, and the Doc said he was through. All we gotta do now is keep him off it for another few months – you know, until he's off it in his head.'

Luciano sighed with relief, smiling his pleasure. 'So, my boy's back, is he? Michael's back . . . Good, that makes me feel good. Now we get him to talk, now we hear his side.'

CHAPTER 7

LYDIA WAS loaded with so many parcels and carrier bags that she could only just squeeze through the door and stagger into her bedroom. She leaned against the wall, kicking off her shoes, and dropped the heavy book of fabric samples on the floor. The place was a tip, full of cardboard boxes of all different shapes and sizes.

She had found her apartment, and would move in when it was decorated to her specification. Every day she arrived at the stores like a military invasion, her campaign mapped out on bits of paper and colour charts which were stuffed in her pockets.

Carolla called her once a week, but he paid no attention to her colour schemes. 'Sweetheart, you're gonna live there, you choose whatever you want. Don't waste the call on giving me a fuckin' rundown of *Homes and Gardens*, all right? How's your body?'

'Waiting for yours, baby.'

'It had better be. You miss me?'

'Every minute.'

*

In Giorgio's room there were so many books there was hardly any space left to walk on. Like Lydia, he had been using his account as if it were going out of fashion. First he had ordered the standard publishers' lists, then he began ordering books to be imported from all over the world, and put all the expenses down to his father. In his own way he was building up a library, his eclectic taste ranging from Raymond Chandler to Pirandello, from anatomy to poisons. One of his greatest interests was the macabre, and he would pore over recipes for herbal poisons for hours. As an aid to his reading he had bought a stand and a head brace with a pointer and small rubber knob on the end, to enable him to turn the pages. At times he looked like a strange variety of garden gnome, his enlarged head nodding vigorously as he flipped the pages. The television set had lasted only two days, when he persuaded Lydia to keep it in her room. He preferred his own small world to that on the screen.

The new housekeeper came in on a daily basis as Lydia was still occupying her room, so Giorgio was surrounded by women. At times he sounded like a little old lady himself. He was always complaining about his bowel movements, or lack of them, constipation being high on his list of conversational topics. He ate like a sparrow and was very faddish about his food, like a lot of children at his age. The only difference was that when he refused his food it sent the entire household into turmoil.

As it drew closer to the time for Lydia to move into her new apartment, the child felt saddened. She had injected new life into his little world, and they had often laughed together. The holy fathers paid courtesy calls, but no more tutors appeared, Carolla obviously having forgotten his son's request. Giorgio wouldn't ever admit it, but he really would miss Lydia's brash voice, her snorting laugh and her perfume. He would also miss the nights when she had drunk too much and would loll at his door, grinning at him, as well as the glimpses of her nakedness as she strolled to the bathroom, knowing she could be seen, that he was peeking. Sometimes as she passed she would purse her lips and give him a cheeky pout, then pop her head round the door and say sternly, 'Close your eyes, you naughty boy, or I'll tell your father.' She would mimic his high-pitched voice and he would flush with embarrassment.

The removal truck had gone, and there was nothing left of her purchases but empty boxes and tissue paper. She wore her mink coat despite the temperature being in the eighties, and all her jewellery, not trusting the removal firm with anything of value.

'OK, Giorgio, that's me ready. I'll be on my way. I'll give Paulie your love, OK?'

He turned his big, luminous eyes on her with his pointer sticking at a funny angle from his head. 'Good-bye,' he said. He turned away and flipped over a page, but she came close to the bed and bent to kiss him. He shrank away.

'I was just going to kiss you goodbye.'

'Save them for my father . . . and would you please give me the front-door key?'

He held out his wizened hand and she could have slapped him, but instead she delved into her pocket and dropped the key on the bed. She looked at him, her head tipped to one side. 'You know, I should feel sorry for you, but I don't. You're a spoilt brat, you don't know how to say "thank you", all you know is, "I want".'

He began to set out his chess-pieces, refusing to look at her. 'I have a right to want, what's your excuse?'

Before she knew what she was going to do, she hit him. His head banged against the bookcase, and his headset fell off. He looked like Humpty Dumpty with blood streaming from his nose.

'Oh, Jesus, oh, my God . . . Giorgio, I didn't mean it . . . Nurse! Nurse!'

Lydia was beside herself. What if he were to tell Carolla that she had hit him? She began to cry, biting her lip, her chest heaving.

'There's no need to cry, Lydia. He's had these attacks before. He's going to be all right, you are all right, aren't you, Giorgio?'

He smiled at Lydia, and she thought it was the smile of the devil himself. In his singsong voice he trilled, 'Yes, I'm all right now, thank you. I'm sure she didn't mean to hit me quite so hard.'

Shocked speechless, the nurse turned to Lydia. It was the housekeeper who said, 'You hit him?'

'I didn't mean to, it was an accident. If he wants to tell his father different, let him get on with it. You two run around as though he was the Virgin Mary – well, I won't. Someone should have given him a good slap years ago, he's a spoilt, foul-mouthed little bastard.' She turned to Giorgio. 'Yeah, go on, smirk at me, talk at me with your long, gibberish words. But I don't give a fuck, because I can walk out of here, and if your father hadda choose between me an' you, I can tell you which one he'd want . . . So screw you . . .'

The door slammed behind her and the nurse and the housekeeper stood, open-mouthed.

Giorgio was rushed to hospital and the fluid drained from his head. This time he remained in hospital for over a month, in a single room without his books and with only the hospital staff to talk to. He wept for the first time he could remember.

The nurse and the housekeeper visited him occasionally, and Lydia came. She stood in the doorway holding a bunch of flowers. 'OK, you little bastard, you win. I'm sorry . . .'

She took his strange, soft hand and gave it a squeeze. He winced. 'Oh, shit, I've not busted your hand now, have I?'

He laughed his odd, high-pitched laugh and from then on she visited regularly. Almost more important to him than her visits was the fact that she brought him the books he wanted to read.

Michael Luciano had exhausted the bookcase in his room and the village newsagent's supply of paperbacks. The men had brought him cartons full, grabbing any that came to hand, and he ploughed through them faster than they could be replaced.

The nights were the most difficult. Poker games for matchsticks bored them all in the end, and there was nothing left to do but read by candlelight, which was in itself driving him up the wall. He put himself on a rigorous exercise programme to tire himself out so he could fall asleep by nine o'clock. Every morning he was up by six, and the guards were boggle-eyed from the fatigue of simply trying to keep up with him. He would bat a squash ball against the side of the cottage for hours on end, and the thudding inside the cottage gave them all headaches. He would then eat an enormous breakfast of cereal, eggs and steak, with lashings of honey in his coffee and spread thickly on his toast. As soon as he had eaten, he would be itching to get back to his exercises, making do with heavy stones lashed together for weights.

He pushed himself almost to breaking point and would not give in until he had completed his punishing programme each day. After that he would take a five-mile run. None of his guards could run with him as they had no hope of keeping up, so at first one of them rode a bicycle ahead while the Citroën cruised behind, but as his fitness improved they had to replace the bike with a scooter.

They had each witnessed this boy weeping and screaming, curled up in the agony of 'cold turkey', and at one time or another each one had been approached to help him get some junk. Now they watched his progress with almost paternal pride, encouraging their protégé, applauding and admiring him.

The battle was not yet won; he still had periods of depressive despair and highly dangerous swings of mood. He would be at his most susceptible at these moments, and his guards were warned to take great care if they saw so much as a hint of the signs. Michael would not want to admit it after going through so much, but at these times, if offered heroin, he would have taken it. Dr Lissoni had schooled the men well, and in doing so had gained the respect and liking of them all. When he left, Michael hugged him like a brother, and they promised always to keep in touch. But his going left Michael with an intellectual void. None of his guards had ever passed an exam in his life, and two of them were illiterate. He had half-heartedly begun to teach them to read, but he was always restless, on the move, and it had been forgotten.

He began to think that he, too, had been forgotten. He would sit by his window looking down the road, waiting, hoping that one of his brothers or his father would visit. At the thought of his father he often found himself flushing deeply; he had betrayed Roberto, let him down, and felt that he did not deserve his love. This was what drove him to despair, the knowledge of what he had done to his father. The favourite son had fallen from grace.

'There he is, can you see him? You can just make him out . . . Here, look for yourself.'

Luciano stood by the open door of the car and trained the binoculars northwards. He had argued that the boy should not be this far from the cottage, but Calleah had assured him that his three guards would protect him. They always sent the scooter out first to check the route. No one knew that Michael was even in the vicinity, there was no problem.

Luciano caught sight of him for a moment as he jumped over a wide puddle, arms raised to the sky and head thrown back in laughter. His jump was short, and muddy black water sprayed over him, speckling his tanned face. Luciano sat in the car and let the glasses rest in his lap. 'He's soaked to the skin.'

Calleah replied, 'After what he's been through I doubt if a bit of a soaking'll hurt.'

Luciano concentrated on wrapping the leather strap

carefully around the field glasses and did not reply. They drove on to the cottage. As the gleaming car passed the first guard, he recognized Luciano sitting in the front seat and gave a small salute.

Michael was wiping the mud off his face when the guard at the door called that Luciano's car was approaching. He dropped the towel and ran to the open door, wanting with every fibre of him to clasp his father in his arms. But he stopped still, not knowing what to do, like a small child who had broken an adult's precious ornament, expecting punishment but not knowing how it would be inflicted.

Luciano stood by the car, slowly removing his sunglasses and placing them carefully in the top pocket of his coat. Then he smiled and opened his arms. Michael's paralysis left him and he ran into his father's embrace, clinging to him tightly without a word. There were no recriminations, no punishments. Calleah, near to tears, sniffed, then blew his nose on his handkerchief.

Luciano ran his hands across Michael's shoulders and arms, feeling the healthy muscles. 'You look good, you look good . . . Now you look like my son.'

Unable to meet his eyes, Michael gazed down at his sandals in shame. Luciano pinched his cheek, made him look up. 'Hey, what's this? You don't look me in the face? You must be proud! You've come through this, and you did it on your own.'

Michael smiled. 'Not quite – I needed help.'

'Sure, but you had to fight, too, you know. And from what I hear you fought like a demon . . . You beat the demon, understand? You beat it and knocked it out of you.'

Lovingly, Michael cupped his father's face in his hands and kissed his lips. 'I love you, Papa, I love you.'

Luciano's eyes brimmed with tears and again he clasped his son in his arms, whispering that he loved him more than his own life. Then he laughed. 'And if I don't take you to see your mama, my life will not be worth living. You ready to see the family?'

Michael hesitated.

'You can't hide here, can't hide away from things you must face. I am here and we must face it together, you and me.'

So Michael accepted his father's suggestion to spend the evening with the family and return to the cottage in the morning.

Although he was in good shape physically, he still needed time to regain his mental stability. Michael was grateful for his father's understanding. The boy's education was uppermost in his mind. 'I don't think this is the time to discuss your future, there's plenty of time for that, but think about it. Maybe, if you want, you can try for another college. It will be your choice, entirely up to you, I will not force you to do anything you don't want to do . . .'

Michael broke down and wept, sobbing like a child as his guilt and shame swept over him. As he sobbed, he stuttered out his apologies to his father for letting him down.

Luciano's voice cut harshly through his tears. 'I have forgiven you, and the family know nothing. They believe you have been ill. That is all, no more, no less, but I forgive you, understand? I don't want to hear about your guilt, your shame. It's over, that part of your life is over, and now we move ahead . . .'

'It'll just take time, Papa, I can't be pushed. Not yet.'

'No one is pushing you, you have to do that yourself. But you are my son, and it is perhaps because you are my son that this happened to you.'

'Papa, don't make excuses for me. Don't you under-stand, it makes it worse? I have to accept what I did and, until I do, then . . . then I'm no good to you or anyone. No good to myself, that's for sure.'

'The junk, Michael, the stuff you scored and brought with you in the guitar case – where did you get it? Here, or in the States?'

'Does it matter?'

'It matters, and I need to know. I've waited until you were able to talk coherently. Believe me, it matters.'

'I arranged it . . . it was arranged for me in the States. The score was waiting for me here.'

'Who arranged it?'

'I dunno, you mean the guy here? I wouldn't even know him if I fell over him, I was so out of it. I just paid him, and the rest is history.'

'What was the name of the dealer in the States?'

'I don't know, there wasn't just one. I don't know.'

'Then you had better think, because I want their names. Michael, understand me, I want their names.'

'Shit, I don't fucking *know*!'

For the first time ever, Luciano gave his son a hard, stinging slap across the face. 'Don't swear at me! Don't ever swear at me!'

Afraid, Michael backed off. 'I'm sorry, but you keep asking me, and I don't know. I wasn't even in Boston for the last few months – I was in New York.'

'Who were you with in New York?'

'You don't know?'

173

Patiently, Luciano repeated, 'I want you to tell me the names of the people you were with in New York, and who sold you the junk in New York.'

Michael suddenly turned on his father, his face contorted with anger. 'Why? Why? What's with a name? You think I don't know what you are, what you would do? Why don't you listen to me? I did this to myself, I bought the stuff, I injected it, and I wanted it. Whoever sold it to me doesn't matter, because *I did it*!'

Luciano moved fast, gripping Michael's shirt-front and pulling him close. 'What am I, Michael? What am I?'

Michael broke down, and this time his father pushed him away, hard. His back hit the wall and he slithered to the floor in a crumpled heap.

'I am your father, do you hear me? *I am your father!* Now get up, get up!'

He dragged Michael to his feet and threw him into a chair. 'What if I were to tell you that your so-called friends, the ones I presume you are still protecting, were paid to make sure that Michael Luciano became involved with drugs? The women, the booze, everything was set up because they wanted to destroy you – they knew it was the only way they could get to me. Tell me what you think now? You still think it doesn't matter?'

Luciano leaned against the wall and watched his son for a few moments, then went to him and gently massaged his shoulders. 'I want you to try and remember everything, right from the beginning. I need to know their names, Michael. I have to know.'

As well as he could, Michael began to recount everything, from the first night he had joined some friends at the small Italian restaurant. At times his memory was confused, days and weeks merging into a single debauched night, but he could remember a few names, and each one his father repeated. The one name he wanted to hear, that of Paul Carolla, Michael could not recall having ever heard mentioned.

Luciano kissed his son, holding him tightly as he whispered, 'I give you my word, I will find out exactly who did this to you, and you will get justice. Now wash, change, and we go to see Mama. But make no mention of anything we have discussed, never say one word to her or your brothers . . .'

Sitting in the car with Calleah, waiting for Michael, Luciano seemed tired. He put his sunglasses on again as though he wanted to hide his face. 'Whatever it takes, we need to find this Lenny Cavataio. The rest of the names from the restaurant, maybe they will say something useful, maybe not, but get rid of them all. They were all part of it. The boy, Andy Gelhorn, make sure he's the first to disappear. I was too lenient, maybe I have been too honourable for too long, my friend.'

Calleah could smell the danger brewing and he was saddened. Their dream was coming to an end.

Graziella was calling her sons to dinner when Luciano entered, smiling. 'Good, I'm just in time.' He walked straight through to the dining room and beckoned the servant to his side. 'Set another place, we are together tonight.'

Again Graziella called Alfredo, who was out in the garden, tinkering with his motorbike as always. Constantino came in and smiled at his father, followed by

175

Frederico, and a look of complicity passed between them. Then Roberto took up his usual position at the head of the table and said laughingly to Graziella, 'Mama, go out and grab the boy by the scruff of his neck. He's got one of his pals out there with him.'

Graziella threw her arms up in despair and marched to the window. 'Alfredo, I've asked you three times, you want to eat . . .?'

Outside, standing with his arms filled with flowers, was Michael. Graziella kissed and hugged her son, squashing all the flowers, then began to weep with happiness. They finally came in, hand-in-hand, and sat down. Michael had his usual seat, next to his mother, who said a short grace before food was served.

It was as though they had all forgotten the last time they had sat down together. They were in such high spirits, laughing and joking. Michael was fit and strong, suntanned, and eating well. His mother teased him about his long hair, which made him look like an American hippy, but he was Michael again.

She couldn't help the fact that, as ever, Michael stood apart from his brothers simply because of his physical appearance. They were so dark in comparison to him. His deep laugh was so infectious that the boys were losing their slight shyness of him.

Graziella watched him with adoring eyes, then squeezed her husband's hand, whispering, 'You promised he would come back and now here he is, as if he had never been away . . . I love you, I love you so . . .'

Michael lay wide awake in his room. The house felt protective, womb-like, safe. He pulled the sheets closer around him and thought about all the things that had happened in the last year. The nights so drugged he could not even recall where he had slept or who with . . . and then he remembered Sophia. He closed his eyes and thought about her for the first time in almost a year; about their childish lovemaking that night in the orchard, his empty promises. He remembered the gold heart and chain he had given her, and how she had gone back to search for it after he had thrown it from the car. He had promised to write and he hadn't, promised to come back to her and hadn't . . . The more he thought about her the more he wondered, had she waited? Was she married by now? She was the last thing he thought of before he slept and the first when he woke.

The following morning, Michael had almost changed his mind and wanted to stay on, but when his father called him into the study he wouldn't hear of it. He wanted Michael to be more sure of himself, and suggested he take his books with him, do some studying and use the next few weeks to make up his mind about trying for another college. It made sense, and Michael agreed; he had, after all, been the one who had said he needed more time.

As he was about to leave, he asked his father if he could stop off in the town and maybe see some of his old friends, just for coffee. Luciano shook his head and told Michael quietly that it would be safer for him to go direct to the cottage. Thinking his father didn't trust him, Michael flushed.

'It is not what you think, Michael. I trust you, I know you will not succumb to temptation again. But think, be more aware than ever before. The same people who tried to kill you may try again. They will attack me through you, because I have something they want.'

Without further question, Michael kissed his father and went to say goodbye to his mother.

Ettore Calleah drove the Don's car through the town. They passed the small coffee shop and Michael asked Calleah to stop. It would only be for two seconds, he just wanted to see if a girl he knew was still working there. He explained that he would only look through the window and not even go in. Eventually, Calleah gave in on condition that Michael remained in the car while he went in to check.

He was gone only a moment. He came straight back to the car and drove off. 'No, there's no one called Sophia there. She left over a year ago, so now we go, too, huh?'

Michael was so disappointed that Calleah laughed and said he looked love-struck. Michael gave him that smile of his. 'I was, a year or so ago. Can we just drive past her apartment? I won't go in, I promise, just see if she still lives there, then maybe I can write? Will you do that for me?'

So they made a detour through the squalid streets of Sophia's district and pulled up outside the old block. The entire façade was clad in scaffolding, and work was obviously under way.

Calleah looked at it and shrugged. 'Place looks empty. Maybe we should drive on.'

Michael closed the window and reluctantly agreed. They resumed their journey, but the Mercedes had been recognized as Don Roberto's, and a glimpse of Michael's face identified him as the Don's son. It was obvious that, far from being a hopeless drug addict, Michael was alive and very well indeed.

Sophia's home, in fact the entire apartment block, had been bought by the Borsalino boys, Juan and Philippe, who were converting it into a processing laboratory for heroin under cover of the 'building works'. They were the ones who had set Michael up at the airport and had moved Cavataio out fast on Carolla's instructions.

But now the Borsalinos put two and two together and came up with five. They believed that Roberto Luciano was with Michael in the car outside the building, that he knew who was responsible for his son's addiction and was going to retaliate. Afraid of the repercussions, aware that they had botched the Luciano assignment, the brothers were equally scared of losing their massive stake in the new refineries. They were Carolla's partners but they needed him, and Carolla had threatened to withdraw from the deal unless Michael Luciano was dead, and soon.

Michael still concentrated on his rigorous training schedule, but now he also spent hours shut up in his bedroom, studying. The four permanent guards worked in shifts, but they had grown lazy. No one came or went, they never had any visitors except Calleah and Luciano himself.

When the lights of the black Mercedes were seen approaching the cottage, nobody worried much about security. Calleah always wore a rough woollen cap and the guard could see only one man in the car, one man in a flat cap. He waved the car past with a casual smile, not even moving from his lookout position.

There was no answer to Roberto Luciano's second call to Ettore Calleah the next morning. When he rang the garage, he found that Calleah had taken the Mercedes out the previous evening but had not returned it. It was not unknown for him to keep the car overnight if he had an early start, but he was not usually late when he knew the car was needed, and it was now past the time he was due at the villa.

Luciano sent a man to Calleah's apartment to see if there was a problem, then decided to cancel his meeting and get down to some paperwork while he waited.

By twelve o'clock they still hadn't made contact with Calleah, and Luciano knew something was wrong. He thought of Michael; there was no phone at the cottage, and the only means of contacting his son was by a complicated system of calling the nearest village and having a message relayed to him. By two o'clock Luciano, carrying a Luger pistol, was on the way to the cottage with a driver and two armed guards.

The journey was a nightmare of tension. They passed the first lookout, sitting high up on the side of the road. He made no sign, and Luciano trained his binoculars on the man's face. As it came into focus Luciano shouted to the driver to move. He didn't even have to climb up and check; dead eyes stared back at him.

The car rolled and jolted as they hit the rough dirt track. They could see smoke curling up from the cottage chimney, but there was no sign of a guard at the gate. The car smashed through the gate and screeched to a halt in front of the house.

The two armed men, guns drawn, leapt out to shield Luciano, but he would have none of it. He pushed them aside and was already running towards the front door. It stood open about two inches and he kicked it back, pistol drawn, screaming his son's name. There was nothing but the echo of his own voice.

Luciano stood in the doorway of Michael's room, his limbs frozen. One of his men went to his side, about to enter the room. Luciano raised his hand to stop him.

'No, wait,' he whispered. They watched as he walked slowly into the room, and the door creaked shut behind him.

Michael lay face down on the bed, his right arm dangling over the edge, a hypodermic needle still protruding from it. When Luciano turned him over, barely an inch of his beautiful face was unmarked. His nose had been smashed, his cheekbones and eyes were puffy and swollen. He had fought hard; his face, bloody knuckles and torn fingernails gave witness to resistance.

Don Roberto, with the body of his son cradled in his arms like a baby, sat in the back seat of the car. As they drove past the tortured and bullet-riddled body of Ettore Calleah, left by the killers, propping up the gate post like a bedraggled puppet Luciano whispered for them to get rid of him, any way they chose. No matter what had been done to him he had betrayed the family.

Signor Maniscolo had tried everything he had ever been taught to reshape the boy's face and remodel his nose, but it had been impossible. Only the silky blond hair remained as it always had been, falling to his shoulders like an angel's. Maniscolo had washed it and combed it around his cheeks to hide as much of his face as possible, knowing he had not been able to recreate the handsome Michael Luciano. He was a mask-like stranger.

Michael's draped coffin had been set in the lounge. One by one, his brothers had come, weeping, to say farewell. Frederico couldn't look into the casket or even go close; the first sight of Michael's hands clasped over the rosary was too much for him.

Graziella, who had been in a state of shock since his death, had given a heartbreaking smile, sure there had been some mistake. This was not her son. Roberto had tried to comfort her, saying she should only remember him as she had seen him that last time, smiling up at her with his arms full of flowers.

He was unprepared for her ferocious onslaught; she screamed at him that it was his fault for sending her son away. 'Can you bring him back to me now? Can you?'

Her voice cut into him like a knife, opening wounds that would not bleed but healed rigid, straightening his body until it was so stiff and unyielding that he could not even take his wife in his arms to comfort her. He could comfort no one because he was without comfort himself.

One guard had survived, Gennaro Baranza. The man was protected day and night in the hospital. Baranza had terrible wounds; his body had been so riddled with bullets after Michael's murder that he had been left for dead. Luciano sat by his bedside, having been warned he might not survive the night. Gennaro's face and head were swathed in bandages, but he knew Don Roberto was there. His breath hissed as he whispered. 'They were Americans . . . *Americani.*'

Like a man possessed Luciano gave orders for his men to remain with Gennaro, but he never mentioned the one name he wanted to hear: Paul Carolla.

Many weeks later, when, to the medical staff's amazement, Gennaro recovered, he was mysteriously removed from the hospital in the middle of the night. Under Luciano's orders, Gennaro was kept in a safe house and every day shown hundreds of photographs. At last he identified one of the killers. The small-time mobster was traced to Chicago, and under torture gave two more names, but he swore Paul Carolla had never been a part of it – this man had, like the other two, been hired by Lenny Cavataio. The three men were silenced and no trace of their bodies ever found. Luciano was now desperate to find Lenny Cavataio, the man he had let slip through his net, and only now realized the importance of his involvement in the murder of his son. Cavataio worked for Paul Carolla, and as no one could trace him, Luciano suspected Carolla must have had him killed, he would never leave such a dangerous witness alive. Luciano in truth felt as if his own life had been drained from him.

The funeral was lavish, ornate. Michael was given the burial rites befitting the son of a don. The mourners came in their hundreds and the floral tributes and wreaths had to be carried in two separate cars.

The Luciano boys surrounded their mother, protecting her from the gaping crowds, while their father stood on one side, greeting the guests. His dark glasses hid his eyes and his strong, straight frame seemed untouchable even by such a loss. His beautiful boy was gone . . . He had not shed a single tear, not even at the open coffin.

In Italy, only the very poor bury their dead in the earth. The ground is too final, so the cemeteries are filled with marble mausoleums, the *congregazioni*. Very ornate, they are like small, private marble houses with wrought-iron grilles for doors, often so elaborately designed and decorated with gold leaf that they seem to beckon the dead into a garden rather than a cold tomb.

The Luciano *congregazione* was the largest and most decorative in the cemetery, built to accommodate the entire family. Already shelves had been carved for where they too would one day lie at rest; their coffins, like Michael's, would eventually be placed on the tiers and sealed.

Roberto stood alone, the yellow light from the wrought-iron lamp casting shadows over the many flowers that were spread outside and inside the mausoleum, covering every inch of ground like a pale, heavy carpet. One wreath seemed to stand out, and Roberto bent slowly to read the card. It was from Paul Carolla. Roberto tore it apart, hurling the flowers across the silent graves. He had come to mourn his son, but instead he raged against the man he knew had set out to kill Michael, to destroy his beautiful boy. Instead of prayer there was a hoarse, whispered curse as the flickering light caught the photograph of his son. Even the sight of his boy's face could not bring the tears he so desperately needed to shed; his anger and hatred turned into a nightmare of fear for his family. He had been foolish to come alone, he was easy prey. He hurried quickly from the mausoleum, looking over his shoulder involuntarily, knowing that if he were hit, his entire family would be taken out within hours.

Everything he had been, everything he had become, paled beside the desire to murder Paul Carolla himself, but beyond revenge was the knowledge of what that single act of violence would cause. His family had to be protected, and he clung desperately to the Mafia code of honour. He would claim his rightful justice, justice meted out within the Organization. They would give Carolla the death kiss and he would be avenged without fear of repercussion.

This fear was Carolla's strongest weapon against him. With his own eyes he had seen that Luciano's vulnerability lay in his love for his family. Luciano should have shot Carolla outside the Manhattan restaurant, but instead he had waited, and so his son had died.

Torn between protecting his living sons and avenging Michael, he had to believe that what he had done was right. There would always be a terrible guilt, a lonely guilt, because he would never admit to a living soul that he had loved too much, that he had been afraid to lose that love . . . that he had been afraid.

CHAPTER 8

SOPHIA HAD decided not to wear her new dress for travelling in. She calculated that to make the best impression she had to be fresh, clean and respectable. After paying for a cardboard suitcase and her train ticket, enough was left over from her frugal savings for one night at a hotel.

She had been preparing for this day since the baby's birth. It was very early, not yet five o'clock, and the nuns were taking mass. The blinds were still drawn on the nursery windows. She put her suitcase down beside the baby's cot and looked at the sleeping child, stroking his cheek gently until he opened his eyes. Then she reached down and picked him up, hugging him tightly. The past few months had been very hard, with little time to spend with him.

'Shussssssh, it's all right . . . It's your Mama . . . Shussssh . . .'

He yawned, sleepily, and snuggled into her neck, making soft gurgling noises. Afraid he would wake the other children, she put him back in the cot. Immediately, he began to scream.

A sister appeared at the door, frowning. Sophia slipped her gold chain from around her neck and dangled the little heart in front of the baby's face. She often let him play with it when she came to see him, swinging it back and forth and watching his plump hands reaching out. It always calmed him, his eyes following its motion as if it were hypnotizing him to sleep.

Sophia stayed until her son slept. She was about to put the chain back around her neck when she changed her mind and slipped it over her child's head.

As Sophia crept out of the nursery, the sister reappeared. She gave Sophia a scathing look, her eyes flicking down to the suitcase and back to the cot. How many times had she seen this happen . . . but she had not expected it of this girl.

'I'll be back in a few days. Take care of him, won't you?'

The sister pursed her lips. 'You know the regulations. Three months, then he's up for adoption just like the others here.'

Sophia's hand tightened on the handle of the cheap case. 'He is not like the others, he is my son. I will be back, believe me. I am going to Palermo on business.'

'You will have to sign the papers, it's the regulation.'

'I know,' said Sophia confidently. 'I have signed them, Sister Matilda, but it is a waste of paper – I will be back for my son.' She walked out.

She was in plenty of time for the train and sat on the platform, bathed in the early morning sun. She felt free, positive that she was doing the right thing.

As the train drew closer to Palermo she was amazed at her own anger. She began to twist her hands and pluck at her skirt. What if they refused to see her, what if Michael refused to believe the child was his?

Her doubts persisted, even after she had booked into

187

a cheap hotel, even after she had bathed and changed. She stared at her reflection, hating the thick-soled shoes, unsure even of her dress. And she looked so thin . . .

'I'm thin because I have to work like a slave,' she snapped to herself, brushing her hair frantically. The thick, heavy waves fell to below her shoulders, and even in her self-critical mood she had to admit that it looked healthy and shining. When she had threaded ribbons through it she nodded her approval. The shoes she still loathed, but she looked presentable.

After a long wait, the bus came and deposited her half a mile from the Villa Rivera. As she walked over the brow of the hill she could see the house below, bathed in golden sunlight. Her confidence was dwindling fast and she rehearsed her little speech as she skirted the high brick wall. She licked her lips as she came in sight of the wrought-iron gates. This was the long-awaited moment. She hurried the last few steps.

As she reached for the bell pull, a guard appeared. He stared at Sophia through the bars of the gate.

'*Buon giorno!* My name is Sophia Visconti and I am an old friend of Michael Luciano. I was wondering if I could speak with him. It's a personal matter.'

The guard was nonplussed. Was she having him on or was she crazy? But something about her heart-shaped face and the determined set of her chin made him speak to her kindly.

'Go on home, girl. Go on.'

Standing her ground, Sophia went into her second speech. 'I refuse to go away until I have spoken to him or his father.'

'Don't you read the papers? Go on, get out of here. Have more respect.'

Another guard peered through the gate and gestured for her to move away. She responded firmly, 'I will not leave until I have seen Michael Luciano. I have come a very long way to see him. Please, it is very important.'

The two men looked at each other and then back at Sophia. Her hands were clenched around the bars of the gate, her face pressed between them.

'Where have you come from?'

'Cefalu. Please let me in.'

The first guard stepped back as his friend pointed to the ornate, black-ribboned wreath hanging high on the other gate. Sophia turned and looked up at it.

'Michael Luciano died three weeks ago; this is a house of mourning. I must ask you to leave. Please go away, no one will see you.'

Uncomprehending, Sophia stared at them through the gate for a moment. As the men turned back towards the dark, shuttered house, she began to scream over and over that it wasn't true, it couldn't be true. In the end they opened the gates and prised her hands away from the bars. She fought like a wildcat, scratching and kicking, trying to bite their hands, as they dragged her away from the gate and down the lane. Her hysteria alarmed them, not because of the violence but because they were afraid her screams would be heard inside the villa.

Between them they pulled her along the lane until they were satisfied that she could not be heard from the house. She still tried to wriggle free, kicking and screaming, until the tougher of the two men slapped her face. She spun away from him and crumpled into a heap on the ground.

His friend bent and picked up her purse. 'Come on,

we don't want to hurt you. Here's your purse . . . Now, go on, go away from here.'

Sophia sat in the middle of the road for more than an hour. When at last she rose slowly to her feet, the men sighed with relief. She dusted her skirt and picked up her purse, staring blank-eyed as she walked back to the bus stop. But when the bus came, she couldn't even lift her hand to hail it. She didn't know how many hours she stood there, but it was dusk by the time she decided to walk on, her mind still numb with shock.

She didn't hear the car as it raced around the corner and certainly didn't mean to walk in front of it. Perhaps she intended to ask for a lift, she never could remember, but the next thing she knew she was lying in a cool, dark room. A sweet-faced woman was holding a damp cloth to her head.

'Don't be frightened. There was an accident, but you are all right. The doctor is on his way to see you.'

Sophia closed her eyes without even asking where she was. The doctor came shortly after that and examined her. She had slight concussion and a very nasty bruise on her temple, but there were no bones broken. He offered to call an ambulance to take her to hospital, but Graziella insisted that the girl remain where she was. She would take care of her.

When the doctor had left, Sophia again felt the gentle hands bathing her face. She opened her eyes.

'There, does that make you feel better?'

Sophia smiled weakly, then her lips began to tremble and the tears flowed.

'Well, little sparrow, do you have a name? What's your name?'

'Soph-ia . . .'

'Well, Sophia, we will get you well. Now, is there anyone I can call, anyone who will be worried about you?'

'No, there is no one . . . I only came today, I only arrived here today.'

Graziella tucked the sheet around her, then gently squeezed her hand. 'The doctor gave you something that will make you sleep. We will talk again after you have rested.'

As white, billowing clouds formed in her head, Sophia lay back, smiling her thanks to the woman. She whispered something that Graziella could not make out, then she was asleep.

The boys each felt the loss of their brother, who had always been the favourite, the golden boy. Michael had looked like an angel, and now he could really be one, forever gliding over their heads, as untouchable in death as he had been in life.

Frederico had destroyed Michael's guitar, set light to it in a desperate attempt to make himself noticed. It was a sad gesture, a silent scream, 'I am here, someone notice me and help me! I am alive!' But it was ignored. Constantino began drinking, alone in his room. It was his own way of calling for attention, but no one gave his slurred speech or stumbling gait a second thought. Alfredo drove like a lunatic, so crazily that he had mounted the pavement and almost killed a young girl.

The one common denominator in their lives was Michael. Now a total outsider with strong emotional ties to the dead boy, although the family did not know it, slept under their roof. Graziella was the first to reach out. By caring for Sophia she broke her own wall of silence.

Alfredo looked up, a concerned expression on his face, as his mother came down the stairs carrying a bowl of water.

'She's all right. She's got a nasty bruise on her temple, maybe slight concussion, but the doctor says she'll be fine. Let it be a lesson to you – you drive too fast, you always have. So now you make sure you take more care.'

It was the first time since Michael's death that Graziella had communicated with anyone, so even the simple ticking-off she had given her son meant a great deal.

Inching open the door, he looked at Sophia, who was deeply asleep. He crept to the bed and looked down at her. She lay with one hand curled by her face, a sweet, heart-shaped face that looked so vulnerable he immediately wanted to protect her. He bent closer, then jumped as Graziella walked into the room.

'Out! Go on, let the poor little thing sleep,' she whispered.

'Isn't she beautiful?'

'I've seen better fed, she's as thin as a rake . . . Now go on, leave us, she needs me to sit with her.'

Sophia didn't even know she was in the room, but Graziella positioned a chair by the bed and sat down, not wanting the girl to be frightened at waking up in a strange house.

Alfredo tapped on his father's study door, then entered. His father didn't even look up, but continued to write.

'You heard I had a little accident? She's all right, though, and Mama's sitting with her.'

'I'm a very busy man, Alfredo, and unless you have something worthwhile to discuss with me, kindly do not interrupt in future. You should know better, and you should know better than to drive at such a ridiculous speed that you hit someone almost on our own doorstep.'

Alfredo closed the door silently behind him. No one could speak to his father since Michael's death; he was unable to communicate with any of them. Alfredo knew that his mother and father were torn apart, and his father was sleeping in one of the spare rooms or on the sofa in his study. It was as upsetting for Alfredo as it was for his brothers.

No matter how they tried, he would not be drawn into conversation. They said it was grief, it would soon be over, but it did not look as though it would end, ever. Until Luciano could direct his anger at the right target, at Carolla, and avenge his son's death, he felt helpless and feared that if he gave way to his grief, he might never be able to pick himself up from it. It was a living nightmare of his own making, and the only way he could survive was to go away from everyone who meant anything to him.

Graziella sat up all night with Sophia and made no effort to speak to her husband. She heard his heavy steps on the stairs at bedtime and listened as he went, as he did every night, into Michael's bedroom. She knew she would have to go in.

Roberto's eyes were anguished, like a beaten dog's,

and he did not have the strength to hide it from her. His face puckered and his voice broke as he said, 'Mama, they took my boy . . .'

Seeing him that way broke her heart. Whatever she had accused him of meant nothing now, her love and pity for him overwhelmed her. She held him then, rocked him in her arms, and at last he let the dam break.

In his room, Constantino could hear the sound of his father weeping. He put his pillow over his head to block out the sound. Frederico, out in the yard below the window, ran into the orchards, away from the dreadful sound.

Alfredo's hands were trembling, rattling the crockery, as he set the tray down beside Sophia. She was sitting up, eyes wide with fear, clutching the sheet to her breasts. The sound of the man weeping had woken her.

Alfredo immediately sat beside her. 'It's all right, it's all right . . . It's . . . it's my father.'

Involuntarily, he put his hands to his face, muffling his voice as he tried to apologize and explain all at the same time.

He could not stop the tears, and they streamed down his face. 'My brother, his name was Michael . . . My brother died three weeks ago, and . . .'

Sophia's eyes widened and she clutched the sheet tighter around her. Her mind was full of shattering glass, each word a splintered fragment . . . 'This is Michael Luciano's house?'

'He was my brother.' Alfredo opened one of the shutters a fraction, then, with his back to her, he said softly, 'Michael was always special. He was cleverer than any of the rest of us, and there was nothing he couldn't do. He went to America . . . and I was glad, because suddenly my father noticed me.'

He turned to her then, looking so young and hurt, the tears trickling down his cheeks. 'I'm sorry, I don't know why I'm telling you this. Maybe because now my father doesn't even know we exist, any of us.'

Sophia replied by holding out her arms to him like a mother. It felt so strange, offering comfort to Michael's brother as if it surpassed her own grief. As he fell into her embrace, the door opened and Constantino stood framed in the doorway. He stepped back, surprised, gesturing to Alfredo to come closer to him. Then in a low voice he asked, 'Did you hear Papa?'

Alfredo nodded as Sophia said, 'My name is Sophia,' in her soft, husky voice. Both brothers turned to her as she continued, 'Sophia Visconti . . .'

Alfredo smiled and bowed, introducing himself, 'I am Alfredo Luciano, and this is my eldest brother, Constantino.'

At that moment Frederico peered into the room, eager to see what was going on. Alfredo slung an arm around the younger boy and pulled him into the room. 'This fat one is the youngest Luciano, this is Frederico.'

Three dark faces, with dark eyes and black hair, smiled in the doorway. They bore no resemblance to their dead brother, Michael.

Sophia remained at the villa for another week, but she never saw Roberto Luciano. At the end of the week, the Don went to New York on business, after instructing Constantino to make sure Sophia would not be there on his return. Constantino was to pay her well, but now, more than ever, strangers were not welcome at the Villa Rivera.

Graziella wanted Sophia to stay a little longer as she seemed very frail, but her son was firm in carrying out his father's orders. He apologized and suggested that the doctor call at her hotel if she still needed him. She thanked him for the family's kindness, but knew she was being got rid of. She knew that the Don was no longer at home, and could not bring herself to tell anyone else why she was in Palermo. If she was going to discuss her child with anyone, it must be Michael's father.

She sat silently at Alfredo's side as he drove her to the hotel. Their arrival sent the manager scurrying this way and that, bowing and scraping, when he recognized Alfredo. He insisted that Sophia occupy the best room the hotel had to offer.

Alfredo stayed for only a few moments, thanking her yet again for being so understanding and apologizing for the accident. She had only to call the family if there was anything she needed . . . Sophia spoke hardly two words; she was still very confused and was worried about the cost of the new room. As soon as he had gone, she went down to reception, where she was received with an ingratiating smile. Nervously, she enquired about the charge for the room and was told that the Lucianos had settled her outstanding bill and paid for the room up to the end of the month. He handed her a packet that Alfredo had left for her, and when she opened it in the privacy of her room she found it contained a small diamond brooch.

In the late afternoon, she went down to reception. The manager gave her a slight bow and asked if she required room service. She hesitated, then shook her head. She had not eaten but found she wasn't hungry.

'I was wondering if it would be possible for me to have my old room back and pay me the difference in cost.'

The manager sighed, suddenly irritated, and flipped through the register. Sophia coughed and he looked up.

'I was also wondering if you need any help. I have to work,' she said.

He smiled, tapping his fingers on the register. 'What kind of work?' he asked.

'Cleaning, making beds, anything.'

He reached over the desk and pinched her chin. 'Aren't the Lucianos looking after you?'

Sophia stepped back. 'Yes, they are looking after me.'

She was a very attractive girl, a bit skinny for his taste, but he might put her behind the desk. It was always good to keep in with the likes of the Lucianos, but at the same time he couldn't help wondering what the connection was.

Michael Luciano's *congregazione* was still decked with flowers and fresh bouquets had been placed in the urns outside. Sophia, carrying a small bunch of wild flowers, stood at the gate, which was locked, and peered between the railings. An elderly caretaker called out to her, waving his arms for her to go away, and came over when she didn't move.

She turned, the tears streaming down her cheeks. 'Please, please, let me see him.'

There was something about the girl's grief that moved the old man. After checking that no one was there to see, he opened the mausoleum and allowed Sophia inside. He stayed on guard at the gate, saying she could only have a few moments, but minutes went by and she didn't come out.

It was the photograph; she hadn't been prepared for that. Seeing Michael's beautiful face, his soft smile, brought the pain crashing down again, swamping her. The caretaker found her slumped on her knees, her face pressed against the cold marble, and almost as white. She couldn't stand; like a small child she lifted her arms to him, and the old man held her tightly. Just before she collapsed she whispered, 'I loved him, I loved him . . .'

The old man walked Sophia back to the hotel. He had given her hot, sweet tea and watched the colour slowly creep back into her pale face, but her burden of grief seemed, if anything, heavier. She had said little and he had asked no questions.

When she thanked him and opened her purse to pay him for his kindness, he refused.

As Sophia passed reception the hotel manager called to her that her old room was free.

'You can help out here on the desk, and make up the beds in the morning.'

She gave a small nod and a tight-lipped 'thank you' and hurried up to her room, slamming the door behind her. She felt so angry, but didn't know why. Locking the door, she threw the key on the bed and began to pace the room. She had missed her opportunity. Why hadn't she said something while she was at the villa, actually in Michael's home? Why hadn't she asked to speak to his father? How would they react now? Would they think she was lying if she suddenly told them about her son, about Michael's child? She stopped suddenly, searched at the back of a drawer for the brooch, and held it in the palm of her hand. They owed her a lot more, and she wanted more.

All night she tossed and turned, going over the past week in her mind. Graziella had been so kind, so understanding, why had she not told her? Her son was a Luciano, albeit a bastard. But doubts hammered at her; would she, in their place, believe such a story from a girl picked off the road, a girl who had seen their wealth at first hand?

By morning she had made up her mind. She had three months before her son would be put up for adoption. She determined to speak to Don Roberto and, if he didn't believe her, she would return to Cefalu and bring her son to them.

She started work at the hotel that morning, which passed in cleaning, sweeping, washing and ironing. Her thoroughness surprised the manager, who told her she could spend two hours on reception. She busied herself polishing the counter, dusting the pigeonholes and tidying the keys.

The bell pinged and she turned. It was Constantino's turn to blush. 'Did you receive my mother's gift?'

He pulled at his tie, feeling out of place in the rundown hotel, knowing he shouldn't have come.

'I was about to write to your mother. I'm sorry, I hope she doesn't think me rude.'

'No, of course not . . . Have you lost your key?'

Sophia looked puzzled, then gave an embarrassed smile. 'No, I am working here.'

'Oh, I see . . . I didn't know; Alfredo said you were staying here.'

He saw the manager approaching and gave Sophia a

small nod. 'Well, I won't keep you from your work. *Buona sera*, Sophia!'

She watched him walk out to his Alfa Romeo and stood, wrapped in thought, remembering her drive in Michael's car. The manager also watched Constantino drive off and gave Sophia a sidelong look. He leaned on the counter.

'That was the Don's eldest son, wasn't it? He'll be in line for a fortune . . . Any time you want to entertain, you talk to me, understand? The Lucianos are a big family, I do a favour for them, understand me? Any time . . .'

Sophia loathed the fat, greasy little man. Her body tensed whenever he came near her. He reached out to pinch her chin and she brought her hand up to stop him.

'Don't touch me, don't you ever touch me, understand? Any time.'

He backed off as if he had been slapped and scuttled into his office. Sophia smiled to herself; it was extraordinary, he would be afraid of her just so long as the Lucianos were in evidence. He had changed her room without argument, given her money and agreed to pay her a reasonable wage. If all this was simply due to her being associated with them, what must it feel like to actually be a Luciano?

That evening she wrote a careful note to Signora Luciano, thanking her for her hospitality and her kindness in sending the brooch and wondering if she might call at the villa before she left Palermo. She did not see Constantino again, but received a short note from Graziella, asking her to tea the following week.

The days were passing, and Sophia knew she would

200

have to make up her mind how to tell Graziella about the baby. The invitation seemed the perfect opportunity.

Sophia had bought a new white linen dress and white gloves, her shoes were polished and she wore her hair braided with blue ribbon. The small diamond brooch was pinned to her collar.

Graziella sent a car to collect her, and the uniformed chauffeur helped her into the back seat. She sat well back, stiffly at first, on the luxurious soft leather. They passed the two guards that had sent her away, but they appeared not to recognize her as they waved the car through the gates.

Now she saw the villa in all its splendour. The long gravel drive had been in darkness when she had first been brought here, but now she saw the banks of flowers, the neat hedges and lawns, the pillared portico bedecked with flowers and the wide verandah curving most of the way around the ground floor.

Graziella was waiting for her guest at the open door. She smiled and waved as the chauffeur helped Sophia out, and hurried down the steps to greet her. As if she were a close friend, she linked her arm through Sophia's and drew her into the house, patting her hand and saying how well she looked as she guided her through the panelled hallway and into a cosy sitting room.

The long shutters were drawn back and the windows opened onto the verandah, where tea was already laid. It was cool and shady, and the roses trailing along the rails gave a heady scent. Sophia noted that the tea table was set for four.

201

She was introduced to Adina, a pleasant-faced servant, who bustled around the table bringing baskets of pastries and home-made cookies while Graziella kept up a steady flow of light conversation about the garden, explaining about certain plants, how she pruned them, and how many gardeners she employed. Sophia sat politely, her hands folded in her lap.

'My husband is in New York on business, and I get very lonely. I cannot tell you how delighted I am that you were able to accept my invitation. Adina, ask the boys to join us if they are taking tea . . . Now, Sophia, you must not refuse Adina's pastries, they are delicious, and you are too thin. Alfredo?'

Alfredo bounded up from the garden, his face and hands streaked with grease. Graziella refused to let him sit on her clean cushions until he had washed, laughingly telling Sophia that her son was in love. Not, sadly, with a nice girl he could marry, but with motorbikes . . . All the time her plump hands fluttered over the tea tray, pouring tea, dispensing sugar lumps, handing plates and lace napkins.

'*Buon giorno! Mama. Come sta?*' Constantino kissed his mother's cheek and then Sophia's hand.

Sophia blushed and replied, '*Molto bene, grazie . . .*' She was very aware of her chapped red hands and quickly replaced them in her lap.

Alfredo, clean now, joined them, and the family put her at her ease with their easy banter and teasing. Frederico, the youngest son, had been put on a diet. He was not allowed any cakes, and sat glum-faced until Graziella allowed him one small slice of chocolate gâteau. Sophia was enjoying the afternoon, and her eyes sparkled.

The dark cloud that suddenly descended was so unexpected that for a moment Sophia could not understand what had happened. Graziella had seemed so happy, surrounded by her sons, Frederico perched on the arm of her chair . . . It wasn't anything anybody had said; Graziella's face changed, one moment wreathed in smiles and the next on the verge of tears, lips quivering. Her small hands, one moment so busy, remained poised in the air as tears trickled down her cheeks.

Alfredo put his plate down quickly and, with Frederico, helped her from her seat.

'It's all right, Mama, come on. Maybe you should rest.' Sophia heard her sobbing as she was guided from the table.

Constantino put his cup down with care. 'I'm sorry, Mama does not see too many people and I think perhaps she over-excited herself. She is still . . .'

'Your brother?'

'Yes, my brother. It's strange, it often happens at meal times, maybe because he was such a strong personality. When we're all together his not being there is more obvious. Mama just seems to be overcome, but it doesn't last long. She'll be all right soon.'

They sat in silence, looking out across the garden. Sophia was wondering desperately if Graziella would come back to see her, she couldn't miss this opportunity. 'Will your father be back soon?'

Constantino started and gave her a puzzled look, as if asking why she wanted to know.

'It must be easier for your mother if he is here,' she explained.

'Not necessarily. It has been difficult for both of them

to come to terms with my brother's death.' Sophia noticed that he never said 'Michael', always 'my brother'. He continued to stare at the garden.

'It must be very difficult for you, too,' she said.

'Yes . . .' He tapped his foot on the verandah. 'I was the second son . . . Now, may I say how very beautiful you look?'

Astonished at the unexpected compliment, Sophia gave a soft laugh. 'Thank you . . .'

He stood up and walked the length of the verandah, stopping at the far end, half in shadow, his hands stuffed in his pockets. 'I wanted to come and see you, but . . . Well, I wasn't sure if you wanted to see me. If I had come to the hotel, would you have seen me?'

Again she laughed, then replied that of course she would. He smiled, pleased, and walked back towards her. 'You have no family?'

'No. My father died when I was a child, and my mother eighteen months ago.'

'I'm sorry . . . The hotel, where you work, are the people running it related to you?'

'No, I work there, that is all.'

Suddenly he laid his hand on her shoulder. 'Where did you come from? The manager said you had only just booked in the night before the accident.'

She knew it was time, her opportunity, and opened her mouth to speak. But Constantino gently caressed her cheek and whispered, 'Forgive me, I have no right to ask you so many questions . . .'

Just then Alfredo came back, and the moment was lost.

He picked up a thin slice of home-baked bread and sat on the railings, a smear of butter on his cheek.

'Are you recovered? No after-effects?'

'No after-effects,' said Sophia, aware of the young boy's scrutiny. He was twisting a piece of string in his fingers. She had noticed that all the boys were highly strung, but especially this one. His heavy-lidded eyes were slightly shifty, but at the same time he was exceedingly good-looking.

Frederico appeared for a moment in the doorway, 'Con, Mama says to see her, and to order a car to take Sophia home.' Constantino held out his hand to take Sophia to his mother. As they passed Frederico, he was grinning, keeping his eyes to the ground. 'Papa just called, he's got to stay in New York.' He suddenly blurted out with a boyish snigger. 'I guess we'll be seeing you again then, Sophia!'

Constantino cuffed Frederico, but he was blushing.

Graziella was lying on a chaise longue. Smiling, she gestured for Sophia to sit with her.

'My dear, I must ask you to forgive me. Please sit with me until the car is brought round . . . You may leave us, Constantino.'

Sophia could not have planned a better opportunity to speak up, but just as she opened her mouth Graziella, as her son had done earlier, began asking questions about her relatives and where she had lived before. She seemed genuinely distressed when she discovered that Sophia was only seventeen years old and had no one.

The moment for mentioning the child came and went. Graziella only detected Sophia's embarrassment when she said she was not staying as a guest in the hotel but was employed there. Nothing in the girl's manner hinted at her inner turmoil; her mind was racing, firing its own questions.

Does she know? Is she suspicious? Why is she asking me all this, why does she want to know . . . ? Tell her, tell her now, the truth . . . Tell her about the baby . . .

'It must be hard for a respectable young girl.' Graziella waited for a reply, but all the girl did was lift her big, dark eyes, as if she were afraid. Graziella knew, of course, that Roberto would not have allowed Sophia in the house again and would not, she was sure, even consider his son's desire to court any girl, let alone this orphaned child, so soon after Michael's death. But Graziella only wanted her son to be happy, for the darkness to lift from the house, the darkness that now crept over her. She gave a long, low sigh.

'Constantino wishes to see you again. As you have no one he can speak to, then it must be your own decision.'

Graziella interpreted Sophia's burning cheeks and obvious confusion, her inability to say a word, to her being simply out of her depth. She smiled.

'You are very young, aren't you, and of course you must be chaperoned. But he wants you to know that his intentions are honourable. No arrangements could possibly be made until my husband returns, but in the interim you are most welcome to come here.'

Sophia remained speechless, wanting to cry when Graziella took her in her arms and gave her a motherly hug. 'He is a dear, sweet boy, but painfully shy. Perhaps when you get to know each other a little better . . .'

Sophia suddenly clung to Graziella, holding her so tightly that she could smell the soft lavender perfume, feel the crushed velvet of the mourning dress against her cheek. There was such desperation in her action that Graziella at first resisted, but then she responded and cupped the sweet face in her hands.

Kissing Sophia's lips, she whispered, 'There has been so much sadness in this house, Sophia. Pray God will bring you happiness.'

Nothing could have prepared her for the events of the afternoon. The realization was dawning that she, Sophia Visconti, was to be courted by Don Roberto Luciano's eldest son. If she wanted, she could be what she had dreamed of, a Luciano. Only her son stood in her way, and there was no escaping the fact that his existence would destroy her one chance.

Sophia sprang from the bed and stripped off her clothes, searching her body for tell-tale stretch marks . . . But her nakedness was perfect, her young skin smooth and tight, her slim figure giving no indication that she was a mother. She stood before the cracked dressing-table mirror, running her hands over her body, then dropped to her knees, clasping her rosary to her lips, and prayed. She prayed that nothing would go wrong, she prayed harder than she had done in her entire life, harder than when she had been so desperate for Michael to come back to her. She prayed that no one would betray her, while the beads of the rosary cut into her hand.

Prayers did not stop the dreams or still the sound of her baby crying for her – she could see him, his tiny arms raised upwards and twice she woke, her body drenched in sweat. She cried for him then, knew what she contemplated doing was wrong, but persuaded herself that it was just time, only time, and one day she would tell Constantino about her son, about Michael.

The following morning, Sophia burnt her small diary. She had no photograph of her child and she was secure in the knowledge that no one in Palermo could possibly know of her affair with Michael or the baby's birth.

She counted the money she had saved and then, instead of going to work, went into town. She window-shopped for hours before buying two dresses, cheap but simple and exactly what she wanted. She would appear virginal, demure and, above all, respectable. Clutching her purchases, calculating what she had left of her meagre savings, she hurried along the street, and came face to face with one of the gate guards from the Luciano villa, the man who had turned her away the day she had arrived in Palermo to see Michael. He gave her a small nod of recognition, and actually passed on before he stopped and turned back to stare. Her hand was shaking, but she held her head up. 'One moment, signor, we have met before, do you remember?'

He gave a furtive look to right and left. 'No, signorina, I do not remember!'

'Then I too will forget, and never mention to Don Roberto your rudeness. I was grief stricken, and . . .'

He interrupted, his face beet red. 'I apologize, signorina, I know now you are a friend of the family, please accept my sincere apologies.'

'I accept.' With that she turned on her heel, so he could not see the relief on her face or the faint smile. She was safe and, feeling confident and enjoying the new-found feeling, she swept into the hotel. She told the manager that she was no longer prepared to do the cleaning but wished only to remain behind the reception desk. She would earn enough for food, and she did not want raw, red hands when Constantino Luciano next called to see her.

Sophia became a regular visitor at the Villa Rivera. Graziella found her a delightful companion and looked forward to her visits. Sophia told her about her mother, how they had left Palermo because of her illness and how she had worked at the convent and the village hotel. She was careful not to embroider her background, knowing it could easily be checked, even telling Graziella about her days in the coffee shop in Palermo.

A routine had developed; after tea Sophia and the shy Constantino would be left alone on the verandah. From time to time he had a slight stutter and flushed easily. At first Sophia had thought him unattractive with his slightly hooked nose, but gradually she came to realize that he was a very good-looking boy. His gentle personality and naïvety charmed her. Constantino had a strength to him, a firmness that she admired. They walked in the orchards and at first simply held hands. Sophia was always aware that they were being watched. He never attempted to kiss her lips, but seemed content just to thread his fingers through hers, and in the end it was Sophia who drew him into her arms, holding her face up to be kissed.

She did not expect to enjoy it so much. Constantino seemed almost as surprised, and held her close.

'I love you, Sophia, I love the sound of your voice, I love the way you move, the way you smell, I love your hair, I love . . . I want you to be my wife.' He clasped her so tightly that she gasped for breath.

When he released her, he looked so flustered that she

laughed, tossing her head, and that was how Roberto Luciano saw them as he was driven up to the house. He was not expected home, he had told no one and so took them all by surprise.

He gave his wife only a brief kiss before demanding to know who the girl was. Graziella had planned how she would tell him, introducing him gradually to the idea of a daughter-in-law he hadn't chosen for his son. Now she found herself blushing as nervously as Constantino.

'You remember the young girl Alfredo brought to the house?'

'Alfredo has brought many girls, I don't remember each one. What are they doing out there?'

'Courting. Now, before you start shouting, let me explain.'

'Courting, here? And you are allowing it?'

'Well, of course I am. He invited her here. He's in love with the girl.'

Even after all their years of marriage he could still unnerve her, almost frighten her with that hooded stare. She broke the silence. 'She is an orphan, only seventeen, and with no one of her own. No family . . .'

'Get her out of my home. I don't like people here, strangers. Ask her to leave.'

'This is my home, too, and I will not. She is a sweet, darling girl, and he loves her.'

Roberto stormed out on to the verandah before she could say another word and called for Constantino to join him. Alfredo, working on his motorbike, whipped round, surprised to hear his father's voice. As always, his stomach lurched. It had been the same since he was a toddler; even if he hadn't done anything wrong he hated that tone in his father's voice.

210

Sophia saw Constantino pale at the sound of the harsh voice. His body went rigid. 'It's my father, he's back . . .'

He straightened his tie, even though it wasn't crooked, then ran his fingers through his hair. He gave Sophia a rueful smile and gestured for her to go ahead; not, she noticed, giving her his hand. But she took it and felt his grip tighten as they hurried towards the house.

Graziella was waiting on the verandah. Even she appeared nervous, patting stray wisps of hair into the heavy coiled bun at the nape of her neck, and explaining that their father was home and they were to wait for him in the drawing room. She gestured for Sophia to go to her side and waved Constantino into the room.

'He's not in a very pleasant mood, perhaps it would be a good idea if you were introduced another time. Do you mind, Sophia?'

Sophia shook her head and was about to return to the garden when Constantino came back on to the verandah. 'Sophia . . .'

Constantino showed his quiet determination, gripping Sophia's arm firmly and leading her into the room.

'Sophia is going to be my wife, Mama, and she will not be hidden until you think Papa's in a suitable frame of mind . . .'

The boys were sitting together on a low sofa. Graziella started pouring sherry into a crystal glass while Constantino pulled out a straight-backed chair for Sophia, touching her cheek as she sat down. Graziella did not offer anyone else a drink, and had just replaced the stopper in the decanter when Roberto Luciano entered.

The tension in the room was overpowering. The Don strode in and took the glass from his wife, without thanks, and sipped. His near-black eyes looked at each of them in turn, lastly at Sophia.

'Father, this is Sophia Visconti.'

The Don continued to stare at her, managing to give a brief, slight nod. 'I hear you are fully recovered.'

Sophia nodded, then looked down at her hands. He terrified her with his hawk-like nose and carved cheeks, his shock of thick white hair, his size and elegance, and she could see that he affected everyone else the same way. He exuded vitality and cold anger. Constantino's hand, on the back of her chair, was shaking.

'I wonder if you would be so kind, Signorina Visconti as to allow my driver to take you home. I have had a long journey and I am very tired.'

He showed no sign of fatigue. His abrupt gesture to his son to remove Sophia from the room was an order, taken as such. Constantino led Sophia from the room as the Don poured himself another sherry.

'Don't be long, Constantino,' the Don ordered, and Sophia saw the fear in her new fiancé's eyes. She stood on tiptoe to kiss him.

He slipped a thin leather jewel case into her hand. It contained a single string of pearls with a small diamond clasp, but she had no time to thank him properly. He opened the front door, saying that the car was on its way. His manner was more apologetic than his words and she knew he was angry. Like his father, he wanted her to leave, but for a different reason. He was furious at his father's rudeness.

'Don't do anything foolish, Constantino.'

With a nervous smile he returned to the drawing room. As the door closed, she heard the sound of breaking glass and Don Roberto's deep voice rising in fury. But she couldn't listen as the driver, already waiting, sounded the horn.

Had Sophia been a witness to the tirade, the bitter, vicious anger of Don Roberto as he confronted his eldest son, she would have felt more than a seed of doubt. She would have believed there was no hope whatsoever.

He had thrown his glass at the wall, his face distorted with rage, yet, when he asked Graziella to see to dinner, his voice was controlled, low and guttural. She walked out, her face taut with anger, but she would not argue in front of her sons.

She knew she had been wrong to allow the situation to go so far without first discussing it with her husband, but she had not expected such fury and did not understand why he was so frighteningly angry.

The Don's three sons sat like guilty schoolboys. Constantino tried to interrupt to ask for his brothers to be excused, but his father turned on him.

'Don't say one word, any of you.'

Constantino fell silent, feeling the tremor of the sofa from Alfredo's nervously twitching foot.

'How many times have I told you never, never, is a stranger allowed to visit this house without my knowledge, without my permission? For you to go against my express wishes . . . You are the eldest, you should know better, should know that when I am away you must take my place. To abuse that position . . .'

Constantino stood up, as nervous as if he were facing his father for the first time in his life.

'I have not abused it, Father, and I never would. I think if you hear of the circumstances . . .'

213

'What circumstances? Your libido is no circumstance! You want a girl, then go to the whorehouse.'

'She is not a whore,' shouted his son.

Luciano's eyes were like a madman's. He prodded Constantino's chest with his finger. 'You know, do you? Who are her friends, who does she know? Where does she come from? *You know these things?* Because she tells you she has no family, because she tells you, you believe her?'

Constantino swallowed and replied bravely, 'Yes, I do.' His voice sounded choked.

'Have you checked out her family, or her lack of one?'

Helplessly humiliated, Constantino shook his head. His face flushed a deep red and, to make matters worse, he stuttered badly as he tried to say that he trusted Sophia.

'Trust is not enough . . .' Luciano reached out and pulled his son towards him, holding him for a moment as his anger subsided. His other two sons looked on, afraid to say a word that might turn his wrath on them. They seemed so young, so naïve, and Luciano knew what a terrible mistake he had made in keeping so much from them. Now he decided they should know the truth.

His sons watched in silence as he turned from them, staring out of the window. 'Michael . . .' And the storm was over, his voice no longer filled with anger. 'Michael returned from America a heroin addict. He had been given the drug by friends, boys he believed were his friends, boys he trusted . . . Boys who were paid to destroy him, by men who wished to destroy me.'

Shocked, his sons flicked glances at each other. Their father slowly turned his haggard face towards them.

'One day we will take revenge for Michael. No matter

how long, we will wait. Death and dishonour must always be avenged, it is immaterial whether in my lifetime or yours. Revenge can be a sweet dish and is often best eaten cold.'

Upstairs in her bedroom, Graziella had not the slightest notion that her sons were being initiated, each swearing an oath to avenge his brother Michael's murder. They listened intently to their father as he quietly explained the intricacies of his company, the importance given to his *capi* within the family structure. He explained how he personally had three *consiglieri*, or counsellors, working for him in the United States. All these men were elected, chosen by men of honour like himself. Even though he was the head of the Luciano family, he was still simply a representative of the Organization, and of the vast wealth attached to him owned only a percentage, the Commission taking the major share.

However, due to his own businesses, set up and flourishing without Organization funds, his personal wealth was formidable and he was not forced to share any of it. The import and export businesses, the canneries and the docks belonged entirely to him, and it was these holdings Paul Carolla wanted. These were the things the Lucianos would fight for, would never allow Carolla to touch. They were legitimate businesses and would one day be run by Luciano's sons. He looked at his heirs and their youth, their innocence, overpowered him. He knew how wrong he had been in sheltering them for so long.

One by one they swore the oath, blood to blood – too scared to meet one another's eyes or ask questions. When it was over their father kissed them each on the mouth, a hard kiss, a kiss of confirmation. Then, before he dismissed them, he said, 'Above all, the most important thing, is to be aware of the dangers. You must watch out for each other, care for each other, love each other, and trust no one outside the family.'

Constantino apologized for bringing Sophia to the house without permission and asked if he could check out her background personally, not wishing to cause his father any inconvenience. He then asked for permission to marry the girl if everything was found to be suitable, although he knew she had no family, no dowry.

Luciano would not give an answer either way, it would need a great deal of thought. As the eldest son, Constantino was in an enviable position and could make himself a very good match that would benefit not only himself but also his family.

'Remember, Constantino, your family always comes first. You must never put your own feelings before those of your family.'

Subdued, Constantino stood up and shook his father's hand, thanking him. He had not given the go-ahead, but neither had he said no.

In truth, Roberto felt so bereft that all he wanted was for the boy to leave the room. He could not help comparing him with Michael. He knew that Michael would not have wished to marry this wretched girl, especially after being offered a part in an organization that would have filled him with pride, as it had Roberto all those years ago. But times were changing and his sons were not like him. He had come from the slums, but his sons had been pampered, spoilt, they did not have the *need* that he had had. They were his own flesh and blood, but deep in his heart he knew he could not, no matter how hard he tried, love them with the same intensity as he had his beloved Michael. His tears flowed freely, he cried for his son, wanting him so much to be alive, and the ache deepened because he knew he would have to protect his other sons with no one to stand at his side.

Graziella tapped on the study door but there was no reply. She was about to return to her room when the door opened and her husband stood there.

'Oh, Mama,' he said, 'I miss him, I miss my boy.'

She closed the door quickly, not wanting anyone to hear, and sat him down, then sat on his knee and wrapped her arms around him.

'I couldn't come home, Mama, didn't know how I could come home . . .'

'Well, you came home all right, and what a row you caused within minutes of getting here. That poor girl must think you are a monster . . . But in some ways you are right, we should have waited, but I didn't realize he'd fallen that hard. He has, you know, and maybe it's what the boy needs, a wife. He's so shy, so nervous.'

'He could have any girl from any major family in Sicily, not to mention New York. And he's just a boy, he's too young.'

'That's as maybe, but he seems set on this girl. Don't think I don't ask myself why; she's no family, no money, no figure . . . She's so skinny, and she's worked herself into the ground since she was fourteen. Then she was scrubbing floors in a convent . . . They thought I wanted a reference for the poor girl as a servant. I've got the best

217

recommendation for a cleaner you could want, but a wife I don't know.'

He laughed, saying his sons might be foolish, but their mother was not. 'So you checked up on her, did you, Mama?'

'You think I don't look out for my boys? She was honest with us from the beginning, she never tried to hide anything. The Mother Superior said she was a good worker, diligent and tidy. You and I had no opposition, just think what you would have done if my mother had refused you permission to marry me! I tell you, you oppose this marriage and you will make your son hate you. On the other hand . . .'

He cocked his head, questioningly. 'And on the other hand?'

'Well, may God forgive me, but if he does change his mind we could make a settlement. She has no family.'

Luciano held his wife tightly, his love for her as strong as the day they married. Arm-in-arm they went to bed, and made love.

Graziella slept in the crook of her beloved husband's arm. The void that had been between them was bridged, and the darkness of grief was lifted from the house.

Sophia was just walking out of the hotel when Constantino's car drew up. He leaned over and opened the passenger door for her. As they drove off, Luciano's personal driver walked into the hotel and met the manager. Together they went up to Sophia's room.

It was a burning hot day, and the fresh breeze along the seafront cooled Constantino and Sophia on their drive to Mondello. They walked down to the harbour, hand-in-hand, and sat watching the small fishing boats bobbing on the water. Constantino hesitantly told her he was to leave Palermo, he had business to see to in Rome.

'He's sending you away from me, isn't he?'

He wouldn't meet her eyes, but she knew. 'So I'm not good enough for you.'

'I want you to be my wife, Sophia.'

'You may want it, but if your father does not . . . Why have we come here?'

'I thought you would like it. There's a small hotel . . .'

She stood up, her hands rigid at her sides. 'Hotel? Is that why you have brought me here, so we can go to a hotel? So I'm not good enough to be your wife, just cheap enough for you to . . .'

He pulled at her hand. 'I meant we could have lunch there, nothing else, believe me. Sophia?'

'I want to go back to town now, take me back now.'

She wanted to scream, this wasn't what she wanted. Everything she had planned was going wrong. She started to run along the harbour, then turned back and shouted, 'You don't love me! You *don't*!'

Constantino hurried after her as she ran to the car. It was locked, so she ran on, then turned tail and ran back to the harbour and down the stone steps to the water's edge. She had nowhere to run to, and she sat down, hugging her knees and burying her face.

Constantino was panting for breath as he came down the steps. 'Sophia, Sophia, listen to me.'

She looked up at him. Her hair was loose, hanging thick and black almost to her waist. Her wide eyes in the tiny, heart-shaped face looked like a cat's, and for a moment he was shocked. Then she launched herself at him, clawing at his face, wanting to hurt him, to hurt this weak, foolish boy who was too afraid to stand up to his father. She hated him and wanted to make him feel the pain she lived with.

Constantino protected his face with his hands, but still she came at him until he caught her wrists, holding her off. Then he pulled her into his arms and kissed her, a wild, frantic, searching kiss. Sophia struggled for a moment longer, then gave in.

Her thin arms were so strong that he could not, even had he wanted, have released himself. He wanted to kiss every inch of her and felt as if he were going to explode . . . With his eyes closed he moaned his love . . .

They sat together on the stone step with the water lapping at their feet. His mouth was dry and his breath caught in his chest. Her dress had come open during their struggle and as she leaned against him he could see one dark, heavy nipple. His hand shook as he reached out to touch her.

She opened her dress further and held his head to her breast. He sucked like the baby she had left in Cefalu while she stared out to sea, at the boats, coloured like rainbows.

Constantino's voice was hoarse with emotion. 'I want you, I want you . . .'

And she replied, 'Then marry me.'

She buttoned her dress and rose slowly to her feet. He looked up and caught her hand.

'I will . . . I'll bring you back a ring from Rome. Do you like diamonds?'

She smiled and nodded. She knew she had caught the

fish at last, when she had all but given up. She laughed, and the dimple appeared in her cheek.

'Yes, I like diamonds – big ones!'

Sophia was singing to herself as she returned to her room. She put her key in the lock and discovered that the door was open. Panicking, she ran straight to her drawer to check her pearls and brooch, but they were safe. She stared around; nothing was out of place, yet she knew someone had been in there, she felt it.

She burst into the manager's office without knocking. 'Someone has been in my room, Signor Tramontera. I said no one was to clean it, I clean my own room.'

He appeared afraid, his eyes shifty as he told her that her room had not been cleaned, but someone had asked to see it, one of Don Roberto's men. So if she didn't like it he suggested she take it up with the Don. Then he told her to get out, he was busy, and it was time for her to go on reception.

There had been little to do on her shift, and Sophia had concentrated on the accounts for the desk till. Sales of the cigarettes and cigars from the small glass case were part of her duties. Tramontera himself always checked her carefully printed figures, and to date she had not made a single mistake.

She was concentrating on her arithmetic when the desk bell rang. She looked up to see Don Roberto Luciano removing his kid gloves. His piercing eyes nearly scared the life out of her, and she was grateful for the emergence of the grovelling Tramontera from the office.

The sweat glistened on his forehead as he kissed Luciano's hand, bowing low. His shabby, shiny suit showed up in marked contrast to the immaculate figure of Luciano.

'Do you have a room where Signorina Visconti and I can talk privately?' It was not a request, and Tramontera gestured towards his own office, stepping back as the Don's bodyguard entered the room.

After checking it out, the man held the door open for Luciano to enter, but the Don gestured for Sophia to go ahead of him. The door was virtually slammed in Tramontera's face.

Luciano looked around the squalid room, then sat in the swivel chair, placing his Homburg and gloves on the cluttered desk. Sophia sat in the other small, hard chair and looked down at her hands, trying to stop herself blushing. Her palms were wet with sweat.

'So, you are Sophia Visconti.'

She focused her attention on the tip of his polished black leather shoe. The creases in his charcoal-grey trousers were razor sharp. She could also see the threadbare carpet, the cigarette ends, the dust.

The Don continued, 'May I take this opportunity to apologize for my behaviour yesterday.'

Although he said the words, there was no trace of apology in his voice.

'My son is very enamoured of you, Signorina Visconti. You met, I believe, a number of times in my absence.'

She nodded, afraid to lift her head, and she saw his foot twitch just a fraction.

He went on, 'You only just arrived here, from

Cefalù . . . My wife tells me you also worked at a hotel there as a domestic.'

The word 'domestic' was given added emphasis, but again she simply gave a slight nod. He could see the way her hands, one moment folded on her lap as if in prayer, now clenched together. He offered his condolences for her mother's death.

'I have been unable to discover your father's name. Your mother never married, is that correct?'

Sophia felt a strange relief. Any hope of his accepting her was over. She was sure that Luciano had checked every detail of her life, sure that he knew about her own illegitimate child, his own grandchild. This man, who sat there like a judge in court, with his power and wealth, no longer frightened her. At their first meeting he had treated her without respect, and now she felt as if all he wanted was to destroy her.

Luciano was fascinated at the way the girl's hands had telegraphed her fear, the long, slender fingers unwrapping themselves, lifting for a fleeting moment as if about to take flight. When she spoke, he was taken aback by her deep, almost husky tone.

'My mother was a good woman. I will not hear a word against her from you or from anyone. My father was killed in the war, and she loved him until the day she died. She had no marriage certificate, but that does not give you the right to insult her memory. I have never had anything in my life that I didn't work for, did not deserve, and if you don't think me good enough for your son, why don't you tell me to my face instead of insulting me by sending someone to search my room, asking questions about me where I worked, as you rightly said, as a domestic. I am proud, Don Luciano. So now you

223

know everything about me, what are you going to do about it?'

Sophia's blazing eyes showed such anger that he was astonished. No woman, apart from his wife, had ever had the audacity to speak to him this way. He stood up, towering above her, and then reached out gently and touched her chin with the tips of his fingers, tilting her head until he could look down into her face.

'Do you love Constantino?'

Sophia knew then that he had not found out – and she had almost been foolish enough to ask him for money!

She was right, Luciano had not as yet sent anyone to Cefalu. Now he could see why his son had fallen for this girl; she had fire inside her, she was exciting and she was a fighter. In some ways she had more fight in her than his own son.

Roberto Luciano gave his consent to the marriage, although he stipulated that it must be a quiet affair as Michael had only been dead six months and the villa was still a house of mourning. Sophia chose her wedding gown with Graziella and between them they organized the buffet and the flowers.

During the frantic preparations, Sophia rarely saw the Don, who was often away on business, and when he was at home seemed preoccupied and distant. At times she felt he was afraid to enjoy himself; she would catch his half-smile, his eyes would begin to light up with laughter, and then fade. She could not help but see the way his sons lived in fear of him; they were such fun to be with when he was not around, but as soon as they knew he was in the house they were all on tenterhooks.

Strangely, Sophia was beginning to hate Michael's name. It made her sick to her stomach, because she was terrified of losing everything just when it was within her reach. Only when she was married, when she was the wife of the Don's eldest son, would she feel safe. By then she would be untouchable, she would be a Luciano.

The gold ring was engraved on the inside with both their names. For the wedding, Sophia wore her large, solitaire diamond engagement ring on her right hand. It had not, as Constantino had promised, come from Rome, but was given to him by his father. It was worth $250,000.

The ceremony had taken place in the local chapel and few guests had been invited because of the family's recent bereavement. Most of them were linked directly with Luciano's business, but protocol demanded that the heads of the Sicilian families be represented.

A small marquee had been erected in the grounds of the Villa Rivera for the reception, and after the buffet a local band struck up the wedding celebration dance. Constantino and Sophia danced together as the guests formed a circle around them, then Constantino was handed a silver rosebowl. The young couple stood side by side while everyone applauded and each guest took a turn to place their tokens in the bowl. Some simply dropped in folded notes, others had placed cash in envelopes. It was the custom to give money so that the bride and groom would be well provided for at the start of their marriage. Sophia's gown was also covered with money, which had been pinned to the fabric.

The rose-bowl was filled to capacity and Sophia's hand was aching, her cheeks flushed from so many kisses. At last the guests started clapping for the couple to dance.

Roberto Luciano appeared distant throughout the day. He was cordial, but restrained. His foot tapped to the music as he sat with his wife. Beside them, Alfredo and Frederico were itching to dance but were not sure if they should.

When the band struck up a waltz, Sophia approached her new father and asked if he would dance with her. Luciano stared stiffly over Sophia's head, refusing to look down and meet her eyes.

'Thank you for my wedding,' she said.

'It is my pleasure. You look very beautiful.'

'I intend to make your son very happy.'

'I hope so,' he replied gravely.

'He loves you very much, but I have no need to tell you?' she hazarded.

'No.'

She continued, 'But I would like to say something that I think must be said . . . He loves you, and you show him very little affection in return. I know you are still mourning Michael, we all are . . .' She felt his body tense and looked up quickly to see his mouth form a hard, tight line.

'You did not know him, you cannot mourn with us. Don't think because my son welcomes you so easily that I have to. I will take my time, be sure, that is the way I am.'

'The way you are, Don Luciano, is cruel. Your sons ache to know that you care for them, love them as you loved Michael, and you never so much as look in their

226

direction. Please, for me, for Constantino, before we go away, show him just a little gesture, anything, so that he knows you care about him.'

This time he looked directly into the heart-shaped face, the wide eyes, and traced her dimple with his finger. 'Well, husky voice, I can tell my son is going to be bossed around just like his father.' Her husky, gurgling laugh was infectious, making him chuckle.

Across the dance floor Graziella wiped her eyes on the big handkerchief Alfredo passed her. It was the first time Roberto had smiled in so long, so very long.

As he joined them, Luciano hugged Constantino and handed him an envelope from his pocket, whispering that the hotel room should be on the top floor as no one passed by, and they need never leave it. Graziella cuffed Roberto, protesting that he shouldn't give such shocking secrets away.

In the envelope were two tickets to Capri. Constantino was overwhelmed. Roberto had booked them the same hotel, the same suite, as he and Graziella had used for their honeymoon. The moment was all too short, yet Sophia understood how much it meant, and also how little she knew Roberto. When he looked at her, there was only warmth in his gaze, but he made her feel as if she had intruded, and she would never do that again.

Sophia lived in fear of her baby being discovered until, five months after her marriage, she contacted the orphanage and was told that Nicodemo was no longer there. He had been adopted, she did not ask by whom. Her hands shook as she replaced the telephone and it was not until that moment that she knew for sure that her secret was safe. The relief surpassed her guilt. Now her new life had really begun.

The child's only possession was a small, heart-shaped gold locket on a chain, the little heart marked by teeth marks where Sophia had bitten on it during labour.

Luciano had spent six months in a desperate bid for incontrovertible proof of Carolla's involvement in his son's death. But Carolla had covered his tracks so well that it had been fruitless. Yet Luciano still believed he would be given justice.

The long delay in the negotiations for a meeting made him aware of his position within the Organization. At last a meeting was called, but not, he learned, at his request. His son's death was low on the agenda of subjects to be discussed. He began to realize how unimportant he was; the real reason for the meeting, involving most of the delegates, was the crash of the Mafia's Cuban gambling sector.

This time they met in Florida. The overall feeling was one of humiliation; they had been literally kicked out of Cuba, and that was worse than the massive losses. Luciano could not help but notice Paul Carolla's absence; he presumed it was out of respect but he was wrong.

All Luciano wanted was justice for his son's murder, but meanwhile he had to sit through many accusations of mismanagement and misappropriation of the members' funds. The atmosphere was highly charged, too much so for any man there to pay much attention to Luciano's personal problems, for that was how they deemed Michael's death. A death that Luciano lived with every second, every hour of every day that passed.

Eventually, when it came to the time allotted for Don Luciano to state his case, they listened with respectful politeness. But most of the delegates were still seething at their astronomical losses, and so their lack of response was understandable. Half of them, too, were involved in some way with Paul Carolla and had hopes of recouping their money through his junk dealing.

Luciano was deeply insulted by an inference that his son was a self-induced drug addict. Without proof, without positive evidence that Carolla had ordered Michael's death, Luciano could not put his request for a hit on Carolla to the vote. There was no proof because Lenny Cavataio had still not been found, so Luciano's case was unanimously dismissed. It was, however, decided to give yet another severe warning to Carolla to stay clear of Luciano, and if he should disobey or try to force Luciano to export his junk, the Commission would withdraw their decision and Luciano's case would be reviewed. Condolences were offered on the sad death of Michael.

As the meeting proceeded, Luciano became increasingly aware of a young man who sat directly opposite him at the conference table. Anthony Robello was an exceptionally handsome man with deep-set amber eyes and a prominent hooked nose. He was tastefully dressed and neither smoked nor drank throughout the meeting. He appeared to be listening intently to every word that was spoken, but made no contribution.

That evening Luciano dined early, sitting alone at a table facing the restaurant entrance.

'May I join you?'

Luciano looked up to see Anthony Robello standing respectfully by his side. He replied, 'Please do, although I'm afraid I have almost finished my dinner.'

Robello sat down, saying, 'Signor Carolla will be joining the meeting in the morning. He has many friends, I am sorry to say. And I am deeply sorry about your son.'

'Thank you . . .' Luciano responded gruffly.

'I am Anthony Robello.'

'Yes, Vito told me about you. Congratulations. You must be even younger than I was when I had the fortune to be chosen. It is a rare occurrence, you must be very proud.'

Robello bowed his head slightly to show that he was indeed proud of the honour. He had recently been made don of a small Sicilian family, a remarkable achievement, as Luciano had said. He was still only twenty-five years old, but what was more remarkable was that his *capi* and soldiers had personally requested that he be honoured as they felt he alone was capable of running their family.

Luciano watched the confident way in which Robello discussed the menu with the waiter. His nickname, the Eagle, suited him. Partly due to his strange-coloured eyes and sharp nose, it also acknowledged that he swooped hard and fast for what he wanted. He already had a history of personal hits that he had carried out skilfully, and some even said he had received the old don's crown because he had systematically wiped out all possible competition. Whatever the rumours, it was known that Anthony Robello was coming up hard and fast in the Organization, and that his men were tough and dependable.

They made polite conversation, then Luciano excused

230

himself. Robello rose in deference to the older man as he left.

Luciano did not expect to see or speak with Robello again, having already decided to leave Florida in the morning. He was surprised, therefore, when there was a light tap on his door a few hours later. Robello gave a small bow and asked if it would be convenient for them to talk privately.

He refused a drink, but accepted a glass of iced water, then came straight to the point. 'I am aware of your powerful connections in Palermo, and of your virtual monopoly of the export trade. I am also aware how valuable your trade must be to Don Carolla and why he wants access to your companies. I am sure you know as well as I do that many of the delegates here will branch into narcotics, the rewards are too rich, too tempting. It is only a matter of time until you can no longer refuse to assist with the trade.'

Luciano raised his eyebrows, but said nothing. Robello went on, 'I have a small family, but a productive one. At the moment I have no resources to buy shipments, and I would say the marketplace is pretty well tied up. However, I am able to offer my hand in friendship, should you need protection. I hope you will feel free to contact me should the situation arise.'

'And your payment – should the situation arise?'

'I need warehouse space, delivery and cargo licences.'

'And your product?'

'Lemons . . .'

He chuckled to himself at the young man's audacity. Of course he would want to use the Luciano companies, just as much as Carolla – but for lemons? Without doubt he would be moving into narcotics along with the rest of them as soon as he had the necessary resources.

The more Luciano thought about it the more he realized just how devious the young man was in offering his protection. If he should choose to do business with Robello, he would need to be protected against him, not by him.

Luciano's voice when he spoke again was soft, but filled with emotion. 'Carolla murdered my son, but I have been unable to prove it. The frustration, the humiliation, has been . . . is hard for me even to speak of. I want Carolla, and I am prepared to go to great lengths. I do not want my sons, my family, to be aware of our plans, and before I continue I must have your solemn oath that you will honour my trust.'

Robello was trying not to show his great excitement. He was sure, very sure, what he was going to be offered. He kissed the blue ring on Luciano's finger, and it was enough, no words were needed.

Luciano continued, 'Firstly, this is what I offer. I will open up my companies for the exportation of any substances, including the bottling factories, the canning factories, and you may have the use of my labour force. My methods will ensure that we can slip through any net any country tries to spread . . .'

Robello listened in awe as Luciano outlined his network of companies and contacts. The young man was being offered untold wealth. The bait was dripping with blood, so tasty that it was all Robello could do to keep himself still. Luciano opened a briefcase and took out folders containing lists of Carolla's outlets, his laboratories, his routes. No name was left out, no soldier, not one of Carolla's workers had been missed.

Robello knew it must have taken months of work and planning, of planting men in Carolla's family, and he was very impressed. He sat back in his chair and studied Luciano with renewed interest, but he was feeling slightly uneasy. If Luciano could so easily infiltrate another don's entire business then perhaps his own would come under such scrutiny.

'I am greatly impressed,' Robello said softly. 'You know Carolla's business well, may I ask why you did not bring this before the delegates?'

Luciano shrugged. 'To infiltrate a man's business does not necessarily give you the evidence of his part in a murder, and can obviously cause friction. Only one man has the proof I want, Lenny Cavataio – a man, believe me, I have searched for. But he is most certainly dead, and I am certain Paul Carolla had to have him silenced – it would be madness to leave such a witness alive. But then Carolla must be insane to believe that I would not avenge my beloved son.' Robello noticed Luciano's face alter at the mention of his son: it softened, and he made a small gesture of apology with his hands . . . and then the dark, heavy eyes flashed in anger. 'Today I asked only for justice. I asked for it, and I was refused. Now I have no option but to take my own justice. As you see, I have been making preparations should such an occasion arise. I would have been satisfied with Carolla's life; now I will destroy him.'

After carefully replacing the files, Luciano offered Robello a cigar and sipped his brandy, as if waiting for a reaction. He smiled to himself; the boy was very cool, but Luciano knew the meat must be smelling very sweet and rich.

He dangled it a little closer. 'I am getting old, my

soldiers are my age, men who have been with me since I first took over from Joseph Carolla. My companies virtually run themselves – my men by now are used to my methods. My needs over the past years have been . . .' He paused and lifted a perfectly manicured hand and let it hover in the air, then laughed softly. 'They are men who would not fare well in a young man's war.'

Still Robello made no move, and Luciano looked sidelong at him, wishing that one, just one, of his three sons had a little of this boy's menace. It was time.

'I want to declare war on Paul Carolla. I want an army, I want to attack, but I need a general.'

At last Robello smiled, but his eyes were hard and glittering, and his sharp nostrils flared. Again Luciano was reminded of the boy's nickname.

'Forgive me, Don Luciano, I do not wish to disagree with you, but I think you have a general. What you do not have is an army. I am my own man, and for the use of my army, what do you propose?'

'I give you Carolla's warehouses, Carolla's men, his shipments, his entire network. When you have it, I give you the freedom to use the Luciano companies as cover. I want nothing – no cut; I just want Carolla wiped out one hundred per cent. Your gain is therefore total. One, you will have his entire business; two, you become in one swoop the major narcotics dealer in the world; three, you will have the guarantee of two years with no problems, an added bonus. I will be the one the syndicate will blame. Carolla will know it is me, Roberto Luciano, who is destroying him. Some bonus, eh? You, my young friend, can become a very powerful man, perhaps one of the most powerful.'

Robello had been made an offer he could not refuse, and his eyes flickered.

Luciano read the boy's thoughts and started to laugh. Robello found it infectious and could not stop his own laughter bubbling to the surface. The next moment, Luciano had gripped his hand. There was no trace of laughter in his voice, no humour in his face. 'It is a deal, yes?'

Robello's smile still hovered on his lips as he nodded. He could not control it, try as he would. It was a deal, and one that he wanted to scream about from the rooftops. Luciano smiled too, slipping his arm around Robello's shoulders as he ushered him from the room. They arranged to meet in one month, Luciano explaining that he required time to complete certain arrangements. As the door closed behind the eager hungry young Eagle, Luciano remained motionless, like a bird of prey himself. Later that night he cancelled his flight to Rome and flew instead to New York, having requested to meet, not with any members of his family, but with a small-time baker. He had offered Robello a deal; he was about to offer another to Leonardo Scorpio, only this one appeared to be personal – he wanted Leonardo Scorpio's daughter.

Luciano's planning for the next meeting with Robello in Palermo was as meticulous as everything else he did. All the men who accompanied him were elderly. They were chosen carefully to act as bodyguards, doormen, office workers. He even took a different driver, an old man who worked in his groves. Each one was hand-picked and obeyed unquestioningly, although some of his younger soldiers wondered why they were not required. His sons asked hesitantly if he needed them to accompany him, but they were told curtly to remain at the villa.

With his 'ancient mariners', Luciano was driven at a sedate pace in an equally ancient black Mercedes. As the car entered the factory courtyard, a Ferrari Dino screeched up behind them in a cloud of dust. It contained Robello and one other man, a squat, surly-faced thug who remained standing by the Ferrari while Robello entered the offices, pausing in the doorway as he caught sight of a big cage. Inside it, snarling over a bone the size of his own head, was a large Canadian wolf. He lifted his head and for a second his pale eyes focused on Robello, then he applied his fangs again to his meal.

Luciano led Robello through his secretary's small office to his own large and sumptuous room.

'How come you have that thing out there? Is it a guard dog, or what?'

'It's a wolf, getting old now, like myself.' Luciano gestured to a chair and Robello sat down, his eyes taking in the room as they had taken in everything during the walk through the factory to the offices. Old Luciano was right, his bodyguard looked as though he could be blown over, and without a weapon. Robello's right foot twitched and tapped. He had been confident when he had accepted the deal in Florida, but now seeing the large, productive factory confirmed to him that there could be no other decision.

Luciano sat behind his desk. Through the clear glass top Robello could see his whole form, sitting easily, yet with that air of stillness to him. One hand rested on the other, and Robello could see the heavy gold ring with the blue stone glinting in the light which was reflected from the steel edge of the glass.

'The best strategy in war is the element of surprise, to hit on every side and give your enemy no time to recuperate between blows. Leave nothing to fate, nothing to chance. So, if you are in agreement, may I show you my plan? It goes without saying that it is open to you to make any changes you see fit.'

He took a file from a cabinet, but it was not the dossier Robello had expected; Luciano took it through to his secretary and asked her to finish the letters, not forgetting the enclosures. Robello was taken aback by the man's calmness; on the one hand arranging a war and on the other dealing with his business as if this were no more than a casual meeting.

The door closed and Luciano returned to his desk, empty-handed. 'I was an explosives expert in the war, bomb disposal mostly. Are you familiar with that area?' He did not wait for a reply but smiled and sat down. 'I think that the days of men spraying bullets at random were more in tune with the old school, the *moustachios*, as we called them. Do you agree?'

Robello made a non-committal gesture and Luciano took a blank sheet of paper, continuing in the same calm manner. 'First we take the refineries. This I have a personal interest in. Do you know of the Borsalino brothers?'

Robello thought for a moment, frowning, then looked up. 'Philippe? Yeah, I know him – used to have vending machines, right?'

Luciano shook his head. 'His older brother, Juan, began working for Carolla two years ago. Now they work together. They were close friends of Lenny Cava-taio, and in the past nine months they've become very much a part of Carolla's team. They run two refineries and may have the evidence I need – they may have made the heroin that killed my son. Juan Borsalino I therefore want myself. A truckload of wood was delivered to the building site that is a front for their laboratory two days ago. The fire should start there, and then in turn will trigger off the device which will blow up the laboratory.'

'How many men work in the labs?'

'Eight, sometimes more. But I am concerned with the destruction of the premises, not the men. Not that it concerns me if they all die, each one of them is responsible for producing heroin that kills thou-sands. Juan Borsalino sees his mistress most evenings, leaving his brother on the premises, so the second device will be timed to go up within minutes of the first . . .'

Robello leaned forward slightly so as not to miss a single word. They talked for over an hour without interruption, without even a light blinking on the tele-phone system. Finally Luciano tore up the now-filled sheet of paper, placed it in the ashtray and set light to it. When the small scraps of paper were burning, he smiled at Robello. 'And then there were none.'

Letting his breath out slowly, Robello gave the Don a look of total admiration. There seemed to be nothing Luciano had overlooked, right down to staking out Carolla's mistress's new apartment and the fact that Carolla had just bought a new Alfa Romeo. Carolla was to be the last; they would let him run from one place to another, thinking he was safe. Carolla had to know before he died that he had lost everything. It was the one mistake Luciano was to make.

Robello kept his driver waiting for more than eight hours. In that time he received careful instructions from Luciano in a small back room of the factory. He could still smell the powder on his fingers, still feel the slight stickiness of the putty they used for the charges . . . it had been time well spent.

The driver watched his silent boss in the mirror and tentatively asked if everything had gone well. Robello pursed his lips as he stared out of the window. 'Yeah, that guy is something else.'

'In the war he was nicknamed the Wolf, maybe that's why he's got that thing in the cage, to remind him of what he was. He's gone soft now, but then he's older.'

Robello's tawny eyes glinted, but he made no reply. Far from being soft, he knew, Luciano was perhaps the most dangerous man he had ever met. He could not rid himself of the feeling even after he had showered and eaten. He knew he could rely on Luciano to keep his word about giving him two years' use of his companies, but was it a fair exchange? Most importantly, did Luciano really want nothing more than revenge, than Carolla?

He lay sleepless, tossing and turning, everything that had passed between himself and Luciano running through his head like endless repeats of a television commercial. One phrase stuck in his mind; when Luciano had said he did not care how many in the narcotics trade died because 'they produce the heroin that kills thousands' . . . Would Robello be as dispensable as the

Carolla men? The more he thought it over the more he began to suspect that Luciano was working a double-cross. Surely no man would be satisfied with the outcome of a vendetta which gave him nothing more than the fat Carolla, not even a percentage of the business which Robello would now inherit. He got up from his bed and paced the room. He was sure that he would have to make one extra explosive device, just one extra, for Luciano.

By morning, Robello was his usual fresh self. He sent two men to check out the Villa Rivera and, most important of all, its owner's movements. He wanted to know if there was a pattern to Luciano's days, what car he used and at what times. He laughed, saying it should not be too difficult as his guys were so ancient that their biggest problem was in making sure none of them dropped dead before they got their boss where he wanted to go.

He knew where he wanted Luciano, and the more he thought about it the more feverish his determination grew. He would be clever enough not to take Luciano out immediately; he would wait until he had taken the blame for the Carolla wipe-out. There would be any number of families then who would want him dead, and not one of them would be able to point the finger directly at Robello . . .

Graziella was preparing breakfast when she heard Roberto laughing. He was out on the lawn, playing with a bedraggled puppy, throwing a pebble which it scuttled after, wagging its stunted tail. Again, his laugh rang out. It had been so long, so very long since she had seen him in such good spirits.

The boys also noticed their father's high spirits and for Sophia, who now lived with the family, it was a new experience. The usually quiet, sober man exuded energy this brilliant, sunny morning.

By the time they all arrived at the breakfast table, Roberto was already seated. He clapped his hands for attention. 'We have a new family member,' he announced, then whistled. The small dog bounded in and ran straight to his side, whimpering. To their astonishment, he allowed the dog to sit on his lap and fed it scraps from his plate. They all tried to think of a suitable name. The dog was so scruffy, dirty and misshapen that the task proved difficult, but there was much laughter as they all offered their suggestions. Graziella laughed; she was the only one to notice that the dog was, in fact, a bitch.

Roberto held the dog upside-down and roared with laughter, saying he was growing short-sighted in his old age. In truth, he looked younger than he had for years. He cuddled the smelly little creature and grinned at Graziella. 'Right, Mama, since you are the most alert of the Lucianos, what do you want to call her, eh?'

'Let me think now . . . She is an orphan, she is ugly, she is dirty, and I know she has fleas . . . What about something that makes her feel special? We'll call her . . . Maria!'

None of them was aware of the reason why he felt so much more alive. His good humour stayed with him, and when he asked his sons to join him for lunch it was like some sort of celebration.

First, he asked Constantino to go to Rome. He wanted his son to take charge of his operations there. Constantino was more than willing to accept. Sophia had been quietly urging him to stand up to his father and ask for more freedom, particularly for them to have a home of their own. As much as she loved Graziella, she felt that the villa was not her home and, as yet, she and Constantino had hardly spent any time alone together since their honeymoon. She had fended off Graziella's constant hints about becoming a grandmother, feeling there was plenty of time for babies. She was now a Luciano, and she wanted time to enjoy her new-found status and wealth. She also wanted to work and, even though Constantino said his father would never approve, she was adamant. Now with Rome on the horizon Sophia was as happy as her husband to accept it and looked forward to finding an apartment and setting up her first real home. Any thoughts she had of her son she pushed so far down inside her that she was almost incapable of picturing his face.

Sophia looked forward to shopping for her new home. She was determined that it would be very special, and part of her happiness was due to having enough money to buy anything she chose. It seemed that her dreams, in the end, had really come true.

Alfredo was not so overjoyed at being sent to New York. It was, of course, a great opportunity, but Alfredo loved

Sicily, loved working in the groves, and actually liked hard labour. He was happiest driving the trucks and inspecting the trees. The responsibility of taking over the American trucking companies was a different matter entirely.

Another reason for his hesitancy was that he had met a young local girl. He had been thinking of visiting her family to ask permission to court her, but this would now be out of the question. His father especially wished him to meet an old friend of his in New York, plus his old friend's daughter. Alfredo knew it was not really a request, it was a command, yet he did not refuse. He quietly accepted his father's arrangements and, like his brother Constantino, prepared to leave almost immediately.

Frederico, like his brothers, learned he was to leave Palermo. His father had arranged for him to be trained to manage the Luciano gambling interests in Las Vegas. Two of the Don's trusted *capi* would take him under their wings.

Graziella's good spirits subsided. She could not believe that her husband was doing this to her, taking all her boys in one move and sending them to different parts of the world. She would be lost, alone in the rambling villa. Roberto was gentle, understanding, but very firm. He wanted his sons to take over his businesses, and how could he expect them to know how to run things if they were tied to their mother's apron strings?

'Don't you want grandchildren, Mama? They'll fill the house again, you'll see. Perhaps you and I should go on a trip, too, it's been a long time. When did we last go away together, can you remember? Well, perhaps we will go to New York, and not just for a holiday. Alfredo is to meet Teresa Scorpio; I think it is a good match, and I would say we might not just be going on a second honeymoon, but also to meet his bride.'

Luciano's plans were Machiavellian in their fiendish complexity. His eyes were alive again, his vigour was renewed and his energy was tireless. He felt it in every fibre of his body.

He knew intuitively that he was being kept under observation. During the final stages he purposely left the villa at exactly the same time each day, wearing the same fedora and dark glasses, and instructed his driver to stop at the gates while he exercised his little dog, Maria, in the long driveway. He would call and whistle for the dog for some time while the aged driver he had hired for Robello's benefit waited patiently.

Robello's men were able to set their watches by Luciano's morning walk, and it was difficult to follow him in his car as it went so slowly. They laughingly reported these facts to their boss. Robello was almost rubbing his hands as he counted off the days on his calendar. They were right, Luciano was getting soft.

As Luciano suspected, Robello was the best man for the job. He had just taken the plan one step further and made small changes to the timing devices to give his men more time to get clear. He didn't intend to lose a single man if he could help it; he was going to need their protection when he took over from Carolla.

Robello had made enquiries as far afield as Brazil,

even arranging to meet Carolla's contacts in Canada. He was going a fraction too fast, foolishly thinking that no one would be interested in why he wanted these meetings, and it was a mistake he would pay for.

One man, a former Gestapo agent and black marketeer, and a major link in Carolla's heroin network, was now residing in Canada. He had been surprised to receive a call from the pushy young Sicilian boss, and was cagey when Robello said he was coming to Canada, hinting that he would like a meeting.

He also paid a high price for Carolla's political protection, so to receive such a call out of the blue from someone he hardly knew automatically made him suspicious. He placed a call to Chicago and asked what his contact there knew of Robello and what the hell he wanted.

It had been part of Luciano's plan to spread the word about a takeover bid in Palermo, but Robello managed to start the rumours all by himself. To fuel the rumour further, Luciano contacted the syndicate's overlords suggesting angrily that they should look into it. The last thing any of them needed right now was for the Anti-Mafia Commission, which had been set up in Palermo, to get wind of a possible vendetta. That sort of publicity would only increase the Italian parliament's determination to crack down on the Mafia families in Palermo, families that their American counterparts depended on.

With four weeks to go, Luciano moved cautiously. His sons had now flown the nest, yet to any outsider it appeared that nothing had changed at the villa. The boys' cars were seen driving in and out as usual, Luciano having chosen workers of around the same ages as his sons for the task. At night the villa was a blaze of light as if the entire family were in residence. And every morning Roberto still insisted on walking his dog.

Graziella was feeling disturbed by the tension and atmosphere of secrecy that surrounded her. She did not ask questions, but she could not stop herself from acting nervously. The sound of the telephone being used at all hours of the night, keeping her husband out of his bed until two or three every morning, confirmed to her that something important was taking place. If the telephone rang, he hurried immediately to his study, and one evening as they were dining alone he was in such haste that he left the study door ajar.

She heard Roberto exclaim, then call her. He was smiling, holding his hand across the mouthpiece. 'Mama, it's Alfredo, he wants to speak to you. Come, come, it's good news!'

Graziella took the receiver. Her son's voice sounded so distant, so far from her, that she wanted to weep. 'Hello? Hello, Alfredo? We miss you, how are you?'

She burst into tears, and Roberto took the receiver from her. 'You hear your Mama crying and she doesn't even know the good news! I'll tell her, we'll be there . . . And you know, this is what I wanted. I am happy for you, she is a good girl, and it is a good family.' He hung up the phone and cocked his head to one side, looking at Graziella. 'You understand? He likes her, he likes this Teresa, and her parents like Alfredo, so . . .'

Graziella couldn't take it in. Her son had only just

246

left, and now he was ringing them about some girl she hadn't even met. 'I don't understand, what girl?'

Taking her in his arms he covered her worried face with quick kisses. 'Alfredo has met with the Scorpio family. They welcomed him, and he is staying with them until he finds a place of his own. They have a daughter, a nice girl, and they like each other, so why waste time? I want a grandson.'

Feeling dizzy, she sat down. Everything was happening so fast. 'You arranged this? Did you arrange this with him and not even tell me?'

'Mama, I just set it up for him to meet her, I arranged nothing. But you will be able to see for yourself. We're leaving for New York; I promised you a second honeymoon – well, now we take it.'

'I know you arranged it, and you know I don't approve of that. We had the freedom to fall in love, why not the same thing for our boys?'

'If Alfredo had not wanted or liked the girl then he would have said so . . .'

He caught her looking at him the way she used to all those years ago, and gave a boyish shrug. 'OK, I admit it. But Alfredo . . . well, he's not every woman's dream, and she is a good girl. A little older than him, but she is a lawyer, did I tell you that?'

'How much older, huh?'

'Oh, maybe four or five years.'

'Then there is something wrong with her. If a girl's not married by that age, then something's wrong with her. She must be nearly thirty – more – and if she's a lawyer, then she can't cook. I know. Remember I worked for a law firm, I know these women.'

He couldn't stop himself laughing, but as he reached for her the telephone rang again, and he turned to it abruptly. She caught his look and knew he wanted her to leave. Sighing, she went to the door, noting the way he did nothing more than give his name until she was out of the room.

The call was from Teresa's father. They were more than eager to arrange the marriage, yet even they were surprised when Luciano told them that he and his wife would be in New York by the end of the week. Graziella, unaware of the real reason behind her husband's frantic schedule, was surprised to find that he had arranged for a couple to look after the villa in their absence. It had never worried him before to leave the villa in the hands of their trusted staff. She did not notice that the couple were of a similar age to themselves; she had too many other things to think about.

Everything was set, everything was ready. Luciano gave Robello his last-minute instructions to hold Juan Borsalino captive. That prisoner was his and his alone. He was to be taken alive, and no one was to touch him.

Robello shook the Don's hand and confirmed their agreement to make absolutely no contact for one month; no phone calls, no letters, nothing. He reiterated that any contact during that time was tantamount to destroying their deal.

The two men kissed cheeks. It was time.

*

That night, Graziella and Roberto took a direct flight from Rome to New York. Waiting for them at the airport were Teresa's parents.

Rosa Scorpio spent the journey describing her outfit and the table decorations. Graziella smiled, trying hard to understand the conversation but, unlike her husband, she was by no means fluent in English.

At dinner they were joined by the introverted Alfredo and his fiancée. One look was enough for Graziella; no wonder they had snatched at her son. The girl was, to put it politely, plain, and her grey dress did nothing to help her looks. She hardly lifted her eyes during the meal, and Alfredo gave his mother a helpless little smile.

Graziella was desperate to speak to her son in private, and suggested he accompany them back to their hotel suite. Alfredo agreed, but as they were about to leave, Teresa asked if he would stay to discuss their honeymoon arrangements.

As Alfredo kissed his mother she clung to his hand, her eyes searching his face. She spoke quietly in Sicilian, asking him if he was sure this was what he wanted; she only cared for his happiness. She then stood almost on tiptoe and whispered, 'Tell me this is what you want, don't marry if you are unsure; it is for life and you are young; don't let Papa pressure you into doing something you will regret.'

Alfredo would not meet her eyes, and instead looked to the awkward blushing girl hovering by her parents. Luciano kissed Rosa Scorpio's hand, and clasped her husband, then ushered Graziella out to their waiting car. He turned back to give his son a brief nod of his head, as if it were somehow confirmation that he was pleased with him.

Teresa had to insist that her parents leave them alone before she confronted Alfredo. She spoke fluent Sicilian, and had understood every word Graziella had said. She smiled, and then gave an apologetic shrug. 'I am sorry for the way my parents behave, they are acting crazy . . . but I think we should talk.'

Her nerves were showing as they sat in the all-night coffee bar. She spilt sugar on the table as she tipped it into her cup. 'I wanted to say that I know you don't love me, because it is impossible. We don't really know each other. I wish to continue studying law; my mother tells everyone I am a lawyer when I still have a year to go before I qualify. My father doesn't believe in women having careers and . . . Oh, God, this is ridiculous! We are both adults and they are treating us like juveniles. All I wanted to say was, if you and I agree together that we don't want to go through with this, then . . .'

Alfredo smiled, and she looked away. 'I know your father arranged this. Maybe he even organized some sort of payoff, but . . .'

Alfredo took her hand and squeezed it. 'I love my father, and if you want to continue to study that's fine by me, too.'

She returned his hand pressure and swallowed. 'I know I'm probably not what you want, but you're the best offer I've had.'

He smiled at her attempt at humour and leaned closer. 'Are you telling me that I'm what you want?'

She turned to him, her small eyes filled with tears, gave him a tiny nod and hung her head.

Alfredo was taken aback that she actually wanted him.

He gave her a big grin. 'Hey, you mean that? You want to marry me?'

Her voice was barely audible. 'Yes . . . Yes, I do.'

For some strange reason her words filled him with confidence, and he was again like a small boy, grinning from ear to ear. She found it hard to believe that such a handsome boy had so little self-assurance. His face had lit up when she had said she wanted him, and it touched her so much she reached for his hand.

'I was dreading meeting you, but from the moment I saw you, I think for the first time in my life, I actually agreed with my parents' choice, and I can tell you I have mostly disagreed with them. Being an only daughter has been very difficult for me. They've been hinting and trying to find a suitable boy for me for almost as long as I can remember, and to be truthful I think my father had given up.'

'You mean they had other guys like me come to the house?'

She laughed, blushing. 'Not quite, but I had Papa hinting every time we went to a wedding, nudging me about so-and-so's boy or cousin or nephew.' Alfredo beamed at her. She did not tell him that often they had taken one look at her and there had been no question of them coming to the house. Instead she asked, 'But what about you? With your looks you must have had plenty of girls in Sicily?'

He chuckled and said casually that there had been one or two, but he was so naïve, had such an air of innocence that she knew he was lying. His lack of assurance gave her more and more confidence, and by the time they were on their second cup of coffee they were totally at ease with each other.

He held her hand as he walked her to the taxi rank, and she couldn't help smiling with pleasure when she saw two passing girls giving Alfredo the eye. He seemed not to notice, chatting away about how he would like a garden and telling her how he had looked after the orange and olive groves at home. He explained in detail how he pruned the trees back and she listened as if it were the most fascinating thing she had ever heard.

The taxi rank was empty, and he waited with her until one of the familiar yellow cabs passed. When she flagged it down, he was disappointed, wanting to continue talking with her. She gave him a small peck on the cheek and giggled, saying they would have plenty of time to talk, their whole lives. His smile dazzled her again as he agreed, then he licked his lips, slipped an arm around her and kissed her softly on the mouth. It was a childish kiss, so gentle, and afterwards he looked at her as if asking for approval.

She touched his handsome face. 'I love you, and I will make you a good wife.'

The day of the wedding coincided with the Luciano hit on Carolla. Robella, acting under Luciano's carefully orchestrated plans, arranged for the first explosion. As Alfredo and Teresa made their marriage vows, Paul Carolla's biggest narcotics factory was blown to smithereens. As Roberto Luciano toasted his new daughter-in-law, the next explosion took place, destroying the second laboratory.

The wedding guests in the small Manhattan restaurant applauded as Alfredo led on to the tiny dance floor one of the young bridesmaids. Graziella touched Teresa's hand.

'He is very happy; that is good, terrific, OK?'

Teresa smiled at Graziella's use of the word 'terrific' and replied to her in fluent Sicilian. The pleasure on her mother-in-law's face made the time she had spent learning it, much against her will, worthwhile.

'I want you to know that I love him.'

'That is good, and I can see he loves you. Maybe he has had a little too much champagne, but it is his wedding day.'

'I was sad that your other sons could not be with us, but it was very short notice.'

Graziella nodded, her attention still on Alfredo as he twirled the delighted girl round and round. Wanting to please her, wanting to be liked, Teresa complimented Graziella. 'You had three sons, you must have been very young . . .'

Before she could finish, Graziella interrupted her, 'Four, four sons. I have four sons.'

'Oh I'm sorry, I thought there was just Alfredo, Constantino and er . . . Frederico.'

'No, four. Michael was the first born.'

Luciano joined his wife and asked her to dance. As he led Graziella to the dance floor, Teresa searched for Alfredo.

'Can I ask my husband to dance with his wife?'

As they, too, moved on to the dance floor, Teresa asked. 'Why did you never tell me about Michael?'

Alfredo paled visibly, and swayed as if about to faint. 'Did my father mention him to you?'

'No, your mother. Are you all right? It's just that you

told me about your brothers and I didn't understand why you never mentioned Michael to me.'

Alfredo gripped her arms so hard it hurt. 'Michael is dead.'

Teresa gave a furtive look around her, afraid someone had heard, seen the way Alfredo stared with such hatred towards his father, but no one seemed interested; in fact many of the guests were looking towards their host, because Luciano and his wife were dancing together like young lovers, their cheeks touching, their eyes closed.

Roberto loved the feel of Graziella in his arms. He tightened his hold and she snuggled closer. It had been so long since they had danced, so long. He looked down into her face, which was peaceful, and lifted his hand to see the time on his watch. By now Carolla, he estimated, would be dead and his filthy narcotics business destroyed . . . At last Michael could rest in peace. Cupping his wife's face gently, he kissed her lips.

Lydia had been waiting for Paul Carolla to return to their apartment, knowing he would be in a difficult mood. During the night he had received a call that Giorgio's pitiful hold on life at long last seemed to be weakening. On his last visit to his son the boy had been ill with a cold. This had now developed into pneumonia and he had been rushed to hospital. Carolla had therefore spent a considerable time in the emergency ward, and even longer discussing his son's welfare with the doctors. He had been shocked to be told that his son had been taking doses of strychnine; not enough to kill him, but traces of it had been found in his blood sample.

As weak as he was, Giorgio dismissed his father's

queries with a smirk, saying he knew what he was doing. Far from killing him, the poison was, in actual fact, if taken in small doses, helping him control his limbs. His lips were cracked, but he gave a lopsided smile. Carolla realized that the present situation could not continue and, as sick as he was, Giorgio seemed to sense it, too, and asked pitifully not to be sent away to a home.

Carolla had persisted in his crazy lies about Giorgio, continuing to tell associates that his son was a normal healthy boy living with relatives. He had always been afraid his son might die when he was in America and then the truth would be discovered. He had therefore been alone at the hospital and had used a taxi to ferry him around the city. By the time he returned to Lydia, he had spent most of the day at the hospital, and a further two hours with Father Orlandi. He was unaware of the mayhem caused by Robello, and contrary to Lydia's expectations of a black mood, he appeared, if anything, relieved.

'I got everythin' arranged. Soon as he's fit enough to leave the hospital, Father Orlandi's gonna arrange a room for him at a monastery. I'm sending them a fat donation, so they'll take good care of him, take care of everything. I'll arrange for his books to be delivered to the hospital, be a nice gesture . . .'

Lydia fussed around him and ushered him to the table, saying she had got him his favourite dinner. He unbuttoned his jacket and switched on the television set before settling himself at her neatly laid out dinner table. Legs spread wide, he did not even notice her new silver candlesticks, the lace napkins, or the new cutlery. He poured himself a glass of wine, as she served the first course.

'I had a driving lesson today, Paulie.'

Carolla slurped his wine, and forked in large mouthfuls of fettucini without waiting for her to join him. By the time she had served herself, he was wiping his plate clean with fresh bread.

'You think he'll be all right?' he asked suddenly.

'You done the best by him, Paulie.'

He pushed his chair back from the table.

'Ah, don't get up from the table, I've got veal marsala . . .'

Stuffing his hands into his pockets, he stood in front of the television set, paying her no attention. Hurriedly, she took another mouthful of her starter, then began to clear the dishes. Behind her, the TV news blared out. She called over the noise, 'I said, I had a driving lesson today. The instructor said what a nice car it was . . . you listenin' to me?'

He was riveted to the television set. Suddenly, he swore and began to thrash his arms up and down, agitating himself so much that it made him vomit. Fettucini and red wine spewed from him and his eyes bulged.

Lydia dropped the plates, thinking he was having some kind of fit, but he was pointing at the TV. She listened to the commentary, '. . . the inferno began early this morning, and it was not until late afternoon that it was brought under control. The two bodies are said to be those of the Borsalino brothers, owners of the new and extensive building project, now, sadly, completely destroyed by the fire . . .'

Still retching, Carolla could do nothing but flail his arms in despair. But the news bulletin wasn't over . . .

'A car bomb exploded early this morning in Palermo

256

Square. One of the bodies in the Fiat has now been identified as Salvatore Pavesi, but the other occupant is as yet unknown. The police wish to contact any persons who saw the two men in the Fiat, registration number . . .'

Carolla slumped onto the sofa, panting, looking for all the world like a fish out of water. Lydia rushed to him with a damp cloth, blocking his view of the television, and he knocked her aside.

'Fuck off out of it, get out of it . . .'

'You all right?'

'Shut up!'

Salvatore Pavesi was also Carolla's man. Carolla's eyes bulged as he continued to stare at the screen. As the news ended, he grabbed the phone and shouted for Lydia to turn the TV off and get out of the room.

No one answered his call, he ripped the instrument from the wall and hurled it across the room. It broke in two and he kicked it, then charged like a mad bull into the bedroom.

'Get out!' he roared at Lydia.

'Where do you want me to go? You told me to come in here.'

'Where's the fuckin' phone?'

'You just used it!'

'I just broke it, and get outta my fuckin' hair . . . Out!'

Lydia scurried into the living room and picked up the broken phone. She pushed it back together and plugged it back into the socket. When she lifted the receiver, she could hear Carolla's voice.

'What the fuck is goin' on? You better get your arse over here, and now! I'll tell you what's fuckin' goin' on, that prick, that cocksuckin' bastard Luciano has started a fuckin' war, that's what he's done.'

Lydia could hear Carolla making call after call. His vomit had stained her white carpet and she could have wept, would have done, had the sudden smell of burning not made her panic. She rushed into the kitchen. The veal was charred and smoke billowed from her new oven.

Carolla smelt the smoke as he ran from the bedroom. At that moment, the doorbell rang.

Vincent Torre was white-faced and visibly shaking when Carolla let him in. He knew his cousin had been killed in the bombed Fiat, but he had brought even more bad news. He was almost incoherent as he gabbled, 'Jesus Christ, Paulie, it's fuckin' mayhem . . .'

Smoke billowed out of the half-open kitchen door and Lydia howled. Carolla turned and kicked the door open; Lydia came out, weeping hysterically and holding up the charred remains of their dinner. Carolla had to slap her face to shut her up.

'What's going on?' she screeched. 'Paulie, what's happening?'

Somehow he pulled himself together enough to fling open the kitchen window. Then he splashed cold water on his face and returned to the living room.

Lydia was still snivelling. 'Oh, Paulie, the kitchen's ruined, and look at the carpet.'

Pulling on his coat he gestured for Torre to follow him, snapping as he walked out, 'I'm being fucked over and she's howlin' about her fuckin' kitchen . . . *Clean it up, you dumb bitch!*'

It was not until Carolla was alone with Torre that he got the facts. As he listened, the colour drained from his flushed, fat face. Torre was so nervous that his hands twitched on the steering wheel.

'The bomb musta been planted when they was havin' coffee, I dunno. But Frankie was in the passenger seat, then Pavesi got in and turned on the ignition. They didn't stand a chance. Around the same time, Cesare . . .'

'What? Was he in the car?'

'No, he was two miles away. He was just walkin' to get his cigars, like he did every morning, an' two guys walked right up behind him. They used a sawn-off shotgun and a fuckin' revolver, an' how about this – broad fuckin' daylight and no one, no one, saw it happen. No one even heard the fuckin' shots.'

'Oh, Jesus Christ, I don't believe it.'

'The fire started at the same fuckin' time, the whole building's wrecked. They're makin' arrests like it's goin' outta fashion . . .'

'I don't believe this is happening, this is fuckin' crazy. Luciano was refused by the Commission, they turned him down. He wanted my balls then, and they refused. He can't do this, he can't fuckin' do this . . .'

'He's doin' it, an' he don't care about the Commission.'

Carolla was thinking fast. He had to get to his second big refinery, warn them to clear the junk in case of fire.

As their car turned the corner, he could see that the street was swarming with police cars. The front for the refinery was a small shoe-repair shop, and from where they parked they could see that its windows were shattered and the police had cordoned off the entire area with blue ribbon. A police car roared past with three prisoners, their faces blackened by smoke, handcuffed in the back. Carolla sent Torre to see how many men had been arrested and watched as he talked with two of the uniformed officers.

He returned to the car and started the engine. 'We better get the fuck outta here, they got the whole crew. They was all in the building, four dead and eight arrested . . . Cops said the place was shattered – another bomb, it was a bomb.'

Torre drove Carolla back to the apartment. The madness of the attacks, the pace at which they were done, gave him no time to gather his men or think tactics. His only concern was to save his own skin.

They pulled up in the small private courtyard belonging to the apartment block and Carolla swore. Parked there for all to see was Lydia's new Alfa Romeo.

He pounded his fist on the dashboard. 'I told that stupid bitch to make sure the car was put away. She's got a fuckin' garage but she's too lazy to walk two yards down the road . . .' He handed Torre the spare keys. 'Here, park it. Anyone could trace me through that fuckin' motor . . .'

As Carolla eased his bulk out of the car and waddled into the building, Torre took the keys across to Lydia's car. He opened the Alfa's door, triggering a massive bomb. The sound was so loud that Carolla's knees gave way and he collapsed on the ground as debris showered around him. Screams went up as windows shattered in the wrecked courtyard, but no one was hurt apart from Torre. The explosion left nothing of him, it was as if he had never been there.

Shaking, Carolla made it to the apartment. He was beginning to gibber, unable to control his speech or his limbs, and had great difficulty opening the front door.

Lydia was at the window, looking down at the wreckage. The police had arrived and the spectators were gathering. 'My car, look what's happened to my car! Oh, Jesus, my car's been blown up . . .'

Carolla merely looked at her and walked into the bedroom. Two seconds earlier and bits of him would have been decorating the first-floor windows, and she was bleating about the car. He began to pack a case, throwing in anything that came within reach, while trying to calculate how many men he was down. In one night he had lost more than half a dozen, plus all the junk that had gone up in smoke.

Luck was on Carolla's side, because there was no way of identifying the body that had been blown to nothing in the Alfa Romeo. He snapped to, realizing the advantage it could give him to be believed dead. He yelled for Lydia to finish packing for him and paced the room, desperately trying to gather his wits.

'You finish packing my clothes, and you listen – listen! Just stop blubbering, will you, and pay attention.'

She was to answer the door to no one until he was safely away. Should the police question her about her car she was to say that Carolla had been driving it, and the last time she had seen him was when he had walked out to the Alfa.

Lydia was terrified of him. 'Do you know who did this to you, Paulie? Who tried to kill you?'

He stared into space for a moment, and spoke quietly.

'Yeah, I know, I fuckin' know . . . He took his time, see, waited until he reckoned I wasn't lookin' over my shoulder. He waited until I got two refineries stashed to the ceiling . . . The bastard, I'm wiped out, I'm wiped out.'

By the time Carolla's car arrived with four body-guards, he was ready to kill Luciano with his bare hands. But he exercised control, supreme control, telling himself over and over, 'Luciano acted without orders, start acting like him and you're dead . . .'

Carolla calculated that this open attack, if he played his cards right, could be turned against Luciano. His old enemy had made a big mistake in not ensuring that he was dead. He knew now that he must at all costs cover his tracks. On being told that Juan Borsalino had escaped and was in hiding he knew that he had to be dealt with first. Then Lenny Cavataio, the only witness left, must be traced.

Hunched in the back of the car, Carolla bit his nails down to the quick. They had travelled miles out of their way until they were sure no one was following them, then headed back to the waterfront, past the docks and into the small back lanes lined with ware-houses.

Carolla kept watch from the back window and as the car drew up he jerked his hand for the man next to him to get out. The man disappeared into the side entrance of the warehouse and was gone about five minutes. When he returned, he leaned in through the window to speak to Carolla.

'He's on the first floor, second room in. He's very jumpy, so make sure he knows it's you.'

Carolla entered the building alone. Juan Borsalino was sitting wrapped in a blanket. He was barefoot and his jacket was torn. Carolla stood at the door and raised his hands.

'It's Paulie, Juan. I'm comin' in, OK?'

'Christ, you took your time, man. I've been waiting in this pisshole all day.'

'Hey, take it easy, you hear what happened? Those cocksuckers tried to blow me to smithereens. I got here as soon as I could. Jesus, it's freezin' in here! Where's your shoes?'

'Under my fuckin' bed, I only just made it out of the goddam building. The bastards, the fuckin' bastards, they got Philippe, you know that? Sons of bitches, they didn't stand a chance, the place went up in a sheet of flame.'

'Hey, Juan, I've not come here for a press conference. We both gotta get out.'

'He was my brother, they killed my brother.'

'Yeah, I'm sorry . . . I got some dough, an' I got you a passage . . .'

'I'm not takin' a fuckin' boat! I wanna fly out. What you got me on a fuckin' boat for? Jesus, Paulie, you know I hate fuckin' boats.'

'You wanted a safe ride, didn't you? You wanna buy a ticket, then buy one! You got me runnin' around after you, what the fuck you think I am?'

'You're the guy that got me into this shit in the first place. I warned you about that bastard. Luciano is one of the biggest dons in Sicily an' you, you fat motherfucker,

263

you thought you could take him on. You should've left his kid alone; I warned you, an' he's traced that bad junk back to me. I want a plane ride, I want some clothes, an' I want them by tonight, Paulie, or I don't mess about. I'm warnin' you now, my brother's dead 'cause of you . . .'

Carolla snapped at him, 'You keep flappin' that mouth an' we'll both be floatin' in the fuckin' dock. I'm here, aren't I? I came as soon as I could. OK, here's your dough, an' here's your ticket.' He handed them to the shivering Juan.

Throughout their conversation Juan had had a Zanotti shotgun resting on his knee, his shaking hands constantly fingering the trigger. Now, as he took the envelope, he placed the gun on the floor by his bare feet, then greedily removed the wad of notes.

It took only two steps and Carolla was behind Juan, taking a thin piece of cheese-wire from his pocket. 'You count it, Juan, and tell me Paulie Carolla isn't your friend.'

Delighted, Juan laughed, then he dropped the envelope as the wire went taut around his neck. The two small wooden handles clicked together as Carolla crossed the wire and jerked hard. The fine, strong metal cut into Borsalino's throat, slashing and garrotting him at the same time. One more hard jerk and the blood spurted. Carolla stepped back fast to avoid getting blood on his shoes. With one single spasm, as though he were having an epileptic fit, Juan lay still. Carolla picked up his money and walked out.

As he climbed into the car, the engine was already ticking over. He settled back in his seat.

'He goin' to the States with you, Mr Carolla?' the driver asked.

'No, I'll book him on a later flight. Bastard got pissed off when I told him he was goin' by boat. I dunno, some guys are never satisfied, no matter what you do for them . . .'

'When I drop you, Mr Carolla, want me to go back for him?'

'Let the cheap bastard walk.'

The bodyguard in the front leaned over his seat and smiled, 'He can't do that . . .'

Carolla looked from one to the other and snapped, 'What the fuck is this? What do you think I did back there?'

'He's got no shoes on! Told me he left them under his girlfriend's bed.'

'Way I heard it, half of Palermo's been under her. Pair of shoes'll make a change.' Carolla laughed at his own wit and the men joined in.

Somehow Carolla held himself together until he was in the safety of the plane heading for Canada. Now there was just Lenny Cavataio, and when he was taken care of, he would demand that the Commission back him against Luciano.

In New York, the wedding celebrations were over. In Palermo, the couple hired by Luciano continued as instructed to run the villa. Every day little Maria was taken for a walk and every day at the same time the

265

Mercedes arrived to drive Don Roberto to his tile factory. Luciano had arranged the perfect alibi, Anthony Robello having not the slightest notion his so-called partner was not in Sicily.

The morning after the wedding, Luciano moved into phase two of his plan. He had arranged a meeting with Vito Nicoli on the pretext of discussing business, but with the real intention of incriminating Anthony Robello. He had to ensure that no possible blame would be attached to himself, but he was working blind as he had as yet received no word about how the war had gone down. There was no one he could call as no one, apart from himself, knew his plans in their entirety.

Vito was waiting in his private salon at the Plaza Hotel, where he and his men occupied a whole floor. The suite was always reserved for him and kept in constant readiness for his visits to New York.

He welcomed Luciano himself and poured him strong black coffee into a fine bone china cup. 'I am expecting a few of the boys, but I wanted to talk to you first. Does the name Anthony Robello mean anything to you?'

Luciano frowned as he stirred his coffee. 'Robello . . . Isn't he the guy who took over one of the families not long ago? Yes, I know, I met him at the last Commission. Young guy with a hooked nose, right?'

'Yeah, that's him. I got a call from a contact in Canada who said Robello had asked for a meet, you know anything about it?'

'No . . . He say what it was about?'

'Could only be one thing. The guy's surrounded by fuckin' gun-happy shitheads, and he'll climb over bodies to get what he wants. They reckon he bumped off Cesare's crew, you know about that? Nobody's sure, but we're still tryin' to find the poor fucker's kids. If Robello's trying to push his way into narcotics in Palermo he's gotta be treading on that slime Carolla's territory. I tell you, his old man was right all those years ago when he give you the family. That Carolla's a mean bastard.'

'You're telling me? That sonofabitch sold my kid the heroin that killed him and I couldn't get any action from the Commission. I'm tellin' you, Vito, the day the Organization moved into the junk business it fouled up, and it's going to get worse, believe me. The Feds are on our backs now, and I for one am sticking out for trying to run my business on the level. We don't need the junk trade and I don't want any part of it.'

Luciano was playing his part brilliantly, and Vito Nicoli was a hundred per cent taken in, relieved that Luciano still wanted no part of the trade. There were too many biting at his heels already. Like any other man, Vito would have liked a part of Luciano's valuable export business to help him smuggle his junk, but that was not why he had asked for the meeting. It was the Robello tip-off that was worrying him.

The doorbell heralded the arrival of more guests. The sixth man to arrive was 'Big Daddy' Scimone. He was blazing as he entered the room, and didn't waste time removing his coat.

'You're not gonna fuckin' believe this – I just got a call from Juan Borsalino's fuckin' whore, she's screamin' blue murder.'

Vito poured coffee and handed it around. 'What's that bitch got your fuckin' number for?'

'All hell's let loose. Carolla's entire warehouse was blown to smithereens yesterday . . . I got a million bucks in that fat prick, and that's only the half of it. Sounds like

267

a fuckin' war is goin' on over there, they even hit his boats. There's bombs goin' off everywhere ... Jesus Christ.'

Luciano put his coffee cup down and waited ... waited ... Everyone began talking at once, Vito asking over and over if Carolla was alive, until Scimone screamed back at him that he didn't know, he had told them all he knew.

Unable to contain himself any longer, Luciano asked about Carolla. Scimone turned to him, a cigar clamped between his teeth, and spat, 'Look, I'm tellin' you all I know, an' if you want the truth I fingered you for this. Stands to reason, you was wantin' Carolla at the last meet, I put this down to you ...'

Vito tried to calm Scimone. 'Where's your manners, Roberto's a guest in my place. I was a guest at his son's weddin'. You think he was dancin' at his son's weddin' an' flyin' over to Palermo to hit that prick Carolla? I tell ya who it is. I'm more than sure it's that kid Robello, it's gotta be him.'

Scimone snapped. 'Who the fuck is Robello? I never heard of him.'

'The kid who took over the Cesare family, the one with the line in snazzy suits. You know how I know it's him? Because I got a call from a contact in Canada askin' me to check him out. I'm tellin' ya, it's gotta be that sonofabitch, he's trying to cut in on Carolla, cut in or wipe him out. Either way I'm takin' a fall. And so are the lot of you.'

The telephone rang. Michele Barzini, one of the men to arrive with Scimone, was given the nod by Vito to pick up the phone. 'Whoever it is, tell 'em to call back,' said Vito, but Barzini, after listening to the caller, said that Vito had better take it. 'It's Carolla . . .' Vito snatched at the receiver.

Luciano swallowed, but showed no trace of the emotion that tore through him like a knife.

Barzini whispered to the men. 'He's in Canada.'

All waited, watching Vito, who said not a word but listened for what seemed an interminable time. Eventually he said into the phone, 'He's here, Paulie, I'm lookin' at him . . . Yeah, I'm tellin' you, he's right here in my apartment. Look, get your ass back here an' we'll talk . . . I said we'll talk when I see you. Yeah . . .'

Vito replaced the phone, then looked directly at Luciano and continued, 'He was pointin' the finger at you, my friend. When I told him you was here it was the only time he went quiet . . . The guy's gone down fuckin' millions, and he's gonna be around with his fat paw out, beggin' for time. I think we gotta have a meet, a big one, and I reckon we gotta have it as soon as he gets to New York.'

Luciano walked from the apartment, telling his driver he would get some fresh air and see him back at the hotel. All his carefully laid plans were meaningless. Carolla was still alive, and he would put two and two together and know it was Luciano. He had been walking on thin ice; now the cracks were showing and he could feel the icy water beneath, waiting to suck him under.

CHAPTER 9

N O LONGER a habitual drinker, Carolla was smashed out of his skull, and had been since he arrived back in New York. He had nightmares of the Alfa blowing up, but instead of his bodyguard disappearing it was his own fat body bursting like a balloon.

The families were getting sick and tired of his irrational accusations against Luciano. He was demanding a meeting of the American bosses. They, in their turn, were growing increasingly angry at Carolla's frantic calls. He was, they suspected, out of control, and his screaming tirades were dangerous. Word was out that the men working for Carolla were talking their heads off. No one wanted to agree to a major meeting, feeling at this stage that it was too risky, but Carolla could not see the reasoning. Although he could not produce evidence to implicate Luciano in his wipe-out, he would not believe anything else.

Luciano remained in New York awaiting the outcome. He was aware that the Organization must have sent representatives to Robello, and prayed long and hard that the boy would stick to the rules and remain silent. Fuelled by Carolla's accusations, the Organization were suspicious and he knew they could quickly turn against him. Would Robello finger him? It was a possibility he was unable to do anything about. If he so much as contacted Robello he was done for.

The heads of the Commission were pressurized into calling both Luciano and Carolla before them. Luciano was ordered to fly to Nevada, where he met six high-ranking bosses. He was accompanied on the flight by two guards, who remained with him while he checked into his hotel and waited while he showered and changed. Then they drove him to a secret address. They treated him cordially, informing him that Carolla would also be brought before the Commission, but Luciano knew he was on trial. What he didn't know was whether they had proof of his participation in the bombings.

With superhuman control he held himself together as he faced the Commission. Not one of them could detect the turmoil inside him. With apparent calmness and self-assurance he was fighting for his life; one crack in his armour would mean the end. He denied all the allegations Carolla had made against him.

Luciano's alibi, that he had been at his son's wedding during the bombing, was convincing. He spoke quietly and confidently, agreeing that he had personal reasons for wanting to destroy Carolla but, as they must be aware, through lack of evidence he had been refused any act of vengeance at the last Commission. Now it appeared that Carolla had been able to instigate an entire delegates' meeting with no evidence whatsoever that Luciano was connected with the war in Palermo.

The Commission heard him out without interruption.

They had written statements from those wedding guests Luciano had so carefully selected, enough high-ranking dons to substantiate everything Luciano said, and their word was irrefutable.

Genovese Rizzio poured a glass of iced water, handed it to Luciano and, keeping his eyes on his face, asked him how well he knew Anthony Robello. With an effort, Luciano maintained his calm and repeated exactly what he had told the men in Vito's apartment.

Rizzio nodded, then pursed his lips. 'I arrived here from Palermo two days ago. I made a point of meeting with Robello before I left. He claims that he knows nothing about the bombing, nothing about Carolla. You know Vito thinks he's behind it, a lotta guys think it has to be Robello. He's not going to admit it, now is he, but the guy is moving into the junk market. You got any opinion? Think it could be this guy? He swears that you were in Palermo, Don Roberto, not exactly pointing the finger at you, but he seemed fucking sure that you were in the city. What do you say to that?'

Luciano shrugged and helped himself to more water. His hand was steady. 'I don't know Robello – I met him once in Havana and that's as far as it goes. How many men were required to set the war up? You think that I could have organized it? Just you tell me how? My best men are here in the States, my sons are scattered – here, in Rome, in Atlantic City. Tell me how, and give me one good reason why I would have done it, apart from the fact that I detest that unprofessional sonofabitch Carolla. What would I gain? I don't deal in junk and I don't want to start now. I warned you at the start that it would cause a fuck-up, so don't come bleating to me.' He paused and sipped the water while they waited silently. 'I leave it to you to find out if it was Robello or not, it's not my business. I've spent years and thousands of dollars greasing the law, the politicians, building up a legitimate business. And for what? So you can haul me in here like some slob that just got initiated?'

Rizzio walked over to him and shook his hand. 'Thank you, Roberto. *Arrivederci*, have a safe trip home, OK? We'll find out if it's Robello. Rest assured, we are more than aware of our need for you and we appreciate your coming here. We will make sure you won't lose out, you have our word. Again, *arrivederci*.'

Luciano picked up his coat and went to the door. He paused, surveyed the men with a cold, arrogant stare, then walked out.

Rizzio sighed, twirled his pen. 'They don't make them like that any more. Pity, the guy's a real Organization man. He's always gone by the rules, and I reckon he's right – we do owe him, and we need him. He's got one hell of a monopoly in Palermo and he's one of the most powerful figures in Sicily, yet he came here. He was willing, throughout this fuck-up, to be brought before us. As yet, Robello is clean. When he was questioned, he denied ever having met Luciano, but my bet's on him. So let's get that slimebag Carolla in, and sort him out good. The guy is out of control.'

Carolla was not well endowed with good features, either mentally or physically, but the one quality he did have was resilience. No matter how hard he was hit, Carolla bounced back. He bounced into the High Commission's special court as if he were going to a party. His sweating face beaming, it seemed that he thought it an honour to be called by the top strata for a private meet. Here he was, broke, owing more than a million bucks to one family alone, and smiling like it was Christmas.

When the Commission refuted his allegations against Luciano, he grew surly, but perked up again when they made it clear that they were convinced Robello was responsible. It was agreed that if it were proved he was behind the bombings, he would be taught a final lesson.

Carolla sprang up, waving his arms. 'I'll fuckin' do it, I'll do it with my bare hands. The prick, the little cocksuckin' bastard, I'll—'

'Siddown, and keep that yapping mouth shut. We decide if he's to be hit, you got that? Robello may be a kid, but he's a don, and he was given the honour by his own family. If he is to be hit, we give it to Luciano, and he will get Robello's business and his soldiers if he wants them. You're out of this, Carolla, until we say different. You've dragged Luciano's name in shit and he has a right to compensation. You should get down on your knees and thank the Holy Virgin that he didn't demand your balls.'

'That's about all I got fuckin' left.'

'You got your life, an' that's more than most of the guys want. Stay clear of Palermo until we say so, understand?'

Carolla decided then and there to screw the Organization just as they had, to his mind, screwed him throughout his life. First his father gave what was rightfully his to Luciano, now they wouldn't lend a hand when he had been almost blown to pieces. They had no right to tell him where he could and couldn't go, he was a free man, and from now on he would work alone. They had cut him loose, and his instinct for survival was so

274

strong that it gave him a new layer of confidence, a tougher layer.

Luciano returned to Palermo only just in time to receive the pre-arranged telephone call from Anthony Robello, one month after the bombing. They arranged to meet at the tile factory at ten in the evening.

Robello arrived with two bodyguards and a driver. This time they all entered the office, although Luciano had stipulated that Robello should come alone. With his men ranged behind him, Robello sat and gave Luciano a brief rundown of how things had gone.

He had, as requested, allowed Juan Borsalino to escape, fully intending to capture him and keep him prisoner for Luciano to question him. However, he had gone into hiding and had then been found with his throat cut by a cheese-wire. Robello shrugged; nobody knew who had done it.

Luciano congratulated Robello on his work and said he hoped no approaches had been made to any of Carolla's contacts just yet, as agreed. He knew full well that they had, even before the bombing.

Robello was very confident. 'I've gone by your rules up to now. I've had the made guys from the US on my back, following me around, and I kept my mouth shut as arranged. I've done everything by your rules, only I didn't expect them to be on to me so fast.'

Luciano shrugged. 'Come on, you knew that would happen.'

'No, no, what you said would happen was that I'd be as white as snow. It would be *you* they'd come down heavy on.'

'You think I haven't been questioned? They figure it was me, Robello, just as I said, so we make no moves, just keep our mouths shut. I'll deal with the Commission when I have to.'

'Yeah, that's just what I have been doing, maybe I've let you deal with them too long. What's this bullshit about you being at some wedding in New York? I know for a fact you were here, in Palermo.'

Luciano looked him straight in the eye and said nothing. Robello tensed. 'Oh, man . . .' He could feel the rug beneath his feet being tugged, just a fraction. He had proof that Luciano had been in Palermo, his men had seen him, hadn't they? But now he was caught, because if he said anything Luciano would know he hadn't trusted him.

Luciano shrugged. 'So we were both in Palermo, so we both let these guys ask as many questions as they like. That's what they're here for and they'll try to trap you into saying something that'll tie you in with the bombing, tie you in with me. You say nothing, you even imply you had my place watched and they'll make the connection, *capiche*?'

Robello nodded. 'Yeah, yeah, I hear you.'

'So hear this – you fucked up, my friend, and you fucked up badly.'

Robello went puce. He snapped that like hell he had fucked up; he had stuck to their bargain right down the line, and now he wanted his payoff.

'You get the payoff, kid, when Paul Carolla is dead. That was the bargain. You'll have everything we agreed, when, and only when, Carolla is out of the way. *Capiche*?'

A muscle at the side of Robello's face twitched. 'I was so sure it was Carolla who took the blast, even the papers said it was him in the Alfa. The guy must have nine lives. Where is he now?'

'That's for you to find out. Why don't you take these goons of yours and get out, and next time I tell you to come alone, you come alone. I've got sons your age, I've been around a long time. You've been producing bodies like a conveyor belt in a slaughterhouse; just give me the one I want and maybe you'll live to see our deal go through.'

Luciano had the boy cornered, and he put the boot in. 'You are going to need me when the time comes, because if you have so much as made a single connection with any of Carolla's associates, you have signed your own death warrant.'

Robello's control was impressive. He said only that the contract would be completed, then he left. He was scared, and Luciano admired him simply because he showed not a flicker of fear.

As the four men passed the caged wolf, it howled and Robello's stomach churned. His men could see the Eagle's chalk-white face glistening with sweat. He had moved too fast and now he had to save himself from being swallowed whole.

'You sure you saw Luciano every day?'

'Yeah, like clockwork. He walks this crazy little dog down his path, waits until it craps and then gets into his Mercedes. Every day I seen him – it's a bitch.'

'What?'

'The dog, he calls it all the time – its name's Maria. It was him all right, the dog goes nuts around him.'

Robello had already made his decision. If he went after Carolla he could lose time; instead he would take out Luciano and the proof that they had ever met. As he thought of it, he relaxed. He had been a good pupil, fast to learn, and Luciano would now discover how good.

Luciano paid off his home minders with enough money to start the small ice-cream parlour they had dreamed of for years. The only thing that made Luigi sad to leave the villa was the funny little mutt, Maria. He had grown quite fond of her, and he shook his head, laughing, when he saw her hurl herself into Luciano's arms.

'She's a street girl all right, Don Roberto. Look at how she switches her affections. You know, I thought she loved me, I was even feeling sad to leave her, but . . .'

Don Roberto laughed as the tiny dog licked his face and snuffled in his ear. 'You know, Luigi, you treat a woman well and she will always come back to you, isn't that right Maria? Eh? We're going to be coming to that ice-cream parlour, and we want chocolate sauce and nuts on vanilla, isn't that right?'

Luigi kissed Luciano's ring in deference. His eyes brimmed with tears. 'I will never be able to thank you. I bless the day we came to you and I pray for you, Don Roberto. I swear to repay your kindness.'

'Just make sure we get free ices, that's all the repayment we want.'

Aware that Robello was not to be trusted, Luciano made arrangements for his younger men to take over immediately on his return. They were to guard the villa day and night, they were not to take in any packages without checking their contents, and, above all, they were to pay particular attention to the cars. He knew that he had pushed the boy to breaking point, pushed him hard enough to try for a hit, and he would more than likely use explosives.

Two days later, Luciano's car was waiting outside the gates of the Villa Rivera. The drivers had already changed over, and the young man polished the gleaming bonnet while he waited, checking for so much as a fingermark. Periodically, he checked his watch and looked up at the house.

Half a mile away, three men observed the villa, sharing a pair of field glasses. One of them said, 'It's a new driver, guy sure is trying to make an impression.'

The driver checked his watch again, then casually opened the right-hand side of the big, wrought-iron gates and strolled up the drive towards the villa.

'What the hell's going on? Is he coming? I can't even hear the fucking dog . . . Come on, come on, you sonofabitch . . .'

The three men watching were so tense they could hear their own wristwatches ticking loudly. 'Jesus, Mother of God, come on, come on . . . Where the fuck is he?'

None of them dared to get out of their car to see what was happening. One of them was sweating so much he kept having to wipe his face on the sleeve of his jacket.

'It's OK, we've got ten minutes yet.'

'I hope you're right, because I want to get the hell out of here before that fucker blows.'

Half-way up the drive, the driver veered to his right to where Don Roberto was standing under a big, full-blossomed cherry tree. It was not simply a matter of trust; he was well aware of the bomb and the timing device attached to it. He had been schooled well and, like Robello, had learned fast. He saw the way Don Roberto glanced casually at his watch.

'Ten minutes an' go, yes?'

'Yep. I've covered it with blankets as you instructed. It's dead, but we got nine minutes.'

Luciano smiled as he heard the sound of police sirens. 'They're cutting it fine. Let's get the show on the road.'

Together they walked briskly to the gates, now in full view of the waiting men, who almost cheered, until they, too, heard the sirens wailing. Without waiting for the explosives to go off they started to drive away. Three police cars came at them, two at the front and one at the rear. The police were out in seconds and the men were trapped. They were spread-eagled over the bonnet of their car, hands above their heads, babbling in terror . . .

The first police car moved on, coming to a standstill close to the Mercedes. Luciano stepped forward. 'There's a bomb in the back seat. It's safe, but get all the men out of the immediate area just in case.'

He waited while everyone took cover. The captured men, still shouting, were dragged to a safe distance. The cool-headed driver remained with Luciano, waiting as he opened the back door of the Mercedes, leaned in and removed the padding from the bomb. It was very crude and, as the driver had said, dead, but Luciano suggested the driver take cover. The crudeness of the bomb worried him.

It took Luciano nearly a minute and a half to remove the wires. As he backed out of the car holding the fuse wire, he was sweating, but he still managed to joke that he would never have made it to the tile factory in one piece – a few thousand, maybe, but definitely not one. There was a collective sigh of relief.

Luciano walked over to the waiting police officers. Again he joked, 'I would call that perfect timing. Thank you for coming so promptly, there was no immediate danger, but you never know. As you can see, it was not a very professional job.'

Maria could be heard yapping in the distance as she ran hell for leather down the drive. She had been shut in the kitchen, but somehow managed to get free. She was barking to gain Luciano's attention, thinking he had forgotten their daily ritual and left her behind. But his attention was not on Maria; he was looking at the three captives who, unlike the police officers and himself, were still yelling in fear and fighting to get free. They were hand-cuffed, with no chance of escape, yet they were desperate to move further away and were pointing to the parked Mercedes.

Two small girls on a bicycle rounded the bend, one pedalling and one clinging to her sister at the back, laughing. Luciano looked at them, looked at the scream-ing captives, then back to the car . . .

Maria ran through the gate and made a flying leap into the back seat of the car, scratching with her paws. Luciano yelled at the top of his voice in a frantic effort to make the little girls stop, but they were so interested in what was going on that they didn't hear him. They were within a few yards of the Mercedes . . .

Seeing Luciano dive in the direction of the children, the police moved closer. The second bomb exploded . . .

The two sisters died instantly. Five police officers and one of the arrested men were killed, and Luciano's driver was decapitated by the flying door of the Mercedes as it was blasted from its hinges.

Graziella Luciano was in church when the assassination attempt took place. By the time she returned to the villa, all that remained in the street was shattered glass and twisted metal, a tow truck already lifting the Don's mangled car onto a trailer. One gate to the villa was being removed, the iron bars twisted and buckled. As her driver stopped, and before she could ask, she was assured Don Roberto was unharmed.

Mario Domino, not Luciano, was waiting for her return. Obviously shaken, she allowed him to guide her into the drawing room and explain what had happened. She did not speak with her husband until early evening and, like Domino, he tried to dismiss the danger, and even the explosion, as an accident. But the relief that he was alive and unharmed turned to anger. 'Someone tried to kill you, and you say it was an accident? Why? Who would do this?'

'They failed, Mama, and now no more questions!'

'Is that all I am to be told, *they failed*, does that mean they will try again?'

He shook his head, and began to unbutton his bloodstained shirt; his bandaged hands made him fumble with the tiny buttons, and he sighed in frustration. She went to him, touching the dark red stains, and he gently wrapped her in his arms. 'It will soon be over, I need you more than ever. This is not my blood, Mama, but it is on my hands, may God forgive me.'

Graziella discovered further details from the news-papers. Luciano himself never spoke of the incident again. However she could not help but notice that the security surrounding her husband was doubled, and the villa began to feel more and more like a prison. Graziella did not know, could not know that until Anthony Robello was dead, Luciano's life was under threat.

Don Roberto Luciano was called the 'Hero of the Rivera Massacre'. The papers ran headlines on the war veteran who defused one bomb and almost lost his life trying to save the Pioti sisters. The two arrested men who survived the massacre refused to say who had planted the bombs in Luciano's car, but they were Robello's men.

The widow of every policeman killed received a large donation and a wreath from Don Roberto. The parents of the two sisters were visited by him personally and, although nothing could replace their daughters, his presence was a great comfort. He also arranged and paid for the funeral, and gave the parents a month's holiday in Capri plus enough money to start their own restaurant.

Anthony Robello was a walking dead man. The Commission had taken his murder attempt on Luciano as proof of his guilt. Carolla also accepted it, and although the Commission had expressly stated that he should stay away from Palermo, he surfaced. He had decided to show Luciano his good faith, that their vendetta was over, and to offer his friendship.

With four men dressed as police officers, Carolla arrived at Robello's home. Since the massacre he had not put a foot out of his villa. He decided to try to talk his way out of his predicament and ushered them into the elegantly furnished sitting room. He was shaking visibly, and blurted out that he was prepared to bargain for his freedom, that he had something to bargain with. In his desperation he made the mistake of not asking to see the police officers' identification. Carolla lagged slightly behind his four men as they entered the room.

Carolla stepped forward. 'I am Paul Carolla. As a don I give you the honour of facing your killer . . .'

Carolla did not wait to hear the desperate, garbled pleas for mercy. He fired six shots and watched gloatingly as the body jumped and twitched. The crisp white shirt slowly turned to deep blood red. Carolla kicked the corpse over and looked down into the dead man's face. 'Better a live fuckin' bastard than a dead gent, eh?'

He bent over the body and removed the monogrammed handkerchief from the pocket of Robello's silk smoking jacket, then with a knife sliced the ring finger from the corpse. He wrapped it carefully in the handkerchief.

The rest of Anthony Robello's body was never found. When his housekeeper called the police on discovering the terrible bloodstains, it was obvious that someone, probably Robello, had been murdered. The house was searched and a cache of explosives and detonators was found, plus a piece of wire that matched those from the Rivera massacre. The chief of police broadcast that they were no longer seeking a suspect in that connection.

The two men caught outside Luciano's villa never made it to their trial. One was found in the washroom with his throat cut, and one hanged himself. The war, it seemed, was over.

Graziella Luciano accepted the packet from the gate guard and tapped on her husband's study door to give it to him. He sighed, removed the glasses that he had recently taken to wearing and rubbed his eyes. 'What is it?'

'I don't know. The guard said it is a personal delivery for you, from Paul Carolla.'

Luciano ran his hands through his thick grey hair and sighed. He did not, however, touch the packet until Graziella was out of the room.

There was a note, with no address on it, that said, 'I give you another ring, with my deep regret that we have not been brothers for so many years. Please accept this, a personal gift from me, in the hope that we may in future be reunited.'

Carolla had signed his name with a flourish. Luciano put the cheap piece of notepaper down and picked up the silk handkerchief covered in brown stains with a grimace of distaste. The rotting finger was dark brown, the nail turning black and the ring was clotted with blood. It looked more like a claw than a human finger. The Eagle was most certainly dead. Luciano, like his wolf, was old and tired, but his teeth were still sharp enough to have played both sides and come out on top. He knew in the end it had won him nothing except, perhaps, his self-respect. Now even Carolla was offering him a truce and on the surface Luciano seemed to accept it. They had both turned away from the Organization, they were both loners, but one day, no matter how long he had to wait, he would make Carolla pay the ultimate price.

CHAPTER 10

NO ONE was ever to discover exactly what happened to Sophia and Michael's illegitimate child after his adoption six months after his mother left the village. The first few years of his life remained a mystery. But five or six years later, the *carabinieri* rounded up a group of street urchins in one of the poorest dock areas of Palermo. The youngest of the boys was half-starved, his blond hair matted and crawling with lice, and he was in a desperate condition. He seemed unable to talk, and either couldn't or wouldn't give his name, but he was already an adept thief. Although too young to be placed in an institution, he was like a vicious animal, biting and scratching the policemen.

The police assumed that the gold locket and chain around his neck was stolen and tried to take it from him. He put it in his mouth, and when they persisted in trying to take his treasure, he swallowed it. He was rushed to the nearest infirmary, where he had to be held down by the two nurses who examined him.

His skeletal frame was badly bruised, deep scars zig-zagged down his back, and open sores on his knees and elbows were severely infected. The locket gave cause for alarm as it could have caused a blockage, so he was X-rayed. The heart and chain were not the only things to show up on the X-ray plates; the child had three broken ribs, his right arm was dislocated, and he had a hairline fracture of the skull. He was also suffering from a ruptured spleen. It was obvious that he had suffered extensive beatings over a long period of time. The examinations also revealed that he had recently been sexually abused.

Father Angelo was doubtful about accepting the child, but seeing the pitiful state of the boy, his pinched, terrified face and shaven head, he agreed to a trial period. So the nameless boy was enrolled in the small orphanage run by the Monastery of the Sacred Heart.

The father collected the boy himself, together with the few clothes he had been given by the hospital charity; an extra pair of shoes, a shirt and a pair of grey shorts in a brown paper parcel. The child refused to allow the robed father to carry it for him, and walked a little apart, his arm still in plaster, clutching it awkwardly. His hair was beginning to sprout again, and both his kneecaps were bandaged. He clumped along in his charity shoes that were two sizes too large.

They caught the train to the northwestern tip of Sicily, sixty miles west of Palermo. The child sat in awed silence, staring out of the window. When Father Angelo unpacked a small luncheon of chicken and fresh bread, the boy snatched the food and sat hunched in the corner, stuffing it into his mouth as if afraid it would be taken from him.

*

Erice was famous in ancient days, particularly among the mariners who sailed the Mediterranean. It was incongruous that it should house the greatest shrine to the goddess of love in the world. A virtual citadel, the small, stone-built, walled town rose nearly half a mile above the sea and still managed to retain a flavour of the Middle Ages.

The drive in the taxi was quite hair-raising, the steep roads curving dangerously. The boy's jaw dropped when he saw the town perched on the hill and he instinctively clutched the father's robe, fearful, as if he were looking at a prison. This was the first indication of the child's insecurity, and also the first natural move he had made towards Father Angelo.

They were met by a plump monk who drove them on the last leg of the journey in a donkey cart, the child clinging to the father's hand all the while, until they arrived at the monastery. Father Angelo thanked their driver, who flicked his whip to make the old donkey trot off to pasture.

The boy was shown into a dormitory containing a row of neatly made beds. His was the nearest to the door.

'This will be your bed now, and see, this is your cupboard for your personal belongings . . .'

The child stood as if rooted to the spot. Unable to tell if he had understood, Father Angelo patted the bed for him to sit on it. But he wouldn't go near.

The father kept trying: 'Now then, you will sleep here, and you will have lots of company. I will take you to meet your new brothers in a moment. We shall tour the whole monastery so you will know where you have your meals, where you go for classes. Tell me, do you play football?'

There was no reply, no change of expression on the boy's face.

His face remained closed as they walked through the arches to the classroom. He hung back at the doorway and looked into the room full of boisterous boys, who fell silent as the father announced that they had a new friend who would be joining them the next day.

The next stop on their tour was the dining hall, already being laid for tea. Brother Thomas, a rotund monk, beamed a welcome at the boy and received an icy stare. Surprised, he looked at the uncommunicative boy.

'Well, what have we here? You are young, aren't you, eh? And what do we call you?'

Patting the child's head, Father Angelo said softly that they would perhaps have to give him a name, as he didn't seem to have one of his own. Taking the cue, Brother Thomas said, 'Well now, let me think, what sort of name would suit a fine-looking fellow like you? What about Arturo? We don't have an Arturo, do we, Father? Would you like to be called Arturo?'

The boy backed out of the room, and Father Angelo guided him to the small chapel. It was cool and dark, with rows of worn, polished pews. The altar cloth was of red silk, and two gold candles flanked the central crucifix. In a prominent position high above the altar were the Madonna and Child. The father crossed himself and was about to kneel when the child screamed. The look of terror on his face as he ran back down the stone aisle was to remain with Father Angelo for a long time. The boy seemed to hurl himself from the chapel, not caring that he banged his injured arm against the wall.

When Father Angelo finally caught up with him, he was curled in a corner, his teeth clenched, chest heaving, making rapid snorting sounds. The father squatted down on his heels and stroked the boy's head. At first the child shrank away from his touch, almost snarling at the outstretched hand, then he calmed down and his breathing relaxed. Picking him up, the father carried him to his private study and put him in a big wing chair, the only comfortable one in the monastery.

Father Angelo sat behind his desk and cupped his chin in his hands, watching the boy. Perhaps this time he had taken on too much, yet he knew that it was God's will that they should give some comfort to this disturbed little creature.

It was obvious that he would need a lot of special care, a lot of time, and Angelo did not have time to spare. There was much to do; the monastery had to provide for itself and the fifteen orphans in its charge, who had to be fed, clothed and educated. There was a small dairy, a bakery, and two fields to be sown and harvested, but otherwise they were dependent on charitable donations. The ten monks worked a fourteen-hour day simply in order to exist, and even before the new arrival they were stretched to the very limits. The buildings were in a constant state of disrepair and the chapel roof had been leaking for years. It was summer now, but soon they would have to find the money to cover the much-needed repairs to the archaic plumbing system. The old boilers were so patched that Father Angelo doubted if they would survive another winter.

Automatically, Angelo began to sift through the paperwork on his desk. He opened one letter of particular interest; a request that the orphanage take in a sick boy who was not expected to live very long.

He read on; in the event that they accepted Giorgio

Carolla, the enclosed cheque would be only the first of many donations. He stared at the amount in disbelief; it was enough to install an entire new heating system, with some left over towards the roof. Just as they were facing a financial predicament he thought they could never overcome, they had been offered a saviour, like a gift from God Himself. Closing his eyes, the father offered up a silent prayer of thanks.

He had forgotten his companion, and had not heard him move. As he opened his eyes, he met the boy's blue ones, peering at him over the edge of the desk. He was so small he could only just see over the top.

Father Angelo stared in surprise as the boy said, 'My name is Luka,' in a hoarse, strangely deep voice. He had difficulty in forming the words, speaking each syllable in a slow, deliberate way. The father swallowed his emotions and replied, 'Then, Luka, that is what we shall call you.'

Luka demanded more time and attention than any child Father Angelo knew. It took weeks just to get him to eat like a normal human being, but he still hid food in his pockets or stuffed it in his mattress, and often made himself sick with overeating. As time went on, some of the monks secretly believed that such behaviour should be punished; Luka not only stole food, he rifled the other boys' lockers, broke their pencil boxes and stole their treasures. If caught, he would merely give a sullen shrug.

He refused to go into the chapel, no matter how much they cajoled him. Father Angelo used all his persuasive powers to get him through the doors, but he would become hysterical, biting and kicking anyone close at hand. On the rare occasions that he spoke, his language was obscene, as if he knew only the speech of the gutters, and seeing his listeners' shocked faces only encouraged him. The boy could be no more than five or six years old, but Father Angelo began to have doubts that they could keep him beyond the agreed trial period.

Luka's hair had grown back, and was washed weekly and combed every morning by whichever brother happened to be on duty. The plaster had been removed from his arm and he had put on weight, although he was still exceptionally thin. No one could understand why, as he ate enough for three boys put together.

In lessons he was so far behind even the youngest student that he quickly grew bored and disruptive, but he seemed to be well liked, despite all his thieving. He was fearless, and prepared to fight at the slightest hint of disagreement, age or size immaterial. Within six months, Luka had become a strong influence, and Father Angelo decided to make one last attempt to get through to the boy. Luka sat tapping his heels against the leg of his chair, though apparently listening to the father's quiet voice. He was still too small for his feet to reach the floor.

'You have continued to steal from your brothers, be it a pencil or a rubber band. You cannot just take what you want if it does not belong to you, just because you want it. You were warned about stealing as you were warned about disrupting the class, but instead of attempting to learn to read and write, you persist in being as tiresome as possible. You still eat like an animal, even though we have taken great pains to teach you how to use your cutlery. You cannot possibly excuse this by saying you are still a very young child; we are fully aware of that and have taken it into consideration time and time again . . .'

Luka sighed and stared out of the window, a half-smile on his angelic face. It was as though Father Angelo's painstakingly slow and careful words with which he tried to make Luka understand the consequences of his anti-social behaviour were directed at someone else.

'Are you listening to me, Luka?' The boy, unconcerned, nodded his head. Father Angelo continued, 'Will you please look at me when I am speaking?'

Luka turned his bright blue eyes on the father and gave him a cheeky smile. Angelo rose from behind his desk and began to pace the room. 'You refuse to go to morning chapel, God knows how Brother Thomas has tried, and you have bitten and kicked him. There is not one of the brothers you have not physically assaulted . . . You find this funny, boy? Are you laughing?'

'I am a naughty boy, naughty boy . . . Luka is a bad boy, you can hurt Luka, you hurt Luka for being bad.'

Astonished, Angelo watched as Luka got to his feet and wriggled out of his shorts, then bent over the arm of the chair, his naked backside raised. With both hands he prised his buttocks apart . . . Sickened, the father quickly crossed the room and covered Luka with a shawl that hung on the back of the chair. As he wrapped it around him, the child suddenly turned, a terrible look on his face. The cherubic features were distorted and the blue eyes were those of a devil.

Angelo hugged him close, wanting to weep. 'Oh, my God . . . Dear, beloved Mother of God . . .' He rocked the boy in his arms, and a small hand gently touched his face.

All the father's adult words about anti-social behaviour fled from him, and he carried Luka to the window. He

293

stood looking out over the meadows. 'Luka, no one is going to punish you that way. That way is past, it must never happen again. Whoever did that to you is a bad person, evil. We are good, we are caring, and we want to keep you with us, but you must be prepared to be a good boy, too.'

The tears rolled down Luka's cheeks and as he buried his head in the musty robe, he whispered, 'Luka be a good boy, don't send Luka away.'

After evening prayers, Father Angelo went up to the boys' dormitory. He stopped beside Luka; the boy was lying quietly in his bed, his eyes closed and his lashes like silky white feathers against his cheeks. With his blond hair spread out on the pillow he looked like an angel. The father leaned close and whispered, 'I know you are awake, open your eyes. I have something that belongs to you . . . from the hospital in Palermo.'

He dangled the gold locket on its fine chain before Luka's face. The imprint of the teeth was clear in its centre. The child's face was filled with delight as he opened his eyes, and he gave a soft sigh of pleasure. 'My heart . . .'

Angelo nodded, smiling, then tucked the locket into the small hand. He had heard from the hospital how Luka had been so desperate to keep it that he had swallowed it, but they had believed it stolen and handed it over to the police. No one had ever claimed it, and it was an easy matter for Angelo to retrieve it from them.

As Father Angelo left the dormitory, he looked back to see Luka smiling up at the heart as he swung it back and forth in front of his eyes, as if hypnotizing himself. His face was a picture of innocence.

From then on, Luka began to settle down. He was still disobedient, still disruptive, and he did not stop thieving, but he made an attempt to study, even taking extra tuition, although he was unable to concentrate for any length of time.

What did change drastically was his attitude. From being surly and watchful he became a sunny-natured boy, his deep, husky laugh ringing out, usually when it shouldn't. He was not a tactile boy, yet his personality grew daily more outgoing, and he endeared himself to the brothers, one by one, with his quick jokes.

Father Angelo had discovered that the best way to make Luka do anything was to ignore him. No one ever forced him, and no threat of punishment ever worked faster on Luka than being ignored. He gradually learned to do day-to-day chores like all the other boys without cajoling. Although no good at his lessons, he earned rewards for good behaviour. He was allowed to choose his own treats, which included playing football and being allowed to help with the fruit-picking and gardening. He would use any possible excuse to escape to the garden and had a natural, instinctive awareness of the earth. It seemed to have a therapeutic effect on him, and his delight in his labours and in seeing things grow was a joy to watch.

The other boys occasionally turned against Luka, usually out of jealousy, but he dealt with them very effectively. One boy, Mario, had lost his pencil sharpener and discovered it in Luka's desk. When he threatened to tell Father Angelo, Luka had cursed him, but not in a childish way. He held up his fingers in the horned sign of the ram, spat at the ground and whispered, 'I am the devil, Mario, and tonight you will feel me crawling inside you and pinching your tongue. When you scream it will be me, that is why I am so special, that is why no one dares punish me.'

It made such sense to Mario that Luka talked with the devil; he never came to chapel with them, never took mass.

This fear of the devil was within them all, and was easy to conjure up in young, fertile minds . . . But the arrival of Giorgio Carolla caused the rumours to run rampant, as if the devil had arrived in person.

CHAPTER 11

GIORGIO WAS brought to the monastery in a horse-drawn cart, accompanied by three men in dark coats and hats. Mario, awake after one of his frequent nightmares caused by Luka, heard echoes of the bell ringing around the stone corridor. He witnessed the whispered meeting at the big gates and saw Father Angelo ushering the men through the courtyard. Two of them carried heavy suitcases and the third held in his arms what could have been a baby, wrapped in blankets.

Giorgio's room was in the main wing which the monks occupied, at the end of a long stone passage. Mario spread rumours about the strange creature in the blanket. Whoever it was had a room entirely to himself and never came out, although trays of food were taken in. Mario became the focus of attention, embroidering what he had seen every time he told his story.

The rumours and whispers grew out of all proportion, and dare-devils would sneak along the passage towards the room. One boy failed to hear the soft footfalls of Brother Thomas. He was caught and, squealing with terror, held by his collar while he was admonished. At supper the brothers laughed when Thomas relayed the story of young Giovanni pleading not to be made to go into the room and look the devil in the face.

'But, Giovanni, that's what you were trying to do, was it not? Forgive me if I have misinterpreted your stealthy, creeping progress along the corridor, but were you not trying to open the door to the private chamber?'

A clever mimic, Brother Thomas rolled his eyes, acting the part of the terrified boy. 'Oh, no, Brother, I had rolled a m-marble along the f-floor and I was just looking for it . . .' He wiped his eyes while he roared with laughter.

The room fell silent as Father Angelo slotted his napkin back into the carved wooden ring. 'Perhaps we should tell the children, so as not to disturb our patient. They will only be fuelled by Giovanni's tales of his capture.'

Brother Marcus sipped his deep red wine then held it nonchalantly against the candle flame as if fascinated by the colour. 'I agree. Should one of the children look into the room he would truly believe that the devil himself was dining with us. He certainly has a vicious tongue, a Machiavellian turn of phrase, has he not? "Did you enjoy our home-made pea soup, Signor Carolla?" I said. "Tastes like piss," he says. "Oh, I thought it a rather pleasant broth," I said. Then he jabbed with his fork at good Brother Emery's chicken and said, holding it in that wizened little hand of his, "And this, I presume, is also the constipated pisser's offering?"'

Brother Marcus chuckled and looked at the faces around the table. 'Well, you have to admit he is right about the chef!'

The remark was received with a general good-natured laugh, but Father Angelo pursed his lips, not liking the

298

turn of the conversation. He spoke rather sharply. 'I will speak to the children. Perhaps if our guest is not satisfied with our own culinary expertise, someone would ask him his preference. He is, brothers, a very important guest, do not let that fact escape you.'

Each man felt somehow guilty for the humorous exchange. In their hearts they knew that Giorgio Carolla was indeed a tragic figure.

The following morning, after mass, Father Angelo asked the children to remember in their prayers a poor invalid who had come to spend his last days in the peace and solitude of their monastery. They were to pray for him and stay away from the private quarters, being quiet if passing through the courtyard. Any boy seen trying to enter the room would be severely punished.

Luka had tried to sneak into the corridor a number of times, but his attempts were always thwarted by passing monks. The boys began to tease him and say he was afraid, and in a fit of temper he swore he would do it that night. Anyone who didn't believe him would eat his own words.

Shaking with fear, Luka crept down the inky-black staircase, then inched along the corridor. Luka felt cold, his teeth were chattering, but he knew if he went back now they would never believe that he'd dared to go through with it. He decided to warm himself up in the big kitchen, then make up a story and return to the dormitory. He made his way stealthily to the kitchen stairs.

The only light in the kitchen was from the fire blazing in the grate. Luka rubbed his arms in the thin cotton pyjamas and scurried to the fire. As he was warming his hands, he heard a loud belch, then Brother Thomas's voice outside the door. Looking this way and that for a means of escape, Luka spotted the pantry door and slipped in just as Brother Thomas entered, followed by Brother Emilio, who carried a tray.

'See, he's hardly touched a morsel, and this time it's chicken *fricassee* . . . he's not even sipped the milk,' Emilio was saying.

'Ah, well,' said Thomas, 'waste not, want not,' and he sat down to finish off the leftovers.

Luka could hear the monks dragging chairs to the fire and he sighed, praying that they would not come to the larder. He pressed his ear to the door and listened to their conversation.

'I have tried to be pleasant, and I got the Lord's book thrown at me, almost hit my head. You wouldn't think he would have the strength. I know Angelo said we must be caring and gentle, but he certainly makes it a difficult task . . .'

The smell of freshly cooked chicken in the pantry was so tempting that Luka crept to the large meat plate and lifted the white muslin cover. He wrenched an entire leg off the chicken and munched hungrily. When he had demolished a quarter of the chicken and his belly was full, he curled up beneath the shelves.

He must have fallen asleep for the next thing he knew he was feeling cold, and no sound was coming from the kitchen. Opening the pantry door, he saw that the fire had burned low and the monks had gone. He warmed his hands before making his way into the stone corridor.

Climbing into bed, he removed the second chicken leg from his pocket and ate it, then slipped the bones beneath his pillow.

In the morning, he was so deeply asleep that he had to be woken by one of the boys as Matins had rung and he would be late getting up.

'I went in, and I saw a creature that was so frightening, so . . . Wait until I tell you what happened last night . . .' But the boys were running helter-skelter down to the chapel and he did not have time to tell the story he had made up.

The last to leave the dormitory, he was crossing the courtyard when a thought struck him. If he went through the vegetable patch, across the field and into the small, private garden that the brothers used, he could peer in at the window and see whatever was in that room.

The winter sun threw long shadows from the monastery walls. On he went, across the field and over the low stone wall into the garden, then sprinted across to the row of windows.

Crouching, he inched his hands up to the window sill and peeked in, then gasped and slithered down again. Staring back at him through the frosted window he had seen the face of a gargoyle, a terrible devil's face, with wide-set eyes and a thick, flat nose above a full pink mouth which flapped open. Although panting with fear, Luka forced himself upwards again to take one more look.

This time the enormous head with the large, limpid eyes saw him, and from that dreadful flapping mouth came a tongue . . . It distorted the face to such an extent that Luka screamed, and the next moment he was running for his life. He fell and grazed his knee, but nothing could stop his mad scramble back to the safety of the courtyard.

Head down and running blindly, Luka did not see

Father Angelo and ran straight into him, collapsing in a heap at his feet.

'Why were you absent from Matins, Luka?'

'I was sick Father!'

'Perhaps I know the reason why.'

Father Angelo dragged Luka into the classroom and sent him slinking into his seat. Then he strode between the desks to stand near the blackboard.

'Quiet, all of you. This morning Brother Emilio came to me with very disturbing news. I am going to ask each and every one of you to tell me the truth, I will tolerate no lies. Last night, someone broke into the kitchen and stole half a chicken, food that Brother Emilio had prepared for luncheon . . .'

The boys stared at the father and exchanged shifty glances as he continued. 'Would the boy who committed this theft step forward? He will not escape punishment, that he must know, but unless he admits the theft publicly I will have to punish the entire school, and there will be no football for a month.' A groan went up from the boys and they looked around, wondering who it might be.

Brother Thomas came bustling into the room, took Father Angelo aside and whispered a fervent message in his ear, then scurried out again.

'I ask the boy responsible to step forward . . . I am waiting . . .'

The class gazed at him silently. Father Angelo's cold, enquiring gaze met Luka's blank look for a moment. 'Very well, you are dismissed. The thief did not confess, and it is too late now. There will be no football for one month. Please leave in single file and stand in the courtyard. Luka, would you please come to the blackboard?'

Luka stood patiently at the front of the class while the other boys filed out, casting glowering looks in his direction. As the last boy closed the door, Father Angelo turned to Luka.

'Do you have anything to say on this matter, Luka?'

'No, Father. If you like, Father, I will ask every boy for you,' Luka replied helpfully.

'I don't think there's any need to do that, do you, Luka?'

From behind his back Father Angelo produced some chicken bones and laid them on his desk. 'What are these, Luka?'

Peering closely at the bones, Luka pursed his lips. 'I think it is a chicken leg, Father.'

'You think? Luka, this was found beneath your pillow. Brother Thomas brought it to me after searching the dormitory. He found it, Luka, beneath your pillow.'

'No!' exclaimed Luka in innocent disbelief.

'Yes, Luka. Now I ask you, did you or did you not steal the chicken from the pantry?'

'No, Father, I did not.'

'Would you place your hand on the Bible and swear to me that you did not take the chicken?'

Laying his hand on the cross of the black Bible on the desk, Luka began, 'I swear by Almighty God I did not . . .' His clear blue eyes looked into Father Angelo's without a flicker of guilt. It was such a direct, pure gaze that the father flushed.

'May I speak, Father?' Luka asked, and received a small nod of permission. 'Well, you know, Brother

303

Thomas is larger than all the others and he does need more food. Perhaps he took the chicken but is too ashamed to admit it, or . . .'

'Or, Luka?'

'Well, this person in the room at the end of the corridor, perhaps he did it. His room is closest to the kitchen . . .'

Sitting down slowly, Father Angelo folded his hands and threaded his fingers together. 'As you have tried to blame our patient you will, instead of gardening today, help Brother Emilio clean his quarters.'

Frightened now, Luka licked his lips, but he was able to disguise his fear as well as he did his lies. He gave a slight shrug and asked politely if he was free to leave. Father Angelo watched as the boy went out, turning at the door to give him a small, sweet smile before closing the door. Angelo bowed his head in prayer and when the door opened again he hoped for a moment that it was Luka.

Brother Thomas asked, 'Well? Did he admit it?'

'Far from it, Thomas, far from it. He accused you.' Angelo smiled, without humour.

'The little devil! Well, I've got more proof, look at this – Luka's pyjamas, covered in chicken grease.'

Sighing, Father Angelo picked up the pyjamas and walked out of the room, telling Thomas that perhaps barring the whole class from their favourite pastime would force Luka to admit the truth.

'I'd force him! I'd give him a good thrashing, because that's what he deserves. Saying I stole it, the little devil!'

*

All the way back to his study, Father Angelo was thinking about what he should do. He was almost in agreement this time with Brother Thomas that perhaps Luka did need a thrashing.

A tearful Giovanni was waiting at his study door. 'It was me, Father, I took the chicken . . . I did it.'

'Were you wearing Luka's pyjamas when you took it?'

'Pardon?'

'What did you do with the bones, Giovanni?'

'P-p-put them under Luka's p-p-pillow so he would get the blame.'

'And why did you do that?'

'I d-don't know . . .'

'What did Luka do to make you lie to me, Giovanni?'

The little boy bellowed between his sobs, 'He was going to send the d-devil out of the secret room to get me . . . Father, oh, please, don't tell him I've told you, please . . .'

Unbowed, unrepentant, Luka was brought to Father Angelo's study. He still did not admit the theft, he did not care about that, but he did not want to be forced to go into the gargoyle's room. Heavy-hearted, Father Angelo took out the cane. He had hoped never to have to do it, especially to Luka, but now he had no alternative.

'Luka, you have lied, you have committed blasphemy, you have tortured Giovanni. This will be only a part of your punishment. You will not play football for the rest of the term.'

'Does that mean, Father, that I don't have to clean the private room?'

305

'That is not a punishment but a lesson in humility. Now take down your trousers.'

Luka's lip curled in a smirk as he dropped his trousers and leaned over the chair. He was given twelve lashes but never murmured, although the beating raised red weals on his buttocks. One of them was bleeding. When it was over, he pulled his trousers up, still with that look on his face, and asked if he could go.

As the door closed behind him, Father Angelo put his head in his hands and wept. He knew the punishment had been richly deserved, yet he felt nothing but remorse. The look on Luka's face had been exactly the same when he had first arrived, the way he had prepared himself to be sexually assaulted, drawing his buttocks apart for penetration. Luka had learned nothing; beneath that angelic face and sweet smile was still a very warped and twisted little boy, a boy filled with deep, abiding anger.

Luka was forced to wait on Giorgio Carolla for one week as an exercise in humility. It would, they hoped, make Luka understand how fortunate he was and how others suffered. They could not have anticipated the relationship that formed between the two very different boys. One weak, misshapen and totally dependent, the other fit and strong. They were, as Father Angelo wistfully noted, like Beauty and the Beast. Luka's delicate, perfectly proportioned face and startling china-blue eyes were more suited to a girl than a boy, in stark contrast to the domed forehead, the flat, wide nose and drooling mouth of Giorgio.

At their first meeting, Giorgio's strangely deep, pain-racked eyes stared hard at Luka, then turned away in embarrassment.

'You talk?'

'What do you expect? Snarls? Gibberish? Because my mouth drools it doesn't make me a mute, and I am not hungry, so you can take that pig swill back.'

'Can I eat it?'

Giorgio shrugged his twisted shoulders and then watched as Luka ploughed through the breakfast, his cheeks bulging like a hamster's. 'Don't they feed you in this prison?'

'Not this stuff, we get porridge and thick bread. You've even got your crusts cut off. How old are you?'

'What are you doing here?'

'I'm on punishment duty. I've got to bring you your meals and clean your room.'

'Are you an orphan?'

'Dunno . . . is that a record player?'

'Yes.'

'You got a lot of stuff in here, it's quite cosy. What you doing here?'

'Dying.'

Luka laughed and munched on Giorgio's toast and looked through his record collection. He picked up some books and raised his eyes.

'You must be older than you look, these are real books . . . Hey, what's this?'

He picked up a slim volume and turned it over in his hands, slowly making out the title. Giorgio could not raise his head, it was very difficult for him now even to turn it, and the weight threatened to snap his fragile neck.

Luka gasped, 'It's poisons! A book on poisons; what you got a book on poisons for?'

'Don't you ever stop asking questions?'

'Can I have it?'

'No, you can't.'

Luka dropped the book back on to the shelf. He looked around the room and discovered a large box of chocolates. Giorgio heard the papers rustle but could not see what Luka was doing. Then Luka brought the box to the bed and offered them as though they belonged to him. Giorgio pulled a face in refusal; he hated chocolates, particularly the kind Lydia chose for his father to give him. They were liqueurs, and hideously sweet.

'Can I have one?'

'You already have . . . Look, would you fix my head-band on, I want to read.'

Luka knelt on the bed and saw Giorgio wince with pain. 'Sorry, did I hurt you? Where's your legs?'

'What little I have are under your knee, you clumsy bugger.'

'Can I see?'

Giorgio's one strong hand clutched the sheet defensively. Luka sniffed. 'You smell a bit, can't you go to the toilet?'

'No I fucking can't, I can't do anything for my fucking self. Now why don't you piss off, take the chocolates, go on, piss off and tell everyone about me. Tell them about the dwarf, the gargoyle. I've got ears, see, both sides of my head like anyone else, and I can hear, it's one of the few things that are perfect, and I've heard them outside my window. So you tell them about me and let them laugh, like everyone else laughs at me. Go on, fuck off.'

'You'd better not speak like that or the monks will

have a fit.' Luka opened the door and peered out, then closed it. 'Oh, no, here comes Father Angelo. Look, don't tell him I ate your breakfast, and don't say anything about the chocolates.'

'I won't have to, he'll smell the alcohol on your breath.'

Father Angelo entered as Luka began frantically dusting a shelf. He spoke in a hushed voice, his hands clasped in front of him, asking if Giorgio was feeling a little better this morning and had he enjoyed his breakfast? Giorgio gave him a weak smile.

Father Angelo turned to Luka. 'So you two have met. Luka will be bringing your food trays, and anything else you want, just ask him. Brother Louis will be here with your medicines at eleven. He will also change your bed and wash you. Luka, don't disturb our guest any more than is necessary, and as soon as you have finished your duties please go straight to the classroom. I shall look in again this evening, Giorgio. God bless you, my son.'

Luka continued dusting until the heavy oak door closed, then tossed the duster aside and returned to the bed. He put Giorgio's headband with the page-turner on his head, taking great interest in how the small rubber knob worked. The battery gave a low but reasonably good reading light. It was now perfected to Giorgio's design, and meant that he needed no one to turn his light off so he could read at night without disturbing anyone. Luka set up the modern book-stand that fitted across the narrow bed, talking non-stop, and Giorgio's head reeled. Luka's energy was exhausting him.

It was not until Luka could no longer legitimately remain in the room that he made to leave. He paused at the door and watched Giorgio's big head with its funny pointer stick wobble as he turned a page, while spittle ran from his slack lips. Luka hurried back and, using the duster he had cleaned the shelves with, gently wiped Giorgio's chin.

'See you at lunchtime, Giorgio, and thanks for the chocolates.'

Giorgio pretended to read until Luka had closed the door, then he inched himself up a fraction until he could see from the window. He watched the blond boy running across the courtyard, and at one point jump high in the air for no reason. It seemed a simple, joyful movement and it filled Giorgio with a longing he had always kept under control, a longing for the chance to make a single jump, to have a single moment of freedom. But he only ever experienced it in his dreams.

Giorgio was ten years older than Luka and obviously far more intelligent, but he was surprised at Luka's lack of learning, and asked what books he read for pleasure. Luka just shrugged as he swished the mop over the floor. He was not the slightest bit interested in books, so why read them . . .

In amazement Giorgio replied, 'Because they're beautiful, you idiot! What about poetry?'

'Bores the pants off me . . . You sure you don't want this chicken? You've got the breast, we only ever get wings and legs. They get them cheap from the local butchers. Anyway, I think real things are more beautiful than words.'

'Like what?'

'Flowers, I grow flowers, and vegetables. These greens

310

you turned your nose up at, I grew them, and if you want my advice, instead of flipping all those pages over with that thing you'd be better off trying to eat and get your strength up. You should be sitting out in the garden, your skin's like a lemon . . .'

'Fuck off, you illiterate bugger.'

'You fuck off!'

'Cunt!'

'Anus features!'

'At least I've got brains in my head. You've only got turds.'

'At least I get my turds into the john, not in my bed, asshole.'

Brother Louis, standing at the half-open door, was so shocked he spilt Giorgio's washing water. He couldn't believe what he had just heard. Giorgio spotted him before Luka, who was still swishing the wet mop over the floor. Giorgio tried to warn him, but Luka continued furiously, 'Turd features, that's what I'm going to call you.'

'Luka . . . Luka . . .'

'Aw, shuddup, creep, or you'll get this mop round your head.'

Giorgio raised his voice. 'Good morning, Brother Louis. We were just discussing Latin translations in today's literal terms. You know the word "fuck" was first used in 1600 . . . to defecate, turd, shit – very interesting, don't you think? The American use of the word "john", meaning lavatory, the English use "toilet", as derived from the French *toilette* . . . The lavatorial heel was first worn by King Louis the Fourteenth, the Sun King. Because he was so small and because no one could see it against the royal-red carpet, the red heel disguised his true stature. It was shaped like the S-bend of a lavatory. Now, "john" is used by modern-day prostitutes . . .'

'Giorgio, please, may God forgive you. These words are appalling . . . And Luka, to hear you using language that is from the gutters . . .'

Again Giorgio piped up, interrupting Louis. 'I am so sorry, Brother, have I done something to offend you?'

'Most certainly, and I assure you I will discuss this matter with Father Angelo. He will no doubt punish this outrageous behaviour. Luka, please go to your class immediately.'

He was again interrupted by Giorgio, his voice even higher. 'In discussing this matter, Brother Louis, will you also give him the Latin translations or just the modern terminology? I should hate Father Angelo to misinterpret what Luka and I were discussing, and which you inadvertently overheard. Luka cannot in any way be blamed for the conversation you eavesdropped on. I did not hear you knock, and although I am incapacitated, I have requested that, to ensure some element of privacy, those entering my room allow me a little dignity. My father assured me . . .'

Luka's mouth dropped open as Giorgio, his pointer wobbling and his one good hand gesturing like the Sun King himself, totally flustered poor Brother Louis into apologizing. He hoped Giorgio's father would not be informed that the monks were not taking pains to ensure their guest was being well treated.

When the confused and flustered brother finally departed he had forgotten to wash and change Giorgio. The mere thought that the monastery could lose its valued guest through any fault of his made him tremble.

Luka had to clap his hand over his mouth to stop himself laughing aloud. Giorgio was elated, but the effort had tired him considerably, though he tried not to show it.

'You were brilliant! I never heard anything like it, you got him so mixed up. Giorgio, you are fucking *brilliant* . . .' Luka paced up and down mimicking Giorgio's high-pitched, haughty voice, laughing so much he had to stop and wipe his eyes. 'Is your father important? Is he? When you mentioned him I thought Louis'd shit himself.'

'I just did, so you'd better call him back. He's going to be in a worse state because he didn't wash me, and if I were to tell tales to my father they'd lose out on the monthly cheque. One of the reasons they are trying so hard to keep me alive is because I'm worth so much to them. Dead, the cheques stop.'

'God, you are so funny. No one in their right mind would pay to keep someone here! You are the best liar I have ever met, in fact, I think you're even better than me . . .'

'The best lies, anus features, are those with an element of truth. Now get the wretched man back. I am very uncomfortable, not to mention stinking.'

Picking up the bowl, Luka said that rather than have the old faggot back he would do it. Without thinking, he pulled Giorgio's sheets back, and for the first time saw his small, twisted body. The wizened legs were no bigger than a three-year-old's, and his curved spine made his left shoulder humped. Helplessly, Giorgio attempted to retrieve the sheet, but his head lolled and slipped from the cushions that propped him up. He wanted to weep. 'Oh, Jesus, why did you do that?'

Luka lifted him back up, gently, held him in his arms and kissed his big, flat face; strange, fluttering, childish kisses of comfort. Giorgio began to shake uncontrollably and murmured that it was all right, he didn't mind.

When at last the trembling stopped, Giorgio turned his head away, unable to look into Luka's eyes. 'I stink, I'm sorry.'

Luka obeyed Giorgio's instructions on how to remove the bottom sheet, but he was not very good at it. In the end he lifted Giorgio on to a large chair and propped his lolling head carefully, then cleaned the bed and remade it with fresh sheets. He opened the window to let the fresh air in, then began to worry like an old woman that Giorgio would get chilled, so he wrapped a blanket around him. Giorgio watched the way Luka moved, the way he gathered the stained sheets and turned the mattress, so agile and quick. When he had spread the clean sheet he picked up the bowl of water and moved towards Giorgio, who lowered his eyes in shame for his disability, embarrassed at his total dependency.

Giorgio's nightshirt was stained so Luka, his face puckering with the effort of working out a solution, suggested washing him on the chair so he wouldn't dirty the clean sheets. He was so gentle, so caring as he lifted off the nightshirt and washed the poor boy. The only people who had ever seen or touched Giorgio's body were nurses and doctors, and he felt ashamed that Luka should be doing this for him.

Luka's eyes blazed with anger. Giorgio's bedsores were raw and, as young as he was, Luka knew Giorgio had not been properly attended to. He rummaged in the medicine box and took out ointment and talcum powder.

'I'll just dab them, and I'll be as careful as I can so you don't hurt. Now, can you just lean on me . . .? That's it, lean on me while I do your bum.'

Giorgio could smell the carbolic institution soap on Luka's neck and see the tidemark of dirt where he hadn't washed properly himself. He had never known such a sudden rush of emotion, like a hot flush rising through his entire body. His face rested on Luka's shoulder and, before he could stop himself, he kissed his friend's neck. It was the first time in his life that he had kissed anyone, just as Luka had been the first person ever to kiss him. In a soft voice he whispered, 'I love you, Luka.'

Luka eased a clean nightshirt over the big head and buttoned the front. He grinned. 'I've never done this for anybody before, so I guess I love you too, you big, ugly bugger.'

He carried Giorgio back to the bed and made sure the pillows were propped in the correct position. Then he picked up a comb from the dressing-table and combed Giorgio's spiky black hair into a semblance of neatness.

'I've got to go now, I'll be late for lessons. You have a sleep, and I'll see you at dinner break.' He bent and kissed Giorgio's wide forehead and gave him a wink as he slipped from the room.

'God works in mysterious ways,' said Father Angelo, staring from his study window.

Brother Thomas pulled at his ear. 'And you still think we should allow it?'

'His doctor saw a marked improvement. If it continues, I see no reason not to allow such a small thing,

315

'I'm sure it gives him so much pleasure. I wrote to his father yesterday to tell him of his son's progress, he'll be delighted.'

In the distance, by the hut in the vegetable garden, Father Angelo could see Luka hammering. He had been working on his 'Giorgio Project' for weeks, in every woodwork class and every spare moment, and had roped in a number of the other boys to assist. They had taken a broken-down armchair and raised it on a platform with a small wheel at the front and two larger ones at the back. Then they attached a pair of handlebars and steering gear to the front. It resembled a go-cart, and Luka was now in the process of attaching leather straps to the steering wheel. While the two monks watched, the boys had a great deal of fun on the trial runs, their laughter ringing out. Then Luka turned to give a thumbs-up signal to the window where he knew Giorgio would be watching.

Brother Thomas pulled again at his ear, not approving of the situation. 'He will not allow anyone but Luka to wash him, and Luka insists he wants to do it. But I sometimes wonder if we should let him become too fond of Giorgio. He is dying, we all know that, and even if he seems to have a temporary reprieve, the boy is very ill.'

'They are friends, and if he dies it will further educate Luka into the real world, help him to understand the fragility of life, to give thanks for what so many misuse and abuse. The realization that there are many, like poor Giorgio, less fortunate than himself has been a great lesson in humility and understanding. It will benefit him in his adult years, perhaps even lead him to embrace the priesthood. We are in these boys' lives for such a short time, and this is not a natural environment where death and birth are part of their lives. To have the opportunity to see God's creatures taken into his bosom, I believe, is a great incentive to them to lead full and honourable lives. Love is free, Thomas, caring sometimes is not. Luka, you must see, is a changed boy.'

Brother Thomas gave a wry smile. 'To some extent, but I know for a fact he's threatened a few of the younger boys. He's so determined to make them accept Giorgio that he tells them if he so much as catches them smiling at him, they will get a beating. He's got one lad so scared that he wouldn't even look at Giorgio. He told me that Luka would raise the devil if he so much as stared at the invalid . . .'

'Ah, well, children can be cruel.'

'You still let that boy get away with murder, you always have, and if you could hear from Brother Louis how he's fallen behind in his maths, you would maybe think differently. And Giorgio is not all he seems; he's got the foulest mouth I ever heard in a child. He gets away with being as rude as he likes because the brothers don't want to upset him and risk losing the monthly donations. He's abusive in religious instruction, and when the day comes for the Good Lord to take him, with his language, he might just be thrown out again.'

'You know what Giorgio is to Luka? His family . . . In that crippled boy is mother, father, sister . . . Giorgio has shown him how to love. I believe it is the Lord's way, and I give thanks every night.'

'What is Luka to Giorgio?'

'Everything he would have wanted. He is a strong, healthy, handsome boy. I believe Giorgio's own intellect protected him, like armour, but with Luka he has no need of it. As we know, Luka is not academically inclined, backward even, but together they make a perfect whole. Together they are one.'

'If you say so, Father, but my own feeling on the matter is that they are too close. If, as you say, they are one, then when Giorgio Carolla dies, which he most certainly will, perhaps Luka's lesson in life and death will be too harsh. He will have lost his entire family.'

Father Angelo opened his desk drawer to indicate that the meeting was over. 'I shall make sure that I am here for him when the time comes, but I will think about what you have said. I appreciate your discussing it with me, I know you mean well. Just be assured that I am aware of the situation.'

Feeling rather like a naughty boy who has been to the headmaster telling tales, Father Thomas left. No sooner had he departed than there was a light tap on the study window.

Luka stood outside. His face was tanned, and even though his hair had been cut almost to the scalp, like all the boys in summer to keep the lice at bay, it seemed like a golden halo around him. His slanting eyes were so blue with the sky and sun behind him. Seeing him, Father Angelo caught his breath. He was astonishingly beautiful. It was as if the Lord had decided that this face was too perfect and had placed a smudge on the cheek like a dab of grey paint from an artist's brush; a dimple appeared like magic when the boy smiled, and now he was smiling broadly.

'Giorgio's chariot is finished, it's safe, and we have all tried it. He won't be able to fall out. Will you come and give your approval?'

Although his instinct was to show pleasure, Father

Angelo looked sternly at Luka, then at his study clock. 'You will be late for geography, Luka. Perhaps if I have a moment, I will see it tomorrow. Now hurry, I am truly tired of your persistent lateness, and even more tired of your poor marks. If they don't improve, your privileges with Giorgio will be curtailed. You may go.'

The dimple disappeared and Luka gave a curt nod. He strode off, his mouth pursed in anger. Father Angelo sighed and collected his books for his tutorial, missing the way Luka paused a short distance from the window, missing the way the angelic face became like a mask, the eyes expressionless.

His low murmur was inaudible, but directed at Angelo, 'You fucking piece of whore's shit, you selfish, cocksucking, motherfucking bastard . . .' The hatred rose to the surface fast, peaked and subsided like a tidal wave.

Brother Thomas had not hidden intentionally, but when he saw Luka he remained in the shadow of the stone archway. He could see the smiling boy clearly, and saw also how Luka had turned to look back at Father Angelo's window. He had not heard what the boy said, but the sight was enough. He felt chilled at the expression of hatred that had distorted the beautiful face, like a fleeting madness.

CHAPTER 12

CAROLLA HAD taken years to climb back after the so-called war. He had lost his own fortune along with many others, but he fought back, and his contacts were still prepared to deal with him. Many who had lost money lent him more in the hope of making up their losses.

Bankrolled, Carolla moved back into action. He started at the bottom; he began to deal in junk at street level to make money fast. His total lack of moral decency gave his dealers the freedom to make their sales any way they chose. He knew they were selling junk to kids at the school gates, enticing them with offers of sweets and records. Jukeboxes were another attraction the kids were drawn to. He laughed, comparing himself to the Jesuits who said, 'Give me a child until he is seven years old and he is mine for life.' He would say instead, 'Gimme any kid, an' I'll have him payin' me for life.' That their lives were cut short by his product never gave him a moment's guilt.

He took over the main dealerships in Naples, and with what he made there he opened new refineries in France. He renewed his contacts in Canada and Brazil, and spread his network to Florida. He had more buyers now than supplies, so he went further and approached two of the biggest narcotics agents in China. He had a nose for junk, and his methods of couriering the raw heroin were inventive and outlandish.

Palermo, as it had always been, was still his best base, and Luciano's export facilities were like an apple constantly dangled before his eyes. He wanted to bite, but he had learned a lesson. His fingers had been badly burned, so he bided his time, knowing the more powerful he became, the more profit he offered the American bosses, the more likely he was to get his bite at that apple. But he would do it from the inside, like a worm at its core, eating his way to the skin. There would be nothing Luciano could do or say about it. In time, Carolla would once again have so much cash that every major Palermo family would want a part of his rackets, but until then he was content to continue as he was.

Occasionally, when he travelled to Palermo, he would stay at the apartment with Lydia. On his last visit, he had collected a letter from Father Angelo describing Giorgio's renewed health and thanking him, as always, for his generous donations. Carolla immediately presumed he was being ripped off, that Giorgio was dead and the father was writing lies. As if his son could be well enough to take lessons with the other kids! They were conning him, and the only way he could find out for himself was to make a surprise visit to the monastery.

Luka had devised a strap which was attached to the back of the wheelchair and enabled Giorgio to keep his head up. It passed under his chin and was padded so as not to hurt him. He made a strange sight, sitting propped up on pillows in his handmade chariot, looking like something from outer space. He still tired easily and was often forced to rest, but his skin was now pink instead of yellow, and he spent many hours in the garden. He wore a sunhat, and Luka had nailed a big umbrella to the side of the chair to shade him. Heat made him uncomfortable, so Luka had put a bottle with a long straw on the other side of the chair so he could sip water whenever he needed.

It had been Father Angelo's idea to bring Giorgio into the classes, and with Luka's encouragement Giorgio had soon agreed. He had proved to have far greater intelligence than any of the boys and this had given him tremendous confidence. His grasp of the classics and his enquiring mind was an incentive for the other students. Luka looked on with pride as Giorgio asked such complicated questions that the class would be brought to a standstill while Brother Louis thumbed through reference books and even occasionally shook his head, unable to answer.

One day they were studying Shakespeare's *Romeo and Juliet* when Giorgio flashed his light on and off, his own system for attracting attention rather than putting his hand up.

'Yes, Giorgio?'

'When the friar gives Juliet the poison, what exactly is the herbal remedy he has concocted? What draught has the ingredients to make Juliet appear to be dead? Surely she would still have a pulse?'

'Well, one must allow a certain amount of theatrical licence, you know, Giorgio.'

'May I suggest that the poison he used was a specific dosage of strychnine. Acute poisoning with strychnine results in total collapse and the rapid lowering of the blood pressure, and death occurs within one to two minutes. With Romeo . . .'

'No, no, Giorgio! I am sure Romeo did not take strychnine. It was a herbal drug, a draught made up by the friar.'

'But that could have been strychnine. In those days it was used in laxatives, even tonics, because its immediate effect was to induce a feeling of well-being. Depending on the dosage, it causes increased reflex excitability in the spinal cord, which can result in stimulating the motor cells, contracting the muscles simultaneously . . .'

'Well, it is very interesting, but I really cannot see what this has to do with *Romeo and Juliet*.'

The entire class was agog, looking back and forth between Giorgio and Brother Louis who, nonplussed, scratched his head. He was saved from any further embarrassment by the bell bringing the class to an end, but to his amazement none of the students wanted to leave. They were thumbing through the text and reading avidly, whereas usually at the sound of the bell they ran for their lives.

After dismissing the class, Brother Louis ploughed through the play himself, then carried the volume of the complete works of Shakespeare with him to supper that evening. He banged it on to the table and enquired if his brothers felt that *Romeo and Juliet* was suitable material for young boys to be reading.

Giorgio continued his dissertation with the boys grouped around his chair. They listened to his theories and were suitably awed when he informed them that he himself had taken strychnine on numerous occasions. He had taken the poison to enable him to appear to his father fitter and more in control of his limbs than he actually was.

Luka remained in the background while Giorgio held forth, which of late he often did. Proudly, he nodded his head in confirmation that everything Giorgio said was true. As he wheeled the chariot slowly across the court-yard towards Giorgio's room, he asked his friend with concern, 'Was that true? Have you really taken strychnine?'

Giorgio's eyes were closed as he said, 'In the olden days, Luka, poisons were as much in use as medicines today.'

The chair jolted, and Giorgio winced with pain. He was feeling badly in need of rest.

'How come you know all this?' asked Luka.

'Books, Luka. You can learn anything you want to know from books, not just stories. You should read more, you really should. Did you finish the Dickens I gave you?'

'Where do you get the books from?'

'Book stores, where do you think? All I have to do is send away and then they arrive. I have accounts, my father arranged accounts in shops all over Palermo, so all I do is send off for them and anything else I want.'

'What kind of things?'

'Well, anything . . .'

'Why don't you send off for a proper chair?'

'OK. I never thought of that.'

'We'll need pamphlets, so we can find out the best there is. Can you get other things, too?'

'Like what?'

'Well, gardening equipment, you know, spades and seeds – and a radio.'

'OK, we'll look through the catalogues when I've had a rest.'

While Giorgio rested, Luka sat in his room thumbing through the mail-order catalogues and listing everything he thought suitable. He also added a number of items for himself. That evening they filled in the order forms and Luka posted the thick envelope himself, climbing over the monastery wall and running to the post office. He was in high spirits as he strolled back, his mind buzzing with excitement at the prospect of receiving it all.

Three weeks later, Father Angelo was confronted with a hand-cart at the monastery gates which was loaded so high the poor carter's knees were buckling The delivery men had had to leave their lorry in the town and help push the cart along the narrow lanes. Signatures were needed on the receipts, and Father Angelo asked them inside so he could talk to Giorgio.

'But it really is totally acceptable to my father. It is the way I bought everything you see in my room. The chair will be so much better, it's battery controlled, and much smaller and lighter. Then there's a special cushion with a hole in the middle for me to sit on . . .'

'Yes, yes, Giorgio, and I am aware of the medical benefits of certain items, but I cannot allow . . .' He paused, running his eye down over the delivery notes. He sighed and paced the room, at a loss to know what to do.

It was not the books, nor the medical supplies, that worried him. It was the puzzles and board games, the gardening tools and numerous articles of clothing and sports equipment, and he could not allow a radio to be played in the monastery. The classical records he had agreed to accept when Giorgio had first arrived, but a second portable player was unnecessary and against all the regulations.

Giorgio sighed sadly, and his eyes filled with tears. 'Am I not even allowed to give the boys small gifts to show my appreciation, Father? The gardening tools are a small thank-you for the hours I have sat watching Father Louis, who is so old and frail. Please, please allow me to show my gratitude. I do, to the Good Lord, every night, but may I not also thank the boys who are so kind and thoughtful?'

Father Angelo acquiesced, allowing Giorgio to sign the receipts. That evening the brothers were up in arms, apart from old Father Louis, who couldn't wait to start planting all the new seeds in his vegetable patch. Brother Thomas was appalled, sitting with a sour face looking time and again at Angelo and shaking his head.

'The items I have not allowed will be returned to the stores. I shall write to Mr Carolla explaining that this is a monastery, not a hospital ward. Giorgio may give the boys small tokens of his appreciation, and I have accepted his new chair and certain medical items he assures me he needs. I have barred the playing of the radio and records outside of the music class, and Brother Matthew will be in sole charge of them. The case of port which he bought for us will be returned, as will the Burgundy and Beaujolais. You will all agree with me, I am sure, that we cannot accept these gifts. However, as the rosaries and prayer books have the name of the monastery printed on them, I think we must accept them. I will write immediately to our dear patron, Mr Carolla, thanking him for the gifts and stating our reasons for their unacceptability.'

Brother Thomas spoke up, 'Of course, we do not wish to antagonize our benefactor, certainly not while the roof to the chapel is only half-completed . . .'

Father Angelo's eyes twinkled. He knew Brother Thomas was about to hint that they could not accept the records or the radio, but three cases of vintage wines were a possibility. He would also, Father Angelo felt sure, offer to be the first to check the contents of the bottles for purity.

'I think you are absolutely right, Thomas. We do not wish to upset our benefactor. We owe our young guest so much, and we do not wish to stretch his good father's charity any more than is necessary. The mere fact that his son has recovered so much is our payment, and the Lord's will. Let us now give thanks to our Blessed Holy Mother for the wellbeing of Giorgio Carolla.'

The soft, light strains of Paganini drifted into the dining hall. It appeared that the new musical equipment was already in use by the young monk, Brother Matthew, whose place had remained vacant throughout the meal.

Riding in his new chair, Giorgio handed out small gifts to every boy in the dormitory as Luka passed them to him, like Father Christmas and his helper. The delight of the boys, being used to so little, was touching. New pencils and sharpeners, notebooks and erasers were inspected and proudly displayed. Giorgio's hand ached from being grasped.

A secret smile passed between Luka and Giorgio, and they departed. Luka whispered that the plan had worked perfectly, as he had known it would. He was the one who had suggested buying gifts for the brothers as well as for the boys, and in that way they had been able to get many of their purchases past 'Holy Customs'. They were delighted.

As Luka carried Giorgio to his bed, they heard Brother Matthew's music, and Giorgio closed his eyes. 'Ah, will you listen, Luka – such beauty.'

Luka opened the window and they listened together. But Luka soon grew bored and began to open more of their boxes. Giorgio whispered, 'Play Berlioz, please, play the *Symphonie Fantastique* . . . please . . .'

Luka excitedly opened up the chemistry set. No sooner was it unwrapped than he delved into another box, and another, feverishly strewing packaging everywhere.

'He heard me, Luka . . . listen, he's playing the *Symphonie Fantastique* . . .'

The opening bars drifted through the courtyard and echoed slightly. Luka couldn't have cared if he were playing Maria Callas singing in her bath, he was trying on a pair of running shoes.

Giorgio spoke softly. 'You know what it's about? An artist, someone with imagination, in a crazy state of mind like Chateaubriand described in *René*. And then he sees a beautiful woman, someone his heart has always longed for, and he falls desperately in love. At the same time his thoughts and his love are linked in the music . . . Hear? It's love, it's his heart, love that knows it's hopeless, but . . .'

He looked at Luka, who had not heard a word. He was trying to see his reflection in the shining lid of a sweet tin. There were no mirrors in Giorgio's room; very few were allowed in the monastery and there were none in the boys' bathrooms or dormitories. Giorgio caught his breath; Luka was intent on his reflection, holding the tin at arm's length to see the cowboy waistcoat with the fringing. He had also strapped the guns, in their ornate plastic holsters, to his legs. He propped the tin lid on the bookcase and stepped back, raising his head slightly. His white-blond hair and blue eyes were caught in the half-light of the small room, as if suspended. It was a magical moment as the music swelled, depicting the occasion when the hero poisons himself with opium. Intent on keeping his image within the shining metal lid, Luka lifted both guns and slowly aimed them at himself as the hero in the music drifted into a narcotic nightmare, a terrible dream in which he believes he has killed his loved one. Giorgio was almost afraid to breathe, not wanting to break the spell.

With the fluidity of a dancer, Luka replaced the guns in their holsters in one movement, still gazing in fascination at his own reflection. He moved closer, closer, reaching for the glinting lid, and studied his reflection. Giorgio saw him touch his face, then slowly trace his mirror image, a smile on his lips . . .

That night, Giorgio could not sleep. He drifted, semi-conscious, and all he could see was the angelic face, the smile and the small dimple on Luka's cheek. In that moment he had loved Luka so much that he had been afraid to speak. It was not a sexual love but an adoration of his beauty, and a sadness. He would not see Luka grow into maturity and, as young as he was, he knew his friend would need someone when he was gone.

*

Luka knew there was something wrong as soon as he entered Giorgio's room. He was puffing at a cigarette, as usual, but his agitation was obvious. Luka remonstrated with him, opening the window and wafting the smoke out with his hand, saying he should always wait as he could catch his bed linen alight.

'Screw the linen – here, stub it out, will you?'

Luka ground it out, then carefully wiped the saucer and wrapped the dog-end in a piece of paper. 'I've come to take you into chapel. Now that you've gone all religious you have to pay for it. You'll be in with old Brother Louis, and then when you've had an earful from him, the rest of them take over. Why do you want to be confirmed? There's nothing to it, you know, it's a waste of time. You could be in the garden with me.'

'My father's coming.'

'*What?*'

'My fucking father's coming, you gone deaf?'

'Oh, shit . . . You think he'll go mad about the things we've been buying? I can start hiding them, and I could take some down to the cellars.'

'Do you think he cares about how much money I spend? He's coming to view the specimen. He expected me to die, and here I am.'

'He won't take you away, will he?'

Giorgio sighed. He was so afraid that would happen that he couldn't put it into words.

Luka whispered, 'We could run off, if you like?'

'Don't be so childish! How in God's name am I going to run? Even the batteries wouldn't last down that hill. No, I'll just have to face the sonofabitch.'

*

Giorgio was still moody and depressed when he was wheeled into the chapel. Luka opened the double doors and bent to whisper to Giorgio, 'They won't part us, Giorgio. If they try, I'll carry you down the hill. Wherever you go, I go – till death us do part, OK?'

Giorgio smiled and flicked a switch. The chair moved off down the aisle to where Brother Louis was kneeling at the altar. His dark brown robes were threadbare and the hem was edged with mud from the garden, as always. The sight of him touched Giorgio.

The old man was so deep in prayer that he didn't even turn as the chair buzzed its way up to him. Giorgio positioned himself just behind the friar, then took out his rosary and prayed. He was not sure if the comfort he had found here of late was actually connected with religion or simply the result of the silence and peace within the chapel. He was still very ill, and tired more easily than ever, but here he felt wrapped in calm, finding the coolness of the chapel soothing in itself.

As Brother Louis finally rose from his knees, Giorgio whispered to him, 'Brother, I am the way I am because I must pay for the sins of my father.'

Louis rubbed his stiff legs with gnarled hands and stood next to the wheelchair, his hand on the rubber arm. 'Do you believe your father to have sinned? Do you believe the Virgin wants some kind of debt repaid?'

'Well, Brother, I have tried to think of every reason known to man that is fair, that I can accept, and I am prepared now to believe that I was born this way because

331

of my father's sins. "He that hasteth to be rich hath an evil eye . . ." Well, he certainly *hasteth* for riches, and also in Proverbs, I don't know which number, it says: "He that keepeth company with harlots spendeth his substance". My father has *spendeth* his substance, in fact he goes further than simply *spendething*, he *lives* with a whore . . .'

Louis had often sat and listened to Giorgio trying to embarrass or shock him, and he said nothing until the boy calmed down. Today, however, he detected more anger than usual in the boy, and touched his shoulder. 'Tell me of your own mother, Giorgio.'

'I never met her. She died, at my birth, probably from the shock of seeing me. I've certainly given a jolt to quite a few people. Whether it caused a heart attack I'm not sure.'

'Are you frightened of dying, Giorgio?'

'No . . . No, I'm not, it would be a relief, or . . . I think it would be.'

'You feel differently now?'

'I don't want to leave Luka.'

'And to you, Luka is – what?'

'Life.'

'So, by not wanting to leave Luka, you are not wanting to leave your life. So really, you're saying you're not afraid to die, you just don't want to go right now, is that it?'

A single, dry sob shook Giorgio's body. 'No one could be so cruel to let me die just when I have begun to live.' Suddenly the words gushed from him and he was a small, frightened boy. He begged Brother Louis not to let his father take him away. Louis gave his word that, as far as he could, he would try to persuade

Giorgio's father otherwise if he suggested he leave the monastery.

Brother Louis could not keep his word, through no fault of his own or anyone else's. When Paul Carolla arrived, he suggested that the doctor should see his son before he did, and remained with Father Angelo in the study, discussing Giorgio's request for confirmation. His hands moved nervously, and he fiddled with his heavy gold and diamond ring. His gold watch protruded from the cuff of his blue-and-white striped shirt. His suit was a dark navy, single-breasted pin-stripe and his shoes were polished Gucci loafers. With a dismissive wave of the hand, Carolla accepted the father's thanks for his donations. Angelo was rather relieved to receive the same gesture when he brought up the subject of the gardening equipment, which could be seen in the vegetable patch outside the study window.

Father Angelo turned to the improvement in Giorgio's physical and emotional health. 'We owe much of your son's improvement to a young boy here, Luka, who has taken a great interest in helping Giorgio. It was Luka who first suggested taking your son out into the garden in a wheelchair, and built the first one himself. We managed quite well, but then Giorgio thought he would like one he could manoeuvre himself.'

'Father, this is a miracle, it's gotta be a miracle. The boy's never got out of bed since he was born.'

They were unaware, as they talked, that Luka was sitting beneath the study window listening to every word.

*

Father Angelo led Carolla to Giorgio's chair beneath a tree, gave a small bow and left father and son together. Carolla moved slowly around the chair to face his son. The domed head and drooling lips were just the same, except that now Giorgio sported a ridiculous pair of sunglasses, tied with a piece of string to stop them falling off.

Carolla sat on the bench that surrounded the tree and drew a large silk handkerchief from his pocket to mop his head. 'Hello, there, how ya doin'?'

Giorgio winced at the gravelly voice and the stench of cologne. 'Thank you for coming, and thank you for settling all my accounts. I really appreciate it. How are you?'

'Me? Hot right now, very hot. The doctor couldn't believe the improvement,' Carolla said, then, 'I can't believe the improvement.'

'Nor can I, I'm taking tap-dancing lessons next term.'

'What?'

'Joke, it was a joke.'

'Oh, yeah, you still got that sense of humour.'

'Could I get some more books, would that be all right?'

'Sure, go ahead, an' if you wanna buy somethin' for the brothers then that's all right too. I tell you what the doc said? He said – now don't go gettin' your hopes up – but he said that because you were so fit, maybe you could stand that operation. You know why you get so breathless and tired, well you wouldn't any more. It's your heart, see?'

'I would have to leave here?'

'Well, they can't do the operation here, now can they? You gotta go to Rome, the big hospital there. You'd

334

have the best surgeon, I'd fly him in from wherever, but if you can take that op, then you'll have it, son.'

'I don't want it if I have to leave here.'

'What?'

'I won't leave here.'

'Don't be so fuckin' stupid.'

'It's *my* fucking heart!'

'It's got a fuckin' hole in it! What are you, nuts? See, the more healthy you get, the bigger you get. You've put on pounds and pounds, and it's puttin' more strain on your heart and it won't be able to cope. You got a hole in your heart, son, but they can stitch it up.'

Giorgio smirked. 'Either way you look at it, I've only got a limited time. Rather like a battery when it runs out, that's it.'

'Listen, we're all on a fuckin' battery. I'm not takin' you away from here. Christ, you wanna come back, you come back. I dunno if they can do the operation anyway, so this is just . . . this is . . .'

'Hypothetical.'

'I gotta go. You know, we hadda walk to this place? No wonder Eros pissed off outta here, he couldn't take the pace on his feet.'

'Wings on his heels, Eros had wings on his heels.'

'Eh, give this to that kid's been helpin' you, it's dollars, but he can change it, OK son? An' think about that operation, maybe we've been too hypo . . . hypothetical. See what comes from the doctors, maybe they couldn't operate anyway.'

'If they can, I would go on one condition.'

'Now you're giving me conditions?'

'If I have to go, can Luka come with me? Will you pay for Luka to come with me?'

'Sure . . . You're gonna get well, son.'

Not knowing whether to shake his son's hand or even kiss him, Carolla just walked off, pausing a few yards away to call back, 'You gettin' confirmed, I like that. That's a good boy! You take care now, Giorgio, eh? You're lookin' good, kid, you're lookin' good.'

A whisper came back, 'Eh, Giorgio, you're lookin' good, lookin' good, kid . . .' Giorgio laughed at Luka's mimicry of his deplorable father. His friend appeared from behind the tree, having obviously been there for some time.

'Here, this is for you.'

Luka kissed the note, held it up to the light and kissed it again, hardly able to believe he had $50 all to himself.

Giorgio watched him closely, then shook his head. 'Did you hear, you cloth-eared, grasping bum-hole, that I may have to go to Rome, for an operation?'

Luka looked down at him then, and in one of his odd, fast moves, he cupped the big face and swooped down, his nose within an inch of Giorgio's. His slanting eyes were mirrored in the black lenses of Giorgio's sunglasses. They flicked from side to side, then he gave a quick, dry-lipped kiss to the pink mouth of the boy he adored. 'You're gonna live a long time, Giorgio, I just spoke to the devil himself.'

336

CHAPTER 13

S OPHIA LUCIANO sat at the centre table in La
Fontanella restaurant in Rome. Everyone from
movie stars to the Kennedys had dined at this
elegant 'Little Fountain' since 1953. One of the leading
eating places, it was on the famous square just across
from the Palazzo Borghese, built in the shape of a
harpsichord.

Sophia was radiant and confident. Her collection this
season was one of the highlights of the Rome boutique
set. Her business, along with her flair and style, had
flourished over the years, growing beyond her wildest
dreams. She was courted by high society, and today's
guests were some of her most affluent clients, the luncheon being a celebration and thanks for their support.

The hostess was wearing a maternity dress designed
especially for her by Nino, the designer who partnered
her in the business. The dress was of hand-printed silk,
with brilliant china-blue ribbons woven into a bold
pattern of lilies. The silk was swathed and gathered to
disguise and flatter her pregnancy. Her gleaming hair
was drawn severely back from her face and coiled into a
simple bun at the nape of her neck. Her heavy ear-rings,
diamond and gold hoops, gave her a gypsy quality, albeit

a very exclusive, designer gypsy. On her wedding finger she wore a large solitaire diamond, and round her neck a single, fine gold chain with small diamonds between each fifth and sixth link. She was perfectly at her ease as she rose to greet her guests, who all remarked on how well she looked considering the imminence of the birth. She laughed as she seated them and the waiters served the chilled champagne.

Nino made a theatrical entrance, laden with spring flowers. He bent on one knee to present Sophia with the bouquet. Flamboyantly dressed, he was a brilliant advertisement for his own designs. Like Sophia, his taste was faultless, and his camp humour and brittle, wicked tongue lifted the party into abandoned gaiety as they gossiped and discussed the Italian collections.

Sophia had come a long way from the convent, from scrubbing floors to feed herself and her ailing mother. She had come so far so fast that sometimes she shook with the fear that it might end and pinched herself to make sure it was not a dream. She was happier than she could have believed possible, and her own success had made her independent of her husband, even of the Lucianos.

Perfectly aware of her in-laws' desire for a grandson, Sophia had promised that, after her first Rome collection, she would begin the long-awaited family. The baby was due within the month. Constantino had presumed that she would now give up work, but she had flatly refused, having no desire to stop even after the birth. It had caused friction, but then, as always, she had been able to win her husband round. Don Roberto had given Sophia's boutiques his blessing and even encouraged her, seemingly proud of her success. Much of it was due to being able to acquire Nino Fabio as designer. She had offered him a partnership, which at first he had refused. When, eventually, he did accept he not only brought his expertise, but many noted clients. The elegant luncheon was proof that the partnership had paid off, and was being covered by many of the upmarket glossy magazines.

Sophia might not have been so vibrant, so happy, had she known that the illegitimate child she had abandoned for the good life was preparing to travel to Rome with Giorgio Carolla. She did think of him, indeed could not help but remember her first-born son as that evening she went into labour . . . Carlo Luciano was born the following morning, surrounded by the best medical staff, a private room bedecked with flowers, and an adoring husband and proud father at her side.

The maternity wing was distanced from the main operating section. The room allocated to Giorgio Carolla, although in the same building, was on a different floor. Paul Carolla and Roberto Luciano were in the same hospital at the same time but totally unaware of each other's presence.

Roberto and Graziella already had a grandchild by Teresa and Alfredo, but Roberto shrugged; it was a girl. Now he walked around the hospital corridors with the tiny Carlo in his arms, smiling broadly and chucking him under the chin, talking at him constantly and giving anyone who would listen details of his weight and size. He was inordinately proud, as if he and he alone had produced this little wonder.

Constantino was now *numero uno*, and to mark the birth Roberto gave him yet more control over his part of the family business.

When Don Roberto called his son Alfredo in New York to pass on the good news, he sounded happier than Alfredo had heard him for a long time, as he gave the details of the birth of his new grandson.

Alfredo flopped on the bed as Teresa came out of the bathroom, brushing her hair.

'How are they all?'

'Fine. The baby's strong, eight pounds odd, and Papa is driving everyone nuts telling them how thrilled he is with his grandson.'

'It'd be nice if one day, just one day, he said something about Rosa, even asked about her.'

'He does, he always does.'

'Don't lie. Maybe your Mama, but not your father, not once. And he never speaks to me, never asks how I am.'

'He does, of course he does . . . Now don't start.'

'Start? Me? You don't think I have a right? Rosa was three years old before he saw her. How many times since then, eh? Once, he's seen her once. She doesn't even know him.'

Alfredo sighed, loosened his tie and rolled over on the bed. 'He wanted a grandson. Maybe next time, maybe . . .'

'Maybe, maybe. They treat you as second-rate. I'll bet any money that Sophia and Constantino will be getting a nice gift for . . . What are they calling the baby?'

'Carlo.'

'What did he give them?'

Alfredo's face flushed with anger. 'I didn't ask. We do all right, just don't start, OK? And don't wait up for me, I'll be late.'

Before Teresa could say another word he had walked out. She sighed, called to her daughter Rosa, and like most nights they sat down to supper alone. The child had heard their raised voices, knew by her mother's terse gesture for her to sit at the table that her father would not be eating with them.

'Your Aunt Sophia has had a baby, a boy.'

Rosa wanted to know more about the baby, but her mother snapped that she wasn't hungry and left the table. Teresa was fully aware of her husband's limitations and wanted, in time, to give him more assistance in the legal matters and contracts he often brought home. He would balk at the idea, for although he did ask her advice, needed it, he would fly into terrible rages at the thought that she was interfering. None the less, he relied heavily on his wife's business acumen; he just refused to admit it.

More often than not he was confused and unable to understand the complex instructions his father sent to him. Import controls and licensing of goods entering the USA were nearly a full-time job in themselves. Teresa had become more and more aware lately of how little Alfredo actually did, and how many other men Don Roberto employed in America. Time and time again she had reason to suspect that Alfredo was given menial tasks to keep him out of the way, but out of the way of what? She was clever enough not to voice her suspicions, but very much aware of the family's wealth and power.

They lived well, the apartment was paid for and

341

decently furnished, she had jewellery and fine clothes and cash in the bank, but whenever she went to Sicily she noticed that Sophia and Constantino lived at a far higher standard. Even taking into account Sophia's successful business enterprise, she was still envious of their sumptuous Rome apartment, the Rolls-Royces, the elegance and social standing which she quite obviously didn't have. Teresa was convinced that Don Roberto favoured them, and was determined that she and Alfredo would get their rightful share.

Alfredo's weakness, his lack of interest in their marriage and their only daughter she swallowed, because she had never stopped loving him from the day she had first seen him. She supposed that he loved her, in his weak-willed way, though he very rarely touched her. She had learned to live without physical love, but couldn't bear the thought of losing him altogether.

Teresa was sure that there were no other women in his life, there were none of the classic signs. He spent most of his spare time watching television or tinkering with vintage cars in the garage.

Teresa was so sure there was no other woman that she talked herself into forcing open his desk and searching it. She prised one drawer open with a penknife, and having started she could not stop. The drawer had a false bottom which contained a stack of chequebooks and statements on accounts she knew nothing about. She made a list of them and put them back as she had found them, then systematically searched the entire apartment.

She found nothing at all in the drawing room or in any of the cupboards, and checked every drawer in the bedroom. Finally, she went through the pockets of every garment in his wardrobe. Close to tears, angry at herself, she went on until she found, in the ticket pocket of a jacket, a packet of condoms. Then she knew she had been wrong.

Alfredo had known within two days of his wedding that he had made a terrible mistake. At the age of twenty he was too young and naïve for marriage, and the arrival of a child, which quickly followed his twenty-first birthday, made him resentful. He tried to discuss his problems with his father, but Roberto had simply told him to get on with his life and, in particular, the business.

It was too much for Alfredo, he simply could not cope with his responsibilities at work and at home. Roberto, sadly, knew it, and manoeuvred Alfredo into a position of respect but which involved little in the way of duties. His *capi* quietly took their orders from Luciano himself or from Constantino in Rome. Alfredo felt emasculated, his wings clipped, and his marriage suffered even more.

One of his father's trucking companies was having consistent problems with vehicle maintenance. With little else to do, Alfredo looked the trucks over, and within minutes was dressed in overalls and tinkering with the engines. He made friends with Pete 'Bomber' Barone, a mechanic, who was as fanatical about motorbikes as Alfredo. The two men began going to race meetings together, then Alfredo bought two bikes and they went dirt-track racing. Alfredo kept very quiet about his part in it and, as a team, they used Pete's name on the tracks.

Within a couple of years, they were well known on the circuit, moving up a step with a more powerful bike and sidecar. They entered formula races and, although not successful for some time, they slowly moved into the top ranks of amateur riders.

After their races, Pete would take Alfredo back to his trailer home near the trucking company, where he kept some clothes. He would clean his hands carefully, then change into his street clothes before returning home.

The night Teresa had searched the apartment, Alfredo made the mistake of wearing a different tie from the one he'd had on when he went out. It fuelled Teresa's suspicions and she connected the secret bank accounts, the contraceptives and the tie with Alfredo keeping a mistress. Having wept herself into a state of near-hysteria, Teresa waited for Alfredo to come into the bedroom.

'Don't put the light on, Alfredo, please.'

'Where are you?'

'Over here, near the bed. Please don't put the light on.'

'Are you OK? Nothing wrong, is there?'

'Where've you been?'

'Oh, just a meeting, over at the trucking warehouse. Shit, I can't see a thing. What's the matter, you sick?'

'You weren't there, I called.'

'I was in the warehouse. Look, what is this, are you checking up on me?'

'Do I need to?'

'What?'

'I said, do I need to? Here, you forgot these.'

She threw the small packet of contraceptives across the room and he squinted at them where they had fallen near the wardrobe. He picked them up and shrugged.

'They were in your jacket pocket.'

Sighing, he threw them on the bed and began to unbutton his shirt.

'Where did you get that tie?'

'For Chrissake, what is this, a fucking trial? What's the matter with you?' He snapped the light on and glared across the room at her.

She hid her face in her hands, her voice muffled with weeping, 'I also went through your desk and found all those bank statements. What have you been doing with all that money? Keeping a woman? Are you keeping a whore? How could you do this to me, to Rosa?'

Alfredo continued to undress, hanging his clothes in the wardrobe. He found the jacket the rubbers had been in. He held it up accusingly.

'When did I last wear this? Eh? Come on, you know everything, so tell me when you last saw me in this? You've been monitoring my every fucking move, so you can tell me, when? Can't remember?'

He grabbed her face between his hands and dragged her towards him, then flung the jacket in her face. 'Look at it, look! It's ten years old, I wore it on our honeymoon. So why don't you and your warped, vicious mind just *stay out of my life!*'

'Like your father makes sure you stay out of his?'

'You keep my father out of this, you hear me? Hear me?'

Rosa opened the bedroom door and he turned on her, grabbed her by the arm and threw the frightened child out of the door, shouting for her to go back to her bedroom. Then he leaned against the door and seemed to deflate. Teresa went over and slipped her arms around him but he pushed her away.

'Leave me alone, just leave me alone!'

'No, not this time. I leave you alone every night, every day. We have to talk, we have to. I only want you to have what is yours.'

'I got it! Look at you, I got it, didn't I?'

'Whatever I am, you made me.'

'Bullshit! You were an ugly bitch before I married you.'

'And you were tied to your mother's apron strings, terrified of your father. Now you're all hot air, you're still afraid of him and you're still tied to your precious mother, *tied* because you're scared of them, you're scared of your brothers.'

Enraged, he grabbed her by the throat and shook her until her ears rang. Then he suddenly found the control to stop himself, and backed away from her.

'I gotta get out of here, I gotta leave you.'

Before she could react, he had walked out and shut the door. Now he would never come back. She called his name and Rosa came to her door, her face as pale as her mother's.

'Where's your father? Alfredo! Alfredo? Get back into your room, Rosa, go on, get back.'

He was sitting at his desk, his head in his hands. There was no anger left in him. He gave her a mournful, pitiful stare and then swallowed, turning his face from her as he mumbled, 'I'm sorry, I shouldn't have hit you. I don't know what came over me, I'm sorry . . .'

'It's all right, it's all right . . . shussssh, now, shussssh, it's all right.' She rocked him gently and stroked his curly hair.

Like a guilty schoolboy he started to tell her what he had really been doing; not, as she had suspected, keeping

346

a mistress, but racing motorbikes with his friend Pete. All the cash he had used was for the bikes.

'I knew you wouldn't approve, and I knew if Papa found out he wouldn't allow me to race, but I love it. I love it, and I won't stop.'

Teresa was so stunned she couldn't speak for a moment. He began to tell her his racing stories, about his bikes, the meetings he went to. Slowly, she eased the conversation round to how much time he spent on the bikes, and what he was doing at work.

'Well, it started as a sort of helping hand. You know how good I am with mechanical things, and some of the trucks needed repairing, losing hydraulic fluid and so on. They're tricky to maintain, and the engineers, the bastards, are real cowboys. Now I sort of take charge of the fleet . . .'

'So who does the contracts? All the work you used to bring home?'

'One of the guys, I'm not sure who, but I don't get into the office much. I mean, I don't mind, don't get me wrong, it's just that I prefer what I'm doing.'

'How do the men treat you? Do they treat you with respect?'

'Sure, it's just that I get on better with the Petes of this world.'

'Pete?'

'My racing partner.'

'Oh, yes, Pete . . . Will I get to meet him now?'

He smiled and nodded, and she opened her arms to him. He knelt before her, putting his head in her lap while she stroked his hair. He pressed his face between her legs and began to inch her thin silk nightdress up, further and further until she spread her legs wide and he

licked the soft hair around her wet, aching crotch . . .
She pushed against him, moaning, ready to scream with
wanting him, wanting to make love with him so
much . . . She tried to pull him upwards, to feel his body
against hers, but he held her legs firmly apart, licking and
sucking until he drove her crazy . . . She was half-afraid,
he had never done this to her before . . .

He pulled her roughly from the chair on to the floor,
continuing to caress her with his hand, making strange
slurping noises and pressing his fingers into her. She
twisted and turned, but he kept his hand inside her as he
lowered his trouser zip with the other . . . 'Oh, yes, yes,
you like this, baby? You like this?' He ripped her nightdress open to reveal her breasts, his tongue flicking in
and out of his mouth, crazy-looking, and again she tried
to push him away from her. He straddled her, pushing
his erect penis into her face, trying to find her mouth,
moaning that she liked it, she wanted it . . . She tried to
twist her head away, but he yanked a handful of hair and
forced her to take him into her mouth, rammed it to the
back of her throat.

'That's it, baby! Suck me, suck me . . . Yes, come on
baby, suck me, *suck it, you fucking bitch*!'

Still she fought, she wanted him inside her, not this
way, not this way . . . She tried to wriggle away from
him, tried to push him down between her legs so she
could take him into her, but he pulled her hair, viciously.
She gave a muffled scream . . .

'You wait, bitch, wait, and then I'll fuck you! Suck
me, suck me and then beg for me, I want you to beg for
me.'

She sucked him as he rode her chest as if she were a

horse, moaning so loudly he didn't hear the door open, didn't see his daughter's face as she stared at them from the doorway . . .

Teresa began to pray for it to end, and finally he thrust himself into her. When at long last he kissed her it was a hard, cruel kiss, his tongue moving in rhythm with his body. His penis felt as though it were ripping her apart, and when at last he came he bit her lip so hard that it bled. Then he flopped on top of her and lay panting, heaving for breath.

Teresa stood in her bedroom, naked, and surveyed her bruised, trembling body. She felt as if she had been mauled and raped by a stranger. She knew now that he went with other women, but what kind of woman would like what he had done to her she would never know. She covered herself quickly with her dressing gown, wanting to pray, to go to church and pray for forgiveness for the sins she had committed, he had committed . . . She felt disgusting, dirty.

He came out of the shower next morning, a towel tied around his waist and another around his neck. His black hair dripped water as he leaned against the door.

'You know, you're right, they treat me like a bum. Not in so many words, but I know they don't give a fuck for what I think. They like me in the warehouses because I'm out of the way, but I just don't know how to go about changing things, you know? There's guys that have worked for Papa for more'n twenty years, they know the business inside out, but me . . .'

Teresa gave him a maternal smile. 'But they don't win

motorbike races and, besides, I think maybe we should take a little holiday; go and see Sophia and Constantino's baby.'

'OK, sounds a good move.'

'And maybe, before we go, you should bring some of those contracts home. You can go to the tracks whilst I look over them, then we can discuss it together, just so you'll have an idea what's going on when you speak with Papa.'

'OK, whatever you say.'

Whistling, he returned to the bathroom and dabbed aftershave on his cheeks. Teresa watched him, his lean, tawny-coloured body, and he caught her looking at him. He smiled, his perfect white teeth flashing. He was full of vitality, his dark eyes shining, as he said, 'My, you were sexy last night, very sexy . . .'

She smiled and walked back through the bedroom, murmuring that she would put some coffee on. He waited until she had gone, then strolled back into the bedroom.

As he bent to comb his hair in the mirror he noticed the packet of contraceptives and gave a half-laugh. He had almost been caught out, and he knew never to bring a packet into the house again.

CHAPTER 14

FREDERICO LUCIANO had always been plump, but now, almost twenty-two years old, he was simply fat. He was smaller than his brothers and balding, even at that early age. He had his father's eyes and hooked nose, but his mother's sweet mouth which gave his face a weak look. However he was far from that as he had been brought up surrounded by friends of his father since his teens, and he was quick to learn. His wonderfully good humour and open manner made him extremely well liked, and he had an unusual ability to command respect for one so young, but he was hungry for power and the good humour could switch to terrifying rages. Frederico Luciano was not a young man to cross.

He was, it appeared, quite able to handle the Luciano holdings in the gambling cities. His latest move was to open two small pinball arcades in Atlantic City. One of his priorities there was to purchase property, because rumours were rife that once the gambling laws were straightened out the city would become another gambling Mecca. Apart from casinos, there would be a need for car parks, garages, laundries and other service premises. He decided to move to Atlantic City to be on the spot.

Frederico's relationships with women were invariably short-term flirtations, most of them with Las Vegas chorus girls and always paid for.

It was at a card game in Las Vegas that he met Moyra Rosenstiel, although she used the surname of James, feeling her Jewish name wouldn't look good in lights. An ex-showgirl, she always had difficulty in getting work because she was so tiny, so she took a croupier course and worked the tables as a fill-in, while waiting for her big showbiz break. She was a sharp little thing, with big, china-blue eyes and bleached blonde hair. Her nose, an LA snub, had done a lot to rid her of the 'Rosenstiel' connection.

It was her wisecracking that had first attracted Frederico to her. He had taken a chair and played for more than half an hour at her table, noting how she dealt the cards quickly and professionally, her twinkling blue eyes darting this way and that, her jokes a constant source of amusement to him.

One night, Frederico had called the pit manager over and told him that he wanted her for a private card game at his apartment, a high roller suite in the casino.

Moyra arrived dressed to the hilt. As soon as Frederico's man let her in she raised her hands in a humorous gesture.

'I'll make sure you get a good game.'

'You want a drink?'

'Not when I'm working, thank you very much, Mr Luciano.'

'There's no game, I just wanted to meet you.'

She hitched her skirt up and put her hands on her hips. 'Look, no offence, but I'm a croupier. That's what I'm paid for, that's what I came here for tonight, and if there's no game maybe the pit boss heard you wrong . . .'

'I told him there was a game, but I wanted to talk with you. Here, it's a good champagne.'

'Thanks, but no thanks.'

'How about dinner?'

'I've already eaten.'

'Tomorrow, maybe?'

Moyra hesitated, then giggled. She picked up the glass of champagne. 'I lied about eating, I'm starving.'

Frederico continued to see Moyra in Vegas, but when he left for Atlantic City he had no real intention of seeing her again. She broke into floods of tears and wept herself red-eyed. She was losing the best meal-ticket she could ever have dreamed of, and knew if she didn't do something drastic, she would lose it full stop. She calculated the price of all her gifts from Frederico in dollars, and was physically sick at the thought that there would be no more. She persuaded him at least to call her, and sat by the telephone for a week until he rang.

She whispered and cooed down the phone to him, telling him she was naked and he could play with her over the line. He was astonished that she could turn him on even from a distance, and after several nights of their sexy phone calls he said to himself, 'What the fuck, why not get over there and see her?' But that wouldn't work as he was so busy, so he sent her a private plane. She knew she was getting to him and this time she wouldn't let him off the hook.

Moyra could eat like no other woman Frederico had ever met. She was in the king-size bed eating a vast breakfast of ham, eggs and brownies, plus currant toast dripping with butter, when the bedside phone rang. She called to Frederico, but he was in the shower, so she picked it up. The call was from Rome and she yelled for Frederico to take it.

He came out of the shower like a dripping Buddha. Her mouth full of toast, she held the phone out to him and said, 'Here, some guy in Rome.'

He pushed her roughly aside and took the call, sitting on the bed, quiet for a moment. Then he laughed and lay back, speaking in Sicilian, and Moyra heard the word 'bambino'. After what seemed an age he said goodbye, making kissing noises, and put the phone down.

'Who was that?'

'My father. You don't answer the phone, Moyra, OK?'

'What if it's for me?'

'You don't get no one to call you. If I'm gonna ring, I'll tell you when, but you don't answer any other time.'

'Why not?'

'Because I say . . . Now get dressed, we gotta buy a gift for my brother, he just gotta son.'

Frederico was in a foul temper, snapping all the way on their shopping expedition. They chose an elaborate silver christening cup and a solid silver teething ring, and strolled along the boardwalk while they waited for the baby's name to be engraved on them. Moyra said nothing, just slipped her arm through his.

'Family's important, you know that, Moyra?'

'Sure, I know. I love kids, I really love kids.'

'Papa sounded like a kid himself, so proud. You'd like my father, he's something else, something else . . .'

'You've got a big family? How many brothers?'

'Two, just two. There was another . . .'

'What?'

'Nothing . . . Let's go an' pick up the silver. You wanna eat?'

'You have to ask?'

'That's my girl.'

'Am I, Freddy? Am I really your girl?'

'Sure you're my girl, you see any others in the apartment?'

'No, just sometimes I don't feel like I was important to you.'

'You're important, OK?'

'You mean it?'

'What do you want from me, a signed document?'

'If you wanna know, yes. I love you, an' I don't see nobody else around for me. Sure I want a signed document, don't you?'

'Eh . . . Don't fuck around.'

'Is that all I am to you?'

'What?'

'A fuck?'

'Don't use that language, you know I don't like you to swear.'

'OK, am I just your screw, then? Is that what I am?'

'Don't say that neither! How many times do I have to tell you I don't like you using foul language?'

'I am though, aren't I?'

'You are what?'

'You know.'

Frederico swore. He knew she was trying to force him to ask her to marry him, and no way did his intentions stretch to that.

Subdued, she pouted as they collected the christening gifts, 'You ashamed of me?'

'Jesus Christ, Moyra, will you let it drop? You keep on at me an' I'll swear I . . .'

'You don't want to marry me?'

'Let's just drop it, huh?'

'OK . . . I won't ever bring it up again.'

Moyra kept her word, but stopped taking her birth pill. Six months later, she became pregnant.

She chose her moment to tell Frederico when he had finalized some particularly tiresome negotiations on two properties. A fire had eventually persuaded the owner to give way and Frederico bought the two charred warehouses for less than the going rate. It was the land Frederico was interested in, not the buildings. She had watched him arrive, seen he was in good spirits and decided this was the time.

'I got somethin' to tell you, and you gotta promise me not to be angry. I'm going to have a baby.'

'Aw, fuck, are you sure?'

She ran, crying, into the bathroom. She refused to come out for three hours, until he finally promised to get a special licence the next day.

*

Three months later, Moyra was rushed to hospital, where she miscarried. The baby was a boy who was christened and buried at the same time. The doctors had told him his wife would be unlikely to conceive again. He asked them not to tell her, then returned to the penthouse and cried, surrounded by toys, the cradle and an ornate pram.

He should have waited, but he needed to talk to his mother, so he called the Villa Rivera and blurted out that he had got married. His father was speechless, unable to comprehend how he could take such a step without consulting them. He fired questions at his son – was she Italian? Was she from a good family? Was she Catholic?

'I'll bring her home to meet you, I just wanted you to know.'

Graziella took the phone and began to tell him about their little Carlo, laughing and saying that perhaps now they could look forward to more grandchildren. When the phone went dead, she presumed they had been cut off.

Suddenly, Frederico had a strangely clear picture of Michael, dancing with his mama beneath the old tree in the garden, as if it were only yesterday. Then he remembered the look of doting pride on his father's face, a demonstration of such adoration it had pained the young Frederico. His father had never looked at him in that way, would never feel like that towards him. Now, after all those years – how many had it been since Michael's death in 1960? Fourteen, fourteen years, yet the memories were fresh and clear. He stared out at the ocean, understanding more than ever before the terrible loss his father must have felt. His own son had never even lived, yet he felt pain for him.

Michael's death had carved his name in all their hearts.

In a way he was glad that he had got away from Sicily, away from the domination of his father, away from Michael's ghost. Here in America he would prove himself, show his father that he was more than worthy of the Luciano name. He caught sight of himself in the mirror, his balding head, his fat body . . . It was hard to believe that Michael was his brother, they hadn't shared a single feature. Even now Frederico was jealous of him, just as he had always been. To his own reflection in the mirror he said what he had wanted to say to his father the night before they had buried Michael.

'I love you, Papa.'

Giorgio Carolla had been on the operating table for more than two hours while his father sat in the small waiting room nearby, a pot of hot coffee on a table beside him. Giorgio had been declared fit enough for surgery, yet it was a terrible catch-22 situation; the hole in his heart had enlarged considerably since it had been discovered, and the deterioration of the muscles had rapidly escalated the weakness. Left as he was he would be dead in three or four months, but the dilemma the surgeon always had to face in these circumstances was that the operation itself could kill him. Although he was stronger than he had been in his whole life, the improvement in his physical condition had further strained his heart, draining that strength from him.

The decision had not been taken lightly. Carolla had sought the advice of several surgeons, but the prognosis was always the same; Giorgio must take the risk or die anyway. Eventually Giorgio took the initiative and agreed to undergo the operation.

Carolla did not count the cost, although it amounted to a fortune. He had never been close to his son, and couldn't make up for it now. Although he felt he should have spent the night before the operation with his son, he had been relieved when Giorgio refused the offer. Luka was the one who had remained with him throughout the tests, and with the nurse as well he didn't need anyone else.

Luka, usually so boisterous, was eerily quiet the night before the operation. He hardly moved a pace from Giorgio's side, he was so terrified that his beloved friend would not survive. Their narrow hospital beds were side by side, and Giorgio watched with his big, heavy eyes as the only person he had ever loved in his life carefully pushed the beds together. Luka placed his pillow close to Giorgio's and pulled the tight bedding from the join between them until the bed was one. He patted the covers gently, always aware of how delicate Giorgio's body was; even the weight of the blankets was heavy to him.

Satisfied at last, he slipped between the sheets, moving closer to Giorgio until they lay within inches of each other. The warmth between them was soothing. Giorgio felt for his friend's hand under the sheet.

'You cold? Your hand's cold, Luka.'

'I'm OK. You OK?'

'Yeah, I'm OK.'

Voices echoed along the corridors as the night staff came on duty.

'You awake, Luka?'

'Yes, I don't sleep until you sleep.'

'What do you do when I'm not around?'

Giorgio had seen the way his friend dangled his precious little gold heart, but he was trying to find an opening for what he knew had to be said. 'I might not always be around, you know that, don't you? If I come through the operation, it's only a temporary reprieve.'

'A what?'

'You understand, Luka. Some day I'll be leaving you, so I guess this is as good a time as any to tell you what you have meant to me. I love you, you must never forget that, because I ran the risk of never being able to love anyone. My father, we know, will be relieved when I'm gone. He may get expansive, over-generous – he may offer you money because, as dumb as he is, he knows what you mean to me. You take what you can, but stay away from him. Go back to the monastery and finish your education . . . Luka? Luka?'

Luka was up and out of the bed. His face, in the darkness, looked like white marble.

'You bastard, you bastard! Why are you doing this to me? You are not going to die, you are not leaving me!'

Giorgio tried to sit up as Luka pulled open a drawer in the dressing table and began hurling clothes across the room.

'What are you doing? Luka, for Chrissake, what are you doing?'

'No operation, I'm taking you out of here.'

Giorgio bunched the pillows behind his head to enable him to sit up. 'Don't be so fucking stupid, I was speaking hypothetically. You know there's a possibility that I won't come through the op tomorrow, you know that. What do you think is going to happen? I get a new heart so I can run with you? I'll never run, Luka, I'll

360

never be whole. If I don't go in, I'll die, don't you understand, you crass idiot? I *am* dying, I have been dying all my life. All it means tomorrow is maybe a few more months, a year. I am never going to get better, Luka, and if it happens tomorrow and I haven't said what I want to say . . .'

'What you got to say that's so important?'

'Learn from me, all that I am, all that I taught you. I learned from books, I lived through the written word, and only you took me outside it. You filled my life, Luka, promise me to fill yours. Don't waste it . . .'

The big moon face cracked. Tears streamed down the wide, flat cheeks and he cried. Giorgio wept because he was so scared – not of dying, but of leaving Luka alone. His frail arms lifted in an imploring gesture like a child to its mother, and Luka went to him, clung to him, his head close to the heart that was wasting away.

For a long time they were quiet, content to lie close to each other, but during the long night Giorgio whispered odd phrases; 'Everything you need is written, Luka. Remember that . . .'

It was near dawn when Luka knew Giorgio was asleep at last, but he remained in his arms, afraid to wake him by moving. Half-dozing, he made plans for when they left the hospital. He now faced the prospect of losing Giorgio, but he believed that God would give him just a little more time and prayed as he had never done before. He prayed with his little gold heart clenched in his teeth, biting on the mark his mother had made during his birth.

When Giorgio was finally taken down to the operating theatre, Luka could not understand why he couldn't go, too. He fought, striking out at everyone who tried to restrain him, and eventually had to be given a sedative to keep him quiet. Finally, he sat on the floor outside the theatre, knees drawn up under his chin, eyes closed, praying. As the sedatives took over, his head slowly drooped. At last Carolla was able to pick him up and carry him to the waiting room, where there was a narrow bed he could lie on.

As Paul Carolla picked up the red blanket to tuck around Luka, he looked closely at the boy for the first time and stood transfixed. His hair was white-blond, his long, pale lashes rested on cheeks that were rosy from being pressed against his knees for so long. Carolla stepped back, confused by his own fascination. He was the most perfect child Carolla had ever seen. The strange thing was that he even belonged to the same species as the poor, misshapen devil that was his son. He stood with the blanket in his hand and startled himself by speaking his thoughts aloud. 'Why aren't you my son? Why?'

He glanced around to see if anyone was within earshot, then covered Luka quickly. He pulled up his chair and sat beside the bed, still staring at the boy. He could not remember falling asleep, but he was jolted awake when the surgeon shook his shoulder gently. Carolla knew by the expression on his face that Giorgio had not made it.

'I'm sorry, sir, we did what we could and we almost won. But right at the end we found another fission and . . .'

Luka stirred, and Carolla stood up, licking his lips. They both looked at the boy on the bed as he stretched and yawned like a cat, easing the sleep from his body. Carolla gave the surgeon a slight nod to indicate that he would tell Luka himself.

Luka sat up as the surgeon left the room. He faced Carolla, his blue eyes so pale they were like pieces of ice.

'Is the operation over?'

Carolla sat heavily on the bed. He had never before had to deal with such a tragic situation, knowing that this child would feel more sense of loss than he, the father, did. Putting out his fat hand to touch Luka, he said tenderly, 'It's over for Giorgio now. No more pain, no more, it's all over.'

Luka's face crumpled and he wouldn't let Carolla touch him. He slid from the bed, shaking with grief, and supported himself against the wall as he went to the window. He pressed his face against the cold window-pane and spread his hands against the glass. Hearing his voice broke Carolla's heart.

'Run, Giorgio, run . . . Run now, go on, you're free now . . . Run . . .'

Carolla could not get Luka to come away from the window, nor could the hospital staff. He clung to the window-frame and spoke not a single word, staring blank-eyed as though he were watching and waiting for someone. It was pitiful, and no one knew quite what to do; he resisted with all his steely strength and they could not move him.

Carolla needed to make the funeral arrangements and to let Lydia know what had happened. Because he had never told the truth about his son, he could not rely on anyone else to handle it for him. His mind was working overtime as he organized the short service and cremation. He felt a certain sorrow, although his real grief had occurred at the time of his son's birth.

They let Luka stay where he was until it was time to leave the hospital. When Carolla returned to the waiting room he found the boy in exactly the same position, his body stiff, his face set. He closed the door and stood in silence for a moment, then pulled up a chair and sat down. 'I've got to take you back to the monastery, Luka. I'm having your things sent over from the hotel, and I'll call Father Angelo to meet you at the station . . . Are you listening?'

Luka did not move. Carolla would often ask himself if he had planned it, subconsciously, but at the time he was just sure that it was the right thing to do. 'If you don't want to go back to the monastery, you can come with me. I'll adopt you, you can be my son. I have to go to Naples on business, then I'm returning to New York. Everybody knows I have a kid, but no one has met him, so they would accept you as my son. I think it's a pretty good deal I'm offering you, kid.'

Luka still did not move. Carolla sighed, got up from the chair, and put it back against the wall. Then, slowly, he moved closer until he could put a hesitant hand on Luka's shoulder. He did not know what to say, had even shocked himself a little at what he had already said, but then Luka turned and looked up into the concerned face. His eyes were brilliant blue now, as if they had absorbed colour from the sky. Without a word he slipped his hand into Carolla's.

Touched, Carolla had to swallow before he could speak. 'So, do I take it we got a deal, huh? Yes?'

Luka tugged his hand but still did not speak. He was not at all certain that Carolla meant what he had said, but he walked out of the hospital and sat beside him, composed and silent, in the limo.

When they reached the apartment, Lydia made up a

bed for Luka in the spare room. He viewed everything with a certain mistrust, but as the night went on, it became more and more obvious that Carolla was serious. He even overheard Carolla discussing it with Father Angelo on the telephone.

Lydia could not believe it, and kept asking if Carolla was serious. She was the only person, apart from Father Angelo and Luka himself, who knew about Giorgio. He could trust the father not to gab, but Lydia?

Luka remained silent for the next two days. Carolla put it down to grief and decided the best way to handle it was to ignore it. When Father Angelo arrived with the papers he took Luka aside, asking if it was what he really wanted. Luka replied with a soft, but very firm, 'Yes'. It was the chance of a lifetime, a great opportunity for the boy he had taken into his care all those years ago, yet he could not help feeling a terrible sense of loss. When he embraced Luka to say goodbye, he felt the tremor in his young body and knew he wanted to weep but was controlling himself.

'Be good, Luka, and remember us in your prayers. Write to me, I am always here for you, no matter how far away you are. I want you to know I am here, should you need me.'

The familiar, musty smell of Father Angelo's robes hung in Luka's room long after he had gone. He curled up on the bed, staring at the ceiling and thinking how strange it was, as if he were entering a new world. Everything was suddenly different and he was outside it all, watching through a long, narrow tunnel, apart from, but still the centre of, all the action going on around him. The loneliness and the emptiness were so immense it hurt him to speak.

Having made the decision, it never occurred to Carolla to change his mind. Just as he always picked himself up from any business troubles, he never looked back. The future looked better than it had for a long time, and he felt a surge of power as if he had been blessed by the Virgin Mary herself.

It was a standing joke that the telephone was an extension of Carolla's right hand. Now he almost drove Lydia insane with his persistent calls to New York. It tickled him that no one thought it strange, no one questioned the authenticity of what he said. So many years his men had heard of his son, and when those close to him were replaced, many believed this so-called son was a figment of Carolla's imagination. In the past he had never encouraged mention of the boy, and many didn't even know he had one. Even though Luka was ten years younger than Giorgio, no one would have dared query or insinuate anything amiss. Perhaps he was even his kid by the whore he lived with. But whatever they thought, it remained unspoken.

Carolla appeared to be in such high spirits and loved saying 'My son this' or 'My son that . . .' He asked advice on the best school for Luka, mentioning that, as he had been educated in Sicily, he spoke little English. When they went out together he would smile and nod at total strangers, and if he met anyone even vaguely familiar he would introduce his son with a pride that made Luka blush in apparent shyness. But, in truth, every time Carolla called him Giorgio, Luka felt as if he were being stabbed in the heart.

Lydia mistrusted the boy from the moment she first met him, and the minute she was alone with him, she warned him. 'Listen to me, you think I don't know what you're after. How much you think you can squeeze outta him before you run off?'

Luka stared, knowing he must be nice to her, knowing no one must ever know what he really felt. He smiled, touching her hand. 'I love him. I never had a father, and he is everything I ever dreamed of . . .'

'Like hell! It's his wallet you dream of, you little bastard.' She saw the way his eyes narrowed, the tiny step back away from her, but the smile never left him. He knew she was dangerous, knew that he had to ingratiate himself with Carolla to such an extent that given the choice between them, he would be chosen. Lydia was in the way.

Carolla was ahead of Luka. Lydia could make him look like a crazy man if she ever told anyone the truth. Perhaps it would be best if, when he and Luka left for New York, she was not around. He did question his own motives, but could only think how it felt being able to say, 'This is my son.'

Carolla gave Lydia a wad of notes with instructions to buy clothes for Luka. She had followed him around like a shadow, but the sight of the cash, the knowledge she had far more than she would need, made her hesitate. So Carolla gave her a further incentive to go shopping by hinting that she, too, would need more clothes for New York.

He watched her walking across the courtyard below, and, as if she sensed he was there, she turned, looked up to the apartment window and waved.

'Is she coming to New York with us?'

Slowly, Carolla turned to him, unsure, hesitant . . . unable to answer.

Luka, as young as he was, knew intuitively this was his moment. Slowly, he lifted his arms, clasping the man who was to become his father and whispered, 'Papa . . . Papa.'

Lydia never returned from her shopping expedition, and the following morning Carolla, carrying only a briefcase, told Luka they were leaving.

As Carolla arrived at the airport, the body of a woman was discovered in the harbour at Palermo. No one had reported her missing, there was no sign of violence and no identification. The dead woman wore no jewellery and was shoeless. Paul Carolla had chosen Luka, as Lydia had been afraid he might do. But she could never have dreamed that, after all the years they had been together, she would be thrown aside. She had never really known Carolla, nor had he the slightest notion of who the boy he had adopted really was. Had he known that Luka was Michael Luciano's illegitimate child, it might have been him thrown into the sea instead of poor Lydia.

Sitting in the first-class section of the TWA jumbo jet, Carolla held Luka's hand tightly as the plane lifted off. A part of his life was over, and he looked forward to a new beginning in a partnership with the boy at his side.

'Eh, can you see Palermo down there? See it? Take a look, I hate to look down from a plane. Makes me wanna puke.'

Luka looked down and gasped, then settled back in his seat as Carolla opened the menu for the first-class luncheon.

'OK, Giorgio, let's see what we got for eats.'

Luka slipped his hand through Carolla's arm. 'You know, Papa, I don't think you should call me that. You can say I changed my name at the monastery.'

'It's on your passport, your name is Giorgio now.'

'No, it isn't.'

About to argue, Carolla sighed, but the small hand patted his arm and Luka cuddled closer. He looked down into the smiling face and pinched the dimpled right cheek. The boy's eyes were so brilliant they seemed to sparkle.

'So what d'you wanna be called?'

'My name is Luka, Luka Carolla.'

CHAPTER 15

TEN YEARS passed without any outward signs of conflict between Paul Carolla and Roberto Luciano. During the 'quiet years', Luciano continued to expand his companies, but gradually passed more control to his sons. The New York shipping and trucking outlets were headed by trusted *capi*, with Alfredo as figurehead.

By 1985 Atlantic City had become a gambling mecca and Frederico's consistent purchasing of real estate there, ahead of the gambling boom, had made the family millions. Moyra Luciano had visited Sicily on a few occasions with her husband and, although Frederico knew his father had never accepted her, he never voiced his disapproval and treated her with respect, as did Graziella.

Constantino, the eldest son, ran the Palermo-based companies. He and Sophia were very obviously the Don's favourites. Sophia's fashion boutiques continued to flourish. She had opened two more shops and moved her headquarters to a large warehouse. Their second son was born two years after Carlo, and christened Nunzio. The children often went to stay at the Villa Rivera, where Luciano was a doting grandparent.

The years had mellowed the Don. On major decisions he still dominated, but he was, everyone secretly believed, ready to retire. Although no one dared voice this opinion to him, it was close to the truth. The threat of a takeover, of pressure from the massive narcotics trade, was always there. But Luciano was by now a formidably rich man, and he had a virtual army working for him on both sides of the Atlantic.

Luciano never spoke of his beloved first-born son, Michael, and never referred to the past vendetta with Paul Carolla. He was well aware, however, that his old adversary was now one of the foremost drug dealers in the States. Everyone knew of the ill feeling between the two men, and it was Carolla and not Luciano who had become high-ranking within the Organization in the States. But in Palermo Luciano still held firm, and Carolla, having been warned over the Robello incident never to cross or begin a vendetta with Luciano again, kept his distance. But it was a permanent thorn in his side that Sicily, being one of the safest junk routes, still remained inaccessible to him yet open to others because of Luciano.

Although Luciano tried to keep tabs on Carolla, he could only move so far, because just as Carolla had been warned so had Luciano – there should be no more confrontations between the two of them. But Carolla had learned his lesson harshly and having been wiped out once, he took care to ensure it could never happen again. The truce between them held, but Carolla had grown far more devious, his overt tendency to violence now insidious and very dangerous.

Luciano was unaware that during the so-called 'quiet years' his hated enemy had been engineering a long-term plan to squeeze Luciano's hold on the docks. For ten years Carolla had been creating a complex network of companies and, by using various names, had been buying every available property bordering on Luciano's. He was surrounding him, nibbling at the edges like a school of fish until he was ready to bite like a shark.

Luka Carolla had been unable to settle in New York for a considerable time. The language barrier was the first excuse his adoptive father used, and even when Luka had learned to speak fluent English he continued to excuse the boy's erratic behaviour as 'culture shock'. Luka had been thrown into the American way of life and he would, Carolla insisted, take time to adapt.

He was expelled from every decent school he was sent to. No one could understand why Carolla put up with the boy's anti-social ways; Carolla had, as all his men knew, a very short fuse. Yet with his son the fuse never seemed to ignite, no matter what Luka did. They could see the way he manipulated his father, always able to ingratiate himself by the simple device of showing the squat little man love, a love that overcame everything.

The years in America had sharpened Luka, clarified his every feature into a strange, beautiful perfection. His eyes were wide, clear, and ice blue, his nose straight, and the dimple, which still appeared with those gentle smiles, could be turned on at will. His strong teeth were small, white and even and, although he remained very slender, bordering on thin, he was immensely strong. A solitary figure, he had made no friends of his own age and appeared not to want them. He regularly worked out for hours on end in a small gymnasium built for him in the apartment. He was obsessive about his clothes, spending hours window-shopping and choosing each item carefully. His natural sense of style – not, unfortunately, copied by his father – was possibly inherited from the mother he had never known, Sophia Luciano.

Although he appeared to dote on his father, those close to Carolla believed otherwise. They had seen that awful, hooded, sly smirk creep over Luka's perfect face when he was unaware of being watched. His strange habit of talking to himself gave him a disturbing eeriness. If caught, he would become very still, too still, like a statue, never speaking or acknowledging that anyone else was in the room. He would remain poised and silent until they left him alone.

Luka had persuaded Carolla not to send him to college. At first, Carolla wouldn't hear of it but, in May 1985, he acquiesced and agreed to allow Luka to join him on a trip to Canada. The deal was nothing special and did not require the usual retinue of bodyguards. There was no imminent danger and it was therefore a good opportunity to introduce Luka to the business.

Carolla had eventually given up trying to trace Lenny Cavataio. Now, twenty-five years after the murder of Michael Luciano, nothing could have been further from his mind than the small-time mobster. Carolla had to think hard even to recollect the name, but he took the call in his hotel suite literally minutes after he and Luka arrived in Canada.

He couldn't believe it; he listened to the drawling

voice with growing fury. Cavataio had heard he was due to arrive and wanted a meet.

Luka watched Carolla closely, fascinated. He could see the effort his father was making to maintain control, the way he stood over the telephone breathing rhythmically. His knuckles were white, but gradually he relaxed his hand.

It was incongruous that Lenny, who had given Michael Luciano the bad junk, was now a hopeless junkie himself. He had been living on handouts and bumming around the clubs, scoring and dealing, for years. Now Carolla discovered that Lenny owed one of his dealers $10,000. It was absurd that Lenny was hitting him for cash that would eventually find its way into his pocket anyway.

'Trouble?' asked Luka.

Carolla gave a mirthless, short laugh. 'Yeah, trouble. Shoulda taken care of it years ago. Go get Johnny in for me – go on, move it.'

Luka went to the adjoining room and told Johnny Moreno he was wanted. They returned to Carolla's suite together. Luka was about to sit with them when Carolla told him to get lost. He went into the bedroom without a word, but he left the door ajar and stood peering into the room through the crack in the door.

His father was talking angrily about Cavataio. 'If he gets to the Lucianos, those fuckin' family guys an' their vendettas . . . I got things goin' down in Palermo an' I'm in strong with the Organization. This crap'll cause real aggravation.'

Luka could hardly follow what his father was saying. Try as he could to piece it together, it didn't make sense.

Johnny Moreno was obviously edgy, muttering about how he hated dealing with junkies.

Carolla snapped, 'You think I like 'em? Only decent junkie is a dead one, an' that's how I want Cavataio. An' I don't want no one else involved. Less people know about this, the better. Just get rid of him.'

Luka had to bite his lip to keep from laughing. The dialogue amused him, just like watching an old James Cagney movie . . .

None of them left the hotel, but Lenny didn't call again until the following morning. The waiting had turned Carolla into a mad bull. But he kept himself under control as he told Lenny the money was ready for collection, and asked where he wanted the drop.

Luka ate his breakfast while Carolla gave Moreno his instructions. He watched Moreno shredding toilet paper into stacks, then wrapping notes around them with rubber bands to hold them together. He placed them in the briefcase to look like the payoff cash. When he left at eight-fifteen, Carolla joined Luka and tucked into ham and eggs with relish, as if the matter had already been dealt with.

'Who is Lenny Cavataio?' Luka asked.

Carolla wiped egg from his lips with a napkin and picked up the coffee pot. 'A nobody. Now eat your breakfast, an' get outta my hair. Here . . . go buy yourself a coupla shirts.'

He tossed $200 on the table. Luka stared at him, then picked up the money and walked out.

*

Johnny Moreno never returned. By the time Luka went back to the suite, Carolla was being questioned by the Canadian police, who had found Moreno's body in his hired car. The hotel key had been inside the car, and the hotel receptionist had told them that Moreno had arrived with Paul Carolla.

Luka was impressed by the way his father handled the police. He was charming and helpful, but unable to give them any reason why someone might want his driver dead.

Only minutes after the police left, Cavataio called again. He screamed at Carolla, refusing to listen to his excuses. Now he wanted $50,000 for his silence.

Carolla was in a difficult situation. The police obviously knew he was in Canada and knew of his connections, so narcotics agents were all over the hotel. It was possible they were also tapping his phone. He felt stranded, without back-up, and any meeting now would be madness. This business was something he had to take care of himself. The more people that knew about the Michael Luciano incident, the worse it looked for him. Luka asked why he didn't just pay the bum off, and was taken aback by his father's blistering attack on his stupidity. Carolla was taking out all his pent-up rage on Luka. He was unprepared for his son's reaction.

Luka was equally angry, but his voice was so controlled he actually calmed Carolla. 'Maybe I am stupid, but I'm not the one with two yards of toilet paper stuffed down my throat – Johnny Moreno is. Maybe you should take more care, choose better guys to protect you.'

Carolla rubbed Luka's cheek and laughed. 'You talk

big, kid, but when I want your advice I'll ask for it, OK?'

Carolla hesitated, not sure how much to tell Luka but needing to talk. What came out was not the real reason Cavataio was blackmailing him. For the first time he actually spoke of what it had meant to him when his father, his own father, chose Roberto Luciano instead of him. 'In front of the heads of all the families, Luka, they told me. How could he have done that to me? I was his son.'

Luka reached over, held his father's face with both hands, and kissed him on the lips. 'Let me do this for you. Let me show you what I can do, then maybe you'll let me be the one to protect you, look out for you. I am your son, I've got more to lose if anything happens to you than any of the made guys you got around you. An' it'll be just you an' me that knows.'

When the third call came from Lenny Cavataio, Carolla had already left Canada. Luka explained who he was and that he had the merchandise. Lenny instructed him to be at a small night-club and to sit on the fifth bar stool, leaving the case on the right side of it. Then he was to walk out of the club.

Luka placed the briefcase on the floor, finished his glass of orange juice and walked out of the seedy club. He waited for over an hour before he saw the case being carried out. The man wore a denim jacket, jeans, sneakers and a peaked cap. He walked twenty yards, then did a

U-turn, looked up and down the street and retraced his steps back past the club. He walked for almost a quarter of a mile, then entered a rundown rooming house. The Lyceum had a large sign in the window, 'Rooms Vacant'. Luka waited a few moments before following his quarry into the house.

The reception area was dark, with a glass booth occupied by a fat woman drinking a glass of beer. She was leaning out to peer short-sightedly towards the lift. When Luka approached soundlessly to stand by her counter, she actually jumped.

'I got somethin' for Lenny, he just came in.'

'So what? He knows the rules, an' I've warned him. It's a single room he owes for, you tell him that, an' you've got five minutes. Third floor, room nine, an' five minutes.'

Luka stayed a little more than five minutes, and he apologized as he left. She grunted and returned to reading her paper.

Cavataio walked in fifteen minutes later. He tried to slip past the woman without her seeing him, but she yelled after him, 'I've told you, no guests. You pay for a single room, an' you pay for tonight, then you're on your way, jerk.'

Without replying or waiting for the lift, Lenny ran up the stairs to his seedy room. The shower and washtub were behind a hardboard partition, and he could hear the water running.

As he drew back the curtain, the water overflowed from the plastic base and on to his shoes – bright, blood-pink water. Tony was hunched, naked, beneath the shower head, his eyes open and his mouth gaping horrifically where his tongue had been sliced out. The sight was made more gruesome by the fact that Tony was holding his tongue in his dead hand.

After staying in hiding for a month, a terrified Lenny Cavataio arrived in Atlantic City. He knew he was a marked man, and learning that one of Don Roberto Luciano's sons was there, he tried to get to see him.

Frederico Luciano was told there was a junkie with some information for sale, and would have dismissed him out of hand, except that the messenger passed him a note that had on it only a scrawled name. No one could tell what he was thinking; he stared at the scrap of paper, his face expressionless. Even after all these years, seeing his brother's name hurt. Michael was like a ghost who would not rest.

Roberto Luciano was reading in bed when Frederico called. Graziella was asleep next to him, and he talked quietly so as not to disturb her. He asked if anything was wrong, but Frederico quickly put his mind at rest.

'No, Papa, everything's fine. But I got a present for you – his name is Lenny Cavataio.'

'How soon can you bring him to me?'

'Next flight out – and, Papa, the guy's a junkie . . .'

A very frightened Lenny arrived at Luciano's Palermo warehouse. The dank gloom of the cavernous building made him blink after the brilliant sunshine outside.

Frederico had ensured that he had whatever junk he needed to keep him straight and for a while Lenny had almost relaxed, believing that his deal was going to come off. But as the heavy doors closed behind him, he began to sweat. He turned to the man who had accompanied him on the flight, but he stepped back, away from his side. On his other side, the fat young Frederico, who had taken such great care of him, also stepped back as if Lenny were contaminated.

'Welcome back to Sicily, Lenny.' Don Roberto Luciano came from the shadows, his white hair glowing as though a small light were trained on his face. Lenny's mouth went dry and he swallowed, but his tongue felt as if it were too big for his mouth. He coughed, and sat gratefully on the orange crate indicated for him.

Don Roberto sat in the only chair and offered Lenny a cigar, which he refused. Luciano took his time, carefully clipping and lighting his cigar and blowing the smoke in a thin circle above his head.

'So Lenny,' Luciano said quietly. 'They got my boy hooked, then what?'

'Carolla had a bunch of real cowboys calling themselves chemists, and they fucked up a whole shipment of gear – you know, overheated it – an' it was useless. Well, useless to sell to the main dealers, but he was able to peddle it on the streets. It was lethal stuff. Then I was told that Michael Luciano would be arriving in Rome and he would be waiting for a fix. I was to give it to him – not all bad junk, I was to give him a good fix an' leave him the bad junk to fuck himself over.'

Luciano leaned closer. 'Who gave the order to kill my son?'

Lenny didn't hesitate. 'Carolla gave the order to kill

380

your boy, Don Roberto. It was like an obsession with him.'

The Don appeared more intent on his cigar butt than anything Lenny had said. He smiled as he dropped the end on the stone floor and ground it out with the toe of his highly polished, handmade shoe.

'OK, Lenny . . . I'll get this written down for you to sign, to be used as a statement.'

'Eh, now wait a minute . . . I never agreed to go . . .'

'What do you expect me to do with this information, huh? Run after Carolla myself? No, no, my friend, times have changed.'

Roberto Luciano walked out without a backward glance. Lenny tried to follow, but, with a small gesture from Frederico, two guards closed in on him. He joined his father outside the warehouse, his own bodyguard a few paces behind him. 'Papa, he'll not last more than a few hours after we hand over a statement and Carolla gets to hear about it . . .'

His father interrupted, his eyes blazed with anger. 'That is my intention, but it's got to appear as if we are, as I have maintained for the past twenty years, prepared to co-operate with the *carabinieri*. I'll make sure Carolla knows we have Lenny, because I'll get his statement delivered to him personally, and I guarantee he'll be in Palermo within twenty-four hours.'

'Papa, let me take him; I got guys in New York.'

Luciano slowly lifted his arms to embrace his son; like a lover he whispered his thanks, but his eyes were without love. Paul Carolla was what he had wanted for so many years; now at long last he would have him, and he would show the Organization that he had been right. Paul

Carolla had murdered his son, and it was Luciano's right to finally make him pay.

Luciano was not the only man to lose a son. Shortly before Lenny Cavataio surfaced in Canada, another known mafioso don was in Rome; he, too, had lost sons in a Mafia war. His name was Tommaso Buscetta, but, unlike Luciano, Buscetta was under arrest.

Tommaso Buscetta was the highest-ranking member of the Sicilian Mafia ever to betray *omerta*. He was arrested in Brazil and taken to Rome in total secrecy. No one knew of his arrest or the subsequent deal to turn state evidence. His first statements to Italy's leading investigating magistrate, Giovanni Falcone, were given in a closely guarded safe house. He talked for months and altogether his statements covered four hundred pages.

Buscetta's revelations precipitated the most intensive assault on the international power of the Mafia ever undertaken. Under heavy guard Buscetta was shipped to the USA to continue his confessions and there, in a superbly protected safe house, the United States Drug Enforcement Administration continued to take down his statements.

Buscetta's arrival in the USA coincided with Roberto Luciano delivering Lenny Cavataio and his statement to the Sicilian *carabinieri*. Two days later, Paul Carolla also received a handwritten manuscript, as did the main prosecutor at the chief attorney's office in New York.

Carolla was eating breakfast when one of his men brought in the hand-delivered statement from Lenny Cavataio. He read it from cover to cover, at first in total disbelief, and then he erupted into a rage, screaming for Luka. Luka, he was informed, had been out all night and no one seemed to know where he was.

Luciano could not have timed it better. By now, Buscetta had also named Paul Carolla as one of the main narcotics dealers. The district attorney began preparations to arrest and charge Paul Carolla. Like many other members of the Organization, Carolla was unaware that Buscetta was in custody.

Two hours after receiving the Lenny Cavataio statement Carolla was tipped off that he was about to be arrested; he automatically assumed it was in connection with Lenny Cavataio. He had still not discovered Luka's whereabouts, and knew he had to move fast, arrange a safe departure from New York and head for Palermo. Cavataio had to be dealt with and fast. He was totally unprepared for the onslaught Buscetta was about to unleash; uppermost in his mind was the desperate need to silence Cavataio because he was not only implicating him in major drug activity, but also alleging that he was the man who had ordered the death of Michael Luciano.

Carolla spent the best part of the day arranging his departure, moving at a feverish pace. The murder connection would have disastrous repercussions within the Organization, since he had denied ever playing any part in Michael Luciano's death; and because he had been believed by the Commission, he could now be in the firing line from all sides.

*

Luka had been showered with expensive gifts on his return from Canada. His grateful father, presuming Lenny Cavataio dead, had bought him a new Porsche and handed over thousands of dollars, proudly announcing that his son was now going to be one of his personal bodyguards.

Luka took his job seriously, enrolling in shooting schools and collecting a virtual armoury in the privacy of his bedroom. He enjoyed playing at being a killer, as if he had become part of one of the thriller videos he watched constantly. He was actually watching one when his irate father kicked the television screen into smithereens. For the first time since the adoption, Carolla turned against Luka, screaming that he had fucked up so badly they could both stand to lose everything. There would be no more money, no Porsches, nothing. As proof, he waved the Cavataio statement in Luka's face, then gripped Luka by the hair and forced him to read it.

Luka could have no inkling that he was reading of the murder of his own father, Michael Luciano. Desperate to make amends, he offered to leave for Palermo that very minute and kill Cavataio.

Carolla turned on him in fury. 'Killing isn't a game, Luka, it's a profession.'

'Yeah, I know.'

'Yeah, you know, do you? You just cost me, you cost me, Luka, an' if you wasn't my son, I'd fuckin' shoot you through that wall.'

Luka was hurt; he wasn't concerned with Carolla's predicament, but with the insinuation that he wasn't a professional.

'I am a professional!' he screamed back, opening drawers to display his carefully stored weapons; the neat row of hand-drilled bullets, the dentists' drills, the martial arts knives. There was enough to equip a small torture chamber.

Luka watched Carolla as he snapped orders to his men to get rid of everything. All the weapons were numbered and could be traced. Carolla's face was contorted with rage at his son's foolishness; his fingers ached to strangle the stupid kid.

Meanwhile, Buscetta's information was being acted upon. The round-up on both sides of the Atlantic was about to begin. Still unaware of Buscetta's treachery, Carolla left the United States only days before a warrant was issued for his arrest.

Luka had clung to his father's side, begging not to be left behind, and eventually Carolla agreed to take him along. With two bodyguards they landed at London Airport, where they stayed for one night only before switching passports and flying to Paris, where they repeated the switch. Carolla's contacts reported the mass arrests in the USA but, as yet, there was no whisper of what was about to take place in Sicily.

After arranging a hide-out, they headed for Sicily, arriving one month after Carolla had received the Cavataio statement. Carolla was still not unduly worried, convinced that Cavataio could be dealt with and that he could then move his headquarters to Brazil, to continue business as usual. His first priority was to find out where Lenny Cavataio was being held. It was all happening as Luciano had anticipated but, like Carolla, Luciano was unaware of Buscetta's treachery. No one could have anticipated the storm that followed the breaking of the news that a major Mafia informer was being held in the USA, least of all Luciano.

Acting on the Buscetta information, the Italian authorities had for months been preparing a massive round-up of Mafia suspects. The Cavataio statement played only a minor part. Carolla's mountain hide-out, like an army dugout from which he could still control his business, safely surrounded by his own men, was to turn into his prison.

Carolla had unwittingly walked into Luciano's web, and also into the carefully laid plans of the Italian and Sicilian authorities in their attempt to break the Mafia stranglehold for all time. No sooner had Carolla arrived than the order was given for the onslaught to begin. Only when he was trapped, cornered in his hide-out, did he learn of Buscetta. He made desperate attempts to pressure the many families he had drawn into the narcotics business into giving him assistance. Representatives came and went under a cloak of secrecy, all promising to do what they could to get Carolla out of Sicily, though their priority was to save their own skins.

With no concept of what was actually taking place, Luka attended the meetings with member after member of the major families. He was thrilled; as Paul Carolla's son he was allowed to stay, he was accepted, and his safety was also of importance.

Unable to move from his hide-out, Carolla became paranoid. His safety was costing him millions as tip-offs from within the police force indicated that something big was going down. The *carabinieri* were rumoured to be bringing in reinforcements by the hundred, and the newspapers began to report the hourly arrests of named men, known associates, from high-ranking officials down to street dealers. As the massive clean-up gained momentum, Carolla began losing men, either arrested or on the run. It became impossible to maintain contact with the people who were supposedly arranging his passage to Brazil; Buscetta had wreaked havoc over there and, as yet, his men had still not discovered where Cavataio was being held.

Roberto Luciano watched the mass arrests with growing admiration. It was something he had never believed possible. He gloated, secretly, as those he had warned against joining Carolla were herded to jail like animals. It appeared to many that Luciano himself was untouchable because, by now, he and his family were legitimate and had never had any part in the narcotics trade. He had wanted justice for his son's murder; it seemed that he was getting more than he had bargained for. It would only be a matter of time before Carolla was hunted down. Luciano knew he was hiding like a dog in the mountains. He waited to see the man who had given the order to kill Michael stand trial at last. He would see Carolla's empire smashed once again, along with those whose greed had made them join him. To date more than four hundred had been arrested in Sicily alone; in the States no one had yet calculated the numbers.

Buscetta's evidence did not worry Luciano. He went about his business as though he were in a different world. Having no relationship with his parents, he felt little compassion or sorrow when he was informed that his cousin had died. The information was brought to him by Emilio Luciano, a boy Luciano did not know existed. He was very shy, stuttering out that his father had been Don Roberto's father's brother. His handsome face flushed pink with nerves as he continued his rehearsed speech. 'I was always forbidden to speak with you, Don Roberto, but now both my parents are dead. I have lived all my life in Naples and I have my degree in electronics. If you find me acceptable, I would be grateful for a position in one of your companies. I come to offer you my respects.'

Don Roberto smiled. 'They are most gratefully received, and if you wish to become part of my family, you will be made welcome.' The boy was shaking as he bent to kiss Don Roberto's hand, but instead he received a warm embrace. He did not expect to be taken into the villa, and could not contain himself when Don Roberto insisted he stay with them on a permanent basis. That evening Emilio dined with the famous Luciano, the man whose name was forbidden to be spoken in his parents' home.

Rosa Luciano was also invited to spend her summer vacation at the Villa Rivera with her grandparents. The invitation had been unexpected, and eagerly accepted, and she was met at the airport by Emilio Luciano, who was now very much part of the family. He was to become an even closer part. With the approval of Don Roberto, Emilio began to court Rosa Luciano, and two weeks after her arrival in Sicily he proposed marriage and was accepted. The panic-stricken nightmare world outside the safe walls of the villa seemed far removed from them all.

The nightmare for Paul Carolla, however, was growing out of control. There seemed no way out; Cavataio had still not been traced and there were no escape plans ready. Only one good thing had come out of it all; Luka had proved himself to be exceptionally useful. Carrying a passport in the name of Johnny Moreno, the driver murdered in Canada, he was able to move around freely and carry messages. With his blond hair and blue eyes he was accepted as a young American tourist. At the same time he was getting to know many contacts within the families.

Acting under Carolla's orders, Luka touched base with Enrico Dante, a huge bear of a man who handled Carolla's finances in Palermo. Dante had been the instigator of the purchase of many of the properties in and around Luciano's territory. He worked under cover at the Armadillo Club, a small, seedy night-club with a warren of rooms, a bar and a dance floor the size of a postage stamp. He looked after a string of call girls and laundered the narcotics money. Massive amounts of untraceable cash in every currency were stashed in the safe.

Dante could not help but notice the well-dressed American boy who sat at the bar, sipping orange juice. The barman had tipped Dante off that the boy was asking for him, but he waited and watched, making no move to speak to him. Luka returned three times before Dante agreed to see him, and was taken aback when he learned that Luka was Paul Carolla's son. He wanted to know if the package they were interested in had been traced.

After an elaborate detour, backtracking and changing cars three times, Luka arrived back at the hide-out. He thoroughly enjoyed the cloak and dagger aspects of the situation. This time he was shaking with excitement; he had the information his father was so desperate for – he knew where Lenny Cavataio was.

Carolla was sweating, constantly wiping his forehead with the back of his hand. Cavataio was holed up in a private hotel, guarded by four men round the clock. It was going to be a bitch to get to him with only a handful of men. The two men he assigned to the job were not eager to accept; to try for a hit in a public place when the entire city was swarming with police was madness. How were they even going to get into the hotel?

Carolla screamed that they could fly through the fucking window for all he cared, but Cavataio must be taken care of. In truth, Carolla was beginning to doubt that he would be able to escape from Sicily, and with Cavataio alive he was in real trouble. The two men departed on foot, heading down the three miles of dirt track from the farmhouse. They had gone more than a mile when they heard soft footsteps behind them.

'I can get you into the hotel, I can even book a room. Who's gonna give me a second look?'

Luka smiled. His face in the darkness seemed as if lit by the whiteness of his hair. The men turned away, not interested.

'It's an order, you take me with you.'

The two men walked on, taking no notice, but neither did they tell him to go back. Like a shadow, Luka followed.

The horrific murder of Lenny Cavataio had been carried out in such a way that it had to be Mafia-organized. The headlines in the papers said that a suspect had been taken into custody and was being questioned. The article went on to state how Cavataio was the main witness against the wanted Paul Carolla, the supposed 'Boss of Bosses', still presumed to be hiding out in the mountains, and that the search for the Mafia leader was being stepped up.

Roberto Luciano read and reread the article, then dropped the paper in the waste basket. His hands were clenched at his sides, his mouth a thin, tight line of fury. He should have ensured Cavataio's safety himself, doubled up the guard with his own men if necessary; this should never have been allowed to happen. In front of him, as if reproaching his father with pale, wide eyes, was his dead son's face. Luciano picked up the silver-framed photograph and kissed the cold glass, swearing that Carolla would not get away, no matter if he had to go into the mountains himself. The noise of helicopters above the house brought him quickly to his feet. He looked out of the window, but the sound subsided as they passed the villa.

The helicopters were heading for Carolla's hide-out. Four armoured trucks were travelling overland; twenty-five officers, all armed, surrounded the farmhouse. One of Carolla's men, caught after the Cavataio murder, had talked.

Luka Carolla, making his way back to his father, was stopped by armed *carabinieri*. They searched his car, checked his passport and told him to head back to the main road: no traffic was allowed beyond the roadblock.

He returned to Palermo, looking up as the helicopters passed overhead. His father, he reckoned, didn't stand a chance. He wondered who to turn to for help. He

arrived at the Armadillo Club as the police opened fire
on the farmhouse.

Carolla offered little opposition, coming out of the
ramshackle building with his hands above his head. The
police discovered that even in hiding he had been
organizing drug runs. Although they found no bulk
heroin, there were obvious signs of a refinery having
been in one of the barns recently.

Carolla believed that with Cavataio gone half the charges
would be dropped. But his confidence diminished rapidly
as the charges mounted up and he became aware of how
much damage Buscetta had done. Cavataio's allegations
about his complicity in Michael Luciano's murder were
nothing in comparison; Carolla was being charged on
more than fifty counts of blackmail, extortion, murder,
fraud and narcotics trading. When his arrest made the
headlines, more people came forward and accused him
of further crimes.

Never had so many defendants been held in the cages
at one time. The figure stood at four hundred and fifty-
three and was rising daily. The press announced, in
blazing headlines, that the forthcoming trial would
herald the end of the Mafia's stronghold on Sicily.

More and more law enforcement officers were shipped
into Palermo as the sweeping arrests continued. The
courthouse was to be specially built to protect not only
those on trial but the judges, lawyers and witnesses. Too
late, Paul Carolla realized his mistake in returning to
Sicily.

*

Mario Domino entered the Don's study. It was almost ten o'clock at night, but he had come without question when he received the call. Domino knew that if his presence was required it was obviously something that could not be discussed over the phone.

Luciano stood with his back to the room, staring into the empty fireplace. Domino unbuttoned his coat and tossed it over the back of a chair, saying nothing, simply waiting to be spoken to.

'What are his chances?'

Without asking, Domino knew he was referring to Carolla.

'He's hired the best men money can buy and, I may be wrong but I doubt it, they will withdraw the murder charge. Without Cavataio or any other witnesses the statement will be dismissed as hearsay. He will not be able to sidestep all the other charges, there are more than fifty . . . I'd say he'll get life.'

Luciano turned. His face was grey, the lines more deeply etched than ever. 'Would you, my old friend, put your life on it? You read the papers today – perhaps it was all premature. More witnesses have disappeared, statements are being withdrawn. He's clawing his way out of the cage.'

Domino hesitated a moment. 'Even if they don't put him away for life here, the United States will want him after our courts are through with him. They'll get an extradition order, that I guarantee.'

Luciano sat behind his desk, rested his chin on his hands. He gave a strange smile; there was no humour in his dark eyes. Domino had to strain to hear his soft voice as he said, 'I want you to call the prosecution counsel, tell him he has a new witness, one who will not be afraid to take the stand, who will not be frightened off. I will ensure that Paul Carolla will rot to death behind bars.'

Paul Carolla's confidence was severely deflated when his chief lawyer, Dr Ulliano, arrived on an unscheduled visit. He was very disturbed; he had heard a rumour, from a very reliable source, that the prosecution had a new witness. Not Buscetta; this was someone who was being held under wraps for his own protection. This someone, so the rumour went, had been allocated an army on a round-the-clock basis. Whoever it was had to be high ranking, perhaps even above Buscetta. But as yet they had no name, the security measures were so tight. The prosecution were asking for an extra week before the scheduled start of the trial to accommodate the new witness's evidence.

Carolla instructed his lawyers to find out the man's name. Legally, it was his right to defend himself; surely they could not allow an undisclosed witness to take the stand. He offered any amount of money to assist them. 'If the guy's got an army protecting him, that's the easiest way to trace him. One of them, just one, is all we need to get him.'

Ulliano spoke sharply to Carolla, his veiled threat ominous. 'Signor Carolla, if we discover this man's identity for our own legal case, and anything directly connected to you should happen to him, then we will hold ourselves responsible. Do you understand? It is imperative that we have your word as a man of honour that you will not instigate any violence or harassment of this witness.'

Carolla lifted his hands in a submissive gesture. 'Just

find out who he is. Like you said, you're working for my defence, so defend me. I am innocent of all charges, I am innocent.'

Deep down, Carolla knew who it was, but actually feared to even say his name. He was afraid that, if it were Don Roberto Luciano, his chance of freedom was over. If Luciano now had proof of Carolla's part in Michael's murder, the Organization would also know that he had lied to them. No matter how many years had passed, their rules, by which many Sicilian families in particular would still abide, made Carolla a marked man, inside jail or out. He knew it was imperative to get messages in and out without his legal advisers knowing, and there was not much time. He had to discover the identity of the witness.

He was still engrossed in his own thoughts when the guard tapped on his cell door to say he should go out for exercise as the cleaner wished to do his cell. The cleaner, Frank Paluso, waited as the jailer unlocked the door. In comparison with most of the cells Carolla's was exceptionally comfortable. He paid highly for the extras, but then unlike many prisoners he could afford them. As he reached into his wardrobe, one of the many privileges, for his coat, the cleaner entered with duster, mop and clean bed linen, Carolla's own expensive pure cotton sheets. Outside the cell the guards were talking to another prisoner while they waited for Carolla.

He spoke to the cleaner, low and fast. 'You name your price. I need to get messages out, and returned to me.'

The mop swished and soaked Carolla's shoes. The man didn't even look up from his work. Carolla reached out and yanked the mop from the man's hands, pushed him hard against the wall.

The cleaner was unafraid, meeting Carolla's snarling face with a disdainful look. His voice was steady. 'I heard you, Signor Carolla, and I would prefer to clean the sewers than assist a man who sells death on the streets, peddles junk to young kids not even out of school. May you rot in hell.'

Carolla spat, 'Nobody speaks to me like that, nobody! You motherfucker, you prick . . .' He was unceremoniously hauled out of the cell, shouting so everyone nearby could hear him, 'I want that guy's name, I want that guy's name . . .'

During exercise, Carolla asked everyone the name of the prison cleaner, the man who had been in his cell. He was told that Frank Paluso was in fact the owner of the small company that cleaned the entire prison. He had firmly refused any bribes during the two years he had been contracted to the Unigaro jail and courthouse. It appeared that Carolla was not the only inmate trying to send messages out. Carolla smirked, saying that everyone had a price. He would get the little bastard to run his errands.

The following day, Dante came to visit. He found Carolla fluctuating between rage and deep, sullen depression. Carolla demanded that Dante do something about the prison cleaner, he needed him, needed more freedom to contact people, and he could not do it through his lawyers. Every visitor was body-searched both coming in and going out, therefore Dante could not carry messages. But Dante also knew that Frank Paluso could not be bought.

Carolla seethed. 'He's got a family, hasn't he? He's

got a wife an' kids? So, he don't like my money, then make him so fuckin' scared he'll do whatever I want him to . . .'

Frank Paluso's youngest son, Juan, aged nine, was shot outside his own home. A car pulled up, a man called the child over to the car and fired at point-blank range. The boy died instantly. The story made the headlines, and not just in Palermo. Dante was terrified, shaking with fear, when one of Carolla's lawyers called to say that his client wished to see him. Dr Ulliano asked if Dante had heard of the tragic murder and Dante commiserated, but said nothing that could implicate Carolla or himself.

Carolla was sitting chewing on a cigar, and Dante noticed that his head jerked spasmodically.

'I brought you some cakes.'

'I'm supposed to thank you? You crazy sonofabitch, what the fuck d'you think you're doing, huh? Who the fuck gave the order to take the kid out? I can't show my face outta this fuckin' cell now, because they put it down to me, an' they got fuckin' guards, three at a time, cleanin' the cells. Any chance I got of sending anythin' out is fucked . . . Jesus Christ!'

Dante swallowed, trying to control his shaking hands. Carolla looked at him. 'You hired someone, didn't you? Who was it? Just who was it? They can't put this down to me, the bastards can't put this down to me. It comes down on my fuckin' head an' I swear to Christ I'll drag you into it.'

Dante was sweating now, and Carolla banged the partition between them with the phone. 'Who was it?'

'I couldn't do it, Paulie, you know I've never had the stomach for that sort of thing.'

'Who did you send? *Who?*'

Dante stuttered, the sweat from his hands making the phone slimy to touch. 'He said he would take care of it, he said he knew what had to be done.'

'*Who . . . ?*'

Dante's voice was a hoarse whisper. 'It was your son, Luka.'

Carolla's eyes bulged, he caught his breath and jolted back as the bell rang shrilly for the visitors to leave. Carolla gabbled that Dante had to get Luka out of the country, send him back to the States, but at all costs keep him away from the jailhouse. There must never be a connection, no one must ever know . . .

But Dante missed the last part as the phones were cut off. All he could see was Carolla's mouth flapping behind the glass partition.

Part Two

CHAPTER 16

Sophia Luciano sat beside her husband, Constantino, watching his driving, knowing that within moments they would reach the brow of the hill from where they could see the sprawling Villa Rivera.

She knew soon that he would tell their sons they were 'home'; it always annoyed her slightly that her husband referred to his father's house as 'home' when they had lived in Rome for the past eight years and had their own spectacular apartment, but she said nothing.

Constantino stopped the car. From their position on the brow of the hill they could see the striped awnings of the marquee, already erected for the wedding.

'Is something wrong?' asked Sophia.

'They must be workmen, see them? On the roof, around the gates.'

Sophia shaded her eyes and replied, 'There'll be a lot of people, darling. They must be completing the marquee, caterers, gardeners. You know Mama will want only the best.'

*

Graziella Luciano was already waiting on the porch, as immaculate as ever with her grey hair coiled in a bun at the nape of her neck.

The guards were opening the fifteen-foot-high wrought-iron gates. As her son's car continued up the long driveway, she waved to acknowledge their arrival, but at the same time gave a curt order to the florist to space the floral displays a little further apart and reminded him that everything had to be completed before five o'clock.

The boys ran from the car and into their grand-mother's arms. Her face wreathed in smiles, her blue eyes warm and brimming with tears, she hugged her grandchildren.

Graziella linked her arm through her son's and smiled a welcome to her daughter-in-law. Sophia blew a kiss with her fingertips and instructed the maid to take care with the wedding gown, which was draped in sheets to keep it clean.

Sophia could hear the boys in the bedroom below. She would have preferred them to be on the same floor as herself, but knew better than to question Graziella's arrangements. She began to unpack the cases, which were already neatly stacked at the foot of the bed.

Sophia snapped open the locks of her case, angry with herself because every time she came here she was reminded of Michael. Over the years Sophia had delib-erately learned where each silver-framed image was placed, so she could never be taken unawares, never be shocked by seeing him.

At that moment Constantino walked in, closed the

door and watched her, smiling. Her curvaceous body was so often hidden beneath her perfectly cut and draped clothes; now she was barefoot and wore only a silk underslip. Her movements were fluid, like a dancer. It never failed to arouse him when he saw her like this.

'You need any help?'

'No, just watch the boys don't get too unruly.'

'Mama's with them, she's bought them new Action Men.'

'She spoils them.' Sophia inspected an outfit she was thinking of wearing for the wedding.

'She loves them.'

She smiled. 'I love you.'

He went to her, but she sidestepped him, laughing.

'No, let me unpack. Your Papa will be home shortly.'

Constantino caught her in his arms and kissed her neck. 'Take your hair down.'

'No, just let me do what I have to do.'

He released her and flopped across the bed. 'It's going to be a full house, and guess what? They are actually using Michael's room.'

Sophia almost dropped a coat hanger. 'What?'

Constantino put his hands behind his head and smiled. 'Yep, the groom is to be in Michael's room. You know, this will be the first time in God knows how many years that we've been all together. I'm looking forward to it, maybe lay a few ghosts to rest.'

'You mean Michael?' Sophia could have bitten her tongue.

'Michael? No, I wasn't thinking of Michael. I know Alfredo and his wife feel slighted that they don't play more of a part in the business; but with the wedding no doubt Teresa will feel happier.'

'What about Frederico's blonde bomber?'

Constantino laughed. 'I think the least said about her the better. What the hell made him marry her I'll never know.'

'Well, he's not actually every woman's dream, darling.' She caught sight of his face in the wardrobe mirror, saw the flash of anger. He was always this way if she said a word against any member of his precious family. God forbid that she would ever say one thing against his parents. 'Where is Don Roberto?' she asked.

He rolled off the bed. 'Mama said he was caught up with some business in town. Should be home by f-f-five.' He stuffed his hands in his pockets and frowned. 'Something is going on. I've tried to c-contact Papa, he's selling off some of the companies, it doesn't make sense.'

Sophia noted the stammer and watched him. He rarely discussed business with her, but she knew he had been worried lately. 'Well, now is your chance to talk to him.'

He nodded and changed the subject. 'You think Mama looked OK?'

'Yes, why? Didn't you?'

Before he could answer, they heard the sound of a car horn. Sophia went to the window.

'It's Alfredo and Teresa. They almost ran in to Mama's flowers.'

Constantino said, 'I'd b-better go down,' but he stood there, his hands still deep in his pockets.

Sophia went to him and wrapped her arms around him. 'Your Mama is fine. She's maybe a little nervous, this is a big occasion and she has a lot to think about.'

He rested his head on the nape of her neck. 'You always smell so good, you know that? Sometimes I look at you when you don't know I'm there, and I still can't believe you're mine.'

She ran her fingers through his hair and cupped his face in her hands. 'If you like, I'll wait up here for you, and I'll let my hair loose . . .'

He drew away as the car horn sounded again, loudly. 'No, you'd better dress. Mama will want you downstairs.'

He hurried out and she heard him calling to his brother. From the window she watched.

Rosa Luciano was still collecting her things from the back of the Rolls-Royce.

Sophia was surprised to see how attractive the girl had grown; of course, she had had Rosa's detailed measurements to make the wedding gown, but it was years since she had seen her. She had inherited Alfredo's dark eyes and black, curly hair, and her features favoured her father rather than her mother.

Teresa made a move to speak to Graziella but was ignored. Sophia couldn't help but chuckle as she saw her sister-in-law make an embarrassed gesture to her crumpled skirt and jacket.

'Aunt Sophia . . . Aunt Sophia . . .' Rosa Luciano rushed into the room. 'Can I see my dress? Can I see it?'

Sophia moved quickly away from the window. 'Can you wait until it's pressed? I want you to see it at its best . . . You know, Rosa, you have grown into a beauty. Let me see you close.'

Rosa beamed, then tossed her head. 'Maybe you should wait until later, when the creases are out of me. We were delayed hours at the airport, and then Mama and Papa argued all the way because Papa insisted on driving, so Mama nearly had heart failure . . .'

405

Sophia kissed Rosa's lips. 'When one is as young as you, and a bride-to-be, there are no creases. They come with age, my darling, and you are as pretty . . .'

Rosa hugged her tight. 'Oh, Aunt Sophia, I am so happy I don't know what to do with myself.'

'I suppose your mother must be very happy.'

Rosa gave a lopsided grin. 'Are you asking me or telling me? You'd think it was Mama getting married, she's made such a fuss. You won't believe this, but she's started telling me the facts of life, keeps bringing me books on the reproductive organs, checking that my periods are regular. In the end I said, "Mama, I'm getting married, not going into labour."'

At that inopportune moment, Teresa walked in. She pursed her lips.

'Shouldn't you unpack, Rosa? You must take everything you want pressing down to Adina in the kitchen.'

Rosa jumped off the bed and winked at Sophia as she loped out of the room. Teresa sighed and crossed to Sophia; they kissed.

'She can never walk from a room, she's so ungainly. I hope you haven't made a dress with a long train, she'll fall head over heels.'

Sophia laughed and assured Teresa that the dress would be perfect.

'Can I see it?' Teresa asked.

'Mama has decided that all the women will spend the evening alone while the men go out. We can all see the dress then.'

Teresa pushed her thick glasses back to the bridge of her thin nose. 'You look very fit, slim as ever. Are the boys well? I hear they spend a lot of time here. How is Constantino?'

'Well, very busy . . . And you?'

Teresa ignored the question and continued, 'It's strange Don Roberto was not here to meet us, he usually is. Was he here when you arrived?'

'No, just Mama.'

'But then, you see her more often than we do.' Teresa's shortsighted eyes flicked around the room, noting everything, the clothes on their hangers, the neat array of shoes.

She had never been sure how many of the family knew the background to her own marriage. Now, with her daughter's marriage, she was confident they would no longer feel like poor relations.

'Well, I'll no doubt see you later. We are on the top floor, it's rather inconvenient what with having to help Rosa dress. I would have thought we'd have the room below yours, the big guest room.'

'Mama put the boys in there. We can keep an eye on them, hear them if they wake in the night.'

'Yes, she told me. Well, I'll unpack, not that it'll take me long. I see you have brought a veritable collection. Perhaps if my suit is not good enough, you could lend me something?'

Sophia mistakenly took the remark at its face value. 'You are welcome to choose anything . . .'

Teresa interrupted her curtly. 'Thank you, but I'm sure what I've brought will suffice.' She left the room.

Moyra Luciano was in floods of tears. Frederico was ready to explode. They had done nothing but argue on the drive from the airport, due to one little slip he had made. After listening to her worrying throughout the

407

entire plane trip whether or not she had brought the right clothes for the wedding, he had suggested that if she hadn't, she should ask Sophia, as she knew what was class. Moyra had taken it as an insult, because Frederico had insinuated that she had no class. The argument had then spiralled into the fact that he would never have married her if she hadn't been pregnant. No amount of reassurances would stop the build-up into her hysterical sobbing.

When he finally calmed her down, Moyra spent the rest of the journey repairing her make-up while trying out her Sicilian, which she had been learning for the past two years. She could understand the odd word, but as for speaking it . . . She fell quiet as they approached the Luciano home.

Frederico was equally nervous. Suddenly he sat up and beamed, his fat face wreathed in smiles.

'We're home, honey. Will ya look at that place, bathed in gold? How many times have I heard Papa say it reminds him of Mama's hair when she was a young girl . . . Golden hair Mama had . . .' Moyra touched her own bleached blonde curls and her stomach turned over.

Frederico's fawn-like eyes changed, became alert, watchful. There were a lot of men about the villa, some even on the roof. He began to count the small black figures. Then he saw his Mama, waiting, and he felt again like a little boy, so impatient for the gates to be opened. His fat hand rested on the door handle, and he opened it before the limo stopped.

'Mama . . . Mama!'

Graziella wept openly, 'I am so happy. Everyone is here; Constantino, Alfredo . . .'

'Where's Papa? He inside?'

Graziella turned to Moyra, her hand outstretched. 'Welcome, welcome . . .'

She did not kiss Moyra and, although apparently welcoming her, her manner was dismissive as she greeted the blushing woman, who stood awkwardly, wondering if she should try out her few words of Sicilian. But she did not get the opportunity as Frederico was drawn into the villa by his mother. He was immediately assaulted by his two nephews, bellowing that Uncle Frederico had arrived.

Next to arrive was Emilio Luciano, the groom, his young face bright pink with nerves. Among the congratulations, the back-slapping, the shouting and teasing, Graziella stood bursting with happiness. These were her boys, her sons, her grandsons. She seemed unaware of the mayhem; she just clapped her hands, hunching her shoulders coyly when one or another of her boys paid her an outrageous compliment.

'Who is this young woman, where's our Mama, eh? You telling me this beauty is our Mama? How come you don't age, huh?'

Poor Moyra remained standing in the hall. She had no idea where she was to sleep or where her cases had been taken to, and she could not understand a word that was said, they all spoke so fast and so loud. She was grateful when Teresa came down the stairs.

'Hi, I don't suppose you know where I can wash up, do you?'

'Hasn't Mama told you? It's always the same when they all get together, you can't hear yourself speak. Ask Mama.'

Hesitantly, Moyra teetered through the drawing-room doors.

'Freddy, which room are we in?'

'Mama, where we sleeping?' he shouted.

Graziella threw her hands up in apology. 'Come, Moyra, you must forgive me,' she said in English.

She ushered Moyra ahead of her as she hurried into the hall, calling for Adina to show their guest to her room. While they waited, she said, 'Moyra, for me, please call Frederico by his name not Freddy. I don't like it.'

She stood in the hall watching as Moyra and Adina went upstairs, tutting at Moyra's high, red slingback shoes and her too-tight and too-short skirt. She would never understand why her son had chosen this one; of all the girls he could have married he had brought this creature home.

Alone, Graziella's body seemed to sag. She sighed, a long, deep sigh; the tension of having to hide her feelings had exhausted her. He should have been home by now, he had said no later than five and it was already past that. The florists, the builders and decorators had all gone, the family had arrived, and still there was no sign of him. He always phoned if he was even fifteen minutes late, why hadn't he called, today of all days?

None of the family, sitting together in the cosy drawing room, had the slightest inkling that anything was wrong. Graziella joined them, giving nothing away. Smiling, she passed around more cakes and pastries.

'This is the first time we are all at home together, so that is what we celebrate tonight, the family.'

Moyra had changed her clothes. She slipped into the room just as Graziella finished speaking and perched on the arm of Frederico's chair. Sophia snapped her fingers at her eldest son to show his manners and give his seat to Aunt Moyra.

'No, er . . . *grazie*,' Moyra stuttered, but only Frederico noticed her attempt to speak Sicilian. He patted her knee, leaving a sticky fingerprint on her clean skirt.

Constantino became aware of his mother's frequent glances at the gold carriage clock on the big mantel. She kept a small smile on her face yet her eyes betrayed her nervousness.

'Are you worried about something?' he whispered, kissing her hand.

'Your Papa is late, I have dinner to prepare. Next thing I know, it's ruined.'

Frederico, wading his way through another slice of cake, asked loudly, 'Eh, Mama, what's with the army of guards out the front of the house?'

Graziella ignored the question. 'If you all wish to change, bathe, then we must come to some arrangement about the hot water. Sophia, you want to go first, see to the boys?'

One by one the sons of Don Luciano looked at each other. Something was wrong and they all knew it. Constantino gave Sophia a small nod of his head to take the boys out; putting her half-full teacup down, she called them and immediately left the room.

Alfredo looked hard at Teresa. She frowned, not understanding.

'Take Rosa up to finish unpacking, will you?'

It was not a request. Teresa put her cup down and

411

beckoned Rosa to go with her. Frederico nudged Moyra, who almost fell off the arm of the chair. 'Go and get yourself ready.'

'But I just changed and I've not had my tea.'

He gave her such a look that she scurried out. Alfredo closed the doors behind her while Graziella fussed with the tea tray.

'Papa w-w-worried about this trial, Mama?' asked Constantino. Graziella nodded, and then excused herself and left her sons together. Constantino walked slowly to the great stone fireplace and leaned against the mantel.

Alfredo shrugged. 'So what was all that about? The way she acted I thought she wanted to talk to us . . .'

Frederico gave Constantino a guarded look. 'Eh, Emilio, you wanna do me a favour? My cigars, I left 'em in my room. Get 'em for me, would you?' The young groom knew he was being asked to leave the brothers alone and he obeyed without question.

Frederico stood up and drew the curtains aside. He looked out at the drive, the guards on duty at the gate. 'What's goin' on? You think this trial business is gettin' to the old man? There's more guards out there than at the National Bank.'

'They got any of our guys?' asked Alfredo.

Frederico snorted. 'They got the rubbish, small-timers. Cages are filled to breaking point with every bum in Sicily. Nice way of cleaning up the garbage.'

'Paul Carolla's no small f-f-fish,' Constantino stammered.

Frederico gave him a strange look and dropped his easy manner. 'Eh, you think I don't know that? Word's out the bastard hired someone to hit his jailer's nine-year-old kid. He put pressure on the guy to take out

412

messages; when he refused, his son's head was shot off. Like to squeeze that cunt's balls.'

In comparison to Constantino, Frederico seemed uncouth. His portly, balding appearance and foul language made him seem older than his brothers. 'Hell of a time for a fuckin' wedding, guest list'll be cut by half. You think anyone wants to come over here right now? She's not havin' a kid, is she?'

Alfredo sprang to his feet, his face twisted with anger, but Frederico spoke first. 'Take it easy . . . But you gotta admit it's a hell of a time for a fuckin' wedding, unless that's the intention. We're all here, all under one roof, an' it looks like he hired a fuckin' army to guard us, so maybe he's worried. I know he was blazin' about Lenny Cavataio because it meant they dropped the murder charge . . .'

Alfredo, calmer now, lit a cigarette. 'Who's he?' He waited, but neither of his brothers answered. 'So who is this Lenny what did you call him?' he asked, a slight edge to his voice.

Frederico burped loudly and replied, 'Cavataio, used to deal in junk for Paul Carolla.'

Alfredo shrugged. He had never heard the name. Frederico realized that the stories about his brother must be true; rumour had it that their father had virtually manoeuvred him out of the business. Now he wondered if the reason the marriage was taking place was that their father intended moving young Emilio up to look after New York. Frederico was so immersed in his own thoughts that he didn't hear Constantino speak. He looked up.

'What . . .? What did you say?'

Constantino kicked at the grate, his hands stuffed

deep in his trouser pockets. 'I said have you talked to him lately? Only I've tried to make contact, few things need sorting out. He's sold two companies without even discussing it with me . . . It has to have something to do with this Cavataio business.'

Alfredo was getting pissed off, unable to follow what they were talking about. 'So who the fuck is this guy Lenny, for Chrissakes?'

Taking a cigar from the box on the coffee table, Frederico searched his pockets for his lighter. 'What you got upstairs, set of marbles? Lenny Cavataio was the guy who fed Michael the bad junk that killed him, I picked him up in Atlantic City, brought him here.'

Alfredo couldn't believe it. He waited impatiently while Frederico puffed his cigar alight.

'He wanted to make a deal. He'd been hidin' out in Canada for a decade, finally crawled out from the gutter to try an' blackmail Carolla. But Carolla wasn't takin' any crap; he tried to get Lenny wiped out. Last thing he wanted was old history raked up, especially as he'd got so high up in the Organization. Whole thing backfired on Carolla because he came to us, understand? Cavataio came straight to the very people Carolla was so desperate to keep him from.'

Alfredo still looked confused. Frederico paused, irritated by his brother's stupidity. 'You follow me? This gettin' through . . .? Carolla was goin' to be charged with Michael's murder. Lenny was singin' his head off, not only about the murder but everything else to do with Carolla's rackets. The Feds were on to him, New York drug squad, and the asshole ran right back to Palermo, hid in the mountains . . .' He laughed, shaking his head. 'Man, did he choose the wrong place.'

414

'So why have they dropped the murder rap? Because it's history or what?'

Frederico sighed, shaking his head at Alfredo as if he were dumb. 'You don't have newspapers in New York? Word is out you spend too much time at the race tracks, you should get your fuckin' act together. Lenny Cavataio was wiped out four months ago. He was found in a sleaze hotel here in Palermo with his balls cut off. Cops were supposed to be guarding him until the trial; they obviously fucked up, so the charges will be thrown out. His lawyers will scream circumstantial evidence.'

Alfredo stared at the thick carpet, 'You bastards should have told me.'

'Maybe you should have got off your arse,' Frederico snapped.

Constantino put up a hand. 'Come on, that's enough. We don't want to f-fight among ourselves. You know how Papa works, Alfredo, he likes to k-keep secrets.'

He was not as tough as Frederico, who said coldly, 'You been slack, Alfredo. Hear your wife kept on appearin' at the company, she was handlin' certain contracts. Papa didn't like that.'

'She's a *lawyer*! Teresa knows the import licences better than me!' He sighed, knowing he had no come-back. 'Ahh, what the hell, I never wanted to be in New York. You think this kid Emilio's gonna take my place?'

His brothers made no answer. Alfredo was close to tears. 'Papa never contacts me. He's been in New York and not even called to see me, and now this . . . No matter what I've done wrong, I should have been a part of this Lenny business. You should have brought me over.' He broke down and began to weep. Frederico tried to comfort him. 'Look, they got Carolla banged up on so many charges the odds are stacked against him. He'll never get free. They'll drop the murder rap, but in the end he's finished. Maybe it'll let Michael's ghost rest in peace. I hope so because, if you want the truth, I've had him on my shoulder too long.' Surprised, Alfredo looked up, wiping his face with the back of his hand.

Frederico gave him a quiet, boyish smile. 'It's the truth, may God forgive me. I've never been free of the perfect Michael, I could never match him in anything I did, and I was glad when Papa sent me to Atlantic City because there I didn't get him shoved down my throat . . .'

Constantino opened the liquor cabinet and poured himself a whisky. He downed it in one. 'I guess we were all in competition with him. Just take a look at the family album perched on the piano; you see me, Sophia, the kids, you see Alfredo, Rosa, Frederico . . . and there is Michael, always Michael, the biggest frame, the biggest photograph.'

Frederico chuckled, then his face lit up in a cheeky grin. 'I used to put his photo at the back; every day I did it. And every time back it would go, and there he was smiling at me, like he was sayin', "Fuck you, you don't get me out of your life that easily . . ."'

Alfredo snorted with laughter. 'I did the same thing, no kiddin'. I used to sneak around the house movin' his picture an' puttin' mine at the front. That's the God's own truth.'

Laughing, Constantino poured three glasses of whisky. 'Well, I want to propose a toast, just for us, a toast no one else will understand. Because maybe Frederico is right; they've got Paul Carolla, they've got

Michael's killer behind bars. He'll never be free, it's over.'

They clinked their glasses together. 'To Michael, may he rest in peace and leave us in peace.'

They drank, and Alfredo threw his empty glass into the stone fireplace. Constantino followed suit, then Frederico. They stood and stared guiltily at the shattered glass.

'Holy shit, Mama's gonna hit the roof. They were her b-b-best crystal.'

Carolla was led into the small interview room. He went straight to the counter and pressed his hand against the bulletproof glass partition. On the other side his son gave a slow smile and laid his hand flat against the glass. Carolla looked at his two guards, then back to his son, and whispered hoarsely into the mouthpiece, 'I know what you did and I want you out of Palermo. I don't want you near me, or near this place. You get out and you stay out, you hear me, Luka?'

Luka held the phone loosely. The only indication that he had heard his father was a slight arching of one of his fine, almost invisible, eyebrows.

When he spoke, his soft voice was a strange echo-like whisper. 'I know the name, I have the name, everything is going to be all right.' Luka put on a pair of mirrored sunglasses and waved a tiny scrap of paper.

Carolla's rat-like eyes darted this way and that. He turned yet again to see if the guards were listening. Could Luka possibly know the name of the witness? All he could see now was his own face reflected in the glasses, his fat, jowled, ugly face looked scared, even to him. He was scared of his own image.

Carefully, Luka straightened the piece of paper and laid it flat against the glass. In his strange, old-fashioned spidery writing he had scrawled the name of the witness for the prosecution.

Carolla's stomach lurched and his bile rose. He tasted it as he retched uncontrollably, but his eyes were riveted on that name: Don Roberto Luciano.

Don Roberto's driver radioed to the guards at the gates that they were arriving in minutes. The message was passed by walkie-talkies to the men on the roof, and the last part of the journey was closely monitored through field glasses.

The villa was ablaze with lights. As the car stopped, Don Roberto sat for a moment, waiting for the door to be opened. His eyes missed nothing . . . He had been giving statements since ten o'clock that morning, a gruelling, painstaking day, a day when memories flooded back and old wounds opened. But now he stood ramrod straight, inches taller than his bodyguards, and smiled.

He patted the man's cheek and murmured, '*Grazie.*' The front door opened as he walked up the white steps and onto the porch.

The family occupied every bedroom in the sprawling villa. There was not one of them who did not know, could not sense the presence. Don Roberto Luciano was home.

CHAPTER 17

DON LUCIANO'S family sat down to dinner. His sons, his daughters-in-law, his grandsons, his granddaughter, his nephew, all sat and talked loudly amongst themselves. Only the throne-like chair was empty, waiting for *Il Papa*.

Graziella was the first to know he was entering the room. Her chair, at the opposite end of the table to his own, was nearest the double oak doors. She saw his moment of shyness, saw his face flush with pleasure to see everyone and knew he was unsure how to greet them.

His sons rose to their feet to shake his hand. He kissed each one and then smiled a welcome to his daughters-in-law, calling them each by name 'Welcome, Sophia, Teresa, Moyra . . .' Then he looked at Rosa and gave her a private smile. 'The beautiful bride Rosa and my nephew Emilio, welcome.' The two young grandsons stared up at him, open-mouthed, and he cupped each face in his big strong hands and kissed them on the lips. 'And, last but not least, welcome to my special boys.'

Graziella lifted her glass in a toast. 'To Papa . . .'

They toasted their Papa and were surprised by his tears. 'You make me happy, it is good to have you all here. Now we eat before Mama's food goes cold.' He took out a clean handkerchief and blew his nose loudly. His youngest grandson copied him, using his napkin and making everyone laugh.

The Don was patient with Moyra, taking great care to speak English to her. She flushed, trying to reply in her halting Sicilian. He congratulated her, and Frederico beamed with pride.

The Don had a private word to say to everyone, making each feel special, whilst the wine flowed freely. Graziella brought out some crackers that had been left over from Christmas and they pulled them, with much shouting and laughter. The Don was the first to put the bright pink paper hat on his head. By the time the ice cream and sweets were served, the Don had one grandson on his lap and a black plastic moustache clipped to his nose. His other grandson was sitting on the arm of his chair, his arm around his grandpa's shoulders.

Only Graziella knew how tired her husband must be after spending so long with Emmanuel. No one else even detected so much as a hint of their Papa's intentions, or felt the slightest suspicion that their world was about to crash.

The following morning the Villa Rivera reverberated with the sounds of the family. Gifts for the bride and groom were being stacked in the drawing room as they arrived. There was a profusion of wedding bells and horseshoes, but only the Don and his wife knew that each parcel had been carefully inspected and rewrapped before being brought into the house. Only they knew why there were men on the roof, men in the orchards and in the stables, and more drafted in to check everyone who entered or left the premises against the list of staff hired to complete the wedding arrangements.

The same tight security enabled Giuliano Emmanuel, the prosecuting counsel, to feel secure in his own home. He was still tired from the previous night, having worked late over the Luciano tapes in the privacy of his own home. It was after ten o'clock when he drove to work, where the security was very much in evidence. It was a considerable time before he could even enter his own office, but he could not complain as the guards checked his identity papers, even though he was tired and irritable. He was the one who had instigated the security measures.

Closing his office door he tossed his briefcase on the desk. Without taking his coat off he poured himself a stiff Scotch and downed it, then poured another and topped it with soda. He carried his drink to his desk, put it down and threw his coat over the back of the chair.

He knew that if he felt drained the Don must feel even worse. They had decided on a weekend break to allow Emmanuel to write up the statements from the tapes. Their meeting places over the past few weeks had changed daily, the arrangements for getting the Don in and out of various buildings without being seen had become almost farcical. All the tapes had to be transcribed before they went to court and by then he had to have prepared a list of any problems with the earlier statements and any further questions.

Removing the tapes from his briefcase he pulled the tape recorder closer and loaded tape number four from the last session. The volume was too high, distorting the Don's voice, and he turned it down. Then he opened his notebook and switched on his word processor.

Emmanuel typed onto the screen: *Roberto Luciano, Statement 3, Tape 4. 12 February 1987.* He worked solidly until after twelve, rewinding the tape when he wanted to confirm or query something Luciano had said, continually cross-referencing and checking against statements he had already compiled from previous days. He tapped the execute key, tapped again; the screen had locked out. He could not execute or even exit from the programme.

Suddenly the screen flashed: *Power failure.* He sat in mute fury, refusing to believe the hated words, desperately wishing them away because, against all instructions, he had not backed up his disks or saved the changes he had made as he went along. The only thing he could do was to shut down the system to clear the hang-up, and lose all the work he had just done.

Swearing at his own stupidity, he reached for the switch as the telephone rang. The bell cut through his anger, startling him. As he reached for it, he knocked over his glass and, in trying to save it from falling to the floor, he dropped the telephone receiver. It smashed against the side of his desk.

He could hear his wife's voice from the dangling phone, asking if he was all right. Yelling for her to hold on, he grasped the telephone cord to pull the receiver up. The curly flex hooked on the edge of his desk and he swore yet again, running his fingers along the desk to release it. Suddenly he reacted as if he had been given an electric shock. He pulled his hand back.

His wife was shouting, 'Hello? You there? Hello?'

Emmanuel quickly picked up the receiver. 'I'll call you back . . . No, I'm fine, nothing's wrong. I'll call you later.'

Nothing wrong? Jesus Christ . . . He slammed the phone down and felt along the side of the desk, heart thudding. He trembled as he touched it again; he knew exactly what it was and he panicked, calling for the guard outside his door to come in. Then he ran to the door and yanked it open.

The man was at the far end of the corridor, holding a whispered conversation with another guard.

'Get in here! Move it!' Emmanuel yelled.

His office was bugged. How it had been done was immaterial, the most important thing was: when? How much of the Luciano tapes, his own phone calls, had been recorded? His face white with fury, nerves on edge, he stared at the word processor. Could someone have tampered with it? Even worse, accessed his disks?

The women were going to do some last-minute shopping. Rosa, who had refused the invitation, was sitting in the garden with Emilio. They looked so young, perhaps too young to be getting married.

As the car passed them, they waved. Only then did Sophia see the car moving into position close behind theirs. She still didn't realize that they were being followed, not until they had left the villa and passed the guards on duty at the gates, when they all understood the extent of the security arrangements for their innocent shopping expedition. All Graziella would say to their questions was that it was what Papa wanted, that the extra hands could be useful for carrying their purchases.

'They had a guard sitting up front with the driver, and then another car trailing them with two more guys. OK, so Papa's uptight about the trial, but they're all round the place, it's like Fort Knox.'

Constantino shrugged. He did not put into words his own thoughts but he had, like Frederico, been very aware of the security measures.

They could not discuss it further as their father appeared. To his sons' astonishment he was wearing a pair of carpet slippers.

'Alfredo's discovered that old motorbike of his. Do you know, he's got that engine ticking over! It was rusty, not been used for ten years, but he's fixed it.' The Don said it with such an air of amazement that Constantino laughed.

'Don't you remember, Papa, he could take any engine apart and put it back together again before he was twelve years old.'

'Ah, yes, you get old, you forget.'

Frederico nudged his brother to broach the subject of the guards. Constantino opened his mouth to ask but the sound of a motorbike revving up turned their attention to the far end of the verandah as Alfredo roared up on the old bike. He stopped beneath them and looked up, his face streaked with oil, his hands black to the elbow.

'You wanna see this thing move? It's a Harley, they're indestructible. Eh, you want a ride, Papa?'

Alfredo didn't dream that his father would agree, but

424

asked as if it were a dare, not really caring one way or the other. When Luciano did agree he became protective, suggesting that perhaps he should watch. But nothing would dissuade his father, he insisted.

Lifting his leg, he sat awkwardly on the pillion. 'You think I'm too old? I ever tell you about the time Michael and I rode into town on his Lambretta?'

He saw the way Alfredo's face changed as he turned away and snapped, 'I am not Michael, Papa, and this is a motorbike. You wanna ride or not?'

Gently the Don put his arms around his son's waist. 'You take care of me, now . . .'

Round and round the garden went the old Harley. Their Papa, his hair standing on end, clung to Alfredo, yelling with sheer enjoyment, waving as they passed the verandah for the third time. 'This is wonderful! It's wonderful!'

At four-thirty in the afternoon the women returned from the town to find Constantino and Frederico sitting on the verandah while Alfredo played tennis on the lawn with the two boys and their grandfather. Graziella noticed that one of her beribboned floral arrangements was looking very bedraggled, with telltale loose soil around the base, but she said nothing.

Nunzio, the younger child, saw his grandmother and ran to the verandah steps. 'Grandpa's been on the motorbike, Grandmama – and he fell off!'

Graziella gasped and Frederico laughed. 'He's fine, Mama . . .'

Don Roberto called the boys back and demonstrated a service, scattering balls all over the lawn. It was all so

425

relaxed that even one of the guards had been cajoled into acting as ball boy. The Don called to Graziella, 'You know, this boy is a brilliant mechanic. He repaired that old motorbike.'

Don Roberto pulled his son into his arms. 'I love you . . . Maybe I've been too hard on you, but we'll work it out. You are my son.'

Alfredo could not remember ever feeling happier. His brothers, watching them from the verandah, felt relieved and united.

Constantino asked Frederico if he had had something to do with it, if he had talked to their father about Alfredo. But Frederico shook his head. There had been little time for privacy, let alone to discuss his brother.

'No, but he's different, don't you feel it? The way he keeps on saying he's getting old . . . Maybe he's gonna hand over the reins, it's not before time.'

'Mmmm . . . Maybe that's what he's gonna tell us tonight.'

Frederico nodded. 'Yeah, maybe, an' tonight we ask him about this army he's got surrounding the place. Must be costing a fortune.'

Graziella smiled at her immaculately dressed husband as she carefully tied his bow tie. 'You'll tell them tonight?'

'Yes, tonight.'

She patted the lapel of his dinner jacket into place, even though it sat perfectly. 'You have been wonderful with the boys, especially Alfredo. He loves you so. They all do, and maybe what you've decided has made you feel free to show your love.'

'It is time Michael rested in peace. Maybe they won't love me too much once they know of my decision.'

There was a hardness to his face. Was all his care and attention to his sons simply to pave the way for what he had chosen to do? Her throat felt dry and she blinked back her tears.

'They were his brothers, they'll understand. And they will stand by your decision, as I do.'

'They have no option.' Gently he touched her face, cupping her chin in his hand. 'Don't be afraid, Mama, and don't tell the women; not yet. Let their men, my sons, tell them. That is the way it should be.'

Graziella called to the women that the men were leaving. Chattering and laughing, they waved casual goodbyes. In a way they were anxious for the men to be gone so they could be alone. Sophia was about to unveil the wedding gown so there was much excitement.

Constantino's two boys, already bathed and changed into matching pyjamas for bed, shouted from the top of the stairs. Constantino made them promise to be good. Seeing their shining faces and damp hair sent him leaping up the stairs two at a time for another hug and a kiss goodnight. Constantino was the last to leave the villa.

Sophia took Rosa upstairs to try on the wedding gown while Moyra and Teresa unwrapped the gifts and put them on display in the dining room. Graziella settled the two boys into the big double bed, tucking the sheets around them and listening to their prayers.

427

The evening was warm and she left the shutters open slightly, noticing as she did so that the guards were gathering at the gates. She checked her watch; it was eight-fifteen, they were not due to change over until after ten o'clock. Just then Rosa's excited voice called out that she was ready. They all hurried to the hall and waited for Rosa to come down the stairs.

Slowly, Rosa walked to the head of the stairs. The waiting women gasped. The bodice was low-cut with a wide, scooped neck, the long, tight sleeves reached a point at her wrists, and her tiny waist was emphasized by tight lacing and a full, hooped skirt reminiscent of a Victorian gown. The heavily frilled hem was cut slightly higher at the front and trailed on the floor at the back. The material was cream satin, shimmering with thousands of tiny seed pearls stitched into a daisy pattern to enhance the daisies of the headdress which would support the veil. It was a fairy-tale gown, perfect for Rosa's dark, pretty looks.

The deep neckline displayed her figure well and added a sensual quality. Teresa knew, in this moment, that her little girl was gone; before her stood a stunning young woman.

Brimming with happiness, Rosa proceeded down the stairs. The skirt swayed, moving with her, and there would be no problems with the train.

She lifted her hands to her flushed cheeks. 'Oh, Mama, I feel so good.'

Emmanuel insisted that his wife and little daughter be given top security and leave Palermo that night. His first priority was his family, and he was terrified that they would be kidnapped.

His office was swarming with police officers trying to discover how the bug had been planted despite the tight security net. They began to sift carefully through the records of every police officer who had been on duty in the past few weeks. Emmanuel had given orders that they all be suspended from duty and a new team put on the case. All the other prosecution counsellors were contacted and their offices checked.

Emmanuel was beside himself. He took the head of the security force aside. The closely guarded secret of his prize witness's identity was now known and it was obvious he was in great danger.

The stony-faced chiefs were overtly evasive when he insisted on giving orders, and he found their procedures tortuously slow. No one would admit to being at fault, insinuating that the entire affair had been mishandled from the beginning. There were arguments and criticisms flying from all quarters, until Emmanuel shouted that if anything were to happen to Roberto Luciano, if so much as a hair of his head were touched, he would hold the police responsible.

It was after nine that evening when Emmanuel received a detailed list of the men allocated to protecting Roberto Luciano. They were trusted men, but the extra guards brought in by the Don could not be verified. Emmanuel had already emphasized the dangers of discussing the situation with anyone but the Don, which delayed the process, until he took it upon himself to be the bearer of the bad news.

Emmanuel knew the entire family was at the Villa Rivera, which relieved him somewhat as he felt the Don, surrounded by his sons, would be safe. Graziella at first refused to tell him the name of the restaurant the men had gone to, even though she knew who he was. He took great care not to frighten her, keeping his voice calm, almost casual, but he was in a catch-22 situation, unaware of how much Signora Luciano knew. He could only say that it was a matter of grave urgency, it was imperative that he contact the Don personally.

When he finally obtained the number of the San Lorenzo restaurant, he tried unsuccessfully to get through. The line was constantly engaged. Frustrated, wishing he had not taken on the responsibility himself, he decided that the safest, to his mind the only, choice left to him was to go and speak to Luciano in person. By this time it was ten-fifteen.

The Don had chosen his favourite restaurant for two reasons. He was, in fact, the owner, and knew the staff; he also knew that the private upstairs room was easy to guard. The main part of the restaurant was closed for the night, and the doors would be locked after their arrival.

Don Luciano had ordered that only a skeleton staff be on duty. The bodyguards would eat downstairs and the drivers, instructed not to leave the cars for even a second, were to return for them at twelve-fifteen. They were not to wait outside because the cars were well known.

The men did not enter the private dining room until

430

the bodyguards had searched it carefully. They did not sit down to dine at the ornate table until nine o'clock.

Having installed his family in a 'safe house', Emmanuel had a long drive ahead of him. He headed for the San Lorenzo restaurant.

After only ten miles, one of his back tyres blew out. The car careered out of control and, with his nerves in shreds, Emmanuel fought it onto the hard shoulder. His hands shook and he had to sit and talk himself down; it was only a tyre, only a blown tyre ... But he was convinced someone had taken a shot at him.

His heart beating fast, he eased the door open. His mouth was dry, his breathing heavy. Then he sighed with relief. It was just a tyre.

Graziella could not join in the banter about who was wearing what for the wedding. She went over and over her conversation with Emmanuel in her mind – was something wrong? Why was it so urgent? Then she pushed it from her mind. She was tired, it had been a busy, full day, and tomorrow would be even busier. The caterers were due at seven in the morning. As meticulous as she was about everything, she wanted to greet them and oversee all that had to be done.

Moyra was teasing Rosa, saying she should be in bed, she needed her beauty sleep. The clock on the landing chimed again and Graziella checked her watch, then collected the coffee cups and stacked them on the tray. Sophia told her to sit down and relax, offering to clear up, but Graziella insisted.

As she held the door open for her mother-in-law, Sophia said softly, 'And I suppose, Mama, you will just pop up and check on those grandsons of yours?'

Laughing, Graziella said over her shoulder that Sophia had read her mind.

At fifteen minutes past eleven a truck driver stopped to help Emmanuel. They eased the ruined wheel off the car and examined the spare by torchlight. It looked very flat.

Quietly, Graziella opened the door of the children's bedroom. They lay facing each other, Nunzio's arm resting protectively across his brother. They looked so tiny in the big double bed, so peaceful and innocent that she couldn't help but smile.

Satisfied they were sleeping, she was about to close the door again when she heard a sound as if a slate were falling from the roof. Creeping to the window she found the shutter was open wider than she had left it. She glanced across the lawn towards the main gate.

In the darkness she could see the tips of the guards' cigarettes like small, glowing dots. They were waiting for the Don's return. As she silently closed the shutter, the latch banged and she caught her breath, afraid she had woken the boys. She turned towards the bed.

Neither child had stirred; they lay in exactly the same position. In the dim light she could see a dark area on the pillow between their heads. Puzzled, she moved closer, until she was standing over the little boys.

The dark stain was seeping into the pillows, between their faces.

Rosa was at the open drawing-room door, giggling at Moyra's teasing, when the terrible scream tore through the house. She was the first to see the stricken, terrified face of her grandmother, her eyes wide with horror, chest heaving, at the top of the stairs.

Sophia rushed past Rosa and was half-way up the stairs before the girl could move.

'Mama, Mama, *what is it?*'

Graziella dragged at Sophia's arm, trying to stop her passing, pleading, sobbing for her not to go into the room.

'What is it, Mama.' What is it?' Teresa could get no answer and she made to follow Sophia when the awful, low moan erupted into a high-pitched shriek, '*My babiesss!*'

Through the open door they could all see the dreadful sight of Sophia lying across the bed, clinging to her sons, their limp bodies beneath her on the bloodstained pillow. They had each been shot in the temple, and the killer had turned their little faces towards each other, hiding the bullet wounds, and slipped Nunzio's arm around his brother.

Now their wounds could be seen. The blood matted their hair, drenching their mother as she sobbed uncontrollably, willing them to be alive, shaking them, fighting Graziella away. She would let no one near her, let no one touch her.

*

Emmanuel waited while the tyre was inflated. The garage mechanic watched the air gauge, bent down to feel the tyre. Satisfied, he began to unscrew the pump. Emmanuel paced up and down, checked his watch. It was almost eleven-thirty.

The Don's driver banged on the restaurant door. He could hear the recording of Pavarotti singing Puccini's *Turandot* while he waited. It was playing loudly, and he stepped back to look up at the brightly lit second-floor windows.

The second driver arrived and waited with him while he knocked again. He knew something was wrong, one of the bodyguards should have opened the door by now, or at least a waiter.

The back door of the restaurant was also locked. Lights streamed from the kitchen windows. The Pavarotti tape continued, seeming even louder now as panic rose in the two men. They kicked at the main door, then fired shots into the lock until it gave way.

The door swung open. Nothing in the empty restaurant seemed out of order; the checked tablecloths and the cutlery were all ready for opening up the next day. No chairs were overturned, nothing was disturbed. But there were no bodyguards, no staff.

The drivers stood together with guns drawn. The first man inched towards the door marked 'kitchen'. It swung back and forth on its hinges as he kicked it.

Pans of spaghetti sauce had been carefully removed from the still-lit hobs. Dirty dishes were stacked in an old-fashioned stone sink and black refuse bags were half-filled, as if someone had been in the process of clearing the rubbish and had just left it for a moment. Had they? It seemed that any moment the chef would walk in, brandishing a wooden spoon, singing along with Pavarotti, whose recorded voice still echoed around the deserted kitchen. The two men said not a word, their panic growing with every passing second. The back door was bolted and barred from the inside.

Emmanuel inserted the coin. At last there was a ringing tone and he waited. His fingers drummed on the window of the phone booth, willing someone to answer. He waited.

The telephone was ringing. The sound, coupled with the operatic aria, was eerie, but before they reached it the ringing stopped.

Once again they looked around the empty restaurant as they made their way up the narrow staircase one behind the other. It was not wide enough for them to walk side by side.

Emmanuel pounded the side of the kiosk with his fist. Unable to get an answer from the restaurant, he had again tried to reach Luciano at the Villa Rivera, but the line was engaged. Frustrated, he ran to the car and drove out of the garage, heading for the San Lorenzo restaurant.

*

Pavarotti finished his aria, which was followed by frenzied, taped applause. He thanked his audience, '*Grazie . . . grazie . . .*' The tape ended as they reached the door of the private dining room. There was silence.

The door was locked from the outside with an old iron catch. The men stood shoulder to shoulder as they inched the latch up and eased the bolt back. They waited a beat, then, with a small nod of confirmation, they were ready.

Guns drawn, they kicked the heavy oak door. It creaked, swung open, then started to close. The first man pushed with his shoulder, his breath hissing. Then he whispered, 'Oh, sweet Jesus . . .'

The intimate dining room was lit by two candelabra on the table and dimmed electric candles around the walls. The red velvet curtains matched the dark-red carpet. The heavy, high-backed oak chairs threw shadows on the rough white walls and on the men still seated in them. What faced them as they entered was a nightmare, a terrible, frozen tableau.

Don Roberto Luciano, at the head of the table, was slumped slightly to one side, his hand still clutching an upright glass of wine. His body was propped up by the high back of the winged chair. On his right, Constantino was sitting well back in his chair, his head turned as if speaking to his father. On the Don's left, Alfredo had fallen across the table, his red wine spilling across the white cloth. Frederico leaned towards Alfredo, his face distorted in a grimace that might have been taken for laughter.

The young bridegroom, Emilio, had obviously risen from the table before he died. He had fallen forwards, then slipped to his knees. The glass of wine that he had perhaps been lifting in a toast lay smashed at his feet. One hand still grasped pathetically at the tablecloth.

Somehow the Don's driver, a man who had been with him for fifteen years, forced himself to check each body. He knew they were dead, but he made himself do it before he broke down, sobbing. Tears streamed down his face in helpless grief. Don Roberto had been like a father to him and he stared at the body, willing him to be alive, willing the nightmare to be some kind of fantasy . . .

Mario Domino, the Don's lawyer and friend for forty years, arrived at the restaurant at the same time as the police. The atmosphere was one of stunned silence. No one could believe what had taken place or voice their feelings.

Sitting in his car, the door wide open, Emmanuel's face was ashen. His hands still gripped the steering wheel. He had been the one to contact Mario Domino.

As Domino approached him, Emmanuel turned. He had to lick his lips before he could speak. In deep shock, his words hardly made any sense. It was not until Domino led him up the narrow staircase to witness it for himself that he realized the extent of the tragedy.

The bodies awaited the arrival of the medics and forensic officers, so the tableau remained intact. Domino bowed his head and sank to his knees. He would remember afterwards how everyone there followed him, how, to a man, they knelt in prayer. Each of them had known the still figure at the top of the table in his own special way.

Luciano, in death as in life, remained a powerful sight.

His open eyes seemed to blaze not with agony but with anger, as if he had known his killer.

As Domino approached the villa, he could see police patrol cars surrounding it. Lights blazed from every window. He put on speed, afraid someone had told Graziella the tragic news before him.

When he learned about Luciano's grandsons, the shock was too much for him and he broke down. He had to weep, release his grief, before he could go to her, tell her there was more tragedy, more death.

The ambulance doors were open and two small figures on stretchers, covered with sheets, were being carried from the house. Uniformed and plain-clothed policemen were everywhere.

Domino walked into the house without being stopped or questioned. He stood in the brightly lit hall; every room seemed filled with men, every door stood wide open. Totally disorientated, he looked helplessly for a face he recognized and was relieved to see Luciano's own physician walking slowly down the stairs.

The man's face was grey. Seeing Domino, he gave a sad shake of his head. 'Why?' he said quietly. 'Who could do such a thing?'

Domino took his arm and drew him to one side. 'You'd better stay, they'll need you. Where is Graziella?'

'Mario.' It was Graziella's voice.

Domino turned to see her standing half-way up the staircase. He held the doctor's arm a moment before going to the foot of the stairs. 'I have to speak with you alone.'

She walked down the last few steps. The men fell silent, aware of her presence. Domino felt their prying eyes. He held his hand out for her and she clasped it tightly, giving such a sweet, sad smile that it broke his heart.

'Thank you for coming, you must be here. I want everyone to leave before Roberto gets home. There is no answer from the restaurant, I've tried to call so many times . . .'

They went into the Don's study and she closed the door behind them. He realized then that she did not know, had not been told, and he was at a loss to know how to begin.

Graziella went on, 'They went to dine together, you see. He was going to tell them about his decision, he wanted to speak with them alone. Oh, God, Mario . . . the little boys are dead.'

Her eyes were blank with shock, translucent and so pale, as if the colour had been drained from them.

'Graziella . . .' his whisper was strained, barely audible. 'There is more . . . So help me God, I don't know how to tell you.'

She looked at him, so distressed herself that only now did she really see him. She saw his fear; he could not meet her eyes.

'More?' she said.

He nodded and his face twisted as he tried to stem the flow of his tears, but they streamed down his face.

Her voice was like steel, loud, harsh. 'Look at me, tell me . . . *Tell me!*'

He gripped the back of a chair and, with his head bowed, his eyes closed, he told her. He felt so inadequate, fought so hard to control his own emotions to enable himself to comfort her, but it was she who gently patted his arm. Her hand felt so light, feather-light.

He turned to take her in his arms, but she stepped back. She gave a strange sigh; once, twice, three times she sighed, then patted her chest as if her hand registered her heartbeat. He had no words of comfort, there were no words, nothing he could do. He stood in wretched misery.

Slowly she moved round to stand behind the Don's desk, stood staring at the row of photographs. To Mario's consternation she sat down, almost businesslike, and picked up a pen, pulled a piece of paper forward and began to write. She wrote quickly, covering the entire page, then calmly read over what she had written before handing it to him.

'Would you please contact everyone on this list, the marquee must be taken down.'

'Graziella . . .'

'No, please listen to me. I want the flowers taken away, the caterers and the guests informed. No one must come to the villa. Tell the guards, then ask everyone to leave. We must be left alone, do you understand? We must be alone.'

Domino found Graziella's strength awe-inspiring. She did not break down once during the entire time he was with her. She made the decision to tell each woman separately, and asked the doctor to accompany her.

She chose to see Rosa first, and sat holding her hand while the doctor sedated the shocked, hysterical girl. The wedding dress was still hanging on her wardrobe door and Graziella was the one who removed it, but Rosa would not let go of the veil. She clung to it tightly, even as she slept.

Teresa repeated her husband's name. The terrible confusion of trying to accept not only the deaths of the children but of her husband and Emilio was beyond her. She smoothed her skirt constantly, chewed her lips, whispering, 'I don't understand, I don't understand . . .'

As with Rosa, the doctor was in attendance. When he asked if she needed anything, she shook her head, looking past him to the waiting, silent Graziella.

'There'll be no wedding, no wedding?' Her pleading voice was pitiful to hear. Her eyes, behind the thick-rimmed glasses, were magnified like a china doll's, blank eyes that slowly, as Graziella waited, began to register . . . As the facts hammered at her dulled senses, her breath caught in her throat, her breathing quickened until she was gasping, her eyes blinked rapidly and then, at last, she wept. Her tears were magnified, like her eyes. Graziella was deeply moved at Teresa's superhuman effort to regain control of herself. She asked, after a while, to be left alone.

Moyra was not in her room. Terrified, she had locked herself in the bathroom, unable to get the gruesome picture of the children out of her mind. Graziella had to cajole and gently persuade her to open the door.

After fifteen minutes the door inched open. Moyra's face was streaked with mascara and she had lost one of her false eyelashes. The tip of her nose was red from crying, which gave her a clownish quality, but when she was told about Frederico she became irrational, ferociously demanding to be allowed home.

'Me an' Freddy are leaving this place, we're going home.'

Graziella tried to calm her, never letting her voice rise, which in itself seemed to push Moyra into a rage. She became louder and louder until she was yelling incoherently. In the end the only way to stop her was a hard slap.

The doctor stood by as Graziella hit Moyra once, then again. Moyra spat at her, fought back, kicking and scratching, screaming at the doctor not to let Graziella touch her. Graziella paid no attention to the disgusting language from the painted, smeared mouth; it meant nothing. Moyra accused Graziella of hating her, trying to get rid of her. They had never liked her, she wasn't good enough . . .

Her face was puce, crazy. 'Nobody hits me, understand, you bitch? *You fuckin' witch! I'll get the hell out of this place!*'

She started throwing clothes into a suitcase, but in the end it was Moyra who quietened herself. She caught sight of her own image in the wardrobe mirror and stared, as if seeing a stranger. Then she began to laugh, pointing at herself, and kept on laughing until her legs buckled beneath her and she lost consciousness.

The doctor carried her to the bed and checked her pulse. He turned to Graziella and said softly, 'Sometimes nature takes care of the unbearable, but be sure someone is here when she wakes up.'

'There will be, doctor,' Graziella replied, and he knew she meant herself. She wrapped the eiderdown gently around Moyra.

As she closed the door behind her, the doctor warned

442

her to take care, that she, too, must rest. She dismissed him curtly, leaning over the banister rail and asking Mario Domino to see him out. Then she went across the landing to Sophia's room and inched open the door.

Sophia was sleeping, face down, her arms splayed out, one hand dangling over the side of the bed.

The doctor repeated his warning to Mario Domino, that they must not allow Graziella to exhaust herself. Her voice made both men turn.

She was standing at the top of the stairs. 'Please leave some tranquillizers, in case any of my daughters need further sedation. Perhaps you could leave two bottles . . . I shall administer them, I shall take care of them. Goodnight, doctor, thank you for being here, Mario . . . Goodnight.'

Domino watched the tail lights of the doctor's car going down the drive as he slowly pulled on his coat. He felt as if Graziella had slammed the door in his face, but there was nothing more he could do. She had wanted him to leave, so, after standing forlornly in the empty hallway for a full fifteen minutes, he let himself out. But he couldn't go; instead, he sat on the stone steps, head in hands, and wept.

Moyra had woken, taken some hot milk, and now rested quietly. Rosa remained deeply asleep. Teresa was grateful, her own sense of loss was too much to share. She wanted nothing but to lie in a dark room, alone.

Graziella checked each of them, persuading Teresa to sip a little brandy. She had still not told Sophia, although she knew she was awake. She had seen the light beneath her door.

For Sophia she had to steel herself, clench her hands until the nails cut into the palms so she was in control . . .

Sophia was not in bed, but sitting at the dressing table, her long, dark hair hanging almost to her waist, her hands folded in her lap. The after-effect of the tranquillizers made her feel woozy, her eyes were heavy-lidded and puffy from weeping. Her lips moved soundlessly, as if she were whispering to herself, or praying. She did not turn when Graziella entered the room and stood quietly behind her. She did not even acknowledge Graziella's hands on her shoulders.

Her dark eyes, that seemed so large, too wide, for her heart-shaped face, stared expressionlessly into the mirror. Graziella reached over and picked up the silver-backed hairbrush; she began to brush the thick, silky hair in long, rhythmic strokes. A few strands of hair crackled with static, and Sophia closed her eyes.

'Mama, tell me it is a nightmare, tell me that any moment I will wake up and it will all be over.'

Graziella continued to brush with long, slow strokes. Suddenly Sophia turned sharply and gripped her mother-in-law's wrist.

'Where are they? Why aren't they here? Where is Constantino?'

The shutters were closed, the curtains drawn. The workmen came and went until there was no trace left of the wedding preparations. The gifts were repacked in their boxes, the cards and telegrams that arrived were stopped at the gates. The ornate, brilliantly coloured floral displays were thrown onto the rubbish heap, but the fallen petals remained to blow about in the cool night breeze and brown to a crisp in the heat of the day.

The Villa Rivera was shrouded, as if allowing only those trapped inside a time for grief. Like animals caged, the press gathered at the wrought-iron gates, their hands clasping at the bars, but they remained closed.

At Graziella's insistence, she was the only one to identify the dead. Wearing mourning, a veil covering her face, she clung to Mario Domino's arm as he guided her through the groups of camera-flashing photographers. Scuffles broke out as the *carabinieri* pushed them out of the way.

As soon as they entered the morgue, Graziella withdrew her hand, preferring to stand alone. Silently, she allowed Domino to walk ahead, following the white-coated policemen along corridor after chilling corridor. They entered the white-tiled, cold room.

The mortician's hands were encased in fine, yellowish rubber gloves. They looked like the hands of the dead as they slowly withdrew each cover, lifting them just enough for Graziella to view the faces. She moved from corpse to corpse, crossing herself and calling each one by name, the only words she spoke. She made no attempt to touch them, no physical contact.

'Roberto Luciano ... Constantino Luciano ... Alfredo Luciano ... Frederico Luciano ... Emilio Luciano ... Carlo Luciano ... Nunzio Luciano ...'

Graziella once again took Domino's arm and he

helped her back to the Mercedes, but she refused his offer to accompany her back to the villa. She sat well back on the seat and he closed the door carefully. Again his feeling of helpless inadequacy consumed him.

Slowly her window slid down. Her face was a mere shadow beneath the veil. 'First I will bury my dead. I want everyone in Sicily to know, to demand justice. You will arrange for me to meet Giuliano Emmanuel. You are to tell him he has a new witness for the prosecution, do you understand? *Grazie*, Mario, *grazie* . . .'

She raised her black-gloved hand a fraction to indicate that she wished to leave. Before he could say a word, the window closed, the car drew away from the pavement, and she was gone.

CHAPTER 18

HOURS AFTER the Luciano murders had been discovered, the bodies of the chef and one waiter were found. They had been bound and shot with a Heckler and Koch P7M8 pistol, a tell-tale sign of a professional gunman – or gunmen. The bodies of Don Roberto's guards were not discovered for a week. The stench of their rotting flesh led the *carabinieri* to a well twenty yards from the restaurant. The one missing man, the second waiter, had disappeared without trace.

Strychnine was the cause of the Luciano deaths. Traces were discovered in every dish they had eaten, and even the wine. The investigation continued; it was calculated that three or possibly four men were involved. Casts of footprints were taken from the damp earth around the well. Fingerprint experts began the laborious task of assessing the hundreds of prints taken from the restaurant, but a week after the assassinations there were still no suspects.

Once the autopsies had been carried out, the bodies were released by the police and taken to the funeral home.

Only Graziella accompanied Mario Domino, who carried two suitcases of clothes for the dead to wear.

She carefully examined each body while two embalmers followed her at a respectful distance. When she stood by the two children, she asked if their wounds could be concealed. They assured her that the plastic they used would most certainly disguise them. She then astounded the men by remaining with them through every stage of the embalming, sitting silently and watching as they washed the corpses, and pumped in the embalming fluid. No one, to their knowledge, had ever subjected themselves to viewing this process, but she was adamant.

Don Roberto was the last to be embalmed. She sat while the men worked on his face, threading clips from his jaw to his nose to keep the mouth firmly closed.

Graziella moved from one son to the next, checking their appearances. She stood looking at the two angelic faces of her grandsons, then turned, calling one of the men to her side. 'He has too much colour. Nunzio is always very pale. A little more powder, perhaps?'

She nodded her approval when the child's face was finished, then stood beside her husband. 'Thank you for allowing me to be with my family. I came for a reason – my first-born son died tragically. When he was brought home, it was as if I buried a stranger, my grief was indescribable. My daughters must see their loved ones as they were, they have suffered enough. Thank you again, gentlemen . . .'

The widows never knew the part Graziella had played. The dead lay in state, their coffins like ornate, satin-lined bedchambers. They mourned together in the privacy of the villa until it was time for the funeral.

At six o'clock, the first mass, the crowds had begun to gather. Men, women and children, they came from the villages, they came from the mountains. They came by train, by boat, by bus, in horse-drawn carts, to bid farewell to *Il Papa*, to show their last respects to their beloved Don. Hundreds slowly gathered in the square in front of the cathedral.

The *carabinieri* had withdrawn their guards from the villa, but as a show of respect sixteen motorbike riders moved ahead of the procession. Many off-duty police came of their own accord and joined the silent, waiting crowds who lined the road all the way from the Villa Rivera to the cathedral square. Every major family in Sicily put aside their private animosities and arrived to mourn a man both loved and respected.

The cathedral choir was joined by a string quartet, a harpist and four leading singers from La Scala Opera Company. The white lilies were in such profusion that the cathedral was heady with their perfume and shimmering with the flames of hundreds of candles lit during the mass.

The first pew awaited the widows. The purple velvet hassocks had all been embroidered with a gold 'L' by nuns from the Lucianos' local church.

By ten-fifteen, the motorbike cavalcade was in position outside the villa. The gates were opened wide and they were given the signal to move on.

A black stallion, draped in purple and with a black, plumed head-dress, was led out by a young farm boy to walk at the front of the procession. The stallion tossed his head nervously, and the boy held on to the wide black ribbons while he took a harmonica from his pocket. The horse calmed as he began to play and they moved forward.

A murmur went through the crowd as the first hearse turned into the street, pulled by six men in black morning dress. The hearse was over a hundred years old and carved in the ornate Sicilian fashion. White roses spelt out *Il Papa* in letters eighteen inches high. The coffin was laden only with white flowers, apart from a single red rose. Black, billowing silk drapes were caught at the corners with white roses.

Following Don Roberto Luciano came the hearse of his eldest son, Constantino. A thick blanket of white flowers covered the coffin, and again a single red rose. In third position came Alfredo's hearse, followed by Frederico's and Emilio's, each smothered in white with one poignant red bloom.

There was a short delay, then twenty village children between the ages of six and eight, wearing their white confirmation clothes, walked ahead of the two tiny, white-flowered coffins. They carried roses, and the white veils of the girls were crowned with white flowers. One small girl at the head of the little procession began to cry. The occasion was too much for her, and her high-pitched sobbing made the sight of the small coffins even harder to bear.

Moving very slowly to the mournful, echoing sound of the boy's harmonica, the procession wound along the silent streets. It was the silence that everyone would remember, although the streets were full of people.

Nor would anyone who witnessed the Luciano funeral ever forget the extraordinary sight of the widows. To everyone's amazement, they walked. Led by Graziella, with Sophia and Moyra together four steps behind, and Teresa and Rosa another four slow steps behind them; they walked slowly, heads held high, in their black mourning clothes and flowing black veils. Each held her black-gloved hands clasped as if in prayer. They seemed bound together, yet separate, facing directly ahead, and even when Graziella led them into the cathedral no one turned.

The boy soprano rose from the choir and sang *Ave Maria*, his high, clear voice soaring, as the women took their seats and knelt in prayer.

The coffins were brought in one by one and lifted onto the stands in front of the altar. As the two children's coffins were carried up the aisle, the full impact of the tragedy hit the congregation, and many wept. Not a single flower adorned the coffins now, and the gold plaques could be seen glinting in the candlelight. During the service, as the congregation filed up to take communion, a wizened old woman swathed in black inched past the children's coffins to lay a small, worn crucifix on the Don's coffin. She sobbed loudly, and no one attempted to stop her; it was as though she wept for everyone there. All wanted to show their shame at the loss of this, their beloved Don, his sons and two innocent grandsons.

The ground was thick with floral displays, covering the small area outside the family mausoleum, hanging from the iron railings surrounding the white-pillared entrance and carpeting the lane leading up to the gates. The crowds remained standing; dark-suited men held them back, their arms linked to allow the five black-clad women privacy for their last goodbye.

As they entered the mausoleum a flash went off. Graziella, the last to enter, turned, her expression hidden beneath her veil, and pointed at the press photographer responsible. One of the guards immediately, without any apparent coercion, was handed the offending roll of film. The doors closed behind the women.

In the gloomy interior of the tomb, the coffins were already in their final resting places on the shelves, though they had not yet been cemented in. The highly polished wood glinted in the flickering light of a single torch.

The women prayed together until Graziella said, quietly, that it was time to leave. Rosa clutched her grandmother's hand and Teresa inched the door open, but Moyra seemed at a loss. She turned to Sophia.

Sophia's body was rigid, she could not move. Unable to look at the coffins of her husband and children, she focused on the picture of Michael Luciano. The photograph had been there for twenty years, protected by the glass and the airtight tomb; it could have been placed there the day before. Michael's angelic face and soft, sweet smile made Sophia's dulled senses scream awake. Hands clenched, the scream surged through her, forming the single word *no*.

Graziella released her granddaughter's hand and her voice was hoarse as she ordered the women out. She caught Sophia as she fell to her knees.

'Get up, Sophia . . . Up on your feet.'

Her grip felt like pincers cutting through Sophia's

skin, pressing against the nerve in her elbow and making her whole body jerk, but Graziella held on. The others stood waiting at the half-open door. Graziella took Teresa's handkerchief, lifted Sophia's veil and wiped her face.

'Let me go first.' Satisfied that Sophia was all right, Graziella almost pushed past her daughters and led them out to face the watchful crowd.

The show, for that's what the funeral was, was still not over. There were further agonies for the widows to endure; they now had to greet and thank the many mourners who were invited to pay their respects at the villa. The lingering crowds saw the show of wealth and power in the Rolls-Royces, Mercedes, Maseratis and Ferraris that lined the route back to the villa.

A row of gilded red velvet chairs had been placed in the lounge, replacing the coffins. For five hours the women sat, still veiled, to receive the condolences of the mourners. When it finally ended the villa seemed slowly to die – no voices, no sound – it was over.

Luka had chosen to arrive in the cool of the evening, knowing that climb as well as he knew any place on earth. He carried a small overnight bag and a long, thin leather case. His shoes were scuffed and white with dust. His straw hat made his head sweat, soaking his hair and dripping on his shirt, even though he had removed his jacket and slung it over his shoulder.

He kept walking, higher and higher, stopping occasionally to look at the wondrous views, but only for a moment. He came to the Chiesa Matrica, the small church of the Mother of God, and gave a small bow of his head as he passed. Continuing along the narrow, cobbled lanes, he eventually reached the rough track he knew so well. It was not far now, perhaps another two miles.

He was not expected, yet he knew that he would not be turned away. The heavy iron ring and old, frayed bell rope were exactly as he remembered, and he could hear the bell ringing in the courtyard. He knew it would take a few moments before anyone could reach the door and open the small, carved peephole.

Father Angelo was painfully incapacitated by arthritis, but when he was told Luka Carolla was at the gate, his eagerness to see the boy made him forget to pick up his walking frame.

Luka knew he had made the right decision. Father Angelo wrapped him in his arms, weeping with pleasure, making him so welcome that Luka was close to tears. Brother Guido, a monk Luka did not recognize, hurried to assist the father. He bent to pick up Luka's bag and was rather taken aback when it was snatched from his hands. Luka hated anyone touching his things, but he apologized quickly, saying that the bag was light and he could carry it himself. He had never let the long, narrow case leave his grasp.

Brother Guido took Father Angelo's arm and the three walked slowly across the courtyard into the cool stone corridor. The father's slow, shuffling steps halted and he patted Luka's arm.

'You shall have your old room, remember it?'

'Yes, Father, I remember it.'

'They closed the orphanage, did you know? Did I write that to you?'

'Yes, Father, you did. Would it be OK if I stayed a coupla days?' Luka spoke in English.

'My, my, Luka, you are American now.'

Father Angelo's sandals made a familiar shushing sound on the stone flags. He seemed so frail, leaning heavily on Brother Guido; his flesh hung on his bones and small tufts of downy white hair sprouted on his otherwise bald head. Luka felt such a longing to hold this old man that he moved further into the shadows, afraid his deep emotion would be detected.

Father Angelo called to two other brothers across the courtyard. 'It's Luka . . . LUKA! You remember Brother Thomas, don't you, Luka?'

Thomas was almost unrecognizable. His girth had shrunk to almost nothing, and his once thick, curly black hair was white above his wizened face. He smiled and waved as he came towards them with another brother who seemed even more elderly. Luka stared hard; it could surely not be Brother Louis, and yet . . . The two old men shuffled closer and Luka realized that it was indeed Brother Louis, not that the old man knew his own identity. His mind was as vacant as his small, washed-out eyes.

Brother Thomas wrinkled his nose and nodded. 'Luka? Well, well, Luka . . . Welcome, welcome. What a fine man you have grown into, and so smart. You look wealthy, you look like an American through and through.'

He bent his head to Brother Louis and shouted, 'It's Luka, Louis, do you remember? Luka!' Brother Louis sucked in his cheeks and smiled, exposing his pink gums. Thomas repeated at a bellow, 'IT IS LUKA!' Then he shrugged, 'He can't hear, he's deaf. He's over ninety, you know. Well . . . welcome, welcome.' The two old men shuffled off.

The smells brought the memories flooding back. Brother Guido opened the door to a cell-like stone room and ushered Luka inside. The room contained only an iron bedstead, a folded mattress and pillow, a small chest of drawers and a wardrobe. While Father Angelo leaned against the doorframe, Guido carefully removed a pressed white sheet and pillow-case from one of the drawers and placed them on the bed. Then he picked up a large white china jug, excused himself and went to fetch some water.

Luka put his bag down and laid the smaller case on top of the chest. He turned and Father Angelo smiled at him, a sweet, loving smile. Luka's mouth trembled, his eyes filled with tears and he took the old man gently in his arms. He could feel how frail, how thin, the father was, just as Father Angelo could feel the strong, fit body of this boy he adored. 'Oh, my son, my beloved boy, how happy you make this old man. You fill my heart. I began to believe I would not see you again before I die, I give thanks to God.'

Brother Guido returned with the jug of water and Angelo smiled his thanks. 'Thank you, Guido, and if you will assist me back to my room, I shall leave this boy in peace. There's a robe and sandals, Luka, should you wish to change, and mass will be in one hour. At supper we shall hear all your news . . .'

Luka nodded and whispered a soft thank-you as they left. He waited, listening to their footsteps, until there was silence. He closed his eyes and sighed; he had come home.

He stripped himself quickly, wanting to be naked, wanting to be cleansed. He poured the cold water into the bowl and picked up a wooden nail brush, its bristles tough and hard. Without soap, he scrubbed himself until his white skin was red raw. Finally he slipped the robe over his head, tied the sash and slipped his feet into the sandals.

He unpacked his clothes from the soft leather bag, carefully hanging or folding the garments, two fine cotton lawn shirts and an identical pair of trousers to those he had been wearing. He produced a duster and polished his shoes, placing them neatly at the bottom of the wardrobe, next to the empty bag. His shaving equipment, in its matching leather bag, he placed on the chest of drawers, next to the long case he had brought with him. He could not resist touching it lightly, almost stroking it. He talked to himself all the while in a low whisper, as if telling himself where to put his belongings. Then he took the case to the bed, lifted the mattress and stowed it underneath.

He laughed to himself as the bells began pealing for Matins and for a moment wondered whether to join the brothers. He decided to make the excuse that he had fallen asleep, but sleep was the last thing he could think of. Instead, he climbed silently from the window and headed for his old vegetable patch.

He walked between the rows of dried and rotting lettuces, noticing the tangled beans and the strawberry patch that had been allowed to run wild. He paused, surveying the fields that stretched far into the distance to the right and left, but ahead seemed to merge with the skyline. He reached the top of the slope, stood caught between earth and sky, and there was the dark, glittering sea stretching to infinity.

He knew what he had done. He knew it then; no amount of scrubbing could cleanse Luka, it was inside him. He lifted his hands, stretching his arms high, but the terrible knowledge was like a rigid hand twisting his heart and he sobbed. 'Forgive me, forgive me, I have sinned, I have sinned . . . Hail Mary, Mother of Jesus . . .'

Father Angelo saw him from his window. Thomas came blustering in, filled with complaints as always, but Father Angelo put a finger to his lips to silence him and beckoned him to the window. Luka's silhouette resembled a holy saint, the blondness of his hair like a halo.

'Luka,' sighed Father Angelo, like a prayer.

Brother Thomas' eyes were not as good as they were, but he could not mistake that figure. How often they had reprimanded him for climbing out of his window at night.

'He always was a little devil, I always said he had the devil in him. You remember the scene we had over the chicken leg, Angelo? You know, I will go to my grave knowing he stole it, but I was never able to find the proof. Well, now I shall have the opportunity to ask him face to face, as a man, and I shall do so. He stole the chicken leg.'

The two aged monks made their way to chapel. As they creaked down on to their worn, arthritic knees in prayer, Luka also prayed. He would give himself a penance; he would not leave the monastery until he had sown and reaped, he would not rest until he had made good the neglected vegetable garden.

The evening after the funeral, the widows were to dine with Graziella. They entered the room one by one to find she was already sitting in her husband's chair; they noticed that she also wore his ring. They were not hungry and hardly touched the food that was placed in front of them by Adina, who had been in service with the Lucianos since she was a young girl. Her eyes red-rimmed from weeping, she moved silently and unobtrusively around, serving and clearing.

There was an air of expectancy, and at last Graziella spoke in halting English, choosing her words carefully, for Moyra's benefit.

'Mario Domino will be preparing the will. It will take time, so in the meanwhile I think you should all return to your homes. There is nothing more that can be done here. I shall cable you as soon as I know when the reading will take place . . . I ask you for your patience and your promise to return as soon as you hear from me.' Graziella hesitated, now obviously highly nervous, and took a black-bordered handkerchief from her pocket to wipe her eyes, although she did not appear to be weeping.

They turned dull eyes to her, trying to assimilate everything she had just said. Finally she said, 'There is something you should all be made aware of, something I have not told you . . . Papa had begun making statements for the prosecution.' She looked at them, expecting a reaction, but received none. It was as if they had not heard. She continued, 'Papa believed in his decision, and trusted that we would all be protected.'

Suddenly Teresa snapped, shaking with shocked rage, 'Protection! Jesus Christ, protection! He must have been out of his mind! It was his fault, his fault this happened!'

'Do you think I have not thought, every minute, every hour, every day since? You blame Papa, then you must blame me. I knew of this decision, I approved and believed what he was doing was right.'

Teresa's face was tight, her mouth a thin, vicious line. 'You knew, you *knew*, and you welcomed us with open arms. You brought us over here, and we saw the guards, we saw them . . . Jesus Christ, Sophia even asked you why! Why was the car trailing us on a shopping expedition, and what did you say? *You said it was what Papa wanted!* You should have told us then; you think Sophia would have left her babies for a second if she had known? We were all in danger, and you never told us . . .'

Rosa's chair fell over as she stood up. 'Is that why I was to be married? To get us all here? Was that why I was to be married? You arranged it, you arranged my wedding!'

Sophia slapped her hand down on the table, '*Stop this!*'

Moyra had not understood. She asked again and again what was being said. Her voice rose, 'What? What are you saying, what?'

Teresa shouted, 'Mama knew, she knew that Papa was standing as a witness for the prosecution.'

'I don't understand.' Moyra's voice was bleating, half-crying.

'Use your brain,' said Teresa, 'Papa was giving evidence. He knew he was in danger, knew we would all

460

be. That's why we were surrounded by guards. He used us, all of us, but worse, she . . .' Her voice caught in her throat as she pointed to Graziella. 'She used . . . my poor Rosa.'

'I make no excuses. Yes, Papa chose the wedding, he chose it because if anything happened to him we would have been together. Paul Carolla murdered Michael . . .'

Sophia twisted the stem of her glass in her hand. Her deep voice was calm as she interrupted Graziella. 'Michael died, Mama, more than twenty years ago. Are you saying that Papa jeopardized the entire family because of Michael? I have lost my husband and my babies because of *Michael?*'

The stem of the glass snapped cleanly, spilling the water across the cloth. They all looked to Graziella for an answer. The tension in the room was heightened by Rosa's muffled weeping.

'Papa did what he felt was right. Who are we to say now that he should not have . . .'

Moyra screamed it, her face red with pent-up anger, 'I'm saying it! I don't give a fuck what anyone else wants to say, *I'm saying it, my husband is dead*!'

Graziella looked at Moyra with contempt. Her voice was hoarse now. 'My husband too, my sons, my grandsons . . . I have asked you to find it in your hearts not to blame Papa, but to pray for justice, and you have nothing but hatred for him. Hate the men who did this, not Papa. All of you carried the name Luciano, carried it, benefited from being the wives of Lucianos.'

Teresa interrupted, swiping at the table, hitting out in anger. 'Rosa was never allowed the chance to become a wife. He and he alone is to blame, and you know it.' Teresa's head jerked back as Graziella slapped her face.

'I wish you to leave. When the will is completed you may return, not before then . . .' They watched her walk from the room. Her slow footsteps crossed the marble hall.

Teresa rubbed her cheek, shocked, hardly able to believe it had happened. She asked no one in particular, 'Michael? He did it for Michael? Justice for Michael? A boy none of us even knew! Well, I spit on his memory, because if it weren't for Michael Luciano, our men would still be alive. I will be glad to leave this house, leave her to her justice . . .'

Sophia folded her napkin carefully. She felt empty, drained, unable to argue. 'If you'll excuse me, I'm going to bed.'

Teresa burst out, 'Don't you have anything to say? Don't you think we should talk this through? I mean, she's asked us to leave, are you going?'

'What is there to say, Teresa? No words can bring back my sons, my husband. I don't care about justice, about Paul Carolla. My babies, my beautiful babies, are dead.'

Sophia, not wishing to wake anyone, did not turn the lights on. In the darkness the house itself appeared to be mourning; strange creaks and groans emanated from the staircase and the shutters.

She inched open the door to the drawing room, crept to the drinks cabinet and poured herself almost a tumbler of whisky. The pills she had already taken were making her feel woozy. As she turned to go back to her room, the fringe of the shawl which draped the piano brushed her arm. She gasped; it felt like ghostly fingers trailing along her skin. She gulped at the whisky, her hand shaking badly, and there he was again, smiling at her. Michael's photograph always stood in front of the others. His face blinded her, obliterating the family shots, blurring the picture of her laughing sons riding a rocking horse.

She whispered, 'I curse you, I curse the day I met you.' The sound of her own voice frightened her and again she drank, wanting to escape into drunken oblivion. But a small voice inside warned her to be careful.

Graziella, her long hair braided, a woollen shawl around her shoulders, walked silently into the room and took the glass from Sophia's cold hand.

'You should not drink if you have taken sleeping pills, it is dangerous.'

'You mean I could sleep and never wake up? Then give me the glass.'

'I'll take you back to bed.'

Sophia backed away, remembering that vice-like grip at the mausoleum, but Graziella kept on coming.

'Stay away from me, leave me alone.'

'Very well, if that is what you want.'

'I want to leave this house.'

As silently as she had arrived, Graziella turned to leave, but Sophia blurted, 'Why didn't you warn me? Because you knew, you've always known.'

'Known what?'

'What this family is, what it was ... You've always known. Is that why you are so strong, why you don't weep? Is that why?'

Graziella stood over her, eyes blazing. 'You didn't know? Don't play the innocent, it doesn't become you. Yes, I have known, just as you have, but perhaps my

463

reasons for accepting it were different. What were yours, Sophia? What made you return to this house? For my son? Was it for Constantino or for what you saw here?'

'I loved him, you know that. He was a good husband, he was a good father, but . . .'

'But he was a Luciano.'

Sophia put her hands over her ears. She wanted to shout, to curse the name aloud.

Graziella pushed the shutters slightly open to let the cool night breeze into the room. 'I tried not to see, not to know. It was all hidden from me, I could pretend that what went on outside could never affect me and, as I chose not to know, Michael died. But perhaps, if I had been more aware of my husband's world, Michael need not have died. When I realized there was a side I didn't know, I made it my duty to know. Mario Domino would have been shot if it had ever been discovered, but I made him keep me informed of everything he could possibly tell me. Papa never knew. He knew most things, about all of you. Remember how he delved into your past when you wanted to marry Constantino?'

Sophia's breath caught in her throat, she couldn't speak. She was suddenly afraid of Graziella; did she know everything? Could it be possible?

The quiet voice continued, 'He always said you were his favourite. You must forgive, Sophia, not blame him. You are not like the others, they are nothing.'

'What about Rosa, Mama? Is she just a nothing? Was the marriage really arranged, or did Emilio love her?'

Graziella's eyes were like stones. 'I will take care of Rosa.'

At that moment Sophia loathed Graziella. Her calmness, her strength, drew what little energy she had left. 'I'll return to Rome in the morning.'

'You must do whatever you think best. I'm sorry you all feel this way, that we are so divided. Together we would be stronger.'

'For what? There's nothing left, Mama.'

Graziella lifted her arms as if to embrace her, but Sophia hurried out, not wanting to be touched.

Left alone, Graziella took stock of the elegant drawing room. Her eyes had grown accustomed to the darkness and she noticed a cushion out of place. She straightened it deftly, then paused, looking at the array of family photographs. Michael's was out of line. As she pushed it back into its place she said to the empty room, to the faces of her dead, clearly and quietly, without emotion, 'It is with me now.'

CHAPTER 19

THE WIDOWS had returned to their homes, and Graziella was left alone in the villa. The rooms were kept dark and airless, the shutters over the windows, every door closed.

Graziella's entire adult life had been taken up with caring for her family; now she thought only of the end of Paul Carolla.

Mario Domino had tried to dissuade Graziella from going to the trials. He made the excuse that there was not one spectator seat available and she had told him curtly that she would arrange it herself. 'The guards are paid a pittance, make sure that they have a seat for me every day, no matter what the cost.'

The first time she saw Paul Carolla she was shocked by his arrogant, audacious manner. She could not take her eyes from him. He became aware of her attention and called a guard over, pointing her out. When she lifted her veil, Carolla gave a low, almost mocking bow of recognition, but then he turned away as if she meant no more to him than any of the other spectators.

The eye-to-eye contact made Graziella recoil in a

spasm, as if she had been punched in the heart, a reaction so strong that she snapped the silver crucifix chain in her hands.

Emmanuel had made many excuses to delay the meeting with Graziella. Eventually he could no longer put off the inevitable meeting when she appeared at his office. He was impressed by her calmness. He assured her that Carolla would be convicted. He still wished to accuse Carolla of the murder of Michael Luciano, but with the many other charges of drug dealing, extortion, fraud and blackmail, sixty-six indictments in all, he was certain that Carolla would never be free.

She listened attentively, then asked quietly if there was any evidence that Paul Carolla had ordered the assassinations. Emmanuel hesitated, choosing his words carefully. Carolla was in jail; if he had ordered the murders, they had no proof, not one shred of evidence. He explained to her that when the news leaked that Don Roberto was to take the stand as a witness for the prosecution, there must have been many people afraid of what he might divulge.

'Did my husband's evidence incriminate others?'

Emmanuel twisted the cap of his fountain pen on and off, then spoke with care. 'He chose only to tell me the pertinent facts surrounding your son's death, possibly incriminating himself more than anyone else.'

'Are you able to use the statements he made?'

The pen twisted and turned in his hands. 'Without Don Roberto's presence the statements could be dismissed as circumstantial evidence. This also applies to the statement made by Lenny Cavataio. As I explained to

467

your husband, all the evidence contained in the Cavataio statement was decreed by the defence counsel as hearsay. Don Roberto knew this, it was the sole reason he chose to offer himself.'

Graziella leaned forward, her black-gloved hand resting on the edge of his desk. 'Firstly, I would like to have the tapes my husband made. Would that be possible?'

Emmanuel nodded. They had been transcribed and he had them on file in his computer. But he was not prepared for her next words.

Hands folded in her lap, she said, 'I wish to offer myself in my husband's place. I am prepared to stand as a witness for the prosecution.'

She paused, searching his face for a reaction, but all she saw was that the nervous hands twisting the fountain pen became still. Emmanuel rose from the desk and walked to the window, parting the slats of the blind a fraction and peering out.

'Did you discuss the statements with your husband, Signora Luciano?'

'I did not need to. I am fully aware of the facts. I am prepared to be your witness and am prepared to repeat in court everything my husband told you.'

He turned and scrutinized her. He wondered how much she really knew. 'These facts, signora, would you be prepared to discuss them with me, now? Or would you require access to your husband's taped interviews first?'

'Are you asking me if I would perjure myself?'

He blushed and returned to his desk. 'I am in the middle of the case. The time required to discuss everything with you would mean my asking for a stay of at least one week. These men have been held in jail for almost ten months, we cannot afford further delays . . .'

'The murder of my entire family is just a delay? How long did my grandchildren's deaths delay the court proceedings, signor? One day? One hour?'

'Please, I mean no insult, but at the time of the tragedy, Paul Carolla was being held in the Unigaro jailhouse.'

'Paul Carolla instigated the death of my son. I know he, and only he, benefited from the death of my family . . .'

'But forgive me, signora, without proof . . .'

'The proof is in the graveyard.'

He sighed, 'Trust me, I give you my word . . .'

'Your word means little to me. My husband trusted you, trusted your word that there would be protection for himself and for his sons . . .'

Again Emmanuel sighed. He was the one who was getting upset. There was no denying that the leak had come from this very office, his office. He asked if she would be prepared there and then to answer certain questions, in front of a witness. If he felt she had valuable evidence, he would accept her for the prosecution.

Hesitantly, Graziella agreed. She waited while Emmanuel called for a stenographer to be sent in.

He began by asking her to state her name, and from then on he was as tough on her within the confines of his office as he knew he would have to be in court.

'Would you state your relationship with Paul Carolla?'

'I have no relationship with him.'

'How well did you know the defendant?'

'He came to my home, to visit my husband.'

469

She could not recollect the exact date but knew that the first time she had met Carolla was in the late fifties. She explained that there had always been friction between Carolla and her late husband.

Emmanuel tapped the side of his desk with his foot. 'So you were aware of ill feeling between the two men as far back as the early fifties?'

'Yes. He came to my home wanting my husband to release him, he no longer wished to work for him. He wanted to start his own business.'

'And what business did Paul Carolla wish to begin?'

'I believe it was narcotics.'

'You believe? Do you have any evidence to substantiate this statement?'

'No.'

'I see. So let us move on to the ill feeling between your husband and the defendant . . .'

'The second time Paul Carolla came to my home, he wanted my husband to assist him, to use the Luciano export companies as a cover for shipping narcotics. He had become very wealthy, and he threatened my husband.'

'Were you a witness to any of these threats?'

She hesitated, and he knew before she spoke that she was lying. 'I heard them shouting at each other, I heard Paul Carolla say that he would make my husband pay for abusing his friendship. My husband refused to assist him in any way. He had always maintained his companies legally, had spent years building up a good name. My husband was a man of honour and he hated drugs of any kind.'

'Signora Luciano, when you say a man of honour, do

you accept the fact that your husband was, up until the time of his death, a known Mafia . . .?'

She interrupted angrily, 'My husband was a man of honour, a war hero, decorated for bravery. A man who despised the trade in drugs, despised Paul Carolla.'

Emmanuel was already certain that it would not work out, but he had to continue. He changed the subject, asking gently, 'Tell me about Michael Luciano.'

She seemed grateful, giving him a half-smile. 'He was my first-born son. He came home half-way through his second year at Harvard. He was very sick. He collapsed and my husband took him to hospital. He remained in hospital for a few weeks, then he was taken to the mountains to recuperate.'

'What happened to your son, Signora Luciano? What happened to him?'

She tried to say it in a matter-of-fact way, but could not. 'My son was . . . murdered.'

'Did you witness his death?'

'No, I did not. My son was shot, killed as a warning to my husband not to stand against Paul Carolla. My son's return, signor, coincided with Carolla's threats, and my husband took my son into the mountains in the belief that he would be safe there.'

Emmanuel was kicking the side of his desk with small, light taps of his shoe. 'These threats, signora, did you actually hear Paul Carolla say that he would . . .' He paused, knowing that Michael Luciano had not been shot, and chose his words carefully. The stenographer waited, pencil poised.

'What was the development of this tragedy? Was anyone ever charged with this brutal killing?'

Slowly, Graziella shook her head. 'No, but it was Paul Carolla.'

'Was it ever proved, the part Paul Carolla played in the death of your son?'

There was a helplessness to her, but she didn't break down. 'No . . . But there was a witness.'

'Do you know the name of this witness?'

Her eyes filled with tears and she gave a pleading look to the stenographer, as if she could help. In the end she lowered her head and whispered, 'No, I do not know, signor.'

Sophia sat in the cool, empty church. She had been sitting there for almost two hours. She wore a lace veil over her face and clutched her rosary.

She had tried to pray but her mind blurred and she could do nothing but listen, her face cupped in her hands as she knelt. Footsteps came and went, voices echoed, there were whispers from the confessional. Twice she had risen and moved closer, only to stop and kneel down again.

She had asked the maid to clear the children's toys away and take them to a home along with their clothes. Constantino's clothes had also been removed.

The church was the only place she went to, and for three days she had come, needing to confess, needing to tell someone, but had been unable to enter the confessional.

The candles she had lit for her sons and her husband were flickering, almost at an end, and she quietly fetched three more.

The confessional was empty and she inched closer,

closer . . . Then she moved quickly to swish the curtain aside. Once sitting in the small, dark booth she forced herself to speak, but her voice was so low that the priest had to ask her to speak up.

She told him, haltingly, that she wished to confess, and the kindly tones of the voice behind the grille calmed her. They prayed together for a moment, then he waited. He began to scratch at a gravy stain on his cassock. He could hear her sighing, but she said nothing.

'I have sinned, Father.'

He leaned closer. Her voice was so husky he could barely hear her. He encouraged her to continue.

'I have sinned, Father.'

'Ease the pain in your heart, say what you feel you need. There is time, take your time. I am just here to comfort you, to pray with you.'

'I had a child, a son. I left the baby in an orphanage; I intended . . . I wanted to go back for him, but first I needed to tell his father, explain to him.'

The priest waited . . . He heard her sighing, then he saw her hand, a delicate white hand with blood-red nails, the fingers threading through the grille. He touched her fingers, gently. His hand felt warm, soft. She withdrew her hand.

'Did you tell the father of your baby? Tell him of his son?'

'I couldn't, Father, I couldn't.'

'Were you afraid? Afraid of rejection?'

'No . . . No, you don't understand . . .'

'I can only understand, be of help to you, if you tell me everything.'

'He died, he died . . . I couldn't tell him, I couldn't tell anyone.'

'So the father of your baby was dead. What did you do then?'

'*Don't you understand what I have done? Don't you understand?*'

The priest quietened her, said he understood, could understand her heartache.

'No, you cannot, you can't understand.'

'Well, my child, tell me what I cannot understand.'

The white hand, the red-painted fingernails, scratched at the grille.

'I wanted so much to be a part of the family, I wanted everything they had, I wanted to be . . .' As disturbed as she was, Sophia still held back, still did not say the name Luciano.

'Do you want to find your child?'

She leaned back. She could smell the mustiness of his robes just as he could smell her distinct, heavy perfume. She answered on a long, low sigh, 'Yesss . . . Yes, that is what I want.'

'Then that is what you must do. Trace this child you harbour such guilt, such deep guilt, about. Your sense of betrayal is natural, you know what you have done in the past and you know the reasons. Find him, ask his forgiveness, and God will give you the strength. Now together we will pray for his soul, pray for you, my daughter, and pray for God to forgive your sins.'

Graziella looked towards her husband's study. She could hear the murmur of voices. She handed Adina her veil and black lace gloves.

'It's Signor Domino, he said it would be permissible. He has three gentlemen with him, signora.'

'In future, Adina, no matter who it is, no one is allowed here, especially not in my husband's study, unless I have given you authority. You may go.'

She waited until Adina had returned to the kitchen before she moved closer to the study door. She paused, listening; she could hear Mario Domino speaking.

'. . . Panamanian companies. Listed alongside are the US State Bonds. We were recycling the proceeds through our bank to Switzerland.'

Graziella walked into the study and Domino froze in mid-sentence.

'Graziella, I was not expecting you to return . . . I apologize for the intrusion, but . . . Please allow me to introduce these gentlemen, they are from America and are handling the legal side over there for Don Roberto.'

Graziella did not offer her hand but remained standing at the open door. Domino made the introductions, first gesturing towards a tall, well-dressed man in a dark-grey suit. His eyes were small, accentuated by heavy, horn-rimmed glasses.

'This is Edouardo Lorenzi from New York.'

Lorenzi gave a small bow. 'Signora . . .'

The man next to him was squat, his face shining with sweat, his collar stained. His plump hands clutched at a large white handkerchief. 'I think you have met Signor Nicolas Pecorelli, a very old and trusted friend, now taking care of the Don's interests in Atlantic City. And, lastly, from Chicago, Julio Carboni, who has been assisting me here.'

The latter was very much younger than the others, but stockily built. He was wearing an open-necked casual shirt. They all appeared to be very uncomfortable, especially when Graziella glanced around the study: the drawers and even the safe door were wide open. Stacked around the desk were files neatly tied with string, obviously ready for removal.

'I shall be in the dining room. If you wish refreshments before you leave, please call Adina.' Graziella walked out, leaving the door open and making it obvious that she wanted the men to leave.

She sat in the cool, dark dining room, in her husband's chair with her back to the shuttered windows. She could hear the men preparing to leave, their hushed voices sounding to her like those of conspirators. Then Mario himself appeared in the room.

'I am sorry, Graziella, I was hoping to have completed everything here before your return. Don Luciano was conducting international transactions. I am not the only lawyer involved with the businesses so we had a lot of work to do. They will be handling all the American issues.'

She had never seen Mario so hesitant. He looked guilty, mopping his brow with a silk handkerchief. 'They have removed only the files necessary . . .'

She stared at her folded hands. 'Perhaps in future you would be kind enough to warn me if you require access to my husband's study.'

'Of course, but I doubt if I will have to intrude again. Forgive me.' He bent to kiss Graziella's cheek but she averted her face.

Hurriedly, he retrieved his briefcase from the study, his eyes darting around the ransacked room, making sure there was no trace of incriminating documents. There was not one room in the villa that had not been thoroughly searched. Now he would begin the marathon job of assessing the Luciano holdings, knowing that many of the territories had already been taken over, that someone had already stepped into Don Roberto's shoes. He had known the moment he had been approached by the three men Graziella had met in the Don's study.

Graziella watched Domino drive away before she picked up the heavy packet of her husband's tapes. She carried it to the study desk and looked around. The room smelled of the men's cigar smoke and of charred papers . . . Sure enough, there in the grate were the tell-tale blackened scraps of paper.

Adina entered with a tray. She had prepared some soup and a small side dish of pasta. She closed the door quietly behind her and paused, listening for the sound of cutlery being used, knowing that Graziella had not eaten for days. As if a ghost crossed her soul, she froze as she heard clearly the deep, warm tones of Don Roberto Luciano. She could not help but cry out, and the study door opened.

Graziella's face was white with anger. 'Leave me alone, leave the house now.'

'My name is Don Roberto Luciano. I give this statement on 10 February 1987. I have certified evidence to prove that I am of a sane, healthy mind and have a witness to prove that these statements are given freely without any undue harassment or pressure from any quarter. I make these statements of my own will . . .'

His voice hurt her, pained her. But she had to listen, had to know what her husband knew and what she did not.

She would hear exactly how her son had been murdered, she would hear, in those same, warm tones, another side of the man she thought she knew and loved.

Teresa looked down into the New York street and watched Father Amberto hail a cab. He was carrying two heavy suitcases filled with her husband's clothes. She remained standing at the window until the cab merged into the stream of continuous traffic on 63rd Street, then turned back into the small room she and Alfredo had used as a study. She went to the desk where she had stacked all Alfredo's unpaid bills and company papers in preparation for work that evening, but now nothing could be further from her mind. She was so angry she was still shaking. She pressed her hands to her cheeks, flushing at the thought of what her daughter had said to the priest. Suddenly she pulled open the door and walked into the narrow corridor.

'Rosa, *Rosa*!'

Her daughter's bedroom door remained firmly closed. Her transistor radio blared, the volume turned up to ear-splitting level.

'Rosa, *Rosa, come out of there*!' Teresa hit the door with the flat of her hand, kept on hitting it until the music was turned off, then she stepped back, hands on her hips, as Rosa opened the door.

'How could you do that? How could you say that to Father Amberto?'

'What?'

'You know perfectly well what, how dare you! I have never been so humiliated in my life.'

'Didn't faze him, he was too busy stuffing the suitcases with all the clothes.'

'I want you to apologize to me, you hear me?'

'Sure I hear, so can half the block. There's no need to act so hysterical, you think he's never heard the word before? All I said was . . .'

'I know what you said. "Check the pockets for rubbers." For *rubbers*! What in God's name possessed you to say such a thing? Search your Papa's suit pockets?' Teresa put her hands over her face. 'What will he think of us?'

'I don't think he'll be saying Hail Marys over it, Mama; it was nothing, forget it.'

'*Forget it*? Why did you say it Rosa, why?'

Rosa shrugged her shoulders and turned to go back to her room. 'Maybe because I can't stand the way you're acting, creeping around the place. Every time I look at you, you start blubbering, and you're taking every mass. It's a wonder your knees aren't calloused.'

Teresa pulled her daughter by the shoulders, her face red with rage. 'How do you expect me to behave, huh? You want me to play music so loud I deafen everyone? You want me to throw open the blinds and have a party? My husband, your father is dead! So help me God, what do you want me to do?'

'I don't know. I don't want anyone else coming here with their prayer books and clasping me by the hand. People I don't know pinching my cheeks as if I was a kid.'

'They're being kind, Rosa, they're trying to help us.'

'No they're not, they're just prying, we don't even know them.'

'They're from the church.'

'But they don't know me, they never knew Papa. He never set foot in church unless you dragged him there. They're just nosy and you are loving every minute of being the centre of attention.'

Teresa slapped Rosa so hard she crashed into the wall. She staggered a moment, then hurled herself at her mother, fists flying, screaming '*Leave me alone!*'

'Fine, I'll leave you alone. I won't cook for you, clean for you, wash for you . . .'

'*You don't have to anyway . . .*'

'Sure I don't have to, and I don't have to give you money every day to go to college. Sure I'll leave you alone. I won't speak to you until you apologize. May God forgive you, and you'll need his forgiveness for what you said to Father Amberto.'

'Why? It was the truth, wasn't it? You think I'm deaf? I heard you two fighting and arguing, I could hear you screaming at each other. He never loved you. He had other women, I know it, everyone knew it . . .'

Teresa couldn't stop the tears. 'Why, Rosa? Why are you saying these things? Since we got home you've been behaving crazy, like I don't know you.'

Teresa searched for a tissue and blew her nose. 'Oh, don't cry, Mama, please, I'm sick of the sight of you crying.'

'Because you *don't* . . .'

'Why should I cry, huh? Tell me why? Cry for Emilio? He never loved me, it was all arranged. I'm glad he's dead because I feel used; I was handed over like a piece of meat.'

Teresa couldn't listen to any more. She walked into her own bedroom and slammed the door behind her.

How little her daughter knew, how little she understood. She took out a photograph of herself on her graduation, wearing her cap and gown, younger than Rosa.

Rosa was sitting in front of her dressing table, trimming her fringe with a pair of nail scissors. Small snippets of hair covered the glass top and fell on to her cosmetics, but she snipped and snipped; anything to stop herself thinking, remembering.

'Rosa, can I come in?'

'No.'

Teresa hovered in the door. 'I wanted to show you something, it's a photograph of me when I was your age, in my cap and gown.'

'I've seen it Mama, Grandmama used to have it on the mantelshelf.'

'Look at me, such a stern little face, with such thick glasses.'

Rosa gave only a fleeting glance at the photograph and Teresa continued, 'You remember Grandmama and Grandpapa? I was brought up in that bakery. Father was always dreaming of going home some day but Mama never wanted to, she felt that they had done so well here in America. Papa was so proud the day I was accepted in college, he thought by just gaining a place I was already a qualified lawyer. He told everyone and they streamed into the bakery with gifts and congratulations . . .'

Rosa blew at the hair on the dressing table, only half listening.

'My father worked in the bakery, Rosa, he didn't own it, and he rented the apartment in the basement. It was dark, airless, and we ran a constant battle against cockroaches. They came in hundreds as soon as the ovens went off . . .'

'Why are you telling me this? I've heard it so many times, about how you used to chase them with a broom . . .'

'Because the man who bought my father the bakery, and bought him the little apartment on the top floor where there weren't any cockroaches, was Don Roberto.'

'So what was Don Roberto going to give Papa for marrying me off? Move us out of this dump? Was that the deal? What was I worth, Mama? A new apartment or a bigger slice of the family business?'

Teresa was too late to stop Rosa ripping her graduation photograph in two, tossing the scraps aside.

Teresa shrieked, 'You don't know anything, you don't know . . .'

Rosa picked up her scissors, jabbing at her mother. The small, sharp blades cut into the back of Teresa's hand. 'Why don't you leave me alone?'

Teresa went into the bathroom and ran cold water on her hand, watching the trickle of blood from the deep cut spread down her fingers. Rosa appeared, shamefaced, at the door.

'Are you OK?'

'Yes.'

'You need a plaster?'

'Yes.'

Rosa opened the glass-fronted cabinet. Her father's shaving brush, razor and cologne were as he had left them. She took out the packet of plasters and opened it.

'This size?' She held a plaster up and watched as her mother dried the cut on a towel, then held her hand out. Rosa gently placed the plaster over the cut. 'You forgot to take Papa's things out of the cabinet. I'm sorry, Mama, and I'll apologize to Father Amberto next Sunday.'

Teresa sat on the edge of the bath. 'I never had a boyfriend, you know. All through college. It wasn't for want of trying. I made the excuse that I had to study so hard that I never had the time. Mama was frantic, it was like an obsession, like there was something wrong with me. Some days when I got home she would have some old women there gossiping, ready to introduce me to their sons, grandsons, uncles ... My father was still proud, informing every customer that his daughter was a qualified lawyer, not that I was. In fact – I never did qualify.'

Rosa interrupted. 'You never qualified?'

'No, I always promised myself I would go back and finish my studies but ... I had you to think of, and Alfredo. He needed me; some of the licences were so complicated, the export and import paperwork was spaghetti to him.'

'I thought you qualified.'

'You thought wrong, you think you know everything – but you don't.'

Teresa took off her glasses and began to clean them on a towel. Rosa noticed the red mark on her mother's nose, the slight rings beneath her eyes – small eyes, watery with tears, the thin sharp nose and small mouth so different from her own. She felt moved by her mother's plainness and continued to stare, blushing as Teresa suddenly looked up and gave a weak smile. The smile accentuated the sharp features, stretching the skin over her high cheekbones.

'You look so like him, I see his face every time I look

at you. You were conceived on our honeymoon, did you know that?'

Rosa nodded. She eased the lid of the toilet seat down and sat, elbows on knees, chin cupped in her hands. There was no escape and, even though she didn't want to listen, Teresa continued, 'I came home one afternoon, I used to walk in through the bakery and down the back stairs . . . One day Mama was waiting, wearing her best dress. I thought, "Oh God, no, not another suitor . . . not someone else's cast-off." "Quick, quick," Mama said, "go and change, put something pretty on, we have company." Of course I refused – in some ways you are very like me – but then Papa rushed up to me, his face bright red. He whispered to me that I had to do my hair, wash my face, he spoke to me as if I were a child, and he repeated, "We have company, we have company, hurry." That was the first time I saw Don Roberto Luciano. Until that moment I wasn't even aware he existed. I don't think my parents ever knew why, but Don Roberto Luciano had come to meet me, wanting me to marry his son, Alfredo.'

Rosa leaned forward, fascinated. 'Go on . . .'

Teresa smiled, pushing her glasses up the bridge of her nose. 'I was furious, I was so humiliated.'

'So what made you change your mind?' asked Rosa.

'Fear. You could feel it, my father was terrified. He was a simple man, he couldn't understand why Don Roberto had come to him in the first place, asking for me, for the daughter they had already begun to think they would never find a husband for. So I agreed to meet him.'

'The following day Alfredo came round, by himself. I

don't know what I had expected, maybe some retard, it was all kind of crazy . . .'

'Go on.'

'I thought he was the most handsome boy I had ever seen, and he was probably even more embarrassed by the situation than I was. I loved him from the first moment, Rosa; then I was scared he would turn me down, so scared that I agreed to everything. I agreed to the wedding taking place within the month and agreed to allow the Lucianos to arrange the guest list, the reception, everything. When I met Graziella Luciano I was even more afraid Alfredo would not go through with the wedding. I knew she didn't think I was good enough. She made the mistake of speaking in Sicilian to Alfredo, she didn't realize I understood every word. She was tearful, telling him he should wait, he was too young.'

'Did he love you?' Rosa could not help the disbelief in her voice.

'Yes, Rosa, he loved me. I asked him if he was having second thoughts . . . Part of me was so afraid that he would admit that he was, but he seemed afraid that I had changed my mind, and so we got married.'

Teresa suddenly didn't want to talk any more; she dropped the towel into the laundry basket. 'My parents were given the bakery, Rosa, and the apartment, and every day Mama said a Hail Mary for Don Roberto Luciano. She died blessing him, still thanking him . . .'

'Mom, did you ever find out why? Why Grandpapa chose you?'

'No.'

'Maybe he saw you some place, and you never knew . . . Mom?'

Teresa gave a shrug of her shoulders. She would never know, never even know how her father knew Luciano, but she said, 'Yeah, maybe.'

Rosa followed her mother into the corridor. 'Emilio said he fell in love with me when he first saw me. You remember that time at the Villa Rivera last summer, Mom?'

Teresa's head was throbbing, she pressed her fingers to her temples.

'You think he would have married me anyway? Even if Don Roberto hadn't wanted it? Mom? I mean he gave your parents the bakery, did he ever say what he was gonna give you?'

'I've got a headache, Rosa, I need to lie down.'

'I need to know . . . *Mom*, I have to know.'

'Does it matter now, Rosa? The boy is dead.'

'I'll go call Grandma . . . I'll ask her.'

'You won't.'

'Why not? You scared I might say something to upset her? She may cut you out of the will, are you scared of that . . .?'

Teresa had taken enough. She rounded on Rosa, 'Yes, maybe I am. Graziella holds the reins, and until I get what is due to me you don't even speak to her. You are her granddaughter, but she'll cut you out like *that*,' she snapped her fingers. 'And that was all he ever had to do, Rosa, that's all Don Roberto ever had to do to get people exactly where he wanted them. If it was for his son to marry me, his nephew to marry you . . . Grow up, Rosa! He manipulated everyone, and Graziella was right at his side. You upset her and we'll get nothing. Right now that may not be important to you, but it is to me, it's all I have left.'

Teresa sighed, 'Oh God, Rosa – you see what you made me do? I'm sorry it had to come out this way, I'm sorry.'

Rosa's dark eyes filled with tears. She whispered, 'I'm sorry too, Mama.'

CHAPTER 20

MOYRA LUCIANO watched Louis Mincelli place the diamond and ruby bracelet into the reinforced cabinet. He laid it on the black velvet between her diamond and emerald Scorpio birth sign and the topaz and garnet brooch.

'Can you make them small bills, Mr Mincelli? I spend forever at the cashiers changing bills, an' car hops expect two dollars just for handing you the car keys nowadays.'

Slowly he counted out the bills, $2,000 in grubby used notes; ones, fives, tens, twenties – then the rest in hundreds, apologizing that he had no fifties.

'That's OK. I see my rings have gone.'

He nodded, stacking the notes in a bundle and drawing an elastic band over them. Moyra placed them carefully in her clutch bag. She liked to feel the wad, it was like a comforter.

The bell pinged as she left the shop and the electrically controlled security bar snapped into place. Mincelli heard rather than saw his wife as she shuffled in with two cups of coffee.

'That was Freddie Luciano's widow,' he said. He

slurped his coffee as his wife shuffled to the display cabinet looking at the new piece. 'I said that was Freddie Luciano's . . .'

'I heard you,' said his wife. 'He was a nasty piece, no doubt be another to take his place – and she'll be back on the streets where he found her, any money on it. What's she doing with all the cash? How much this week?'

'Two grand, it's worth double. She wants it held for a week, said she might come back and reclaim it.'

'That's what they all say.'

Moyra parked the car in the underground lot beneath the casino. She checked the time, knowing Mr Simonie would be on his break.

She did not enter the casino by the vast boardwalk entrance, but from the smaller street side, which meant she didn't have to walk past the casino manager's office. Mr Simonie, the man who had bowed and scraped every time he saw her with her husband, was now less than cordial.

She waved her way through the slot-machine punters, giving a small wave of acknowledgement to the cashier, and headed for the row of lifts. The two security guards recognized her, and both said a polite, 'Good afternoon, Mrs Luciano.' She stepped into the lift and pressed the button for the apartments on the top floor, the courtesy apartments for the high rollers.

Frederico Luciano had been given a number of these apartments to use as he pleased, and he never paid a nickel for them. Frederico didn't have an office; he did his business from the apartments or from some place in the centre of Atlantic City where she had never been. She had no idea of its location.

Her footsteps soundless on the thick-piled carpet, she passed the gym, the keep-fit rooms and the deck leading to the open-air swimming pool and walked along the corridor towards the private suites. She breathed a sigh of relief at having escaped the hawk-nosed Simonie.

The apartment commanded a spectacular view over the ocean, not that Moyra cared. She headed straight for the bedroom, kicking off her stilettos, threw her clothes off and took a shower. Afterwards she sat, wrapped in her dressing gown, eating a doughnut she had brought with her, all the while watching the time for when she could get dressed up and go into the casino. She felt safe there, moving from table to table. She never played for high stakes, sometimes winning a few dollars but mostly losing, playing well into the night just to keep her mind busy.

But she was unsure how long she could keep it up. They had written four short, cryptic notes requesting her to vacate the apartment, but she had simply ignored them. She had been to the bank three times, demanding access to her husband's accounts. The exasperated manager eventually showed her the lawyer's letters freezing her husband's assets; the documents authorized in black and white the closure of Frederico Luciano's accounts and the transfer of all monies to a bank in Palermo.

Moyra had no bank account of her own. Frederico had never kept her short of cash, so she had never needed one. All she had after his death was the cash she had found in the apartment. Money was running out fast.

The realization that she had been nothing but an appendage, a nonentity, destroyed her confidence. To

490

begin with she had approached a few familiar faces and, although there was a polite, if strained, conversation and an expression of condolence, not one person had taken the slightest interest in her circumstances.

The more Moyra thought of her situation, the worse she felt. She contemplated calling up a few of the girls she had danced with in Vegas, but decided against it. Too much time had passed. So for something to do she half-heartedly surveyed her wardrobe.

His suits and shoes were as he had left them. Finding nothing in any of the pockets she opened the cases she had brought back from Palermo and began tossing out her still unpacked clothes. She was looking for his small black address book, which she knew was in the case because she had put it there herself. She tossed his wallet aside and then bent down to retrieve it. She sat on her heels and opened it. She knew there was no money in it, because she had taken what was there while in Sicily, but there had been a few cards, mostly gambling club memberships. But the wallet was empty.

Moyra began to search in earnest for Frederico's address book, littering the room with her clothes. Had she taken it out? She was sure she hadn't, but, just in case, she checked the drawers of the bedside table. They were empty. There had never been anything of value, just photographs, dry-cleaning bills and a few family letters, but they were all gone.

Panic set in as she crawled across the floor to her dressing table and dragged out every drawer. Her heart was thudding; someone had been in the apartment and must have gone through everything.

It was a few moments before she realized the telephone was ringing.

'Moyra? Moyra, is that you?'

'Yes, it's me. Who's this?'

'It's Teresa. Are you OK?'

'Who?'

'Teresa, your sister-in-law. Moyra? Are you there?'

'Oh, Teresa . . .' Moyra sat down on the edge of the bed, cupping the phone in both hands. 'I'm so glad you called me, it's so nice to hear your voice.'

'Have you heard from Graziella?'

'No, I've not spoken to anyone. Is the will gonna be read then?'

'I don't know, that was why I called.'

'Why don't you and Rosa come visit me, just for a weekend? I got a huge apartment . . . Teresa? Could you put me up when they kick me out? Hello?'

Click, the phone went dead, but just hearing from Teresa had made it all real again. She was in line for a good whack, she knew it. She laughed out loud. 'Jesus Christ, somethin's gotta give, it's been a helluva day so far.'

Rosa walked into the study. 'Did you talk to Moyra?'

Teresa nodded, searching over the desktop. 'Yep, she's not heard either, maybe I'll try Sophia later.' She was getting angry, banging open the drawers and slamming them shut. Suddenly, she sat back. 'Someone's been here, there's not one file left with the Luciano name on it, not one letter. Alfredo's diaries, his address book, they were all here because I put them on the desk myself.'

'You gonna call the cops?' asked Rosa.

Teresa shook her head. 'What's the point? Nothing of value's been taken.'

492

'Must have been of value to someone otherwise they wouldn't have bothered breaking in and taking whatever they took, right?'

'Unless they thought there *might* be something – I'll call Sophia.'

The ringing of the telephone seemed to be part of Sophia's dream. She struggled awake.

'Sophia? It's Teresa, did I wake you? I never checked the time.'

'That's OK, Teresa, how are you?'

'Broke and waiting, you seen Graziella?'

'No ... I've had things to do, you know, the boutiques.'

'All right for some! Look, I'll tell you why I rang; one, to see if you've had any news and, secondly, we had a break-in here ... Hello? You still there? Can you hear me?'

Sophia closed her eyes. 'Yes, I can hear you.'

'I said we had a break-in, all Alfredo's papers, photographs, some of the files I had from the trucking company and the gasoline ...'

Sophia interrupted. 'I wouldn't worry, Constantino's desk was cleared out weeks ago, same thing, just papers.'

'Worry? Someone's been inside our apartment.'

Sophia threw back the duvet. Naked, she eased her legs over the side of the bed, feeling for her slippers with her bare feet. She held the phone loosely. 'Don Roberto had a lot of connections, Teresa, people that don't like anyone outside their circle knowing what they're involved in. They were probably just checking there was

493

nothing incriminating, no names, no unfinished business. Just forget it happened.'

'I spoke to Moyra in Atlantic City, they want her out of her apartment in the casino. All this waiting is getting everyone down. Maybe not you, but if you could have a word with Graziella, kind of hurry things up . . .'

'I'll call her tomorrow. How's Rosa? She coping all right?'

'Rosa is fine, will you call me soon as you hear anything? If we haven't heard by the end of the month we are going to Sicily, whether Graziella likes it or not. We've waited long enough.'

There was a brief pause on the tape. Then Don Roberto continued. 'Nevertheless, I intended to gain enough evidence to convict Paul Carolla if necessary. But it became exceptionally difficult. Witness after witness disappeared and I had to wait a considerable time until my son recovered enough to be questioned. You must understand he was an addict, he was very sick.'

Graziella sighed, resting her head in her hands. How many times had she played this tape? Too many to count, over and over again, and every time she heard the words . . . 'You must understand he was an addict, he was very sick,' she wanted to weep, because she did not know, had not known, Michael was addicted to heroin. She blamed herself for not standing against her husband. If she had known she would have demanded to see him and would have taken care of him – she should have been the one to nurse him, she was his mother! But always, as in everything – she had to obey her husband.

The tape continued, her husband's voice speaking

494

calmly with no sign of emotion. 'Michael had fought to stay alive, fought with his bare hands. His nails were torn out by the roots. A hypodermic syringe, containing enough heroin to kill four men, had been forced into his arm. One guard, the only one to survive, was found with bullet wounds to his chest and groin. Gennaro Baranza had been left for dead, but he survived and was able to describe my son's killers. They were not Sicilian but American . . .'

There was a slight pause on the tape, a rustle of papers, then Emmanuel spoke. 'These Americans, I need their names. I will need to question them.'

Don Luciano answered, 'I'm afraid that will be impossible. Paul Carolla made sure they could never be traced, even their bodies have never been found.'

Graziella switched off the tape. The palms of her hands were sweating, leaving an imprint where she had pressed them against the polished surface of the desk. How many lies had her husband told her? Too many even to assimilate. She knew now why Michael, brought home in the velvet lined coffin, wore the cotton gloves on his hands, why his face was that of a stranger. He had not been shot as Graziella had been told. He had not died quickly but fighting for his last breath, clawing at his killers like a pitiful animal.

As Graziella prepared to replay the tapes Adina brought her breakfast tray, putting it down wordlessly and removing the untouched tray from the previous evening. She received only an impatient *grazie* from her mistress, who was still in the same clothes as the day before.

The second tape began with a short introduction from Emmanuel stating the day and time of the recording. The Don described how he had tried without success to gain the evidence to have Paul Carolla eliminated. He made no excuses about his membership of the Mafia, but described how, at a meeting of all the delegates, he had been refused justice for his son's murder.

Not once had Don Roberto mentioned the name of any other member, only Paul Carolla, until he brought up the story of a young don, Anthony Robello, nick-named 'The Eagle'. Luciano explained how the young man had approached him, offering his condolences and also the help of his own family should the time arise for Luciano to need backing. 'I decided to take the justice I had been refused. This was a personal one-to-one vendetta, but one that had to be very carefully orchestrated so that I, though not necessarily Robello, would be totally blameless.'

Graziella felt chilled. All this had occurred when? After they had buried Michael? When they were still grieving? When? The tape gave the answer.

'I arranged that in one day, beginning in the early hours of 4 November 1963, Paul Carolla's refineries, factories, warehouses and two fishing boats would be systematically destroyed.'

Graziella turned off the tape and thumbed through her diary. The date, 4 November, was familiar to her but she could not at that moment recall why. She checked her notes at the front of the diary and discovered that it was the wedding anniversary of Alfredo and Teresa . . . The day Don Luciano had pinpointed for the destruction of Paul Carolla was his own son's wedding day.

Graziella understood now why Alfredo's wedding

had been arranged in such a hurry, why he had chosen that mouse of a girl, Teresa Scorpio. Don Roberto had arranged Alfredo's wedding as a cover for his attempt to destroy Paul Carolla. In his desire to avenge one son he had used another.

Graziella pressed her fingers to her temples. She recalled that the couple Don Roberto had hired to run the villa during their absence resembled the Lucianos so much that no one would even know they had left for New York. She remembered how her husband had laughed about it. She switched the tape on again and felt the hairs on her arms prickle; by coincidence, she heard Don Roberto's laugh again, this time emanating from the tape recorder.

The laughter stopped. His voice was soft and menacing. 'In one day my friend Paul Carolla lost millions. His men were rounded up like cattle, Carolla lost everything but his life.'

There was a long pause, Luciano could be heard to sigh . . . Emmanuel interjected asking if he wished to take a break.

'No, we have little enough time as it is. I sigh, my friend, not from tiredness but from . . . what is that quote? All the best-laid plans? Ah I forget, I forget . . . well, my well-laid plan backfired, leaving me not only in a vulnerable position but in a very dangerous one. I was, understandably, the most obvious suspect. But, I had, thank God, a perfect alibi. I was at my son's wedding in New York . . . I was in New York!'

There was a long pause on the tape. Graziella knew it had not been turned off, she could hear the rustle of papers.

'Please continue. I have made a note of the dates and

will verify that the police records of the explosions coincide . . .'

The Don interrupted, his voice harsh with controlled anger. 'Understand, *amio*, I am not on trial, *capiche*? Be sure, my friend, if I incriminate myself I am more than aware of it. I am here for one reason only, Paul Carolla. There are many who will be afraid, many, but I have no interest in any other man. I have waited twenty years.'

Emmanuel interrupted hesitantly, 'But you must understand my position. If you incriminate yourself, I must make . . .'

'You make sure, my friend, that there are no repercussions either to myself or to my family, is that clear? Do I make myself clear? Now, do you wish me to continue?'

There was a pause and the tape clicked. Graziella knew there must have been some kind of agreement between the two men. With another click the tape continued and there was that laugh again, a cold, hard laugh. 'Robello's attempt on my life made Carolla offer me his friendship, a truce. Now I will tell you why I have mentioned this entire episode. This was given to me by none other than Paul Carolla, a gift to show his good intentions. The box was delivered to my home with this note.'

Graziella could hear something being placed on Emmanuel's desk.

'It is not a bomb, my friend, it is the severed finger of Anthony Robello. You will see, still attached to the finger, his family ring. It resembles a bird's claw, no? His nickname was most apt, no? The remains of Anthony Robello were never discovered, but the note, in Paul Carolla's handwriting, is all the evidence you need.'

Graziella couldn't listen to any more. She ordered her

car and left immediately for the library in the centre of Palermo.

Graziella was in the library for three hours, reading newspapers dating back to the time of Alfredo's and Teresa's wedding. She read for herself about the destruction of Paul Carolla's refineries. The headlines screamed of a Mafia vendetta and the biggest ever narcotics haul. She also read that twelve men had lost their lives in the series of bombings.

She found the issues that covered the assassination attempt on her husband. She remembered reading them, and remembered how proud she had been when they had called him a hero. She also remembered how he had asked her not to question him, the blood on his shirt, blood she had been so terrified was his. And he had said, what was it he had said? . . . 'It is not my blood, Mama, but it is on my hands, may God forgive me!'

Graziella turned the pages of the newspaper, and stared at the picture of the two little girls, the sisters who had been riding their bicycle past the Mercedes when the bomb intended for Luciano had exploded. 'It is not my blood, Mama, but it is on my hands, may God forgive . . .'

Everything felt tainted; behind the façade of husband and father had been a man Graziella did not know existed. She had lived surrounded by death and murders. Worse, she had lived off the proceeds. Graziella bowed her head and whispered over and over. 'May God forgive me . . .'

*

Mario Domino was relieved to hear from Graziella. He had tried to contact her for the past two weeks but she had refused to answer his calls. She had not checked the piles of work he had been diligently overseeing, nor had she answered any of his hand-delivered letters.

'Are you well?'

'Yes, Mario . . . Will you find a man called Gennaro Baranza? I must meet him as soon as possible.'

He felt the chill in her voice. 'Graziella? You must meet me! I have done considerable work on the tax situation, but we must discuss the sales of the companies.'

'Another time, I have to go to court. Remember, Mario, Gennaro Baranza, he used to work for Don Roberto. It is a very important matter.'

'But Graziella, this must be given precedence over everything else! You must consider . . .'

There was a silence on the line. 'Graziella, are you there? Please, this is insanity! I have laid off all the men as you instructed, but don't you understand what you are doing? All Roberto built, everything he spent his life building . . .'

Before Domino could say another word she had hung up. Graziella had given him only one instruction: 'Get rid of everything, sell everything.'

She wished only for the cash to be accumulated for her daughters-in-law and her granddaughter. Domino had begged her to wait, to take advice, but she was adamant that nothing must remain. She even instructed him to include the Villa Rivera in the sale.

The following morning, Mario Domino set out early to drive to the Villa Rivera in the hope of catching Graziella

500

before she left for the trial. There was only one guard at the wrought-iron gates and he opened up without even asking Domino's name.

Adina grew upset as she told Mario that Graziella rarely, if ever, ate, and most nights never slept.

'She plays the tapes over and over . . . I hear his voice, like a ghost through the house. I don't know what to do, she is making herself ill, she is so thin, so . . .'

'Has the doctor been to see her recently?'

'No, signor, she sees no one. She will not allow me to answer the phone . . . And look, see all these letters and cables? She does not even open them. She listens only to the tapes. Signor, what is on those tapes? What makes her act this way?'

Domino sighed, patting the servant's shoulder. 'Perhaps the truth.'

Going down the long drive Domino remembered the day Don Roberto had discovered his wife's visits to his office. At first Domino had tried to deny that they were a regular occurrence, and Don Roberto had snapped that there was nothing that was not reported back to him. Domino had been afraid; this was a man he had worked for all his adult life and yet he terrified him.

'Your wife, Don Roberto, feels greatly that she is in some way to blame for Michael's death, that you did not allow her to nurse him. If she knew more . . .'

'Understand this, Mario, Graziella is my wife, she is the mother of my sons. You will tell her nothing, nothing, unless I give you permission.' Then he had given that charming smile of his, 'You may call it jealousy; even after all these years I have not forgotten you were once to be married. I am sorry if I spoke curtly, forgive me . . . She may come to you once a month, I will give you certain information she may be told, no more, no less.'

In the courtroom Carolla stared at Graziella. He could not tell if she was looking at him from behind her black mourning veil.

Carolla's sweating face, his obsession with cleaning his nails, filing and picking at the cuticles, drew her attention. She stared . . . kept on staring. Had Michael's death, in the end, joined Luciano and Carolla together? If she had known the truth, known the way her son had died, nothing would have stood in her way, no matter what the cost. She could not, like her husband, have waited. Why had he waited? And why, if Carolla was unlikely ever to be freed, had Don Roberto chosen to be a witness? He must have known the dangers, not only to himself, but to his family.

When the trial closed for the day, Carolla had still not taken the stand, had never used the microphone that linked his cage with the courtroom. He had sat impervious to the proceedings.

Graziella returned to the villa, more determined than ever to uncover the truth. Mario Domino was already waiting for her. This time she did not refuse to speak to him.

The study was cold. She did not turn on the light, preferring to sit in the shadows. Domino opened his briefcase and took out some files.

'Did you find Gennaro Baranza for me?'

'Yes, he lives with his son in Mondello. They run a small hotel; I have the address and phone number. He is very frail. May I ask you why you wish to see him?'

She looked up, her face paler than ever. 'You know, every day at the trial I look at the men in the cages and I know many of them must have worked for or been known to Don Roberto. I hear of prostitution, blackmail, kidnapping, extortion, murders, and I think of this place, I think of my life. I listen to his voice and he is a stranger to me . . . I have lost four sons but, worse, I have lost all respect for him, Mario.'

'Then you do him a great injustice.'

'Do I? How much of his fortune was built on fear, how many died to make my family worth being murdered for? You want to hear what I have been listening to? Hear him laughing when he describes how he arranged his son's marriage as a cover for murder? Do you want to hear what he did, how he used me, how he used his sons?'

'Throw the tapes away, don't listen to them.'

'I will listen. Because even at the end he lied to me. He said he could not rest, could not die in peace without giving Michael the justice he deserved. It was *lies*! Carolla had to *know* that it was Don Roberto Luciano who put him in jail. Michael had nothing to do with his decision, Mario, it was for himself. He wanted to prove to Carolla that in the end he had beaten him.'

'That is not true, Graziella.'

'No? How much proof did he need for the courts, for the law? Everyone would have known what we were. If he had given evidence, he would have implicated himself and his family, Mario, he would have destroyed them

503

anyway. Well, he succeeded, and now I want nothing, nothing to be left. My granddaughter, my sons' wives, none of them must know the truth. I want them to live their lives without fear, I want them free, Mario.'

Mario picked up his papers and carefully rearranged them in order, stacking them in his briefcase. He snapped the locks, resting his hands on top.

'As you wish. I will contact you as soon as the transactions have taken place. But understand, you will be giving the very people you despise access to your husband's legitimate companies. Companies that were to have been your sons' inheritance.'

'Mario, I know about my sons, please don't think me that naïve. They were part of it too, Frederico more than the others. And you, like my husband, fed me a pack of lies . . . Well, no more lies, I want to go to my grave in peace. Now you must excuse me, it has been a very long day.'

Mario looked at her sadly. 'I have always loved you, you must know that. I would protect you with my life, but I could not go against his wishes.'

'Because you were afraid? Tell me, Mario, were you afraid of him too? Who were they, those men? Why did you search this house?'

'For your own protection. I had to make sure there was nothing here, nothing anyone else would need, or want – nothing incriminating, do you understand? Even though it is against your wishes, I am simply trying to do what I believe is in your best interest. At the same time, your demand that I sell everything, whether at profit or no, has caused nothing but suspicion. I am trying to transfer all monies to a Swiss bank account so that you are not taxed as you would be if it is paid here in Palermo. You would be losing millions of lire in death duties and taxes . . . And then today one of my clerks . . .'

Domino had to sit down as he could not get his breath. 'I have sixteen men in my offices, all working towards finalizing the will for your daughters and grand-daughter. Today, however, we have come across certain discrepancies . . . One of the buyers, I believe, though I cannot be sure, is acting under orders . . .'

Domino's harassed face went grey and Graziella fetched him a glass of water, holding it for him while he searched for his tablets. She watched as he gulped at the water, then slipped her arms around his shoulders.

'Forgive me. I have misused you, tired you and never said one word of thanks.'

Mario smiled at her. 'You and your daughters will, I assure you, be well taken care of.'

'What will you do, Mario, when it is all over?'

'Retire, live out my old age in blissful ignorance of everything occurring in the world. I have always wanted a garden, did you know that? And I have always lived in an apartment with not even a window box.'

Arm-in-arm they walked to his car, both surveying the once beautiful gardens. He laughed. 'Perhaps you could hire me, I could come here and take care of that lawn. It is so neglected.'

Graziella smiled. 'I made this my world, Mario. I thought it was safe and secure. I know about Michael, Mario. I know, and I should have been told.' She cupped her face in her hands. 'I know now that the only innocent was Michael. Papa used the others, didn't he? Constantino, Alfredo, Frederico?'

Mario agreed sadly. 'He was a hard man to refuse, Graziella, and yet he was so easy to love. I loved him like a brother, but you were right, I was always afraid of him. No, not always . . . Do you remember when he came back, after the war? He was different then, he had changed.'

He paused, even now hesitating to tell her the truth. But what was there to fear now? 'He wanted out, Graziella, and he tried, but they wouldn't free him. He knew too much, was too valuable.'

She stepped back from the car, shutting the door. Mario continued, 'I'll be in Rome for a few days. If you need me, the office will know where I am. Take care now, and rest.'

She waved as he drove away, but her mind was churning over what he had said. It was true, after the war Roberto was changed. As the weeks had passed into months and Roberto had still made no effort to find work, she had become concerned. The boys had been just toddlers then and the black-market eggs and chickens that had been delivered throughout the war by her husband's friends had stopped.

Graziella stood in the cavernous hall, now filled with antiques and paintings, statues and the finest carpets. How different it had been then. She sat on the stairs and closed her eyes, picturing her husband as a young man, working outside, mending fences, cutting wood for the kitchen fire. But the packages stopped coming.

Graziella put her hands over her ears. She could hear herself, hear the words she had shouted and see the children clustered around her as her voice rose to a screech, demanding that Roberto find food for his hungry children. Unlike the starving families all over

Sicily, it was the first time the Lucianos had been short of food. Where had the supplies come from? She had never asked because she had known it was the black market, just as she knew when she pressed his white shirt and best suit that he was not going to try to find work in town because there was no work. Sicily was desperately impoverished after the war . . .

Graziella stood and whispered to the empty, marble hall, 'I have always known . . .'

She paused for a moment by the open, carved doors of the dining room. The only sound was the soft ticking of the marble clock. She walked the length of the room, skirting the polished table, the rows of baroque chairs with their plum satin upholstery, past the priceless paintings, the solid Georgian silver candelabra. She walked beneath the crystal and gold chandelier and continued slowly by the inlaid, glass-fronted cabinets filled with ornaments and treasures. Everywhere was lavish opulence.

She sat in her husband's carved chair, her hands clasping the arms, feeling the lions' open mouths with her fingers. 'I have always known,' she whispered again. Graziella returned to the study and picked up the single sheet of notepaper with one line of Mario Domino's meticulous handwriting. *Gennaro Baranza. Hotel Majestic, Mondello.*

Adina could not believe it when Graziella burst into the kitchen.

'We are going to Mondello . . . I need you.'

'Mondello?' Adina smiled. She had been born in Mondello, and had not been there for many years.

'But, signora, you have no driver.'

'I know, that is why I need you. You will have the map and you will direct me. I am driving.'

'Oh, no, signora! Please, no, don't drive.'

The single guard on duty had just enough time to open the right-hand gate before the Mercedes screeched past, right over his foot. As he hopped up and down in agony, the car jolted to a halt. He watched fearfully; it seemed to be coming back towards him . . . With another jolt it stopped, and Graziella leaned out of the window.

'No one is allowed into the villa until I return.'

'*Si*, Signora Luciano.'

He watched the car weave down the road in a haze of dust, the gears grinding horribly. Graziella, her face set with determination, was at the wheel; Adina sat beside her, clutching her rosary, eyes tightly closed, until she heard Graziella laughing . . .

'This feels so good, I feel good now, Adina. Now, the map is in the glove compartment . . .'

'*Si*, signora, but please . . . Don't take your hands off the wheel, I'll find it.'

CHAPTER 21

SOPHIA HATED the smell of the cab. It made her sick to her stomach and the lurching, erratic driving threw her from side to side.

For the latter part of the journey she had to direct the driver along narrow, cobbled streets until they reached the tall, open gates to the warehouses, now converted into factories. She could see her seamstresses hanging out of the windows, calling to the men at work on the heavy machines in the building opposite. The women would have recognized her yellow Maserati but they ignored the taxi.

As she left the shadow of the building and emerged into the bright sunlight, she heard a frantic whisper, 'It's Signora Luciano!' The girls ducked quickly back to their work.

Sophia entered the building by a small side door marked 'S & F Designs' and climbed the narrow staircase. She had to clutch the wooden rail to help her up the old, uneven steps.

At the first landing Sophia flattened herself against the wall to allow two men to pass, carrying files and artwork. They thanked her politely. Before she could start up the next flight of stairs two more men came down, carrying armfuls of dresses. She watched from the window as the men loaded everything into an S & F delivery van. Through the van's open doors she could see that there were already two filing cabinets inside.

The last of the stairs up to the top floor were expensively carpeted in a pale peach. She pushed open the freshly painted door with the tasteful gold S & F logo and entered the showroom. The reception was filled with fresh flowers.

'*Buon giorno*, Signora Luciano.'

'*Buon giorno*, Celeste. *Come sta?*'

The girl appeared rather flustered. '*Molto bene.*'

'Is Nino here?' asked Sophia.

'*Si*, signora, shall I call through for you?'

'No, *grazie.*'

Sophia continued through reception and into the outer corridor. She passed her own office and approached her partner's. Nino Fabio flushed when he saw her.

'What's happening?' Sophia wanted to know.

'I've tried to contact you for weeks.'

Sophia stood by his empty desk, opened her handbag and took out a cigarette, tossing the match in the waste bin, then looked around the room. 'What's going on?'

'Guess it must be pretty obvious. I'm moving out.'

She inhaled, letting the smoke drift from her nostrils. 'I can see that. Where are you moving to?'

He seemed very nervous. 'I tried to reach you, to tell you personally, I've had a good offer. So, with this new collection for Milan, I accepted. I've wanted to go for some time now . . . Well, now I am able to.'

'You've never mentioned this to me before.'

'I tried to contact you.'

She sighed, growing angry. 'Well, you must know why I haven't been available.'

'Well, of course I do . . . I wrote to you, did you receive my letter, the flowers?'

'Yes.'

The receptionist brought two cups of coffee, put them on the desk and left without a word. Sophia said, 'I see everyone is aware of your sudden departure except your partner. What were you going to do, clear everything out and then write to me?'

'I have tried to contact you, Sophia.'

'I heard you the first time. How many people are you taking with you?'

'The ones I brought with me.'

'I see . . .' She picked up her coffee, shaking so much that she had to hold it with both hands. 'Pretty low, isn't it? Sneaking out of the back door?'

'I am not sneaking, Sophia, and if you had spent a little more time here you would have known that, financially, we are in trouble anyway. And since . . . since . . .'

'Since what?'

Nino was really edgy. 'Since your husband and . . .'

'My husband had nothing to do with this business,' she snapped.

'Maybe he had more to do with it than you were ever aware. Look, Sophia, please; I don't want to go into detail . . .'

'What do you mean, more than I was aware? This is my business, my husband had nothing to do with it.'

'Your husband, Sophia, was very much a part of this business. You were quite simply never made aware of it.'

511

His overpowering cologne was making her nauseous.

'The deal, or my deal, was to make sure you never knew . . .'

She interrupted. 'Deal? What are you talking about, what deal?'

Nino raised his manicured hands to stop her. 'OK, you might as well know it all. You were an innocent, my love, married, a woman with more time than she knew what to do with . . .'

'Don't tell me about my life, Nino.'

'You wanted to open a boutique, wanted to prove something to yourself, right? Think about it, Sophia; why would a young designer walk away from a big fashion house to start work with a partner with no credit?'

'Why don't you tell me why, Nino?'

He shrugged. 'Money. After I refused, I was paid a visit by your husband. He offered me more, a lot more, Sophia, but it wasn't an ordinary offer. The only way I could have left you was to slit my throat.'

Sophia's mind whirled. She could hardly take it all in; Constantino, sweet, kind Constantino?

Nino continued, 'Now don't get me wrong. We've had a lot of fun together, but two boutiques and a couple of half-hearted fashion shows a year have hardly helped my career.'

Sophia's throat had constricted and it was a few moments before she could speak. 'So . . . my husband paid you on top of what you were earning from the boutiques, is that what you are saying? He paid you on top of our contract?'

Again Nino sighed. 'I also run a lucrative mail-order

business.' He paused, cocking his head to one side. 'You wanna see for yourself?'

He led Sophia into their own small workroom where eight machinists made up the bales of cloth chosen by Sophia. The walls were covered with Nino's designs and notes.

'All these girls worked for how many weeks on one wedding dress, remember? Now, who do you think was running the boutiques, organizing the stock, while nothing was being made up? New orders came in from left and right and were ignored, right? Eight girls working flat out . . . That costs, Sophia.'

The wedding dress had been Sophia's gift for Rosa. Sophia felt dizzy, trying to fight the picture in her mind of little Rosa swirling around the hallway of the Villa Rivera.

They walked out of their own building. Two warehouses away, Nino opened a door with no sign on it, ushering Sophia ahead of him. The noise of sewing machines was deafening as they walked through to the main workroom. Thirty-two women looked up, but continued their work. Nonplussed, Sophia followed Nino along the narrow aisle as he held up see-through briefs and négligés, hideous brassières and suspender belts, tossing them aside on his way to the back of the room.

They arrived at the open glazed door of an office. Nino turned and waved his hand at the workroom.

'This is what covered the costs of your enterprise, Sophia, all of this . . . Come on into the office.'

A small, balding man in shirt-sleeves held up by armbands stumbled to his feet. His head was in a cloud of cheap cigar smoke. He looked first at Nino, then at Sophia.

'Signor Silvio, this is Sophia Luciano.'

Sophia spent the rest of the morning looking over the two sets of accounts: one for her boutiques and the other for the lingerie mail-order business. Nino pointed to the figures.

'Hookers and cat-houses are the main buyers. We distribute to all the markets, the street traders.'

Somehow she kept her control, giving no sign of what this meant to her. She had been so proud of owning the shops independent of the Lucianos. The accountants, the salesmen, even her own business manager, were all involved, and she had been kept oblivious.

Signor Silvio's body odour was overpowering. 'The situation now, Signora Luciano, is that we don't know whether you wish us to continue. We've had no one directing us for six months. Nino Fabio has been overseeing everything here, but as he is leaving we are not sure who will be responsible for the salaries, the outgoings . . . We still have orders to fulfil, but we must bring out a new catalogue. We can get better deals, cash transactions as we have in the past, for photographs, et cetera . . .'

Sophia stood up and straightened her skirt. 'This factory will be closed. Please pay everyone a month's salary.'

Nino poured a large vodka and handed it to Sophia. 'You will never survive without the sweat shop. Your shops have been running at a loss for years. If you want to continue, Silvio's a good, hard-working man. And consider the girls; you'll put them out of work, and hundreds of street traders . . .'

'Why didn't you ever tell me, why?'

Nino's face hardened. 'Maybe I value my life.'

The neat vodka burned her throat. 'Now . . .'

He gave a shrug. 'Now obviously things are different. If you wanted you could find a buyer easily, but I want out, Sophia. Do you think I wanted to design that cheap shit downstairs?'

Sophia drained her glass and poured herself another stiff measure. 'What about all the designs we worked on?'

'We?' Nino's face twisted. 'Picking the fabric, my love, is not designing. Face facts, you've been allowed to play at business for years, now why don't you grow up? I am taking my designs and I am walking out of the door. If you don't like it, then . . .'

'Then what, Nino?'

'I've been treated like a piece of meat for too long, Sophia. You can't make me stay; if you try I'll leak the story of your whores' factory to the press. It'll ruin any chance of you holding on to the clients, clients that I brought with me. I doubt if they'll still be interested anyway, not after the things they've read in the papers about the . . . the . . .'

'Not interested after what, Nino? Not after my entire family have been murdered?'

He sighed. 'You said it, not me. Look give me a break. I've been trapped here, now I want out. Is that such a bad thing?'

'There is nothing I can do to stop you.'

Suddenly, he eased up, realizing she was telling the truth. 'I appreciate it. It's a big chance for me, I will get

515

my own label. Sophia, I can never even say that I worked for you, do you understand? I want to go to the States, if it gets out that I was connected with the Lucianos it could blow any chance of a visa. Your family name and the obvious connection, it's been plastered all over the papers . . .'

'Just go . . .'

He didn't need telling twice. She could hear him outside the office, laughing and joking with Celeste, then there was a strange silence. She wrote a brief note and then buzzed through to Celeste to come to her office.

'Will you type this out, please, and put it on the notice board?'

Celeste pinned the notice up and the girls gathered around. Sophia was giving them a month's notice with six weeks' pay. It was very generous, but then some of the girls had been with Sophia and Nino from the beginning.

Sophia found out later that Nino Fabio had withdrawn all the cash from their business account. He had also removed bales of silk fabrics and all the racks of evening dresses destined for her boutiques. Trying to assimilate exactly what stock she had and what she would require to stay in business, she discovered Nino had removed vast quantities of stock from the boutiques themselves and she was therefore forced to give notice to all her sales staff. Sophia paid them off using her personal account, certain her bankers would cover the monies.

She foolishly continued to write cheques, not caring that she did not have the resources to cover the costs.

Her bankers became alarmed and requested an urgent meeting. Sophia could not even give her apartment as security and she handed over the keys to her husband's garage knowing the fleet of cars would be, like the apartment, part of Constantino's estate. Within two weeks she was millions of lire in the red, and cheques were still outstanding. Sophia was warned that she would face bankruptcy, and her bankers were also concerned over the alarming discrepancies in her business account. They suggested she speak urgently to the executors of her husband's estate.

Sophia did try to contact Graziella, but receiving no reply, she was in some ways grateful not to have to discuss her financial situation, sure that at any time Constantino's funds would be released. Sophia's only thoughts were to trace her son, and she arranged to fly to Sicily from Rome and from there travel by train to Cefalu.

Adini brought the tray of lemonade. Her hands were still shaking. Graziella was sitting, perfectly calm, with her eyes closed and her face tilted towards the sun. They were at a small roadside café, waiting for the car to be repaired.

They were just outside Mondello, and had been waiting for two hours. Across the road the mechanic could be seen, lying beneath the Mercedes. They could also see three large dents. They had not had three accidents; just one rather complicated one with a bollard and a tree.

Adina sighed. The thought of travelling any further with Graziella at the wheel was disconcerting. She rarely managed to get out of second gear and the car tended to leap-frog along. They were only eight or so miles from Palermo, and yet the journey had taken most of the morning.

'This Hotel Majestic, do you know it, Adina?'

'No, signora, I have not been there since I was a child. I know only my cousin, my stepsister. It is a very popular resort now, not like when I was a girl. It was just a fishing village, but the lido . . .'

'I know, I know. We used to bring the boys when they were young. Go and ask about the hotel.'

Adina crossed the road and held a lengthy conversation with the mechanic. Eventually she returned to Graziella.

'He knows my cousin.' Adina sat down and drew her chair closer to the table. 'He also knows of Antonio Baranza, the old man's son. They don't like visitors, the old man rarely goes out. Maybe we should talk first to my cousin?'

'As you wish. How long will the car be?'

'Not long. We made a hole in the carburettor. I have directions, it will be no problem. The Majestic is on the far side of the square, not far from my cousin.'

An hour later the Mercedes leap-frogged through the square, causing many of the old men, sitting with their beers in the shade, to chortle.

Adina, having said she knew no one, spent much of the journey leaning out of the window addressing what appeared to Graziella to be the whole town. Knowing the street was too narrow for the car, Adina suggested they park in the square. She would go and speak to her cousin and return immediately. Graziella watched her, shaking her head. She was at it again; '*Eh, Giorgio, buona sera, come sta?*' She talked to all and sundry, so it was half an hour before she returned.

Graziella was furious, but Adina paid no attention. She seemed very nervous, waving her hands around as they headed out of the square and on to a smaller road on the north side.

'The Majestic is a café, signora. They rent out rooms. They have a few tables in front and a small bar, mostly used by residents. Not many tourists.' She dropped her voice to a hushed, conspiratorial whisper, 'They will not speak with you, will not let you see the old man. His son tells everyone he is senile, but my cousin knows the woman who helps in the kitchens. Sometimes she takes the old man for a walk; she pushes his chair along the harbour. There is a small bar with tables outside. She will take him there this afternoon and if you are waiting there, she and I will—'

'You know this woman?'

'*Si*, signora, we were at school together. The Carboni family run this part of town, signora. My cousin's sister works for Alessandrini Carboni. Baranza's son also works for the Carbonis.'

'I shall wait, Adina, but not for long.'

Gennaro Baranza wore a straw hat, one side looking as if a dog had made a meal of it. He also wore a strange pink pair of ladies' sunglasses perched on his bulbous nose. The rest of him looked shrivelled as he hunched in the wheelchair.

The plain-looking woman pushing the chair waved to Adina, who hurried to join her. They talked as they wheeled the old man towards Graziella and parked him in the shade.

Graziella was at a loss how to begin. Looking at the trembling man in the moth-eaten straw hat she felt she had wasted her time. Then she heard his voice, very faintly.

'I wept for your family, signora.'

She whispered, 'So you know who I am?'

'*Si*, signora, I know. We met, many times. I was only a young man.'

'Forgive me, I did not remember.'

Again he lifted his shoulders. One of his hands was crippled but the other plucked at the knitted shawl across his knees. 'My son tells people I am senile, but I forget nothing. Perhaps only what has to be forgotten.'

'You knew my son Michael?' Graziella asked.

'*Si*, I knew him well. He taught me to read and write. We spent six months together in the mountains. I loved your son, he was . . .' He touched his heart with his good hand. 'An angel's soul.'

They fell silent for a moment, then Graziella sighed. 'I did not know he was addicted to heroin. I only discovered this recently.'

'Don Roberto said he would cut out the tongue of any man who told you. You will only have good memories, signora, the others you would not be able to push away. They would haunt you, believe me.'

'I have only memories, Gennaro, of all my sons. I have lost four sons.'

She leaned forward. 'Tell me how Michael died. Tell me everything you know.'

She could not see his eyes behind the pink sunglasses but he averted his face, as if he could not bear her to look at him. 'I do not remember, my mind sometimes is as dead as my body.'

'I do not believe you.'

'Believe me, signora, the day your son died I have every reason to forget, for in some ways I died too. I was left for dead. Maybe it would have been better if I had died. All that is clear is the pain, pain that is with me day and night.'

Graziella sat back and fanned herself with her handkerchief. Even in the shade the heat was overpowering. 'Would you like me to push you a little further along the harbour?'

For all his frailty, Gennaro was no lightweight. Graziella found it hard to push him, but at last they reached the top of the harbour. She turned the chair to face the sea.

Gennaro smiled, cocking his head to one side as he looked over the brilliantly coloured fishing boats in the harbour. 'Who was King Lear?'

Graziella looked down at the old man. 'King Lear? He was a character in a play by Shakespeare. Why do you ask?'

They fell silent for a moment, then Gennaro began to talk in his croaking voice. 'The Don carried his son like he was a baby, wrapped in the sheet he had taken from the bed. No one knew what to say to him, or what to do for him. Standing in the doorway with his son, he cried out.'

Graziella hesitated, then she said kindly, 'King Lear was a mighty king. His favourite daughter died and he carried her in his arms. I think the line is, "Howl . . . howl . . .".'

Gennaro's face puckered into a heavy frown. 'A daughter, not a son, eh?'

Graziella turned his chair so he faced her. 'You remember the men who killed my son? All I ask is for you to tell me what you know. I would never make you go to court, never force you to be a witness. This is just for me, Gennaro, for me, for Michael's mama . . .'

He gave a heavy sigh. 'They were American.'

'Did you know their names?'

'No. I was shown many photographs.'

'Who showed you?'

'Don Roberto. I recognized their faces, but I did not know their names. But he found them. One by one, he found them.

'Don Roberto.' He gave a hard chuckle, 'He found every boy from America who had so much as smoked a cigarette with Michael. Not one escaped.'

'Did these Americans admit that Paul Carolla ordered the death of my son?'

Gennaro averted his face, refusing to answer. She snatched his sunglasses from his face and stepped back in shock. One eye socket was empty, the lid a mass of scar tissue.

His voice was plaintive. 'My glasses, signora, please.'

She held them away from him. 'They didn't all escape, did they? Lenny Cavataio survived, do you remember him?'

Gennaro grimaced. 'He was the last, the one who knew everything, but he too is dead. My glasses, please, signora.'

She handed them to him but he could not manage to replace them. She did it for him, then rested her hand gently on his shoulder.

'Forgive me . . . I owe you an explanation. I am trying to understand why, if my husband knew of Paul Carolla's part in my son's murder, why he waited so long. Why did he wait?'

Gennaro stared straight ahead, she had to stoop to hear him. 'Don Roberto had three more sons, his family. When he found Lenny Cavataio, only then did he have the evidence, the right to demand justice. But it was too late, Carolla was already in jail.'

Graziella bent even closer. 'If what you say is true, why did he take Lenny Cavataio's place as prosecution witness?'

Gennaro looked up into her face. 'I don't know, signora, but standing as a witness in Carolla's trial signed his death warrant. He would have had more respect if he had taken a gun and shot him. Perhaps, in the end, he waited too long.'

She gripped the arms of the wheelchair as Gennaro tried frantically to turn it. She could feel his panic.

'Who ordered the deaths of my sons, my grandsons? *Tell me!*'

Running towards them along the sea wall came a small boy. He shouted and waved as he came closer. 'Grandpapa! *Grandpapa!*'

Gennaro looked at the child as he jumped down from the wall. The child sensed his grandfather's fear and started to scream, pulling Graziella's hands from the chair.

She pushed him roughly aside. 'My husband could have forced you to stand trial, you witnessed the death of my son. You owe him; pay your debt to me. Was it Paul Carolla?'

Adina could hear Graziella's raised voice, the screams of the child. Panic-stricken, she ran towards them.

'Signora! Signora!'

As frail as Gennaro was, he faced Graziella. His voice rasped as he shouted, 'Stay away from my family! Go away!'

Gennaro's son was panting with fear, as his father was wheeled towards him.

'You crazy, you foolish old bastard! What did she want? What did she want?'

'Whatever, does it matter? She's a woman, what can she do?'

'So what did she want?'

'Tell me, do you know who King Lear was?'

His son spat at the ground and ordered the old man inside, calling after him that from now on that was where he would stay. Gennaro's body ached from being pushed over the cobbles, his head sent shooting pains through his eye. But he turned and called out, 'You have this hotel, you have money for beer, all from the Lucianos.'

'And you are crippled from the Lucianos.'

'But I can read, and I can write . . .'

Safely restored to his shuttered room he heaved his skeletal frame from the chair to the bed and sighed with relief. Tossing his sunglasses aside he massaged his eye socket with his good hand. A bullet was still lodged in his skull, another in his spine. Many times he had wished he had died that night, the night he had seen the Don's car drive up the mountain track. The sentry, high on the mountainside, had flashed his torch, presuming the Don himself had come to visit his son. The passenger wore a similar fedora, the driver was the Don's personal body-guard, Ettore Calleah . . . But as the car drew up outside the cottage two men had sat up from the back seat and two machine guns rattled. Two guards, one of them Gennaro's brother, had died instantly. Gennaro had run back towards Michael's bedroom, calling out a warning. He had just reached the door when the bullets tore through his body.

He had been unconscious for perhaps seconds, per-haps minutes, but the men had presumed him dead. In his semi-conscious state he had seen them, watched them torture and beat the boy he called 'Angel Face'. There was nothing he could do, he could not even call out, he just lay in his own blood where he had fallen and heard the terrible screams.

Gennaro remembered as if in a haze Don Roberto's hoarse voice refusing to allow anyone near his son. He had wrapped his beloved boy in the bloody sheet and carried him like a baby.

Gennaro had been too ill, almost near death himself to see Don Roberto, but he had heard that terrible howl of grief, and no one at that mountain hideout would ever forget the sound, it chilled the soul. He slipped his hand beneath his pillow and took out a small hardbacked book. An inscription inside read, 'To my poetic friend,

525

and student, from Michael Luciano.' The book was in English, and so Gennaro had never been able to read it, but he knew the title by heart: it was *King Lear* by William Shakespeare.

CHAPTER 22

S OPHIA ARRIVED in Cefalu. But having made the decision and carried it through, her confidence ebbed dramatically. How was she to begin? She sat in the small hotel room trying desperately to form some plan of action. She had not registered as Luciano but had used her maiden name of Visconti.

From the tiny, high balcony she could see the harbour, the cobbled street where she and her mother had lived and the hotel where she had worked as a maid. Above the rooftops she could see the church spire but, to her consternation, there was a new glass and concrete hotel where the orphanage had been.

She threaded her way among the tombstones, unable to find her mother's grave. She had not been able to afford a headstone. Eventually, she laid the flowers she had brought beside a small wooden cross that bore no name and whispered a plea for forgiveness, for her Mama to forgive her.

Walking from the cemetery up the narrow street, she found that little was familiar. Twenty-five years had brought many changes. She evoked curious stares from

527

the locals; the woman in the fine clothes was a stranger to them.

It was growing dark as she stood outside the convent, looking up at the high roof, the small windows. A pale face peered down from one of the upper rooms. She had been there once, frightened and lonely, an outcast.

The coolness was as Sophia remembered. The stone walls, the floors, the heavy oak doors had not changed. In a whisper, the sister had asked her to wait in the corridor. After a short while, she returned.

Sophia followed the sister down a familiar narrow passage, pausing at a small door, where she knocked. Without waiting, she opened the door and ushered Sophia inside.

The Mother Superior was seated behind a large, ornately carved desk. She wore small, rimless glasses. She could smell heavy, sweet perfume but could not see the woman visitor's features clearly as she was wearing a mourning veil.

'Signora Visconti, please sit down.' She watched with interest as the delicate lace veil was slowly lifted.

'Sister Matilda? Do you remember me? It's Sophia.'

They talked of the time when the Mother Superior had been simply Sister Matilda. There had been many changes since then; sadly, the orphanage no longer existed, but they had a new school and a new wing for the poor and needy girls such as Sophia had been. It was hard for Matilda to recall Sophia as a young girl, but when she told her the reason for her visit she remembered very clearly. Sophia wished to trace her son, the child born in the convent.

Sophia was devastated when the softly spoken woman explained that the adoption records had been destroyed in a fire.

'Is there no other record? Not even in the church register?'

The Mother Superior apologized; he would be impossible to trace. She offered to show Sophia the new buildings and, almost without realizing she had agreed, Sophia followed her.

She caught the sleeve of the Mother's gown. 'He had a locket, a small gold locket. I put it around his neck. He used to like me to swing it back and forth and would reach for it with his little hands . . . I'd swing it for him until he slept . . .'

'I'm sorry, Sophia. If you recall, you left the baby at the orphanage to enable you to go to work . . .' The Mother's eyes glinted behind her spectacles, and Sophia could hear the coldness in her voice. 'I believe when you left Cefalu you must have signed papers giving permission, if you did not return for your child, for him to be adopted. Did you sign such documents?'

Sophia nodded. 'Is there no one I can speak to, no one who would possibly remember? There must have been more than one set of records. The doctor . . .'

'He died more than ten years ago, God rest his soul.'

Sophia wanted to scream aloud but simply followed the black-clad figure, who was proudly showing her the gymnasium.

'Our benefactor was a very generous man. All this he donated and, of course, the new chapel. We are dependent on charity, as you must be aware . . .'

They walked across the small courtyard and back to the main building for coffee. The Mother, although aware that Sophia was crying, did not acknowledge her distress. She asked calmly, 'Why now, Sophia? You released him, and may God forgive you, but would trying to trace your son be fair to him? Unless there is a particular reason to find him?'

Sophia's voice broke. 'He is my son.'

'He was your son when you left him. I know you were just a child yourself, but you made the decision.' She folded her white, smooth hands as if in prayer. A gold wedding ring was her only adornment.

Sophia had to get out, she couldn't stand the cold, pious woman's voice another second. 'Thank you for your time,' she said, searching frantically in her handbag for her chequebook. She wrote a cheque and handed it over the desk. 'Please accept this as a gift.'

The Mother smiled her gratitude as her white hand drew the cheque closer, out of politeness trying not to look directly at the amount. But suddenly she picked up the cheque and stared at the name printed beneath Sophia's signature.

'Luciano? Sophia Luciano?'

Sophia cursed herself for being so foolish.

'Ahhhhh, perhaps I understand.'

Sophia was puzzled. The Mother probably knew of the murders, but . . . Nothing could have prepared her for what was to come. The cold, aloof face broke into a grimace that was meant to be a smile.

'Our benefactor, Sophia, was Don Roberto Luciano.'

Sophia started to interrupt, but fell silent when the Mother Superior raised her hand. 'Please don't, please listen. We were visited by Constantino Luciano. He enquired about you and specifically about your child. He wished to have the baby placed in an orphanage of his

530

own choice. He did not see the boy and, as the father was not named on the birth certificate, we agreed to let the baby go. You may think whatever you choose, but we had the assurance that the child would be well provided for. This was also verified by the young man's lawyer, a Signor Mario Domino. Don Luciano never came here personally, although the donation was in his name. I have prayed for his soul. Pray with me now, Sophia, pray that God will give you strength and for the Holy Mother to forgive your sins.'

On her knees, her eyes closed, Sophia prayed. She knew Mario Domino would help her; she was sure that he, of all people, would know where her child had been taken. She wept tears of relief, praying, not for forgiveness, but for her son.

Moyra moved from table to table, searching for one with the right feel. Eventually she took a seat at a blackjack table because she liked the look of the young croupier. She always preferred to play with a male rather than a female running the game.

She stashed her $20 blue chips at her side and placed her drink carefully on the wooden edge of the table, away from the green baize.

As the coach approached Atlantic City, Teresa was having withdrawal symptoms. Why she had allowed Rosa to cajole her into the trip she couldn't think. At least her daughter seemed happier. She was giggling at the amazing collection of blue-rinsed pensioners aboard the 'All-In Trip to Atlantic City, Including a Free Roll'. The roll referred to was the small, wrapped tube of disks needed to play the slot machines in the casinos. They each had one, although Teresa doubted if she would play.

They had taken the night bus and would return at the same time the following evening. Teresa became more and more sure that it was a mistake as they entered the mammoth Atlantic City terminus. Hundreds of buses and coaches could be seen spilling out their aged passengers, while more waited to take them on the local trips to the various gambling establishments. The temperature was in the eighties, although it was almost seven-thirty in the evening, and the heat was overpowering.

Moyra nodded to the croupier for a card. She was drinking steadily, downing her vodka martinis as fast as her chips were removed.

'Card.' At last she got blackjack and scooped up her winnings. She smiled at the croupier, who gave her a small wink of congratulation; very small, because if the pit manager had seen it, he would be instantly removed.

Teresa could not believe the noise from the vast array of slot machines all being fed and churning out chips. Lights blazed and bells rang to the constant accompaniment of muzak and loud voices.

She enquired at reception for Mrs Moyra Luciano. The desk was frantically busy; American Express cards thudded through the machines, cashiers changed chips, and attractive desk clerks answered phone after phone. Eventually Teresa was told that Mrs Luciano was not answering.

Rosa wanted to use her free tokens, but Teresa suggested a walk along the boards. She found it very chilly in the casino where the air conditioning was going full blast. Rosa laughed and told her mother that it was all a ploy on behalf of the casino to make the punters keep warm by working overtime on the one-armed bandits.

Arm-in-arm, Teresa and Rosa headed along the boards, stopping at a few shops on the way to buy candy. They enjoyed looking at the very expensive articles in some of the plusher shops. Rosa promised herself that she would buy up everything as soon she received her inheritance.

Moyra had been winning consistently for the past hour, and downing the vodka martinis. She had changed the small chips for $50 red ones which were stacked at her side and filled her small handbag.

The reception desk seemed even busier than before. Teresa was knocked this way and that by bellboys careering along with trollies stacked with suitcases. When she finally caught someone's attention, she found that Moyra had still not returned. Teresa was getting frustrated and tired; why had she been so stupid as to arrive unannounced?

She threaded her way through the slots, panicking slightly when she couldn't find Rosa and spotting her eventually playing a machine with two T-shirted boys encouraging her. Stony-faced, she joined her daughter.

'I was looking for you.'

'I'm playing my freebies.'

The two boys caught Teresa's cold look and shambled off. 'Don't make a spectacle of yourself, Rosa, remember who you are. You know these places are full of hookers . . .'

'Oh, Mama, give it a rest, just enjoy yourself.' Rosa lost her last disk and asked if she could go and watch the high rollers.

Teresa looked at her watch; it was almost nine-thirty and she suggested they go for a bite to eat before trying Moyra again. If she wasn't in her apartment by then, they would get the next bus home. Rosa's moody pout reminded Teresa of her husband.

'Don't throw one of your tantrums, not here, Rosa, because I have had enough of this place. If it weren't for you, I would never have come.'

'But you did! Now we're here, why don't you just ease up?'

'Maybe because I have more respect for myself. You should think about who you are. We've got to keep a low profile, people will know who we are. You don't have any respect for yourself or me.'

'Because I played a few slots, because I laughed with a couple of boys?'

Teresa marched towards one of the slot machines, unwrapping her coins. 'You want me to play? If that's what you want, I'll play. Now, what do I want? Three cherries . . .'

'Yeah, why not? One of them could be mine.'

Teresa had put the disk in the slot and actually pulled the handle before she realized what Rosa had said. 'What do you mean by that?'

Rosa smirked. 'Ohhhh, you are lucky! Hold the cherry, Mama!'

'What did you mean by what you said?'

Rosa pushed her face up close. 'I meant I am not a virgin, cherry lost, understand? Oh, Mama, look! You are lucky, you've got two cherries now. Hold it, *press hold*!'

Not really realizing what she was doing, Teresa obeyed. She searched her daughter's face, was she serious? 'You are joking with me, Rosa? Did you and Emilio . . .?'

Rosa gave her an odd half-smile. 'Yes, Mama, we did it . . . *Quick!* Put another disk in! You want to know where, when? In the orchard, that day you all went shopping. We did it then.'

'You're lying . . .' Teresa pulled the lever.

'I'm twenty years old, how long did you want me to hang on to it? *I am not a virgin!*'

Flushing, Teresa looked around to see who might have heard. Just then, up came cherry number three, and there was mayhem. Bells rang, lights flashed, and $200 began to spew from the machine. The coins overflowed the cup and rolled on the floor. A recorded voice boomed out 'Jackpot! Jackpot!' Teresa's face was a picture of confusion.

Rosa shouted above the bells, 'I lied, Mama! I lied!'

Teresa started to laugh. 'I won, Rosa, I won! Do you know this is the first time in my life I have won anything? *I won, I won!*'

From nowhere came a scantily dressed girl with a camera. She clicked away, a rigid smile on her face.

'Photo, you want a photo of your lucky night? Come on, ladies, smile!'

Rosa hugged her mother and smiled at the camera. Teresa blinked as the girl took a single photo, for real this time, and handed her a ticket.

Rosa laughed. 'Low profile, Mama?'

Teresa beamed at the reception clerk. She still couldn't get over the fact that she had won $200. She asked if Moyra was back and one of the nearby girls called over to say she had just seen Mrs Luciano go up.

As Teresa moved away, the girl lifted one pencilled eyebrow. 'Well, almost going . . . I think she needed assistance.'

Having changed her winnings into $50 bills, Teresa was in a very good mood. She felt even better as they walked along the corridor, past the gym and the swimming pool.

Teresa saw the casino security guard standing in the centre of the corridor. She asked rather haughtily, 'Which is Mrs Luciano's apartment?'

'That one, but she got company!'

He pointed, and Moyra's apartment door burst open. She could be heard shouting at the top of her voice, and running out from the apartment was a young guy she had picked up. The so-called nice guy so eager to help her back home had been trying to steal her winnings, but he hadn't bargained for the fact that drunk or sober Moyra wouldn't be that easy to take. The boy ran straight into Teresa, almost knocking her off her feet. The security guard wasn't sure if he should chase after the boy or see if Moyra was in trouble, but he chose the latter and followed Teresa and Rosa.

Moyra slammed the door in the guard's face and leaned against it to stop herself falling over. Her right cheek and her mouth were swelling as the shocked Teresa watched, and a trickle of blood ran down her chin.

Moyra seemed completely unaware of her injuries; she was still trying to stand up, trying to focus her glazed, drunken eyes on the open bedroom door. Her dress was torn, exposing one breast, and her panties were round her ankles. One gold shoe hung from her ankle by its strap, the other foot was shoeless.

'Fucking bastard picked the wrong girl, fucking cunt!'

Her knicker elastic snapped and she fell forward, but pulled herself to her feet and staggered towards the bedroom. Stumbling to her knees she crawled around the floor, searching for something, then gave a triumphant yell. She held up her handbag, then lost her balance completely. Wads of $50 and $100 bills fluttered around her. She grabbed a fistful.

'Never got a cent, prick . . . Never got so much as one dollar . . .'

Rosa and Teresa stood rigid, staring at Moyra as if she were a freak show. She clawed at the bedspread, so drunk she had to haul herself to her feet, then she peered at the two of them. She still couldn't focus.

'Who the fuck are you? How did you get in?'

Teresa pulled at Rosa's arm. 'Come on, we're leaving.' But Rosa yanked her arm free.

'We can't leave her like this! Moyra, it's Rosa, and Teresa . . . Moyra?'

537

Teresa looked with disgust at Moyra, 'She's drunk out of her mind.'

Rosa picked up some of the money and moved closer. 'Did he rape her? What do you think happened?'

'Whatever it was, I am not interested. I just want to go back to New York.'

Moyra's face was a mess, her lip cut and swollen and a dark bruise forming on her cheek. She squinted at Teresa. 'There's a fridge, get me some ice, would you?'

Teresa folded her arms. 'You should be ashamed of yourself.'

'You mind?' said Moyra, pointing to a Chinese silk dressing gown, then she burped loudly. 'I feel like I been hit by a truck, but I gave as good as I got. He was after my winnings, I won tonight.'

As Teresa threw the garment at Moyra her voice was icy. 'You didn't wait long, did you? Frederico's hardly cold in his grave.'

'Whether he's hot or cold or turning somersaults doesn't make any difference, he's still dead! I just needed a screw. Don't give me any crap about waiting, I've waited, that's all I've been doing, waiting. That bitch, that mother superior in Sicily, doesn't answer my calls, my cables. What goes on in life is my business.'

'It's family business. You are a Luciano, and if Graziella knew you were carrying on . . .'

'*Carrying on?* What's with you? Don't come on to me like you was the Pope's sister, we all know about your husband. You makin' him into some kinda saint now? I don't give a shit about being a Luciano, that's past, that's past . . .'

Teresa ushered her daughter from the room before she turned back and said to Moyra, 'You may as well know, Moyra, if we haven't heard from Graziella by the end of the month we're going to go back to Sicily. I was gonna suggest you do the same, but now I think you should stay as far away from us as possible.'

Moyra didn't wait for them to leave before she let rip with a stream of abuse. She had no intention of letting the sour-faced Teresa Luciano get to Graziella first. If they were going at the end of the month, so would she.

Sophia knew now that Constantino had not only manipulated her business venture but had known about her child. She felt like a puppet, but who had really pulled the strings?

There was no one Sophia could turn to for confirmation or comfort, and that realization added to the suffocating weight that hung on her, like some predatory creature with tentacles, wrapped around her mind and body. The Valium didn't help: it made her feel she should give way to the dragging sensation, take it a step further and sink into complete oblivion.

Moyra felt wretched, her head thudding, her bruised face aching, her lip agony, but she was a survivor. She knew instinctively that Teresa was bound to talk about their scene. If it was to Graziella there could be trouble. She knew it would be best to get in first so she decided to make Sophia her ally.

That was her sole reason for calling Rome. She left the phone ringing and ringing, muttering to herself, 'Answer, come on, answer . . .'

At last the ringing stopped. 'Sophia? Sophia, is that you?'

'Who is this?'

'It's Moyra . . . Freddie's wife . . . I gotta talk to you, I had no one else to call . . . Hello?'

Sophia fell back on the bed, the phone falling with her.

'Listen, I gotta talk to you. I just had this terrible thing happen to me, please don't hang up, please just listen to me . . . There's no one else I can talk to, I was so lonely . . . Sophia? Jesus Christ, you hang up on me and I swear I'll kill myself.'

Convinced that she heard Sophia laughing, Moyra became irate. '*You think it's funny?* Well, maybe things are different for you, maybe you had it easy.'

Suddenly Sophia sat up, shouting furiously, 'Don't say that, you don't say that to me!'

Oblivious, Moyra continued, 'I'm not sayin' Freddie wasn't a good husband to me, I'm not sayin' that, but he wasn't easy to live with. And I know the family, especially Graziella, never approved of me.'

Sophia couldn't understand what Moyra was saying. She was still angry, everyone presumed that she had it easy . . . She spoke rapidly in Italian, shouting that no one understood her, she had more troubles than any of them knew about.

Moyra yelled, '*Shuttupppppp!* I can't understand what you're saying. All right, maybe I was wrong about Graziella, all I'm sayin' is, I was Freddie's wife, OK? And if Teresa starts telling lies about me . . . Can you still hear me? It's just that I might sound slurred because I got a cut lip, which is the reason I'm callin' . . .'

Sophia tucked the phone into her neck and reached

540

unsteadily for a cigarette. She noticed that her pills were scattered all over the floor. 'You shut your lisp?' The words wouldn't come out right . . .

She tried again, but Moyra interrupted.

'Christ, you sound as if someone gave you a crack . . . Look, I'll come right out with it. Teresa was here, she came in an' I was with this guy, he was tryin' to screw me outta my winnings . . .'

'What? Speak slower, I don't understand.'

'I – had – a – guy – in – the – apartment, OK? And Teresa and Rosa walked in just as . . . he was trying to rape me.'

'Are you in New York?'

'*No*, I'm in Atlantic City.'

'I am in Rome.'

'*I know, I called you!* Jesus Christ, look, I needed someone, I was feelin' like I wanted to die. I was gonna commit suicide . . . Suicide, understand?'

Sophia started to laugh. If only Moyra could see all the yellow pills.

'Oh, yeah, go on, laugh! Even funnier now, my lip's bleeding all over my Chinese . . .'

'He was Chinese?' Sophia was picturing Teresa bursting into the room while Moyra was being raped by a little Chinese man . . .

Moyra held the phone at arm's length but could still hear Sophia convulsed with laughter on the other end of the line. 'Are you nuts, or drunk? Look, forget it, I'll try the Samaritans.'

But Sophia's laughter was infectious and Moyra began to giggle. 'I guess it was funny. You know, Teresa's got a face like a dried grape . . . You'll be seeing her sooner than you thought, she's coming out at the end of the month, with or without Graziella's invite. Will you be there?'

Sophia wanted to tell someone, anyone, about her son, but she hesitated and Moyra got in first.

'I lost my baby, Sophia, he was only five months. I can't have any more kids and I guess all I got is this money. Freddie's money, and it's mine. Sophia, you don't mind me calling ya?'

Sophia's lips trembled and her voice was just a husky whisper. 'No, I don't mind, Moyra. In a way, you couldn't have called at a better time.'

Mario Domino's apartment in the centre of Palermo was empty. He was, in fact, very close to Sophia's home.

Even at that early hour he was already at work in his hotel room. He always stayed at the Hotel Raphael which resembled, in some respects, his own apartment, furnished as it was with fine antiques. He was sitting at a Louis XIV desk, with his papers stacked at his feet and by his elbow. He had opened the windows to the balcony even though his room was fully air conditioned.

On many of the documents he wrote the initials 'P.C.' in red felt-tip. He had traced the buyers of more than ten of Luciano's subsidiary companies to a bank here in Rome, to a box number, and had hired two men to wait for someone to collect. That person was, as he discovered later, Enrico Dante. The name on the sale contracts, however, was Vittorio Rosales, which Domino believed was fictitious. All the information the bank could give him was that enough money was available in the account to cover all the sales.

Domino subsequently identified Dante as being in the

pay of Paul Carolla. The two were partners in a thriving night-club, the Armadillo, in Palermo.

Domino splashed his face with cold water and patted it dry, staring at his reflection in the bathroom mirror. Often he would suddenly remember inconsequential moments of his life, flashes that would take him unawares and leave him desolate. He heard now the familiar laugh and could see Don Roberto sitting at his big, carved desk. He was drawing circles on a piece of paper to explain the purchase of a ceramics factory. Domino believed it to be a waste of time until Luciano held up his drawing.

'You see, my old friend, the big outer circle is filled with the little companies, like an army. They confuse the enemy and protect the inner circle. That inner circle is really all I care about; it is legitimate, and the most powerful. If anything happens to me the piranhas will be snapping at my heels. They will have to bite through the outer circle and, as they bite, you will have time to ensure that the centre stands firm and remains strong for my sons.'

Domino sighed. The piranhas had become sharks, the inner circle was broken and the massive holdings Luciano had fought to keep, the docks, the warehouses, the ships, all were closed.

The pain in Domino's chest never seemed to leave him now and the tablets had no effect. He made a note in his diary to go for a check-up on his return to Palermo.

Domino was a very worried man, having discovered not only the Carolla connection but the banking scams. On top of all this, he had been further disturbed to unearth many discrepancies within his own company; men he had trusted had been systematically siphoning off the huge amounts of cash that should have been directed to the Lucianos' Swiss account. He felt like weeping, everything was out of control and he knew it. He was incapable of handling the situation.

Domino was a very wealthy man, his prized art collection and carefully chosen antiques were his children. He took out his calculator, assessing the possibility of covering some of the losses himself. He had let Graziella down, let down her daughters and her granddaughter. His fingers flew over the calculator, then froze as his arm went rigid with pain . . . He could not get his breath and the pain grew steadily worse.

Domino was found that afternoon by the maid. His body was driven back to Palermo the following day. Graziella arranged the funeral, contacted his relatives, and awaited the arrival of his niece at his empty apartment.

With Adina's help, Graziella had removed all the photographs of her family, knowing the press would try to bribe the housekeeper, because the Lucianos were still front-page material.

The study was full of files, so many that she knew she could not begin to sort them out. Instead she instructed Domino's company to bring them all to the Villa Rivera. She locked the door behind her and walked from room to room with Adina.

It was strange; she had only been in Mario's home on two or three occasions, and here was a side of him she had never really known; the artistic side of him, the art lover. She had never thought of him as being anything but Mario, their faithful friend. Yet here was such taste, such carefully arranged rooms, but for whom? Who had ever come here to admire his collections? Who had enjoyed searching out the lovingly collected antiques and knick-knacks? She could remember no one, man or woman, who had ever been part of his life, except herself.

'You know, I never realized how rich he was. Somehow he always remained the poor law student to me – and he was so poor, Adina. Well, until he met Roberto.'

Domino's niece and a distant cousin stared around the apartment in awe. They had never seen such wealth. But they were to receive none of it; Domino's will left everything he possessed apart from the paintings to his university, to create a scholarship fund in his name. He had detailed every item.

The one thing that was never settled was the ownership of the paintings, which alone were valued at L125 billion. He had bought them as an investment for Roberto Luciano, but the widows never received them. The works of art were held by the government, pending verification of their rightful ownership; several of the Old Masters were known to have been stolen. The rest of them disappeared without trace.

The Luciano estate was dwindling fast. With Domino out of the way the frauds and embezzlement escalated. The documents taken from his apartment were first delivered to Domino's firm. Graziella signed a new power of attorney with the firm, stipulating that everything should be cleared up within the month. She had waited long enough and wished to settle the inheritances without further delay.

Amongst the papers was a small black diary for the year 1960. One of the entries, written in Domino's meticulous hand, was only pertinent to Sophia Luciano, because it referred to her son. 'Child removed from Cefalu and taken to the orphanage of the Sacred Heart, Catania.'

Domino had chosen the largest city in Sicily, next to Palermo, to ensure that the identity of the baby would never be discovered.

Graziella and Adina had just returned from Mario Domino's funeral. There had been few people there and the majority of the weeping and wailing had been from his relatives when they realized they had been left out of the will. Graziella had therefore not been in the court that afternoon, nor had she read the newspapers.

Emmanuel straightened his tie, checked his hair, then drove up the long drive of the Villa Rivera. He felt sick to his stomach and had no idea how to begin to tell her.

Graziella offered wine but Emmanuel refused. He seemed unable to sit still; he had taken his pen from his pocket and was tapping it on the polished surface of the dining-room table.

'Signora, I have little time, I must return to my office, but I wanted to see you, to tell you personally . . . Today there was a new development in the court.'

He adjusted his tie again and took a deep breath. 'I don't know if you are aware of the fact, but here in Italy there is a law stipulating that no man can be held in prison for more than eighteen months without trial. As you know, the court process has been lengthy; hundreds of men are charged, some separately, some in groups. The law also says that it is every prisoner's right to have all his statements and the charges against him read aloud to him before sentences can be handed down. Do you understand?'

'Yes, I understand. I studied the law before I was married. Do you know about Mario Domino?'

'Please, Signora Luciano, let me finish. Forgive me, but my time is very limited and I must get back. Today the defence counsel demanded that the laws we have just discussed be upheld. That means that every one of the prisoners you have seen at the jail, including Paul Carolla, wish their statements to be read. The majority of the prisoners have been held for a considerable time; for example, Paul Carolla has been in jail for more than sixteen months.'

Her voice was hoarse, her eyes frightened as she interrupted. 'How long will it take for these statements to be read?'

Emmanuel licked his lips. 'At a low estimate, more than one and a half years. If the law is upheld, most of the men will have to be freed.'

'Paul Carolla?'

'Yes, signora, Paul Carolla would be freed.'

She sat back in her chair and lifted her hands in a gesture of disbelief. Emmanuel continued, 'That is why I am here. I wanted to tell you myself, and to assure you that everything possible is being done. However, the judge does not have the power to dismiss these demands, it has to be turned over to the government. It will be up to them to make the final decision. I am sure, signora, very sure, that they will refuse. The trial will continue as if nothing had occurred, until we hear from the judge.'

Graziella rose to her feet. Her control was super-human. 'I am well aware of how the government works . . . Thank you, signor, for coming to see me personally. As you said, you are very busy, so I do not wish to delay you any longer . . .'

Adina entered the hall as soon as she heard the bell ring, but Graziella was already ushering Emmanuel out. As the door closed behind him, he was still apologizing.

Graziella's face was like a mask. 'They are going to free Paul Carolla.'

CHAPTER 23

COMMISSARIO JOSEPH Pirelli was on his fifteenth length in the Olympic-sized public swimming pool; swimming always cured his hangovers. Reaching the shallow end, he stood, heaving for breath with his hands on his hips. At the far end of the pool, wrapped in a white bath towel, Judge Ricardo Orsini gestured to Pirelli, then pointed to the steam room.

Pirelli squinted through the thick steam and saw the outline of Orsini lying on a bench. Pirelli had been celebrating the end of a long and tedious homicide case. His desk cleared, he was due to leave Milan for two weeks' holiday with his wife and son. He had intended going into his office later, but was now officially on his long-awaited leave. He sat opposite Orsini, leaning his elbows on his knees, wondering which bastard at the office had told Orsini where to find him. He waited.

Orsini sat up and looked at Pirelli. 'There's a big problem in Palermo; got a call this morning, you been following the trials?' Pirelli shrugged; it was difficult not to, the trial was front page in every newspaper.

'It's not official,' continued Orsini. 'Carolla's counsel are causing havoc, it's a mess.'

Pirelli watched the heavy man swing his legs down from the bench, his body glistening with sweat. 'I'm sorry, Joe. I want you to take over the Juan Paluso investigation. The murdered boy's father, Frank Paluso, is getting a lot of press, he's even tried to take out a private summons against Carolla, now the government has stepped in and they want the case closed. I know about your leave, and it'll be made up to you.'

Pirelli sighed, 'What if I refuse?'

Orsini wrapped the towel around his belly. 'Tell me that when you've read the reports. The boy was the same age as your son; these bastards are killing children. The offices in Palermo are understaffed and now with this hitch in the trial proceedings, Carolla could be freed. I know your desk is cleared, but even if it wasn't, I'd suggest you take the case over. See you outside, say ten minutes?'

Pirelli joined Orsini in the car park. The judge was wearing an expensive silk suit and immaculate shirt and tie; his thinning hair was combed and oiled. Pirelli, his shirt creased, his tie trailing from the pocket of his crumpled linen suit, looked as he had felt before his swim, hung over. He had forgotten a comb so his thick, curly black hair stood up on end and, adding to his youthful appearance, he had his rolled towel and wet swimsuit tucked under his arm. Pirelli's staff always laughed about his famous frown. When his brows met in one dark line it usually meant he was ready to blow; they met now, in fact, almost overlapped, he was so angry.

Orsini opened the trunk of the silver Alfa Romeo and took out his briefcase. Pirelli towered above him, glowering. Orsini handed him a file. 'I'm sorry, Joe, I'll be in my office if you need to contact me, but the sooner you get there, the sooner you can get back. There's everything you need. An apartment's been arranged, and they've set up an office . . . leave as soon as you can, OK?'

Commissario Pirelli seethed as he watched the Alfa drive out of the parking lot. He didn't even open the file, but walked to his own car, a beat-up Fiat. His temper was held in check as he drove to his apartment. He parked in his allotted space beneath the apartment block and opened the file. Clipped to the pages of the report was a large eight-by-ten-inch black and white photograph of the murdered child. His bicycle lay across his legs, his right hand clutched an ice-cream cornet, his skull and right side of his face was a congealed mass of blood; it formed a circle, dripping into the gutter.

Pirelli opened his front door and was greeted by the sight of his son Gino wearing a snorkel, swimming mask and flippers.

'Where's your mother?'

The distorted voice from behind the swimming mask said she was shopping. Pirelli sighed with relief and, as the flippered feet padded after him, he hurried into the bedroom. He showered and changed, tossed his clothes into an overnight bag, and was ready to leave within fifteen minutes. He went into the kitchen where their cleaner was mopping up, not assisted by the small frogman. He had a whispered conversation with her, and then hurried into the drawing room. There he wrote a brief note, knowing all hell would break loose when his wife knew that yet again he had been forced to cancel their holiday. He suggested that she and their son go on to the hotel where he would join them later. In a postscript he wrote that the case was urgent, so he had already left for Palermo, but would call as soon as he arrived.

Pirelli returned to the car park. His six-foot-two-inch frame bent almost double as he squeezed into the Fiat. He drove out, forgetting the ramp at the exit; he always forgot the ramp and always hit his head on the roof of the car.

Pirelli caught the afternoon ferry to Sicily and then drove on to the Palermo Police headquarters, arriving late at night. As there was only the night-duty staff, there was no one to assist him or direct him to his office. He strode off in search of his apartment, and realized he had not eaten since breakfast so stopped at a small café. By the time he finally reached the address of the apartment that had been provided for him, he discovered there was no one to give him the keys. He booked instead into a nearby hotel, where he collapsed in a state of total exhaustion. The celebrations the night before, his hangover, the fifteen lengths at the swimming pool, the long drive, the guilt about, yet again, ruining the family's holiday arrangements, all made him moan out loud.

Tired as he was, and it was now four o'clock in the morning, he couldn't sleep. Downing a few miniatures from the courtesy fridge in his room, he watched some awful cartoon on the television. As a last resort, he looked over the case that had, before he had even begun, caused him so much aggravation. Looking again at the photograph of the pitiful little boy put everything into perspective. Somebody had brutally destroyed his life, someone had looked into that eager, innocent boy's face, as he accepted the ice cream, and then killed him. Pirelli closed his eyes, thinking, as he drifted to sleep, what kind of human being could live with himself, could live with that on his conscience . . .

Luka Carolla strolled through Erice, wearing his monk's robe and leather-thonged sandals. He carried a straw bag slung over his shoulder, filled with packets of seeds, wrapped in sacking, ready for planting.

He paused for a moment at a vegetable stall and touched the ripe, dark plums, then stepped inside the fly-filled shop. There were cigarettes and sweets, jars of herbs and row upon row of tinned foods. The little shop attempted to stock everything possible. Luka asked for a kilo of plums and flipped through the rack of newspapers while he waited. A headline caught his eye: 'Mafia Trial Continues.'

Luka busied himself looking at the herbs, but his eye kept being drawn back to the papers. At the last minute he bought two. He folded them into a square and tucked them in his basket beneath the plums.

The old lady beamed toothlessly. '*Americano?*' she asked.

'*Si, Americano. Grazie.*'

*

Luka opened the newspapers, turning each page as if frightened the walls would hear the rustle of the paper. He read of the prosecution's attack on his father, who maintained that he was innocent of all charges. He read part of the lurid article on the so-called 'Boss of Bosses', Don Roberto Luciano.

A tap on his door made him spin round. 'Yes?'

'It's Father Angelo, Luka. May I speak to you?'

Luka kicked the newspapers beneath the bed and opened the door. The walking frame inched into the room, then Father Angelo held out his hand for Luka to help him sit on the bed.

'Is something wrong?'

'Does there have to be for me to visit you?'

'No, of course not, Father. But I was about to begin work. I must finish the garden. You know yourself I am late planting. I will only just catch the last of summer.'

'When did you last take confession?'

'I have given myself penance, Father.'

'You have? And since when have you been father confessor to yourself? As a boy, Luka, you were the same; if you lied or stole, you always made amends by working. Come to me tonight.'

'Very well, Father.'

Luka helped Angelo rise and assisted him to the door. There the old man stopped.

'I can successfully manoeuvre myself now. God bless you. And, Luka, remove the newspapers, you know I have never approved of them being brought into the sanctuary. If you wish to read papers, do so when you are outside our walls. This is not a hotel, even if you choose to use it as one.'

Luka followed him into the corridor. 'Do you want me to go?'

Father Angelo paused and shuffled round to face him. 'Far from it. I think you have come here for peace, perhaps you should think about staying here. In the remaining few years of my life nothing would give me greater pleasure than to see you ordained.'

Luka laughed. It was an extraordinary laugh, possibly because it was heard so infrequently. It was infectious, and Father Angelo chortled. 'I see the idea amuses you? Let it not be said that I gave up trying. I always believed you were destined for it, but I must admit I was the only one.'

Luka walked sideways, pressing his back against the wall, keeping pace with Angelo. 'You believed I had a vocation?'

'Odd as it may seem, the answer is yes. One day, when you triumph over the dark side, you will perhaps see for yourself.'

Luka stopped following. As Angelo continued at his slow pace, his voice echoed back, 'It is still within you, Luka, I can feel it . . .'

He looked back. Was the boy still there? But the corridor was empty. Luka's door closed soundlessly behind him.

Later that afternoon, as Luka toiled in the garden, Guido lifted the lid of one of the dustbins near the kitchens. Discovering the torn newspapers, he furtively took them into the library. The missing sections frustrated him but he pored over the rest of them, then returned them to the bin. He could see Luka working and, under the pretext of taking clean sheets for his bed, he went into his cell.

He searched quickly. There were few places to hide anything, and he soon found the missing articles. He scoured them, nervous of being caught, and quickly replaced them. When Luka walked in, he had his hand on the clean sheets, about to strip the bed.

Guido flushed guiltily. 'Ah, you are here . . . Well, you can assist me, I have brought you clean sheets.'

'Thank you. I can change the bed myself, I know where the laundry is. There is no need . . .'

'Oh, but you are a guest, I insist.'

He lifted the mattress to pull the sheet free. He did not see the gun case, but Luka did. He moved quickly, gripping Guido's wrist until it hurt. 'Please leave my room.'

Guido rubbed his arm vigorously. 'I'm sorry, I did not mean to intrude. Forgive me.'

Luka's eyes did not waver from Guido's face until the door closed behind him. He waited a few moments, then in two strides he was by the bed. He threw the mattress aside; he had to find another hiding place, and find it fast.

The chapel was dark. Luka crept between the familiar worn benches and reached the altar. Looking quickly around, he stepped into the crypt.

The ten-foot-high cross was more than a foot thick. It was held against the wall at the back by two heavy wooden battens. Deftly he climbed up, tucked the gun case into position and was just sliding back down the cross when the door creaked open. There was a muffled howl and the sound of hasty steps.

Brother Louis ran this way and that, straight into the wall at one point, before he was able to reach the corridor. Arms flapping in panic, he ran, calling for Father Angelo. 'Christ has arisen . . .'

Between bouts of hysterical weeping and praying, he insisted that he had seen the figure of Christ at the back of the crypt. No one paid him much attention; these states of his were not uncommon. Last time he had insisted he had seen a circus in the courtyard.

With Louis in such a state Luka had a perfect excuse for not going to confession. He had been lucky, but he believed his luck was running out.

The newspaper article's headline ran: 'Legal Loophole Causes Uproar in Court.' Enrico Dante could not believe it. There had to be a mistake, but on his visit to the jailhouse later that day, Paul Carolla's confidence appeared fully restored.

Carolla was sitting opposite Dante with the telephone in his fat hand, beaming. 'I'm gonna walk, they got no fuckin' chance an' it's all legal. One more month an' my time is up. Are my guys worth their fuckin' dough? They came up with this weeks ago, but until we were sure we had a chance they kept it quiet. You should have been in court, fuckin' uproar.'

Dante had been running all of Carolla's businesses during the trial. He had been handling the contracts, the transfer of the monies, siphoning much of it into his own pockets in the certainty that Carolla would never be freed. Now, when Carolla came out, he would have a lot of explaining to do.

'Eh, you OK? What's the matter?'

Dante's voice was an octave higher than usual. 'Nothin', Paulie, it's the best news, maybe make up for some of the bad . . .'

Carolla's face changed, the rat-like eyes hardened. Suddenly his whole attention was on Dante. 'Everythin' goin' through OK? You got problems?'

'No, no, everything's on course, just gonna be a bit of delay. The lawyer, the Lucianos' executor, he's dead.'

'Who the fuck bumped him off?'

'It was a heart attack. Domino had agreed prices but nothin's signed and sealed.'

'How long before you get it sorted?'

'I dunno, Paulie, few days maybe; there'll be a new executor.'

'What you know about a cop called . . . Pirelli?'

Dante squinted and dabbed his neck with a handkerchief. 'Pirelli? Never heard of him. He with the Palermo outfit?'

'He wants to question me about that Paluso kid . . . You say you don't know him? What they done, brought someone in from outside?'

'I'll find out, Paulie.'

'Yeah, you do that. How come I'm gettin' more information inside this shithole than you're gettin' outside?'

'I was in Rome.'

Carolla stared hard, saw that Dante was uncomfortable. 'Yeah, I bet you were. Well, just as long as you're not spreading my dough around you'll be OK.'

Dante pushed his chair back and Carolla snapped that he wasn't through yet. He asked if there'd been any word on his son, did Dante know if he'd left Sicily? Dante confessed yet again that he didn't know.

Carolla banged the glass between them with his fist. 'Find out, I don't want him anywhere near. I'm gonna walk outta here, hear me? Find him, there's a monastery at Erice, check it out an' do it fast.'

Carolla hung up the phone and called the guard to take him out.

Dante was reeling. Carolla freed! No one had ever thought he would get out of this one. He sighed: the man had the luck of the devil . . .

Pirelli felt the sweat trickling down his back. His shirt was sticking to him and the apology for a fan was turning at snail's pace. He loathed the city, and this building in particular, with barely any air conditioning. But it wasn't the heat that was getting to him. So far he had been allotted two officers who seemed young enough to be his sons. They were eager to please, but inept.

Pirelli checked every statement, and all he had come up with so far, after questioning the one witness to the shooting of the child, was that the driver of the unidentified blue or grey car was, possibly, young. This slim piece of information was arrived at after making the man repeat what had happened over and over again.

Pirelli had asked about the driver's clothing. Was he wearing a coat? A sweater? Were his hands heavy, hairy? Eventually, the witness stated that it might have been a denim jacket, and the hand was small and slim. Further prodding elicited that the man might have been blond, and was perhaps wearing mirrored sunglasses. That was why he hadn't seen his face . . .

Pirelli had so far not managed to arrange an interview with Carolla; permission had been refused because of his court appearances. Hearing the possibility that Carolla might be freed, he put the pressure on.

He was rewarded with a six o'clock meeting, but was told that Carolla's lawyer would be with him. Pirelli gave the Palermo murder chief a sardonic smile. 'Fine, he can have the bloody army with him, all I want is to talk to him. It's been like getting an audience with the Pope.'

The meeting took place in a guarded room. Carolla was already seated when Pirelli entered.

He briefly acknowledged Dr Ulliano, Carolla's attorney, who remained standing. Before Pirelli could open his mouth he gave a small, helpful speech about how his client had already assisted in every way possible in a case that obviously had nothing to do with him whatsoever, as he was locked in his cell at the time of the crime.

Pirelli lit a cigarette and tossed the match in the ashtray. 'I am fully aware of Signor Carolla's incarceration, but we have important new evidence which could involve him. We now have a good description of the killer.'

Pirelli saw the dark eyes harden, the quick glance from Carolla to his attorney. He continued, 'You stated that Frank Paluso was cleaning the cell, with the door open. You asked if he would take a message out, is that correct? Knowing it was against the law? Now, it is quite obvious that this message was not to be read by your legal adviser . . .' Pirelli nodded towards Dr Ulliano.

560

Carolla pursed his lips. 'Look, you got my statement. I admitted I wanted the guy to take out a message . . .'

'Just the one message, or did you hope Paluso would become a regular carrier?'

Carolla leaned forward. 'You read my statement, it's all in my statement. I wanted to get a message to my business associate, that was all.'

'And when Paluso refused?'

Carolla laughed and spread his fat hands. 'I got uptight, I admit it. I said a few things, maybe made a few threats. You get that way inside.'

'So you made a few threats . . .?' Pirelli turned the pages of Carolla's statement, then picked up a notepad. '"You got family? You got a wife? You got . . .?" Do I need to continue? You admit you made these threats?'

Carolla shrugged and shot another glance at Ulliano. 'Like I said, in the heat of the moment I might have said certain things, but I don't remember.'

Pirelli stubbed his cigarette out carefully. When he spoke, his voice was very soft. 'You don't remember. You made a threat against a man's wife, his family, and two days later, two days, his nine-year-old son, nine years old, Signor Carolla, was shot at point-blank range. It blew his head off, have you seen the photos?'

He pushed the gruesome picture of the murdered child across the table, but Carolla averted his face, turning to Ulliano. 'What the fuck is this? Get this guy outta here.'

'I say when this interview is over, Signor Carolla, I say, understand? You made a threat, and two days later . . .'

Carolla rose to his feet. 'I've had enough, this is bullshit. You say you got a witness, a suspect, then you

561

know I'm innocent. I got an alibi, one not you nor anyone else can do anythin' about. Go bring in your witness, and go fuck yourself.'

With care, Pirelli packed away his papers. 'That is exactly what I intend doing, I am referring to your suggestion about the witness, *not* the latter! Thank you for your time, Signor Carolla. I will need to question you again.'

Ulliano asked meaningfully if there was any possibility that one of Carolla's visitors could have misconstrued something he'd said? Carolla shook his head and started biting his nails. He could see his son's face, the mirrored glasses, the crazy hat . . .

Ulliano picked up on Carolla's hesitation. 'It's just that, should we not get the law passed, you know that's a possibility, anything at all that might assist us . . .'

Carolla snapped that they would cross that bridge when they came to it. 'It's illegal to keep me in here longer than eighteen months. You know it, I know it, and I'm gonna walk, understand?'

Teresa was out of breath as she reached their flat on the top floor, clutching the bag of groceries. She fumbled for her keys, then jammed her elbow against the doorbell.

The door opened and Rosa stood there, a towel wrapped around her head.

'Didn't you hear the bell?'

'I was washing my hair.'

Rosa made no effort to help her with the shopping but went straight back to the bathroom.

Teresa almost missed the cable. She dropped the groceries and ripped the envelope open. 'Rosa! Rosa!' She ran down the corridor. 'Rosa, it's come, it's here! It's from Graziella, look, look . . . We gotta go to Palermo, first flight. Jesus Christ!'

Teresa stared, open-mouthed. 'What have you done? Dear God, what have you done?'

Rosa backed away from her. She had cut her hair, hacked it into jagged pieces, the top so short it was like a crew cut. But worse, it was bright orange – at least, some of it was.

Rosa ran her hand over her hair. 'I cut it.'

'I can see that! Why? Why did you do it?'

Rosa shrugged, keeping well away from her mother. Teresa waved the cable at her. 'We are going to Sicily, we gotta get to Palermo . . . and you *cut your hair*!'

'It's *my* hair, Mama.'

'You're my daughter! You're Graziella's granddaughter, what's she gonna think?'

Rosa picked up the cable, which said little. '*Return Palermo urgent. First plane. Graziella Luciano.*'

Moyra didn't know whether to laugh or cry. She had kissed the cable, done a lunatic dance around the apartment, but in the end she had wept with relief. At last all the long months of waiting were over. She was Frederico Luciano's widow, *now* she would receive what she was entitled to.

Sophia's return from Cefalu had proved frustrating to the point of her wanting to scream. There was continued pressure from her bankers, still desperate to sort out her financial predicament. She was fending off the threat of bankruptcy, repeating over and over that her husband's estate, the entire Luciano estate, had not as yet been finalized. She assured the bank it would be settled any day.

Sophia made continuous and frantic calls to Mario Domino's apartment, desperate to speak with him to trace her son. His phone remained unanswered. She rang the villa, and the phone was either left off the hook or unanswered. Sophia had to leave her own telephone off the hook as the press continued to hound her, going to great lengths to try and gain an exclusive interview with the 'Murdered Babies' Mother'. The publicity surrounding the trial never ceased: it continued to be front page news, it was on television, it was on the radio. It seemed an interminable time had passed since the Luciano assassinations, and in death Don Roberto had become the most notorious Mafia leader in history. No longer was he referred to as a war hero, an honoured and respectable man. Day after day the reporters raked up his past, and when the prosecution councillor, Giuliano Emmanuel, displayed the dismembered hand of Anthony Robello, causing an uproar in the court, it intensified the pressure from the Press. They broke into Sophia's apartment, they waited like vultures in the apartment lobby, they tried various disguises when groceries were delivered in an attempt to gain an exclusive inside story. She was near to breaking point, and had decided that she would try one more time to contact Mario Domino or Graziella, and if she did not succeed then she would leave for Palermo that night.

As before Graziella's phone continued to ring and

ring, but just as Sophia was about to replace the receiver it was answered. She almost wept with relief. 'Oh Mama, I have tried to speak to you, I have to see you, I kept on calling but you . . .'

Graziella sounded distant, interrupting Sophia, saying little except that she must be at the Villa Rivera the next day.

'You will come, Sophia? It's important.'

'Oh Mama, I need to speak with you . . .'

'Until tomorrow . . . everyone will be at the villa tomorrow.' Graziella hung up, Sophia slowly replaced the receiver. She was a little afraid. The fact that her financial situation would be relieved meant little as she knew she would inherit a vast fortune. The fear was having to tell Graziella about her child; how would she react? She decided to leave for Palermo immediately and contact Mario Domino personally, and the prospect of at last being able to locate her son via Domino made her fear subside – at last the waiting was over . . .

Pirelli was staying in a rented apartment in the centre of Palermo. The vast rooms were sparsely furnished with heavy, fake baroque antiques. But at least the mosaic-tiled floors were cool to his bare feet.

He padded around the kitchen, making himself a mug of coffee and a sandwich, then carried them to the cavernous dining room and put them on the huge, oval table. His gun holster was empty and the sweat stains on his shirt disgusted him, so he peeled it off and chucked it in a corner. His body was tough and muscular, he looked younger than his forty-one years, but tonight he felt much older. He was tired, his eyes hurt, but he was determined to go through the list of Carolla's visitors over the past sixteen months before getting some sleep. The faster he got on with the Paluso case, the sooner he could return to Milan. His wife had hardly spoken to him since he cancelled their holiday.

He settled down among the litter of empty beer bottles and overflowing ashtrays on the table. He had brought two copies of the list of visitors; the original, to check the signatures, and a typed transcript to decipher them. He began working backwards; the visitors around the date of the murder were obviously the most important. He would soon discover if the same names recurred over the months.

Luka Carolla stood staring at the neat rows of bamboo canes. It was finished. Whatever he had hoped to feel at the completion of his task, perhaps relief, did not happen. The summer was almost over, already a chill wind blew from the sea. The sky appeared to telegraph his darkness, black clouds gathering: winter would come, and the frost would destroy all his months of labour.

He returned to his cell and packed his few possessions, adding the robe and sandals at the last minute. His heart began to pound as he crept along the dark stone corridor. The heavy oak door of the chapel creaked open and he winced. Had anyone heard? But the silence was as heavy as the darkness. He put his bag down and moved soundlessly up the aisle.

The crypt was lit by a little shaft of moonlight, breathtakingly beautiful. The Christ figurine on the mighty cross shone, the wounds showing as deep shadows. Luka moved closer and closer.

Brother Guido, watching from his hiding place behind the carved screen to the right of the cross, was almost afraid to breathe. He had been praying when Luka entered, and knew he should have made a sound to let him know he was there, but he had bent lower until he peered like a thief through the fretwork. The boy's beauty was almost ethereal. He stood with his face slightly tilted, his body straight, poised like a statue, and Guido dared not move.

The sound was very soft, like a moan on a slight intake of breath. Guido realized it was a word; Luka was saying 'No . . .' repeating it as if in terrible pain. Guido could not stand it a moment longer; he stood up.

He could not recall, later, if he had actually spoken Luka's name, but the boy's reaction was like an electric shock. He snarled like an animal, lips pulled back. His face twisted like a cat's and he spat, hissed . . . He began moving backwards into the darkness.

Guido was terrified, especially now he couldn't see him. When Luka spoke, his blood ran cold.

'I know what you are, and I know what you want, but I won't bend over for you, you stinking, fucking faggot.'

The door opened and closed, but Guido could not move. His whole body felt hot and tears streamed down his face.

Enrico Dante was thinking how he should go about tracing Luka when the young man walked into his office.

He sauntered in, wearing the mirrored sunglasses, smiling as if he were expected.

'Jesus Christ, what in God's name are you doing here?'

'I read the papers, they're gonna free him.'

'If they find you, he won't be. You get out on the first plane, understand? They got a new cop on the Paluso murder, and they say he's got a witness.'

'I need money, I got no money.'

Dante broke into a sweat. He didn't want the kid around either. The last thing he wanted was for someone to make the connection . . . He fumbled with a set of keys and went to the safe.

Luka moved round the desk. 'I guess it would be very convenient for you to get me out of the way, nobody to keep tabs on you.'

Dante wanted to slap his sneering face. 'Grow up, schmuck, we all know about you. You better get one thing clear; if they don't come through an' get Carolla off, he's gonna need somethin' to bargain with, like who did the hit on that kid. So don't play the big hood, you're still wet behind the ears. Take your dough and clear off, and I mean clear off . . . *capiche*? You're history.'

He pressed a button on his intercom and called in one of his men. He nodded to Luka. 'See this kid gets on a plane.'

Pirelli breezed into his office and Bruno di Mazzo, his young assistant, shot out of his chair.

'We got a suspect an' he matches the description we got out of our witness. He visited Carolla in jail, twice, wearing mirrored sunglasses. Blond hair, mid-twenties.

He had to show his passport at the prison for his visiting rights.'

Pirelli grinned. 'Our suspect is Paul Carolla's son.'

CHAPTER 24

LUKA SAT in the departure lounge with twenty minutes to go before his flight. The stewardess took up her position to check the passengers through to the plane. He joined the queue.

What was there for him in New York? Where would he go? He didn't even know if the old apartment was still available. He still had a few traveller's cheques, plus the money Dante had given him, but that wouldn't last long. He had no bank account of his own, having always been dependent on his father for money.

There was a safety deposit box he knew about, but he discounted that as too difficult. The safe in Dante's office had been stuffed with money; most of it, he was sure, belonging to his father. Yet Dante had given him only a paltry few hundred dollars. What if his father meant to cut him off, never see him again?

'Your ticket please,' said the stewardess. Reacting automatically, Luka almost handed it to her. Then he hesitated, turned and walked away. He had no need to claim baggage, he carried all he possessed in his holdall.

He picked up a cab outside the terminal. On his way back into Palermo he stopped at a chemist's, then had the cab drop him at a cheap garage, where he rented a beat-up Fiat. He drove into the seedier part of Palermo and booked into a motel. He was still wearing his straw hat and mirrored sunglasses. He picked up the pen to sign his name in the register, then changed his mind and wrote the name 'Johnny Moreno'.

The room stank of stale body odour, the sheets were wrinkled and the floorboards were only partially covered by a threadbare, stained carpet. But Luka didn't care, the adrenalin was pumping around his body, a good sensation.

He hung his clothes on the bent wire hangers and laid the monk's robe in a drawer. Then he turned to the cracked washbasin. There was no shower or toilet in the room. From the chemist's bag he took two packets of hair dye, read the instructions carefully and mixed it in the plastic tooth mug. Stripped to the waist, he put on the rubber gloves and, with care, applied the dye.

His breath caught in his chest when he saw the dye like a bloody cowl over his head; frantically, he began to wash his hair, ducking his head under the water, shaking out the shampoo and sending the frothing, red dye swirling around the basin.

The shampoo stung his eyes, dripped down his chest. Like a blind man, he fumbled for the towel and covered his head as if he was afraid to see himself. Finally, he let the soaking wet towel slip away and tentatively edged around the room until he was close to the mirror, then took a surreptitious look at himself. He turned to the right, to the left; bent his head a fraction. The dye had taken well, and he congratulated himself. He felt cleansed, and Luka Carolla was now, to all intents and purposes, Johnny Moreno.

Graziella knew Paul Carolla could only legally be held for one month longer and she fully expected him to be released.

In a small velvet bag right at the back of the safe was the Luger. She felt for it, touching the soft velvet and carefully removing it. The gun felt icy cold to her hand. She placed it gingerly on top of the wills stacked on Don Roberto's desk.

Opening the third desk drawer, she took out the cartridges. She knew exactly how to load the gun, she even knew how to fire it. She had also calculated that she had only one possible chance, the moment they brought the prisoners out. Paul Carolla, handcuffed, was always last in line. He occupied a cage on his own, close to the defence counsel's bench. The procedure was always the same; before the lawyers took their seats, Carolla would be put in his cage. His leg shackles were then locked on, while the cell door was closed. Her seat was directly opposite him. He was always slow, looking around the court, and it would be her only opportunity. She dared not miss.

Enrico Dante kicked off his shoes and unbuttoned his flies. His trousers were half-way down his legs when he became aware that someone was in the room. He froze, listening, the hair on the back of his neck rising.

The curtains moved. He yanked them apart so hard

572

they almost came off the rail. The window was open; he slammed it shut, trying to remember if he had left it like that. Hissing with relief, he took off his trousers, holding them underneath his chin by the turn-ups while he straightened the creases. He opened the wardrobe door and started to scream . . .

Luka's arm shot out, gripping Dante by the throat, forcing him backwards. Dante didn't recognize him. His throttled scream gurgled in his throat, as he backed helplessly towards his bed. The backs of his knees struck the mattress and he fell as Luka released his hold.

Luka jerked his arm and the knife slid into his palm. With one flick he had it open, revealing the long, razor-sharp blade. He knelt over Dante, held the knife to his throat and saw Dante's eyes register recognition.

'I guess I missed the plane.'

Dante was blubbering with fear. He touched his neck and brought his hand away, covered in blood. 'Oh, sweet Jesus . . . You're makin' a mistake, if Carolla had his way you'd be fuckin' dead. I'm tellin' you, if this deal doesn't come off, he's gonna finger you, son or not. He's gonna use you to bargain with the prosecution, he knows you hit that kid. You're gonna need me.'

Luka suddenly tucked the knife away. 'With my father dead, you'd be in a good position, huh? Means the same for me, too.'

Dante stared, and Luka smiled. 'I'm his son, every-thing he has is mine. Whatever you've got I guess is yours.'

Dante said nothing, watching Luka carefully, hardly able to believe what he was hearing.

Luka continued, 'So what I'm saying is, either way we

could both be hurt, understand? I mean, there's no love lost between us, you said he wanted me out of the way, that's what you said, isn't it?'

Dante couldn't speak.

'If he was dead we'd both benefit, right?'

Dante swallowed and found his voice at last. 'You'd never get away with it, you'd never . . .' He shut up fast. What did he care if Luka got away with it or not? If he got caught, with Carolla dead, Dante would be even better off. He changed tack. 'How would you do it?'

Luka pursed his lips. 'Maybe in the courtroom, but I'll need your help.'

Luka was smiling. 'I don't mean help with the hit, I work alone, I am a professional, understand? We always work alone.'

Dante nodded, thinking to himself, *This kid is nuts, a real case*, but he felt safer with the knife out of sight. 'Sure, Luka,' he said aloud. 'Anything you need.' He straightened fast as Luka dived towards him.

'No! Not Luka, never call me Luka! I am Johnny Moreno, my name is Johnny Moreno, remember that, OK?'

'Sure, Johnny, I'll remember.'

'OK, I'll come by tomorrow, tell you what I need.'

Dante had no idea what he should do. The boy was obviously a maniac, but should he tell Carolla that Luka hadn't left Sicily? Not only that he hadn't left, but that he was going to attempt to kill him? He kept coming back to the fact that with Carolla in prison he was in a good position, with Carolla dead, a better one. The kid would either get himself arrested or killed. In the meantime, no more visits to the prison, he would play along with whatever Luka wanted and wait for the outcome.

The kitchen garden had run wild, even though Adina had done her best to keep it cultivated. The strawberry runners caught at the hem of Graziella's skirt as she walked the fifteen paces back from the tree. She held the gun as her husband had taught her, both arms outstretched. He had laughed to see her wince, blinking at the sound, but now she kept her eyes steadily focused on the bark of the tree. *Keep your arm steady, remember the muzzle of the gun is where the bullet will come from. Hold it steady on the target. Your eyes are the gun.* Luciano's voice was like a whispered encouragement in her head . . . Fifteen minutes passed, shells littering the ground, before she heard a dull thwack as the bullet found its mark.

Sophia Luciano pulled up at the gates of the Villa Rivera. There was no guard, and one gate stood half-open. She opened the gates fully to allow the car through, and then she heard the shots.

Running back to the car, she drove to the house. As she ran up the front steps, two more shots rang out. She shouted for Graziella, pounding on the door, but there was no reply. She ran towards the back of the house as another shot rang out. She screamed in terror as Graziella's head appeared over the fence.

'Oh, it's all right, it's the guard. We are having trouble with some wild cats, they are chasing the pigeons. I

575

didn't expect you until this afternoon. Go to the front and I'll open the door.'

Graziella opened the door. Still wearing her dressing gown, she kissed Sophia warmly and insisted on taking her case.

'Mama, where are the gate guards, where's Adina? Are you here alone?'

'Adina will be back shortly, she is getting some groceries. I have to go to the trial so you'll be left to your own devices.'

Sophia asked when the others were expected. Graziella seemed agitated, constantly looking at the big kitchen clock. 'They sent cables to say they were on the way, so we shall all dine together this evening. You don't mind me leaving, do you?'

Sophia shook her head and apologized; she should have called.

'Is the will finalized, Mama?'

'I think so, but we have had problems. Poor Mario . . .'

Sophia interrupted. 'I have to speak to him, I'll come into Palermo with you.'

'Oh, you don't know? I should have called you, but I have had so much to do. Mario's dead, Sophia.'

Sophia was trembling. 'No, Mama, tell me it's not true, he can't be, he can't be . . .'

'But it is, he had a heart attack.'

She ran from the room, leaving Graziella nonplussed. But as she was about to follow, she heard the tooting of a taxi horn.

Adina had arrived, laden with groceries. The driver had to make four trips to the back door with them all. The kitchen table was stacked high.

'Are you going to the trial this morning, signora? If so, I can ask the taxi to wait.'

'No, I shall drive. Sophia is here, take her some coffee, she's very upset. I just told her about Mario Domino, I had no idea she was so fond of him.'

Adina began unpacking the boxes. 'Maybe she has had too much death, signora.'

Graziella nodded. 'Maybe.'

'The taxi can wait, signora. Please, for me, take the taxi.'

'No, I am taking the other car.'

'The Rolls-Royce, signora? Oh, no, please, why not the Mercedes?'

'It's run out of petrol.'

Adina tapped on Sophia's door. Receiving no answer, she eased it open. Sophia was sitting on the bed, holding her head in her hands.

'May I speak with you, Signora Sophia? She is driving the Rolls-Royce, the Don's car; she is unsafe. She must not drive, she has no licence and she doesn't know how to reverse. We went to Mondello, no more than twelve kilometres, it was terrible. We hit a tree and a bollard, we could have been killed . . . signora? You must stop her, please.'

Sophia, not having taken in a word, slowly raised her head. 'What do you think has happened to Mario Domino's papers, his personal papers? Would they still be in his apartment?'

'I don't know, signora. There are boxes and boxes of documents from his company locked in the study. We have only one man who comes and goes as he pleases, we have no driver, no gardeners . . .'

Sophia said, almost to herself, 'I needed to speak to Mario Domino.'

'I am sorry, signora.'

Sophia gave a soft laugh, almost a cry. 'So am I, you'll never know how sorry I am, nobody will.' She gave Adina a sweet, gentle smile and the dimple appeared in her right cheek. 'I'll help you get rooms ready.'

Luka stood in line, waiting for the guards to search the spectators as they slowly filed into the courthouse. He would have to be much earlier next time if he wanted a good seat, close to the cages. But, for now, the further away from Carolla the better; even with his hair dyed, he could not afford for his father to recognize him.

Graziella did not have to wait in line, her seat reserved. She had sat in the same seat since the opening of the trial, and paid highly for the privilege. All the guards knew her, and she was no longer subjected to the humiliating search.

Both Graziella and Luka timed the delay before Carolla was brought up the steps from the cells below; both paid particular attention to the moment Carolla waited for the cage door to be opened.

Luka asked the man sitting next to him if he had been to many sessions, and he nodded. Luka asked if it was always the same routine, and again the man nodded, jerking his head towards Carolla. 'He's an arrogant bastard, always stares around the courtroom. If he gets onto the stand today, you'll see one hell of a performance.'

Both Luka and Graziella intended to kill Carolla but his days in court could soon be over, so the question was, when?

Commissario Pirelli had received a fax from the States. Paul Carolla had married Eva Gambino in New York, 19 April 1945, but there was no record of a child. Eva Gambino Carolla had died in Sicily in 1949. The prison records stated that Giorgio Carolla, Paul's son, had visited him on two occasions, in January and February 1987. The records stated that he had produced a passport for identification, but no passport number was recorded. So who visited Paul Carolla?

Detective Sergeant Francesco Ancora, in charge of the murder investigation of the two Luciano children, approached Pirelli. He had received verification of a ballistics report that directly linked his investigation with the Paluso murder. The report stated that the bullets, or the tiny fragments salvaged from all three corpses, were possibly fired from the same gun. All fragments had matching grooves, which could have been drilled by a dentist's diamond drill.

Due to Paul Carolla's court appearances, his legal advisors refused to allow their client to be subjected to further harassment. Carolla had already been subjected to hours of interrogation and had freely given statements regarding the Paluso child, but confronted by this new evidence, the judges agreed to allow Pirelli a second interview with him. The meeting would take place the following morning before the trial began. Pirelli was confident he would discover the identity of the man calling himself 'Giorgio Carolla'.

Dante's heart pounded. He hadn't heard Luka enter his office.

'You move like a cat.'

Luka smiled, liking the description. 'I've been in court all day. Main problem is getting the gun into the courthouse, but I think I've found a way round it. That is, if you can get me what I want.'

Dante began to sweat. 'You name it, I got contacts. Just tell me what you need.'

Luka beamed. 'This is it . . .'

Dante stared at the single sheet of paper, then looked up. 'How the fuck am I gonna get hold of this?'

Luka smirked. 'There's one in the museum and there's one in a case at the Villa Palagonia; I've seen it on display. It'll need a lot of readjustments, but we've got all night, and that's all we've got because I'm gonna do the hit tomorrow.'

Graziella Luciano did not leave the courthouse until the end of the day's session. She would tell no one of her decision. She alone would take the justice denied her family, denied her son Michael Luciano, and she would take it the following morning.

Teresa let the curtain fall back into place. 'Here's Mama now, I can see the Rolls coming down the hill.' She said it to no one in particular. At that distance she had not seen that Graziella was actually driving herself.

Moyra drummed her long red nails on a small table. 'You'd think she would have been here.'

Rosa cocked her head to one side and asked, 'Why?' Moyra shrugged and said she didn't know why, it just would have been nice. She looked at her hands and frowned. The table was dusty.

'That old servant needs someone in to help her, the place is really dusty. My room's still got the sheets over everything.'

Sophia took a cigarette from a solid gold case and lit it with a gold Dunhill lighter. Her gestures were fluid, like a dancer's, and she slipped the lighter and case back into her soft black kid clutch bag.

'How many do you smoke a day, Sophia?'

'I don't know, too many. Can I get anyone a drink?'

Teresa looked at her watch. It was not five o'clock and she murmured that it was too early for her.

'Is that one of yours?' asked Moyra.

'One of my what?'

'I like that dress, it's nice the way it drapes to your body.'

'No, Yves St Laurent, last season.'

'Ohhh, excuuuuuse me . . .'

Sophia looked quizzically at Moyra, not understanding.

Moyra turned her attention to Rosa. 'How's college, Rosa?'

'I left . . . What's five letters, "Almost with warmth but no affection"?'

Teresa stood up. 'Tepid . . .' She couldn't bear to look

581

at her daughter. The new haircut had caused considerable interest, if not amazement. Moyra had suggested
that she sue the salon, but Sophia said she quite liked it,
though not necessarily the colour.

There was a bang and a sound of scraping metal
outside. Teresa looked through the curtains again. 'My
God, it's hit the gatepost, the car . . . I don't believe it,
Graziella is driving, she's driving the car.'

Sophia smiled. 'You'd better believe it. You should
see what she's done to the armoured Mercedes . . .'

'Well, why isn't there a driver? There's not even a man
at the gate, and it's quite obvious no one's been tending
the garden, it's in a dreadful state. How could she let the
place go?'

All four women looked expectantly at the double
doors. They heard Graziella's voice, then footsteps going
up the stairs. Adina suddenly appeared and Sophia asked
for a bottle of champagne and some sandwiches, then
went into the hall to call her mother-in-law.

Sophia returned and lit another cigarette. 'Mama's
tired, she'll see us at dinner, eight o'clock . . . And she
would like us to dress.'

'Who else is coming? Mario Domino, is he coming?'

'No, Teresa, he's dead. Didn't you know? He died a
week or so ago.'

Teresa took off her glasses. 'Nobody told me. Why
didn't Mama tell me?'

Sophia's head began to throb. 'Maybe she didn't think
you knew him that well. Does it really matter?'

Teresa pursed her lips angrily. 'Well, he was supposed
to be seeing to Papa's will. I just thought I should have
been informed.'

'Well, now you have.'

Rosa looked up at her mother and raised an eyebrow slightly to shut her up.

'Who're you talkin' about?' asked Moyra.

'Papa's lawyer, Mario Domino.'

'What about him?'

'He's dead, Aunt Moyra, like everyone else connected with this family.'

'That will do, Rosa,' snapped her mother, and Rosa knew she had really been out of line as Sophia also stared at her.

Adina brought a tray of glasses and a bottle of champagne. Sophia gestured for the maid to put it near her. She opened the champagne, pouring four glasses.

'I said I didn't want a drink,' snapped Teresa.

'I know, this is for Adina.'

Adina accepted the glass, embarrassed, and did no more than touch it with her lips before she quietly left the room.

'Well, as she's not coming down I shall go and have a wash. Do you want to come with me, Rosa?'

'No, I'm having a drink.'

Teresa walked out, closing the door behind her. Moyra peered at the plate of sandwiches. 'She's all on edge . . . Is she always like this, Rosa?'

'No, Aunt Moyra, she's not, but she's had rather a lot to be on edge about lately. You know, like the death of her husband.'

'Rosa . . .' Sophia gave her an angry look.

'Sorry . . . Sorry, it's just that I can't stand the way we're all creeping around each other when we all want to freak out . . . Well, I do. This house is like a morgue. I wish I hadn't come.'

'I don't,' Moyra said as she poured herself another

583

glass of champagne, 'I don't, because I need the money I got comin' to me, and I need it bad. I been waitin' for that cable like a dog for a bone . . . Cheers!'

'Well, at least you're honest. How's Grandmama, Sophia?'

'She's all right, I think, but I hardly spoke to her. We'll no doubt hear more tonight, at dinner.'

Sophia opened a small gold pill box and washed one down with champagne. Then she walked to the door and pivoted on her perfect shoes. 'I'm just going to lie down.'

Moyra sipped her drink, still inspecting the sandwiches, peering between the slices. 'You want one, Rosa?'

'No, thank you. Your underslip is showing at the back.'

Moyra leapt up. 'Shit, is it? How's that, better?' She hitched the slip up from the back and then pulled it down again. At least the suit was grey and the small bodice underneath was in pale grey silk, but her ample cleavage was on show. It was not exactly what one would expect a widow to wear, but this was Moyra's demure look, which might have succeeded if she hadn't worn dreadful red slingback shoes.

Moyra smiled. 'About that night in Atlantic City, you won't say anything, will you?'

'No, why should I? I think I'll go and have a bath.'

'Ah, don't leave me alone. I hate being alone in this place.'

'You're not, we're all here . . . See you later.'

Rosa sauntered out without bothering to close the door and Moyra hurried after her.

She ran up the first flight of stairs as fast as her tight skirt would allow and was just about to start up to the

584

next landing when she saw Sophia through the half-open door of the bathroom. She was staring at herself in the mirror as she ran water into the basin. Moyra was struck by her sister-in-law's beauty, the perfect jawline, no sagging chins, the way her thick hair was so silky and worn, as always, drawn into a tight bun low at the nape of her neck. As Sophia bent her head to splash the cold water on her face, Moyra was really impressed because she realized that Sophia hardly wore a trace of make-up.

Afraid of being caught watching, Moyra hurried up to her room, calculating on her fingers how old Sophia was. She had to be at least forty-one, possibly more, and yet she looked no more than thirty. Moyra lay on her bed and wondered if Sophia had had a face-lift. If so, she would like the name of her surgeon.

The table could easily seat fourteen, and the five places set at one end looked cluttered compared with the long stretch of starched white cloth at the other. The settings were of the best silver, with five cut-crystal glasses grouped around each place, and an eight-branch candelabra in the centre. Decanters of red and white wine were placed within reach. The table glittered as if for a banquet. The heavy silver cutlery, all monogrammed with a large 'L', was highly polished and the fine bone-china dinner service, Graziella's wedding gift from her husband, shone as if it, too, had been polished.

The four women were waiting for Graziella to appear. Sophia looked sophisticated and stunningly beautiful; the black Valentino gown enhanced her creamy complexion and dark, slanting eyes.

Teresa had made a great effort, but her black dress was ill-fitting and old-fashioned.

Rosa wore a simple black dress in a shiny satin material, with short sleeves. It was cheap, but somehow Rosa's prettiness made it acceptable. She wore no jewellery, and with her hair springing up in uneven tufts she seemed much younger than her twenty years. Her eye make-up was unnecessarily heavy for her large brown eyes, and emphasized the fact that she wore no foundation or lipstick.

Moyra's make-up, on the other hand, was about an inch thick. Her curly, permed hair was stiff with lacquer and she fairly glittered with expensive fake *diamanté* jewellery: rings, bracelets, necklace, and long drop earrings. Her black dress was frilled at the neck and hem over a stiff layered petticoat. Although it was unintentional, the seating arrangement had left her slightly apart from the rest of the women.

Graziella entered like a duchess. Adina seated her before the women could make up their minds whether or not to stand. The wine was poured and Graziella lifted her glass in a toast.

'To you all . . . Thank you for coming, and God bless you.'

Graziella hardly touched her wine, but the rest of the women toasted her and drank. The conversation was very stilted, while Adina served thick lobster bisque and hot rolls. They began to eat.

The furnace gave the room a terrific heat. The loud clanging of the gunsmith smelting and reshaping the firing chamber made the waiting men wince. Luka watched every single stage, asking eager questions, at one point even wearing the protective mask so he could stand even closer to the man as he filed the metal.

The old man, nearing eighty, was a master craftsman, painfully slow and methodical. He took great pride in his work, holding it up for inspection at each stage. Special bullets would have to be made, of course; the weapon was so old that none of the ammunition he had in store would be suitable.

Dante looked at his watch. 'How much longer?'

'Four or five hours,' said the old man, and Dante swore.

'I am a professional, signor, I have got to remake the firing pin and then there will be adjustments. It's the length of the barrel that's the problem.'

'Just do what you have to, signor. As you said, you are a professional, I understand.' Luka patted the man's shoulder encouragingly, then walked casually over to Dante. 'When he's finished, maybe it's best he's not around.'

Dante snorted, shaking his head. His voice was very low. 'He's eighty years old; he won't talk, believe me.'

Luka's eyes glittered. 'I too am a professional, signor, and he's a fucking witness.'

Graziella waited until Adina had set down the coffee tray and left the room. She did not want to discuss the will until she was sure they would not be interrupted. Then she began, in Sicilian.

'The defence lawyers requested that the entire testimony

of the accused be read aloud to the prisoners. If the government will not give the judge the power to deny them this right, Paul Carolla will be freed.'

Teresa said sharply, 'But isn't he also wanted for narcotics trading in the States? I don't believe this country will allow the defence their so-called rights, even if it is the law; this trial is not just front-page headlines in Palermo, it's worldwide.'

'What did she say?' asked Moyra. Rosa whispered to her but she still couldn't understand. She turned to Sophia. 'Does this affect the will? I don't understand, I mean, isn't that why we're here?'

Graziella spoke in her halting English for Moyra's sake. 'Ah, yes, the will. Mario Domino died, and as he was handling the entire estate there have been considerable delays. Please excuse me one moment.'

She left the room and Moyra leaned forward. 'Wasn't he a bit old to be handlin' everything? I mean, it's not just Papa Luciano's will but Constantino's an' Alfredo's an' . . .' She stopped speaking as Graziella entered with a bulging file.

'I gave Mario the power of attorney, and at his suggestion began to liquidate all the assets.'

Moyra interrupted. 'What is she saying? I don't understand.'

'Mama, Moyra cannot understand. Speak English.'

Graziella gave Moyra a small smile of apology and began again in English. She told them that Mario Domino assumed that as women, they would not want to handle the companies themselves but would prefer the freedom of money, and in this way she could divide it equally between them.

Teresa was greatly concerned, and she interrupted her mother-in-law sharply. 'Wait a minute, Mama, liquidate all the assets? Are you serious? I mean, there was surely not enough time to arrange sales, auctions . . . How much work did Domino do before he died?'

Frowning, Graziella turned to Teresa. 'This man I would trust with my life, are you saying he would cheat us?'

Moyra sighed and threw her napkin down, saying to Rosa, 'I don't understand. Is the will to be read or not?'

Graziella pointed to Rosa and told her to translate anything she said if Moyra didn't understand. Then she turned to Sophia and spoke in Sicilian. 'Constantino, as you know, ran the export companies. I have decided that as you, Sophia, were Constantino's wife, this should be handled by you, and I have therefore organized all the sale contracts for you to look over while you are here.'

Teresa was at it again, not liking what she was hearing. 'The export? Does that include Alfredo's company in New York, Mama?' But she received no reply as Graziella turned over pages in her file, passing a number of papers to Sophia, who took them and began to sift through the assortment of documents.

As Teresa was about to interrupt again, Sophia looked up, 'Mama, these don't make any sense. These are old contracts for the exporting of fruit and vegetable oils. They're two years old. Where are the legal rights to the docks and warehouses?'

Teresa leaned forward. 'Surely, Mama, Domino cannot have begun negotiations without conferring with us? Alfredo's business depended upon the cargoes, and the company is at a standstill in New York. Who has been

589

overseeing the trade during the past months? I have tried to get into the office myself, but they've changed the locks, so who has been doing that? Domino?'

'I left everything to Domino. I want none of you involved in this. It must be sold, I want everything sold, nothing that can cause you trouble.'

Moyra flapped her napkin at Sophia. 'What did she say? Is that the will?'

Teresa was trying to control her temper. 'But, Mama, who is taking care of the legal side?'

'Mario Domino is doing everything.'

Sophia took her mother-in-law's hand. 'Mama, Domino is dead. Now why don't you let Teresa have a look at all this? Then we can discuss it tomorrow. Right now you can't say I have this and Teresa has that, because we don't know what we have . . .'

Moyra half-rose from her chair. 'I know that Frederico had millions stashed in the bank plus shares in three casinos, a hamburger joint and two pinball arcades and . . .'

Teresa snapped at her, 'Moyra, we have to do this stage by stage.'

'Well, what has been going on for the last ten months! I mean, where's all Frederico's money, money that, by rights, is mine? I'm his widow.'

'We're all widows, Moyra,' said Sophia, 'and I think Teresa should look over the contracts and see what Mario had so far accomplished.'

But yet again Teresa spoke up. 'Mama, I don't know Sophia's situation, but the past months have been very tough for me and for Rosa. Alfredo, unlike his brothers, left nothing but debts . . .'

Graziella responded with pride, 'No, that is not true! No Luciano ever had debts, this I know.'

'You didn't know, Mama, but you do now because I am telling you. I paid off what I could, but right now they are probably taking our apartment. I need to know what actual money I am going to see, you know, hard cash. Because I more than anyone else, know exactly what the turnover for the New York side was.'

'You know nothing, you don't know, Teresa . . . No, you don't.'

'*Yes I do!*' Teresa shouted, now. 'Because I saw the contracts, all the licences! But if you're gonna hand it to Sophia, that's your business. I disagree, but that's something we can discuss.'

'What . . . What she say?'

'*Shut up*, Moyra, just for a second. We'll tell you all you need to know in a minute.'

'Oh, fine, talk away, talk over my head . . . What do you think I am? I seen Frederico's bank statements, I know what he had. What I don't know is why I couldn't have had it straight away. We don't even own the apartment, it's crazy! Freddy had more real estate than he had hot dinners.'

'What is she saying?' asked Graziella.

Teresa hit the roof. 'Mama! I am taking these files, all of them, into the study. I am going to go through them, now, tonight, OK? When I've got a better idea of what's going on, why don't we all talk it through? Anyone against this?'

Sophia put her hand on the top of the file and gave Teresa a warning look. 'Is it all right, Mama, for Teresa to do this?' Graziella nodded, but Sophia could see a muscle twitching at the side of her mouth. She knew Graziella was angry and she knew that something was very wrong. The atmosphere in the dining room was electric; even Moyra realized something was up.

Teresa gasped as she read the first page of the file, which listed part of Don Roberto's liquid assets. 'Oh, my God, I don't believe it, I don't believe what I am reading . . . $40 million . . . *$40 million!*'

Sophia looked from her mother-in-law to Teresa, who was hugging Rosa. Moyra was scrabbling over the table trying to read the good news for herself. Graziella turned to Sophia and whispered for her to come into the study.

Graziella unlocked the study, gesturing for Sophia to enter ahead of her. 'I always keep the door locked . . .!'

Sophia looked around the study aghast; boxes of files lined the walls, some stacked on top of each other, crates half opened took up most of the floor space, and the desk was littered with folders and loose papers.

'Oh, my God, Mama, what's all this?'

Graziella shrugged helplessly. 'After Mario's death, his company took over. I signed the power of attorney to them, they became the executors. But then, when I knew you would all be here, I told them we had waited long enough, I wanted everything returned to me. As you see, much of the work has not as yet been finalized. Some of these crates contain Mario Domino's papers from his office and his private study. It was impossible for me to go through everything.'

Graziella searched the desk top, and then handed Sophia a sheaf of telexes. 'I don't understand these, they are from the American brokers . . .'

Sophia lit a cigarette, inhaled deeply, and began to read the telexes. Graziella hovered at her side. 'There are more, and then some cables, and these statements, so many! It was impossible for me to read them all.'

'Mama, did Mario Domino leave any notes I can look over?'

'He was ill, you know. At the end he didn't know how sick he was, it was his heart.'

Sophia sighed. 'Mama, you should have contacted us. How could you have allowed this to happen?'

Graziella gestured to the room, 'My disgust allowed it to happen. Sophia, don't think me that much of a fool. May God forgive me, I was ashamed of the name Luciano! But now I realize I was wrong, and I have tried since Mario's death to rectify my mistakes. As you see, perhaps I have left it too late!'

Teresa, with Rosa and Moyra at her side, tried to decipher the complex array of papers in front of her. There appeared to be large cash deposits placed in banks in New York and New Jersey; these were within days broken down into $100,000 to $300,000 sections, then again, within days, split into smaller deposits of $10,000 and placed in various small banks as far afield as Jamaica, Tokyo and Hong Kong. From there Teresa traced that again, and within a month they were switched to a list of named guaranty trusts and wired directly to Swiss banks. No sooner deposited in various Swiss banks, it was returned to New York banks. The money was therefore on a strange turnaround during the entire period that Mario Domino acted as executor of the estate. The bulk cash was still kept moving in and out of accounts; next it shifted to the Bahamas, to Nassau banks. Domino then listed how the monies eventually joined together, making vast lump sums accumulating more each transfer and currency, at a rough estimation $100 million. All the monies finally ended up again in Switzerland, split between Credit Suisse and Banca Della Svizzera Italiana ... Domino had begun making notes of one further transfer, the last, and moving the entire fortune into one main account, but the page was strangely incomplete!

Moyra had amazed Teresa: she was like a pocket calculator, and it was Moyra who came up with the final sum. There was, she estimated, at least $30 million ... this, added to the amount Teresa had first read, $40 million, made them all rich beyond their wildest dreams. However, Moyra continued to search the documents, and it was Moyra who sowed the first seed of doubt that all was not as it seemed.

It was true they had lists of the monies due to them, money taken from Constantino, Frederico and Luciano himself, but there was not amongst the papers in front of them the number of the said Swiss account that contained the entire Luciano fortune. Teresa was about to call for Sophia, when she walked into the room with Graziella ... one look at their faces was enough. No one spoke; they waited as Graziella sat down, and it fell to Sophia to break the news.

CHAPTER 25

THE WOMEN sat in silence, unable to really comprehend that their entire fortune could not, at this time, be traced. The monies had disappeared after the death of Mario Domino. Moyra had actually laughed, as if it was some terrible joke, but something inside her told her that it was not, and she fell silent. Teresa gestured for Sophia to continue.

'As far as I can make out, there's enough for us to live comfortably, if not in luxury. The bulk cash, deposited for us, may one day hopefully be traced, but that leaves us with the assets remaining here in Sicily. Much of it has been swallowed up in taxation and according to Domino, a great deal of the problem arose from within his own company: massive fraudulent misappropriation of monies connected to our family has taken place within Domino's company, and within the Luciano companies. We still retain bulk shares in New York, and we have the brokers' lists and suggestions for when to sell. Now is not a good time.' Teresa was near to fainting, she was shaking, her mouth felt dry, and she could hardly speak. 'Sophia, the company, is that still ours?'

Graziella took over, calmer now, and speaking good English. 'The main company, Teresa, the import-export section, is dormant and has been for seven months. All the workers were paid off . . .'

'Jesus Christ, I don't believe it.'

Teresa put her head in her hands as Graziella continued, 'Everything is up for sale, the warehouses, the factories, the docks and the ships.'

'Where are the ships? I mean, are they just sitting in the dock?'

Graziella's face tightened with anger and she ignored the question. 'The section of the dock we own outright will be auctioned, but due to the delay . . .'

'What caused this delay? Are you telling me there are warehouses full of cargoes just sitting there rotting? Who decided to pay the men off, for God's sake?'

'I did,' replied Graziella. 'Please allow me to continue without interruption, Teresa. I have already put the villa up for sale, all the land and orchards, the groves. You will be able to see that the offers are substantial and, as I have told Sophia, there will be more than enough for you to return to your homes.'

Teresa's voice was hoarse from trying to control herself, but she was panting. 'Sophia, what did you mean by "fraudulently misappropriated"? Is that just a nice way of saying we have been ripped off, everything stolen from us while we just sat over in the States *waiting like idiots*?'

Graziella slapped the table with the flat of her hand. 'Mario Domino did everything humanly possible. He and his company worked with the lawyers in America. He had to fight to . . .'

Teresa jumped to her feet. 'He was an old man, what in God's name did he know? Jesus Christ, Mama, on one sheet of paper there's $40 million in *cash*! Where the hell has it gone? You want me to believe this bullshit about

596

misappropriation? It's *theft*! What I want to know is, who in Domino's company was handling our affairs after his death? Who had access to *our* money, money that belongs by right to me, to my daughter, your granddaughter? Do you think I want to go home and live, how did she say? In *comfort*? After what we have been through, comfort isn't enough, it's not enough!'

Moyra too now sprang to her feet, screeching hysterically. She was beginning to understand that there was no fortune.

'Where's my money, what about Frederico's money? That was mine. I don't believe you, nobody can just walk in and take what was mine.'

As she broke down sobbing, Graziella stood up. 'The most important thing to us is that we will have justice. Don Roberto was an honourable man, we will have the justice he wanted. It is not over. I brought you all here because . . .'

Teresa hurled the papers from the desk. 'Too damned right it's not over, but let me tell you, Mama, I don't give a goddam about his honour! He should never have done what he did, and you should never have allowed this to happen. *I don't care about justice*, do you hear me? I am forty-five years of age, I can't have any more children . . . All I had was my inheritance, and you have thrown it away. *Screw your fucking justice . . .*'

The slap was so hard it sent Teresa reeling, then she leaped forwards and gripped Graziella's wrist. 'What gives you the right, *what right have you to slap my face*?'

Graziella jerked her wrist free. 'Because I am Don Roberto Luciano's wife and I am now head of the family. You never speak to me like a gutter woman, you never swear in this house, is that clear, Teresa? This is my

597

house, my home. You insult my husband's memory, you insult yourself.'

Moyra was moving along the table as Teresa ran out of the room. 'Well, don't try it on me, because I don't give a shit, about you, about your family.'

Graziella's face became like a mask. She froze Moyra in her tracks. 'As soon as we have sold everything, then tell me how badly off you are. This family welcomed you, all of you, cared for you, loved you . . . I did everything to protect you, believe it or believe it not. You should all be ashamed. You have no pride, no honour.'

In the silence she stared from one daughter-in-law to the next, only seeming to lose confidence when she faced Sophia. The dark eyes were glittering, she looked like a cat, her lips drawn back over her perfect white teeth, clenched teeth. There was no hysteria in her voice, it was low, husky.

'I don't think, Mama, that any of us are concerned right now with honour. The fortunes, the money you sneer at our desperation for, would have eased the loss, the emptiness. Papa put his faith in justice; well, I hope he turns in his grave when Paul Carolla walks free from the court. Papa's death wasn't honourable, Mama; it was a tragic, sickening murder, but he had lived a long life, unlike my babies. I have lost too much for being a Luciano and would, if you offered me the chance to live my life again, walk away from this house, walk away from being what I am now, one of the Luciano widows. And I'll walk out with nothing, just as I walked in, but that doesn't mean I don't think what has happened to the others an outrage. Our men were killed so there could be no retaliation. With the men gone, we are nothing . . . Well, be content with the crumbs they throw to you,

Mama, but don't ask me to be. I have too much pride, maybe too much honour. Goodnight.'

As she left the room, closing the door quietly behind her, Graziella bowed her head. Moyra rose unsteadily to her feet, trying to keep herself as calm and poised as Sophia. However, when she met the cold blue eyes of Graziella, her voice faltered.

'I'm not ashamed, I'm not ashamed of anything I ever done, but I won't leave here without my cut, without my share of what I know is mine. You never liked me, I was never good enough, but I was a good wife to your son an' I loved him. Now, because of his father, I'm a widow; I got no daughter, I got nothin', so I'm gonna fight, because that's all I got. Goodnight, an' I hope you don't mind, but I'm taking a bottle with me.'

'Grandma, can I ask you something?'

Graziella paused and waited as Rosa continued, 'I know Mama loved my father, but their marriage was arranged, wasn't it?'

Graziella said nothing, she was too tired to think that far back and wondered why the girl suddenly wanted to know.

'Grandma, did Papa Luciano arrange my marriage too, did he?'

Graziella took Rosa's hand. 'Let me tell you something. Alfredo loved your Mama, I know because he told me so. Just as your Emilio loved you, and asked for your hand. He needed no encouragement – he loved you, Rosa.'

'You shouldn't have slapped Mama, she didn't mean what she said. You don't know things, it's been very hard for her.'

'It's been hard for all of us, child.'

'But it's different for you, you're old.'

'Yes, but it's not over, not yet. Now, goodnight, I'm tired.'

Rosa left the room without kissing her grandmother and Graziella, left alone, felt alone. She had not expected such anger, such desperation from her daughters-in-law. She did feel guilty, knowing she had not handled their inheritance or overseen Mario Domino's work properly, but her belief that they should be free of all ties to the Mafia lay beneath her decision. She was glad now she had said nothing of her intentions for the following day in the courtroom.

Teresa had not retired to bed. She remained in the study, checking the hundreds of letters and contracts. Moyra, unable to sleep, saw the light beneath the door hours later when she crept down the stairs. She peeked around the door.

'What you doing? Can't you sleep either?'

Teresa was elbow-deep in papers and the entire study was strewn with documents and files. 'It's a mess, and it'll take weeks to get things sorted out. But here, I found the will. Want to read it and have a good cry?'

Moyra closed the door and picked up the will. 'Look I know Frederico had money, I know he didn't have no shares, why is it I don't get his cash?'

'Frederico, like Alfredo and Constantino, all named their father as executor and main beneficiary, as he did them, and Graziella, if she should outlive him, as his heirs. So when they all died, it all came to her.'

'You mean my husband didn't leave me nothing?'

'On the contrary, you were a beneficiary, but not sole heir. That would be the family, they would have to be taken care of first.'

'You mean he left you money, too?'

Teresa pushed her glasses back up her nose. 'Come on, Moyra, don't play games with me, we're all big girls. And if you want to be useful, start getting this bunch of papers into date order, 1988, '87, '86 . . . I'm trying to see what we'll be left with.'

Moyra leaned close to Teresa. 'Can I ask you something? If Papa was acting as witness for the prosecution, he was doing it because of Michael, right? 'Cause this Paul Carolla killed him, right? Now I know that, but I still . . .'

Teresa took her glasses off and rubbed her head wearily. 'You still what, Moyra, what?'

'Why did they do it? Who did it? I just don't understand. The cops don't seem too eager to question us, even find out who murdered them, and this Paul Carolla couldn't have done it because he was in jail, so who?'

'We were used, Moyra, as a warning, a warning to anyone who was even thinking of talking.'

Teresa turned back to her work and Moyra's legs turned to jelly. Teresa muttered, 'They've got invoices in with the payments, I can't even get together how many men we've still got on the payroll. Moyra? You OK?'

'Yeah, I'm OK, but maybe I just never heard it vocalized before. You think they're gonna come after us? I mean, if we start meddling with all these papers an' things?'

Teresa laughed. 'No, Moyra, we're just women. The men were the heart of the family and they took the entire

601

heart out. They left no one to carry on what Papa had begun or to avenge his murder. All we have to do is wear black until we die, and keep our mouths shut.'

Moyra watched Teresa looking through another file, flicking the pages back and forth. She squinted through her glasses and tapped the folder. 'This is an offer to buy the tile factory, dated May 1985 . . . Now, here . . .' She searched the desk and picked up another sheet of closely typed headed paper, 'Here, the same company's offer to Mario Domino, nearly two years later, for less than the original price and, by your elbow, you've got all the company's sales ledgers and export orders. For two years the business expanded, so how come they offer less? Domino was stalling. There's writing all over the contracts. All these are offers from a man called Vittorio Rosales, and the only address I can find for him is a box number in Rome.'

She pointed to the contract so Moyra could see. 'Can you tell me what you think Domino's written in the top right-hand corner? He's underlined it and then ringed it in red. What do you think it says?'

Moyra took the contract and held it under the desk lamp. 'I think it's Parolla . . .'

'I think it's P. Carolla.'

Both women turned in surprise as Sophia walked into the study. 'I couldn't sleep,' she said, excusing her interruption.

Teresa took off her glasses and rubbed her eyes. 'Most of the contracts that are ready for signature, in some cases already signed by Mama, and the new power of attorney, are in the name of Vittorio Rosales. You ever heard of him?'

Sophia shook her head. Teresa sucked the arm of her

glasses and explained, 'I think I've just come across something important. Rosales could be a front for Paul Carolla.'

'What? Are you serious?'

'Yeah. Domino's notes gave me the tip-off, look for yourself. See the writing at the top right-hand corner? You tell me if that's not P. Carolla.'

Sophia checked the documents and agreed. Teresa was shaking with tension. 'If I'm right, this means Carolla had good reason to order the murders of our men. Even before he was arrested he was buying up the companies. And as you can see, he's been continuing even from jail ... Look for yourself at the dates. That prosecution counsellor said he doubted if Paul Carolla ordered the deaths of our men. He would have wanted Papa dead because he was giving evidence against him, but Alfredo, Constantino, Frederico couldn't act as witnesses, so why have them murdered?'

Sophia clenched her fists. 'My babies weren't witnesses.'

Teresa nodded. 'Right, so why have them killed? It doesn't make sense. We all accepted what the police told us, what the prosecution counsellor told us, that our family was used to warn anyone else from coming forward. But if Paul Carolla stood to gain the entire Luciano company ... if we can prove he is Vittorio Rosales ...'

'How can we do that?'

Teresa held up one contract. 'We do it by checking out the only address we have, a box number in Rome. But we have to do it fast, because all these documents are ready for exchange. Tomorrow we revoke the power of attorney to give us more time.'

Sophia folded her arms. 'Won't the other families retaliate when they find out it was Carolla?'

Teresa was tapping away at her calculator. She shrugged. 'When, if . . . Right now, that's only part of it. I'm concerned with tracing the so-called liquid assets that were based here.'

'Mama said one day she came back to the villa, Domino was in here, with three Americans. He said they worked for Papa in America. There were documents removed, papers burnt. If they had access to, or could gain access to Papa's money, they simply took it, and there is nothing we can do or prove otherwise.'

Teresa snapped. 'That's the cash, Sophia. What *I'm* concerned about is the missing money from here in Sicily – that's got to be traceable, and I'm not talking about a few hundred dollars, but thousands. Maybe somewhere among those crates we'll find the missing details of our Swiss bank account. The more I check over old Domino's work, the more I realize he was fighting to save our inheritance, and he was no fool. That system of moving the cash around was for a purpose, he didn't want anyone getting their hands on it . . .'

Moyra moved closer to Sophia, as usual two or three conversations behind. 'When they say other families, are they the ones that have already had a share of the will?'

Sophia gave Teresa a covert look. 'Yeah . . .'

'So what do you mean when you said . . . what you just said, "retaliate" . . .?'

Sophia, sorting through one of Domino's crates, ignored the question. 'Teresa, are there any more boxes with Domino's personal papers in?'

'There's one in the corner, mostly junk, old diaries, and four more behind me.'

604

Sophia bumped into Moyra. 'Sorry.'

'What did you mean?'

Teresa crooked her finger for Moyra to come closer. 'I am going to tell you this once, Moyra, and not again. When Papa died, the organization he belonged to took their percentage. They don't wait for wills, they come with their hands out, understand? But if they find out that Paul Carolla owns the Luciano holdings he becomes a very powerful man, *capiche*?'

Moyra pouted thoughtfully. 'OK, I'm with you so far, but if what we have is worth so much, how come these other people aren't offering us good money for it too?'

Teresa sighed. 'Because, Moyra, Paul Carolla cum Vittorio Rosales got in first. Papa has been selling up for years, not openly, and in small sections.'

'So are we gonna get them back?'

'Not the cash, that may never surface, but we will have something to sell, Moyra.'

Moyra nodded, then patted the stack of documents nearest to her. 'How much do you reckon it's all worth?'

Teresa shrugged. 'Maybe ten million, maybe fifteen million, twenty million. Who knows?'

'Dollars or lire?'

'Dollars, Moyra! Now, would you get out of my light, I want to carry on working?'

Moyra grinned. 'Well, that's better'n a kick in the face, what do you say, Sophia? Sophia?'

Sophia didn't mean to snap, but she told Moyra to get out of the way because, right on top of the crate, she had found the stack of diaries. Her heart was beating rapidly as she shuffled through them . . . 1980, 1979, 1976 . . .

'I've made a note of Rosales' box number for you, Sophia,' said Teresa.

Sophia's hand was shaking. She had found it, a small diary bound in black leather, dated 1960. She stood up, slipping it into her pocket. 'Yes, I . . . I'll leave tonight.'

'Well, there's no need to rush . . .'

Sophia was already on her way to the door. 'The sooner, the better. Just write down everything you want me to find out, while I go and get ready.' Her hand was on the door knob, she couldn't wait to read the diary.

Teresa stood up and said in rapid Sicilian, 'You must be careful, is there anyone who can help you? I mean, we don't know anything about this guy, and if he does work for Carolla . . .'

Sophia turned, her eyes blazing, and replied in the same language, 'If I discover that Paul Carolla gave the order to kill my babies, then I hope he is freed, because I'll kill him myself.'

Unnerved by the look on Sophia's face, Teresa sat back. Moyra, not understanding but aware that something strange had been said, asked, 'What did she say?'

'Nothing important. Moyra, do you mind if I say something personal? That perfume you use, could you spray a little less on? It makes me feel ill.'

Domino had made no detailed entries, just lists of figures and occasional initials. Sophia licked her finger to help turn the pages, looking for the actual date of her marriage.

There it was, just a single line, 'S & C wedding'. She turned to the next page; how long was it after the wedding that she had called the orphanage? She jumped as Moyra knocked and peered around the door.

'This is the box number in Rome, Vittorio Rosales. Sorry, did I make you jump?'

'Yes, yes, you did. Goodnight, and thank you. Tell Teresa I'll return as soon as I know anything.'

She almost pushed Moyra from the room and locked the door after her. Then she snatched up the diary. She was trembling, and couldn't suppress the half-moan when she found the entry.

Moyra peered over the banisters as Sophia moved like lightning down the stairs, opened the front door and left.

'Holy shit,' she muttered to herself, 'these foreigners are really something else.' Maybe she would be all right after all, they certainly weren't letting the grass grow under their feet.

At eight o'clock the next morning, Graziella left the villa. She was wearing her black crêpe de Chine dress, a lightweight black coat and her widow's veil, and carried a large black leather clutch bag. In her black-gloved hand she held her rosary.

Luka Carolla, carrying a small bundle under his arm, left his hotel at eight-fifteen. He walked to the public lavatory and changed into his monk's robe. After carefully folding his own clothes he wrapped them in brown paper and hid them on top of the cistern. He stepped down from the toilet seat and picked up his walking stick. As he walked along the street, he began limping, leaning heavily on his cane. He turned down a side street and through an alley which brought him out on to the square, facing the Unigaro jail and courthouse. It was now nine o'clock, and the court session was to begin at ten.

Dante received the phone call at nine-thirty. He was told exactly what Luka had done, his address, and the clothes he had changed into in the lavatory.

It had taken most of the night, both working on the weapon and practising with it out in the woods. He admitted, grudgingly, that Luka was something else. He had fired over and over at one small mark on the chosen tree. He had even made Dante stand and bend to Carolla's height, arranging some logs to give him the height he needed, as he would be firing downwards. He missed on six tries, but by the seventh he had got the angle right. The tree was splattered with bullets. He then loaded one of the specials he had worked with the drill himself. When he fired, the trunk of the tree seemed to explode, leaving a gaping hole. They had all inspected it, Luka being the first there.

'Jesus Christ, it'll blow him through the courthouse wall!'

Dante had been stunned, but Luka had laughed, saying casually that it would have to, he was only going to get one chance, one shot.

*

Pirelli knew something was up the moment he stopped his car in the courtyard outside headquarters. Detective Sergeant Ancora was waiting for him and ran to meet him. There had been a meeting in the committee room. The defence and prosecution counsels had been closeted with the Judge and three government officials. There would be no acquittal, the clauses had been revoked and Carolla didn't stand a chance in hell of being freed. Ancora was almost jubilant – he laughed, as pleased with the result as the prosecutor Giuliano Emmanuel, but the bad news was Pirelli would have to forgo his interrogation of Carolla until after the day's session was over.

'They say Emmanuel's gonna throw the book at him today, and his defence lawyer's requested that their client should not be told. Seems they want the slob to retain his confidence on the stand!'

Pirelli slapped the steering wheel in frustration, then he shrugged. 'Maybe I'll take in the trial myself, anything comes up that's where you'll find me, OK?'

Ancora would have liked to sit in on the court session himself, but the Fiat, in a filthy cloud of black smoke from the exhaust, was already on the move.

Graziella's heart was pounding as she made her way slowly to her seat. She was one of the first to be allowed into the court that morning.

Luka propped the cane against the wall as the guards ran their hands down his body. They would not meet his gaze as they were embarrassed to be searching a father from the Holy Mission. He had the audacity to lean against the guard as he reached for his cane, then asked in a throaty, watery voice if it would be possible to have an aisle seat at the far side as his leg gave him pain if he could not stretch it out.

He was shown to an end seat four rows in front of Graziella. She sat staring straight ahead, her face hidden by her veil. As Luka eased his body into his seat, he placed the cane against the seat in front, right on the outside edge. The man who occupied the seat was unaware of the cane, as it did not touch him, just rested close.

Paul Carolla was five-feet-nine-inches tall, and Luka knew he had to slightly raise the tip of the cane, which even now pointed to the empty cell at the end of the line, Paul Carolla's cage.

Graziella opened her handbag, purposely dropping her rosary. She bent down as if to retrieve it, shielding the moment when she opened her handbag and took out the gun. She rested it beneath her bag as she sat back in her seat.

Paul Carolla had been prepared for his meeting with Pirelli. When it was cancelled, he knew something was going down. He had been in solitary for months and Enrico Dante had not paid him his regular visits. Like an animal he could smell the danger, knew without being told that the legal loophole, his chance of freedom, had failed. Now he was desperate to bargain. He had ranted and raved and bribed the jailers to get a message to his lawyers, but panic really set in when no one came. Now he knew that at any moment the bells would clang for the prisoners to prepare to leave their cells for the courthouse.

After eighteen months, the prisoners in the cells below the court were accustomed to the routine. The guards opened up each cell only as the prisoner's name was called out, then he was linked to the others by leg irons and placed in single file. They were also hand-cuffed.

As they waited for their names to be called, Dr Ulliano's clerk was arguing with the guards that he had to speak with his client. It was against the rules so there was considerable shouting and much gesticulation, but at last he was given permission to make his way along the narrow corridor to the last cell, which was still locked, as Carolla would be, as always, the last in line.

Carolla had shouted himself hoarse, demanding to see his lawyers before the session. Now he stood with his face pressed desperately against the bars. At last he saw the clerk hurrying towards him.

'You wanted to see me?'

The clerk knew the law had been revoked but was under strict instructions not to tell his client. They wanted him to be as confident as possible on the stand. They knew Emmanuel was going to hit him hard and if he knew he was not to be freed, he might break down.

'You got any news for me? There's rumours flying around down here, you heard anything yet?'

The clerk shook his head. The bellows of the prison guards as they brought the men out of their cells pushed him closer to Carolla.

'You would be the first to hear, Signor Carolla. You know this is irregular. If you continue to abuse the privileges you have been granted they will not allow me to see you as frequently . . .'

'I been thinkin' about what Dr Ulliano said, an' I got a name, but I want your word you will only use it if we don't get the injunction . . .' He was sweating with fear

611

that the other prisoners would overhear, and had lowered his voice so much that the clerk had to press his face against the bars to hear him.

'A name?'

'He said if I could give you a name, someone who might have been responsible for the Paluso kid . . .'

The line of prisoners was moving out fast as cell after cell was emptied. The shouting and the noise of the roll call made it almost impossible for the clerk to catch what Carolla was saying.

Carolla became so agitated he grabbed the young man's hand through the bars. 'You trace my son, trace Luka Carolla . . .'

The clerk could hardly believe his ears. Was he naming his own son? It was too late to ask again, as the guards ordered him to leave. They were opening the cell next door. But the clerk knew Carolla was not playing games with him, because he was weeping.

In the robing room the clerk joined the rest of the lawyers. He took Dr Ulliano aside and helped him into his robe, saying, 'He's come up with a name for the Paluso boy.'

'What, are you serious? Can you trust him?'

'He's named his son, Luka Carolla.'

'*What?*'

'That's what he said, what do you want me to do about it?'

The guards were calling the lawyers to stand by for the beginning of the session. Ulliano began gathering his things together.

'Get over to police headquarters, get Commissario

612

Pirelli to see me during my lunch break, but don't say why until I've spoken to him.'

He strode out, heading the group as they proceeded through the underground passage to the courthouse. Ulliano's clerk was already running towards police headquarters as Pirelli edged his way to the back of the courtroom. Unable to get a seat, he stood up at the back.

Luka twisted the handle of his stick gun. Now the safety catch was off, and his finger was on the trigger within the handle of the cane. His hands were steady, the cane not moving so much as a hair's width. He waited.

They were now filling the next to last cage. Carolla was about to be led in.

Graziella felt for the safety catch on the Luger and released it.

The guards were locking the cage next to Carolla's. She turned her head to look at the prisoners' entrance where Carolla was standing between two guards, in leg irons and handcuffs. The signal was given to lead him into the court.

As always, he was flanked now by two more guards to front and rear, hemming him in among them. As he shuffled towards his cage, there were catcalls from the prisoners. Many of the men cheered and some tried to touch him.

Carolla walked in silence, looking neither right nor left, his head slightly down. But always, as he reached his cage, he stepped aside to allow it to be slid open and, like a ritual, he glared around the court. That was the moment.

The door began to slide back. One guard stepped aside, the other moved to Carolla's left, and he was completely clear. Now he turned his head and his small eyes flickered.

Graziella rose to her feet, sending her handbag clattering to the floor.

Luka's hand never wavered. Both guns fired together as if the split-second timing had been rehearsed. Carolla was hit in the face, the impact blowing his skull apart.

Graziella's bullet went wide, hitting the cage bars and splintering the wall, but she, rather than Luka, drew the attention towards her. Spectators rose from their seats, and Luka turned like the rest of them to see what was happening.

Pirelli couldn't see what was going on, all he knew was that a gun had been fired and Carolla was hit. He began pushing his way down the aisle, holding up his ID card.

It was pandemonium. People tried to run from the court while the guards grabbed Graziella. Within seconds she was overpowered and the gun taken from her. Above the screams and shouts the guards tried to call for order. The defence and prosecution counsels had not yet entered the court, and remained safely outside. The prisoners screamed and clanked their chains while Luka carefully steered himself closer and closer to the exit. He had the audacity to ask a guard if he could do anything for the shot prisoner.

The guards asked the people to remain quiet, stay in their seats, it was all over . . .

Luka made his way back to the public lavatory and changed his clothes within minutes. By the time he returned to his rented room his whole body was shaking.

There was no remorse, only a feeling of exhilaration. He was drenched in sweat, which dripped from his hair and glistened on his body as he stripped. He ran water into the small wash bowl and stuck his head beneath the tap. When he swung his head back the water was dark red. His stomach lurched and he vomited.

His brain would not function; Dante would have to wait. He was too tired, he needed sleep, he had to sleep.

Luka took out the little gold heart and swung it above his head until his eyelids drooped and he fell into a deep, dreamless sleep.

CHAPTER 26

SOPHIA HAD waited an hour until the orphanage was open, then a further half-hour before the father who ran it was able to see her. He apologized for keeping her waiting. She explained her reason for being there and he excused himself, explaining that he could not, personally, help her as he had only been at the orphanage for ten years. He returned with an elderly sister who carried a file with dates and lists of names on the front cover.

Sophia was icy calm, outwardly, but inside her heart was beating so rapidly that she felt faint. She waited as the file was opened; page after page was turned, the sister showing the open pages to the father. He leaned over the desk, reading, his face furrowed in a deep frown. He did not look at Sophia but asked the sister if there were any further information, was anything ever resolved with regard to the incident? She shook her head and gave Sophia a forlorn look.

'Was my son brought here? Please tell me, please . . .'

The sister looked at the priest. Something was terribly wrong.

'We have a record of your son for the first five years of his life, the years he was with us.'

Sophia leaned forward. 'Was he adopted? Can you give me names?'

The priest nodded to the sister and she pressed both hands flat on the desk, as if needing the contact to enable her to speak.

'I recall your child, even though it was a very long time ago. He was perhaps four, almost five, when I came here. We used to take the children on picnics after Sunday school. There was a fair, run by gypsies. The children did not have money to go on many of the attractions, but some of the fair people were very kind and gave them free rides ... Your child, he was very wayward, irrepressible, and he was angry when we had to leave, and ran back to the fairground. His absence was not noted at first, there were fifteen children ... We returned to try to find him, and when it became dark the police were contacted. We did everything possible; the fair was forced to remain for an extra week for the police to continue their investigation ...'

Sophia's voice was almost inaudible. 'Is he dead ...?'

'We don't know. No body was ever found, he disappeared without trace. As you can see, we tried everything humanly possible to find him. The police searched for months.'

'You have been very kind, I thank you,' Sophia said eventually. She had very little money on her and did not dare write a cheque, so she slipped her diamond ring from her finger.

'Please accept this; it is worth a considerable amount, it is all I have. When I left my baby, he wore a small gold heart on a chain. Did ... When he was brought here, did he still wear it?'

The sister thought for a moment, touching the crucifix

at her own neck. 'Yes, yes, I remember . . . He used to move it like so before he slept.' She lifted the cross and dangled it, letting it swing back and forth.

Sophia drove out of Catania, feeling cocooned in her own misery. She had made no effort to trace the owner of the box number; nothing could have been further from her mind. In a daze, she headed back to Palermo, almost letting the car run out of petrol.

She pulled in at a petrol station and found herself listening to the attendant's radio blaring pop music. It was followed by a news flash. Paul Carolla had been shot dead during the morning's court session. The impact of it cut through her dulled senses and she sat, electrified, hearing that an elderly woman had been arrested and charged with the murder.

Teresa had discovered photographs of Dante and read the notes Mario Domino had attached to them. Excited at having discovered, without Sophia's assistance, the identity of the said Vittorio Rosales, she carried the notes with her as she went to the kitchen.

'Rosa? Moyra? Where are you?'

The television set in the kitchen was on; a newscaster was giving a rundown of the latest headlines. Teresa paused at the mention of Paul Carolla and turned up the sound. A moment later, Moyra came in.

'You callin' me?'

Teresa turned to her, shock on her face. 'Oh, my God, Moyra, I think Mama's shot Paul Carolla.'

*

618

Commissario Pirelli was trying to assimilate the morning's events. He knew Carolla had actually named his son, giving the Christian name as Luka, not Giorgio, yet there was still no trace of him. There was no record of Eva Carolla giving birth to a child in America, but what about Sicily? As he reached for the phone, there was a tap on the door. Without looking up, he called, 'Come in,' expecting it to be his assistant. There was a long silence; when he finally looked up, he dropped the phone quickly and rose to his feet.

'My apologies, signora, you wish to speak to me?'

Sophia Luciano hesitated in the doorway and Pirelli walked around to the front of his desk. 'Can I help you?'

She came a little further into the room. 'I was not sure who I should speak with. My name is Sophia Luciano.'

The deep, husky tones of her voice made the hair on the back of his neck rise. He had actually read of men struck by bolts of lightning, but he had never suspected it could happen to him. She was the most beautiful creature he had seen in his whole life, and her vulnerability, her shyness, made him want to hold her. He could not, would not, ever be able to forget this first meeting.

He gestured to a chair, pulling it out for her to sit down. 'You must be here about Signora Luciano, but I'm afraid I'm not handling the . . . er, please sit down, signora. I can find out where she is and then I'll take you to see her.'

He offered coffee but she refused, sitting with her head slightly bowed. 'I heard it on the news. I came straight here, I wasn't sure where I should go . . .'

The feeling of loss, the terrible emptiness in her

demeanour, overwhelmed him and again he had the urge to take her in his arms. His mind was working overtime, trying to remember which Luciano she was, was she the mother of the two little boys? But he didn't ask, he excused himself and left the office.

Outside, he let out his breath as if he had been holding it the entire time he was with her. He hurried along the corridor and straight into the red-faced Detective Sergeant Ancora.

'Commissario, a Luka Carolla was booked on a flight two days ago, but he never got on the plane. There was a seat reserved in his name . . .'

'In the name of Luka, not Giorgio?'

'Yep, so it means he's still here, he's in Sicily, unless he has another passport or took off from Rome. I'm checking there.'

Pirelli nodded, then caught Ancora's arm.

'Which one of the Luciano widows was the mother of the two children?'

Ancora paused, chewing his lip as he tried to remember. 'Sophia Luciano, married to the eldest son, Constantino.'

'She's in my office, I'll take her down to the old lady. Who's got her, do you know?'

Ancora told him she was with the Mincelli team on the top floor, then bustled off to his own office.

Sophia was still sitting in exactly the same position. Pirelli closed the door. 'You will be able to see her in a few moments, all the statements have been taken, and . . . I doubt very much if she will be held.'

Her dark eyes were so frightened that he busied himself with the pens and pencils on his desk.

'But she killed Paul Carolla?'

'No . . . She tried, but she did not kill him. There was another gun fired at the same time. I have no details yet, and perhaps I shouldn't have told you.'

'Someone else shot him?'

'It appears so . . . I am sorry. When I take you to her, you will obviously learn more.'

She nodded and whispered her thanks. He offered her a cigarette but she refused, then opened her handbag and took out her own cigarette case. She clicked it open.

'I smoke only these, they are very expensive and difficult to find, and I pretend to myself that it helps me not to smoke so much. Would you care for one?'

Pirelli had already put his own Marlboro in his mouth. 'No, *grazie*.' He fumbled for a light and she beat him to it, holding up her gold lighter. Her cigarettes were a strong Turkish blend. She exhaled and let the smoke drift into a haze around her head.

'Did you see her?' she asked.

He loved the sound of her husky, throaty voice, it was so sexy. He could not take his eyes from her. He was behaving like a schoolboy, he knew it, and he flushed. 'No, I did not see her, but I believe she is greatly shocked. The officer said he is not sure if it is from the attempt to kill Carolla or from learning that her gun did not kill him.' He quickly wiped the smile off his face, realizing the stupidity of trying to make a joke of it.

'Have they arrested anyone else?'

Pirelli shook his head. 'Not to my knowledge.'

She searched for an ashtray and he moved quickly to place one near her. She stabbed the half-smoked cigarette out and stood up. He had not realized how tall she was,

621

almost his height, and his eyes flickered down to her high-heeled shoes. At the same time he could not help but notice her perfect legs.

'You have been very kind to me. May I see her now?'

After making a brief phone call, he went to the door. She moved towards him, seeming to sway slightly, and he reached out to clasp her elbow. For a brief moment she leaned against him, sending shock waves through his body. 'Are you all right? Would you like a glass of water?'

'No, *grazie*, no . . .'

She followed him up to the next floor and was introduced to the detective in charge. Pirelli waited, while she asked what would happen to Graziella, then walked slowly away. He didn't want to leave her . . .

He overheard the officer's reply, 'She'll be charged with attempted murder and possession of an offensive weapon, but with mitigating circumstances. I doubt if Signora Luciano will be imprisoned, but she'll have to stand trial. If you want to see her before bail arrangements are made it's all right with me. If not, you can come into my office and we'll sort it all out. Then she's free to go.'

Ancora greeted Pirelli, beaming. 'Eh, Commissario, we got it, Eva Carolla had a son, born in Rome, 1949, she died in childbirth, they're getting all the particulars sent over, means he's not as young as we thought, in his early thirties. Joe? Joe, d'you hear what I said?'

Pirelli nodded. They were getting closer, he could feel it, but all he could think about was Sophia Luciano. The phone on his desk rang and Ancora answered, then held it out to Pirelli. 'It's your wife.'

Pirelli made a face and took the call. Ancora smirked to hear him making excuses about why the case was taking so long, and saying that he hoped to have it cleared up shortly . . . He interrupted her to ask about their son but, as she talked, he could only picture Sophia in his mind, her two little boys and the overwhelming sadness that enveloped her. He closed his eyes, remembering her musky perfume, then forced himself to concentrate on whether his own son should take extra violin classes or not.

'I thought it was the guitar. Oh, that was last term? Well, do whatever you think best . . . Yes, I'll see you at the weekend.'

He hung up and stretched, walking to the window and peering through the blinds to the street below. Sophia Luciano was helping her mother-in-law into a Mercedes 280 SL.

Pirelli turned. 'I call that one hell of a lady.'

Ancora shrugged. 'If my grandmother had started taking pot shots at people I don't know if I'd call her that, I'd put her in a home where she couldn't do any damage.'

Pirelli stuffed his hands in his pockets and wandered around the offfice: 'They got any suspects for the shooting this morning?'

'Nothin', they're still scraping Carolla's brains off the floor. It'll be a while yet, they've got to check every single person in the courtroom. You were there, weren't you?'

'I was right at the back, I couldn't see anything. Then when the shots were fired, it was chaos.' He opened the file drawer and flicked through the files. In theory he was still only heading the Paluso murder, but he had retained

623

the files on the Luciano children. He slid the drawer slowly back in. 'While you're with me, who's taken over the main Luciano case?'

'My old chief, Mincelli. Poor bastard, he's got the Carolla shooting as well. Guy's goin' nuts, but this'll take precedence. Eh, Joe . . . A word of advice. Stay out of the Luciano business if you want to go back to Milan. You'd be here for . . . Joe?' But Pirelli had already left.

Sophia drove Graziella home, waited with her while the doctor gave her a sedative, and sat beside her until she slept.

The act of madness touched them all, and their own guilt that not one of them had accompanied her to the trial. They arranged legal representation for Graziella and were assured that it was unlikely she would stand trial given the mitigating circumstances and Graziella's age. Teresa handled everything.

When they had exhausted the subject of the shooting, the shock was tempered and they were left subdued and listless. They ate dinner in silence, until Teresa brought up the point that, no matter what had occurred, their main objective was to settle the family business. Sophia apologized for not being able to discover anything in Rome, giving the excuse that no sooner had she arrived than she had heard the news, and so returned.

Teresa flipped her notebook open. 'Well, as it turned out, it would have been a wasted effort anyway, because old Mario had already done the investigating. I found these photographs; don't know who took them, but on the back someone's written, "Enrico Dante alias Vittorio Rosales". Dante works for Paul Carolla, he's also partners with him in a night-club in Palermo called the Armadillo. We were right about Carolla, and this is the man who's been doing the buying for him and who's waiting to exchange contracts. Mario obviously got on to it and refused to complete. Now is our chance to get them back.'

She showed them several columns of figures. 'So, in this first column is what we might make from the sale of everything I've been able to verify as legally ours, the second is what we might be able to get back, with a little help. Some of these are the ones Dante was negotiating for Carolla, a couple are US-based, trucking companies, etc. The third column is what I can see as a long-term prospect. That is, if we run the Luciano business ourselves.'

Sophia paid little attention to the figures. 'Do you think you'd be allowed to do this?'

'Whether or not we would be allowed is nobody's business but ours. Besides, I know enough about it, on the import side, anyway. When Alfredo was alive I used to run . . .'

Sophia threw up her hands in a gesture of impatience. 'And Papa was alive, and Constantino, and Frederico . . . You were protected, Teresa, you never ran anything. So maybe you did a few figures, jiggled a few contracts, you're living in some kind of fantasy world. Papa wanted us to have the cash and get out. This is what Mama wants, what Mario Domino was trying to get for us – out, Teresa! And that is what we will do. We'll sell all of it, lock, stock and barrel.'

'But you don't understand, the companies are worth three times that amount. Dante, or Paul Carolla, was ripping us off. I agree, if that is what you want, what we

625

all want. We will sell, but not until we know what we own. There's no point arguing about who's doing what, OK? Agreed, Sophia? Moyra?'

Too tired to argue, Sophia shrugged and gave in. Moyra gave the thumbs up, her attention on Teresa's columns of figures. 'Yeah, all right by me. Things don't look so bad, not bad at all. What d'you say, Rosa?'

Rosa leaned on her elbows, bored and only half-listening. 'I'll go along with everyone else. Sooner we leave here the better.'

Teresa picked up her notebook. 'Then it's agreed. I don't think it's necessary to tell Graziella about any of this, let her rest. You stay with her, Rosa.'

'Where are you going, Mama?'

'Dante's club, might as well do it straight away. Moyra, Sophia, you'd better come along with me.'

Sophia rose to her feet, muttering under her breath. 'Do we have an option?'

Dante had closed his club, paid off the staff, and was moving as fast as was humanly possible. His man, Dario Biase, returned; the old gunsmith had been taken care of. Dante enquired about Luka; he was still at his hotel, he had not been out of his room since the killing.

Dante had never been capable of cold-blooded murder, he had always hired someone else. Working for Carolla, he had never had to deal with that side, but now he was in a dilemma. The gunsmith was no longer a problem, and the only two witnesses connecting his involvement with the murder of Paul Carolla were Luka, and this broken-faced ex-boxer Dario Biase. Dante smiled.

'I'm gettin' out, Dario. I'll come back when the heat's off. I suggest you do the same. There's a club up in Tipani – you take your wife and kids.' He stacked bundles of lire on his desk and the big, broken hands couldn't grab it fast enough. Dante reached down to stop him.

'Wait . . . you'll get ten times this, but I want Luka taken care of. Neither of us can trust him, he's crazy.'

The big hands didn't move.

'How many kids do you know who could kill their own father?'

The watery eyes blinked, then Dario nodded his agreement. As a further incentive, Dante repeated, 'Ten times this amount, I'll be waiting.'

Dante waited until he heard the heavy plodding footsteps pause at the front entrance door of the club, waited until it banged shut, then he fetched a black holdall and started loading it with the lire. The gun went in last. Just as Dario Biase would be the last witness left, he would also be the first man Dante had ever killed personally.

Dante was feeling confident, and decided whilst he was waiting for Dario to return that he would finish stock-taking in the bar. He carried the bag into the dark area of the bar, putting it down near the till. He paid little attention to the rattling of the door chain at the fire exit, believing it was some punter who didn't realize the club was closed. Then his mind raced; no punter would try to come in the back way . . . The door rattled again and he stood poised, listening, finally making his way slowly through the curtained archway towards the fire exit to see who was there.

He called out that the club was closed. There was silence, and he listened, then took a heavy bunch of keys from his pocket and unfastened the padlock, pushing the doors open slightly . . . He stepped out and looked up and down the back alley. He could see no one. As he was about to relock the doors he heard a noise, this time inside the club, in the bar.

Dante moved slowly backwards, standing half-hidden behind the curtains, and peered through the gloom. There was only the working light behind the bar . . .

He squinted, screwing his eyes up to see more clearly. He looked over the tables, the stacked chairs, and moved further into the room, almost to the edge of the dance floor.

'Hi, OK if I help myself?'

His heart stopped for a moment. Luka appeared from behind the bar. He was holding a glass of orange juice, raised slightly as if in a toast. 'You see the news on the television?'

Dante smiled nervously. 'How did you get in?'

Luka sat on a high stool and sipped his juice. He was wearing just a shirt, no jacket, and it was obvious he wasn't carrying a gun. 'I came through the front door – it was open.'

Dante swore under his breath, that fool Dario couldn't have shut it properly. He kept a frozen smile on his face.

Luka delved into his pocket and brought out a bullet, holding it between his thumb and forefinger. 'Here, you want a keepsake? We made two, just in case, but . . . Is he taken care of? The gunsmith?'

Dante poured himself a brandy. 'Yeah, it's done. I've been stuffing a bag with some dough for you.'

Dante had inched further behind the bar as he talked. He had to get to the bag, to the gun; it was propped up beside the till. Luka's pale, wide eyes looked at Dante, then at the bag.

'How much d'you put in there for me?'

'A few thousand dollars, could be more. Should last you a while, and later we can get down to sorting through the rest.' He bent down for the bag, his back to Luka. 'You want to count it?' His hand was in the bag, feeling for the gun. Through the bar mirror, Luka could see every move he made.

Luka quickly shifted his glass to his left hand, flicked his arm up a fraction and down again until he felt the knife slide down his arm. He cupped it in the palm of his hand. They stared at each other, then Luka smiled warmly. 'I guess I can trust you, what's a few thousand dollars between friends?'

As Luka said the word 'friends', Dante fired, through the bag, through a wad of dollars. The glass of orange juice slipped from Luka's fingers and rolled on to the floor, intact. Luka didn't even feel the bullet smash into his shoulder, he was moving so fast. The knife sliced into Dante's stomach, ripping through the muscle, the blade so fine and sharp it was like a razor.

The gun was still in Dante's hand inside the torn bag. He tried to hit Luka with the bag, but the boy was too fast, dragging it away from him. Dante began howling and gibbering, clutching his belly, blood streaming between his fingers. He made a desperate run to get clear of the bar, knocking bottles to the floor.

Luka kicked the bag away and swung up and over the bar, ending up facing Dante. He fired twice; aiming once at Dante's throat and again into his heart. The big man wouldn't go down; the impact of the bullets at such close range threw him backwards into the rows of glasses, but he was still standing. Luka was about to fire again when, in slow motion, Dante died on his feet. He gurgled as his lungs filled with blood, oozing from his mouth as he crashed backwards and finally lay still.

Luka stared at himself in the splintered mirror, reflected hundreds of times. He was fascinated to see his shoulder covered in blood, spreading over his shirt, dripping down his arm . . . He had been hit, and only then did the burning pain cut through his brain like a scream.

The bullet was lodged deep in his left shoulder blade. Part of his shirt-front was covered with bits of the bag and dollar bills. He knew he had to get out, and fast; three shots had been fired, someone must have heard. He hurried to one of the tables to collect his own bag, and carried it back to the bar. The pain was so fierce that he felt dizzy, it was useless trying to salvage any of the cash Dante had stalled him with. Instead he went to the office, kicking open the door. He put the bag on the desk and went to the safe. The door still stood wide open . . . He was just about to start filling his bag when he heard the chains on the fire-exit door rattle . . .

He turned towards the bar and heard the door rattle again. Then a woman's voice called, 'Is anyone there?' He switched off the one light behind the bar and picked up the gun. Again he stumbled . . .

Another woman's voice, 'It's open, Teresa, it's open . . .'

*

Moyra pushed the door further open, then peered into the dark corridor. 'Hi, is anyone here? Hello . . . Anyone here?'

Luka entered the cloakroom, leaving the door open no more than a crack, and stared out. Moyra appeared in the doorway from the main room.

Behind her was Teresa, who called in Sicilian, 'Hello? Anyone here?' They peered around in the gloom, then she whispered to Moyra, 'You see an office? Maybe there's someone in the office. Hello?'

Moyra made her way to a door marked 'Private'. She knocked and waited, then swung the door open wider. Teresa remained standing on the dance floor until, after a moment, Moyra came out.

'There's a safe, an' it's open, wanna take a look?'

'OK. Soon as you see someone, yell.' She hurried into the office.

Sophia walked in. 'Where's Teresa?'

Moyra pointed. 'In there. There's nobody here, she's havin' a look around. Seems like someone had a good party, look at the state of the place.'

From his vantage point behind the bar, Luka could see Sophia clearly. He gritted his teeth, wishing they would all get the hell on with it. The pain was beginning to burn and the blood dripped down his hand, making a pool on the floor by his feet. He was losing a lot, and fast.

Sophia looked around, puzzled that the doors should be unlocked, wondering why there was every sign that somebody was there and yet there was no one. Something on the bar gleamed where it caught the light, and she walked towards it. It was Luka's bullet, and she was

631

just reaching for it when Teresa called from the office doorway.

Her voice was full of excitement. 'Sophia, I found them! There are papers on the company, the warehouses . . . Everything's here.'

Moyra rushed over. 'What are you going to do with them?'

'Without these he's got no proof of anything.'

Teresa went back to the office and Sophia turned away from the bar. She was only a few feet from Dante's body. As she did so, her foot struck Dante's bag. She bent down and picked it up, then stood up quickly. Her hand was stained and sticky, but in the darkness she couldn't tell what it was . . .

'Sophia, come in here . . . Hurry!' Teresa called from the office. The safe door was wide open and she was eagerly removing file after file. 'Holy Mother of God, you should see what some of these are . . . Look at this!'

Sophia said quickly, 'Just take our contracts, Teresa, nothing else. And hurry.' Her eyes had become accustomed to the gloom and she could see her hand was stained with blood. Moyra picked up Luka's bag and handed it to Teresa. 'Here, put everything in this,' she said.

Teresa brought out stacks of lire and dollars. Moyra hovered at her side. 'Why don't we take some of the cash, make it look like a robbery?' she suggested.

'No,' said Sophia, overhearing. 'Take the contracts and nothing more. You leave the money, *leave it*. Let's get out of here.'

She went around behind the bar. Now she could see all the broken glass. She inched forward, the glass crackling beneath her feet. She screamed.

Moyra almost fainted with shock. She and Teresa ran to the dance floor. Sophia, still behind the bar, was backing away and pointing in horror.

Teresa leaned over the bar and then turned away. The sight of the body made her sick to her stomach. As Moyra scurried towards them, she snapped, 'Just get the rest of the papers, Moyra, and hurry.'

Moyra ran back to the office as Sophia tried to pull Teresa away. 'We've got to get out of here.'

Teresa stepped back. 'Do you think I don't know that? Who is it? Did you see who it was?'

'No ... Come on, please, let's go, please,' said Sophia.

Teresa glared, telling Sophia to pull herself together, and called out to Moyra to hurry. Then she walked around the bar to look down at the body. 'Is this Dante? Sophia?'

'I don't know, how do I know? I've never even met him.'

After a moment's hesitation, Teresa rolled the body over and slipped her hand into the back pocket of the corpse's trousers. She flipped open his wallet. 'It's Dante.' She touched his hand. 'And he's still warm. This must have only just happened. What do you think we should do? I mean, do we call the police, or what?'

Carrying the bag stuffed to bursting with papers and anything she could lay her hands on, Moyra hurried out of the office. She had almost reached Sophia's side when she slithered on the still-wet bloodstains and her high heels gave way beneath her. She screamed and, panic-stricken, all three turned and ran for it.

*

In the first car, Teresa and Moyra suddenly screeched to a halt, waving frantically for Sophia in the car behind to stop. She pulled up behind them and Teresa ran back to talk to her.

'You're not going to believe this, but she left her handbag in the office.'

'She *what*?'

'Look,' Teresa replied, 'you go on ahead with her, she's hysterical. I'll go back and look for it. Go on, I'll be all right.'

They switched cars and Teresa made a U-turn, heading back towards the Club Armadillo.

When Moyra and Sophia arrived home, they shut themselves in the study. Moyra began tipping the files from the bag they had picked up in the club. There were stacks and stacks of papers and, to Sophia's fury, bundles of banknotes.

'I told you not to take any money.'

'I didn't mean to, I just swept everything into the bag. I swear I didn't mean to take the money . . . It's not much, it was an accident.' She tipped out the rest of the contents of the bag and screeched as part of Luka's cane gun fell on her foot.

The front door slammed and Teresa ran into the study. 'I searched everywhere, you must have been wrong, there was no bag. Are you sure you took it with you?'

Moyra's hand flew to her face as she tried to remember, then she hurried up to her room to see if it was there. She even went out and checked the car. When she returned, Teresa screamed at her, 'How could you be so stupid?'

Moyra had found no trace of her bag and she was close to tears. Teresa snapped, 'What's in it? Come on, think.'

'Well, everything . . . My wallet, passport, my cards . . . I know I had it with me, I know I did.'

'What the hell did you take it into the club for?'

'How was I to know we'd find a dead body? We were just goin' to talk with the guy that owned the place . . . You think I'd leave it there on purpose? It's your fault, I packed all the things in that bag an' I musta forgot it wasn't my own. How the hell do I know how I did it? Are you sure it wasn't there?'

Sophia was turning over the strange horse's head on the short piece of cane. She checked the handles of Dante's bag, they were covered in blood.

Teresa gasped, 'Look at the handles of the bag – give it to me, Sophia – it's blood. Is this his bag?'

Sophia's voice rose. 'I don't know, how would I know whose bag it is?'

Teresa paced up and down, 'What if this bag belongs to someone else, someone who shot Dante? What if it happened just before we got there?'

Moyra began to cry.

'Shut up, Moyra. What I'm trying to work out is if we disturbed the killer.'

Sophia's nerve went and she couldn't get her breath. 'Oh, God, we should have gone to the police.'

Teresa shouted, 'Don't you understand? Don't you see that if we disturbed the killer, he could still have been there?'

Moyra screeched, 'He could have killed us!'

Teresa wanted to shake her. 'He could also have *seen* us, he would have seen us taking the papers from the office.'

Moyra yelled, 'My handbag! Oh, my God, he'll know who I am!'

'Shut up, Moyra!' shouted Teresa. 'For Chrissakes, try and pull yourself together. If he was there, he saw us take the papers.' It was her turn to feel dizzy and she sat down quickly. 'Jesus, what a mess. We'd better think straight, or Moyra had, because we have to find her bag. Go over exactly where you went, what you could have done with it.'

Moyra mimed entering the club, going into the office, and was sure that she'd left it on Dante's desk. Teresa shook her head, there was no handbag there because she'd checked. All three knew then, at the same moment, that they were in trouble, because now it was obvious that if the killer were there, if he had seen them, he would find out quickly who they were with the help of Moyra's handbag.

Moyra was crying again. 'Maybe we didn't disturb him, maybe he'd already gone.'

'Great, Moyra! Now if the law gets there, they find the safe open, a dead body, and *your fucking handbag*!' Teresa felt something sticking in her back. She had sat on the top part of the walking cane. 'What's this?'

Sophia pointed. 'It was in the bag.'

Moyra howled, 'What are we gonna do?'

Sighing, Teresa said, 'Go back, we've no option. Go back, maybe I missed it. We'll take two cars, just like before. You two remain outside while I search. You hear or see anything, blast on the horn . . . Right, let's go. Gimme the bag.'

'What bag?' asked Moyra.

'The bag we found there, for Chrissake! Give it to me and I'll leave it there.'

Luka Carolla was in trouble. He had managed to get himself back to his own rented room, but he could not staunch his wound. He had torn a sheet up to make a small pad, but the blood was even seeping through that.

Alone in the squalid room, he was frightened that he would bleed to death. The bullet had to come out and the wound needed cleaning, but he could not go to a hospital, they would ask questions. He was very aware that the gun he had used to kill his father was in the bag the women had taken, just as he had taken Moyra Luciano's bag. The contents were now spread across his bed . . .

Sophia's hands were clenched on the wheel, the engine still running. 'You see anything, Moyra?'

'No . . . Oh yes, look, look, it's a patrol car!'

The ambulance screeched past them, bells ringing. Sophia gritted her teeth. 'That's an ambulance, Moyra, just calm down.'

'No, *look*, that's a police car, isn't it? Toot the horn . . . Oh my God, I can't believe this is happening to me. *Toot, Sophia, toot the fucking horn! There's two police cars heading right this way!*'

Sophia watched in horror in the rear-view mirror as

the patrol cars headed straight for them. They looked as if they were going to stop, but then slowed down to make a left turn down the alley beside the club. Sophia's nerve gave way; the cars, the sirens, made her shake. She pressed and pressed the horn.

Moyra yelled, 'OK, let's get out of here! Drive off, Sophia, drive!'

'Where's Teresa? We don't know if she's found your bag!'

Moyra pointed. 'There she is, it's OK, she's carrying a bag . . . For God's sake get us out of here . . .'

Teresa threw the bag into the back and jumped into the driving seat. Moving fast, Sophia and Moyra pulled out ahead of her and disappeared down the street. Teresa could not get the engine started . . . She was driving the old Mercedes and the battering Graziella had given it must have caused some damage to the engine. Once, twice she turned the key, but there was nothing but a low growling sound from the ignition. Teresa began to shake as yet another police car passed her, sirens wailing. She tried to calm herself, talk herself down.

'Don't flood the engine. Keep calm, next time it's going to go. Lick the key, lick the key, that always helps.'

Teresa spat on the key, replaced it, turned it, gave a silent prayer . . . The engine caught.

Moyra was waiting beside Sophia on the steps of the villa. Teresa drew up, the Mercedes backfiring. 'Did you find it, did you get it?'

Teresa shook her head, hurrying to enter the villa. 'No, I didn't,' she said.

Sophia caught Teresa's arm. 'Then what's that you've brought back with you?'

Teresa pushed her away. 'It's something that's got my fingerprints all over it. I'll lock it in the study, we'll burn it tomorrow.'

As they let themselves in, Rosa rushed to greet them, pointing to the dining room and gesturing them to silence. Teresa paid her no attention, thinking she was referring to Graziella. She entered the study and shut the door.

Rosa gripped Sophia's wrist. 'There's a man in there, he's in the dining room, I didn't know what to do. He's weird, he says Moyra knows what it's about.'

Teresa, white-faced, came out of the study, 'Rosa, get back to bed.'

Sophia and Moyra seemed frozen with fear. Teresa said angrily, 'Rosa, get up the stairs *now*!'

'But Mama, who is he? He's in there, just walked in when I opened the door.'

'What?'

Sophia found her voice. 'There's someone in the dining room. He told Rosa it's something to do with Moyra.'

Luka was sitting in the Don's chair, a balloon glass of brandy in front of him. He was very pale, and his wound still seeped blood through the makeshift pad. His right hand, with Dante's gun in it, rested on the bandage. Close to him on the table was Moyra's handbag.

He half-rose to greet them, but the pain was so bad he sat back instantly. 'Which of you is Moyra Luciano?'

'I am.'

'This, I believe, belongs to you.'

Teresa held Moyra back. 'What do you want?'

'I have a bullet in my left shoulder. You will have to take care of me.'

'What makes you think that we'll agree?' asked Teresa.

'Because you were also at the club, so I'll make a deal with you. I'll take the cash you stole and walk out of your lives as soon as I am fit. The papers you can keep, I have no interest in them.'

'What's to stop us calling the police right away?'

'If you wanted their involvement, they would already have been called.'

Sophia shook her head. 'We didn't mean to take any money. You can have what we took now, but you cannot stay here.'

Luka looked pointedly at Teresa and she hesitated, then eased open the door. She looked out to see if the coast was clear. 'Put him in the small room at the top of the house. I don't want Mama to know he is here.'

Angry, Sophia turned to her. 'You agree? Are you agreeing to this?'

'Why not? It seems we all need each other right now, unless you want to discuss this evening's mess with the police. I don't think they would be too co-operative, especially after the Graziella episode . . . He gets the cash, we get the documents . . . It's a deal, mister—?'

'Moreno, Johnny Moreno.'

CHAPTER 27

LUKA WAS shown up to the small bedroom at the very top of the house. It had been a maid's room at one time, and contained only a single bed, a wardrobe and a tallboy. There was a small handmade rug beside the bed.

Sophia brought a pair of pyjamas from Michael's room, and Teresa found fresh bed linen in the laundry room. Moyra crept around the kitchen pouring boiling water into bowls, fetching bandages and antiseptic.

Luka put the gun underneath his pillow. He was wearing just the pyjama bottoms and the stained bandage on his shoulder was stiff with his blood.

Teresa dipped a clean cloth in hot water. 'You'd better take that chain off, I'll have to disinfect the whole shoulder.'

Luka removed the gold chain with the small gold heart and tucked it beneath his pillow, watching Teresa as she moved back and forth.

She checked his bandages and said, 'I'll have to soak them until they come away easily, I don't want to rip the wound.'

*

Sophia was creeping up the stairs carrying a bottle of brandy and a tumbler. 'Is this what she wants?' she whispered to Moyra.

Moyra whispered back, 'He's got the gun under his pillow. Maybe if we give him enough of that, he'll pass out, then we can take it.'

Sophia passed her the brandy. 'I am having nothing to do with this. I still say we should go to the police.'

She stopped as she heard Luka moan and Teresa came to the bedroom door. 'I'll need some help, the bullet's still in him and I don't know if I'm even doing the right thing or not. He's lost so much blood and he's in agony. Did you check your handbag, Moyra? Is everything in it?'

Sophia snapped, 'Why don't we stop all this nonsense and call a doctor? If he's still losing blood he could die, then what would we do? Has he taken anything, Moyra?'

'He's not going to die,' Teresa said sharply, 'I just want him fit and out of here as soon as possible. Now which one of you will help me? My eyesight's not so good and we need fine tweezers to get the bullet out.'

Moyra backed off fast. 'Don't look at me, I couldn't, I really couldn't. I mean, I'll do anything you ask but I'm not good with the sight of blood . . . I'd better check everything's in my bag.'

Sophia sighed and said she would help, but she was still against them keeping him at the villa.

Moyra met Rosa on the landing below. The girl was desperate to know what was going on and Moyra, knowing she shouldn't but unable to stop herself, told her everything. Together they searched through her handbag.

*

Luka lay with his eyes closed, his wound streaming blood even though it was padded with clean lint. The room was heavy with the smell of antiseptic and steam from the bowls of hot water on the tallboy.

Sophia picked up the tweezers and joined Teresa at the bedside, leaning over the bed. 'Mr Moreno? I've brought some brandy. Maybe it would be better if you had a few drinks, this is going to be very painful and we have nothing to stop the pain.'

He shook his head, and Teresa switched on the anglepoise lamp, directing the light into the gaping wound. 'Can you see the bullet, Sophia?'

Sophia nodded. She could see that the skin around the wound was red and swelling fast. The bullet was buried at least an inch and a half deep. She leaned closer. 'Are you all right?'

Luka nodded, gritting his teeth. Sophia didn't bother dabbing with the lint; she poured the antiseptic all over his shoulder, then looked at Teresa. 'OK, I'm going to have a try.' To Luka she said, 'Are you sure you don't want some brandy?'

'No, just do it.'

Teresa looked away as Sophia began probing the wound. Luka winced and tears rolled down his cheeks. The pain was excruciating.

Sophia could not clamp the ends of the tweezers around the bullet, they were too narrow, and after two attempts she gave up. Luka gave a long, shuddering sigh and passed out.

Sophia washed the tweezers and stretched them as far as she could. 'I'll have another try, at least he won't feel it, he's out cold.'

Luka did not stir when she slipped her hand beneath the pillow and brought out the gun.

'Steady the light,' said Sophia. 'OK, you ready?'

She worked for fifteen minutes and finally eased the bullet out of the wound. She held it up, then dropped it into a bowl. Teresa quickly padded the wound as the blood drenched Sophia and the sheet. Then she bent to feel for the pulse in Luka's neck.

She freaked. 'Jesus, Mary, Mother of God, I can't feel anything . . . I can't find his pulse . . . Sophia, there's no pulse.'

Sophia pushed her aside and touched Luka's neck. Even she had difficulty finding a pulse because it was so faint. Blood still oozed from the wound.

'It needs stitches, it'll never heal open like this. Get me a needle and cotton, anything. Go on, hurry.'

Dante's body was not discovered immediately, due to the fact that the police found another corpse first in the car park at the rear of the Armadillo Club. The body was identified as Dario Biase, ex-boxer, doorman and bodyguard of Enrico Dante. The bloody footprints led the police from the car park to the back entrance of the Armadillo. The doors were open.

It was obvious that Dario's throat had been cut near the club fire exit and somehow, bleeding badly, he had staggered down the alley to the car park where his body was found by a bunch of kids.

The club looked as if it had been ransacked. Discovering Dante's body behind the bar, robbery became the first motive.

*

644

Sophia had stitched Luka's wound with white cotton. She poured more antiseptic over it and then carefully wrapped heavy pieces of lint around his shoulder.

She smoothed his hair back from his sweating, white face. 'I think he's started a fever. We'll take it in turns to sit with him. I'll do the first shift, you get a few hours' sleep and take over. Where's Moyra?'

'She went to bed. I'll wake her when it's her turn.' Teresa inched open the door, afraid to make any noise, and whispered, 'I'll hide the gun in my room. If we can get him to eat, we can keep him drugged – I've got a few sleeping pills, we can break them up and put them in his food.'

Three hours passed. The fever was worse and his pulse was even weaker. When Moyra came up to do her shift, she was loath to take on the responsibility, but Sophia was tired and needed rest herself.

Sophia's mind was in turmoil and she could not sleep. She had used up most of her supply of Valium, so she crept down into Graziella's room and searched her dressing table.

'Is that you, Sophia?'

'Yes, Mama. Go back to sleep, I'm just looking for those tablets. Remember, the ones you gave me, have you any left? I can't sleep.'

She returned to her room with almost full bottles of both Valium and Mogadon. Her hands shook as she tipped out the tiny yellow pills. She was so drugged that Moyra had to shake her awake. The boy, she said, was shivering, and she was worried. One moment he seemed cold and the next he was sweating. He looked terrible, and she was scared.

Sophia rinsed the cloth in iced water and held it gently to his neck, his chest and right shoulder. She noted that the bandages were still clean, and knew it was a good sign – the bleeding had stopped.

Rosa slipped into the room. 'How is he?'

'I think he's doing fine.'

Rosa approached the bed and looked down at Luka. 'He's very handsome, isn't he?'

'What?' Sophia was winding the bandages to be washed so they could use them again.

'How old do you think he is, Aunt Sophia?'

'Oh, I don't know, and I think the less we find out about him the better. Did Teresa tell you what happened?'

'No, Moyra did. Mama's still in the study working. What's his name? He's American, isn't he?'

Sophia crossed the room to pick up Luka's clothes. 'Johnny Moreno.' She checked the pockets of his blood-stained clothes; they were empty. Rosa picked up Luka's gold Cartier watch and turned it over in the palm of her hand, but there was no name engraved.

'If his fever starts up again, you'd better call me,' Sophia said as she rested her forefinger against Luka's neck to check his pulse. His skin was soft, warm. 'It's strong,' she whispered, and the memory of her babies swept over her, their tiny cold lips, how cold their skin had been in their satin-lined coffins when she had kissed them for the last time. Sophia could not lift her hand from Luka, as if she needed the comfort of his life beneath her fingertips; she closed her eyes until the memory faded. Rosa was concerned, a little afraid.

'Are you all right, Aunt Sophia?'

She watched as Sophia removed her hand from Luka, placing it against her own wrist. She then touched the pulse at her neck. 'I think I am very tired,' she whispered.

The photographs of the Luciano children were on Pirelli's desk, a computer printout left on top of the photographs for him to read. Giorgio Carolla, born in Rome, at the hospital of St Paul. Pirelli, having to date been unable to trace the existence of Giorgio in the United States, now surmised he must have been taken there illegally and subsequently changed his Christian name to Luka. Giorgio Carolla, alias Luka, was now the main suspect.

Further evidence had now surfaced in connection with the murder of Paul Carolla. Most of the spectators in court on the day of the shooting had been traced, but amongst those still to be interviewed and eliminated from enquiries was the priest. The priest had signed the requisite register for court attendance as Brother Guido, and the address . . .? 'The Monastery of the Sacred Heart.'

Commissario Pirelli whispered a few Hail Marys, hoping he was right, as he checked back through his personal notes accumulated from the prison visitors' logbook. The address alongside G. Carolla was, as he suspected, 'The Monastery of the Sacred Heart, Erice'.

The long, uphill walk from Erice station took its toll on the overweight Detective Sergeant Ancora. Pirelli had to wait a full five minutes before his sweating, red-faced companion joined him, his coat slung over his shoulder and a handkerchief clutched in his hand.

They were shown into an anteroom beside the main gate of the monastery. The bells were ringing, the echo thudding through the small, bare room. It contained only a wooden bench, a table and a bookcase.

Ancora was still panting, his shirt wringing wet with perspiration, yet the cell-like room felt chilly. It also smelt damp and musty. They waited for more than fifteen minutes until a young priest approached them and introduced himself as Father Guido.

Guido did not notice their reaction to him. They showed him their ID cards and asked if he had been in Palermo at all in the past few days. He said he had not. He seemed very nervous, twisting a rosary around his fingers and blushing when asked if he could verify his statement. He assured them that he could as he had not left the monastery at all, and had many witnesses to prove it.

Watching him carefully, Pirelli told him he was investigating the whereabouts of Luka Carolla.

Guido's hands trembled as he whispered that, although it was unusual, he had become familiar with the trial taking place in Palermo and he was aware that Carolla had been shot. He was able to tell them that Luka Carolla had been staying at the monastery up until the week before the killing, but he could give no information as to his present whereabouts.

'Did you ever hear Luka referred to as Giorgio, or was he always called Luka?'

'Always, I never heard the name Giorgio mentioned.'

'Is there anyone here who would know more about him?'

Guido nodded, but told them it would not be possible to talk to Father Angelo as he was giving the last rites to a dying monk, one Brother Louis. All he could tell them was that Luka had been raised at the monastery before going to America with his father.

He gave a detailed description; strangely detailed, adding that he was very strong physically and that he had done a great amount of work in the gardens.

Pirelli asked when it would be convenient to interview Father Angelo and was told that it was in the hands of the Lord. Pressed by Pirelli, he eventually said it could be in two or three days.

As they were about to leave, Pirelli asked Guido if Luka had brought much luggage. He described the leather holdall, then he hesitated a moment and said, 'When he first arrived, he carried a case, a small, flat leather case. I remember it because I offered to carry it into his cell, but he refused.'

'What size?'

Guido demonstrated with his hands an object about twelve inches long.

'Did you see him leave?'

Again there was the deep flush as Guido shook his head. 'I am afraid not. You could see his cell if you wish.'

They inspected the small, bare room and Pirelli asked if it had been cleaned recently. Guido told him he had washed and swept the room himself directly after Luka's departure.

'I don't suppose there is a photograph?' Pirelli asked.

Guido shook his head and apologized. They did not, to his knowledge, have one in the monastery.

On his return to Palermo, Pirelli discovered there were further developments concerning the weapon that was used to kill Carolla. They were now working on the assumption that the priest was the killer and the walking cane had some sort of single-firing mechanism. The guard who had searched Luka described the cane as best he could, recalling that it had a brass head, some sort of animal, but he couldn't quite remember what. The guard was asked to assist in the construction of an identikit picture.

Pirelli mulled over the possibility of the gun being a customized special. They knew Luka Carolla had carried what appeared from Guido's description to be a gun case. They also knew that Luka had been in Erice directly before the assassination, so it was possible that the gun had been purchased locally.

Ancora hesitated. 'There's another possibility, that the Luciano women hired the guy. They'd have the connections.'

Pirelli was incredulous. 'You serious?'

'Yeah. I doubt it, but you never know. They're all the same, they close their eyes, see only what they want to see. And then, when one of them gets shot, they scream blue murder . . .'

'The whole family was wiped out.'

Ancora shrugged. 'Read the papers, Joe. That old boy, Don Roberto, must have wiped out more than a few families in his time.'

'OK, I'll do you a favour. You check the gunsmiths

out and I'll save you a journey; I'll go and see the Lucianos.'

The only reason Pirelli had decided to go to the Villa Rivera was to see Sophia Luciano again.

Teresa's back was aching but she continued working. She looked up and yawned when Sophia entered.

'Who's with him now?'

'Rosa. Where Moyra is God only knows . . . She got us into this and she's the one sleeping like a baby. Did you tell Mama anything?'

'No, of course not, and we shouldn't,' Teresa replied. 'She has enough to worry about. I don't think I can stop the sale of the villa, it's about the only deal that Domino really saw through, and the price is acceptable. You know, we are in a very different situation now, with Dante dead, and Carolla, and all the documents back in our hands . . .'

Sophia didn't seem very interested. 'What do you think the boy was doing here? Not at the villa, but here in Palermo?'

'We'll ask him when he comes round. I think maybe we should lock the door on him, too, what do you think?'

The doorbell rang and Sophia peeked through the blinds. She let them snap closed. 'It's the *carabinieri*. It's probably about Mama.'

'Ask them in, offer them coffee, anything, but give me a chance to warn the others. And Sophia – don't say anything about our guest, promise me?'

*

Sophia gestured for Pirelli to follow her into the dining room. Apologizing for the darkness, she opened the shutter slightly. The light cascaded around her and she blinked, putting her hand over her eyes.

'Is it cold out?'

'No, very pleasant, fresh. I always like the cold, sunny days.'

She stared at him as if she hadn't understood what he had said.

'How is Signora Luciano?'

Sophia sat as far away from him as possible, right at the end of the table. 'She is well, very tired. It is good that we are all here for her.'

He wanted to ask her out for dinner, but didn't know how to approach the subject. She was wearing a dark-maroon cashmere dress that draped her figure softly, and he noted she wore no jewellery. She was no longer wearing the red nail polish and her nails were very pale.

Sophia was desperately hoping the others would hurry and join them, she hated the way he was scrutinizing her. Did he know?

'That is a very nice painting.'

She turned to stare at the large oil, a puzzled expression on her face. 'You like it?'

He looked properly at the painting, it was quite dreadful, a group of men slaughtering a pig. 'No, I don't know why I said that.'

'It's a pig being slaughtered.'

'Yes, I see that now.'

He stood up as Teresa entered, Rosa and Moyra behind her. He shook hands with each of them and when he realized Moyra did not speak Italian he switched to English for the rest of the interview.

Sophia, Teresa and Moyra sat at the long, polished table like schoolchildren, their hands clasped neatly in front of them. He tried to put them at their ease, smiling and assuring them he had not come to arrest Signora Luciano, but they remained silent. He refused coffee, but asked if they minded if he smoked. Teresa assured him they did not mind and Sophia accepted a cigarette from him. As he leaned across the table to light it for her, Teresa and Moyra could see that her hand was shaking. Uneasy looks passed between them.

'Have you run out of your Turkish cigarettes?' Pirelli enquired.

Sophia inhaled the smoke. 'Yes, I must get some. Thank you . . .'

'I know a good tobacconist, I'll have some sent to you.'

'That won't be necessary.'

He opened his briefcase and took out a small notepad, then searched his pockets and brought out a fountain pen. 'I apologize for calling on you unexpectedly, but I wondered if you would mind answering a few questions?'

He hesitated, looking around, and Teresa placed a heavy crystal ashtray in front of him. He thanked her and continued, 'We are trying to trace a man we wish to interview. His name is Luka Carolla.'

He looked at each of them in turn, but there was no reaction. He went on, 'Have you ever heard of him? Possibly even met him? He is Paul Carolla's son.'

Sophia shook her head and seemed to look to Teresa for permission before she spoke. 'I never met Paul Carolla. This man . . . Luka? Is he suspected of the murder of my children?'

Pirelli gave her a concerned look and chose his words

653

carefully. 'I am afraid that investigation is not the reason I am here, this is an entirely different matter. At this moment we simply wish to interview Luka Carolla. I am aware of the past relationship between Paul Carolla and Roberto Luciano, and so far we have been unable to trace Luka Carolla.'

He paused, finding it strange that they did not look at each other but directly at him, waiting expectantly.

'Carolla's son had apparently been visiting a monastery. It was also the only address the lawyers had for him, but unfortunately he has left.'

The women froze as Graziella walked into the room and Pirelli rose to his feet. He kissed her hand and gestured for her to be seated, drawing out a chair next to his own.

'Are you arresting me?'

'No, no, signora, it is a very informal call. It's just that we have the name of a possible suspect in the Paluso killing. You remember Juan Paluso was shot?'

Graziella listened as he told her of the search for Luka Carolla, asking if she had ever seen him or knew of his whereabouts. Graziella told him she was not even aware that Carolla had a son, she had never met him nor heard his name mentioned.

Teresa noticed that Pirelli made no notes but doodled on his pad continuously. He was a very charming man, and his relaxed manner did ease the tension in some ways. He told them that the police had only just discovered Luka Carolla's existence themselves when Paul Carolla had suggested that his son be questioned.

Teresa leaned forward. 'You mean Paul Carolla implicated his own son?'

Pirelli nodded and tapped the edge of his notepad

with his pen. 'I think at the time Carolla would have implicated his own mother had she been alive. The case was going against him; the tragic murders of your family, the death of the Paluso child and the mounting accusations in the press placed him under enormous pressure within the confines of the jail?'

Sophia's cigarette ash dropped on the table and she brushed it away.

Pirelli returned to his doodle. 'When the case against him built up momentum, his advisers suggested that if he did have any information that could lead them to the killers, prove that he had no connection, it would obviously place him in a better position to make some kind of deal with the prosecution. However, he continued to refuse, continued to claim that he knew nothing, until the morning he was shot. That morning he demanded to speak to his lawyer, but he was due in court; there was no time to make a statement. In fact, it was his lawyer's clerk who eventually spoke to him, and all Carolla gave him was a name. According to the young clerk he seemed very emotional, almost desperate. The name was that of Luka Carolla, his son. Perhaps, if we do find him, it will mean nothing, but we have to trace him . . .' He went on to tell them what he felt the eventual outcome of the trial would be, that he was sure the jails would be full to bursting point.

Graziella brought the subject round to Carolla again, asking if Pirelli had any knowledge of who had killed him.

'I am not on that investigation, signora, but I believe they are making headway.'

'So, they make headway in finding the killer of the man who murdered my children, but there seems to be no one continuing our investigation. Why have we not been visited before, kept abreast of what is happening?'

'As I have said, Signora Luciano, I am not . . .'

'Yes, you are not involved . . . Who is? I do not believe the *carabinieri* know anything. This trial will end, but still the murderers walk free, just as it has always been . . .'

Pirelli saw the hatred in her eyes, washed-out blue eyes like chips of ice. He looked at the still faces of the women and bowed his head. 'I believe that the man who shot Carolla was a professional. Ballistic reports have suggested that the gun was special, a custom-made, single-shot gun, possibly disguised as a walking cane. The killer carried it undetected into the courthouse. Perhaps he was hired by one of the families that suspected Carolla was cracking under the strain. It was even suggested that the Luciano family . . .'

'Ah, now we have it, you are not here to question us about this Paluso murder. The reason is, you think we are involved, you believe we had something to do with the man who murdered Paul Carolla.'

Graziella pushed her chair back and stood up. She was shaking, her whole body trembled, and the others rose from the table almost in unison. Teresa put a protective arm around Graziella's shoulders; the old woman was, for a moment, unable to speak.

Her chest heaved, but she pushed Teresa's arm away and turned to face Pirelli, who rose slowly to his feet. 'My daughters had no knowledge of my attempt to kill Paul Carolla. This I have said in my statement. No one assisted me, no one knew of my intentions, and I swear before God and the Holy Virgin that it is the only criminal act I have ever committed in my life . . .'

Pirelli interrupted her. 'Please, Signora Luciano, I had no intention of . . .'

Teresa could not keep quiet. She looked at him with contempt. 'No intention of what, Commissario? Why don't you actually ask us, ask us if we hired an assassin to kill Carolla? Do you think if we had even considered it we would have let Mama go into that courtroom? What do you take us for? What kind of people do you think we are?'

Pirelli stared hard, then reached for his raincoat. 'You must realize, these questions are bound to be asked. Whoever killed Paul Carolla escaped because of the hysteria surrounding Signora Luciano's attempt. I had no intention of insulting you, and I apologize, but I am investigating the death of a nine-year-old child.'

Sophia stepped forward then. 'And my children? They don't concern you, do they? They were as innocent as this Paluso child, and because of who we are . . .'

Pirelli threw his coat down and faced them. 'Who you are is of no concern to me. What your family was is of no concern to me. I am pursuing this investigation to the best of my ability . . . Now, I have apologized, I did not mean to insult you, any of you. Thank you for your time.'

Pirelli put his hand out to shake Graziella's but she turned and walked towards the door. She paused and said, 'My daughters will show you out, Commissario.'

Teresa picked up his notepad and glanced at it. The doodle on the page was a picture of a walking cane . . . She closed the book and held it out to him.

'There was one more thing I wanted to ask you,' said Pirelli.

The three women stood side by side, waiting. Pirelli

flipped his notebook open and turned a few pages, then snapped it shut and said questioningly, 'Enrico Dante?'

Teresa pressed her hand into the small of Sophia's back.

Pirelli continued, 'He was an associate of Paul Carolla, does his name mean anything to you?'

Teresa shook her head. 'I have never heard of him.'

He looked at each of them, then strode into the hall. Teresa opened the front door and he walked out without another word being spoken.

As the door closed behind him, he went slowly down the steps, paused a moment, then continued along the gravel drive. He had left his car outside the gates. He stopped suddenly and turned back to look at the sprawling villa, the gardens, the groves. The bonnet of a dark blue car, a Fiat similar to his own and in no better condition, was just protruding through the bushes. It was Luka's hired car, hidden as best he could manage under the circumstances.

Pirelli gave it no more than a cursory glance. His mind was elsewhere, because he knew that what Sophia had said was right. The Luciano murders were, to him, on a par with the hundreds of Mafia vendetta murders that occurred all the time.

Returning to headquarters, Pirelli opened the filing cabinet and flicked through it, withdrawing the file with the photograph of Sophia Luciano's children. Removing everything else from his noticeboard, he pinned the photo up.

'So it's true, you're taking on the Lucianos?'

Pirelli gave Ancora a puzzled look. 'How do you know, I've only just thought about it.'

Ancora shrugged. 'Well, the rumour is that Milan's given the go-ahead for you to stay. I thought it was just a rumour, I mean, I know you want to get home.'

Pirelli smiled, shaking his head. 'I guess somebody read my mind!' Ancora was surprised. For a man desperate to go back to his wife and kid, Pirelli appeared to have accepted the extra workload without complaint, unless there was some other reason keeping him in Palermo; but he made no comment. Instead he got on with the job in hand, placing two reports on the desk.

'I think, though I'm not sure, that the weapon was a shooting cane, made in the early eighteenth century. The top part is a horse's head, and it comes apart in three pieces.'

Pirelli snatched the paper.

'You've found it?'

Ancora shook his head. 'No, but there's a report on a theft from the Villa Palagonia. It was broken into, and the only thing stolen was this old shooting cane.'

Pirelli frowned, then reread the report of the stolen gun. 'It hadn't been fired for sixty, seventy years. If this is the one, someone must have worked his butt off.'

Ancora nodded. 'Stolen the night before Carolla was shot. We've got men checking out all the gunsmiths capable of carrying out that kind of work.'

Pirelli was leaving, fast. At the door he turned, 'You get over to the Villa Palagonia, take the identikit of Luka Carolla, see if he was there.'

He paused, frowning. 'Also get some ID from records, those two corpses at the Armadillo Club. Take their mug shots with you and see if anyone recognizes them . . . and start checking out car-hire firms, garages, see if our boy hired a motor.'

Ancora sighed, Pirelli certainly knew how to give orders. He wondered what Pirelli himself was going to be doing.

In fact, he was faxing the police in the States, on the basis that even though Luka Carolla was an illegal immigrant, he must have been educated there at some stage. He requested a check on schools and colleges, etc., in the area of Paul Carolla's last known address. Luka born 1949, accompanied by his father . . . somebody somewhere must have a record of the boy as a teenager and he needed a recent photograph.

'He only took a couple of mouthfuls,' said Sophia. 'Moyra crushed up two Mogadon and sprinkled them over the soup . . . Did you hear me?'

Teresa opened the desk drawer. 'Yes, yes . . . this was in his bag, Moreno's bag. Remember the one we brought the papers in from the club? Now, watch.'

She picked up the first part of the cane, the section with the horse's head, then slotted the second piece into position. 'It's a single-bullet gun, see? The horse's head is where you fix the bullet, the safety catch is the ear, and you fire it by pulling the head back . . . Acts as a trigger. Moreno is the killer, Sophia, he has to be. It's almost exactly the weapon Commissario Pirelli described, isn't it?'

Sophia had to sit down. 'What are we going to do?'

'Keep it. As soon as he's well, he's out, we pay him off, just as we agreed.'

'Pay him off with what? Moyra only took a few hundred dollars, which I told her not to do . . . God! I said, don't take any money. Do you think he'll be satisfied with a few hundred dollars? He could blackmail us, think of the hold he has over us! If we keep him here, we are as guilty as he is. We have to call the police.'

'Fine, you want to call Pirelli? Go ahead, explain why you never told him about Moreno when he was here. You were at the club, you knew the same as all of us that he had to have shot Dante. If he also shot Carolla, then we should give him a goddam medal! Call Pirelli, go on, get me arrested while you're at it.'

Teresa's eyes frightened Sophia, because beneath all the bravado there was something else, she could feel it.

'What have you done?'

Teresa backed off and Sophia knew she was right.

'I did it for us, I couldn't resist it.' She took her glasses off and rested her head in her hands. 'I did it for us.'

'What?'

Teresa fumbled with the dial of the safe and swung the door open. It was stacked with bundles of bank notes, dollars and lire in thick bundles.

'I took all the money from Dante's safe when I went back for Moyra's handbag.'

Too shocked to speak, Sophia stared at the cash, then at Teresa's frightened face.

'How much is there?'

At least Sophia was not shouting. Teresa felt more confident. 'Enough to start clearing up the docks and warehouses. I've been making lists of everything that has to be done, costing it and . . .'

Sophia interrupted. 'I don't want any part of it, Teresa. I will stay for Mama, but as soon as the hearing is over, I'm leaving. You stole that money and it's on your head.'

'Fine, it's on my head, I'll handle it. I'll make sure we all get what's due to us, and that is all I care about, Sophia. This is family business. Maybe it's different for you, you don't need . . .'

Sophia leaned over the desk and spat, 'The family is in the graveyard, Teresa. Don't presume that you know anything about me, what I need or what I don't need. Just leave me out of it, and get rid of that boy upstairs, or, so help me God, I will call the police.'

It was after midnight, and Rosa sat reading by Luka's bed. Her bookmark slipped from between the pages and she knelt to retrieve it. As she straightened up, she saw something glittering beneath the bed. She had to lean right under the bed to reach it.

The small gold heart was covered in fluffy dust and she blew it clean, dangling it on the fine gold chain, then dropped it into a small glass bowl on the chest of drawers.

CHAPTER 28

COMMISSARIO PIRELLI began to live up to his reputation, and sarcastic rumours were spreading that, given the opportunity, he would be taking over every unsolved case. The investigation into his original case was merging and expanding, because his main suspect, Luka Carolla, remained at large – his whereabouts unknown. The bullet discovered at the Armadillo Club had similar grooves and matched the fragment removed from Paul Carolla's skull. The one clear print taken from the bullet, a right thumbprint, was also verified as belonging to the same person as the right thumb and forefinger prints discovered on the glass of orange juice at the Armadillo Club, but so far they had been unable to match the prints with any on record.

No sooner had the report been delivered to Pirelli than it was returned with a query. He wanted to know if the same drill that made the grooves in the Carolla bullet was also used on the bullet fragments taken from the Paluso boy and the Luciano children.

Ancora had also been working flat out, and had further information. The tour guide at the Villa Palagonia identified from mug shots not only the deceased boxer, Dario Biase, but also Enrico Dante. Both men had been at the villa on the day the shooting-cane gun had been stolen. However, when he was shown the identikit picture of their suspect Luka Carolla, he was doubtful that it was the man he had seen waiting in the back of Dante's car; that man had been dark haired, not blond.

Pirelli felt it was imperative that they return to the monastery. This time he would insist that he speak to Father Angelo. His frustration and tiredness made him snap angrily at Ancora that they had wasted enough time. Ancora had never worked so hard in his entire career; if Pirelli was exhausted, he was almost on his knees, but at least he would be able to sit down on the train journey to Erice.

The winter timetables had now come into operation and, as they arrived at the station, the only train that day to Erice was about to leave the platform. Pirelli sprinted to the train, yelling at the top of his voice for the guard to wait. He ran alongside the moving train and jumped aboard, leaving his overweight detective sergeant lumbering behind him, stranded on the platform.

Luka opened the bathroom door, wearing a towelling robe that had once belonged to Roberto Luciano. It swamped his slender frame, making him look even more youthful and boyish. He was shaking with the effort of bathing and drying himself, and he clung to the door handle for support.

Teresa offered to help him, but he recoiled from her, so she stepped aside as he entered the small room. She had opened a window, and Luka sat on the freshly made bed. He lifted the pillow and searched beneath it.

'I have the gun, Mr Moreno.'

He turned to her with a puzzled expression, then touched his neck. 'My chain, my gold chain . . .'

'Is this it? Rosa found it, she thought it might have belonged to a maid.'

'No, it's mine.'

She watched as he twisted the chain around his fingers, nervously.

'How long do you think you need to stay here?'

'Until I feel strong enough to leave.'

'We had Commissario Pirelli here asking questions . . . It's all right, he knows nothing, but we know you killed Dante. Did you kill Paul Carolla?'

Luka lay back and closed his eyes. He could feel her looking at him. This one was different from the others, this one had cold eyes, and he didn't like her.

Teresa moved closer to the bed. 'The police think there is a connection between the two murders. If you did kill Carolla, we will never give you away. I think we might even congratulate you.'

He opened his eyes and turned to face her. His voice was soft. 'I did not kill this man. I have never heard of him.'

She gave a humourless, twisted smile. 'I think you did. I don't only have the gun from under your pillow, I have the other one, too, the one that looks like a walking cane. It was in the bag we brought from Dante's club . . .'

She was caught by the expression in his strange, ice-blue eyes. 'What bag? I don't have a bag, you must be mistaken.'

Teresa raised her eyebrows and smiled. 'No? Don't lie to us, Mr Moreno.' She turned and left.

As he heard the key turn in the lock, his body curled

into the foetal position. The chain was wrapped so tightly around his knuckles that it broke the skin. 'Please, don't lock me in . . . Please don't.' The surrounding darkness was like a heavy cloud of blackness.

As Teresa was passing Sophia's room, she tapped on the door. 'Can you come down to the study? I need to talk to everyone.'

Sophia was lying on her bed, the room in darkness. She said she would need a moment to wash. Moyra and Rosa were already seated like expectant schoolgirls as Sophia came into the study. Teresa sat behind the Don's old desk; she seemed a little irritated that Sophia did not sit alongside the others, but stood staring out of the windows.

'OK, now, the reason I called this meeting is because this afternoon I want to take you all around the docks and the warehouses, so we can all assess how much work will need to be done. We will have to pull every string we know to get men to come and work for us . . .'

'Who's paying them?' asked Moyra.

'We are, but obviously we'll need to come to some arrangement. They do owe us; for years Don Luciano took care of them . . .'

Graziella walked slowly and sedately into the room, carrying a rather wilted plant. She placed it carefully on the desk. 'My husband is dead, Teresa. You are not the head of this family, I am, and I refuse to agree with this venture.'

'This venture, as you call it, Mama, will hopefully provide financial security for our future. If we attempt to sell the company in the present state, we take a loss. We have the deeds returned, the power of attorney is now in my hands, all I am trying to do is salvage what is left of our inheritance. We need you with us, Mama, would like you to be with us, but if you refuse that is your prerogative. I am going ahead whether you approve or not . . .'

Graziella looked to Sophia but she remained staring out of the window. Whether she did change her mind or not, they couldn't tell, but she accompanied them when Teresa drove them to the docks.

The total standstill of the once busy company was tragic. The stench of warehouses full of rotting oranges left in their cargo boxes was like an open sewer, where rats scurried across dank floors. The cargo boats rusted in their dry docks. Lines of trucks, their tyres slashed and canvas tops ripped, stood forlorn, their paintwork blistered by the sun. Engines had been stolen, almost every removable part had gone. The appalling and wanton neglect was heartbreaking.

The once flourishing tile factory remained shuttered and thick dust from the tiles covered every inch of the place, even the offices. Windows were shattered and the place had been broken into so many times there was hardly a room left intact.

The women were silent, but their sightseeing tour was not over.

They drove out to the massive canning factory, towering above the desolate yards, then to the groves themselves. Again they were witness to the sad rows of delivery trucks and warehouses filled with empty crates, but worse was the mile upon mile of dying trees, orange, lemon and olive, their fruit rotting, fly-infested and stinking. The watering sprays had rusted, the irrigation canals were filled with dead fruit and the flies hummed in a thick cloud above the trees, a black, ominous cloud.

Graffiti could be seen, written in the dust and painted across the walls: '*Mafioso finito; Bastardo Luciano* . . .'

Teresa made no attempt to keep their spirits up. Her face was set, rigid with determination, as she strode from one nightmare to another, making notes and murmuring to herself as the women trailed after her. Graziella flicked her fan, always lagging slightly behind, taking long, lingering, sad looks, bewildered by the wreckage, the terrible waste. She could not understand how it had happened, how this flourishing business now lay like a paralysed soldier, left to die of neglect in the trenches. That was the pervading feeling; their men had died, and everything that had been built up over forty years had been left to die too. All respect, all honour, had gone.

When they returned to the villa, Rosa slipped upstairs to unlock Luka's room and check his bandages. The rest remained in subdued silence in the study. Teresa was as tired as anyone, perhaps even as depressed, but she never let it show. She flicked open her notebook.

'First we will need men to clean, remove the garbage, check the trucks over to determine what we can use, what we have left.'

Moyra brushed the dust from her skirt. Even her hands felt gritty. 'It's not a house, Teresa. You can't just get a crew of people in with mops and buckets.'

Ignoring her, Teresa continued, 'The trees need to be pruned, cut back almost to their roots, and the sprinklers repaired before next year. They look worse than they are, but they'll not harvest for a couple of seasons, if not more.'

Sophia flung her hands up. 'A couple of seasons? And in the meantime, what do we do in the meantime? What happens when we clean up the docks, the warehouses, the ships, what happens then? We have no product. It's madness, as Mama said, we'll never be able to start again.'

Teresa snapped, 'We don't, and we're not! We are simply preparing to sell. I don't want to hear what Mama thinks. It's Mama's fault we're in this situation, and if she wants to get us out of it, go tell her to find the so-called Swiss bank account with our inheritance, OK? . . . Can I continue?'

Sophia sighed, and Teresa, behaving like a school mistress, tapped the desk with a pencil. 'Right, I have a list of every export company in Palermo, and we will approach them. Maybe then we will see if we are taking on too much or not. You don't think I am about to open up and start production? I am fully aware of our financial position, and I know that it would be impossible. We decide either to sell, depending on the price offered, or we lease space. We have export licences, we have the space for goods in New York, the warehouses Alfredo ran, we have a delivery and trucking company, we have the Luciano name and that, along with everything else, is worth a lot more than we have been offered to date. Now does it make sense? I am trying to put together the best possible package for a deal, and to make those that have already offered up their price. In other words, I am doing exactly what I would do if I were trying to sell an apartment for the highest price possible.'

No one argued, no one said another word. Teresa sat smugly behind the desk. 'All you have to do is exactly what I have planned.'

*

Pirelli was sweating from the long walk up to the monastery, even though there was a bitterly cold wind blowing. Brother Guido welcomed him and showed him to the same room near the gates. Father Angelo would be with him shortly, he said, and Brother Thomas was also coming to speak to him.

The small bookcase beneath the crucifix caught his eye and, just for something to do, he looked over the worn, leather-bound prayer books. He took one out and traced the embossed gold cross with his finger. He was about to replace it when one of the other books fell to the floor. It fell open at the first page, and he saw the inscription inside: 'Giorgio Carolla, 1974 . . .'

Brother Thomas shuffled into the room, carrying a brown manila envelope that looked dog-eared and well used. 'I wondered when you would return, Commissario. I did not get the chance to speak with you last time you were here. Please, shall we be seated? I am Brother Thomas. You wish to discuss Luka? Luka Carolla?'

Pirelli sat down. The old man's robes had a heavy, musty smell, and the father himself looked as though he could do with a bath. His fingernails were black and his feet, encased in thonged sandals, were filthy. The old man's eyes were like peas, small and a muddy greenish colour; sly eyes. His whole manner was furtive; he looked constantly at the closed door, lowering his voice secretively and sucking his breath noisily between his gums. 'I knew he was bad, a liar. He stole a chicken leg once, you know . . .'

Pirelli listened to the old man's rambling tale about some incident he could make neither head nor tail of, about a theft committed by Luka in the orphanage. He was very patient, and when they heard the slow footsteps

670

approaching, Thomas pressed the worn envelope into Pirelli's hand, saying he was not to mention it.

Father Angelo moved painfully slowly, and Guido helped him to the chair. Pirelli didn't show it, but he was getting more depressed by the minute. Thomas had proved incoherent, and he was sure this elderly man would be even worse.

'You may leave us, Guido.'

Pirelli sat back. The voice, though wavery, was direct, the old man's eyes were clear and bright. As the heavy oak door closed behind Guido, Father Angelo folded his hands.

'So, you wish to know about our son, Luka, is that correct?'

'Yes, Father, it is of the utmost importance.'

Father Angelo nodded, lifting his hand slightly. 'Perhaps I should begin at the very beginning, yes? When he first arrived here?'

'If you wouldn't mind. I think the more I know of him the better.'

The dirty sheets from Luka's room were still in the tumble dryer, and Sophia busied herself unloading it. As she folded one of the pillowcases, she noticed the stains on it. She threw it into the waste bin, presuming the dark-brown marks to be blood. It was not until she went in to check on the sleeping Luka later that evening that she noticed his hair was very much lighter than it had been. She leaned further over him and was so startled when Rosa walked in that she sprang away from the bed.

'You frightened me.'

Rosa looked at her suspiciously. 'What are you doing?'

Sophia put her finger to her lips for Rosa to keep quiet. Luka was still asleep. 'Come and see, here . . . Look at his hair, it's dyed. He's blond, see?'

Rosa leaned over to look, then agreed. She whispered, 'Why has he dyed his hair?'

Sophia did not reply. As they left the room quietly and locked the door behind them, Luka opened his eyes. He was able to get out of the bed with ease, and began to walk up and down the room. He had heard them talking, and stared at himself in the mirror; the roots were beginning to show blond, and he swore softly to himself.

He knew his time was running out, he had to leave, and he began to stretch the fingers of his left hand. The pain still lingered, but he slowly took off the bandages and began to exercise . . .

Pirelli licked his lips. There was only one glass and he was thirsty, but he said nothing. He waited, but Father Angelo was staring silently at the blank wall.

'Please continue, Father . . . I am sorry if this distresses you.'

'Luka never returned here. I received a number of letters, I have brought them for you to read if you wish. I signed the adoption papers, releasing him from our care. I believed it was for the best, I believed Luka would have a great opportunity . . .' The tears started to trickle down his face. 'I did not see him again until his return this year . . .' He reached for the glass of water, taking small sips. 'Would it be possible for you to tell me why you are so interested in my son, Luka? Do you believe he has committed some crime?'

Pirelli coughed and licked his lips again. 'Yes, Father, I believe so.'

'He came to me, he came here for help, I know that now. You see, as a boy, whenever he had done wrong, he would attempt to make up for it by working. Painting, digging, anything . . . He came and worked here for a while and I knew, I knew something was terribly wrong.'

Pirelli rang the bell by the door, wanting someone to take Father Angelo away, dreading to cause him further distress. He helped the old man to rise and placed his walking frame in front of him in readiness.

'There is something . . . there was a darkness to Luka, I always felt it but was never able to unlock it. He had been sexually abused as a child, do you understand what I am saying?'

Pirelli nodded, with one eye on the door. Guido overheard the last few words as he entered the room.

Father Angelo acknowledged Guido's presence but continued, 'Whatever happened to him made him terrified, violent even, and, for the first few years he was here, we were unable to get him to enter the chapel. I believe whatever sins were committed against Luka were within the confines of a holy place. May God forgive me, but that is what I believe.'

Guido, flushing deeply, would not meet Pirelli's eyes. He fussed with the walking frame, preparing to assist the father from the room. Almost as an afterthought, Pirelli asked, 'Did you speak to Luka before he left, Father?'

The old man shook his head. 'No . . . No, I did not, Brother Guido was the last one of us to see him.'

He inched towards the door, pausing again with his back to Pirelli. 'Luka did not even bid me goodbye . . . Have a safe return journey, Commissario.'

'One moment, Brother Guido . . . Could you spare me a few minutes?'

The young monk's hands were tense as he waited until Father Angelo was out of the room. 'I really must help the father, he is frail, the courtyard . . .'

'I can manage quite well,' came the distant voice, so Pirelli closed the door.

'You were the last to see him, you never mentioned this before . . .'

'I did not think it was important.'

'Maybe not, but there again it might be. Brother Guido, I believe Luka Carolla is a very dangerous man. I am sure he has killed at least one child, and he possibly murdered his father, Paul Carolla.'

Guido gasped. His eyes blinked rapidly and he slumped into the chair, putting his hands over his face as he spoke.

'The night Luka left, I was in the chapel, close to the crypt. I was kneeling in prayer and he didn't see me.'

Pirelli rested his hand on the monk's shoulder, encouraging him to continue.

'I saw him enter, and put down his bag, the small leather bag I told you of. He moved up the aisle; I was about to call out, say something to let him know I was there . . .'

'But you didn't?'

Guido shook his head. 'He stood so still, facing the cross, and . . . his face, it was like watching a statue, I have never seen such stillness, such . . .'

Pirelli released his hold and moved away. 'What happened then?' He repeated himself, this time more sharply. 'What happened, Brother Guido?'

'I stood up, revealing my presence, and he reacted like

a wild animal. He hissed . . . a terrible hissing sound, and backed away down the aisle into the darkness, until I could no longer see him. He then said something blasphemous, I beg you not to ask me to repeat it. I heard the doors open and he was gone.'

'Taking only the small bag? You didn't see the other case you described?'

Guido sobbed, 'No . . .'

Pirelli bowed his head, making the sign of the cross before following Guido up the stone steps to the crypt. He edged around the massive wooden cross and looked up. At first he saw nothing, but then Guido switched on his torch.

Pirelli walked into the ballistics section of the forensic laboratory. He handed over the gun case he had taken from the monastery. 'I want that checked out now, and I want the rifling matched against the bullets used in the Luciano children's murder, and the Paluso murder, and I want it done by tonight.'

The technician moaned, but carried the case to a long trestle table where three men were working. Pirelli followed.

'Did you come up with anything from the report I sent back?'

The assistant took a file from a cabinet. 'Right, the unused cartridge found in the Armadillo Club was the same type used to blow Carolla's head off. The fragments taken from the corpse had the same drilled grooves as the unused bullet and we verified that they had been made with a drill found at the gunsmith's. Similar grooves, also made by the same type of drill but not the same one, were on the bullet fragments taken from the Luciano and Paluso children.'

Pirelli interrupted, 'Got any idea of the type of gun used in the kids' murders? Could they have been fired from a .44 Magnum? The gun I brought in? It's loaded, two bullets in the chamber.'

The assistant slammed the filing cabinet shut. 'Look, we are already working overtime down here. There's more fragments of bullets around here than you've had hot dinners. If the gun you brought in is the one, then when we've checked it out I'll let you know. It's not our job to make guesses, I reckon that's yours.'

Pirelli gave the assistant a hard look and turned to walk out. The man called after him, 'What about prints from the weapon you brought in? You want it checked for prints?'

Pirelli hesitated, then gave a tight nod. He had been so eager to bring his find in that he had forgotten. 'Yeah, no one's touched it.'

'Except you, right? You must have handled it to find out it was still loaded?'

Pirelli flushed. 'Yeah . . . You've got my prints so you can eliminate them, and . . . you're doing a great job.'

The assistant muttered some obscenity under his breath as Pirelli walked out.

Pirelli was irritated to find Ancora using his typewriter again. 'Don't you have an office of your own?'

Ancora grinned. 'Not any more, it's a shoe box at the end of the corridor. Had a good day?'

'Yep, and it's not over. Take a look at this lot . . . One of the brothers at the monastery gave it to me, very furtively. There's an old photograph of Luka, aged twelve, maybe thirteen. Get it blown up, may help. And he's got very distinctive blond hair all right, almost albino, blue eyes. He's about five ten and a half to eleven. According to Brother Guido, he's also pretty strong.'

Ancora looked at the photo and wrinkled his nose. 'Jesus Christ, is this a kid in the wheelchair?'

'Yep. That, my friend, is Paul Carolla's son, that's Giorgio Carolla.'

Ancora's mouth fell open. Pirelli nodded to the photo. 'Luka was adopted by Carolla when he was twelve or thirteen, no one is too sure of his exact age. They've got no birth certificate. But Carolla adopted him and took him to America after that poor, malformed creature died.' Suddenly he picked up the phone and dialled through to Records. 'It's Pirelli. Do you think you could have a go at tracing the records of a kid? All I've got is that he was blond and his Christian name was Luka, I've no surname, but he was in a bad way. He was brought in with a bunch of kids working the waterfront, four of them were charged with theft, rolling drunks and hanging around outside the gay bars. The kid was too young to be charged, maybe five or six years old, and he was in need of hospital treatment, they sent him over to the old Nazareth hospital in 1965 or '66.'

'You got an arresting officer?'

'Nope. You got what I got, see if the Nazareth can give any information.'

'The old place burnt down ten bloody years ago!'

Pirelli laughed, said he was just testing them out. He knew it was a long shot, but he was pretty desperate, and

677

maybe, just maybe someone visited the boy before Father Angelo took him to the orphanage. He swivelled round in his chair, and only then noticed a memo in the in tray from Bruno di Mazzo. He picked it up, read it carefully, and then leaned back closing his eyes. 'Sweet Jesus, I don't fuckin' believe it! You read this?' Ancora shook his head. 'It's from Bruno, got it out of the Luciano file. It says here, the chef from the San Lorenzo – the restaurant where all the Lucianos were poisoned – the chef was shot, according to ballistics, with a Magnum .44!' He thumbed through the report, then back to the original page. 'Only the chef was shot. How old is this? When was this report done?'

Ancora shrugged. 'Must be months back, what, eight, nine months old? Two of them shot with a Hecklar and Koch pistol.' He sneezed, and sniffed loudly. 'I think I'm getting a cold . . . They found the bodyguard stuffed down a well, but he'd been cracked over the head. There was no trace of the extra staff, the washer-up, but they reckon he must have been a plant, you know, to get them into the place. There were three, possibly four men on the hit, judging by the footprints around the well. Joe . . . Joe, you listening?'

Pirelli was standing poised, his mouth open. 'You're not gonna believe this . . . I just brought in a weapon from the monastery, and it's Luka Carolla's and it's a Magnum .44 . . .'

It was Ancora's turn to gape. 'You're kidding?'

'No fucking way . . . Get back to the labs, they've given no details of the bullet in this report. Find out if it was marked, you know, with drills, like the others.'

Ancora got on the phone as Pirelli started to pace the office. He was sweating; the Paluso boy, the two Luciano children, Paul Carolla, the restaurant chef; had their killer left his calling card on all these murders, the tell-tale scratches on the bullets? Could the same man have been responsible for the poisonings of Roberto Luciano and his sons?

'Eh, man, take it easy . . . Take it easy, this is crazy,' Pirelli said aloud.

'That's the first sign, talking to yourself.' Ancora was getting no reply. He dialled again.

Pirelli half-smiled, then pointed to the wall where the photographs were displayed. 'I want all the Lucianos up there, I want Paul Carolla up there . . . I want to see all their faces, you know why?'

'Sure, you want a rise.'

Pirelli laughed and perched on his desk, pointing to the wall as if the photos were already pinned up. 'I think they were all, and I mean all, killed by the same man.'

'What are you, crazy?'

'No, I'm not, but I think their killer must be.'

He got up and crossed the room to stand directly in front of the Luciano children's photo. 'Look at the way he's positioned those two children – shot them and then turned them to face each other, put their arms around one another as if they were sleeping.'

The two men stared at the pitiful sight of the dead Carlo and Nunzio.

Pirelli hesitated. 'The Luciano children were killed at what time? They reckoned nine, nine-fifteen, yes?'

'They weren't discovered until eleven o'clock, I think. Lemme check . . .'

Pirelli rubbed his hair until it stood on end. 'The Luciano men were not discovered until after eleven . . . The chef, the staff, you got a time on them?'

Ancora's hands flew over the files, slammed one drawer shut and opened another. He took out a file and thumbed through it, turning one page after another. He threw his hands up in the air. 'There's no time, this report's only half finished, the incompetent bastards.'

Pirelli snatched the file. 'I'll deal with this personally, you get back on to New York. Tell them we're out by about sixty years on Giorgio/Luka Carolla, grovel, send our apologies but we've got to have a recent photograph of him.'

'OK, will do.'

Almost as an afterthought Pirelli paused at the door. 'You heard about the Luciano women? The docks are swarming with men clearing their warehouses.'

Ancora nodded. 'Yeah! Rumour has it they must have some big shot behind them paying out a lot of dough; smells like trouble to me.'

Pirelli hovered at the door. 'Who do you think it is?'

Ancora shrugged. 'That's the problem with this city, we can see trouble coming but we're too busy to do anything about it. These women should watch out for themselves, something's going down . . . You want a word of advice? Don't get involved, Joe, we've got enough on our plate. You start looking for . . .'

Pirelli had already left. Ancora sighed, turning to look at the notice board, then glancing back at the confusion of papers, photographs and telexes covering the desk. Pirelli was very good at unearthing evidence, but it was always down to Ancora to check it out. He had to admit that, like or dislike Pirelli, he had certainly moved things forward at a gallop, although Ancora had an uncomfortable feeling that the horse was beginning to veer out of control.

CHAPTER 29

FOR FIVE days, work went on around the clock. The canning factory was cleared and swept, the machinery put back into running order, and the tile factory, the offices and warehouses were made ready for occupation. The delivery trucks and even the typewriters were repaired.

Teresa worked herself into near exhaustion. Rosa and Sophia worked well as a team. Sophia was a good delegator and extremely well liked. Moyra continued to surprise them all; she was a tough negotiator and even though she couldn't speak Sicilian she haggled like a market trader. With her wild gestures and mime act she appeared to have total control over her army of cleaners. The cleaners carrying mops, brooms and buckets would be ferried by Moyra from one place to the next. Wheeling around in one of the heavy trucks, Moyra seemed to be having the time of her life. At the end of the day she would pay out in cash, and the women soon learned that if they were slack in any way, pay would be deducted. Moyra also took great delight in the wolf whistles and catcalls from the men working, and she created a wonderful diversion, her blonde curls trapped under a cloth cap and wearing heavy overalls, but with her make-up,

681

perfume and even her false nails still very much in evidence.

All of them kept a tight rota for taking care of Luka, their so-called house guest. Luka was warned not to make any attempt to leave his room as they were worried Graziella or Adina would discover him, and Adina especially had been told not to clean the top floor because they were storing papers and documents.

Luka's door was always locked, and to date they had been successful; neither Adina nor Graziella was aware of his presence in the villa.

Graziella's first reaction to Teresa's suggestions changed radically. She now accepted the work had to be done and she played her part willingly, half afraid to even admit she was actually loving every minute of it. Graziella was even allowed to drive the armoured Mercedes – but only the armoured Mercedes, as the women deemed it safest. Graziella would drag poor Adina on frequent shopping trips to town in the heavy car and then on their return they set about making packed lunches for the workers. Moyra would arrive for the pick up, giving a blast of the truck's hooter, and Graziella and Adina would carry the baskets and load up.

Moyra would occasionally encourage Graziella to accompany her, and to see Graziella perched in the big truck's cabin always made the workers cheer. Graziella enjoyed being a part of it all, but at the same time, she knew not to meddle. Teresa's flashes of temper and her impatience with everyone made Graziella's own hot temper rise.

One afternoon, Graziella realized that Adina was eager for a ride in the truck and so helped her up into the cabin. She waved them down the drive and returned to the villa. She decided to take a nap and was about to lie down when she heard a creaking sound. A little afraid, she listened: someone was moving across the floor above her bedroom. She crept to her door, inching it open.

Luka made his way down the stairs, checking each room and trying to familiarize himself with the layout. Moyra's room he recognized from the sweet smell of her perfume, then he came to Rosa and Teresa's room with its two single beds. Sophia's room had been left with the curtains drawn; he saw the pill bottles, the unmade bed.

He continued along the landing, and was almost caught. He moved quickly into the nearest room, where he left the door ajar and peeked out, listening, but all was silent. Then he looked around at the small, neat bedroom with the sports equipment, the old posters on the wall. This was a strange room; it smelt stuffy, airless.

Luka knew he could not be seen, but through the gap he saw Graziella turn and stare towards him, at the partly open door. He had no idea that it was unusual, that he was in Michael's room and that Michael's door was always closed.

Slowly, Graziella crossed the landing and pushed the door wider, wider . . . There was no hiding place, he was caught, trapped, in the centre of the room. The scream or shout he had expected didn't come.

'Who are you?' she whispered. 'Who are you?'

'Don't be afraid,' he stuttered, 'I won't harm you. They know about me, I work for them. They said I could stay here, do you understand me?' Luka had spoken in English and was afraid she had not understood.

'Teresa? Did she say you could have this room?'

'No, no . . . Upstairs. I had a fall – see, I've injured my shoulder.'

'But you're American?'

'Didn't they tell you about me?'

She was staring at him, moving closer and closer. 'No, nobody told me. How did you get in?'

'They gave me a key.'

'They should have told me, you gave me a fright. What is your name?'

'Johnny.'

'You are in my son's room.'

When Adina arrived home and let herself into the kitchen, she was surprised to discover Graziella sitting with a strange-looking boy, each enjoying a large dish of pasta. However, when Teresa returned, hours later, there was a different Graziella waiting, an irate one who didn't wait even for her to take her coat off.

'I want to talk, Teresa. I don't mind you using Papa's study as your own, but when you want someone to stay, you ask me. You don't let strangers come to this house without my permission, you understand? You don't know where he came from, who he knows, and you should never let anyone have a key.'

Teresa was so stunned she was hardly able to follow Graziella's meaning. 'Wait, wait, Mama, what are you talking about?'

'You know, don't act so dumb. The boy, Teresa, the American student. I found him in Michael's room. Nobody goes in there, nobody.'

'I er . . . I'm sorry, Mama. I'll go and talk to him.'

'You do that. If you think he should stay until he's

better, then we talk it over, but he never has a key to this house.'

That night Teresa announced to the rest of them that Johnny Moreno, an American student, had been hurt in an accident at the factory, and was staying with them until he recovered.

Sophia looked hard at Teresa as she stubbed out her cigarette.

'He needs a few more days, OK?'

It was the first time she didn't back down. 'For now, Teresa, but not for much longer.'

The workers applauded as the freshly painted sign, 'Luciano Export Company', was hauled into place. It was hard to believe that the dockland warehouses were the same ones that only days ago had resembled rat-infested sewers. They had been painted, the doors repaired and the cavernous interiors swept and washed clean. Sophia calculated that the cost of the paint alone must have been astronomical.

A navy-blue Alfa Romeo was parked near the main warehouse, beside the white boundary markings. Its two occupants looked on all the activity with as much interest as Sophia. One of the men was using a camera with a telephoto lens and, as Sophia turned, shading her eyes against the sun with her hand, the camera clicked rapidly, bringing her face closer and closer each time.

*

That afternoon the two men also took photographs of the olive groves, the vineyards and the tile factory, then drove to the headquarters of the Corleone family in the mountains. Still wet from the processing, the photos were displayed to illustrate that, to all intents and purposes, the Luciano family was back in business. The question was, who was injecting the cash to get things started again?

Luka was wearing a dressing gown over a shirt that Rosa had left out for him. He watched as Graziella slowly entered the room, smiling and indicating the tray she was carrying.

'I have been baking, fresh bread, can you smell it?'

Without waiting for a reply, she put the tray down and drew up a chair for him. She gestured for him to eat. 'Now you are *my* guest, so eat, build up your strength.'

Luka found it disconcerting to eat with Graziella watching every mouthful, but her warmth and wonderful smile eventually helped him to relax while she chattered. 'Teresa said I was not to talk with you, that she would see to your meals, but they are out all day.' She pointed to the apple pie. 'That was my son's favourite,' she said, then folded her hands in her lap.

As Teresa opened the front door, she heard Graziella on the stairs and looked up. Alarmed, she called, 'Mama, what are you doing?'

Graziella gave Luka a mischievous smile and hurried down to Teresa. 'I've been having a rest, now I am coming downstairs. Is that all right?'

Teresa tossed her coat on to a hall chair. 'The sign is up, it looks wonderful.'

Rosa bounded in and caught her grandmother in her arms. 'You would be so proud, Grandmama, it's in bright red and gold letters.'

Outside, Sophia and Moyra stood like conspirators on the shady porch. Moyra whispered, 'I saw her pay out so much cash. This time she handed it over for the new tarpaulins on the reconditioned trucks.'

Rosa called them to dinner. Moyra held Sophia back for a moment. 'You ask her about the money, I wanna know where it's all coming from.'

'Why don't you ask her yourself?'

'No, you do it. You'll be better at it than me.'

Teresa was unfolding her napkin. 'What was that, Moyra?'

Moyra took her seat. 'Nothing, just saying I was hungry.'

Throughout dinner, Teresa talked to Sophia about dressing them all for their 'sales pitch'. She wanted all the women to wear the most elegant and expensive clothes. Sophia was sure that she could get dresses for them all from her warehouses, and perhaps a trip to Rome would do them all good.

Teresa pursed her lips. 'I don't think we can all go, but you could take our sizes and bring everything back, couldn't you? I trust your taste.'

Moyra pouted, 'Oh, come on, Teresa, we could all go just for one day. It'd be fun. Look at my hair, the roots are showing through, and my nails, I need to go to a beauty parlour.'

Rosa joined in and cajoled Teresa until she half agreed. Sophia was running her fork along the tablecloth, leaving small tracks. She had hardly touched her food. Moyra gave her a knowing look and a light kick under the table.

Sophia tucked her feet beneath her chair and continued raking the cloth with her fork. 'What about accessories? Do we have enough money for those too, Teresa? Shoes, handbags . . . where will the money come from to buy them?'

Teresa caught the edge in her voice. 'Oh, come on, Sophia, you can't kid us that you are that broke. Can't you get some of your contacts to give us things for free?'

'I have about a $20,000 overdraft, Teresa. On my business account I am close to $300,000 in the red. Yes, sure I can run to a few thousand more to dress us all, why not? I was just wondering if there was any cash in the house; perhaps you have some we could use.'

Coldly, Teresa tilted her head towards Graziella as an indication to Sophia to stay quiet. Graziella cleared the dishes and carried them into the kitchen. As soon as she had left the room, the atmosphere, already tense, became icy.

Teresa pushed back her chair, threw her napkin down. 'In future, watch what you say in front of Mama, and, for goodness' sake, stop running that damned fork up and down, it's getting on my nerves.'

Carefully, Sophia laid the fork down. Moyra glanced at Sophia, then asked, 'Where's all the cash coming from to pay the workers? We're not stupid, we've all seen the cash going out, and it's a lot. So where did it come from, Teresa?'

Teresa shrugged. 'All right . . . When I went back to look for Moyra's bag I took everything from the safe at the club. I had to get things started. What did you expect me to do? If you all feel so damned guilty, when we sell, we'll pay it back, all right, Sophia? All right?'

Equally angry, Sophia snapped back, surprising Teresa. 'Whatever we feel about what you did is immaterial at the moment. What we want settled is Moreno. I don't like him being here with Mama. We made a deal with him, now let's pay him off.'

Rosa stared at her mother, shaking her head. 'What money? What's going on, what money?'

Moyra leaned across the table. 'How much was there, Teresa? I mean, was it enough we could all just have upped and got out of this mess?'

Teresa sighed. 'Let's just say it was a lot. You can see where it all went. It's not as if I took it for myself, I did it for all of us.'

Sophia banged the table. 'Teresa, for God's sake, tell them about the gun.'

'What gun?' Moyra demanded of Sophia. 'The one from under his pillow?'

'No, the other one. Tell them, Teresa.'

Rosa began to ply her mother with questions. Sophia got up and walked out, slamming the door behind her in her impatience. Teresa half-rose to follow her, then sat down again. Both Rosa and Moyra looked on expectantly.

'In the bag I brought from Dante's was another weapon, rather like a walking cane. It fires a single bullet.'

Moyra yelped and put her hands to her mouth as Sophia walked back into the dining room. She placed the three parts of the cane on the table. 'Commissario Pirelli said that they believed Paul Carolla was killed by a specialist gun, possibly disguised as a walking cane. Well, what's this?'

'Holy shit!' Moyra threw her hands in the air. 'Why haven't you said anything about this before?'

Sophia slotted the horse's head into position. 'Because Teresa didn't want me to. But now Moreno is well enough to leave.'

Teresa looked up at her. 'Have you finished? Personally, I don't give a damn if he killed Paul Carolla.'

Sophia shouted, 'None of us gives a damn about Carolla, Teresa. That is not the point.'

Teresa shouted back, 'Well, what do you want me to do?'

Sophia said fiercely, 'Get rid of him, pay him off. What else do you think I want?'

'I can't. I spent the last of the cash today.'

Sophia ran her hands through her hair. 'Well then, we have no alternative, do we, Teresa? We have only his word that the gun is not his, only his word that he shot Dante in self-defence. If we go to Pirelli, explain the circumstances . . .'

Moyra pulled the walking stick towards her. 'Hang on, just hang on a second. Don't I get to speak? First, the money. So Teresa stole it, so what? Is anybody doing anything about the lawyers embezzling all they could get their hands on? Is anybody doing anything for us? No? OK . . . Whatever the kid upstairs did or didn't do, let's pay him what he's owed and get on with our lives.'

Sophia shouted, 'She can't! Don't you see, she's spent his money.'

Teresa gave Moyra a smile, thankful that she was on her side, then shrugged. 'Sophia, you leave Mr Moreno to me. You all go to Rome.'

690

'Fine, I'll go, but don't expect me to come back.'

Teresa's eyes narrowed. 'That's what this is really all about, isn't it, Sophia? You want out? Well, it's your decision, you do exactly what you want, just so long as we can trust you. Can we trust you, Sophia?'

Sophia felt sick. Her voice was hardly audible as she said, 'You can trust me, Teresa. I hope for your sake you can also trust Mr Moreno.'

As Sophia left the room, Teresa turned to see her daughter staring at her. Rosa could hardly believe that this was her mother; she was changing before her eyes. The metamorphosis was chilling.

'I think I'll go to bed, Mama.' She gave her mother a small kiss on the cheek. She was confused, trying to assimilate everything she had just learned.

Teresa caught her daughter's hand, gripped it tightly. 'Everything I am doing is for all of you, Rosa.'

'Is it, Mama? Sometimes it doesn't look that way.'

'Go to bed, Rosa, before you say something you'll be sorry for. And don't think, don't ever think for one moment, that I prefer things the way they are. But life goes on. I intend to make it go on the best way I know how.'

'And you don't care how or what you do, is that it?'

'If you want to side with Sophia we'd better get the air cleared now. What do you want, Rosa? You want to go to the police?'

'I don't know ... Goodnight, Aunt Moyra ... Mama.'

Moyra said she was going to bed, too, then patted Teresa's shoulder, leaned close. 'I'm with you. He's just a kid, you an' me can handle him.'

691

Left alone, Teresa remained sitting in Don Roberto's chair at the head of the table. Her hands caressed the carved wooden lions on the arms of the chair.

Graziella was in the hall, carrying a hot drink for herself. 'Can I speak to you, Mama?'

Teresa chose her words carefully. 'You said that we could have your jewellery if we needed it. I'm afraid, Mama, I do. We are almost ready to sell and we've run out of cash. I want to do the job properly, and . . .'

Graziella opened the safe, took out a large leather-bound box and unlocked the lid. Together they examined the splendid jewels, the diamond pin worn by Luciano, the brooches, the rings . . . Teresa picked out the long strand of perfect pearls. Graziella said not a word until she had carefully relocked the case and put it back in the safe.

'Now, are these real? How much do you reckon they are worth?'

Teresa held the pearls under the desk lamp. She could not tell if they were good fakes or the real thing, but they certainly were large and appeared perfectly matched. Graziella flushed, not liking to see the pearls handled in such an uncouth way; it repelled her. Her old class and breeding reared its head as she said flippantly, 'Oh, $25,000, hopefully more, but that is what my husband paid for them in 1950. They must be worth considerably more now.'

Teresa felt the barbed sweetness and had the grace to blush. 'Thank you, Mama, they will be put to good use. I'm sorry I had to ask.'

Teresa received a light kiss, but she could not rid herself of the feeling she always had – she was not good enough, and never had been, for the Lucianos.

Teresa knocked softly and waited. Luka opened the door, then stepped aside. He half-smiled, as though amused by Teresa's visit.

This was the one Luka didn't like, and he was very uneasy with her. Her eyes were hard, unfeeling eyes.

'Sophia believes you killed Paul Carolla. She wants us to hand you over to the *carabinieri*.'

'I have never met this Paul Carolla. You tell me you have my bag, a gun, but that is my word against yours. I went to Dante's club, he tried to kill me, and I shot him in self defence.'

She fetched the Bible from the dressing table and held it out. 'Swear on the Holy Bible that what you say to me is the truth.'

He placed his hand over the gold cross etched into the black leather cover. 'The whole truth and nothing but the truth, so help me God . . . I was to give Dante a packet of heroin. He received the heroin, but when it was time to pay me, he tried to kill me.'

Teresa put the Bible down and took from her pocket a slim leather case. 'These pearls are worth $50,000, a lot more than I took from the safe.'

Luka didn't even touch them, he just smiled. 'Give me the $50,000 cash, and I'll be out of here.'

'When you leave this house, I don't want ever to see you or hear from you again. You'll have the cash tomorrow night.'

*

Sophia could not sleep. She tossed and turned, got up and searched for her pills. The bottle was empty, so she threw it into the waste bin and searched her bedside drawer for Valium. There were only a few tablets left; she could feel herself breaking into a cold sweat. The more she thought about it the more desperate she became.

She dressed and crept down the stairs. The clock on the landing chimed ten-thirty. They had all taken to going to bed early, mostly because they were so exhausted. All she could think of were the long hours stretching ahead. She went into the study, drummed her fingers on the desk wondering if it was too late to call. Then she picked up the phone and asked the operator to find the number of Don Roberto's physician; she was sure he would see her.

The doctor answered the door wearing a smoking jacket. His face registered such concern as he let her into his surgery that she said immediately, to put him at his ease, 'I am sorry to call you so late, I should have left it until tomorrow . . .'

'Are you ill?'

'No, no, *grazie*, but I suppose you have heard of Graziella's situation? She has great trouble sleeping, and tonight seemed more restless than ever. I wonder if you could give me something to help her sleep, a prescription I can take to an all-night pharmacy, Mogadon? I think you prescribed some before . . .'

He began to write out the prescription, then paused and looked at Sophia. 'How have you been keeping?'

'Oh, I'm fine . . . and could you also give me some Valium, for my sister-in-law? She is very tense, you heard about the court incident? I think she said ten milligrams is her usual ... She meant to bring some from New York, but she forgot.'

He nodded, about to say something, then continued writing. It seemed to take forever, but eventually he tore the slip of paper off the pad and handed it to her. 'Tell her not to make this a regular practice, they can be addictive. At the same time, I can understand the strain you must all be under, especially after ...'

Sophia couldn't wait to get out. 'Yes, it has been ... a difficult time for us all, and I thank you again for your care and understanding that night. Graziella sends you her best wishes.'

As he showed her to the door, he said, 'Please convey my sincere good wishes to your family. Should you need me at any time, please feel free to call.'

As Sophia left, he locked the surgery door and went through the hall to his own apartment. His wife was watching television.

She looked up. 'Everything all right?'

He sighed and lit a cigar. 'Yes, Graziella Luciano has trouble sleeping. It was her daughter-in-law, Sophia.'

'It's a wonder to me any of them can sleep after what they've been through. You just missed the second part; the blonde woman is not his real wife, and her husband is the father of the baby found on the doorstep ...'

Sophia Luciano was forgotten as the soap opera continued.

Sophia took two Valium and replaced the cap. She leaned back, in the driving seat, closing her eyes; just knowing she had the Valium calmed her. A tap on the window made her heart feel as if it would explode.

'Signora? It's me, I'm sorry to make you jump, I was sitting in the bar across the road.'

Sophia pressed a button and the window slid down. 'Commissario Pirelli, how are you? I'm sorry I didn't recognize you . . . I have just been to the chemist for my mother, Graziella.'

'Would you join me for a drink?'

'Thank you, no, I must take her medicine back.'

'Please, just one small drink, or a coffee? There have been a few developments and I'd like to keep you informed. I was going to come by tomorrow.'

This posed a dilemma for Sophia. She knew she would be in Rome the following day and didn't want Pirelli to find Graziella alone in the house with Moreno. But still she hesitated.

Pirelli smiled. 'It'll take no more than a few minutes, and I hate drinking alone.'

The bar was rather seedy, so Pirelli changed his mind and they walked a block to go to another. About half-way Sophia paused at a café with tables still outside.

'Why don't we sit outside, I would prefer a cappuccino.'

'Won't you be cold?'

Sophia shook her head; she was wearing a dark mink coat. He drew out a chair for her and signalled for the waiter.

'Are you hungry?'

'No, just coffee would be fine.'

'A pastry?'

She smiled and shook her head and the waiter took the order for two coffees plus a brandy for Pirelli. He was feeling the chill in the night air but said nothing.

Sophia opened her cigarette case and Pirelli smiled. 'You have replenished your stock, I see.' She didn't seem to understand. 'The Turkish cigarettes?'

She remembered, and tilted her head back as he struck a match for her. He kept it alight while he took out a Marlboro, and burnt his fingers. She flicked open her lighter with a soft, low laugh and he gave her a boyish grin, putting his elbow in a dark, congealed mess of spilt coffee. He wiped it off with a paper napkin.

'I'm afraid this is probably not what you are used to. My apologies.'

Again that delightful laugh. He wanted to lean over the table and kiss her. 'The bar is nicer, if you would prefer . . .'

'This is fine, Commissario, really.'

The waiter brought their coffee, shivering as the evening was getting really cold. Sophia snuggled into her fur coat. She was beginning to feel light-headed . . . She raised a hand and called the waiter back.

'I've changed my mind, I would also like a brandy.'

Pirelli promptly handed her his and she thanked him, sipping it and feeling it warm inside her. He offered sugar and she shook her head. He put two spoonfuls into his own coffee and stirred it.

'You said there were some new developments, Commissario?'

He tilted his head. 'Joe, please . . .' He had no intention of telling her what he had so far discovered, nor of visiting the villa as he had told her; he simply wanted to be with her. He coughed and fingered his tie.

'Yes . . . They are connected to your case, specifically to your children.' He wanted to reach for her hand when he saw the way the sadness, that had lifted for just a few moments, swept over her face. She turned away, her perfect profile motionless.

'I think we found the gun today.'

'Do you know who it belongs to?'

'Not as yet, but it won't take long. It was a Magnum .44, and we have a strong lead on the killer. We think the same man also killed Paul Carolla.' He had said more than he had intended, but he carried on, 'We believe it is Luka Carolla, Paul Carolla's son, signora, and any day now we will arrest him.'

Sophia turned to face him. What he was saying was that the American boy hiding in the villa could not have killed Carolla. Moreno had, after all, been telling them the truth . . . She relaxed slightly, and sipped the brandy.

'So you have been able to trace him? When you came to the house you were trying to find him.'

Pirelli pursed his lips, careful now. 'We can trace anyone, find anyone, especially now with all the computer equipment. Data is easier to pass from country to country, town to town; fingerprints can be faxed in two seconds.'

He had changed the subject purposely, wondering if she would still ask after Luka Carolla, but she had a frown on her face. 'You mean you can trace, for example, a child, missing for years? Does all this computerization help with that?'

Pirelli thought for a moment, then nodded. 'I guess so . . . What it actually does is give more people access to information. The computers themselves cannot do the tracing, it's the short cuts. You pump in data, everything you know, about your lost child for example, send it to Rome and they can disperse it all over Italy, over the world if necessary. That would have taken years in the old days, but now . . . a few hours.'

'And does everyone have access to these computers?'

'No, no . . . But if, say, we take this lost child again, if it becomes an investigation, then of course we can use all the facilities open to us . . .'

Sophia nodded, then looked at him. 'You have coffee froth on your top lip.'

He raised his eyebrows and wiped his mouth. 'Clear?'

She nodded, stubbing out her cigarette. He could detect her change of mood; she was deep in thought, but he had no conception of what she was thinking of, the possibility of tracing her son, of asking Pirelli to help her. She decided against mentioning it, but the seed had been planted. It was just not possible with the situation at the villa to even consider it now, but at some time in the future . . .

Pirelli tried to lift her mood. He laughed. 'It's not as bad as spinach caught between the teeth, you know, that feeling when you get home and find one tooth black with spinach? What always amazes me is why nobody ever tells you . . . I mean, everyone must have noticed, but said nothing . . .'

Sophia giggled, and he leaned over to her. 'You have the most infectious, wonderful laugh . . . Will you have another brandy?'

She agreed, saying that afterwards she really must go.

The waiter was just bringing their bill when they sent him back for more brandy. They had not spoken for a while and Pirelli was racking his brains for something witty and original to say. Sophia was feeling the effects of the Valium and the brandy, simply enjoying the sensation of not caring.

She realized he had asked her a question and looked at him. 'I'm sorry, did you say something?'

'Nothing that is worth repeating, you were miles away.'

She tilted her head, it was a habit she had, and her eyes were sparkling. She leaned forward on her elbow. 'You know, once, I guess I was about fifteen, I used to work in a café like this one, cleaning the tables and washing the dishes.'

'You did?'

She laughed, letting her coat fall open as if she didn't feel the night air. Her cheeks were flushed, he didn't think anyone should be so beautiful . . . She crooked her finger for him to come closer and he could smell her perfume, a light scent of fresh flowers.

'One of my earliest memories is of my mother . . . Have you ever heard of a Toni perm? They used to call them that after the war, Toni.'

He nodded, though he had no idea what she was talking about, he just loved the sound of her husky voice, loved the fact that she had beckoned him closer. With both elbows on the table he was close enough to see her flawless skin, her perfect white teeth. His mind was working overtime, thinking how he could make the move to kiss her. He had never wanted to hold a woman so much in his entire life. Yet his expression was one of serious attention.

She was saying, 'My Mama was so desperate to have her hair permed, she had long, dark, straight hair, like mine.'

'How long is your hair?'

'Oh . . . ' she gestured with her hand almost to her hip and continued talking, but he was seeing her lying, naked, with her long hair splayed across a pillow . . . She wore it in such a severe style, drawn back from her face, but he liked that. He sighed, he liked everything about this woman. He realized she was still talking.

'. . . So they agreed, and she was in there for hours and hours. I was only about six or seven. She came out with all these curls and she looked so pretty, so happy, but then . . . she strapped this billboard around her, you know, a sandwich board? She was advertising the hair salon. I had to give out the leaflets to the passers-by while she strode up and down the street, up and down . . .'

He smiled. 'She must have wanted that perm very badly.'

His heart was thudding in his chest as two tears, two absolutely perfect, pear-shaped tears, rolled down her cheeks. 'Yes, she did. I don't think she felt any humiliation. I did. As young as I was, I felt it so deeply. I was so ashamed, but for her, you understand?'

Pirelli nodded, and she continued, 'Well, I stuffed these terrible little pamphlets into every bin I could see. All the time men were jeering at her, women pointing and sniggering. "Mama," I said, "take it off, please, people are laughing, look," and she answered, "Yes, I know, but I have got the best perm in Sicily for nothing." But it wasn't – I paid for it, she paid for it.'

She sat back, turning her face away. 'I have no idea why I told you that. Maybe so you would understand, I have not always had wealth, not always eaten in the finest restaurants. We were very poor, my Mama had nothing, not even a husband . . .'

'And you used to wait on tables?'

'Yes . . . it was a roadside café.' She breathed in deeply, staring ahead for a moment before she looked back to him. 'I must be very boring, and I must go.'

Pirelli jumped to his feet and went into the café to pay the bill. She waited for him outside, he could see her with her back to the brightly lit window. On a sudden mad, frivolous impulse, he pointed to the vase of flowers on the counter and delved into his pocket. 'How much?'

Highly embarrassed, Pirelli presented the flowers to Sophia, only realizing as he did so that they were plastic. 'Well, I have managed to make an utter fool of myself.'

She held them in her arms, smiling. 'No, I am touched. They will keep for ever . . . Thank you.'

He walked her to her car, remonstrating with her for not locking it, but she pointed out that he had been with her and so was partly to blame. He opened the door for her.

'Would you have dinner with me, Sophia? Can I call you Sophia?'

'I'm going to Rome . . .'

'For ever?'

'No, but I don't know how long I will be gone.'

'Will you be there for Christmas?'

She was very close to him, bending to get into the car, and she straightened. 'Christmas?' Her large, dark eyes lowered and he could see her thick, dark lashes.

She uses no make-up, he thought, then he heard her whisper, 'Oh God, it will be Christmastime soon . . .'

Her eyes were like a frightened child's as the grief engulfed her. At first he did not understand what had distressed her to such an extent.

Her voice was a soft, pleading moan, 'My babies, my babies . . .'

Suddenly he understood what a nightmare Christmas would be for her, the holiday with all the tinsel and mayhem. It was for children, and Sophia's were gone. He hardly realized he had taken her in his arms, he was holding her tightly, saying over and over that it would be all right . . . it would be all right, he was there . . . She clung to him, the soft fur feeling like silk against his cheek. He wanted to hug her and never let her go.

He never knew how it happened, but suddenly he was kissing her; to comfort her, his lips had found hers . . . She turned her face away, pressing her cheek into his coat. His body was on fire, he had never experienced such passion, or tenderness. She remained in his arms for an eternity, then he gradually felt her drawing away; not forcibly, it was simply that the moment was over.

He helped her into the car and tucked her coat in to be sure it would not get trapped in the door. 'Will you have dinner with me?'

She searched for the car keys, without replying.

'I'll come to Rome, to Turkey, wherever you want.'

She put the keys in the ignition and started the car. When she turned to him it was as if she were a stranger. He was desperate to keep her with him a few moments longer.

'I hear you and your sisters-in-law are starting up the business again. You must promise me to take care, great care, and if you ever need me . . . Look, let me give you my card, this is my direct line, any hour of the day or night. And this is my home phone number, I have a rented apartment.'

He was talking fast, scribbling his number on the card. He handed it to her through the window and her hand felt icy cold to his touch. She didn't look at the card but slipped it into her pocket.

'You have been very kind, but I think it best if we forget this ever happened . . . Goodnight.'

She drove off fast, and he stood like a lost soul, completely devastated. Around his feet were the plastic flowers. Ancora would have looked with disbelief to see him, his arms half-raised, as he said aloud, 'Oh, Sophia Luciano, what are you doing to me?'

Sophia tried to enter the house soundlessly, and had crept to the foot of the stairs when Teresa came out of the study.

'Where in God's name have you been?'

'Out, I needed some air.'

'You've been gone hours, it's half-past two in the morning.'

Sophia paused on the staircase, looking down at Teresa. 'You are not my jailer. If I want to go out for some air then I will.'

'No you won't.'

Sophia kept her voice low, but the anger was all there. 'I don't want a stand-up row with you, here on the stairs, we'll wake the whole house, but just who do you think you're talking to? What right have you to speak to me as if I was a child?'

'Right now, every right.'

'You do . . ?'

'Where did you go?'

'I went for a drive, and this you will really love, I had

704

a brandy – no, two brandies – with Commissario Pirelli. You want to make something of that?'

Moyra came to the study door. 'If she doesn't, I do. You tell him anything?'

Sophia threw her coat off. 'What do you take me for?'

'You threatened us that you would tell him, maybe you did. We don't know what you've been doing for the past three hours.'

Sophia wanted to slap Moyra's cream-covered face. The fluffy pink dressing gown wrapped around her voluptuous body really got to her.

'I was sitting in my car, he came up and asked me if I would like a drink because he had some information. He was going to come here tomorrow, so rather than have him in the house with your precious Moreno, I agreed to have a drink. They have the gun that killed my babies – the gun, not the killer. They also believe that whoever killed my sons also shot Paul Carolla, it's the same man, the one he was asking about when he first came here. Paul Carolla's own son, Luka . . . And they are about to make an arrest, which leaves that creature upstairs in the clear.'

Teresa sighed with relief. 'You think he was telling you the truth?'

'Why would he lie? And aren't you relieved? It means that Moreno was telling the truth.'

Teresa turned to Moyra. 'You believe her?'

Sophia came back down the stairs towards Teresa. 'Are you accusing me of lying? *Well, are you?*'

Sophia's breath hissed, she was so angry.

Teresa raised her hands in a submissive gesture. 'And you never mentioned Moreno?'

Sophia sighed and spelt it out for them. 'I did not

mention Moreno, I never said a word about the gun, I said nothing . . . Now, would it be all right if I went to my bed? I'm tired, it's been a long day.'

'I'll come to Rome with you tomorrow.'

Sophia continued up the stairs. 'Won't that be nice!'

None of them gave any thought as to why Teresa had changed her mind about accompanying them to Rome. They simply accepted it, but the truth was she had to sell Graziella's pearls to pay off Luka.

They all waited impatiently as Teresa gave last-minute instructions to Graziella; she was to send Adina up to Luka's room with food trays, and he should remain in his room until they returned. The car was only just out of the villa gates when Graziella, ignoring Teresa's warnings, went to see him . . .

Luka had had little contact with women in his life, let alone women of Graziella's age, and he found her delightful. Perhaps it was because she represented no threat to him whatsoever. He relaxed totally with her, and accepted her invitation to sit in the garden.

As they descended the stairs to the second landing, she tapped him on the shoulder, and he looked up.

'Your hair, why do you dye your hair?'

She saw the way he recoiled, running his long, tapering fingers through the strange-coloured, fine hair. The natural blond growth beneath gave it a mousy look.

'I . . . I just did it for a lark. It'll grow out.'

CHAPTER 30

THE MORNING paper ran yet another article accusing the police of doing nothing to find the killer of the jailer's son. This one named Joseph Pirelli as the man heading the investigation, with insinuations that he had been in Palermo for some considerable time and made no arrest; they suggested he should be replaced and shipped back to Milan.

The article did not bother Pirelli; he had suffered many times at the hands of the press and simply chose to ignore it. The Chief of the Palermo Police, however, did not. He walked in unannounced, carrying the paper.

'You read this?'

Pirelli nodded. 'I was coming down to see you.'

'Up, Joe, I'm three floors up. Mind if I sit down?'

He tossed the newspaper on the table, took his horn-rimmed glasses from their case and looked over the many photographs pinned on the wall. 'That the wall of death everyone's talking about?'

The shiny-suited figure remained firmly planted in front of the notice board. 'There's a few officers getting pissed off about your using the forensic and ballistics team at all hours, giving them no time for any other cases. There's a backlog building up ... You've got

Ancora, the young whatsisname, Bruno di Mazzo, and now Mincelli and his men working alongside you, that's more than ten men. How long do you reckon this is going to go on for? If you know your suspect, haul him in.'

'I'm trying, believe me I'm trying. We just can't get a trace on him.'

'I've read all the reports, Joe, and you need that boy picked up fast. So we'll get all the help we can and try to flush him out.'

Pirelli was getting uptight. 'Every uniformed man's got the identikit picture, every hotel, hospital, we've had men . . .'

'I know, I know how many men, Joe, and you've found no trace. So we'll pull out all the stops and try and flush him out. This city is a sewer, Joe, and it's getting clogged up. You can't have much more time. I'm sorry, but I need my men back as soon as possible.'

Pirelli had known that sooner or later he would lose some of his men, but he didn't think it would be that fast. 'You cancelled all leave?'

'Yep, and it's not gone down well. You wanted to go back to Milan for the weekend? Can you get your wife to come here? We can't afford the time.'

'OK,' said Pirelli. 'But I'm still not sure about the press.'

'You're not sure, Joe, if he's even still in Sicily, right? We go to press.'

Left alone, Pirelli noticed the flashing light on the intercom and picked up the call, sitting back and lighting another cigarette.

After weeks of enquiries, Pirelli's friend had come up with a radiographer from the old Nazareth hospital who

708

708

remembered a child being brought into the X-ray department, one fitting the description of the boy now known as Luka Carolla.

Pirelli left the office early to meet the elderly Signora Brunelli. As he waited for her in the small, neat apartment he wondered if this was a waste of time. What good would anything he learned now be to him in the present situation? He lit a cigarette and searched for an ashtray, finally dropping the match into a dolphin-shaped bowl.

Signora Brunelli walked slowly into the room. When he had helped her to sit down she admitted being surprised at his visit, and asked why he was so interested in a patient she had seen more than twenty years ago. With total honesty he told her that he didn't really know, it was just that anything he could find out about the young man he was trying to trace might, in the long run, help his investigation.

Signora Brunelli stared at the faded photograph of the orphans that Brother Thomas had given him. Her hands shook as she took out a magnifying glass, and studied it for a considerable time, moving the glass from one face to the next.

'The boy ringed with red, the blond child . . . I am sure he is the one I X-rayed.'

Pirelli nodded as he took the photograph back. 'It was, as you so rightly said, a long time ago. You must have had hundreds, if not thousands, of patients. Do you remember them all?'

'No, no, of course not, but sometimes children stay in your mind longer, particularly children in that little mite's condition. Also, and possibly the reason I recall him, is that he had swallowed a . . .' She pursed her lips as she tried to remember, then nodded her head. 'Yes, it was some kind of locket. They had tried to take it from him and he had swallowed it. It showed up clearly on the X-ray. We were worried that it might cause a stoppage of his bowels, but there was no need to operate.'

'You have an exceptional memory, signora.'

'Thank you, it is just that this child was so pitiful. You see, I don't know if you are aware that the boy had been sexually abused, more tormented, I would say. It was so horrific, he was not more than four or five years old, and his body was skeleton thin, covered in scars and bruises. He looked as if he had been subjected to nightmare treatment.' She shook her head. Even now, all these years later, the memory disgusted her, upset her.

Pirelli remained silent for a moment before asking if she had spoken to the boy.

She looked at him in surprise. 'Oh, no, Commissario Pirelli. The child was dumb. I may be wrong, of course, but I am sure the boy was a mute.'

Luka Carolla had begun to take on a different perspective. Although Pirelli felt deeply saddened by what he had learnt, he knew that it was a typical history to spawn a psychopath. He had no inkling that he would get his biggest lead to the boy just one hour later.

As he drove back to headquarters, the engine of his Fiat began to make strange noises. He carried on, but used the back streets in case he was going to break down.

He stopped and lifted the bonnet, then realized that it was his lucky day. Not fifteen yards away was a small repair shop and spare-parts yard.

There were a few Fiats for hire at special cheap rates, looking in even worse condition than his own. Pirelli wandered across to a mechanic and showed his ID. The man turned out to be the owner, and asked Pirelli if there were any word on his car.

Pirelli looked at him, puzzled. The owner persisted, 'It's been five days, haven't you traced it yet? Aren't you with the police?'

'I am, but not traffic. What's the problem? Late back is it?'

'Yeah, more'n five days late. American, and he's not at the address he put down.'

The driving licence particulars were in a neat, clear print. The car had been hired by Luka Carolla.

Through the window, Adina watched the car pause yet again. Three times it had cruised past the villa gates. This time it turned into the drive.

A young man wearing dark glasses and a navy-blue suit stepped from the Alfa Romeo. He walked casually up the steps to the porch and rang the bell.

'Who is it, Adina?' Graziella made her way slowly down the stairs.

'Shall I answer, signora?'

'Yes, yes, quickly . . .'

The man leaned against the doorframe and smiled. 'Signora Luciano, allow me to introduce myself. I am Joseph Rocco, my father was a great friend of Don Luciano. May I come in? Thank you, thank you . . .'

Graziella could not recall the young man's father, but she gestured for him to follow her into the drawing room. She offered sherry, coffee or tea, but he refused.

He sat in the centre of the sofa and placed his expensive leather briefcase on the floor beside his highly polished black shoes. His eyes, behind the dark glasses, roamed everywhere while his lips smiled and his charming voice discussed the weather and other mundane subjects. All the while his eyes were darting, noticing . . .

'Sadly, my father died more than two years ago. I now work for the Corleones, I handle their real estate business. May I give you my card, Signora Luciano?'

Graziella gazed at the neat white card, then tapped it against her hand. 'If you have come to discuss business then you must speak with my daughter-in-law. Are you interested in leasing the factory? Is that why you're here?'

'Pardon?'

Graziella continued, 'Teresa is at the tile factory. If you would like to leave a message, I will make sure she receives it.'

'Yes? Ah, then perhaps you would tell her I called, and that I would like to talk to her as soon as possible. My clients are the purchasers of the villa, and they would like to discuss immediate occupancy. There has been some delay in finalizing the agreement, so I shall look forward to speaking to her. Thank you for seeing me.'

He removed his glasses. His eyes were strangely unfocused, far-sighted, with deep-red pressure marks around the sockets. Without the glasses he seemed a little vulnerable. He replaced them quickly, and with a small bow and a slight click of his polished heels he saw himself out.

Luka watched from an upstairs window as Rocco drove slowly away from the villa. For a moment he had thought

712

it was the *carabinieri*, but then with some relief he had recognized Rocco. He was, as Carolla would have described him, a professional.

Sophia's luxurious apartment was the first thing Teresa suggested should be sold. The cash released by the sale could be used to cover the bankruptcy order against S & F Design Company. Amongst the many other outstanding bills were a number of orders, but not enough to contemplate reopening the shops.

They raided the stock rooms, sorting through hundreds of garments, mostly one-offs discarded by Nino. Sophia picked and discarded, criticized and praised, until she felt all four were walking advertisements for her own fashion label. They needed two taxis to take their new wardrobes back. Then they descended on the beauty parlour. Sophia noticed that Teresa, even under the hair dryer, continued to read through all her bankrupt-business documents.

There were not enough hours in the day. The time flew past, and for once Moyra had been right; they would have to spend at least another day in Rome. Teresa suggested Rosa and Moyra went shopping; even though she still had to sell Graziella's pearls, there were important things she wanted to discuss with Sophia. No sooner had she returned to the apartment than she rounded on her.

'You'd better tell me the truth, because before I go into meetings with lawyers and accountants on your behalf I want you to explain these figures. They don't make sense. You call yourself a business woman? Before you get one cent from the estate, and that includes me releasing this apartment for sale, explain this load of garbage, I can't make head or tail of most of the accounts.'

Sophia clasped her hands together and gave a small shrug of her shoulders. 'I was used, Teresa, just forget the whole thing, what's the point?'

'Point is, Sophia, this is now family business.'

Sophia gave a short humourless laugh. 'That's exactly what it was, Teresa; he ran it all, just like he ran everything in our lives. He used me, used my company to launder money, he paid Nino to work for me, he used me.'

'Who are you talking about?'

She said it with such hatred that Teresa was taken aback. 'Don Roberto Luciano, who else? But, even worse, he made Constantino part of it, my own husband . . . Look, take a look at just what my business really was.'

She handed over the second set of accounts and then waited as Teresa with her ever-present calculator went over the books. The lists of whorehouses, sex shops, prostitutes, mail-order catalogues, the pornography out-lets, the girls employed with no union wages, no taxes, and a network of export contracts for worldwide distri-bution. Sighing, she eventually closed the book and moved to Sophia, putting her arms around her. 'I'm sorry . . . come on, shusshh, don't cry.'

'I just feel such a fool.'

'Was this Nino involved in it all?'

'Yes, from the beginning. He knows everything, and if he wanted he could use it against me.'

'Did he take the machines?'

'I don't know, I don't care.'

'You should, they are worth a lot of money. I don't

714

want to rub salt into the wounds, but the facts are your own business ran at a loss from the word go. Maybe if you wanted, you could start a cheaper range; off the rail they call it, don't they? And if you do, you'd need those machines.'

'Well, I don't have them.'

'But you do have Fabio's designs, you own them, so you wouldn't need initially to go to the expense of acquiring a designer – that is, if you want to start again. Do you?'

'I don't know.'

'Well, there's no need to think about it now, but whatever you do decide, I'll help in every possible way.'

Sophia kissed Teresa's hand. '*Grazie* . . .'

'Fine. Now, will you call Graziella, tell her we'll be late. And then book us a table at the best, the very best and most fashionable restaurant in Rome? All those beautiful gowns, we might as well show them off . . . OK?'

Left alone, Teresa slipped the illegal accounts into her briefcase and locked it. She felt compassion for Sophia, perhaps in some ways more now than ever before. She had been foolish and inadequate, and Don Roberto had used it to his advantage. It was one more lesson, one not to be forgotten or forgiven.

Later that evening they stood together, admiring themselves in their new finery. They looked affluent, sophisticated and confident, their gowns, the best of Nino's winter '87 collection, nails painted, hair coiffed, in full war paint. Sophia had even given them each a piece of her jewellery. They were almost dizzy from their busy schedule and looked forward to ending the evening with a sumptuous dinner at the Sans Souci restaurant. It was a celebration of their release from the pressure of living at the Villa Rivera and of a new beginning.

The uniformed chauffeur of the hired Mercedes raised his eyes in admiration, bowing to each of them as she stepped into the car. Moyra, with her voluptuous figure, wore a revealing, tight-fitting gown; Rosa a short, ruched organza; and Teresa a severe, high-necked crêpe gown with fitted sleeves. Her hair, with Sophia's encouragement, had been lightened almost to blonde, and was set off to perfection by the diamond ear-rings and bracelet. Sophia herself wore a swirling taffeta gown with a vast, frilled wrap, sequinned in diagonal lines. They were all so different in style, but they had one thing in common: all the gowns were black.

The Sans Souci was located just off the Via Veneto. The small bar was dimly lit but shimmered with mirrors and wonderful tapestries. As the four women entered, the *maître d'* hurried to greet them, bowing and kissing Sophia's hand.

'Signora Luciano, we have missed you greatly. You have your usual table . . .'

As if they were royalty, he ushered them to the central table. Waiters scurried to draw their chairs out for them, and the other diners turned and stared. The whisper flew around that they were the Luciano widows.

They were viewed with awe – and were, indeed, awesome under the glittering chandeliers. Even the women had to acknowledge Sophia's beauty, with her blue-black hair coiled like a snake at her neck. As she slipped her black silk cape off, her shoulders were revealed, creamy white. She had lost a lot of weight, and her slim shoulders gave her a fragility in direct contrast to her dark, strong eyes and high cheekbones.

Under the pretext of reading the menu she took covert glances around the room. Many of the diners she knew, and knew well. She had dressed many of the women, yet not one of them acknowledged her, not one person smiled. If anything they averted their faces, but the whispers continued, the story of the murders and the fearful Mafia connections. Not one group in this exclusive dining room could concentrate on their own conversations; the Luciano women dominated the scene as if sitting on a small, spotlit stage.

A group of laughing people arrived, and for a moment a hush fell as attention was drawn away from the centre table. Then the buzz of whispers began again at a feverish pitch.

Sophia leaned close to Teresa. 'The party that just arrived, the small man leading them is Nino, the designer I told you about. But don't look, don't even turn your head . . . Tell Moyra . . .'

Nino stared. The centre table he had specially booked was now no longer available. He was on the point of causing a scene until he saw that one of the occupants was Sophia Luciano. With blatant, pointed rudeness he ignored Sophia, although he came within feet of her as he led his party to a table near the wall. After he was seated, however, he could not help but look at her constantly, as if drawn by her, but not once did she incline her head towards him.

Nino knew she was bankrupt, everyone in the fashion world knew it, and he had presumed she was out of business. He had also expected some sort of retaliation for his betrayal of her.

He had made a considerable amount of money on the machines and stock, but he had never thought of sending her so much as a thank-you note, nor considered that at the time she was probably in deep shock from the tragic murders. Nino was so wrapped in his own thoughts that one of his guests had to squeeze his hand to get his attention. They wanted to know who the occupants of the centre table were.

Nino swivelled round to face the widows squarely and flipped his napkin in their direction. 'Sophia Luciano . . . God knows who the others are – perhaps a schoolteacher, a whore, and a virgin.'

His companion laughed, covering her mouth with her hand, then passed his remark to her neighbour. The general laughter that followed was obviously directed at the Luciano women, and intruded on every other table in the room. In no time the other diners had caught on, but only Sophia felt the full brunt of the backstabbing, insidious laughter, knowing the way they would be gossiping about her. The widows sat like royalty, apparently impervious, and continued their meal, talking quietly, but each of them was aware of the attention. At one point Sophia reached out to Teresa and asked if they could leave; she could not stand being ogled for another moment.

Teresa gripped her hand, a smile frozen on her face. 'Let them discuss us! There is not one woman here to hold a candle to you, you look magnificent. I think,

Sophia, you are the most beautiful woman I have ever known.'

Touched by the direct gaze and the extraordinary compliment, Sophia gently caressed Teresa's cheek. 'Thank you, oh, thank you, Teresa.' She had the sweetest of smiles on her face, but her hand felt icy cold and her dark, wide eyes were one moment fearful, the next sparkling too brightly. Teresa noticed that she began to run the tines of her fork up and down the tablecloth, leaving small but deep tracks.

Moyra had captured Rosa's attention, explaining how she had caught a card player cheating at her table in Las Vegas. Teresa interrupted, asking if it were true that in all the casinos there was a hidden floor above with cameras and high-powered lenses.

'Oh, yes, they can zoom in on a table and pinpoint a player's hand; then they contact the pit manager by radio to tip him off . . .'

She stopped; Sophia had risen from the table. Teresa put out a hand to restrain her, but she was too late. She whispered to her not to do anything foolish, then turned with an embarrassed smile as the people at the table behind them grew silent.

Sophia moved like a dancer between the tables as if mesmerized, her hands slightly raised in front of her. She came to a standstill at Nino Fabio's table.

Teresa half-rose from her seat, knowing something was going to happen, but then sat back, watching in awe as Sophia smiled at Nino's guests. They all watched as Nino, very flustered, introduced Sophia to his table. She leaned towards him slightly, placing her hand on his neck; it was not a caress, it was a pointed gesture, as if feeling his pulse.

Nino sat back, his face white, his own hand at his throat. He could still feel her cold fingers and would take a long time to forget the expression in her eyes. It would take even longer to forget her tiny whisper when she had touched him: 'So, Nino, you are still alive . . .'

As Sophia returned to her own table, Teresa watched Nino's friends eagerly asking him what she had said to him. He stared after Sophia, his face pinched and terrified, his right hand still pressed to the pulse at the side of his neck.

Sophia received a similar reaction from Moyra, who leaned over to ask what on earth she had said to him. Sophia just smiled and lifted her champagne glass in a toast. 'To our future.'

Nino did not relax until the Luciano women had left the restaurant. Someone said it was actually Nino Fabio who coined the phrase '*Bella Mafia*' the description given of the four elegant women below their photograph in the papers next morning. *Bella Mafia*, all that was left of the once powerful Luciano family.

That night at the Sans Souci was the night Moyra got her first taste of a lifestyle she had only read about, perhaps dreamed of. It was unlike Las Vegas glamour or the hustle of New York, unlike anything she had ever known, because she felt inside her it was where she belonged.

The night was important for Rosa, too, because it would always stand out in her memory as the night she decided she wanted never to be poor, that her mother was right to fight for their inheritance. The night of the *Bella Mafia* was the night that Teresa tasted not just the most delicious food in the world, but the untouchable quality of wealth – the so-called sweet smell of success, of power, had been tantalizingly close, almost at her fingertips. To make it real would be a hard, rough climb, but she knew it was attainable.

That night, Sophia felt able to cope with her bereavement and her betrayal for the first time. There was now a possibility of starting her business again, of having the finances to do it, and the knowledge of how foolish she had been in the past gave her a renewed energy. She was determined never to allow it to happen again. She had Teresa at her side and, no matter what their differences had been, and no doubt would be, she was a powerful ally. Uppermost in her mind, hidden from the others, was Sophia's determination to begin the search for her son. She would, she decided, ask Pirelli to assist her; she would have no back-street detectives, she would instigate a full-scale investigation.

That evening would always stand out, because Teresa detected another side of her sister-in-law. They never discovered what she said to Nino, but it had been something that frightened him and, although Teresa knew she now had Moyra and her own daughter very much on her side, perhaps she had underestimated Sophia. But for now it appeared that she had been accepted as head of the family.

After selling Graziella's pearls, Teresa, Moyra and Rosa returned to Palermo. Sophia insisted on staying in Rome to finalize the sale of her apartment and deal with the bankers. She also wished to visit Nino Fabio.

Teresa had slept heavily, having not arrived back at the Villa Rivera until late at night. She was taken aback to find Luka sitting at the breakfast table in the morning, but said nothing.

He was drawing the layout for a kitchen garden for Graziella. Sitting opposite him, Rosa was buttering her toast.

Teresa sat down and Graziella immediately pointed at her head. 'Your hair, what have you done to your hair?'

'It's dyed, Mama,' said Teresa rather frostily.

'Well, I can see that, and I hear Moyra has gone white. I don't understand why you can't all be natural.'

'Perhaps, Mama, none of us has been blessed with your natural beauty. Some of us need a little assistance, me more than others. Moyra's hair, Mama, is not white, it's platinum, and mine is natural blonde.'

Graziella looked at Rosa. 'Well, if you say so, but Rosa's hair looks better without that dye. Do you see what we did to Johnny's hair? Adina cut it.'

Teresa nodded. 'I have eyes, Mama, and I really don't want to have breakfast as if I was sitting in a hair salon.'

Graziella pulled a face at Luka. She asked, 'Has Sophia had her hair cut?'

'No, Mama, she'll be back as soon as she's arranged to sell her apartment.'

'Oh, we had a visitor, he left you this.' Graziella handed over Rocco's calling card. 'He wanted to speak to you, about business. I said you were at the tile factory. I didn't like to tell him you were away. Papa never allowed outsiders to know our movements, it's safest, and I didn't like him. Maybe we should think about hiring someone to take care of the gates, so we know who is going in and out. Do you agree?'

Teresa murmured her agreement and read the card. Luka watched her, saw the way she turned it over in her hand. 'This'll be about the sale of the villa, I told you it was about the only thing Domino had settled. I doubt if we can get out of it, unless you particularly want to. It's very large just for you.'

Graziella blinked and looked down at her cup. The thought of being left there alone hurt her more than she could have imagined. Rosa leaned over and grasped her hand.

'You won't be alone, though, Grandmama. Wherever we go, you'll be coming too.'

Graziella smiled her thanks. Teresa gave Rosa a sharp look, 'It's settled, then, and it's a fair price.'

'There's your money, Mr Moreno. Want to count it?'

Teresa tossed the envelope on the desk. Luka slipped it into his back pocket. He hesitated, then said quietly, 'Joseph Rocco works for the Corleone family.'

'Thank you, Mr Moreno. What time will you leave?'

Luka's voice was soft, persuasive. 'Signora Luciano, please take care. Check Rocco out for yourself before you do any business with him – if not for yourself, for Graziella.'

'You seem to be on very familiar terms with my mother-in-law?'

He stared down at a spot on the carpet. 'One kilo of heroin will make a million dollars. The people who want your space, your legitimate trading name, will be junk dealers, and when they are made aware that you intend shopping around for the highest offer, the only valid contract will be the one to protect your life. The Corleones have sent their representative, Joseph Rocco, to see you personally. They can offer you, Signora Luciano, any price they choose, and you would be wise to take it.'

Teresa was unnerved by his quietness, but more by his knowledge of what she was trying to do. 'Did you go through *all* our private papers, Mr Moreno?'

Now he looked up, stared directly at her. His eyes, a moment ago so pale, were now a brilliant blue, but totally expressionless. She could not tell what he was thinking; as if behind his mask something scanned an inner dimension where words did not exist. Then a small, tantalizing, cherubic smile moved on his lips – Luka almost gave himself away, but he knew he must not alienate Teresa, she had to need him.

The sound of the doorbell interrupted them. Teresa crossed quickly to the window, but he was ahead of her. He lifted the blind, then let it snap back into place.

As Joseph Rocco was ushered into the study, Luka hurried across the hall, through the kitchen and into the garden. He found Rosa standing by his freshly dug vegetable patch.

She smiled at him. 'You certainly did a lot of work while we were away.'

He stuffed his hands deep in his trouser pockets and kept his distance from her, staring over the fence. He could see Rocco's waiting car, the bodyguard leaning casually against the porch, cleaning his nails.

Rosa moved closer. 'When are you going?' she asked.

'Today, maybe this afternoon.'

For a moment she looked disappointed. But he was paying no attention – he had spotted the nose of the car he had hired, partly hidden in the bushes. His whole body tensed and he cursed himself. He had forgotten he had left it there.

Luka knew he had to get rid of the car, and fast. He was so wrapped up in his thoughts that when Rosa innocently reached out to touch the gold heart at his neck, he reacted instinctively, twisting her roughly away from him.

He berated himself for his own foolishness, but she smiled and said it was all right. He took her hand away from her reddening cheek, concerned at first, but then he found himself staring curiously at her, fascinated by her soft, fresh skin. Her arms slipped around his waist, pulling him towards her. Not knowing what to do he offered no resistance, then bent his head and kissed her. It was a soft kiss, childish, passionless.

Graziella appeared at the kitchen door, wearing an overcoat and carrying a trowel. Luka waved as if the embrace had never occurred, then hurried across the garden to her side.

Dressed and ready to go to the tile factory, Moyra waited for Teresa in the hall. She checked her watch and listened at the study door. Hearing Teresa, then the lower tones of Rocco's voice, she opened the door a crack.

'Teresa, I'm ready to go when you are.'

'Go into the dining room, wait for me there.'

The door was firmly shut in Moyra's face. Her high heels clicked on the marble floor as she headed for the kitchen.

From the kitchen door, Moyra called to Luka, 'Teresa said you were leaving today.'

He came towards her and stood rather awkwardly at her side, without speaking.

'You married, Mr Moreno?'

He gave a lovely laugh and shook his head silently.

'You got real lady-killer eyes, Johnny, as blue as the sky, as deep as the sea.'

Luka thought for a moment, then said, 'Your eyes are like soft blue flowers.'

'What kind of flowers?'

He had never played this kind of bantering game before. He thought a moment, then replied, 'Forget-me-nots.'

She closed her eyes and leaned against the doorframe, enjoying the warmth of the winter sun on her face. He could see the powder and rouge on her cheeks, the uneven coating of mascara on her lashes and the glossy, shell-pink lipstick outlined in a darker colour. He could also see the tiny lines beginning to show around her pouting mouth.

'You know why they are called forget-me-nots, Moyra?'

She shook her head and her blonde curls caught the sun, bubbly, lovely curls without the usual stiffening lacquer – Sophia had told her it was old-fashioned.

Luka leaned closer until he could smell her perfume. 'Once, long ago, Moyra, a young man fell in love with a beautiful lady, and on the bank of a river she saw these small blue flowers. It was dangerous, but as she said she liked them and because they matched the colour of her eyes, he climbed down to pick her a single flower. The closer he went to the river, the steeper the bank became. He reached out his hand . . .'

Moyra watched him lift his hand as he leaned further and further out from the step . . . 'He caught a single flower . . . then he fell, tumbled into the wild waters. As he was swept away he held up his hand, with the little blue flower, and called out, "Forget me not!".' He half-fell forwards, looking back to smile at her.

'Is that a true story?'

He nodded.

'What happened to him?' she asked.

'He was swept away in the water. He drowned, Moyra.'

'You're having me on.'

Luka laughed. 'No, it's a true story Giorgio told me.' He sprang to his feet, knowing he had made a mistake.

'Who's Giorgio, then?'

Luka looked down into her upturned face. 'My brother.'

Joseph Rocco had left, and Teresa stood in the hallway, her face drawn and pale.

'Rosa, take your grandmother into town to get the groceries. You too, Moyra . . . I've got some paperwork to see to and I want to call Sophia. We'll go over to the factory this afternoon.'

A very disgruntled Moyra teetered out of the house, while Rosa helped Graziella down the front steps. Luka knew Teresa wanted to talk to him privately and he waited.

As soon as they were alone, she gestured for him to follow her into the study. Luka could see that her hand was shaking, and when she spoke her voice was strained, edgy. 'Joseph Rocco laughed at my proposition. The Corleones want us to finalize the sale of the villa – we can't back out, even if we wanted to. With the villa they want everything else. They will cover our debts and pay what they feel is a substantial amount to ensure that the Luciano women live in comfort – comfort, not luxury. What they offer is an insult. Worse, the amount decreases with every day that I do not agree to their terms.'

She started twisting her wedding ring around. Finally, she looked directly at him. 'He said that no other family would oppose them, that I was only wasting time by approaching them. He said I had no alternative but to accept their offer. I want to fight them, Mr Moreno. Their threats frighten me, but if need be, I'll go to the government.'

'They *are* the government. Take whatever they offer.'

Joseph Rocco had succeeded in frightening her and Luka wondered what else he had said. He watched as she poured herself a brandy and downed it so fast that it made her cough, but he was surprised when she faced him, because the fear was gone.

'If I personally go to the major families and offer them a group buy-out . . . Obviously there is now no question of us being able to lease sections, I will have to sell everything, but . . . what if I tell them about the Corleones' offer? Tell them that not only are the Corleones cutting them out, but that if they are allowed to take over, it will put the rest of them out of business?'

728

'You approach even one of them and it'll backfire. Someone will talk. You'll never get away with it.'

Teresa rubbed her head. 'OK, what if I have no intention of selling to any family in Palermo, but instead offer it to . . .' She flipped through her notebook. 'Here, there's an offer sent to Mario Domino from a man called Michel Barzini. It's not top money, but it's ten times the Corleones' offer. Have you ever heard of him?' Luka's eyes narrowed and he nodded. Teresa asked, 'Who does he work for?'

Luka shook his head. 'I've heard of him, he's a middleman, you know, a negotiator. Maybe the Americans were interested in forming a group to buy out the company. Barzini works out of New York, but I don't know which family he is affiliated to.'

Teresa began to pace the study. 'But if we all travel to New York, we can get to him? If necessary, ask for his protection? Then, if he agrees to buy us out, on whoever's behalf, they will handle the situation here. All I want is a fair price, our rightful inheritance, and I haven't come this far to be cheated, robbed, after all we have done.'

Luka stuffed his hands in his pockets and cocked his head to one side, watching her keenly. 'So you will sell to the Americans but not the Sicilians?'

'Yes.'

'If the Corleones suspect, you will all be in danger, you know that?'

Teresa agreed. 'We can stall them for a while, make up some excuse, maybe hint that we have other offers to consider.'

'When are they coming back?'

'We have to see them in two days.'

'Get them to come to you, here at the villa. Don't, whatever you do, go to them, you'll be forced to sign everything over there and then. There'll be no negotiations and they won't take into consideration that you are women. They want the Luciano company, full stop.'

'Yes, I know.'

Luka remained impassive. Teresa continued, wringing her hands nervously, 'If I am to put us all at risk, we will need someone to protect us, someone we can trust. You and I are bound to each other, you know everything there is to know about our situation, just as I know enough to have you arrested and charged with murder. As an incentive, you will be paid ten per cent, so whatever we make, you make. When we get safely to New York, when the deal is done, you will be free to do as you wish.'

Luka did not reply. She opened a drawer, took out the gun he had taken from Dante's club and laid it on the desk. 'Do we have a deal, Mr Moreno?'

Her eyes were bright, alert, her whole body tense and waiting. The effect these women had already had on Luka intensified. They were unaware that they had eased the torment he had always lived with, a torment he had never known how to control. Luka had lived half his life in some kind of shadow, locked deep inside him, and only now was it beginning to lift. Here in the villa the shadow seemed to be disappearing, as if he were at long last being allowed to step into the sun.

Sophia Luciano arrived back at the villa earlier than expected. She threw her coat over the rail and went in search of Teresa. She found her in the study, talking earnestly to Luka.

Sophia stood in the doorway and addressed herself to Luka. 'Do you mind leaving us? I need to talk to Teresa.'

Luka left quickly, giving Sophia a smile, which was ignored. But as he passed her, she caught his arm. 'Your hair . . .'

He ran the flat of his hand over the cropped crew cut. 'Graziella and Adina cut my dye off . . . You like it?'

Sophia raised an eyebrow, 'Graziella?' She turned to Teresa, 'He's making himself very much at home here, isn't he?' She turned back to Luka. 'Close the door, please.'

'Did you arrange to sell your apartment?' asked Teresa.

'Yes, at least that was simple enough. It's on the market . . . But Nino Fabio refused even to see me. I left a message that he could not refuse, suggesting that he come round to see me. By the time I got back to the apartment this was waiting, it's from his lawyers. He wants his designs returned, all of them that are still in my possession. I wouldn't even have them except they were left in my office . . .'

Teresa read the lawyer's letter. 'He wants his chunk of flesh, doesn't he? Not satisfied with ripping you off for years, he's trying to block you starting up again. Did you find out if he was the one who stole the machines?'

'How could I? He wouldn't even see me. He wouldn't have dared treat me like this when Constantino was alive.'

Teresa settled her glasses on her nose. 'Listen, right now we have more important things to discuss. If you feel bad about the way Nino Fabio treats you, then wait until you hear the latest. The fact that we have no one protecting us, no man to look out for us, that we are just women, means we got screwed out of our fortune and, Sophia, it means they are still doing it. Only now, they're not doing it behind our backs, they've come right out with it. Seems we have really sent some shock waves through the families. They think there must be someone behind us, you know, overseeing all the work and so on, perhaps even financing us, and they . . .'

Teresa chewed her lip, trying to hedge around the subject. 'The one thing Domino had virtually settled was the sale of the villa and the orchards. We agreed a good price. We cannot get out of the sale, it was agreed and signed by Graziella, and Domino banked the deposit. Where, in God's name, that's gone to I don't know, I can't trace it.'

She handed Sophia a card. 'That's Joseph Rocco, the card says real estate, it's a joke. He's a front man for the Corleone family, and they, Sophia, are the ones who have bought the Villa Rivera.'

Sophia scanned the card. 'So? Does it matter who we sell to? You said yourself it's a good price, and by the time we sell all the company . . .'

'No, Sophia, that's all we get. You see, they reckon it's such a generous offer that we should also include in the sale all rights to the waterfront properties, the ships, the entire company . . . Unless we accept it, starting from Monday, the price will go down . . . They want vacant possession by the end of the month.'

'They can't do this. Look, why don't I call Pirelli and ask him to help us?'

'Do you want to put Mama in danger? Rosa? We all

will be if they get to hear that the police are involved. We need someone to protect us, so I've hired Johnny . . .'

'Oh, no, no way . . .'

'Listen to me, just listen! We know we can trust him, because he has to trust us. One call to your precious Pirelli and he'll be arrested for Dante's murder.'

Sophia folded her arms. 'Sounds like you've already made your mind up, whether I like it or not.'

'You can back out. I've not even discussed it fully with the others because it is dangerous.'

'Did Moreno suggest this?'

'No, I put it to him, to see what he thought, and . . . Look do you want to know what we're going to do or not?'

Sophia nodded and gestured to Teresa to continue.

'OK, we stall the Corleones, give us time to leave Palermo. We get to New York and we sell to—'

'Wait a minute, what do you mean, stall?'

'We just make up excuses, ask them to come and see us, tell them we are still thinking about the deal. Then we get out fast. There's a guy called Michel Barzini, he's already made a reasonable offer to Mario Domino. This way we are clear of Sicily and they won't want to get involved in a fight with the States. Even if they did, we wouldn't be part of it.'

White-faced, Sophia said, 'Dear God, Teresa, if they found out! Wouldn't they send someone over to the States? They'd get us, wherever we were . . .'

'I know, and I've thought of that. We only agree to sell if they give us protection. If we are approached, we tell the Corleone family we had no option, Barzini threatened us. We have to play the innocent widows, incapable of dealing with the situation. That's how they think of us, so we play it to the hilt. Johnny thinks the only way we could possibly get away with it is to make sure the Corleones believe we are acting completely alone, have no idea what we are doing, no one behind us.'

'But, Teresa, we *are* alone, for God's sake.'

'Apart from Johnny, he'll look out for us until we get away.'

'One kid, there's five of us, how can he protect us, Teresa?'

Teresa shouted, 'So what do you suggest? Have you got any better ideas? Or do you just want us to accept the offer and get out? Haven't you been cheated enough? Used and betrayed enough? I have, and I won't take any more, Rosa won't, Moyra . . .'

'Do they know all this?'

Teresa walked to the door and yanked it open. 'No, but they will. We'll put it to the vote.'

'You have to include Graziella.'

'Fine, if that's what you want. Let's get them in here.'

Luka listened at the door and could tell by the raised voices that they would be closeted together for some time. Keeping out of sight of the study windows, he made his way towards the main gates, until he reached the shrubbery. He free-wheeled the Fiat out into the lane before starting up the engine and driving towards open country.

Luka had been correct. He returned almost an hour later and the women were still gathered in the study.

He hummed to himself as he made his way back to his room. He let himself in and lay on the bed, then sat up as he remembered the newspaper. Quickly, he retrieved it from beneath the mattress. He had taken it before Graziella had awoken, intending simply to read it, but had been shocked by the front-page story: 'Police step up hunt for suspect Luka Carolla.'

Luka skimmed the article, finding nothing that even hinted at any knowledge of his whereabouts, and his confidence was such that he almost laughed. Only almost, because what really worried him was the identikit picture and the description.

He tore the paper into scraps, feeling sure that Teresa couldn't have seen it, nor Rosa nor Moyra. They had been in Rome. For a moment he panicked; had it also been featured in the papers there? He began to wonder just how safe he was at the villa.

Teresa was sitting in the Don's old chair with Moyra, Graziella and Rosa facing her.

'Well, it's up to you, all of you, but we don't have much time. We've got to arrange all the travel, the removal, get everything cleared from the villa. I think if we go to Rome, fly from there, we have a greater choice of flights and we can drive all night, cross by ferry . . . We can be in New York within twenty-four hours.'

Moyra was twirling a curl around her fingers. 'You think this Barzini character will look after us?'

Teresa shrugged. 'We have all they want, plus we'll give them a fair price.'

Graziella pressed her hand to her knees. 'How much do you think we would receive from this Barzini?'

Teresa took a deep breath. 'I'd ask for twenty million, accept fifteen million.'

'Dollars or lire?' Moyra wanted to know.

'Dollars, Moyra. Don't be so dumb. Dollars, that's a good split between us.' Teresa was getting impatient. 'So, let's put it to the vote and get it over with. The more time we waste the less we have. So, if you all agree . . .'

Graziella was worried. 'We all travel together? Stay together?'

Teresa nodded. 'Yes, Mama, we stick together, it's safest.'

Moyra put her hand up as if she were in school. Teresa asked, 'Does that mean you're in?'

'No, I wanted to ask a question. How soon after we got to New York would we get the money?'

'As soon as Barzini agrees to pay us.'

'And we split it between us?' Moyra looked at Sophia as if for confirmation. She turned from the window.

'You all have to know how dangerous it is, you must know. Don't let the money persuade you, any of you.'

Rosa leaned forward. 'Without doing this, what do we get?'

Teresa sighed. She had expected them to be much easier, couldn't understand why they were hesitating. 'We split the proceeds from the sale of the villa. It'll be about one million dollars, Moyra – between us. Then what we can accrue from the smaller businesses . . . In all, I don't know. Maybe we would clear two million.'

Moyra's mind was working overtime. 'You can't buy a decent apartment in New York for that. I'm in.' She smiled having made her decision, and leaned back in her chair. 'Yeah, I'm in all right.'

Rosa followed suit, nodding to her mother. 'Me too, I'm in.'

Graziella stood up, 'Yes, I agree . . . and I think I have something that will help us.'

They all watched as she went to the safe. She turned the dial and paused. They virtually chorused the combination, having opened the safe so often.

Graziella took out a brown envelope. 'These are passports, for me, for anyone. All in different names. Papa and I used them when we went to America.'

Teresa smiled and held out her hand for them. 'Thank you, Mama.' She appeared to be scrutinizing the passports, saying casually, 'That leaves you, Sophia. Are you with us or not?'

'I guess I have no option. Yes, I'm in.'

They all watched as Teresa phoned Joseph Rocco, asking if he and his contacts would be patient as they had so much last-minute packing to do, and if they would pay Graziella Luciano the courtesy of coming to the villa rather than meeting in their offices. For the plan to work, it was vital that nothing was signed. To their relief, it was agreed. The widows had just one week to organize their trip to the States.

CHAPTER 31

COMMISSARIO PIRELLI had missed the press interview and the television news extra. He eased the tension with his Chief by saying he had not wanted to waste valuable time. They now had details of Luka Carolla's driving licence, which had been faxed to the States, and a description of his car. A flood of telephone calls were still coming in from the public.

Telexes coming in from New York were now more informative, and Pirelli had received confirmation that Luka Carolla had been educated in the States, having entered the country as the dead gangster's legitimate son. The confusion and delay had been caused by misinformation on his age and name. Pirelli was now hopefully awaiting further details and a more recent photograph.

The Fiat hired by Luka was found abandoned on the outskirts of Palermo, stripped of tyres and seats, but it was a jubilant Pirelli who received verification that the thumb and forefinger prints from the left hand, found on the driver's door, matched those taken from the glass in the Club Armadillo. He was sure they were Luka's.

Further forensic investigations reported a smear of blood, the common type 0, rhesus negative. Was their man wounded? They wasted time looking for their man in the hospitals, used valuable hours handing out Luka's description to doctors who might have treated him. Then, at long last, there was a positive reaction to the photofit picture.

By the time Pirelli and his men arrived at the small hostel, the room was already being stripped. Everything that could be removed was taken to the forensic laboratories, the rest checked for dabs. They had a long, arduous task ahead of them as the room had been rented to three occupants since Luka's stay.

The owner of the hostel, sweating with nerves, was driven to headquarters, where he was questioned for more than three hours. He had little information to give, having only seen Luka Carolla twice – once when he signed him in, and once when they had passed each other in the hallway. But Pirelli now had his most vital lead to Luka, his signature in the register as 'J. Moreno' . . .

Another piece of information further confused and delayed the issue. Luka, alias Moreno, the hotel owner assured the police, was not blond but dark-haired.

A major hitch developed for the widows at the last moment. Graziella received a summons to appear in court on the charge of attempting to murder Paul Carolla. Her lawyer said there was no way round it; she would have to appear, which might mean her travelling back to Sicily. After a hurried discussion they decided, as a precaution, that they would all leave the villa, but that Graziella and Sophia would stay in Rome.

Teresa turned to Luka, who was privy to the discussion, and suggested that he should go with them in case of any trouble. He hesitated, wanting to leave Italy more than they could ever have imagined; but they all turned to him and in the end he agreed. Graziella would travel back to Palermo for the hearing, then fly direct with Sophia and Luka to New York.

Sophia was worried that someone would get to know about the court appearance but Teresa refused to alter the arrangements. When they were alone, she told Sophia that she should now use her friend, Pirelli. It was vital that Sophia and Graziella be protected until they could leave Sicily.

Liza Pirelli arrived in Palermo to spend a weekend with her husband. She kept up a constant stream of chatter, hardly drawing breath for the entire journey to the apartment. Once installed she walked from room to room, complaining of the dust, the musty smell. She began to unpack while Pirelli opened his son's jigsaw puzzle. She slipped her arms around his neck. 'Are you pleased to see us?'

He kissed her affectionately. 'You'll see just how pleased tonight . . .'

She giggled provocatively; he had forgotten how pretty she was. She sat with her chin cupped in her hands, looking at him. 'Are you going to be here for Christmas, Joe?'

He shrugged. 'I hope not, we should wrap it up before then.'

'I've read about the Carolla boy.'

He sighed. 'You and thousands, but we still can't

trace him. He must have good contacts, somebody must be shielding him.'

Liza wrinkled her nose. 'You wouldn't think they would, knowing what he did.'

He gave her a glum smile. 'You never can understand people, my dearest, particularly in this city. The place is a sewer.'

His son rode his bike into the dining room and piped up, 'See, I need a bigger bike . . . Mama says no, but by Christmas I'll be even taller.'

Pirelli gave him a wink and tapped his nose. 'We'll see how many inches you can grow in three weeks. No promises, though.'

He could see Sophia, hear her voice, 'My babies, my babies . . .' He put his arms around his son, hugging him tightly, thinking what it must be like for Sophia, losing both her sons, finding them . . .

Liza shouted from the kitchen that everything was so ancient, she had never seen such an old gas cooker. Pirelli heard the gas pop and ran to see if she was all right. She turned with the box of matches in her hand.

'Are you OK?'

'Yes, minus an eyebrow. Have you cooked anything on this since you've been here?'

'No . . .'

'I didn't think so. Never mind, I'll get it sorted.'

He put his arms around her, kissed her cheek. 'I know you will, and I'm sorry about the holiday. Maybe at Christmas we can go skiing.'

They held each other, looked into each other's eyes. 'You look tired, why don't you have a lie down? And I'll come in and further exhaust you.' He laughed, loosening his tie.

As they reached the old iron bedstead, the phone rang. He pulled a face.

'Don't answer it, Joe, let it ring.' Liza tugged his hand, pulling him towards the bed, but he picked up the phone.

It was Ancora, who apologized, but he had a good fish on hook, a con doing life who wanted to make a deal. He knew Luka Carolla.

Pirelli sighed. 'Can't you handle it?'

'Sure I can, just thought you'd like to be in on it. The guy is called Tony Sidona, used to work for Carolla. He was picked up as an accessory to the Lenny Cavataio murder.'

Liza was kissing Pirelli's neck, undoing his shirt. 'I'll be there, wait for me,' he said.

As soon as she heard the words, she flopped back, arms outstretched. 'I don't believe it, I come for a weekend, I'm only here two minutes and he's going out!'

He kissed her, grinning. 'But I'll be back. Get in the kitchen, you hussy.' As he reached the door he turned again. 'I love you, see you later, OK?'

Tony Sidona would only talk after it was agreed that the government would review his case, and he insisted on having it in writing, with his lawyer present. Pirelli, tired, wanting to get back to his wife, agreed to everything. He was becoming more and more irritated by the arrogant Sidona by the second.

'Let's hear what you have to say, and make it quick.'

Sidona nodded to his lawyer. 'OK, you won't back down?'

'We've agreed to have your case reviewed, you know what that means, you'll get an early parole. So, let's go.'

'And it's agreed that anything I say won't be used against me?'

'Yes,' Pirelli hissed, getting really angry. Ancora saw the eyebrows meet and wondered what had got him into such a foul mood. Then he remembered that Liza had arrived and understood.

Sidona received a brief nod from his lawyer. He began. 'OK . . . Carolla came to Palermo with me an' another guy. His kid, this Luka you're looking for, I can tell you, nobody liked. He was a pain in the ass, real weird. He used to hang around the New York apartment, get in everyone's way, always just hanging around.'

Pirelli began to relax, offering Sidona a cigarette which he accepted but stuck behind his ear. 'Did you ever see Carolla mistreat his son?' he asked.

Sidona shook his head. 'Carolla used to try everything to off-load his kid, get him some kinda work. He wasn't heavy in the brains department, got kicked out of every school.'

Sidona spent ten minutes trying to remember the names of the schools, until at last Pirelli got one that he could check. He still had no recent photograph of Luka Carolla. The meeting was worth this information alone.

Sidona continued, 'Put him in a pizza parlour, kid was a fiasco. Tried him in a few gambling joints, you know, runnin' the bets. Fucked up.' He rubbed his head. 'There was one time I saw him lay into Luka. He found a cupboard full of weapons. He shelled out dough like a peanut vendor to the kid, never asked what he was spendin' it on, until he opened this fuckin' cupboard an' found a fuckin' arsenal in there.'

Pirelli stubbed out his cigarette and lit another. 'Did he have any drills, dentist's drills?'

'I dunno, but he had everythin' you need for customizin' his toys. Carolla beat the shit out of him over that. Next the kid gets this knife, a martial-arts knife, you know, a butterfly thing? Every time you looked at him the kid was flicking it open, made some kind of sling in his sleeve. I didn't think he could use it, looked more like it was some kinda circus act, openin' and shuttin' it, slidin' it down his arm into the palm of his hand, and the blade was like a fuckin' razor. He had plasters all over his fingers where he cut himself.'

Pirelli interrupted to ask, 'Do you think Luka cared for his father?'

'Oh, yeah, I guess so.'

Pirelli looked at his watch and gestured for Sidona to continue.

'So, now we got this kid round our necks, and he's a fuckin' nightmare. Questions, questions . . . Jesus Christ, he never stopped talking. We discover that Lenny's holed up in this supposed safe house, hotel or whatever, and he's got two guards day and night. I mean, no fucking way could we blast our way in, they got one guy inside the room, one outside, another on the reception desk.'

Sidona looked at his lawyer. 'You sure I'm OK sayin' all this?'

Pirelli said, 'We made a deal, go on.'

'Well, I can't get in the hotel, right? One look at me an' I'm gonna cause suspicion, same went for my partner. I lived in New York for twenty years, but I still sound like a Sicilian, know what I mean? But this kid don't have no accent, and he's got the freaky blond hair. Christ only

744

knows who his mother was because he certainly didn't take after Paulie Carolla.'

'This partner, he got a name?'

Sidona considered a moment. 'Look, you wanna hear about Luka Carolla? I don't know his name, understand me?'

Pirelli sat back. 'OK, go on. Can't blame me for trying.'

'Well, the kid walks straight in, all American innocence. He's a student, gets a room. Second floor, balcony. So we climb in that way. Now all we gotta do is make it to the next floor and to Cavataio. Fuckin' kid does it again, he walks out of the elevator, we're in it behind him, and we put it on hold. Luka walks up, asks if he's on the fifth floor, dangles his key. My partner takes the guard out, kicks open the door, one guard, three of us, right? Fuckin' guy backed off so fast, he didn't even try to protect Lenny. Dropped his shooter as soon as he saw we meant business, yelped that he had two kids and a fuckin' white rabbit – you know the score.'

At no time did Sidona hint that he had any part in the killings, other than as an accessory. 'My partner saw to the guard, then hit Lenny Cavataio. One bullet, here . . .' He indicated his right ear, and his voice dropped. 'He was dead, we could have walked out. No problem. But the next minute Luka's pulled Cavataio's pants down. I said, "What the fuck?" He said, "Gettin' a small present for my father." He cut his testicles off, I'm not kiddin', just whipped them off with this fuckin' knife.' He shook his head from side to side.

Pirelli stubbed out his cigarette. 'Go on, then what?'

'Well, he wasn't satisfied with just that, he had to show

whoever found the body that no one talked against his father . . . He slashed out Cavataio's tongue. There was all this blood, me an' my partner standin' there wantin' to get the fuck out of it, but he wouldn't leave, he was like crazy . . . He's got these eyes, eyes that go really pale, you know, freak's eyes. We both turned and walked out, left him in there. We got as far as the elevator and the two relief guys walked straight into us. I made it to the next street before they picked me up.'

Pirelli said, 'So you were in jail when they brought Carolla in?'

'Yeah, that's right. And if he was mad about Cavataio givin' evidence, you should have seen the guy go stark staring mad when he was told about Luciano taking his fuckin' place.'

'You ever hear anything about Luka's visits to Carolla?'

'No, we was in different blocks, he was segregated. Lot of the cons had it in for him.'

'You know if Carolla ordered the deaths of the Luciano family?'

Sidona pulled a face. 'Come on, Carolla was a made guy, lotta contacts, but he wasn't that important. That was a Godalmighty hit.'

'Who would you say organized it?'

Sidona became shifty and tucked his hands beneath his chair. 'I dunno . . .'

'Two little boys shot, an entire family wiped out.'

'Look, I dunno anything about that, OK? I made a deal to tell you about Luka Carolla, that's all, no more.'

'Which US family do you think could have played a part in it?'

'Oh, shit, I dunno. I swear on my mother's life, I dunno.'

'Would Luka Carolla know these American people? I mean, could he have been involved in any part of it?'

Sidona was sweating, and ran his hands through his hair. 'He met a lot of family over here, must have had the contacts in the States, he was Carolla's son.'

Pirelli leaned forward and gripped Sidona's knee tightly. His voice was a low whisper, hardly audible to either Ancora or the lawyer.

'One name, gimme one name you think might know something about the Luciano murders.'

Sidona was scared, they could smell it. He leaned forward as if to speak, then sat back. Pirelli held his knee tighter, leaned closer. Sidona licked his lips and finally leaned forward, close to Pirelli's face, whispered, 'Michel Barzini, maybe.'

Pirelli was finished and he put an arm around Ancora's shoulder. They headed for the parking bays. 'You know, I think we've gone about as far as we can. We've got enough evidence to put him away for the rest of his life.'

Ancora opened his car door. 'What's sick about it is, we find him, any lawyer's going to plead insanity. In the end, how can you say that's justice for what he's done? They had it right in the old days, hanged, drawn and quartered. For this creature I'd do it personally.'

Pirelli slammed the car door. 'Yep, but first you have to find him.'

Pirelli thumped the bonnet of the car and watched it drive away before he moved over to his own car. He was tired, perhaps that was why he felt so depressed.

As he drove out of the car park and into the square the workmen were already hauling the twenty-foot Christmas tree into position to beat the rush-hour traffic. Christmas? He heard her soft, pleading voice, 'My babies, my babies . . .'

One week after the call to the Corleones a black Mercedes Benz turned in at the driveway of the Villa Rivera. The Mercedes was followed by an English Jaguar, also black. The meeting was about to take place. Teresa hurried to the door and called to the women to be ready and waiting, as their visitors had arrived.

Luka studied the men in the cars. 'You've got the *consigliere*, don't know the other guy with him. In the second car is Joseph Rocco and a couple of made guys.'

'What does that mean?'

'Well, you're not important enough to get the big man himself or his under-boss. The *consigliere* is their counsellor, like a lawyer.'

'Can we trust him?'

'Yeah, they've sent him to do the deal. His name's Carmine something or other . . . I'll get up to the roof to see if they've got anyone on foot.'

The two cars stopped in front of the villa. The men in the Mercedes remained seated until Rocco got out and opened the door for them. The *consigliere* and his companion looked like respectable bankers, white-haired, wearing dark suits, sombre ties and whiter than white shirts.

Luka eased open the window of the bedroom above the porch and crawled, flat on his belly, towards the edge of the roof.

748

'Stay with the cars?' an incredulous voice asked below. Luka peered over as Rocco turned away, hands on hips. 'Stay with the cars? Me?'

'Yeah, you . . .'

'How long do you want me to wait? I got business to see to, I got a property deal goin' down. You want a car hop, get one of the guys to do it.'

No one replied and the four men disappeared under the porch. Rocco stared after them, his face tight with anger. He called, 'I can't wait long, I don't wanna lose this deal . . .'

Adina ushered the men towards the dining room. The two bodyguards stood back politely and remained in the hallway. They stood like sentries, arms folded, as Adina came out and went to the study door and tapped.

'Signora, your guests are here.'

The women filed in, led by Graziella, who took her husband's position at the head of the table. Only she was veiled; the others, bejewelled and sophisticated, formed a line beside her to greet their visitors. Graziella's hands were shaking as she tried desperately to remember all her instructions. Teresa gave her a brief nod to begin.

'Please allow me to present my daughter . . . Sophia Luciano, widow of Constantino, mother of Carlo and Nunzio . . . Teresa Luciano, widow of Alfredo . . . Her daughter Rosa, who lost Emilio Luciano, her fiancé . . . And Moyra Luciano, the widow of my youngest son, Frederico. I am Don Roberto Luciano's widow, Graziella Rosanna Di Carlo Luciano.'

Teresa gave her mother-in-law a tiny smile. She had done it perfectly. Unexpectedly, Graziella continued, 'I

749

am sorry that Don Camilla could not be present himself, he must be unwell? Please give him our condolences. And you are . . .?'

Graziella was majestic, and Teresa was impressed. When the two men introduced themselves she stretched out her hand to be kissed. Then Teresa seated them all around the table and took over the meeting. She spoke deferentially, her head slightly bowed.

'Signori, I thank you for coming. I now speak for all of us, and would like to say how very much we appreciate Don Camilla's most generous offer. We will vacate the villa by the end of this month, and hope that our request for an extra three weeks will not inconvenience Don Camilla. We are unable to leave before as the apartment we have purchased here in Palermo is being refurbished. We wish the Corleones well, may they have a full and happy life here at the Villa Rivera.'

'*Grazie*, signora, *grazie* . . .'

Luka continued to watch Rocco from behind the shutters as he inhaled the cigarette smoke and tilted his head to blow a perfect smoke ring, then wandered towards the fence by the kitchen garden. He leaned his elbows on the fence, looked around and walked back to his car. He started the engine and reversed the Jaguar towards the lane that led to the back of the villa. The car stopped, then moved forwards a fraction and it looked as though Rocco was going to drive away, but then he stopped again, suddenly. Rocco turned and stared at the garages, the old stables.

Luka was not sure what to do; if Rocco entered the

garage he would see the packing cases, and the women's luggage in the cars, ready for their departure. Would he be suspicious? At this very moment the women were turning down the Corleone offer, lying through their teeth and pretending that they were going to offer the companies to the other families, and remain at the villa for another month. If Rocco told them what he had seen, they would be in trouble.

Teresa smiled, passing over the deeds to the villa, and both men nodded and smiled in return. They presumed that, by handing over the deeds, she was agreeing to the completion of the sale of the entire Luciano holdings. Their faces fell as Teresa said, 'We also take this opportunity to refuse our dear friend Don Camilla's offer for the Luciano companies. We will leave all the financial arrangements for the sale of the villa and its contents to our lawyers, who have worked so well on our behalf during this tragic time. If you wish to speak to them, they await your instructions.'

'Signora, did you understand Don Camilla's offer?'

'Oh, yes,' Teresa answered, 'Signor Rocco made it most clear, but . . . after discussing it with the lawyers and with Don Scarpattio and Don Goya, we were persuaded by Don Dario and Don Bartolli that the Luciano holdings were of such value to them all that each should have the chance to purchase sections of the waterfront areas, particularly as that will also give them access to the cargo vessels and cold-storage warehouses. As the factories are not at present productive, they, too, would make valuable storage areas. Then, of course, the vineyards and groves, sadly destroyed by drought and neglect, could, we have been assured, be productive again in two years.

'According to our lawyers the contracts do not include the American holdings. You must understand, we are just five women who have no interest in the complexities of the business and have simply placed everything in their hands. With the subsequent offers from America you will understand our confusion and accept our apologies for the delay. Until we are told by our legal representative to accept Don Camilla's offer we must, sadly, decline at this stage to sign any documents. Thank you again, and please give our most respectful good wishes to Don Camilla. We hope he will pay us a visit before we leave. If you wish to discuss the matter again, we will be here. I would also like to take this opportunity to thank your associate, Joseph Rocco, who was kind enough to suggest that we approach the other families. As I have said, we are dependent on the advice of others and appreciate all the help and kindness that has been shown to us.'

Teresa stepped away from the table and held out her hand to assist Graziella. Both men rose quickly as the women left the room, just as they had entered, together.

Joseph Rocco cupped his hands around his face and peered through the Rolls-Royce window, puzzled. He squeezed past the crates and went to the trunk of the car, opened it, and looked at all the cases. He even read the label on one, then, leaving the trunk open, he went further towards the back of the garage and bent over a packing case. He read the neatly written shipping labels, with the date clearly visible. He whistled through his teeth; there was not actually anything suspicious, he knew the women were vacating the villa. He squeezed amongst the crates again, lifting his jacket so as not to snag it. Suddenly the heavy, electrically operated garage doors moved back into place . . .

'Eh, what is this? What's going on?'

He had no cause for alarm, he didn't even attempt to run the last few feet towards the closing doors. Only when the heavy, stinking blanket covered him did he start fighting, trying to free himself and reach his gun. He lost his balance, falling against one of the crates, and rolled to one side, frantic to get away from the blanket, to get it off his face.

The first blow hit the side of his head and dazed him, but he managed to stagger to his feet. At last he was able to pull the blanket off his head, but the next blow thudded into his scalp. He sank slowly on to his knees, still conscious, and moaned. The third blow, the shovel coming down blade first, almost decapitated him.

Luka panted, wheezing from the effort. The pain in his shoulder was excruciating, and he was afraid he had reopened the freshly healed wound. He put the shovel down and bent over Rocco, knowing without checking his pulse that he was dead.

Adina closed the door behind the Corleone representatives, who paused only a moment when they realized that Rocco's car was missing, then they drove off hurriedly.

The men were silent, completely controlled; it was a minor setback and would be simply dealt with. The widows would now be forced to agree to the offer, it was no longer negotiable. But then, it never had been, that was just Don Camilla being courteous, a show of respect for the women. Now they would find out that they had been very foolish to abuse that respect.

A short time later the women were preparing to leave, and were doing a last-minute check on the rooms. Moyra slammed the lid shut on her make-up bag and scuttled down the stairs. 'I'm just gonna put this in the trunk, then I'm all packed. Only I wanted to put this in last so it's accessible.'

No one was listening to her, they were all so intent on doing their own last-minute packing.

As Moyra pressed the button to operate the garage doors, she noticed Joseph Rocco's car parked outside. She paid little attention, just waited for the door to swing up and over.

She stepped forward and froze . . . Her mouth opened like a goldfish, her eyes popped wide. Her shriek was so long in taking off that Luka had time to reach her side. He put his hand over her mouth.

'Shut up, Moyra, shut up! Moyra, if I take my hand away, will you keep quiet? Moyra?'

'Mmmmmm, mmmmmmm . . .' She nodded as best she could.

He took his hand away and she screamed blue murder, pounding her fists at him, trying to get out of the garage. He pushed her roughly to one side and pressed the button to close the door.

'Oh, no, no, don't hurt me . . . Oh my God . . .'

Luka was covered in blood, his hands, his shirt, even his shoes and trousers.

Teresa was ticking off items on a list when Moyra, white-faced, lurched into the room. Her voice was high-pitched, verging on hysteria as she stammered, 'Teresa, w-will you c-come with me. . .'

'What is it? What's the matter?'

'I can't tell you, just come out to the garage.'

Teresa turned away from the shrouded body, feeling sick.

'I had to do it,' Luka explained, 'he was opening the cases, he knew we were leaving. But they don't know he came back here, they drove off . . .'

'What . . . What are you going to do with him?'

Luka had wrapped the body in an old blanket. 'Put him in the trunk of his car. I'll drive it some place and dump it.'

Once the bloodied figure was out of sight the tension lightened. Teresa asked Luka quietly, 'Why didn't you just knock him out?'

'Look, I did what I had to do, there's no need for the others to ever know about it. Especially Graziella. But if he had reported back what he saw here you'd never have got away and . . . Maybe it'll work out for the best.'

'What do you mean?'

'Well, they're not going to think a mere bunch of women did it, are they?'

Moyra let out a shriek, 'Oh my God, Teresa, look! It's the truck from the factory, they'll see the car!'

Coming down the drive was one of the Luciano

755

trucks, ready to take the crates into storage. Teresa turned to Luka. 'Hide the car, move it round the back, hurry! And you'll have to burn everything you're wearing, don't let Graziella see you like that.'

Luka could not take the car any great distance as he had to get back to the villa, so he drove by the back streets as much as possible to a multi-storey car park on the outskirts of Palermo. He tossed the ticket away and parked the car on the fifth floor. Just as he was getting out, the car phone rang. He was startled at first, then smiled and picked it up.

The voice was distorted at first because of the concrete building. 'Joseph, is that you?'

'Si . . .'

'Where the fuck have you been? Hello? I dunno why you use this make, you never get a good line. I told you to get one same's I got . . . Rocco? You there?'

'Si . . . I gotta go, leave town for a few days.'

'You kiddin' me?'

Luka laughed, then raised his voice to a singsong, 'I'm kidding . . .'

The voice went silent, then after a moment the man said, 'Who the fuck is this?'

'Leave the Luciano women alone, pass it around. They are protected, understand? Joseph Rocco's dead.'

Two hours later Rosa, Moyra and Teresa left the villa. All the crates had been taken and they were still on schedule. Luka had burned his clothes on a bonfire in the garden, together with the stained blanket and spade.

Graziella thought nothing of his behaviour as she knew there was a lot of paperwork to be burnt, all the private letters and papers from the Don's office.

Graziella, Sophia and Luka gave last-minute instructions to Adina, before they, too, were on their way.

Adina crumpled her sodden handkerchief. This was the end of an era and she knew it.

'*Arrivederciiii*, Signora Luciano, *arrivederciiii*.'

Graziella gave her a small wave. 'Goodbye, Adina, this is goodbye.'

Sophia turned the car and headed slowly down the driveway. Adina waved frantically. 'Write to me, take care . . . God bless you . . .'

Luka turned round in the back seat, put his fingers to his lips and blew her a kiss. He could not see her face, did not hear her cry as the car disappeared through the gates.

The last time Adina had seen Michael Luciano alive was the day he was driven back to the mountain hideout. As the Mercedes moved off down the drive Michael had turned, lifted his fingers to his lips and blown his mother a kiss. Adina felt chilled to her soul; it was, she was sure, a bad omen.

CHAPTER 32

COMMISSARIO JOSEPH Pirelli was now in receipt of a photograph sent from the United States. It had been taken at the last college Luka was known to have attended, when he was fifteen years old. After mid-term he had simply never come back.

The few boys that had known him could be questioned, but none had continued their friendship with him after he left. In the opinion of the education authorities he was a disturbing influence and really required psychiatric treatment.

Pirelli called a refresher meeting of everyone involved in the case. They crowded into his stuffy office, some perched on the edge of the desk, some standing or leaning against the walls. Pirelli was standing in front of his notorious 'wall of death', where the photographs of Luka's many victims were pinned up.

Pointing to the photos, he began quietly, 'I am sure, I would stake my entire career on it, that one man is responsible for all these murders. Any day now they'll pull the rug from under us – we've had more manpower, more hours on this one investigation than any other case in this city. But if you divide those hours among these faces here, it doesn't add up to much for each victim. But if we find Luka Carolla, it will end this investigation.'

Pirelli tipped his overflowing ashtray into the bin and was about to continue when his phone rang. His face lit up as he listened, then he smiled broadly and replaced the phone. 'We got our break, security guards at Rome Airport are holding a guy, he's got a ticket in the name of Moreno, Johnny Moreno.'

Teresa, Moyra and Rosa's plane had already taken off. They didn't even see the young student arrested. The guards took him out of the departure lounge and he was held in the airport customs area to await the arrival of Commissario Joseph Pirelli.

The two remaining first-class tickets, originally bought for Sophia and Graziella, Teresa had handed out to two hitchhikers who could not believe their good fortune. However, they had not been on the flight, but had changed them for tickets to Los Angeles.

In his entire career, Pirelli had never felt such severe and draining disappointment. He took one look at the student in custody and knew he was not Luka Carolla, not Johnny Moreno. Pirelli kicked at the wall with frustrated rage, and his foot went through the partition. A terrible coughing fit forced him to sit down, and his face changed colour as he hacked and spluttered into his handkerchief.

Pirelli was still raging when he called his Palermo headquarters. Ancora had to ask him to repeat himself, then he too felt the disappointment. 'I'm sorry Joe, but it means one thing, he's still around. Why do you think he didn't get on the plane?'

Pirelli snapped that he had probably got cold feet. Ancora asked if Pirelli would come straight back, and he replied that he would probably take a short trip to Milan, to his own home, to change his clothes and maybe take a short nap – he was exhausted.

Ancora chortled. 'Yeah! I heard that one. Give your wife my best!'

'My wife, you fat slob, is in Palermo, she's staying there until this bloody case is wrapped up. An' you can do me a favour, let her know I'll be back late, she'll hit the roof when she knows where I am so tell her I'm . . . tell her anything, OK!'

Safe in Rome, Sophia and Luka made up Graziella's bed. Already the apartment showed signs of Sophia's imminent departure. All her personal belongings were packed, the sale agreed subject to contract.

Luka was to occupy what had been Sophia's sons' bedroom. The bunk beds were all that was left to remind her of the children. There were no toys, no clothes, everything had been taken away.

Graziella was preparing for bed later that night when Luka passed her door on his way to the bathroom. He stopped and watched her in her white cotton nightdress, brushing her hair. The long braids she usually wore coiled in a bun were now loose. She placed the silver-backed brush on the dressing table and picked up a worn black Bible. She had not noticed him and he moved on, soundlessly. By the time he had washed and cleaned his teeth, Graziella's light was out, although her door was still slightly ajar.

Sophia jumped. She had not heard Luka enter the kitchen. 'I couldn't sleep, do you want a drink?' she asked.

He shook his head and sat down opposite her. On the table were a tumbler of whisky and a small pill bottle. He bent his head to read the label, but she picked up the bottle and slipped it into her pocket.

'Do you mind me sitting with you?' he asked.

She shook her head and shrugged slightly. The ashtray was full of half-smoked cigarette ends, and he watched as she picked it up and emptied it into a waste bin.

'Rosa was telling me you're having a lot of trouble with a designer, is that right?'

She sighed and rinsed the ashtray under the tap. He could see that her hair, now uncoiled, reached almost to her waist, like Graziella's. It was dark and silky, and he had an almost uncontrollable impulse to touch it, but he didn't move. Sophia dried the ashtray with kitchen paper and brought it back to the table.

'Maybe I can sleep now . . .'

'You haven't finished your drink.'

She looked at the tumbler, picked it up and drank, then took it to the sink. As she held the glass under the running water, he was fascinated by her movements, her hands with their long, delicate fingers and almost white nails. They were unlike Moyra's, they weren't fake, but perfect ovals with large half-moons at the cuticle.

She dried the glass carefully and reached up to put it

761

away in the cupboard. Her satin dressing gown parted, opening to the thigh, and he knew she was naked beneath it. As she turned back to him, the top of her gown opened just a fraction and he looked away. He couldn't see, but he knew that the crease between her full breasts would be showing. He wanted so much to turn and look but he didn't.

'What did Rosa tell you about Nino?' Sophia wanted to know. She was twisting her long hair around her fingers.

'Nothing much, just that he had, I think she said, "ripped you off".' His legs were shaking and he squeezed his buttocks together, feeling himself harden. He dropped his hands into his lap beneath the table. His whole body tingled with heat and he knew his cheeks were turning red.

'Well, you could say that. Probably my own fault, I was very foolish. My husband warned me not to trust him.'

Luka had changed his position on the hard chair. 'Do you . . .' he pressed his erect penis between his hands . . . 'Do you want to tell me about it?'

She bit her lower lip and unconsciously ran her hands down the satin of her dressing gown, outlining her breasts, and tightened the sash. The whisky and the Valium were making her slightly woozy, but completely relaxed. 'Not now. I think I'll go to bed. Will you turn off the lights? I think everywhere's locked up, but I suppose you'll check.'

As she left the room he came, soaking his pyjamas. The relief made him sigh, a quiet moan of pleasure.

In the darkness of the children's room, hurrying to

get out of his semen-filled pants, he tripped and fell to the floor, landing on his bad shoulder. He winced with pain and kicked his pyjama bottoms away, angry at his own clumsiness. Then he stripped off his shirt and checked his wound, easing away the sticking plaster that held the small dressing in place. It was clean, and he tossed the lint into the waste bin.

The gold heart at his throat glittered and he touched it tenderly, then took it off. He held the locket above his head, swinging it, until his eyes drooped and he slept.

Luka overslept and found Graziella sitting alone at the breakfast table, but before he could ask about Sophia she walked in, already fully dressed. He quickly busied himself pouring coffee so she would not see that he had blushed. He could smell her perfume, a soft, powdery smell, not too strong. He asked if she had already had coffee.

'Yes . . .' She leaned over to kiss Graziella. Her gleaming hair, scraped back from her face and tightly coiled, made her face look severe. She wore a smart, charcoal-grey suit and dark-grey stockings, but her white silk shirt was open at the neck and he could see, as she bent over Graziella, a minuscule fragment of her white lace brassiere.

'Will you take care of Mama, Mr Moreno? I shouldn't be more than a few hours. Did you sleep well?'

Luka nodded. Always immaculate himself, he was angry now that he had come to breakfast in such a hurry.

Sophia walked into the lounge and began putting papers into a slim, black leather briefcase. Luka pushed his chair back and followed her. He saw her close the case, then open a drawer and take out a bottle. She unscrewed the top.

'Would you like me to drive you?'

She turned with a guilty look, her eyes wide and startled. Three tiny yellow pills dropped to the floor and rolled. Immediately Luka was on his knees picking them up, his hand close to her slim ankles, her fine kid shoes. He wanted to touch her . . . When he stood up, he was near enough to feel her warmth and smell again the soft, powdery perfume.

'I have a headache,' she said guiltily. Her confusion gave him confidence.

'I'll bring the car around to the front entrance.'

He hurried to his room before she could argue. Quickly he combed his hair, changed his shirt and put on one of the suits he had taken from the Villa Rivera. The suit did not fit particularly well as it had been one of Alfredo's, left after the funeral. As he passed reception, he noticed the doormen's office door was open and one of their grey uniform caps was lying on the desk. He took it.

Sophia appeared not to notice the effort he had made. She didn't smile when he doffed the cap, turning to face her in the back seat.

'I'm your chauffeur, do I look OK?'

The hat was a trifle large, but he took it off and stuffed tissues in the inside band, then tried it on again.

'Could we go? I don't like to leave Mama for too long.'

She sat to one side in the back of the car, her eyes closed, legs crossed. Luka tilted the rear-view mirror a fraction in the hope that she would open her legs a little

. . . Her elbow was propped on the armrest, her hand covered her brow. She sat like that for most of the journey, only occasionally dropping her hand to give him directions.

Sophia was in her lawyer's office for more than three quarters of an hour, and when she returned to the car her mood was more distant than ever. She sat in the back seat again.

'I have to go to Milan, Nino Fabio is working from there. You can either drive me there or go back to Mama, and I'll make other arrangements.'

'No, I'll take you.'

Sophia reached for the car phone and dialled. Graziella answered and Sophia told her she would be gone longer than she had anticipated as she was on her way to Milan. Graziella assured her she would be all right, she would go out and buy some groceries.

Luka drove out of the city and on to the highway, heading for Milan, watching her as she opened the small bar in the back of the car. He watched her drink the vodka and take another of her little yellow 'aspirins'. Then she lit a cigarette and caught him watching her.

'I wish you would stop looking at me, it's very unnerving. I can see you doing it, you know. If you're spying on me, it's really not worth it. You can tell Teresa that I take about four a day, Valium, and a sleeping tablet now and then . . .'

They did not speak again for the rest of the journey. Once they got to Milan she was able to direct Luka down the back streets to what had once been warehouses and were now converted into luxury apartments and a few offices. They drew up beside the tall building, freshly painted and yet retaining many of the original features.

Luka made no effort to open the car door for her, but watched her as she entered the building. He waited for half an hour, then left the car and entered the building himself. It was now past two o'clock in the afternoon.

Luka checked the company names on the door, then walked down the stone corridor and called the old cargo lift which was still in use.

At the third floor he pulled the lever to stop the lift on the white markings and stepped out into a white-painted, cavernous space. A number of doors led off, but there was no indication of which was Fabio's workroom. Only the tell-tale potted plants gave away the fact that the building was no longer a goods warehouse.

He followed the murmur of voices through a room filled with dummy models to a door at the opposite end. On the other side was a carpeted reception area with a shiny black desk and more potted plants. A flamboyantly lettered sign, in gold, told Luka that he had found 'Nino Fabio'.

To his left he could hear the low hum of machinery. However, the voices, louder and more distinct now, led him straight on to where the space had been divided into offices and showrooms designed by Fabio and painted in bright yellows and peaches. All the doors were glass-panelled with signs: Design Department, Export Department, Showroom . . . Luka paused, turning this way and that until he heard Sophia's voice. She was in the room at the very end, with Nino's name on the closed door.

*

Nino threw the rolled-up drawings across the room. He loved to throw things around to make a point. 'If I let you have the entire '86 – '87 collection my reputation will *suck*! All that frilled and swathed crushed fabric is dead! I'm not doing this to get back at you in some perverse way. Why should I? I'm doing this for my own self-preservation . . . I hate those old designs. You start bringing them out under any label and they are still old Nino Fabio. The answer is no. If you want to open a boutique, fine, go ahead, get another designer, if you can find one. But this one, sweetheart, is not yours to be had.'

'You know I don't have the finances for that, Nino.'

'And that's my fault, I'm sorry. But all I can do is warn you. If you go ahead then I'll sue you, my company will sue you. You can't win, Sophia . . . You want some advice, don't bother. You could never have succeeded without me to begin with.'

'Please, just release a few of them, so I can start again. My lawyer's drawn up a very fair deal, you'll get a percentage.'

'Sophia, please, we've said all there is to say. Everyone will be coming back from lunch. I don't really think you want this spread over every gossip column, because you know that's what will happen if these boys get to hear. The walls have ears.'

Sophia stubbed out her cigarette. 'I don't appear to have any record of the sales of the machines, taken not only from my own premises but also from the warehouse used for the so-called mail-order lingerie business. Where are my machines, Nino?'

He shrugged. 'I haven't the slightest idea. I haven't

been there since the day I saw you there. Maybe the manager, De Silvo, took possession of them, I don't know. I can't help you.'

'I see, so you won't mind if I look around your machinists? If I find one, Nino, then I'll have to charge you with theft.'

'You look wherever you like, be my guest. I don't have your machines, Sophia, I have nothing belonging to you and I don't want anything, just as I don't want you trying to resurrect your business behind my back. You use one design, one, and it won't be you charging me with theft but the other way round. Is that understood?'

Nino and Sophia turned in surprise as Luka walked in. He went straight to Sophia and took her elbow.

'Your car is waiting, Signora Luciano . . .'

Sophia stood in silence as they descended in the lift, her hands clenched at her sides, her face set. When Luka raised the iron bar, she ducked under it and hurried out to the car.

By the time Luka was in the driving seat, Sophia was blazing. 'How dare you interrupt me like that! How dare you walk in like that!'

His blue eyes were angry as he leaned over the seat and pointed at her. 'You are a Luciano. You want that dickhead to sign papers, there are ways of getting him to sign. But you never beg, never beg, not you . . . You don't need him.'

He watched her open her handbag, searching frantically.

768

'And you don't need those.'

'Mind your own damned business! I don't need you or anyone else to tell me how to run my life, you hear me?'

She looked past Luka and her face altered. She cowered back in the seat. 'You see that man, the fat one? Where's he going, can you see?'

De Silvo was talking to a small, oily man in a fur-collared coat. They were so engrossed they paid no attention to the parked car. They entered a building further down the courtyard.

Luka started the car and they moved slowly up the yard to park directly outside the door De Silvo had entered. After a moment Sophia got out, about to follow, when Celeste, the girl who used to work for her, came out. She was wearing a blue-printed wool maternity dress.

'Signora Luciano?'

Sophia smiled and, to the watching Luka, they appeared to be having a friendly conversation. Celeste leaned forward and kissed Sophia on both cheeks. Sophia remained standing there as the girl walked back towards Nino Fabio's.

Finally she got back into the car.

'You OK?'

She made no reply. She was white-faced, and as they turned out of the yard she said, 'Stop the car, I'm going to be sick.'

She stumbled out of the car, lurched towards a wall and bent over as she heaved and vomited. Luka stood beside her, watching her, then handed her his clean handkerchief.

'Sorry, I'm sorry . . . Will you help me back to the car?' She was very unsteady on her feet and struck her head as she bent to get into the car.

Luka passed her handbag to her, then climbed into the driving seat. He sat watching her through the rear-view mirror as she freshened her face and carefully repainted her lips. Then she lit a cigarette and sighed, telling him to drive around for a while with the windows open as she needed some fresh air.

Luka asked her to tell him about Nino Fabio. She found it relaxed her just to talk, telling him how she had started up the business, wanting to have something that was her own. 'You know what it makes me feel like? Used, I have been used, and what is worse, Nino knows, knows I won't do anything about it.'

'Why not?'

'How can I? Now? You tell me, do you think I could go to the police now? As it was the place was illegal, they couldn't have been paying the girls union wages, not to mention the taxes . . .'

'So it was important to you?'

She sighed and stared out of the window. 'Yes, yes . . . It was important.'

'You want to start up here again?'

'Yes, of course, why else do you think I went to see him? But I need his designs, I don't have the money to find another designer, a good one. And in Milan every-one knows what everyone's doing, it's very hard to break into the fashion business and be taken seriously.'

'But if he did them when he was working for you, then you own them, they must have been part of your company?'

'Yes . . . I don't know any more.'

Luka murmured that she would have money from the sale of the companies. She lifted her hands in a small fluttering gesture, twisted her rings around. 'You said, "Remember you are a Luciano" . . . Well, it would be hard to forget, but I want to, I want to forget, Johnny . . . I want to forget so much, sometimes I just want to go to sleep and never wake up.'

She remained with her head resting against the back of the seat, her eyes closed. There was a helplessness to her, a vulnerability that made him ache to hold her.

Driving back through the centre of Milan they hit the traffic. Trams and buses converged to a virtual standstill in the Via Pontaccio and the turning into the Via Mercato.

As they travelled at snail's pace, Sophia looked out of the window at the Piccolo Theatre.

'You like the theatre?' Luka asked.

Sophia shrugged and lowered her window. 'Yes, occasionally. Maybe you should turn off, left at the top and past La Scala, head out that way.'

Joseph Pirelli wandered along the Via Brera and paused outside La Scala. He loved the opera and was looking forward to the forthcoming attractions. He had decided to fly back to Palermo that evening and was simply killing time. He wondered if he could possibly catch half the programme and checked the time, but decided against it.

He was deep in thought, standing on the edge of the pavement, as the Rolls passed him. As he looked up,

Sophia saw him. She gave a smile of surprised recognition. Pirelli hurried after the car, but didn't even have to run as the traffic was so congested.

'Signora Luciano, hello . . .'

She smiled and he walked beside the car. 'What are you doing here?'

'Some business, I used to have a boutique.'

'Do you have time for coffee?'

'No, thank you, I have to return to Graziella.'

Pirelli paid no attention to her chauffeur in the grey peaked cap. 'Please, I am getting a plane to Palermo at seven, just a coffee.'

Sophia looked at her watch. 'No . . .'

'There's a good coffee shop, on the corner near the Piazza del Duomo . . . please.'

There was a break in the traffic and the car began to pick up speed.

'I'll be there, I'll wait for you . . .' He watched the car merge into a throng of vehicles, every one of them tooting their horns, and eventually disappear.

Sophia sat back, realizing she had not had anything to eat since her breakfast. She said to Luka, 'Take me to the Piazza.'

'No, we've got to get back, it's late.'

'Just take me there, I know we have to get back. You can get yourself something to eat.'

'No.'

Surprised, Sophia laughed. 'Do as I say and don't argue.'

'What about Graziella?'

He was beginning to make her angry. 'Graziella is

772

perfectly all right. If you're worried, you can call her. And it's Signora Luciano to you.'

Luka pulled out of the traffic and parked at the kerb. 'You don't want to see him, we'll go back now.'

Sophia's hand was on the door. 'Go and get something to eat, pick me up in an hour, is that understood?'

She was out of the car before he could argue. White with anger, he forced the car back into the stream of traffic, almost causing an accident with another motorist. They began shouting abuse at each other.

Pirelli was waiting inside the coffee shop. When she entered, his face creased into a smile. He had not expected her to come.

He pulled out a chair for her and helped her off with her coat. It was another fur, but he was not interested in the coat and had no idea it was sable. He tossed it on a vacant chair.

'You look very beautiful.'

She smiled and picked up the menu. 'I didn't realize how hungry I was, I've not eaten since early this morning. It was a long drive.'

'You drove from Rome today?'

'Yes, well, my chauffeur did. He was furious that I made him stop.'

Pirelli blushed. 'I'm glad you did.'

They ordered, and he told her he had been on a fruitless mission to Rome, and had simply travelled to Milan to check out his apartment. He made no mention that his wife and son were in Palermo and Sophia assumed he was a bachelor. She realized that she was pleased to see him again.

'How long are you to stay in Palermo?' she asked.

'I went there originally for one case, but it has escalated. Could be months, who knows.'

Luka ate a hurried sandwich, drank a cup of coffee and returned to sit in the car. He checked his watch frequently. The hour was almost up when the car phone rang.

Sophia told him to go back to Rome without her, she had decided to stay on. She had already called Graziella, so it would be best if he went as soon as possible.

Luka was beside himself. 'I'll come to the café.'

'Don't, because I'm not there.'

'Where are you?'

'I'm at the opera. See you tonight.'

The phone went dead. Luka sat there, unable to believe it. The opera? His knuckles whitened from gripping the steering wheel, full of impotent rage, a mixture of jealousy and suspicion. Why had she gone with that man, who was he? Was he her lover?

Thinking it over, he talked himself into an icy calm. He would prove to her that he was the most important being in her life, he would do something for Sophia!

He reversed the car and headed back for Nino Fabio's warehouse.

Ancora tried to make contact with Pirelli, first ringing his Milan apartment and then the Milan police headquarters. They had not seen him since that morning and presumed he was on his way back to Palermo.

Ancora replaced the phone and began to type out a

short report on the body, now identified as Joseph Rocco, a known mafioso, which had been found in the multi-storey car park. He was a member of the Corleone family.

He had been dead for more than twenty-four hours, his death having been caused by a blow to the head. There were also deep lacerations to his neck. As yet the type of weapon had not been determined.

The gun, however, was without doubt the weapon they had been seeking. The cane with the horse's head divided into three separate parts, becoming a single-firing gun when assembled. Rocco's body was clothed, but his trousers had been pulled down to his ankles and the walking-cane gun rammed up his arse. As yet Ancora didn't know if there were any prints on the gun.

Sitting in the opera house, Pirelli and Sophia watched it fill to capacity. The opera was *Rigoletto*, and Pirelli seemed enraptured. Sophia sat in the darkness, half of her wondering why on earth she had agreed to come, unable to comprehend why she would even have a cup of coffee with him, let alone accompany him to the opera. The more she thought about it the more ridiculous she felt. Johnny would be half-way home by now . . . She began to think of her best way to get back to Rome, and her head began to throb. She turned to Pirelli . . .

At that moment he turned to her and smiled. She felt strangely comforted by his shoulder touching hers.

'I have to leave . . . Please, you stay.'

He didn't stay but followed her along the row. When they reached the foyer, he asked if she was all right.

'Yes, yes, I'm fine, but I must go home. It was stupid of me to stay. I'm sorry, you go back, please.'

Crestfallen, he nevertheless took her arm and they walked outside. She felt the comfort of him again; his hand on her elbow was firm. She eased her arm away, wrapping her coat around her.

'It's cold . . .'

He didn't know what to do or say. Feeling self-conscious he said, 'Yes, er . . . My apartment is close by.'

She gave him a look and turned away. He coughed. 'Er, we could go back there, and I can check on the trains.'

Before she could reply, he had flagged down a taxi and they were heading for his apartment, she had no idea where. Her confusion growing, she sat as far away from him in the taxi as she could.

Pirelli said nothing, just stared out of the window. In some ways he was just as confused as she was, almost afraid to meet her eyes in case she could see the turmoil he was in.

They walked up the three flights of stairs to his apartment. It was not special, not luxurious, there was no doorman in evidence.

Once inside Sophia kept her coat on, standing in the middle of the neatly organized lounge while he threw his coat off and checked the timetables. Eventually she sat on the edge of the sofa and lit a cigarette.

'Do you have any brandy?'

He immediately put the book down and fetched her a glass of brandy. She seemed uninterested in the apartment, unlike most women he had known, neither looking around nor remarking on the taste. She was simply there . . .

He handed her the drink and she cupped the glass in both hands, sipping, not meeting his eyes. He had trouble catching what she said, 'I think . . . I think I should call Mama.'

He watched her cross the room to the phone, put her glass on the table. She turned to look at him and their eyes met; she smiled and carried on dialling. Pirelli lit a cigarette and inhaled deeply; his hand was shaking like a teenager's.

'Mama? It's Sophia . . . No, Mama, I'm still in Milan.' Again she turned to Pirelli, and seemed to be searching his face for the answer to some unspoken question.

'Something has come up and I'll be delayed . . . You OK? No, he's not, he should be back shortly. No! No! Nothing to worry about . . . Yes.'

After another glance at Pirelli she turned her back on him. 'In the morning, Mama, I'll be home then . . . Yes, plenty of time.'

She replaced the phone, slowly, but did not turn. She began to ease the fur coat off.

Pirelli went to her, taking the coat and, as it slipped down to her arms, he bent his head and kissed her neck. Her only response was a slight tilt to her head, as if allowing him more area of her bare neck to kiss . . . The coat fell to the floor. He stepped back, and she turned.

He wished he could say something but he was bereft of words. Slowly she cupped his face in her hands . . . She was so tall, she didn't have to reach up, she simply bent her head and she could feel him shaking. She rested her cheek against his and all he could say, as if on a sigh, was her name. She slipped her jacket off and began to unbutton her shirt, her cheek still resting against him, then she lifted his hand to place against her heart.

'Tell me you love me . . .'

He could feel her heartbeat through his hand, feel the softness of her silk slip, the curve of her breast. He was drowning in the heat of it . . . Carefully he slipped her blouse off, his hands gently brushing her shoulders, then worked the zip of her skirt down until it fell to the floor . . . Then he wrapped her in his arms, holding her softly, nestling in his embrace. He kissed the lobe of her ear.

'I love you, Sophia.'

She seemed to collapse against him, and he picked her up and carried her into his bedroom. He laid her down on the bed he usually shared with his wife, although it might have been a cloud he was floating on. Nothing seemed real, nothing he had ever dreamed of felt like this. She turned her face into the pillow, feeling as if her mind was not part of her body, not part of the craving she felt. She wouldn't look at him.

Pirelli unbuttoned his shirt as he drew the curtains down, knowing she didn't want the light, perhaps didn't want to see him. He kicked off his shoes and peeled his socks off, then, still wearing his trousers, he moved soundlessly to sit on the bed beside her.

'You know, I never believed it possible to feel this way about someone. The first moment I saw you . . .'

She turned and touched his chest, tentatively at first; then her fingers dug into his flesh, into the thick, dark, curly hair, and she clawed him, pulling him down. He felt her biting his lip and he gripped her face, drawing her towards him, kissing her more roughly than he believed himself capable of . . . He tore the straps from

778

her underslip, pulling it away from her, and gasped at the beauty of her heavy breasts.

She was unbuckling his trouser belt and suddenly he felt her hands on his erect penis, pulling at him roughly, drawing him upwards as she lowered her lips around it . . .

He pushed her away. 'No . . . no . . .'

She flopped back on the bed. 'What's the matter with you, Commissario, don't you want me? Don't you want to fuck me?'

He couldn't believe he had done it; his slap jerked her head back violently. She came at him, trying to punch him, lashing out at him.

He gripped her wrists. 'Look at me, look at me! Do you think I want you like this? You think I want this?'

Her eyes blazed. 'Just fuck me, hurt me, *make me feel! Make me feel something!*'

He walked away, picked up his shirt and threw it at the bed. She covered her face with it and sobbed, her shoulders heaving. He stood and looked at her, helpless, not understanding. He tried to take the shirt away, but she would not show him her face. At last he sat on the bed and stroked her belly gently, until she lay quiet.

He took the shirt away from her and began to take the clips out of her hair, pulling it loose, while she lay with her eyes closed.

'I dreamed of seeing you like this, with your beautiful hair spread out. I love you, Sophia.'

Like a child she lifted her arms to him and he held her, rocking her back and forth. He tilted her head, kissing her lips, softly at first, then her arms tightened and her tongue explored his . . .

They made love, gently, and he came into her within a few moments.

He smiled down into her face. 'Thank God, we've got all night . . . all night.'

And all night they made love, sleeping only an hour or two in the early morning. He made breakfast and brought it to her and they ate it, sitting side by side in the bed. He ran her a bath and soaped her body, towelled her dry, then held her tightly.

'What am I going to do, Sophia Luciano? You have me wrapped around your little finger, you know that? From the first moment I saw you.'

She laughed and went back into the bedroom, opened the curtains, flooding the room with light. She dressed while he showered and changed, and she sat in her fur coat, waiting for him. Her Turkish cigarettes made the whole apartment smell sweet. It was as if nothing had happened from the moment they had walked in.

'We will be in Palermo for the hearing, Mama's case comes up this week. Will you be there?'

He nodded, realizing he had not called his office. He checked the time. 'I'll get a cab to the airport.'

She stubbed out her cigarette. 'Can you be there? Only, Mama is afraid of the press, she's afraid, and we only have . . .' She was about to say Johnny, but then she said they only had their chauffeur.

'I'll be there . . . Will you be returning to Rome or staying in Palermo?'

'I'm not sure, it depends on the case.'

While he phoned for a taxi, Sophia looked around the room, then stood up to look at a photograph. Her back was towards him while he spoke to the taxi company and thumbed through the timetables at the same time.

'Who is this?' She was holding the photograph.

He touched his lip; it was swollen where she had bitten it. 'My wife, and my son.'

She felt as though he had punched her, but she replaced the heavy frame carefully. 'How old is your son?'

'Nine . . . Well, eight, nine next birthday. Sophia?'

She picked up her handbag, refusing to look at him.

'Sophia, Sophia, I would have told you . . .'

She gave him a cold, dismissive look. 'But you didn't . . . goodbye, Joe.'

On her return to Rome, Sophia was confronted by an irate Luka who demanded to know what she had been doing. She tossed her coat over the sofa and looked at him. She felt tired and irritable and his manner annoyed her.

'We had better get a few things straight; you work for us, you don't give me orders and you don't ask me where I've been or what I've been doing because it's none of your damned business.'

'I am supposed to be protecting you, looking out for you. If I don't know where you are, how can I do that? Who was that guy you were with?'

Sophia walked into the bathroom without bothering to reply. She ran a bath, stripped, and stared at her reflection in the mirror. She felt different, yet there was nothing to show for it. Only the silk underslip showed any sign; she threw it in the waste bin.

Soaking in the bath with her eyes closed, she thought about Joe. She knew he would help her when she asked him to trace her son, she knew he really cared for her.

What she refused to admit to herself was the possibility that she cared for him . . .

Pirelli took a bit of ribbing from Ancora. He was tired from lack of sleep and his lip was even more swollen. No one believed he had walked into a gate, and Ancora knew that Liza Pirelli was staying over in Palermo, so he didn't pry, he didn't dare! Pirelli's famous eyebrows gave the signal for no more jokes at his appearance. He was angry, and deeply frustrated: the facts were that no matter how much incriminating evidence they uncovered against Luka Carolla, they were still unable to get so much as a trace on his whereabouts. Officers were being pulled off the investigation and there was still no sign of him. Bruno di Mazzo was the first, then Mincelli and his team.

He went over the reports of the Rocco murder and examined the walking-cane gun. It had been wiped clean, no prints.

Too tired to think, Pirelli drove himself home. It was almost nine-thirty and he found Liza sitting watching television, her feet propped up.

'Hi, you OK?' He gave her a warm smile.

'What have you done to your lip?'

'Had a bit of a run-in with a couple of guys at the airport, it's OK. Anything to eat?'

She rolled off the sofa and went into the kitchen. 'Did you get to the apartment?'

'Yeah, just a quick look in. Crashed out for an early night. Everything's fine.'

'Good. Can we go out to dinner, then? Save me cooking?'

He sighed and agreed half-heartedly. He was so exhausted he could barely stand up. She stood on tiptoe to kiss him and he gave her a small hug. 'Oh, is that all I get? Away for two days? You haven't even asked me about your son.'

'I'm sorry, just that things are really getting on top of me. Is he OK?'

'He's fine, but you'll have to get him a new bike for Christmas. His has been stolen.'

Pirelli yawned his way through dinner and, try as he could not to think of her, his mind was full of Sophia. When he finally got to bed and his head hit the pillow all he wanted was to sleep and dream of her. Liza snuggled up behind him, kissing his neck, but he caught her hand.

'Not tonight, Liza, I've got a terrible headache.'

She rolled over to her own side of the bed. 'Great, isn't that supposed to be my line? You know, the sole reason I am here in this Godawful apartment is to be with you. What happens? You go back to Milan. When do I get to see you? Joe? Joe!'

He was deeply asleep, dreaming of Sophia with her hair spread across the pillow . . .

After a solid nine hours' sleep, Pirelli presented himself at the magistrates' court for the hearing of Graziella Luciano's attempt to murder Paul Carolla.

Luka and Sophia sat with Graziella on a hard wooden bench in the marble-floored corridor outside the court. Graziella was nervous, twisting her handkerchief round and round in her lap. Sophia asked if she would like some water, and Luka went to fetch it.

He filled the paper cup from the dispenser and returned along the corridor past another court in session. Posted outside the court were the lists of the day's hearings, and beside them notices requesting information on bail jumpers and other wanted felons, arsonists, petty thieves – and there, partially hidden, was the photofit picture of Luka himself.

The poster asked anyone who had seen or knew the whereabouts of Luka Carolla to contact the nearest police station. There was a brief description of him: his blue eyes, his height, with blond or light brown hair.

A woman was standing directly behind him, reading the notices over his shoulder. He excused himself and went on along the corridor. His bladder felt as if it were about to explode, and his hands were shaking. By the time he returned to Sophia and Graziella, his face was ashen and his fingers, holding the small paper cup, felt frozen stiff. They were still waiting for Graziella's legal representative to arrive.

'I've just asked how long we might have to wait. Apparently they do each case in order, so we might be a considerable time,' Sophia said to Luka, but her whole attention was on Graziella.

'Why don't I go and see about arranging a nice restaurant for lunch?'

Sophia hesitated, looked at her watch. Then she shrugged. 'Why not?'

He hurried away, passing Pirelli, who was in deep discussion with Graziella's lawyer. He didn't even glance in Luka's direction as he passed, because Sophia greeted him. He shook her hand, his eyes searching her face.

'Mama, you remember Commissario Pirelli?'

'*Si* . . .' Graziella shook his hand.

Pirelli couldn't take his eyes off Sophia. 'You've got one of the easiest magistrates. I've talked to him, and just had a long conversation with your lawyer. I don't think there's going to be any problem. I've also arranged with the Clerk of the Court that you can leave by the back door, so tell your chauffeur he can park right beside it. I won't be in the court but I will come by later. Could I have a word in private?'

Sophia excused herself and left Graziella with the lawyer. She and Pirelli went into an interview room and closed the door.

'Can I see you after the hearing?'

She wouldn't look at him. 'There's no point . . .'

'I see. What do you want me to do?'

She sighed. 'It has nothing to do with me. You are married, it's best we don't see each other.'

'Do you want to? Just tell me, do you want to? I mean, I don't know where I am with you.'

'I don't know what I want, Joe.'

'Oh, well, that's great. So we just forget it happened, yes?'

'Yes.'

'Fine, well that's that . . .'

He went to the door and his hand was on the handle when he stopped. 'I meant what I said, I love you, Sophia.'

She remained still, giving him no encouragement, just looking at him. He ran his hands through his hair and gave her a helpless look. 'What do you want me to do?'

She came to him, touched his face lightly. 'Joe, I

don't know what I feel for you . . . What I could feel for you . . .'

He pulled her to him and kissed her. She rested against him, feeling his strength, comforted by it, secure in his arms. 'Joe, it would be so easy for me to say yes, I want to see you again, but you are married. It would all become a tangled mess. Why continue if it'll get even more complex, more complicated . . .'

He gripped her arms. 'Because I can't stop thinking about you, because I want you every minute. I want you right now . . . and because I love you.'

She made no reply.

He was beginning to get used to making a fool of himself. He released her and leaned against the door. 'What if I was to leave my wife?'

'That is your business, don't expect me to tell you what to do. If you want to leave her, then . . .'

'Just tell me if that's what *you* want me to do?'

'No, I won't tell you anything. What happens if you leave your wife and then we . . . then we don't work out? You make me responsible, you blame me! I have had enough heartbreak, enough to last me the rest of my life. Don't give me any more, Joe, please. Maybe, maybe I came to you because I needed you, at that moment.'

'You don't need me now?'

Her eyes filled with tears. 'Oh, Joe, I have such a need inside me. You filled me, gave me something, but, don't you understand, what if I take it from you? Take whatever you offer me and then it turns out not to be enough? Think what my life has been like over the past year; I lost everything, and I don't know if it's love or just the fact that you filled the need. I have to try and make myself whole again. I'm only half alive, I'm filled up with Valium and booze. I don't even want to live any more . . . I am being honest with you, I don't know what I want, and you are too good, too kind . . .'

His whole life was turned upside down. He gave her a faint smile. 'I'm sorry, you're right, you'd better get back to Signora Luciano. If you need me you've got me, with or without ties. I mean that, all you have to do is call. I'm sorry, I guess I behaved like a kid.'

She kissed his cheek, whispered her thanks and walked out. He remained in the room, trying to compose himself. He couldn't rid himself of the terrible sense of loss.

He lit a cigarette and sat at the table, knowing he had to pull himself together, but he couldn't. 'How come,' he asked himself, 'how come it happens to me now?'

Luka sat in the car outside the court. He now knew that Sophia had been with the Commissario, the man named Pirelli. What had she told him? How much did he know? Why had they gone into that room to talk together? He was so deeply engrossed in his own thoughts that he cringed when someone tapped on the window of the car.

A court clerk bent to speak to him. 'Signora Luciano is just coming out. You take the first left, down the narrow alley and there's a sharp right turn. If you take that it leads back on to the main road . . .'

Luka already had the engine running as Sophia helped Graziella into the back seat, then sat next to Luka.

'There's the *paparazzi* at the front, so hurry.'

787

Luka didn't need to be asked twice. The Rolls-Royce Corniche screeched along the narrow alley.

As Pirelli had predicted, Graziella was fined and given a suspended sentence. By late afternoon they were ready to leave for New York. There was no trouble with customs; Signora Gennaro, with her son and daughter, were not even questioned.

Luka and Graziella between them had chosen the passports. The photograph in Anthony Gennaro's passport did not really resemble Luka, but the fact that it was a family passport enabled them to pass straight through the security net and the customs.

The steward moved quietly from seat to seat, asking the passengers to fasten their safety belts. They would be landing at JFK within ten minutes.

It had been a good, quiet flight and they had all slept, Graziella resting her head against Sophia's shoulder.

Sophia had not questioned Graziella about the exact time Johnny had returned from Milan, but he had not reached the apartment until early morning. Luka had remained in Milan, had returned to Nino's workrooms and waited for him to leave. He had then followed him to his home and waited until he went out for the evening. He had been watching Fabio for hours, like a shadow in a corner of the dark, seedy gay club. Finally he had introduced himself as an art student.

Later that night they had returned to Nino's warehouse.

The body was not found until the receptionist arrived for work the following morning. She noticed that the light was on in Nino's office and presumed he had come in early, as he often did.

She opened the mail and brewed coffee before tapping on Nino's door. Receiving no reply she called his name, then opened the door and looked into the room.

The white carpet was covered in bloodstains, so much blood that it looked as if someone had dropped a tin of paint. She even entered the room to take a second look. Entire footprints of bare feet showed where someone had walked through the blood, even the splayed toes were distinct. The footprints led to the doorway where she was standing. Stepping back, not entirely comprehending what she was seeing, she registered that the marks disappeared into the black carpet of the reception area.

There were more bloodstains in the small private bathroom, smeared across the mirror, over the hand basin, the footprints clear again in the white floor tiles. It was obvious that someone had made an effort to wipe hand prints away, but there was blood on the taps, blood sprayed over the wall.

As the office began to fill with machinists and cutters, the scene became surreal. Everyone stared into Nino's office, asking what had happened, and no one knowing. The police were called and immediately cordoned off the area while they tried to trace Fabio to discover what had happened in his office.

Two hours later a young assistant, passing through

789

the area where the life-size dummies were stored, began to scream hysterically. People came running, but all she could do was point towards a group of dummies. Nino's body, almost drained of blood, was positioned on top of a male dummy, holding it in his dead arms. He was as waxen and lifeless as the white plastic body he appeared to be humping.

CHAPTER 33

GRAZIELLA WAS distressed at seeing the small apartment that Teresa, Rosa and Moyra occupied. She had no comprehension of the high cost of living in New York and to her the place was little more than a slum, although, ten years before, Perry Street, West Village was considered a good neighbourhood.

Gasping for breath, she was saying she could not climb the stairs again, not if someone was to pay her a fortune. She wept, throwing her arms up in Sicilian fashion as she went from room to room, shaking her head at the small kitchen, asking over and over why, why she had never been told, why had Alfredo never let her and Papa see the state they were forced to live in.

Teresa wanted to scream, having tried to explain the difference in the cost of living, how much the 'slum' cost to run. Graziella demanded that she find a better place; it would be impossible for them all to stay in such cramped conditions.

Sophia could not help but agree; she was leaning against the front doorframe gasping for breath herself, having carried her own suitcase up the stairs.

Teresa pinched her elbow, whispering, 'Am I glad to see you. Moyra is driving me nuts.'

Sophia made no reply but walked into the small hallway of the apartment.

Moyra staggered in and put down two more bags. 'Oh, boy, you all came with enough luggage. Well, I've done my share; Rosa can go back down again.' She dumped the cases and cornered Sophia. 'I couldn't have stood her another minute, she does nothing but get at me. I've nearly whopped her a couple of times.'

Luka brought up two more cases, and the narrow hallway was full. With Graziella's wailing it seemed like bedlam.

It was late evening by the time they made sense of everything, having allocated rooms and moved furniture to create space. Sophia was sharing with Moyra; Teresa and Rosa were together, and they had given the almost demented Graziella a tiny boxroom of her own.

Everyone seemed to accept Luka as a part of it all. He had fetched and carried, pushed furniture around and been very willing to assist in every possible way, but he refused to eat with them as he wanted to go out and arrange a room for himself. He would return in the morning.

Supper was a noisy affair as they all talked at once, arguing about their accommodation. Graziella made Teresa more and more irate by turning her nose up at the food, saying it was like plastic, that if they had to live in the slums there was no need to eat like the *Americani* . . .

Teresa pounded the table in fury. 'Mama, you think we'd be living in this place if there was anything else?

792

We've got no other place, we live as we are until we get things organized, OK? *OK?*

'There's no need to shout, Teresa. Mama is confused. We have been in and out of Palermo, back to Rome . . . Maybe instead of arguing you should ask how it went in court.' Sophia pushed her dreadful hamburger around her plate. 'Mama had to pay a fine, or I did.'

'I presumed everything had gone well, otherwise you wouldn't be here. You always did live in a sumptuous place, Sophia, while some of us didn't. Well, you take a look around. Alfredo was Don Roberto's son, but you take a good look at the way we had to live. And you know something? Compared to most places this is a goddam palace, so I don't want to hear any more about it being a slum. You want to see slums then you walk four blocks . . . What am I doing? My God, am I crazy? We all get together and we're talking about the housing situation. This is crazy . . . Mama, I'm sorry, OK?'

Moyra had managed to eat her hamburger and now helped herself to more fries. 'Listen, I lived in more places than any of you. You think I don't know about high living? Once in Miami we rented a place that made the Villa Rivera look like a pigeon loft. Frank Sinatra stayed there before us. Mirrored bathrooms . . .'

Teresa interrupted her. 'Moyra, will you shut up? All I've heard from you since you arrived is what a dump this is. Don't you think we should talk about the reason we're all here in my *slum*, huh? Can we talk about what's really important?'

Graziella folded her arms. 'You know something, Teresa? What you think is important is not always right. What's most important is the home, that is the heart, that is the place you live from, you grow from. The family and the home are one.'

Teresa looked as if she were about to explode. Sophia slipped her arm around Graziella's shoulders.

'You are right, Mama.'

''Course I'm right. I don't like this place, my bed is next to a wall, who wants to wake up looking at a wall, huh?'

'OK, Mama, you want my room? Take it, have my room.'

'I don't want your room, Teresa, I want out of this place. It closes in on you. Tomorrow when we have had some sleep we look for a new place.'

Sophia helped Graziella to her feet and was elbowed away.

'And don't treat me like I was an old lady, show me some respect. I have left my home; you think I don't feel it in my heart? Don't you know what I lost, what I left behind?'

'You had no choice, Mama.' Teresa was fighting to control her temper.

Graziella leaned across the table. 'I had a choice, Teresa, don't think I did not. That house died, may it rest in peace.'

Teresa threw her hands up in the air. 'What do you want for us to do, Mama, weep for the house now?'

'No, just remember I gave you my home.' She walked to the door, then paused. 'Where's the bathroom?'

Sophia roared with laughter as she led Graziella down the small, obstacle-strewn hallway.

'Well,' said Rosa, 'Aunt Sophia seems in better spirits than when we last saw her. I wonder if the pills are working overtime.'

'You show respect, Rosa, or you'll feel the back of my hand.'

Rosa looked at her mother and continued to pour the wine. She had noticed just how familiar her aunt had been with Luka, and if she had noticed it so had Moyra. As she filled her own glass she said, 'Johnny seems to be a part of the family now, maybe a very close part. Seems very friendly with Sophia.'

Teresa collected the dirty plates, saying nothing, but she did bring up the subject of Johnny when Sophia returned.

'So, how did our Mr Moreno work out?'

Sophia accepted a glass of wine and smiled. 'He worked out just fine. He drove the Rolls – oh, we left it at a long-term garage, Teresa. We can pick it up any time . . .'

'Did you find out anything more about him? Like who he worked for?' asked Moyra.

Sophia shook her head. 'No, but he took good care of us. So what's the next move, now we're all here? What do we do now?'

Moyra put in, 'He's got a brother, I know that.'

Rosa turned to her, surprised. 'He has? He never mentioned him to me. When did he tell you?'

'At the villa, I was tellin' him about . . .'

Teresa rounded on Moyra. 'Can we just stop the chitchat and get on with the important things, OK? Now, I've made contact with Barzini; he's the one we discussed, the guy who made the offer to Domino to buy us out. I haven't contacted anyone else as he seemed pretty eager to speak to us.'

She went on to outline the plan, and she was still

giving instructions the next afternoon as they headed towards Central Park and the Plaza Hotel.

As the hired limo drew up outside the Plaza, the uniformed doorman held the door open for them. Teresa stepped out first, turning to assist Graziella.

They were all wearing black, and Graziella was veiled. They looked rich, they looked like old money, nothing flashy or too fashionable about them, but their clothes were obviously designer quality.

People turned to stare as, one by one, they stepped out of the limo and crossed the sidewalk. Then, in their now well-rehearsed group with Graziella leading, they entered the Plaza Hotel.

Ignoring reception, they walked sedately to the lifts and Teresa asked for suite six. She murmured softly to the lift operator that they were the Lucianos, and were expected. He bowed slightly as they stepped out on to the plush red carpet of the sixteenth floor.

A man in a light-grey suit and pink-tinted gold-rimmed glasses was waiting for their arrival, and he moved towards Graziella.

'Welcome, Signora Luciano. We met in '79, but you will have no reason to remember me. My name is Peter Salerno.'

Graziella nodded, but didn't speak. She leaned on his arm and he gestured for them to follow him through the open door of the suite. He guided them into a very large, sun-filled room.

Pink silks lined the walls, and pale oyster sofas and matching chairs were in profusion. The air was sweet with the scent of large, ornate flower displays on white marble pedestals. Small glass-topped coffee tables were placed conveniently around the seating area and in the centre of the room was a low, white marble table with dishes of sweetmeats and glasses for the champagne, which waited in silver ice buckets. A white-coated waiter stood by, ready to serve them.

The man they had come to meet, Michel Barzini, could be seen through an archway, talking on the phone. He was in his late fifties, a very small man, no more than five feet five. His hair was sandy grey above a pinched face on which he wore rimless, tinted glasses. His suit was a light, shiny grey, and his black shoes were so highly polished that the light glinted off them. His rose-coloured cravat sported a large diamond pin in its perfect folds.

He made a small gesture to acknowledge their arrival, then turned his back to finish his call. Within a moment he put the phone down and hurried with open arms to greet his guests.

'Forgive me, forgive me ... Welcome, Signora Luciano.'

He kissed Graziella's hand, then turned to do the same to each of the women as they were introduced. He patted their hands in condolence and gave each a sorrowful look then invited them to sit down. Graziella, about to accept the offered champagne, was immediately silenced by Teresa.

'Thank you, nothing.'

The waiter was dismissed and no one spoke until he had drawn the carved white doors across the archway. Peter Salerno sat in a high-backed chair while Barzini chose a soft one, facing the women. He addressed himself to Graziella.

'Your husband was my dear friend for many years, he was like a brother to me. If you have a problem, I am honoured that you come to me.'

He had a rather flamboyant way of speaking, using his hands theatrically, often removing his glasses to emphasize what he was saying. His small, pale, short-sighted eyes seemed to roll up in his head when he leaned back, making him look like a blind mole. Then he would lower his head, the pale eyes would refocus, and he would replace the glasses.

The small man's ego was powerful, and he seemed to enjoy his audience of black-clad, dependent women, their obvious deference to his maleness.

The white Art Deco phone rang shrilly, and Barzini leaned towards Salerno and told him quietly not to put any calls through. Salerno moved quickly from the room, to return a few moments later, unobtrusively. Barzini looked enquiringly at him, but he gave a small shake of his head, then took his seat again.

Barzini smiled. 'Ladies, you have my undivided attention . . .'

He looked at Moyra's legs, then slowly up past her knees to her curly blonde hair, her glossy lips, but she too sat with her head bowed. Lastly, he focused on Teresa.

She had opened her briefcase and unloaded a thick folder of documents. Her face was drawn, a little haggard, and when she lifted her eyes he was surprised at how unflinching the contact was.

He knew instinctively that this woman was not afraid of him. But when she spoke, her voice was totally submissive.

'Our situation was very confused after the death of

our loved ones. My mother-in-law used an old family friend, Mario Domino, to arrange our affairs. He was very elderly and, sadly, incompetent . . .'

She went on to give Barzini a detailed and concise history of the women's predicament and financial situation. She gave very clear costings of the worth of the Luciano companies. Salerno made notes of everything she said.

Moyra took small, sneaky looks around the apartment; the vases, the paintings, the thick carpet that virtually buried the toe of her shoe. This was money, she could feel it, smell it from the silk-lined walls.

Sophia kept her head down, staring at the ghastly pink carpet. She found the ornate suite distasteful, cloying, and she did not like Barzini at all. She could feel his mole eyes looking her up and down, undressing her and making her skin crawl.

Rosa was fascinated by the way Barzini's eyes rolled back in his head. She too had felt his scrutiny, but became transfixed with the way his small but cruel hands smoothed the creases of his trousers and fingered his diamond pin. She smiled secretly, knowing the mole creature fancied himself.

Teresa was explaining their treatment at the hands of the Corleones, how they had offered nothing more than an insult. She told him that she knew without any doubt that every family in Palermo would have wanted to lease their properties, if she had been allowed to do what she had intended.

The black, polished shoe twitched, and Barzini flicked a small look to Salerno. Then he removed his glasses. 'You seem very sure. Have you ever had a hand in running an import or export company . . . Teresa, yes? I hope you don't mind my asking you this, Teresa, it's just that without experience you could have been mistaken about the financial worth of the Luciano holdings . . .'

Teresa gave him a wonderfully innocent gaze, hesitated, then sighed. 'I have not, but facts are facts. There have been, over the past twenty years, many offers, and they did not decrease. They could not be expected to, considering the company was very profitable and continued to expand until the death of Don Roberto. These offers, of course, were not necessarily to ship food. The Luciano company was a highly regarded, legitimate business, and I suspect the families wishing to buy us out needed the cloak of legitimacy to enable them to export narcotics . . .'

Barzini leaned forward, then off came the glasses again. His eyes rolled back . . . 'Believe me, I have no wish to offend you, to offend any of you. Pray God, I don't. But Roberto Luciano was standing as a witness for the prosecution . . . No matter what vendettas have come between brothers, that was an act of madness.'

Teresa's mouth turned down and she dropped her act of innocence a fraction. 'Believe me, we know more than anyone what that madness led to. But we come to you for help, because you loved Roberto Luciano as a brother. We feel that we can trust you . . . He stood against Paul Carolla, a man who for over twenty years tried to make him part of the narcotics trade. Carolla knew that with our warehouse space, our cold-storage facilities, our factories . . .'

She reeled them off, one after the other, and Salerno wrote each one down. Not even so much as a look passed between him and Barzini. The only hint that what Teresa was saying was of the slightest interest to Barzini was when his hands became still. He no longer twitched, no longer fingered his cravat or his trouser creases . . . He was, it appeared, still totally relaxed, but Teresa was sure he had fallen for the bait. Could she reel the fish in?

Totally alert, Sophia was listening to every word. She sat half-turned towards Teresa, caught, like Moyra and Rosa, by what she was saying.

Teresa continued, 'All we want is a fair price, what the company is worth, and we come to you, a man loved by our beloved Papa, to ask you to get this for us.'

He sprang to his feet and crossed to Graziella. Taking her hand he helped her to rise, making it appear as if Graziella had instigated their departure. He kissed their gloved hands in turn, leaving Teresa until last.

As they walked to the door, he asked her casually if the documents that she had brought with her were all that was necessary to instigate a sale. She smiled and said yes, everything, proof of ownership, land leases, only the widows' signatures were required.

She handed the file to Barzini and he ushered them out, pressing the button impatiently to call the lift.

His small hands clutched the folder triumphantly, and it was not until the lift was just closing that she mentioned to him that the folder only contained copies of the original documents . . . The doors closed and the lift started moving, so she missed his reaction.

Barzini turned to Salerno and smiled. 'I think the little blackbird just handed us a gold mine. Everything comes to those who wait.'

Sophia snapped angrily, 'How could you do that, Teresa? You never actually said it, but it was clear enough. You know, if they buy us out, what they'll use the company for, the very thing that Papa fought against his whole life.'

'Do you care?'

'Yes, I care. You may be able to live with it, but I can't.'

'You tell me how you're going to live at all, because right now we've got *nothing*. You're the one who needs cash to start up in Rome, you! Well, you'll have it.'

'Have you no morals?'

'Don't give me morals. I'm not dealing in the stuff, I won't have anything to do with it. Whoever buys the company will do what they like – what do you think the Corleones would do, export Italian sweets? Grow up, Sophia, just grow up.'

Moyra was beginning to get irritated by Sophia. The smoke was getting in her eyes and she waved it away with her hand. 'We don't have much choice, Sophia, and if you've got any better ideas then we'll listen. Just come up with them fast.'

Teresa said coldly, 'We haven't got rich yet, and we haven't done the deal. But we'll need your signature. Are you saying you won't give it?'

Sophia gave her a disgusted look and stubbed out her cigarette.

'Yes, I guess that is exactly what I am saying. There's got to be some legitimate trader who'll give us a fair price.'

'Grow up, Sophia, for Chrissake, *grow up*. What straight guy is going to want to put a cent in a company with our connections?'

Moyra stamped her foot. 'Oh, stop it, you two! I don't understand what gives with you, Sophia. You lose your husband, your two kids, and now you take some crazy moral stand just when it looks like we're gettin' out of the shit.'

'Maybe because I had two kids, Moyra, maybe because I have been a mother, that's why.'

By the time they returned home, Moyra and Sophia were not speaking. They couldn't get away from each other in the apartment, and tempers, already frayed, were at breaking point.

Graziella insisted on preparing dinner and nearly blew up the small kitchen as she didn't know how to light the gas stove. She clattered around as she cooked up a huge pot of spaghetti.

Luka arrived, almost hidden behind a bouquet of roses. Graziella took them in her arms, laughing delightedly. He had also brought wine, mozzarella cheese and fresh-baked bread. He was drawn into the kitchen to taste the spaghetti sauce.

Sophia could hear Rosa calling for her to come and eat. A radio had been turned on and Moyra, out of a perverse sense of fury, sang at the top of her voice. Teresa tapped on the bedroom door and entered.

'Are you coming to eat? Mama's cooked and Johnny's arrived.'

'I'm not hungry.'

Teresa closed the door and sat on the edge of the bed. 'I've been thinking about what you said in the car. If you want out, that's your business, and we'll see if we can somehow raise enough for you to return to Rome and start up again.'

'With what? Even if I get a stake, I've no designs, I've

not even a workroom, and I used every last cent to pay off Mama's fine at the court. I'm broke, Teresa, but I still cannot agree with what you're doing.'

Teresa sighed and looked at Sophia seriously. 'Do you want a word of advice? I wouldn't go back into the fashion mainstream, you should use more off-the-rail designs, you know, chain-store things. That's where the dough is.'

'You know about a lot of things, Teresa, but don't tell me how to run my business.'

'Maybe someone should have told you a long time ago, then you wouldn't have bankrupted yourself. Those silk things, you know? Those swathed tops were lovely, but who can afford $5,000? Your market's too small.'

Sophia lit a cigarette. 'A lot of women can, Teresa. I used to, and the women I want to sell to can afford to spend $60,000 on one season, and that's not accessories, that's just dresses.'

Teresa's mouth turned down at the corners and she snapped, 'So don't fuck up our chances of wearing them. If Barzini arranges a buyer we accept it, and start living. You won't stop me, stop any of us, is that clear? Now let's go eat!'

Sophia remained silent during the noisy dinner. Graziella had cooked enough for twenty and she watched and listened.

Just as Rosa was about to clear the table Graziella asked her to remain seated.

'Well, Teresa, what do you intend to do if he offers a good enough price?' Graziella waited, her head cocked to one side. She had said it so quietly, yet they all heard her clearly.

'I suggest we accept, get out and cut our losses.'

'So do I,' said Moyra, but she didn't dare say another word as Graziella reached over and clasped her hand for silence.

'I know Sophia does not approve . . . So, Rosa, what do you think?'

'I don't know.'

'You don't know . . . So, we have two against, two for, and one don't know.'

'There's Johnny's vote, if that's what you're taking. He's in for a cut too.'

Graziella nodded. 'As his signature is not required on the documents, I don't think we need to know right now.'

Teresa sighed. 'So you're against it too, are you, Mama?'

Graziella pursed her lips. 'You are right about certain things; the difficulty of finding a legitimate buyer for one. Also, if we divide up the sales instead of one bulk buy-out, we will lose a considerable amount. Then there is the time involved, and the dangers, because it is imperative we move fast. That is a danger, too, but perhaps it is one we can use to our advantage. There is even a possibility of a clause being arranged by lawyers forbidding the use of Luciano companies for shipping narcotics, but then they are not likely to admit that the cargo contains illegal substances and will, I am sure, go to great lengths to ensure that they are disguised by whatever legal cargoes they will be shipping. So we are left with the question, do we let Barzini arrange a buy-out by whoever he represents, or do we refuse because of our moral obligation to my husband?'

Teresa had heard enough. She pushed her chair back, but Graziella slapped the table with such force that the plates jumped. 'Sit down, *sit down* . . . Give me the respect of at least listening to what I have to say.'

'I was just going to put some coffee on.'

'The coffee, Teresa, can wait. What we are discussing here cannot, and without my signature and Sophia's you can't sell. I would rather die than let this man use our name, I would prefer to see everything wiped out.'

Teresa was about to interrupt again, but Sophia touched her hand. 'Listen to Mama . . . Go on, Mama, finish what you have to say.'

Graziella continued, 'We know the routes the ships use, you know the layout of the warehouses and the chain between the Palermo, Brazil, Colombia and Miami bases. Let us say we sell to whoever Barzini brings into the deal; we sell, take our money, your inheritance, and you are free. If the companies are being used by narcotics traders, what would the drug enforcement agencies need? What information would enable them to arrest and charge these so-called importers? Not in small swoops, but a net could be spread to draw the big fishes as well as the little ones, and we could give them the information to set up the trap.'

They remained silent, looking at Graziella, waiting for her to continue, but she shrugged as if to say, 'That's it.'

Sophia leaned back and lit a cigarette. 'Well, Mr Moreno, if you are getting a cut what do you suggest we do? Better still, save all our skins by offering to give the information to the police.'

'All right, if you want me to.'

Sophia gave a soft laugh. 'I was joking.'

'I wasn't. I could do it, see that the right people received whatever information you want to give.'

806

Again Sophia laughed. 'My God, I think he's really serious.'

Luka flushed pink. He couldn't cope with her sarcasm. 'At least none of you would be at risk.'

'Thank you, Johnny, I appreciate it. We all appreciate your offer, but until we decide what we are going to do our acceptance would be premature.'

Graziella smiled warmly at him and he swallowed, but looked yet again at Sophia. She was turning her gold cigarette lighter over and over on the cloth, in deep thought. He could see the sweep of her dark eyelashes, so long they seemed to rest on her cheek.

She rose from the table. 'If Barzini comes up with a good enough deal we accept, do whatever Mama wants.'

Luka followed Sophia into the hall.

'I have something for you,' he said.

Sophia opened her bedroom door. There was a small suitcase, closed, on her bed.

'What is it?'

'Something you wanted. Goodnight.'

Teresa and Rosa finished drying the cutlery.

'Where's Johnny?' called Sophia from the hall.

Rosa dried her hands, her face tight with anger. 'He's left, he's gone.'

The telephone rang and Teresa hurried into the small room she used as a study.

Sophia searched her handbag for her address book, then picked up the telephone. Teresa was still on the phone in the study, and just as Sophia was about to hang up she heard a man's voice saying, 'That is an awful lot of money, Signora Luciano. I don't know if my friends would be prepared to go to that.'

Teresa's voice was clearly audible.

'In that case, Mr Barzini, am I to presume you are no longer interested?'

'I will have to discuss it further.'

'You won't take long? I think I mentioned our financial situation.'

'Gimme a few hours, maybe less.'

Sophia walked straight into the study without knocking. Teresa put the phone down and looked up with a tiny smile.

'I hope to God you know what you're doing!' Sophia said.

'I do . . . Was that you on the extension?'

'Yes, I'm sorry, I didn't mean to listen in, but I was about to call Rome. Johnny just presented me with a suitcase full to bursting with Nino Fabio designs, it's sort of crazy . . .'

Teresa looked puzzled. 'How come? I thought that was what you wanted.'

'Because before we left Rome, Nino flatly refused to let me have even one design, and now I've got a suitcase full.'

'Are they any use?'

'Well, of course they are. His last collection was a smash in Rome and Paris. He's climbing up, but it just doesn't make sense. I mean, how the hell did he get them?'

Teresa agreed that Sophia should call and find out and handed her the telephone.

'What's the code for Rome?'

'I don't know, call the operator. I bet you think

differently now about wanting out? With your share you could open a boutique here as well as in Rome. Between us we could get a good business going.'

Sophia doubted that she could ever work with Teresa who, since her return to New York was more strident than ever. 'We'll see how things turn out. First let me speak to Nino.'

Teresa, Rosa and Moyra remained in the bedroom looking through Nino's designs. Teresa kept looking at her watch, then the bedside clock. She was worried Barzini was trying to call them and Sophia was still on the telephone.

She was relieved when she heard the extension ping, knowing the phone was now free.

'Teresa?' Sophia called from the hall.

'We're all here, in your bedroom.' Sophia joined them.

Teresa asked, 'Did you talk to Nino?' but before Sophia could reply the telephone rang. She snatched it up, then composed herself before she spoke.

'Yes, speaking . . . Oh, yes, as I said when we met . . . Yes, everything.' She looked at the others and gave them the thumbs up, then continued, 'Thank you very much, I can't tell you how much we appreciate this . . . Yes, thank you . . .' She put the phone down and flopped on the bed. 'We did it, Barzini has agreed!'

'How much? How much? Teresa, *how much*?' Moyra shrieked.

Teresa was half-laughing and half-crying. '$15 *million*! Happy Christmas!'

CHAPTER 34

SOPHIA DID not get the chance to tell Teresa what she had learned about Nino Fabio. They were all so excited by the Barzini deal that even if she had wanted to, she felt that until she had spoken to Luka she should say nothing. Making the excuse she was going to buy champagne to celebrate, she left the apartment.

Sophia paid off the cab and walked into the rooming house. A scruffy man behind the reception desk was picking his teeth. He tossed Luka's key to Sophia and watched with interest as she headed up the litter-strewn stairs.

By the time Sophia reached Luka's door her nerves were in shreds. She tapped on the door and called, 'It's me, Sophia. I have to talk to you.'

He swung the door open wide, smiling, and she brushed past him.

'How did you get those drawings? You'd better tell me.'

'Do you want to sit down?'

'No, I just want you to tell me the truth, tell me how you got his drawings.'

'Oh, yeah . . . I also got you this. He signed it, just in case there should be any trouble. It's not a lawyer's document, but it should suffice.'

She snatched the single sheet of paper from his hand. 'What did you do, Johnny? Tell me!'

He skirted the room with the naked, dim light bulb and single bed, as if cowering away from her. Eventually, he stood with his back to her, looking out of the grimy window over the iron fire escape. 'I thought you wanted the drawings, I thought that was what you wanted.'

The neon lights of the hotel sign outside lit his frame with an eerie, bluish light, off, on, off, on . . . One moment she could see him clearly, the next he was in shadow. She sat on the edge of the bed, rubbing her hand over the rough grey blanket. 'You know, I think I am going crazy. I don't think this is real, I don't think I am here . . .'

'It's a dump of a room,' he said softly.

'I need a glass of water.'

He left the room and she remained sitting on the bed, patting the blanket. Her head was throbbing. She stared around, more for something to do, anything but cave into the terrible sinking feeling in the pit of her stomach. It was a dump, but his clothes, everything belonging to him, were neat and tidy.

He returned, carefully carrying a paper cup, holding his breath in case he lost so much as a drop. She coughed and he went to take her hand. She drew away from him.

'Please don't touch me . . . Don't . . .'

She could hardly hear his voice as he whispered, 'Sophia . . .' His eyes were pleading, childlike.

'Did you kill him?'

'Yes.'

811

She went to put the paper cup down on the bedside table and it toppled over. The next moment Luka was kneeling at her feet, both arms wrapped around her legs.

She protested, 'Please don't do this . . . Please don't.'

He pressed his face against her thighs and shuddered. She lifted her hands, arched her back as if to push him from her, but instead she stroked his hair with gentle, soothing strokes. His arms tightened around her.

'I did it for you, to prove that I cared, that I was important. When I saw you go off with that man, I didn't know if you were going to betray me, and I had to do something to prove to you . . . I did it for you.'

Sophia eased herself away from him and he sat back on his heels.

'I need a drink, do you have anything I could drink?'

He leapt up and hurried to the door. 'I'll get you some more water.'

She was relieved he was away from her and stood up. 'No . . . No, I'll be all right.'

'You sure?'

'Did anyone see you?'

'No, no one.' He tried to take her hand but she snatched it away from him. 'I did it for you . . .'

Her voice sounded alien to her, as if someone else was speaking. 'I have to go, they're waiting for me. Barzini called Teresa, he's offered a lot of money. *Please stay away from me, don't come near me!*'

'Shussssh, someone could hear you.' He opened the door a fraction and looked out, then closed it and locked it.

'When we get the money,' said Sophia, 'you take your share and then you must go away.'

'What are you going to do?'

'It doesn't matter what I am going to do.'

'Yes, it matters. I did it for you.'

She felt her anger rising and she snapped at him, 'What do you think I can do with the designs now? Do you think I can still use them? How the hell could I use them, don't you think it would look suspicious, do you think I could even contemplate using them after I know what you've done? Don't say it, don't dare say it again, I never asked you to do anything for me . . .'

His voice was plaintive. 'But no one can possibly connect you.'

'No? Are you stupid as well as crazy? Won't connect me? I was there, *I was there!* The police will want to question me, the people who work for Nino will notice the designs are missing!'

'But there were hundreds, I didn't take them all.'

'Don't you understand, you've destroyed any chance of my being able to use even one of them!'

He gestured for her to keep her voice down and she clenched her hands at her sides. 'I could have paid him, understand? I could have bought them legitimately.'

He sat on the edge of the bed with his head in his hands. She wanted to hit him, slap his face, kick him. She had never known such blind fury against another human being.

'I should go straight to the police and hand you over . . . Give them the drawings, let them deal with you, you stupid—'

She paced the room, her anger easing the horror of the situation. How could she, even if she wanted to, give him away? It would only cause more trouble, involve all of them, Teresa, Rosa, Moyra . . . Graziella. The more her mind churned over the facts the colder her anger became, blaming him, hating him. She stood in front of him and pulled his hair to make him look up at her.

'As soon as Barzini pays us you get out of our lives, or, so help me God, I'll tell the police.'

It was a hopeless threat; she was cornered and she knew it.

'You crawled to him, you begged him, and he laughed in your face. He made you vomit in the street, he made you foolish, inadequate . . . Now . . . Now it's different.'

She stepped back. His face was impassive, his voice calm, yet his blue eyes blazed. 'Feel what it is like, Sophia, feel it inside you, know that you have had him destroyed, just like that.' He snapped his fingers. 'I would do it again for you, any time. No one can hurt you, no one. You can have anything you want, anything.'

As he stepped towards her she moved away, went to the door, trying to get out. It was locked; frustrated, unable to leave, she turned just as he clasped her to him. She tried to break free, tried to claw at his face, but he twisted her arm behind her back.

'You can have everything again, Sophia. I'm going to give it to you.'

She offered no resistance, letting her body relax. 'You can't give me back my babies, you can't find my son, you . . . you . . .' She looked up at him as he released his hold. 'You cannot give me anything, there is nothing to have that I want.'

'But I love you, I love you.'

'Your love disgusts me. Now, move away from the door and let me go.'

Luka kissed her, a passionate, longing kiss, but she did not respond. He could feel her teeth, her lips . . . When he broke away, he looked into her dark, angry eyes, which were filled with such hatred that he let go of her shoulders and fumbled in his pocket for the key. She stood directly behind him while he unlocked the door and would not meet her eyes as she passed him.

As she made her way down the stairs, she wiped her lips with the back of her hand. She knew he was following her, but she didn't turn back. She didn't turn until she reached ground level, then she looked up to see him staring down the stairwell. The light from the naked bulb behind him encircled his head and shoulders, and at that distance she could not see his expression. He was like a statue, so still, his pale skin and blond hair making him appear ghostly.

Sophia let herself into the apartment. As she closed the door, Rosa appeared.

'You went to see Johnny, didn't you?'

With her hand on the doorknob, Sophia sighed. 'Rosa, it's none of your business where I've been.'

Rosa flushed with anger. 'Are you two lovers?'

'No.'

'Don't lie to me, he can't take his eyes off you. What happened in Rome?'

Sophia opened the door. 'Nothing, and take my advice, stay away from him.'

'Because you want him?'

Sophia slammed the door shut and turned to Rosa. 'Don't be childish, and don't be so rude to me. I'll forget it this once, but don't you ever insinuate that there is anything between me and that creature . . . And I mean it, Rosa, stay away from him.'

Rosa turned and ran into her own room as Teresa came out of the bathroom.

'What's going on?' she asked.

'Nothing . . . I just want to go to bed, all right?'

'Fine by me, I just thought you were having an argument. No need to snap my head off.'

'I'm sorry . . . Rosa seems to think I am having a thing with Johnny.'

'What? Are you serious?'

'Don't let her see too much of him, Teresa. Believe me, I know what I'm talking about. The sooner we get rid of him the better.'

Teresa hesitated, remembering the Rocco murder, but how could she tell Sophia? He had bound Moyra and Teresa to him. She changed the subject.

'Moyra seems to think we should have a turkey. I sort of drew the line at a Christmas tree. You know, she's pretty dumb, she doesn't think . . .'

With a hint of amusement, Sophia shook her head. 'Right now, Teresa, Christmas is the last thing I can think of. Goodnight.'

Moyra was in bed, leaning up on her elbow. 'Pretty dumb, huh? You know you can hear every word anybody says in this slum? Well, she don't know me, and she don't know anythin' about me. Soon as I get my share I move, you won't see me for dust.'

All Sophia wanted was to be alone, the small apartment was suffocating her. Her hair fell loose as she removed the pins and Moyra sat up in the small single bed, hugging her knees.

'You got beautiful hair . . .'

Sophia smiled and started to brush her hair. She closed her eyes and remembered the night with Joe Pirelli . . . She would have given a lot to have him with her. She put the brush down and rested her head in her hands.

Moyra settled back. It was cold, and she pulled the duvet up to her chin. 'I could do with some hunk to keep me warm, it's freezing. They said it'll be snowing soon, on the weather forecast.'

Sophia poured a glass of water and opened her handbag, taking out her bottle of Valium. She tipped three in her hand and took them with one swallow.

'What are you taking?'

Sophia banged the glass down. 'Vitamins, Moyra, all right? And are you going to watch every move I make?'

'OK, OK! No need to bite my head off. I was just wondering if they were sleeping pills 'cause I wouldn't mind a couple myself. You think I can sleep in this bed? It's like a board, I'm not used to a hard . . .'

Sophia walked out. 'I'm going to the bathroom.'

Breakfast was not a happy affair. No one had much of an appetite for the eggs and sausages Graziella had cooked, they were all too worried about the meeting with Barzini. The weather outside was freezing and Sophia, generous as ever, offered one of her furs to whoever needed it. Moyra was wearing the mink before she had finished speaking . . .

The telephone rang, but Teresa made them wait. 'We don't want to look too desperate. I'll answer it.' She disappeared into the study.

Moyra studied herself in the hall mirror in her new

finery. 'I'd do that, Teresa, knowing our luck he'll ring off . . . Oh, Sophia, this is real nice, is it male or female? They say the males are best, don't they?'

Rosa pulled a face. 'Whatever, it's disgusting walking around with dead animals on you. I don't know how you can, you've got about fifty pelts there, that's fifty hearts, lungs . . .'

Sophia lit a cigarette and said nothing. Although Rosa was having a go at Moyra, she knew the criticism was really aimed at her.

Moyra didn't seem to care. She went on, 'You've got leather boots, they had feet once, you know. You just wanna pick an argument.'

Teresa came out of the study. 'We're to meet him at a restaurant called the Four Seasons, at one o'clock sharp. Sophia, have you got a coat that would fit me?'

'Oh, Mama, how could you?'

'Quite easily, Rosa, I'm not going to freeze.'

Barzini and the four women sat at his usual central table at the Four Seasons restaurant. He ordered coffee for his guests and asked that his respects be passed to Graziella, who had not accompanied them.

As soon as the formalities were over, Teresa asked that the money be paid in the form of a banker's draft, within twenty-four hours. In exchange he would receive all the documents relating to the Luciano holdings in Palermo, duly signed over to him.

Satisfied, Barzini excused himself, saying he needed to go directly to his bankers to arrange for the draft to be prepared.

Barzini had made no mention to them of any of the other parties involved in the buy-out.

Graziella had not accompanied them because she wanted to speak privately with Luka. She first made him coffee, then drew up her chair to sit close to him.

'Johnny, I want to talk to you about Rosa.'

He looked surprised, thinking that perhaps Sophia had said something. 'Rosa . . .?'

'She's very young and I think she has a liking for you, a crush, as we used to call it in my day. I don't know what they call it now, but I'm sure you understand what I mean.'

'I didn't know.'

Graziella smiled. 'Maybe not, but you are also very young and I ask you not to encourage her in any way. You see, Rosa must make a good marriage, we are dependent on her, you understand. Only Rosa can carry the Luciano blood . . . Only through Rosa can we become a family.'

He wanted to cry; in a perverse way he had felt that they wanted him, loved him. Graziella detected his sadness and brushed her hand against his cheek.

He caught it and kissed it. 'I want to stay with you all . . . I can work for you.'

'We won't need you, Johnny, and, as I said, you must live your own life. You don't want to be surrounded by women.'

He rested his head on his arms. She touched his hair, brushing it softly. 'What of your family? Moyra says you have a brother, is that right?' She continued to stroke his hair, blond hair . . . He lifted his head and she let her hand fall back in her lap.

He pushed his chair back and smiled. It was a soft, intimate smile. Then he rose to his feet.

'I'll drop by later, I have to collect something for Teresa.'

Graziella heard the front door close behind him but she wasn't thinking of Johnny, of Luka. She opened her dressing-table drawer and took out the photograph of Michael. She stared at it until she could hear his voice, see him clearly, sitting at the old dining-room table, see him leaning close to Roberto, smiling once more that beautiful smile . . .

She heard the key turn in the front door and quickly replaced the photo, telling herself she was being foolish. All the same, she could not rid herself of Johnny's smile, of Michael's smile, because there was something uncannily similar.

Rosa was carrying two grocery bags full to the brim. Moyra's arms were full of brightly coloured parcels, all decorated with Christmas trimmings.

'This is gonna be the best Christmas we ever had, we got everything you can think of . . . Turkey, puddings, yams, crackers, we got crackers to pull, we got presents for everyone, because . . . *We're in the money* . . .' Moyra was irrepressible. She dumped the gifts on the small table in the hallway and swept Graziella into her arms, then they waltzed up the corridor.

'We're in the money, we're in the money . . .'

It was tea-time, just after four o'clock, when the doorbell rang. The bell rang again, and Teresa walked out of the study calling that she would answer, it was probably Johnny. Teresa opened the door wide.

Three men in hideous cartoon masks pushed the door so hard that it caught her shoulder and she fell back. The next moment her hair was gripped, almost torn from her head, and a gun was placed against her neck.

'Keep it shut, now walk . . . move . . . Get the others.'

Graziella came to the kitchen door and the third man dragged her out to join Teresa in the hall. Graziella struggled and he knocked her over. As she fell, screaming, Sophia hurried into the corridor.

'Keep it shut. Put your hands above your head an' you won't get hurt.'

Sophia made the mistake of screaming for Rosa. The gun hit her on the right temple and she fell face forward, landing at Graziella's feet. Teresa was still being dragged along the corridor, hauled so roughly by her hair that her legs went from beneath her.

'Please, don't hurt us, please . . .'

Moyra was next into the corridor. She opened the door and, seeing the men's nightmare faces, slammed it shut again. She tried to lock it, but it was forced open. Screaming her head off, Moyra was dragged out by her dress, which split at the seam. She was pushed and kicked until she stumbled along the corridor.

They were herded at gunpoint into the study. Rosa, still in the bathroom, could hear the screams. Terrified, she dropped the hair dryer, locked the bathroom door and ran towards the fire escape. As she raised the window, she heard shots fired, dull, thwacking noises from a silenced gun, which split the lock and literally blew the door open. Hysterical with fear, Rosa hunched against the window, and the man reached down and dragged her into the hall by her legs. Rosa sobbed in terror as she was manhandled into the study to join the others. She couldn't get to her feet, and was kicked in the ribs until she rolled towards Sophia.

The main man, the only one to have spoken so far, trained his gun on them and backed away. His voice was muffled by his wizard's mask. 'Now keep nice and quiet and nobody will get hurt. You – come here.'

Teresa was yanked towards the desk and her hip banged against the corner. She gasped with the pain.

'We want the papers, and you won't get hurt. Just hand them over.'

Teresa clutched the edge of the desk. 'What papers?'

The man backhanded her and her head snapped back. 'You know, bitch, you know. Now get on your knees . . . *On your fucking knees!*'

He twisted her arms behind her back and she sank obediently to the floor. Rosa started to scream. She was kicked in the stomach so hard that she retched as she buckled over. The second man took some rags from his pocket and sat on her to tie her hands behind her back. Then he made her kneel beside her mother.

The main man was tipping out the drawers, sifting through the papers. 'You know what we want, now don't waste any more time. *Where are they?*'

Weeping, Teresa shook her head. 'I don't know what you want, what papers? There's nothing kept here . . .'

Moyra yelled that Teresa should give them what they wanted, then shrank back in fear as she was forced, like Teresa, to her knees. Her head only just came to the top of the desk.

Her hair was gripped by the main man, his hideous mask leering at her. 'That's a good girl, you tell your

friend, *tell her to give us what we fuckin' want*! Tell her!'
He smashed her head against the desk, catching her just
above the right eye.

Moyra curled up and sobbed, pleading, 'Oh, God,
Teresa, give them what they want . . .'

About to ring the doorbell, Luka paused. He had noticed
that the lock was not quite caught. He inched the door
open as Moyra screamed.

It had come from the study. Opening his jacket he
took out a gun. Now he could hear Rosa's cries, then
Moyra's voice shouting to Teresa to give them what they
wanted. He moved silently to check out the kitchen,
then the other rooms, until he was certain they were all
in the study. Then he backtracked down the corridor,
into the bathroom and out on to the fire escape, following the iron balcony around the corner to the study
window. He flattened himself against the wall and peered
through the blind.

Teresa, a gun at her head, was being forced around
the desk. Rosa and Moyra still knelt in front of the desk.
Sophia stood at the far end of the room with her arms
around Graziella. All the men had their backs to the
window . . .

Luka inched forward a fraction. Only a small gap in
the blind enabled him to see into the room. Twice he
raised his gun, but Teresa was in the firing line. Now she
was handing the main man a folder of documents. He
put his gun down and felt in his jacket for a pen, then
struck Teresa across the back of the head as he instructed
her to sign. As she bent down, Luka fired.

The shot shattered the window, hitting the main man

in the back of the head. He fell forward over the desk, sending his gun spinning almost into Moyra's hands. The two other men turned immediately to the window. More glass shattered as Luka quickly fired. This time the bullet clipped raider number two in the left arm.

Moyra picked up the first man's gun in both hands and fired, hitting the third man in the thigh, and his body hurtled backwards. Luka kicked the remaining glass out of the window before they realized who he was, and jumped into the room.

Still holding the gun, Moyra had gone into shock. Her eyes wide with horror, she backed away from the body sprawled across the desk. 'He's dead, Teresa . . .' She looked at her hand, which was covered in blood. 'Oh, God, he's dead, we've got to get the police.' Sophia untied Rosa, who was shouting for someone to get the third man's gun before he tried to use it. Luka took on the second man who was gripping his injured arm. Without another shot being fired the two surviving men were overpowered.

Teresa ripped the mask off the dead man, then turned to the man wounded in the thigh. Before anyone could stop her, she had him by his hair, dragging him to kneel at the desk as she had done.

Luka whispered to Sophia, 'Get Graziella out of here, take her out.' She obeyed in a state of bewilderment.

Teresa was like a woman possessed. Her fear gone, she was in a state of blind fury, pulling the man's hair, dragging his mask off. 'Who sent you? You, who sent you?'

Looking up, he spat straight in her face. She slapped him so hard that he slid to the floor, then she stormed around the desk and kicked him in the groin. Howling, he dragged his knees up, then gritted his teeth at the pain from the bullet wound.

The desk phone pinged as if someone was using an extension. Teresa yelled to Rosa, 'Go tell Sophia to get off the phone! Don't call the police, not yet!'

Rosa ran from the room, shouting, 'Sophia, Sophia, don't, don't!'

Moyra had wet herself in her fear, and she stood shivering, her dress torn and soaked. 'What are you going to do? What are we going to do? Oh my God, I shot him, I shot him!'

'Moyra, Moyra!' Teresa shouted, but Moyra's shoulders began to heave, her body shook uncontrollably, and Teresa had to slap her hard to bring her to herself. She clung to Teresa. 'Oh, God, what have we done?'

'We've done nothing, you hear me, Moyra? We've done nothing. Come on, pull yourself together, stop it . . .'

Luka calmly finished tying up the two men. They knew now that something was going to happen to them, and there was no question of spitting in Luka's face. Luka sat on the desk, pushing the dead man aside, and waited as Teresa ushered Moyra out.

'Go on, Moyra, see if Rosa is OK. And, for God's sake, don't let them call the police until we find out who sent them. Go on, Moyra!' Teresa returned to the study and shut the door.

Moyra ran to Sophia. 'I can't take this! It was bad enough before, I mean, I don't sleep . . . I keep seeing him on the garage floor, and now this. Jesus Christ, Sophia, we're all gonna go to jail. *I'm gettin' out, I'm gettin' out . . .*'

She ran to the front door. Sophia called to Rosa to stop her and between them they dragged the hysterical woman back. Sophia could see the frightened face of Graziella, who was cowering in the kitchen.

'Rosa, stay with Mama, and you, Moyra, keep quiet, just keep quiet. Come on in here . . .'

She pulled Moyra into the bedroom and handed her a glass of water, then made her stick out her tongue for a pill. 'Swallow it, go on, it's all right, it's only Valium.'

'I need more'n one, we're gonna be in terrible trouble. I mean, I shot that guy, oh fuck, I shot him! I mean, that's two . . .'

'Just keep quiet, Moyra, come on, lie down.'

'I don't wanna lie down, for Chrissakes, I wanna get out of here! I shot that guy, an' I helped carry that Rocco into the trunk of his car . . . I mean, I could get years, I'm going to prison, I know it . . .'

'Rocco? What are you talking about?'

Moyra howled again, covering her face and rocking back and forth. 'Oh, God, I can't tell you, I promised . . .'

Sophia went to the door; she could hear the low murmur of voices coming from the study. She turned back.

'Tell me about Rocco, Moyra. What happened?'

Both the injured men had lost a lot of blood, it was thick on the rug. They both still knelt in front of the desk, their hands tied and their own rags stuffed into their mouths. Teresa was dialling on the phone. Although her hands were shaking she was extraordinarily calm. As she waited for the number to start ringing, she took the gag out of the mouth of the second man and held the receiver to his head. At the same time, Luka held a knife to the man's throat.

Teresa came into the kitchen carrying one of the rubber masks and dropped it on the table. Rosa wept, and Teresa immediately put her arms around her daughter and kissed her.

'OK, it's OK, shusssssh . . . It's over, everything's all right.'

'All right?' screeched Moyra. 'All right? Jesus Christ . . .'

Teresa gestured to Moyra to keep quiet. 'We've found out it was Barzini, he was acting on his own. His partners have agreed to pay us, but he was trying to get the money for himself. He has the draft ready, but was going to keep it. No doubt we'd have been got rid of, and he'd be $15 million richer.'

Sophia held her head in her hands. 'I don't believe I am hearing this. There's a body in there, and two more men shot, one of them by Moyra.'

Teresa snapped, 'Just listen, all of you.'

They waited, watching her every move.

Finally, Sophia banged impatiently on the table. 'Teresa, what is going on?'

'Johnny will take care of the men. He may need one of us to help him. He'll dump the dead one in the alley across the street. The other two we can help down to their car, it's parked out back, and Johnny will drive them to the nearest hospital.'

827

'What about the police, why not take them to the police?' Rosa tried not to let her voice sound hysterical, but she was shaking with terror.

Luka walked in, went immediately to Graziella and hugged her, saying quietly that it was all right now. He then laid a hand on Sophia's shoulder, but she shrugged him away.

'I don't think we should bring the police into this,' Luka said. 'They came here to get the documents for the Luciano holdings. Barzini will be expecting his friends to arrive with the contracts, signed by you all, but we'll be there instead – and we won't have any trouble getting in.'

He picked up the rubber mask and smiled. 'He's alone apart from his wife. One guy is his bodyguard, the other's the driver, and the dead man's his cousin.'

Sophia glared at them all. 'This has gone far enough, are you all crazy? Mama, for God's sake, make them see sense! We can't go to Barzini, we can't do anything but—'

Luka moved to her side. 'Call the cops? Is that your answer to everything? I just saved your life, all your lives, why don't you trust me? Trust me . . .'

Graziella made them all turn to her. She had been so quiet, sitting with her arms folded over her ample bosom. 'Johnny is right, Sophia. No police. I want to see this man, tell him to his face. We have that right, nobody should be allowed to do what he did, and to women . . . Then maybe we do the right thing, what Sophia suggests.'

The dead man had to be removed from the apartment, but he was almost six feet tall, and weighed at least seventeen stone. It was also still daylight. Luka remained calm, suggesting they find a wheelchair, and, fast-thinking as ever, he knew just where he would get one. There was a crippled war vet begging at the subway station and if they paid him enough, he was sure they could borrow the chair to get the dead man out of the apartment without too much suspicion.

Sure enough he returned with the chair within half an hour, and laughed when telling them that the so-called cripple virtually sprang to his feet when he saw the money Luka offered!

The frightened women remained grouped in the kitchen, looking like guilty children, and Luka knew they were having second thoughts.

'What are you going to do with him?' asked Teresa.

'Maybe leave him at the subway, he could earn some dough!'

She tried not to show her fear, snapping angrily, 'It isn't funny, Luka. What are we going to do with him? What about the others?'

Luka took her hand and gripped it tightly. 'Take it easy, I'll handle it, I'll wheel him into one of the back alleys, and dump him, then I'll come back for the others. Now, let's get him into the chair – Rosa, Moyra come on . . . we need a coat and a hat!'

Luka went into the study, closing the door behind him, and when he came out he had a set of car keys. 'They came in Barzini's car, it's a Lincoln parked out back. When I've dumped the body, I'll come back for the others, so just keep the door closed, and get some buckets and cloths to clean up afterwards.'

Teresa opened the front door and gave the signal that the coast was clear. Rosa was delegated to help Luka wheel the body out of the apartment. Graziella came into the hall. 'Johnny! . . . *Johnny!*'

Luka turned. 'You make sure you take the chair back!' Luka nodded, and then he and Rosa wheeled the dead man out. He now wore one of Alfredo's hats pulled down over his head to cover the wound.

It was a long, tough ride down as both the chair and the man were heavy. Luka pushed from the back, easing the wheels down each stair, as Rosa guided it from the front. As they came out onto the street, it was still only five-thirty in the afternoon, but it was already quite dark. People hurrying home from work crowded the pavement, and Luka took over. He instructed Rosa to go back inside, concerned that she would catch cold as she wore no coat. She watched him slowly wheeling the dead man along the street, at one moment leaning forwards to tuck a scarf further around the body, and then he disappeared in the throng of passers-by.

Luka continued for a further few yards before he turned back as if heading towards the apartment block, but then he turned down a ramp leading into the underground car park beneath Teresa's apartment block. He smiled to himself since they were in luck – the men had parked Barzini's Lincoln in a far corner, with the bonnet facing forwards. Luka wheeled the dead man round to the rear of the car and fumbled with the keys to find the correct one to open the trunk.

Luka returned and told the women that the beggar plus his chair were now installed back in their usual position in the subway. He had been gone almost an hour, and now he took the first of the injured men down to the car park at gunpoint. He had checked the bandages well so as not to leave a trail of blood.

The man had to lean heavily on Luka for support, and was in agony, hardly able to walk. He even thanked Luka, repeating over and over that he was only doing a job and that he meant no harm, and was sorry he had frightened the women. As Luka helped him into the back of the car, the man relaxed, believing he was going to hospital. Luka fired a single shot into his temple, using the man's own gun and silencer, then he propped him up in a sitting position before returning for the last man. This one had a flesh wound to his left arm, and although he had lost a considerable amount of blood he was not as disabled as his friend had been. Luka tied his hands behind his back, slipped a coat around his shoulders and went down the four flights of stairs yet again with the same gun and silencer pressed hard into the man's back. It was now almost seven o'clock.

Luka drove out of the car park, and headed towards the East Side, stopping at a hardware store, and from there he drove to a derelict building site. Barzini's Lincoln was eventually returned hours later to Barzini's own allocated space in his private parking bay beneath his hotel.

Luka had hurried back to his rented room, and afraid to leave any evidence of what he had been doing during the past three hours, he stuffed his dirty clothes into a plastic rubbish bag. He then caught the nearest subway train for two stops, and when he left the train he dropped a parcel wrapped in newspaper onto the rails. Luka, as he had promised Teresa he would, had taken care of everything.

He decided it was too dangerous to hire a car and that he would use Teresa's husband's Buick, still parked in the garage beneath her apartment. Luka would drive the women to the Barzini meeting.

The women washed and changed after cleaning the study. The bloody rug was rolled up ready for Luka to take to the incinerator unit in the basement.

The women waited, and waited. However, their initial terror had subsided and Teresa paced the hallway waiting for Luka.

Sophia joined her and whispered, 'I have to talk to you.'

Teresa looked at her watch. 'Where is he? What is he doing?'

Sophia caught Teresa's hand. 'I know about Joseph Rocco, Moyra told me. We are getting in deeper and deeper, this is becoming madness.'

Teresa ran her fingers through her hair. 'You think I don't know that? But what do we do?'

'He made you an accessory, you and Moyra.'

'I know, but it's too late to do anything about it.'

'No, it isn't. The only way we are going to get out of this is to come clean. We go to the police, because there's something I haven't told you.'

Before Sophia could continue, Luka returned. He had changed into a clean shirt and jeans, and handed Teresa the plastic sack containing his stained clothes and the hat and overcoat he had used. She took it from him and together they stuffed the bloody carpet into another sack. Her hands were now covered in blood. The bag began to split, and she tried frantically to stuff everything back in, calling out for someone to bring her another bag. Then she saw Luka's shirt; it was drenched in blood, and she looked at him in horror as he opened up another strong black bin liner.

'What have you done? Johnny?'

'Go and wash your hands, I'll take this down to the incinerator and then we're all set. Everyone ready? And I got you this, it's a very simple mechanism . . . Just withdraw the safety catch here, then it's ready to fire. It's loaded, so don't mess around with it, just put it in your handbag.'

She said nothing, but took the small .22 gun and hurried into the bathroom. She scrubbed her hands under the running water until they were almost raw, then dried them and put the bloodstained towel into the laundry bag, replacing it with a fresh one. She checked the bathroom and took a last look around the study to make sure it, too, was clean. Sophia walked in.

'Teresa, please just give me a few minutes. It's about Nino Fabio . . .'

Teresa shook her head. 'Not now, I can't take in anything more right now. We've got to go, tell me later.'

'It can't wait.'

Teresa snapped, 'It'll have to! If we're going to meet Barzini, then we have to leave right now. If we leave it any longer, we'll never be able to go through with it. We must go now, right now, because we're all so hyped up we can maybe pull it off.'

At eleven-thirty they left for Barzini's apartment. Sophia and Moyra sat up front with Luka, who was driving. In the back seat sat Graziella and Teresa, with Rosa between them.

Luka drove carefully, unhurriedly, often meeting Teresa's eyes in the rear-view mirror. In the silence, tension built within the car. Teresa could feel the outline of the gun in her bag and found it a comfort.

They drew up outside the Plaza and Luka walked around the car to open the doors for Graziella and Sophia. As he returned to the driving seat, Teresa told him quietly to wait. He hesitated, asked if she were sure she didn't want him along, and she shook her head.

The five well-dressed women were not as eye-catching as they had been the first time they arrived at the hotel. Then they had all been wearing black; now they were dressed to merge easily with the many people thronging the reception area. They separated as they approached the lifts. Teresa nudged Moyra.

Moyra walked straight up to the lift attendant, who stood by the intercom linked to the private suites. Opening her bag, she took out a small piece of paper and asked him to read what was written on it for her. As she did so, she tipped everything out of her bag, and the attendant bent down to pick up her compact and lipstick . . .

The attendant didn't even see the four women walk into the second lift. They were on the third floor by the time Moyra had replaced everything in her bag and given the attendant a large tip. Luka made no effort to get out of the car and open the door for her.

'Well, I did my part. They must be on his floor by now, if not inside the suite.'

He turned, and his strange eyes seemed to look inside her head. Then he straightened and looked to the front again, his hands on the steering wheel. 'They should never have taken the old lady in with them.'

'Listen, that old lady is tougher than you think, than any of us think. You're not married to a man like Don Luciano without having a lot going for you. Besides, she wanted to come, she said so herself.'

Moyra sat back in the car and closed her eyes. 'Teresa wouldn't let me go in with them. I was glad at first, now I dunno. I think I am going to have a heart attack.' She leaned forward, gripping the back of Luka's seat. 'Will they be all right?'

Luka looked at the clock on the dashboard. 'I'll give them fifteen minutes. If they're not out by then, I'll go in after them.'

They made it to the door of the suite without seeing anyone. As Rosa pressed the buzzer, Graziella and Sophia put on the masks. Teresa, a fraction behind them as some of the wispy grey hair on her mask had caught on her handbag, jerked it free, and only just had time to get the mask in place before they heard the lock on the door click.

Barzini peered through the spyhole, and they could hear him swearing at them for being so fucking stupid, then he swung the door wide. Before Teresa could even start her well-rehearsed speech, Graziella began a tirade against him in Sicilian.

Barzini was so startled that he stumbled backwards and overturned a small Venetian urn. The floral display cascaded over the floor.

Teresa moved Graziella firmly aside. 'Good evening, Mr Barzini.'

She ripped off her mask and threw it at him. It caught him square in the face. Sophia closed the door and put the chain on it. Her hand was shaking so much that twice she missed the small aperture.

Teresa watched Barzini squirm, could see his mind reeling, trying to assimilate what had happened, desperately playing for time . . .

Rosa cut the telephone wires and replaced the scissors in her bag. She then followed her mother and Sophia into the drawing room.

Graziella went in the opposite direction, opening doors and looking for Barzini's wife. She found the room and locked the bedroom door from the outside, then returned to the drawing room and held up the key.

She sat on the sofa, and somehow her appearance gave Barzini the guts to smile. Half-joking, he said, 'Eh, come on, girls. I don't know what these men told you, but . . .'

He still had the mask in his hand. He tossed it aside. He had composed himself, even made as if to offer them drinks.

Teresa put a hand on his shoulder. 'You give us the banker's draft and we leave.'

'I swear I don't know what you're talking about, I don't know what this is all about. Now why don't I get you ladies a drink and we can talk this through?'

She bent down and whispered to Rosa to give her the scissors. Rosa slipped them from her bag as Barzini turned his attention to Sophia, repeating that he knew nothing about the men who attacked them.

Teresa was at his side, and as he looked round to see what she was doing she snipped at the lobe of his ear with the scissors. He screeched and backed away, his hand to his ear.

'What the fuck! Are you crazy?' Blood trickled down his hand and he took out a white handkerchief, pressing it on the wound.

'We just want the banker's draft, Mr Barzini.'

'Jesus Christ, you cut my fucking ear, you cut my ear!'

Teresa gestured to Sophia, who got up and went to Barzini's desk. She began to pull the drawers out and tip the contents on the floor.

Barzini turned on her in fury. 'You leave that alone, you don't touch anything . . .'

Teresa opened her bag and took out the gun. He stood helplessly watching, dabbing at his ear with the handkerchief. 'I don't believe this is happening, I don't believe you women could be so stupid! You know what you're doing? You know what you're fuckin' doing? You think you'll get away with this, think I make the decisions? I got partners.'

'We know you do, Mr Barzini. Did you ever think that we might have too? And we're not taking anything that you and your partners weren't prepared to give.'

Teresa handed the gun to Rosa and joined Sophia in searching through Barzini's papers. She picked up a small book and flicked through it . . .

Barzini moved to the desk to try and take it. 'You crazy bitches!'

With both hands shaking, Rosa pointed the gun straight at him. He froze, teetering on the spot, afraid to move even a step, while Teresa flipped through the book.

When she spoke her voice was very calm. 'Empty your pockets.'

Barzini took off his jacket and flung it aside. 'You're making a mistake. Believe me, this doesn't stop here.'

Teresa searched the pockets of the jacket and opened

his wallet. She took out a folded white envelope and just by the look on his face knew she had found it. The draft was for $15 million – but it was made out to Barzini.

'You get the documents when you've cashed the draft. That was a nice restaurant you took us to, book another table, say one o'clock tomorrow. We don't want any drafts, just the cash, and in return you'll get exactly what we agreed to. If you don't turn up . . .'

Suddenly Teresa had lost it. What if he didn't turn up, what if he went and cashed the banker's draft himself and took off?

Graziella rose from the sofa and walked sedately towards Barzini.

'If we do not receive the money we will ask for a meeting with my husband's associates. We will tell them of our treatment, we will tell them, do you understand? You made a grave error of judgement; do not believe we are alone.'

As they walked out of the hotel, Luka was already opening the door for Graziella.

They were still describing what had been said and who had done what to whom when they let themselves into the apartment.

Luka listened attentively, then asked to speak to Teresa alone. They went to the study and closed the door. 'He never intended to pay you off, right?'

'It looks that way. The banker's draft was made out not to us but to Barzini. I suppose the intention was for him to cash it and pay us, only he would have kept it for himself.'

'You sure? What if it was his payoff for getting rid of

you? You've come away with nothing, how do you know he'll stick to the bargain now?'

'We couldn't do anything else, the draft was in his name.'

'There's all-night banks ... You shouldn't have walked out, I told you to take me in with you. You fucked up, you could get every one of those women hit, you know that, don't you?'

Teresa felt her legs shaking. Luka leaned close, but his eyes were so pale and dead that she backed away from him.

'You needed me, he had to be scared, understand? You have to put the frighteners on him. You needed me, why won't you trust me? I saved your life, all your lives, for Chrissake.'

Teresa clutched the desktop to give her strength. 'And we saved yours, so I guess we're quits.' She knew a lot of what he said was true, but she hated hearing it, hated to be told. It felt as if he were trying to take over. 'You're going to get a slice of $15 million, and you've earned it. But then what happens? I have to look out for my daughter, my family. What happens next, Johnny? Are we going to live under the threat of blackmail, is that what we can expect?'

'Has Sophia been talking to you?' Teresa shook her head and he went on, 'Then why? Why are you turning against me? I don't understand, you need me.'

Teresa rubbed her head. 'I'm sorry, I guess I'm all confused. And you're right, I made mistakes.'

'Yes, you did.'

She gave him a hard look and adjusted her glasses. 'At the same time, can you blame me? How come you know so much, Johnny? You're just a kid, and we keep on

839

trusting you, but we know nothing about you and . . . You made me and Moyra accessories to murder.'

He lifted his hands in a gesture of amazement. 'You know why I had to do that! You know, you and the rest of them are all accessories to murder, it happened here, right here. What did you want me to do, then? Run? I saved your lives.'

Teresa sighed. 'I know, I know . . . It's just that I feel responsible and it's getting out of control, Johnny. I don't think I can handle it, not alone. I am on my own, the others follow what I tell them to do, and I keep listening to you, but . . .'

He was sitting on the edge of the desk, swinging his foot. 'It works both ways, Teresa. You go down and you take me with you. Reason I know so much is that I was a runner, you know, a messenger boy. I kept my eyes and ears open. My father was small-time, but part of the mob. I was running messages before I was thirteen, cleaning the cars, that kind of thing. But because I could keep my mouth shut they liked me.'

Teresa took her glasses off. '"They", Johnny, the anonymous "they" . . . Exactly who, Johnny?'

'Well, sometimes it was the Gennaro family, and they kind of passed me around. They shipped me out to Sicily almost a year ago, I was supposed to be a courier, you know, bring stuff back for them. By then my father was dead. I was in deep trouble over the Dante thing: I mean, I can't go back; I blew it, they'd have me shot. It was heroin, I told you, and so without you I wouldn't have stood a chance of getting out of Sicily. I guess I need you! So, *you* hire me now, I work for you. You own me, because if you wanted you could turn me in at any time.'

'That works both ways, Johnny.'

'Right, but I don't want to take over. I'll take whatever orders you give me. I want to work for you, you've become my family. I've nobody else.'

Sophia walked in and he turned. She leaned against the doorframe. 'It's three o'clock in the morning. I think Johnny should leave.'

Luka was off the edge of the desk fast. He wouldn't look at Sophia, he just muttered that he would come back to drive them to the meeting with Barzini.

'I'll walk you down, Johnny, I need some air,' said Teresa.

Sophia watched them standing in the street below. She closed the curtain and turned to Graziella.

'Would you like a sleeping tablet?'

'No . . . Get to my age and you don't need much sleep. It was a full day, huh?'

Sophia laughed, folding her arms. 'I would say, Mama, that is putting it mildly. Er, do you have any pills, it's just that I've run out.'

Graziella opened her bedside drawer and held out the bottle. As Sophia reached for it she saw Michael's photograph.

'He was your favourite, wasn't he?'

Graziella closed her eyes. 'He filled my soul and broke my heart. They always say the first-born is the one, the one that touches you most, lives inside you more than the others. Maybe because the first one is so frightening, and so wonderful . . .'

She stopped. Sophia had left the room.

*

Sophia poured a tumbler full of whisky, then sat at the kitchen table. She took the first pill, then a second, and felt a hand on her shoulder. Graziella took the pill bottle, carefully screwing the cap back on, then pulled out a chair and sat down, reaching for Sophia's hands. She could feel the weight around Sophia, it filled the room, but she could think of no words of comfort.

'I want to sleep, Mama, and never wake up. I don't think I can take any more, it's as if we're caught in madness.'

Graziella sighed. 'Yes, I would never have believed any of the things that have happened to us were possible. Sometimes I lie awake and it is as if I am in a different world . . . I guess I am, I am in America, and the past is the past. But you know, I remember the good times more and more, and they are a comfort to me.'

Sophia reached for her hand. 'Mama, there is something I have never told you, the time was never right. Sometimes it is as if nothing in my life has ever been right. You remember that night when Alfredo brought me to the villa, after the accident? I had come to Palermo from Cefalu, because . . .'

She stopped because Moyra had appeared in the doorway. Her tear-stained face, devoid of make-up, looked like that of a lost child.

'I can't sleep, I'm so scared, I can't sleep.'

Sophia sighed as Graziella held out her hand to Moyra, drew her to sit beside them.

'Where's Mama?' asked Rosa as she came into the kitchen. Her face was drawn and pale. Graziella patted her knee, treating Rosa like a little girl. Rosa sat on her grandmother's knee and buried her face in her shoulder.

'Grandmama, I am so glad you are here.'

Graziella smiled. Surrounded by her daughters she felt loved, more importantly she felt needed.

'You know what day it is today? Grandmama?'

Moyra sprang up. 'It's Christmas Day, it's Christmas Day!'

She ran from the room and came back with the little gifts she had bought for each of them. 'Happy Christmas, Sophia.'

Sophia tried hard to smile as she reached for the bright little parcel, but her face crumpled and she sobbed, holding it to her face.

Rosa's lips trembled. 'Don't cry, Sophia, don't cry.'

She burst into tears and Moyra, who had been close to weeping for most of the night, started sobbing. Graziella looked from one to the other, saying nothing, but she rocked Rosa in her arms and began to sing.

Teresa wrapped Sophia's coat around her. They had walked a long way and she had not really intended coming to the trucking company. It was still locked and barred, with lethal-looking wires threaded over the tops of the walls.

'This is where my husband used to work. It's the only part of what we have left that I couldn't include in the buy-out. I didn't know why at first, but I also retained the leasing rights to Pier Number Three at the docks. It's one of the biggest.'

Luka looked up at the unlit warehouses and shoved his hands deeper in his pockets.

Teresa smiled. 'You think I'm crazy if I say to you that I want to go into business? I want to plough my share of the money into starting this place up again. I need help, of course, people I can trust.'

'What about the unions?'

'Oh, that's all old hat now, Johnny. Things are changing. The Mafia's stranglehold on the unions is virtually over. This is where all the gasoline used to be brought to, and you can imagine how much money changed hands over that . . . The Lucianos were paid a percentage of every gallon they sold, did you know? They had so many fake companies it was a full-time job just keeping track of the names. Old Papa Luciano was always going on about his legality, but I know for sure he made millions out of the gasoline scams.'

This was beyond Luka, he had no idea what she was talking about. He couldn't quite make her out, standing hunched in the cold, her thin nose red, but somehow she touched him with her earnestness.

'Money is what counts, Johnny. We can go into straight, legitimate trading because of that pier, but if I have to use other methods to succeed, then I will. Are you interested?'

He laughed. 'You want the Lucianos back in business, is that it?'

She looked down at her shoe, kicked at the road. 'I need to know who Barzini's partners are, what business they're in. Could you find out?'

Luka had not the faintest idea how to go about it, but he nodded.

'Sure . . . I could find out for you.'

'I'd better get back.'

'Yeah, get a cab. We've walked quite a way.'

'No, I'll walk. I know these streets like the back of my hand. I was born not far from here. See you tomorrow.'

She walked away, but stopped and turned back to him. 'You know, I thought you were in this for the money, but I don't think you are. I think you really care about us.'

'I never had a family. I'll look after Barzini for you.'

She smiled and continued on her way, calling good-night over her shoulder. She was sure Moyra had said that Johnny had a brother . . . Odd he never mentioned it.

Exhausted, Teresa climbed the stairs. She hoped they would all be sleeping – she couldn't face any further arguments, she only wanted to sink into her bed and sleep.

She heard them as she turned on to their landing. At first the high-pitched wail frightened her, then she listened in disbelief as the chorus of voices, out of key, bellowed together, 'Hark, the herald angels sing, Glory to the new-born king . . .'

CHAPTER 35

COMMISSARIO JOE Pirelli spent Christmas in Milan, and it was the worst Christmas he had ever had. The investigation into the murder of the Luciano family and the Paluso child had, to all intents and purposes, been forced to end.

The only suspect, Luka Carolla, it had to be admitted, had probably left Italy. The expenses incurred had been phenomenal; the extra men covering the airports and stations, hotels, garages, hospitals, the circulation of thousands of photographs, the forensic and ballistics experts, all had to be paid for.

The judge in overall charge of the cases decreed that Carolla would remain on the wanted list, with the right of extradition if he was found in the United States. There was nothing more Pirelli could do and, although he balked against it, he had no option but to leave Palermo. The case, as with hundreds of other Mafia-linked cases, would remain open on file.

Pirelli, with his wife Liza and son Gino, returned to Milan on Christmas Eve. They shopped for a tree and gifts, including a new bike for Gino. When they finally arrived home, Liza sent Pirelli out to fill a bucket with earth for the tree, while she unpacked.

One of the cases was full of dirty laundry that she hadn't had a chance to wash in Palermo. As she tipped it into the laundry basket, in the bathroom, she noticed the pair of sheets she had put on the bed before she left.

Although it was against the rules, Pirelli dug the earth from a flowerbed. When he carried it back to the apartment, Liza was waiting.

First, she produced the ashtray with the lipstick-stained Turkish cigarette stubs, then she threw the dirty sheets across the room.

'Since when have you bothered to change a bed? I'll tell you when; the day you brought a whore back here, you bastard!'

Pirelli said nothing and Liza's voice rose to a screech, 'You call yourself a detective? No wonder that guy got away, you can't even bring a woman here and clear away the evidence! Well, you spend Christmas here, get your whore to keep you company, because that's all the company you'll have! I am leaving . . .'

Pirelli slumped into a chair and lit a cigarette, still saying nothing. Liza faced him, hands on hips, eyes blazing.

'Well, aren't you going to say something? Even try to make an excuse?'

He shrugged, refusing to look at her. Frustrated by his silence, she stormed into the bedroom and slammed the door. He could hear her crying. Slowly, he stubbed his cigarette out and followed her. She was curled up on the unmade bed, sobbing. He sat beside her.

'Liza . . . Liza, listen to me . . .'

'How could you bring someone into our bed, how could you do that to me?'

'I have no excuse, it was unforgivable, and I'm sorry.'

'Oh, you're sorry? *Sorry?*'

'Yes, I am. If you want me to leave, I will. Do you want me to leave?'

'*Yes!* Get out and leave us alone. I hate you!' Then she added, 'Who is she? Do I know her?'

'You don't know her.'

'How long has it been going on?'

'It happened only once. I'm sorry.'

'Who is it?'

'You don't know her. I couldn't understand it myself, all I can say is that I'm sorry, I am ashamed, if that makes you feel better.'

'Are you still seeing her?'

To Liza's astonishment, he appeared close to tears. He shook his head, unable to meet her eyes.

'Do you love her, this woman . . .? Joe?'

She went to him, pushed his shoulder. 'Are you in love with this woman, whoever the bitch is?'

He caught her hand and she tried to pull away, but he held on tightly. 'Listen to me. I have said I'm sorry, that it's over, but I can't talk about it.'

'Oh, fine! You bring a woman back here to our apartment, sleep with her in *my* bed, then tell me you don't want to talk about it! Well, fuck you.'

She broke free and slapped his face. He turned his head but did nothing else to defend himself. Liza punched him, wanting to hurt him, but he ducked and gestured towards the door. Their son was peeking into the room, his little face scared.

Liza snapped at him, 'Go to your room, Gino, I'll come and see you in a minute . . . Now, Gino, do as I tell you!'

The boy slunk away and Pirelli closed the door. He stood with his back to his wife and sighed. He asked, 'What do you want me to do, Liza? You want me to leave?'

She took a tissue from the box on the dressing table and blew her nose. 'I don't know . . . I just don't know how you could have done this to me.'

She seemed so helpless, her face tear-stained, and he felt terrible. He went to her and rubbed her shoulders comfortingly. 'Believe me, I don't know why it happened, but it did and there's nothing I can say that will make it any better.'

'Don't you love me any more?'

He stroked her cheek. 'I love you, Liza, I love you . . .' He flushed guiltily and gave her a sheepish smile. 'Look, I'll try to make it up to you. We'll go on that holiday, the three of us. Now that I'm through in Palermo we can go straight after Christmas. What do you say?'

'I don't know, Joe. Right now I don't know what I want, I'm so mixed up, so . . . I still can't believe you lied to me.'

His face tightened. 'I haven't lied, Liza, believe me, I haven't lied to you. It is over, I won't see her again.'

He held her in his arms, kissing her hair, her neck, as she clung to him, crying. He hugged her tightly.

'Don't, Liza, please don't.'

*

Christmas was strained, with Liza referring to his 'one-night stand' at every possible opportunity. Even when they made love she asked if she was as good as 'the woman', which was how she always referred to Sophia. Pirelli was sure that he wouldn't think of her half so much if Liza didn't bring the subject up continually. He knew he had to see her again, he even contemplated leaving Liza, but the thought of losing his son changed his mind.

He was torn by guilt, depressed, even maudlin at times. The sense of failure pervaded everything. He had failed, he had not found Luka Carolla, and even though no one could fault his work he could not put it out of his mind.

He had decided not to go back to work after the Christmas break, but to take the holiday owing to him. That was his intention until he received a call from an old friend.

Detective Inspector Carlo Gigante was in charge of the Nino Fabio homicide and he called Pirelli to ask a favour. Could Pirelli help trace Sophia Luciano, as he needed to question her? Pirelli wanted to know why, but Gigante refused, saying he would prefer to leave it until they were in the office. Pirelli agreed. He had no idea that Sophia was in New York.

Michel Barzini was a very worried man. The men who had supplied him with the cash to pay off the widows were now eagerly waiting for the documents giving them full rights to all the Luciano holdings. He had made a gross error of judgement in trying to gain the documents and frighten the women off and retain the money for himself. As their paymaster, if it was discovered that he was in trouble, it could jeopardize any other transactions they put his way, not to mention his life.

He left his suite at the Plaza and walked two blocks to his underground car-parking space. Engrossed in his own thoughts, he walked down the ramp and headed towards his car, fumbling in his pocket for the car keys. He stopped to select the ignition key without even looking at the Lincoln.

As he opened the car door, the parking attendant, who was washing one of the other cars, called something out to him. He looked round, but the attendant had bent down out of sight to wash the hub-caps. Barzini slammed the door and started the engine, then turned and slung his arm along the back of the seat as he reversed out. He heard something fall off the rear seat and, pushing the gear lever to the park position, he leaned over to see what it was.

In the dim light of the car park he could not see clearly, so he opened the glove compartment and took out a torch which he shone on the floor behind his seat . . . Unable to see, even with the torch, he put his hand down to feel what had fallen. He grasped some kind of fibre and pulled.

The material was human hair, attached to the severed head of Harry Barzini, his cousin. The eyes stared sightlessly, the mouth hung slightly open.

The attendant stood up from behind the Cadillac when he heard Barzini scream. He stood on tiptoe and could see Barzini's chalk-white face in the gloom. He continued polishing as he watched.

The rear seat of the Lincoln was caked with dried blood. It was everywhere and, now his eyes were accustomed to the dark, Barzini found he was covered in dark blood-stains himself. Panic-stricken, he struggled out of his jacket and threw it over the dismembered head. Then, with the head wrapped in the jacket, he fumbled to open the trunk of the car.

The attendant had worked his way round to the hood of the Caddy. As Barzini swung the trunk of the Lincoln open, the stench made him retch. He yelped like a terrified dog. He became hysterical, gibbering and shaking, and the head slipped from his shaking hands, rolling like a ball beneath the car.

Barzini had to get down on his hands and knees, lie on the oil-streaked concrete floor to retrieve it. His fingers inched towards the ghastly, glaring face. He drew it close by some strands of hair. Panting with the horror, the hideous feel of the hardening skin, he threw it into the trunk and slammed the lid down, but it sprang open again. He forced it down until the lock caught, then ran back to the lifts.

In a state of shock, Barzini was so disturbed he didn't realize that the whole incident had been watched by the parking attendant. He had not seen exactly what had happened; but what concerned him was that the Lincoln was parked half-way across the exit lane. He threw down his polishing cloth and walked over to the car.

The hysterical Barzini got back to his apartment just as Salerno was about to let himself in. He dragged Salerno inside. 'Get some guys, have my car towed away, dumped, set alight. But nobody gotta find it, understand me?'

'What happened, you had an accident?'

'Just fuckin' listen . . . The Luciano women are crazy motherfuckers. They gotta get paid.'

'What? I thought it was all paid off by now.'

'Just do what I tell you.'

'Your friends aren't gonna like this. The deal was straight cut, what's gone wrong? You try something?'

He knew by Barzini's face that he had, and shook his head. 'When are you gonna learn, Mike? They already got gear bein' shipped from Colombia into Palermo but they got no place to store it and ship it, so you're in shit if they don't get the Luciano property. What the fuck made you do it, what'd you try on?'

'Just get out of here and do what I tell you. Get my car towed out.'

As Michel Barzini climbed into a taxi at the front of the Plaza Hotel, police cars were arriving at the entrance to the underground car park. His car was cordoned off, and a sheet covered the open trunk, concealing the remains of his relative.

Salerno never even made it to the car, but turned tail as soon as he saw the cops. He had no idea of Barzini's plans and all he could do was wait for the inevitable knock on the door. But there was no wait; the police were already at Barzini's apartment by the time he returned. Salerno overheard Elsa Barzini telling them that her husband was lunching at the Four Seasons.

Barzini was ten minutes late arriving at the Four Seasons. He was sweating, but otherwise seemed composed as he walked up the wide staircase.

Teresa was waiting, watching the small man heading up the stairs, carrying a black leather attaché case. He nodded to the *maître d'*, who led him to his table. He sat down, the sweat showing on his forehead.

Teresa smiled, said she hoped everything had gone smoothly, and apologized for having already ordered the wine. She held back until the waiter had poured Barzini a glass, hoping he approved of her choice. She had, she told Barzini, been informed by the *maître d'* that the fresh poached salmon was delicious. Then she passed him the thick folder of documents. He checked them thoroughly, at the same time draining his glass – but if that was an indication of what he was feeling she could not tell. He gave no hint of what he had discovered. That would come later. But the sweat now streaming down his face gave him away. It formed a shining film across his upper lip.

He looked up and stiffened as the waiter refilled his wineglass. Two uniformed police officers had entered the restaurant and were walking up the wide staircase. One called to the *maître d'* to join them. Barzini's eyes, behind the glasses, blinked furiously. The *maître d'* turned towards his table and pointed; the officers headed towards Barzini.

He turned, with a look of loathing, to Teresa. 'You bitch, you set me up, you fucking whore!'

As if it were all taking place in slow motion, the two officers walked towards the round centre table, Barzini's regular table, closer and closer . . .

Suddenly, Barzini erupted into motion, hurling the big table up, sending the glasses and crockery cascading to the floor, and making an insane dash for the stairs.

854

Barzini ran into the street, into the traffic, zigzagging among the screeching cars as they swerved to avoid him. As the officers gave chase he ran directly into the path of a yellow cab . . . His body was thrown into the air, over the front of the cab, and into the path of a delivery truck coming the opposite way. He bounced like a rag doll and finished up trapped beneath the truck's rear wheels.

Teresa saw it all through the vast windows overlooking the street. She slipped the documents into Barzini's case and clasped it under her arm, putting her handbag on top. In the commotion, with people running in and out of the restaurant, no one noticed her leave.

She walked straight to the waiting car and slipped into the back seat.

'That was Barzini. Cops walked in and he ran for it.'

Luka grinned. 'How come, food that bad, is it?'

She smiled. It was strange that she felt no guilt, no remorse; just the opposite, she was almost elated. She clutched the briefcase.

'Convenient, eh?' Luka said as he drove out into the main stream of traffic.

'You could say that. I think we'd better get home.'

Pirelli was in the middle of a coughing fit, his face gradually turning puce. His office door opened and Inspector Carlo Jesus Gigante smiled at him.

'That sounds good; OK if I grab you for a few minutes?'

Pirelli gesticulated wildly, coughing so much he had

to lean over the side of his desk. When he looked up, his eyes were watering. 'Oh, man, I'm giving up before it kills me.'

'You said that four years ago when we worked together. Any hope of some coffee?'

Thick black coffee was brought in and the two men lit up, filling the air-conditioned office with fine blue smoke that drifted out through the air vents.

Gigante offered his condolences on the Palermo situation and Pirelli shrugged. 'I'll get him one day. How's things with you?' He was desperate to ask about Sophia, but he bided his time.

Gigante shrugged. 'Oh, so-so. As I said, I'm on the Nino Fabio case and I need to find Sophia Luciano.'

Pirelli half-smiled, unsure who Nino Fabio was. 'You mind if I ask why?'

Gigante filled him in on the details, then took a notebook from his briefcase. 'I spoke to nearly everyone, and she no longer lives in Rome. On the day of the murder she had an afternoon appointment with Fabio, and everyone within earshot heard them having one hell of a row. There's a very nasty, snide entry in his diary. Apparently, he had seen Sophia and her sisters-in-law at some restaurant, and from there on referred to them as *bella mafia* ... Anyway, Nino refused to help her. Interesting now, all Fabio's drawings, designs, whatever you call them, are missing, as is Signora Sophia. So, what can you do for me? Know any way I can get in touch with her?'

Pirelli poured more coffee. 'I know she was in Palermo just before Christmas, for Graziella Luciano's court hearing. But I don't know where she is now.'

He asked the date Fabio had been murdered and

discovered that it was the night he and Sophia had spent together in Milan, but said nothing. Gigante spilt coffee on his shirt and swore, taking out a grubby handkerchief to wipe it down.

'That suspect you're after, still no idea where he's run to?'

'Carolla? If I knew, I wouldn't be here.'

Gigante gave Pirelli a sidelong look. 'Well, it's because of him that I'm here, that and trying to trace Sophia Luciano.'

Pirelli was like a bird of prey. 'You got something on him?'

'Maybe . . . We had a lot of women to question, you know, the machinists and the designers. There were more than thirty. One of them, Celeste Moranna, was in hospital having a kid, so I didn't get to her until two days ago. That's why I called you. She came into the station.'

Gigante stopped and wiped his shirt again. Pirelli was trying hard to keep his cool, not to push him, but he was hanging on his every word. 'Go on, she came to see you and . . .?'

Gigante pulled a face. 'It's gonna stain. OK, we knew Sophia Luciano was having a row with this Fabio guy, but no one had seen anyone with her. Every witness said she was alone. But this Celeste saw her outside the building and said she was talking to a chauffeur. One girl thought she had seen someone looking around, but didn't know who he was. She said he went into the executive suite, but she didn't see if he left with our Signora Luciano or if he had anything to do with her. All Celeste could say was that she had seen Luciano talking to a chauffeur outside Fabio's place.'

Pirelli sighed. 'Get to the point, what's this got to do with Luka Carolla?'

'Well, she's sitting in my office, right? I ask her to describe the guy so I could check if it was the same man the other witnesses saw. Well, she starts to hum and haw, then she gets up and walks over to the notice board. She points at the identikit picture of Luka Carolla.'

'What?'

'"Hang on, I think this is him," she says, "but this photograph is more like him!" The photograph, Joe, is the one you sent round after the identikit, they're both pinned up on my board.'

Pirelli rocked backwards and forwards in his chair. 'How much can you depend on this witness?'

'Not that much. It was a good three weeks after the event, but she came in of her own volition. There's no material gain – I mean, she doesn't even work at Fabio's any more.'

Gigante rummaged in his briefcase again, eventually pulling out a dog-eared folder. He tossed over some large black and white photos of the corpse. 'The guy that did it was a real sicko. You can see by the stains on the carpet, Fabio bled to death. We found him in this tableau. Not a pretty sight, parked among his dummies.'

Pirelli looked with disgust at the photographs; they helped cover the fact that his mind was reeling. He had seen the chauffeur, but not paid him much attention, could not recall seeing his face. His shirt was sticking to his body, he was sweating so much. Jesus Christ, had Luka Carolla been driving Sophia Luciano's Rolls? There was a knock on the office door, and a female officer entered, excusing the interruption. 'Sorry, Commissario, but I thought you'd want to see this; it's just arrived.'

Pirelli was presented with a telex forwarded from Palermo.

He scanned the page, then slumped back in his seat. 'Whatever I said in the past about the NYPD, forgive me Lord . . . Listen, listen to this, my friend.'

He paced the room as he read aloud, '. . . Aware that you are, etc., etc., etc. . . . Manhattan State Bank . . . private boxes . . . one box listed as number 456 . . . after extensive enquiries was found to be owned by Paul Carolla, now deceased. The last will and testament of Paul Carolla, etc., etc., North East Side, named his son, Giorgio Carolla, as his sole heir. On 28 December 1987, the ownership of the box was transferred to G. L. Carolla, to await collection . . . and to be handed over on signature and legal verification of said G. L. Carolla . . . This occurred . . . G. L. Carolla took possession of the contents of private bank box 456, property of the Manhattan . . . *Jesus Christ!* 28 December 1988 . . . That's one week ago!'

Gigante thought Pirelli was about to kiss him. 'What the hell does that mean?'

'G. L. Carolla is Luka Carolla, and I've got to be there before those bastards let him slip away . . .'

In New York the women moved quickly. The money had been divided up and each had taken her share to a different bank. Teresa said nothing about the fact that she still had all the documents. After discussing it with Johnny, she decided to wait and see what happened after his phone call.

Luka put a call through to Paul Salerno from a pay phone, requesting him to arrange a meeting with

Barzini's so-called partners. He was careful to make no mention of the Luciano women, sure that Barzini's phone would be tapped. Teresa stood beside the phone booth, listening.

'My clients are still interested in doing the same deal. They still have the documents, due to Barzini's unfortunate accident, and wish to do business.' Luka could not repress a smile as he continued, 'You see, they still have no cash, they need to move quickly.'

Salerno did not mention the fact that he was sure Barzini had cashed the banker's draft and paid the widows. He simply stated that he was not in a position to deal, but would contact the parties involved. It would take a few days to set up.

Luka tried to close the conversation by saying abruptly that he would call again, but Salerno was not easily put off. He said, quietly and courteously, that he would require payment for his efforts. Luka finally agreed to two per cent of the final sum.

Teresa inched the door further open and whispered, 'Make sure he knows we don't have the documents at the apartment.'

Luka gave her the thumbs up. 'My clients wish it to be known that all the documents are in a safety-deposit box and not at their apartment, is that understood? I have the key, so it would be a waste of time trying to get them . . .'

'Who is this?'

'That is no concern of yours, I am acting for my clients. I'll call you again, on this number, in three days.'

Putting the phone down, Luka smiled at Teresa. 'You hear? I think he's gonna play ball, he's got no option . . .

Put it there!' He held out his open palm, but she wasn't smiling.

'Why did you tell them we hadn't received the money?'

Luka lifted his eyes to heaven.

Teresa persisted, 'You shouldn't have lied.'

'Oh, come on, think. Barzini cashed the banker's draft, right? It will be your word against theirs, and what would you prefer: $15 million or $30 million? They'll have to pay you twice; trust me!'

Teresa was still unsure, and suggested that they should make no mention of the money business until they had heard back from Salerno. Luka slipped his arm through Teresa's; he couldn't keep his secret any longer. 'I've got a surprise trip organized; what would you say to a weekend trip to Long Island? Maybe now would be a good time to leave the city. I have got something to show you, all of you.'

'You think we should leave?'

Luka skipped in front of her, his hands stuffed into his pockets for warmth, his cheeks flushed pink from the cold. 'Trust me, I'm gonna look after you, and I have got a big surprise.'

Teresa arrived home laden with boxes. 'Happy belated Christmas, Rosa, Mama, Sophia . . . and even you, Moyra. They're from us.'

'Us?' said Sophia as she came to her bedroom door.

'Yes, Johnny and me. He'll be by later, he's arranging a surprise trip. We'll all leave early in the morning, spend a few days out of town. Where is everyone?'

Sophia shrugged. 'Out shopping. Look. I'm sorry to ask you this now, but as we're alone, maybe it's a good idea. I'm thinking of going to Paris, and I just wondered how long you sort of wanted us to stick around?'

Teresa stiffened. 'Well, that's up to you, there's no strings attached. It'd be nice if you came away with us; it'll be a sort of celebration. Besides, I think it's a good idea, just in case any more men in masks decide to pay us a visit.'

Sophia cocked her head to one side. 'But we've got nothing they want, unless Barzini wants his cash back. If he does he'd better hurry, the rate Moyra's spending her share.'

Teresa was not amused; she snapped, 'We still don't know what happened in Palermo. You can joke, but all I'm doing is looking out for us, but you go to Paris, you . . .' The telephone rang, and she froze in mid-sentence. Before Sophia could answer it, she had snatched up the receiver.

Sophia was about to return to her room, but Teresa waved her hand frantically for her to stay. She answered in English, but then switched to Sicilian. 'Yes, but she's not at home right now . . . yes, she is staying here . . . of course, yes . . .'

She covered the mouthpiece, 'It's someone enquiring about you, I said you were not here. It's a detective from Milan, Gigante. Do you know him?'

Sophia shook her head and Teresa said into the phone, 'Yes, yes, I'll tell her as soon as she returns. Do you have a number where she can call you?'

Teresa wrote the number on a used envelope. As she did so, she covered the mouthpiece again. 'He's in New York . . .' Then she asked Gigante, 'May I know what

862

this is about? Oh, I see . . . Well, then, I will get her to call you.'

Sophia was at her side. 'What does he want?'

Teresa gestured to her to keep quiet. 'Yes . . . I will, thank you.'

Replacing the phone, she turned to Sophia. 'He's in New York to see you. He's been trying to contact you. He didn't make it out to be that important, something to do with Nino Fabio. I thought it was best to tell him you were out to give you time to think, because you will have to get rid of him. The last thing we want right now is the police coming round. What do you think he wants?'

She could see that Sophia was shaking and her face was white as a sheet.

With a searching look, she asked, 'What's it all about?'

'I'll show you,' Sophia replied. Going to the bedroom, she opened the suitcase full of Nino's drawings. 'Johnny gave them to me, remember? I tried to tell you about them.'

'Yes, I remember. But why come all the way to New York to talk to you about them? Oh, shit, did he steal them? Did Johnny steal them?'

Sophia bit her lip. 'I presume so . . .'

Teresa snatched her glasses off and rubbed her eyes. 'The stupid boy . . . My God, this is all we need, and it's your fault. You know he's got this thing about you, never mind going on about him and Rosa . . .'

Sophia slammed the case shut. 'Do you think I have encouraged him? Me? I was the one who wanted you to get rid of him at the very beginning, he's the one that's got us into . . .'

Teresa interrupted. 'I don't want to hear that now, Sophia. If it wasn't for him we could all have been shot.

What's past is past . . . So, first, are they worth money? These drawings? Is that why the detective is here?'

'*Yes!* I told you that, of course they are worth a lot of money. It's almost his entire collection, but . . .'

She was trapped. The detective wasn't just in New York to enquire about the theft of the designs but a murder that Sophia found herself involved in. Her mind was so scrambled that she was at a loss, she couldn't think what she should admit to knowing . . .

Teresa was pacing up and down the cluttered room. 'OK, let's take it stage by stage. Do they know about your connection with Fabio?'

'Yes, of course. I went to his factory when I tried to buy them from him. Johnny was with me, he was driving the car, I told you this.'

'Did anyone see you there?'

Helplessly, Sophia shrugged her shoulders. 'I don't know, I can't think . . .'

'Well, start thinking. Who saw you there?'

'No one, I didn't see anyone, not until I was leaving. A girl who used to be my receptionist, I spoke to her. I talked to her outside the building, so they know I was there.'

'So she also saw Johnny?'

'Yes, I just said so, he was driving the car.'

Teresa sighed. 'Well, first you have to get rid of the drawings, burn them, do anything, but get rid of them. They can't be found here, or anywhere near us. Next, you call this detective, seem very willing to see him, and tell him you saw Fabio but you left. You know nothing about the drawings, don't even mention them, come on real innocent.'

Sophia sat immobile.

'Are you listening, Sophia?'

She nodded. 'Yes, yes, I'm listening'

'OK. Take them down to the incinerator, get rid of every one. Then, before he calls again, you'll have to speak to him, otherwise it'll look suspicious. The last thing we want right now is some bloody cop from Sicily hanging around, especially after what has happened . . . All right?'

'Yes . . . Yes, when should I call?'

'I don't know. Look, if I'd started asking all sorts of questions it would've sounded suspicious. Is there anything else? If there is, you'd better tell me.' She looked searchingly at Sophia, then asked again, 'That is all there is to it?'

Sophia picked up the case. 'I'll go down to the basement.'

Luka lay on his small bed, staring up at the light bulb. He had arranged every detail of the weekend trip with care, and he chuckled, doubting if any of them would ever return to New York. The small holdall containing all Paul Carolla's papers was neatly stashed by his bed, and he put his hand out to touch it, pat it, then slid his hand inside to touch the folded papers and bundles of banknotes. Then he rolled over on to his belly and pulled the pillow over his head. He wanted to laugh out loud – Paul Carolla's dream of the good life was now contained in one small holdall.

He saw clearly the fat, potbellied man who had fathered him for twelve years. He could smell the cigar smoke, even feel the way the fat hands used to grip him, hold him in that bear-hug . . . He giggled, hugging the pillow.

CHAPTER 36

PIRELLI UNPACKED his overnight case and went down to the lobby of the cheap Hotel Redmond, then down some steps leading to a bar which was open to the public, with another entrance from the street.

Gigante was already sitting on a bar stool. He ordered a beer for Pirelli and munched on a handful of courtesy peanuts from a convenient bowl at his elbow.

'I put in a call to the Luciano place. They didn't know where Signora S was, but she's in New York. I left the number here for her to call . . .'

Pirelli sat on a stool and flicked open a new packet of duty-free Marlboro. It was too late to do anything that night, so after finishing their drinks they took a walk along Fifth Avenue, window-shopping. Jet-lagged, the pair decided on an early night after a light supper and a few more beers.

It was after ten but, tired as he was, Pirelli couldn't sleep. He picked up his book and tried to read, but couldn't concentrate. He was going to see her and was unsure how he would react. He threw the sheets aside and took a can of beer from the fridge. As he snapped it open, the light on his phone blinked. The operator informed him that there was a call for Mr Gigante, but there was no reply from his room. Mr Gigante had requested that, if he was not available, his calls should be put through to Mr Pirelli. Did he, she asked, wish to take the call?

Pirelli reached for a cigarette. 'Sure, who is it?'

'The caller would not give her name, Mr Pirelli.'

'Put the call through.' He knew it would be Sophia . . . The husky voice asked if he was Detective Gigante.

'No, it's me, Sophia, it's Joe.'

There was a long pause, then, 'Joe?'

'Yep. I'm here on an investigation, we came together.'

'I was asked to call, he wants to see me.'

Pirelli paused and inhaled deeply, letting the smoke drift from his nostrils. 'I want to see you, too.'

She did not reply. Eventually, he asked, 'Sophia, are you still there?'

'Yes . . .'

'I can't discuss Gigante's case, you understand?'

'Of course . . . Well, I'll call him tomorrow. I'm sorry I rang so late.'

'It's not that late . . . How are you?'

'I'm fine.'

He wanted to ask so many questions, but he knew it would be highly unethical. He thought fast, then said, 'Sophia, he'll ask your whereabouts the night we went to the opera. He knows we were together, but nothing more . . .'

Again he waited. When she spoke, her voice was faint. 'Is it about Nino Fabio?'

'Yes, you know about him?'

'Yes, I called Nino's office. Is that what he wants to

see me about?' Sophia, with Teresa right at her side, could not at this stage mention that she knew Nino Fabio was dead.

'Yeah, that's what Gigante wants to talk to you about.'

'Why?'

'I can't really discuss it.'

'No, I guess not.'

'I'll come to see you with him.'

'Oh, are you on the case, too?'

'No, but I'll be with him.'

'When does he want to see me?'

'Soon as possible.'

'Tomorrow?'

'Yes . . . about nine?'

Again there was a pause. 'Make it a little later.'

Teresa gripped Sophia's arm and whispered, 'Don't tell him we are going away, tell him we will be out shopping for a few hours. Tell him as little as possible.'

'Hello, Joe . . . My sister-in-law and mother-in-law are going out shopping, so the apartment will be empty later, it will be easier to talk.'

'OK, how much later?'

Teresa whispered again, 'Say ten.'

'About ten?' said Sophia.

'I'll tell Gigante.'

There was another long pause, then Pirelli said, 'I have missed you, Sophia.'

Silence. 'You hear me?' he said.

'Yes, I hear you . . .'

'I'll see you tomorrow morning, then?'

'Is there a reason for you to come tomorrow?'

Pirelli stubbed out his cigarette. 'Yes, I have some questions I need to ask you.'

'What about?'

'It would be best to tell you when I see you.'

'Until tomorrow, then.' Her voice was very soft.

'I still love you,' he said quietly.

The phone went dead; she had hung up. He held the receiver a few moments longer before he replaced it.

Teresa stared hard at Sophia. 'Well? What's it about? Was that Gigante?'

Sophia shook her head. 'No, it was Commissario Pirelli, they're together. They are coming here at ten.'

'Yes, I heard. Did they say why they wanted to see you? Is it about the designs?'

Sophia shrugged. 'I guess so, and I was seen at the warehouse, so they'll want to question me.'

Teresa squinted. Without her glasses, Sophia's face was blurred. 'Johnny must have been out of his mind, what are you going to do?'

'Well, be here, you heard me. They're all destroyed now anyway – they won't find anything. I can join you wherever you're all going. It's best if I'm here alone.'

Teresa pursed her lips. 'Is there something you're not telling me?'

Sophia shook her head. 'No . . . I'm tired, I'll go to bed.'

Teresa watched her leave the room. Sophia never ceased to amaze her; she appeared unruffled by the fact that the police were in New York. Teresa was very concerned, but at the same time relieved that the rest of them would have left by the time the police arrived.

*

At eight the next morning Luka had hired the limo to take them to Long Island. All their cases were ready and waiting, and Luka began to carry them down to the car, shouting back that they should hurry as he was double-parked.

When they had gone, Sophia leaned against the door and sighed. She had done it, it had been so easy, a simple promise that she would join them and they had believed her. Already the empty apartment, the silence, felt good.

The doorbell rang, shrill and continuous. It was Luka. He stood outside like a man possessed. As Sophia opened the door, he struck it hard with his fist.

'Why aren't you coming? Why?'

She backed away from him. 'Because I have to stay here, didn't Teresa tell you?'

'You have to come with us! I have it all arranged, you have to be there, you can't stay.'

He tried to drag her to the door, but she pulled her arm away.

'I can't.'

'You don't understand, I have something for you, for all of you. You have to come.'

'Johnny, I don't *have* to do anything.'

'Yes.'

'No!'

'Yesss . . .' He dragged her towards the door and this time she pushed him forcibly away from her, but he wouldn't let go. She hit him and he fell against the door. He kicked at it several times in temper.

With his back to her he muttered, 'I have got something for you.'

'Johnny, I can't come, I have to wait here.'

When he turned back to her, his eyes were vivid blue and crazy. 'What'll you tell him?'

'Enough so he won't come back again. I burnt the drawings.'

He glared furiously at her. 'You shouldn't have done that.'

'I had to, if he found them here . . . Don't you understand, he's coming to question me about Nino . . .'

'I'll come back for you, wait for me.'

'That won't be necessary.'

'Why not?'

'For goodness' sake, because I will find my own way to wherever you're going.'

'You won't go away, you're not thinking of leaving?'

'No . . .'

'You remember he is your enemy, keep saying that to yourself, he's the enemy.'

'I'll remember that.'

She turned and walked into the kitchen, pausing a moment because she did not hear the door close behind him. She retraced her footsteps to the hall and found him just coming out of the study. He was holding a small gun.

He came to her side. 'I bought this for Teresa. You see the small lever at the trigger? Lift it, and it is set for firing. There are only four rounds.'

'I don't want it.'

'Take it.'

'Please, why don't you leave . . .?'

He held out the gun again. 'It is for your protection, you must be protected. He is the enemy, always remember that.'

She finally took it and smiled reassuringly. 'I'll be all right.'

He seemed unable to drag himself away. Gently, he lifted a stray curl from her face, a fine wisp of hair. Then he stroked her cheek. 'I'll come back for you, wait for me. Promise you'll wait for me.'

She nodded, wanting him to leave. He bent his head and swiftly kissed her lips. She sighed, averting her head.

'Don't, please don't . . .'

The thick, rough, toweling gown was open in a deep V, and he could see the crease of her breasts. He pulled the cord of her dressing gown and stepped back as it opened, giving a low, faint moan. Slowly, she turned to look at him, making no attempt to stop him as he lifted the fabric away from her breasts. His hand was cold, his touch light, and made her nipples stand erect. Her heavy breasts were swollen as if with a desire she didn't even feel.

'You are so beautiful,' he whispered.

He got down on his knees, kissing her belly, moving the thick robe aside to rest his face against her stomach. 'I love you, I love you . . .'

Somehow she expected more, expected to feel his hands on her thighs, touch her, but he clung to her like a child.

'They are waiting, Johnny, you have to go.'

He got slowly to his feet, leaned towards her, kissing her like her sons had kissed her. 'I'll come back for you, wait for me. Promise you will wait for me?'

'Yes, I'll wait . . .'

She sighed with relief when he left but made no

attempt to cover herself. She let the heavy gown fall to the floor and stared at her reflection in the hall mirror.

Sophia lay in the deep, soapy bath. The silence soothed her, the perfumed oils relaxed her . . .

Her hair washed and wrapped in a towel, she returned to her bedroom. She picked up the gun from the dressing table and ran the cold metal of the weapon over her skin, tracing her thigh, her belly, her breasts. Then she held the gun to her temple, slowly drawing the silver barrel across the high bone of her right cheek until it rested against her lips.

One bullet and it would be over, that was all she had to do, pull the trigger. Her finger tightened, then relaxed as she smiled at herself. She was in control of her life, she could end it if she wanted.

Slowly, she put the gun down. She began putting her make-up on, carefully smoothing the foundation over her perfect skin. She brushed her cheeks with blusher and lightly powdered her face before outlining her eyes and applying mascara. Lastly she painted her lips . . .

Joe Pirelli shaved, brushed his hair and changed his shirt twice. Satisfied that he looked better, he dabbed on some cologne. He put on his thick, long leather coat, and was still surveying himself in the mirror when Gigante walked in.

'You had breakfast?'

'Yep.'

'You ready?'

Pirelli turned with a boyish smile. 'Yeah, I'm ready.'

He locked his room, then said, 'I'll see you outside the Luciano apartment at twelve then, and don't be late.'

Gigante nodded, unaware that Pirelli had lied about the time of the meeting with Sophia. He wanted some time alone with her first.

Gigante walked into the lift. 'How do we work it, I talk first? Hit her with the element of surprise, et cetera?'

Pirelli nodded, pocketed his key and they stood in silence while the lift descended to the ground floor. Gigante noted the way the Commissario checked his appearance in the mirror.

'You're certainly making a great effort; what are you after, another night at the opera?'

Pirelli laughed. 'Nah, I want to impress the law over here. I've got a meeting with the New York Attorney General, he's supposed to be one hell of a guy, Italian. What are you gonna do?'

'Oh, I'll do a bit of shopping, get the wife and kids something. I'll see you at twelve.'

The pair of them walked silently past reception and out into the frozen street. It was thick with slush and more snow was falling heavily.

Sophia checked her watch. It was nine-thirty, time she dressed for the arrival of Pirelli. She had already packed her case and arranged for a flight to Paris that same afternoon.

The doorbell rang. 'Who is it?'

'It's Joe.'

Sophia looked through the peephole and could see he was alone. She tightened her bathrobe and opened the door.

874

'You're early.'

'Yes, and I've also lied. I told Gigante to come at twelve, is that all right?'

She hesitated, then gave a slight nod to confirm that it was. 'Do you want coffee? I was just about to dress.'

He stood leaning against the door. The snow had wet his hair and it formed small curls on his forehead. His thick fur collar was turned up around his ears.

'Yes, coffee would be fine.'

She gestured for him to take off his coat and to follow her into the kitchen. He left it on a chair in the corridor and ran his hands through his unruly, damp hair.

'Are you sure you don't mind me coming? I mean, without Gigante?'

She turned and smiled. 'I suppose you have a reason. Black or white?'

'Black, no sugar. Oh, I got you some cigarettes, the ones you like.'

He tossed a packet of her Turkish cigarettes on the table and pulled out a chair. She smiled her thanks and continued filling the percolator.

He sat awkwardly in the kitchen chair, feeling foolish. He knew he should not have come. He watched her as she passed to and fro, fetching cups and saucers, putting them on the table in front of him. Suddenly he reached out for her, catching her hand.

'I had to see you, didn't know if the brain would function the first time if I was to arrive with Gigante . . . I also wanted to find out if everything was all right. Where are the others?'

'Just shopping, I told you they were going shopping. Do you want to see them?'

'No . . . are they all together?'

'Yes.'

'You've had no trouble?'

'No, should I have?'

He smiled suddenly. 'I've missed you, Sophia.'

He turned her hand over and kissed the centre of her palm. She withdrew it quickly and gestured to the coffee. He sat back, watching her every move, until he had to look away. He couldn't trust himself, he had to resist the urge to get up and hold her . . .

She asked, casually, 'What does he need to ask me, did he tell you?'

'Better wait for him to tell you himself. I'm sorry, but if he knew I was here, he'd throw a fit. I told him I was having a meeting with the Attorney General . . . It's only partly a lie, I'm having lunch with him.'

'Is that why you're here, in New York?'

Pirelli nodded. 'I got a possible lead to Luka Carolla. I reckon he's here, in New York, I got a tip-off. Someone using his ID picked up the contents of a safety-deposit box; no idea what the contents were, but the box was previously owned by Paul Carolla.'

She seemed uninterested, more concerned with the coffee. He continued, 'I was virtually off the case, I'd already returned to Milan . . .'

She turned. 'You mean they closed the case? Even though you hadn't found the killer?'

'Not exactly, but we aren't looking for anyone else. The case remains on file, but since this tip-off . . . Can I help at all?'

She stepped back quickly as if afraid he would touch her. 'No, it won't be a minute. I think I'll go and get dressed.'

As she passed him, he again reached for her hand and

held it. She gave in, leaning against him slightly.'Don't, Joe, whatever happened between us was a mistake, it is over.'

He still held her, resting his head against her side. 'Didn't it mean anything to you?'

Tentatively she lifted her hand, touched his head. 'Yes, at the time, of course it did.'

Pirelli looked up at her. 'I'll leave my wife, if that is what you want.'

She drew away. 'If that is what I want? What I want shouldn't make any difference. If you want to leave your wife, that is your business, it's nothing to do with me.'

He didn't mean to sound angry, but he snapped, ''Course it is!'

Equally angry, she turned to him. 'No it isn't ... What you're saying is, if I want you, you will leave your wife. I can't make that decision, I don't want to make that decision. It's yours, Joe.'

'But if I did leave her, where would that leave us?'

'There is nothing between us.'

He felt as if she had slapped his face. 'I see ... Well, I'm sorry. I must come over as a real prick. You see, part of me, something inside me, believed you felt something, maybe even wanted me, because I wanted you ...'

'Then you were mistaken. I'm sorry, too.'

Pirelli stood up. 'Look, I'll leave, come back with Gigante.'

He was at a loss how to control his emotions, because he could not believe it was happening. Always so assured, so on top of situations because he had to be, he was unable to understand the desire to break down and weep like a teenager. But he was able to ask, with some semblance of control, if he could make a telephone call.

Sophia nodded and pointed to the study. He made sure he didn't touch her as he passed.

She stood at the kitchen door and watched as he walked to the study. The coffee percolator bubbled and frothed and she poured a single cup, then went back to the hall to overhear his phone call. She had missed part of it, but heard the name 'Barzini'. She moved closer.

'Yeah, I reckon he could be working for him. May have been a runner, so if you could get me Barzini's known contacts, say over the last couple of years . . . What? When? How did it happen? Shit! Well, get me what you can and I'll be in at three this afternoon, local time.'

Pirelli let the phone fall back on to the hook. He had just been told that Barzini had been buried that morning. He stared, glum-faced, at the black phone, then walked into the corridor.

'Everything all right?' asked Sophia.

He nodded and walked down the hall to fetch his coat.

'Your coffee's ready.'

'What?'

'Your coffee . . .' She waved towards the kitchen.

He gave her a lopsided smile. 'I'd better skip the coffee, I'll see you later.'

She walked to the front door and reached for the latch. He was close; as she turned, he tossed his coat aside and drew her into his arms. She struggled slightly, resisting as he kissed her neck, drawing her robe away from her . . . He kissed her shoulder, then cupped her breast and gave the nipple a swift, light kiss.

'No . . . No, please don't.'

He grabbed her hair roughly, drawing her head back

and kissing her lips. She couldn't stop herself, couldn't prevent her arms encircling him . . . He lifted her off her feet.

'Where's the bedroom?'

She clung to him and he didn't wait for a reply. He crossed the hall, kicked open a door and laughed. 'First time lucky!' He carried her to the bed and laid her down, holding her arms when she attempted to cover herself. 'No, no . . . let me look at you.'

He slipped the robe away from her, gazing at her, then took her hand and pressed it against his erection. 'Do you want me the way you tried before? You want me that way? You call the shots, because I'll have you any way you want, take anything you want to give me . . . Just tell me, tell me you want me.'

She held her arms out to him and he knelt on the bed, holding her gently. His voice was muffled with emotion. 'I love you, you know that, don't you? I love you, I ache with it, hurt with it . . .'

She was close to tears. 'It can't work, it can't . . .'

He tilted his head and looked at her as he loosened his tie, threw it aside and began to unbutton his shirt. When he reached the third button, he tapped his chest. 'You know how to knife a man in the heart, kill him? Want to know exactly where to place the knife? Here, third button of the shirt. You hit bull's-eye the first time I laid eyes on you.'

She couldn't stop herself smiling up at him, wanting him closer, wanting him to hold her, but he kept his distance . . . She ran her eyes over his muscles, his tight, firm body, then he unzipped his trousers. She closed her eyes, not at the sight of his erect penis but she knew he could see it in her face, if he looked at her, he could see she wanted him. Not until she felt his hand draw her arm away could she meet his eyes.

'I want you,' she whispered.

He smiled and took her face in his hands, kissing her sweetly. Then his tongue traced her lips and she pulled him to her, feeling him against her, the rush of heat sweeping over her until her legs wanted to open for him, curl around him . . .

The coffee was cold, but he didn't care. He gulped it down, then looked at his watch. He was dressed only in his shirt and underpants, and she laughed.

He grinned. 'It's not funny, I've got to get out of here and down to the street before Gigante arrives. It's almost twelve now.'

'I'd go just as you are, he'd never suspect anything.'

He suggested she get her drawers on, his friend wouldn't appreciate . . . or perhaps would appreciate too much . . . being introduced to her semi-naked. They returned to the bedroom and he slipped his trousers on.

'You just have to tell him the truth; we met in Milan by accident and went to the opera, had supper . . .'

She smiled as she brushed her hair, teasing him, 'What if I were to tell him what we really did? I guess that's the real reason you're here, so I won't get your story wrong? Well, maybe I will tell him we spent the night together. What would happen?'

He slipped his shoes on. 'He'd want the graphic details and then get me in the shit. Besides, he's not really interested in you, I've already given you an alibi. He's just after the driver of your car.'

He saw her expression change and looked at her,

puzzled. He was about to leave, but he hesitated. 'It's your chauffeur he's trying to trace.'

She took two steps away from him. 'My God, why didn't you tell me this before? Before you made love to me? Why?'

'Because what just happened was more than I'd bargained for, more than I believed possible.'

She folded her arms. 'Well, now you've had more than you bargained for, what do I expect next? Not just from Gigante, but from you? Do you have something you can't discuss in the privacy of the bedroom with me, only with your sidekick? Are you going to change identities, become someone else?'

'What happened between us is our business.'

'Why are you here, Joe? To fuck me, or what?'

He turned on her, his face flushed with anger. 'I am here in New York to continue the investigation into the whereabouts of Luka Carolla. I am hunting a killer, Sophia, the possible murderer of your two sons. Whatever I feel for you, whatever my hopes are for us in the future, have to be kept separate. I am in the bedroom with you, right now, because I had to see you.'

'Why? To make sure I don't say the wrong thing? You certainly went about it in the right way, in fact you'd have got away with it, but you slipped up, didn't you?'

'My priority is to track down a murderer. That I happen to be in love with you complicates . . .'

She snapped, 'I'm a complication now, am I? You came early to soften me up?'

'That's not true and you know it.'

'Make me know it even more, Joe. Tell me why you will be coming here with Gigante? Tell me.'

He stared at her, feeling the fear behind the anger.

He tried to hold her, but she backed away . . . Her voice betrayed her as she asked again why Gigante wanted to know who was driving her car.

Pirelli opened the front door. 'I'm sorry, I can't discuss it. You'll have to wait for Gigante, this is not my case.'

The look on her face made him close the door again. 'All it was . . . I was worried about your safety, about you . . . Now come here.' He pulled her close, kissed her, and she stiffened. He went on, 'Don't think I have betrayed you, all I am doing is trying to find the killer of your babies. Let Gigante ask his questions.'

'Please go, please.'

She averted her face as he tried to kiss her. He released her, but still could not leave. 'OK, you win. Gigante believes the driver of your car was Fabio's killer.'

Sophia gasped, staring wide-eyed in stunned, faked, amazement. 'What?'

Pirelli looked at her and gave a dispirited shrug. 'That's why I was so afraid for you, for your family . . . Who was he, Sophia?'

'We just hired him, there must be some mistake.'

It was late. Pirelli walked out, saying over his shoulder, 'I'll see you in a few minutes.'

Sophia closed the door, her heart thudding. If they knew about him . . . The trembling faded as she applied her make-up. 'They just want to question me about the driver of the car . . . But they must know more. They? Joe . . .' Had he told her the truth?

She hurled her lipstick across the room. If there were more that Pirelli hadn't told her, then he had simply used her, betrayed her. She reached for the Valium to ease her confusion, but let the bottle fall into the waste bin.

'There's nothing more anyone can do to you, Sophia,' she whispered to herself. 'There is nothing that can hurt you. You tell them just enough to get rid of them and then go . . . get out.'

Pirelli stamped his feet. It was cold, the snow was still falling, the light flakes making the pavement wet. Slush filled the gutters.

Gigante was late. Pirelli checked his watch then, with relief, watched the yellow cab draw up.

Gigante paid off the driver. 'Sorry, I took the gear I'd bought back to the hotel. Everything go all right?'

Pirelli nodded. 'Barzini was killed in a road accident, he was buried this morning. I tell you, this case is some crazy scene, sent to torment me.'

Gigante frowned, 'Barzini?'

'The guy the con in Sicily thought had arranged the demise of the Lucianos. He was a Mister Fix-It, I'd hoped to get to Luka Carolla via him. Somebody must have hired the kid. Now that he's back in New York I thought he might be hanging around Barzini's mob.' He checked his watch. 'We should go up, we're late.'

Pirelli and Gigante walked up the stairs side by side. As they reached the apartment, Pirelli ran his fingers through his hair.

When Gigante was introduced to Sophia he flushed to the roots of his thinning hair. Pirelli had not exaggerated her beauty . . .

Pirelli sat in silence, listening as Gigante took Sophia's

statement. Her voice was quiet, her familiar, wonderful husky tone, and she hardly looked in his direction once.

'And you didn't see anyone at Fabio's workroom?'

'No, I think it was lunchtime. There was no one in any of the workrooms – or perhaps there was, but I didn't see anyone the whole time I was there.'

Gigante tapped his notepad and shifted position. 'If I was to tell you that someone was there, that they saw you, and you were actually accompanied by . . .'

Pirelli watched the way she smiled, shaking her head. 'They must have been mistaken. But then I presume there must have been someone in the offices or you wouldn't have known that Nino and I were arguing . . . But I saw no one, and I was not, as you said, accompanied.'

Gigante asked her where she was between the hours of ten-thirty and twelve midnight on the evening she had visited Nino.

Sophia didn't even give a flicker towards Pirelli. 'I met Commissario Pirelli, quite by chance, and we went to the opera together. It was *Rigoletto*, and we left halfway through, before the last act. We then dined together, until after midnight.'

Gigante raised an eyebrow to Pirelli, but he was staring down at the carpet.

'Do you know Celeste Morvano?'

'Yes, she used to be my receptionist. When I closed my company, she went to work for Nino, although I didn't know that at the time. In fact, I was not aware of it until I went to Nino's workshop. She was pregnant, she had actually told me that she would not be working after she had left my firm. She obviously lied, but then I am getting used to people using me, lying to me.'

She did not look at Pirelli, but he knew she was

insinuating that he had lied to her. He coughed and shifted his position in his chair slightly.

'How did you arrive at the warehouse, or Fabio's workroom?' asked Gigante.

'By car, it's a white Rolls-Royce Corniche. It used to belong to my father-in-law, Don Roberto Luciano.'

'Did you drive the car yourself?'

'No, I used a chauffeur.'

'Did you know the driver well?'

'No. He had worked for my mother-in-law for some time, at the Villa Rivera.'

'Do you know his name?'

Sophia hesitated, then nodded. 'His first name was Johnny, but I can't recall his other name. I am sure my mother-in-law could give you his full name.'

Pirelli looked up, his eyes narrowed. She gave no hint to either man that she had any previous knowledge of what she was being asked. He had to hand it to her, she was being exceptionally calm, but the name 'Johnny' struck him as being one hell of a coincidence. He waited to hear what Gigante would ask next, but he did not seem to pick up on Luka Carolla's alias.

Gigante continued, 'So you talked to Celeste outside the building, is that correct?'

'Yes, she asked how I was and I asked if she was well. As I have said, she was pregnant.'

'Did your driver enter the building at any time?'

'He came to collect me and take me down to the car.'

'Do you know if he returned to the building?'

'No.'

'You seem very sure?'

'Well, I can't say he didn't, I mean, I don't know his exact movements, but he had no reason to return. When

885

I told him to go on to Rome, after I had agreed to meet Commissario Pirelli, he returned directly, or so I presume.'

'You don't know what time he arrived in Rome?'

'I'm sorry, I don't. But I am sure my mother-in-law, Graziella Luciano, can give you the time.'

'He was staying at your apartment?'

She hesitated, licking her lips. 'No, he was not, but I did ask him to check if she was all right, I didn't like to leave her alone for long, after everything she has been through. I cannot give you his address but, again, perhaps my mother-in-law can provide it.'

'Do you know if he knew Nino Fabio?'

'I doubt it, he was simply a driver.'

'So when you went to the opera with Commissario Pirelli, what happened to the car?'

'As I said, the chauffeur returned to Rome, to my apartment there.'

Gigante closed his notebook. 'I will have to question your mother-in-law and I would also like to trace the driver. Do you have any idea of his whereabouts?'

'No, I'm sorry. I presume that after we left Italy he would have taken work elsewhere.'

Gigante looked at Pirelli and the room was silent for a moment. Pirelli got up and leaned against the side of the desk.

'Do you know how Nino Fabio was murdered?'

'No, I discovered he was dead when I called from here to suggest the possibility of renegotiating the purchase of his designs.'

'I have already discussed with you my need to trace Luka Carolla, he was the adopted son of Paul Carolla . . .'

Sophia nodded, then turned away, unwilling to look

him in the face. He continued, 'You were also aware, I think, that I believe Luka Carolla is involved in the deaths of your children?'

Her hands clasped and unclasped. 'I am sure you and your associates are doing everything possible to ... Would you excuse me, I need a glass of water.'

Both men stood as she left the room, then Gigante moved to stand beside Pirelli. 'Why not get her down to the precinct? She's all alone – won't look good here, you know.'

'You think she is lying?'

Gigante nodded. 'She's too cool, nothing seems to register and she doesn't ask the right questions. I think she is covering something. I'm not through with her yet, but I want you to have a go with her, so I can sit back and listen.'

Sophia came back into the room carrying a crystal glass of water and a chilled bottle of wine on a tray, with two glasses. 'Can I offer you some wine?'

Pirelli stuffed his hands into his pockets. 'Would you prefer to come with us down to the local precinct? We have been given an interview room, perhaps it would be more convenient . . .'

'Will that be necessary? Surely, if you need to question me further then I should contact my attorney. Is there any need for me to do that?'

Pirelli crossed his legs, his hands still in his pockets, and looked at Gigante. 'As far as I am concerned, whatever I have to discuss with you does not require the presence of an attorney. Whether Detective Gigante thinks differently . . . He is taking your statement, but if you are satisfied . . .'

Sophia gave a small shrug and sat down. Gigante

could not help but glance at her perfect legs as she crossed them neatly, patting her tight skirt into place. She gave no indication of how nervous she was; quite the opposite. She appeared composed, and her eyes did not waver when she looked at Pirelli.

'There is really nothing more I can tell you.'

Pirelli lit a cigarette and pulled an ashtray closer. As he pocketed his lighter, he looked at Gigante, then started talking. 'Sophia, I sincerely believe that you, and perhaps your relatives, are in danger. In some ways your statement to Detective Gigante, as it stands, could have serious repercussions, but I want to make you aware of the facts. If at the end you wish to call an attorney to perhaps rethink your statement, it is entirely up to you . . .'

Sophia swallowed and flicked a look at Gigante. Pirelli went for it. 'I am sure Luka Carolla killed your children, just as I am sure that he was involved in a number of other homicides. I am also sure that he is a very sick young man.'

There was no reaction, she kept her eyes downcast. Pirelli realized that he should try to break the cold atmosphere, be more relaxed. He poured himself a glass of wine and sat very much at home, behind the desk.

'I want you to understand, even if this entire interview seems unethical, that there is a reason, a motive, if you like, behind my being here. I think you should be made aware of all the facts I am in possession of, in order that you should know as much as I do myself. Because there may be some link, something I have overlooked, and because I believe you and your family are in danger. I repeat to you that you do not have to say anything. I also give you my word that anything you do say, outside of

888

your statement to Detective Gigante, will be strictly between us. You see, I want to find Luka Carolla before he kills again, and there is no doubt in my mind that he will kill. To date I have managed to piece together something of his life and, with the aid of the Palermo psychiatric unit and a doctor from the old Nazareth hospital who attended the suspect when he was no more than six or seven years old, I know that Luka Carolla has the classic background to spawn a psychopath. But without being able to test the subject we can only presume the worst, that he has a compulsion to kill.'

The snow was falling, thick and heavy, the windscreen wipers screeching under the load. Luka drove into the private road and smiled at Graziella through the mirror. She was looking excitedly from the window of the Buick and Teresa, in the front, sent her window gliding down.

'What is this, a hotel?'

'No, it's a private residence.'

The neatly clipped hedges of the drive opened on to a sprawling, snow-blanketed lawn before the white-pillared house, circa 1894. It had belonged to Paul Carolla, although he had never actually lived there. It had been his dream, his step into high society, his proof of his success.

The house had been ready for occupancy the week before he fled the States. It had remained waiting all those months, and now Luka had inherited the entire spread. He owned the prestigious house, the vast gardens, the stables and yards, outright, although he had been unaware of his father's intentions, unaware that he owned The Groves, until he had opened Carolla's safety-deposit box. Situated in the green belt, the most affluent and sought-after location known as the Hamptons, it was worth at least $12 million. This was where Paul Carolla had wanted to live out the rest of his life, but he had never even spent one night here.

The women stepped from the limo, wide-eyed with wonder and delight. Luka was beside himself, almost weeping he was so thrilled with his secret. It was marred only by the fact that Sophia was not with them.

The snow swirled around him and he laughed, wiping it from his face. With an elegant, sweeping bow, he proudly handed Graziella the front door key, the key to what seemed a magical Christmas card.

'It is yours, it's my gift, my gift to you all. And here, the deeds, signed over to you, everything in your name, Mama Graziella Luciano.'

Graziella clapped her hands to her face and said that she couldn't possibly accept such a gift, but Teresa, at her side, laughed and said that if Graziella didn't want it she, for one, would gladly accept on her behalf. All Graziella could say, over and over, was '*Bella, bella* . . .'

Although the house had been made ready for occupation over a year ago, it had stood empty since then, and the beds needed to be aired, the rooms dusted. But everything was new, there was still a lingering smell of paint, of new carpets, and everything was so tasteful, so elegantly luxurious.

Moyra stood in the domed hallway, looking up at the chandelier. 'Now this is what I call a home, this is what I see myself in . . . Oh, yes . . . You can put my shoes under the bed, Johnny.'

Teresa slipped an arm around Graziella. 'Well, Mama, this is more in your line, isn't it? Do you think this place is fit for the Luciano women?'

Graziella nodded, the tears streaming down her face. 'This is what Papa would have wanted for you all . . . Oh, yes, this he would be proud of . . . *Bella, bella* . . . Johnny, come, let me thank you.'

She took him in her arms and held him, kissing his face until he drew away. 'For you, Mama, it's all for you, and for Sophia too. Now, let me show you around.'

Teresa slipped her arm through his. 'This must have cost a fortune, are you serious? I mean, are you giving it to us?'

He nodded, looking more boyish than ever. 'We can be a family, all of us together . . .'

Teresa smiled, and they walked up the stairs to see the bedrooms. She tried to calculate the value of the property, knowing it must have cost more than Luka's share of the money, and wondered how he had got it together so fast. 'Who did it belong to? It looks as if it was recently renovated,' she asked.

Luka smiled happily. 'It belonged to some rich banker, who died before he could move in. It was sold lock, stock and barrel.'

'Is it leased, Johnny? Have you taken a lease on it?'

He shook his head. 'No, I bought it . . . Now, this is the master suite . . .'

The women followed him from room to room, but Teresa began lagging slightly behind, touching the tapestries, looking at the ornaments, the paintings, and feeling the thick wool carpets beneath her feet. She said nothing about the cost, not wanting to spoil Johnny's surprise. And it certainly was a surprise.

Pirelli had been talking for almost two hours. The bottle of wine had been consumed, his cigarette packet emptied. Sophia had not interrupted once, but had sat with her eyes slightly downcast, as if concentrating on a small spot on the carpet. Her glass of water was still half full, and although Pirelli had offered her cigarettes she had smoked only the one she had lit at the beginning of the interview, stubbing it out after a few moments. Her hands remained clasped in her lap.

Pirelli had told her everything he could possibly recall that appertained to his investigation and his search for Luka Carolla. Now he felt drained, his voice was hoarse. He could hear the ticking of his wristwatch and looked across to his friend Gigante.

The only movement in the room had been when Gigante refilled their glasses and shifted his weight on the rather uncomfortable straight-backed chair. Neither man could tell what Sophia was thinking: her composure was admirable considering the fact that he had left nothing to her imagination, describing in detail the appalling murders, the strength the killer needed to be able to inflict such wounds. Even Nino's death seemed to leave her unmoved. He had expected more, hoped for more, and now he felt depressed and sickened, so emotionally drained that his head throbbed. He felt as he would have thought Sophia would feel. He wanted to shout at her, but all he could do was look helplessly at his friend.

The silence within the room was ominous, and he

sighed. Slowly she looked up to meet his eyes, then she looked down again. After what seemed an endless delay she smoothed her skirt, pressing her palms flat against her thighs. 'I . . .'

He leaned forward, waiting.

'Everything you have told me shocks me, frightens me more than I can put into words, but I cannot see how I can help you. Believe me, I sincerely wish that I could, but even knowing everything I am still unable to give you any assistance. I have never to my knowledge met Luka Carolla; however, taking into consideration all you have told me, I will most assuredly take precautions and warn my family.'

Pirelli met her eyes; they seemed so dark, expressionless, and he found it hard to believe that they had been making love only that morning. He moved a fraction closer.

'Sophia, I'm not through yet. Now, you have told us how you went to Nino Fabio's, and about the argument, his refusal to co-operate with you. As my associate said before, we are interested in tracing the driver of your car. We are sure you had nothing to do with the murder . . .'

She continued to stare into his face, even when he gave a small smile at his reference to the possibility of her involvement in the murder. Because, unknown to Gigante, they were lovers, she did not give an inch.

'You have also stated that you met Celeste Morvano outside the building. But what we have not told you is that Celeste, when brought in for questioning, was unable to give a detailed description of your driver. But she saw a wanted poster, an identikit and a photograph on the wall of the police station and stated that the man in the photograph and the man driving your car were one and the same. She swore this under oath, and that is why we are both in New York.'

Sophia continued to look directly at him, waiting. He seemed to be trying to look inside her brain, find some chink in her exterior calm.

'Sophia, the photograph, the picture Celeste picked out, was of Luka Carolla.'

A reaction at last, a sharp intake of breath, the only sign that his words had affected her. She seemed to shake her head slightly; Pirelli waited for something further but she bowed her head, concentrating on her hands in her lap. He wanted to see her face, but she did not look up.

His voice was very quiet. 'The other piece of information I have withheld, until now, is that Luka Carolla uses an alias. Once, when he checked into a hotel before Paul Carolla was killed, another time when he booked a flight out of Italy, he used the name Johnny Moreno; the same Christian name as your driver.'

Both men watched her intently. She didn't make a single move, she was so unnervingly still; they glanced at one another . . . When she eventually spoke her voice was huskier, even deeper than before, but without a tremor. She lifted her beautiful head.

'Do you have this identikit picture? Or was it a photograph? I think, if I could see it, I would be able to tell you if the driver . . . if the driver was . . .' Her voice faded and she almost whispered the name. 'Luka Carolla.'

Gigante took the photograph from his briefcase and passed it to her. She studied it, then handed it back. He then passed her the identikit picture and again she spent some time looking at it, giving Pirelli the opportunity to look at her.

Her profile seemed carved in stone, the jaw and cheekbones with faint shadows to accentuate the curves. Her full mouth with the dark lipstick was open a fraction and he saw her tongue lick her top lip. It was a small movement, one he would have missed if he were not watching her so closely.

Suddenly she looked up, her eyes so dark it was as if they were all pupils, without irises. 'I am afraid there is no resemblance, Celeste must have been mistaken. But then, I am sure that at the time she spoke to me the driver was actually in the car. It has a tinted windscreen ... But there is no question that this man, in the photograph, was my driver. His hair was reddish, he was perhaps younger, but I am sure when I speak to my mother-in-law, she will be able to give you his name, and no doubt the address of his family.'

Gigante looked to Pirelli for his lead; there was nothing more, no further questions. He rose to his feet, placing his empty wine glass on the tray.

'Thank you for your statement, Signora Luciano. I presume if it should be necessary for me to contact you again, and Signora Graziella, I will find you at this address?'

Sophia stood up, and told him she would be staying with Teresa for a while until she found alternative accommodation, and would certainly forward any new address. She walked with them to the door, thanking them both for coming to see her, then shook both men's hands.

Pirelli held her hand a fraction longer, trying to get through to her, but she pulled away. 'If you need to speak to any member of my family, please call. We have almost come to believe that there is no justice, but now

I think differently. You have my admiration, Commissario, and my thanks for all your work. It is deeply appreciated, God bless you.'

Gigante was too close for Pirelli to say anything personal. All he could do was smile; he received, in return, a frozen stare. Sophia was untouchable, her hand resting in his was cold, alien. He had a strange feeling in the pit of his stomach that she was, as from now, unreachable specifically by him. He knew he could never, would never, be allowed to come close to her again.

The men walked slowly down the stairs, hearing the door close behind them. She had waited until they were almost half-way down before she slid the chain across the lock.

Unhurriedly, as if in a trance, she went into the bathroom. She didn't retch, the vomit seemed to spew out of her belly in one long stream . . . She cleaned her teeth and returned to the bedroom, put the phone back on the hook. Then she sat at the study desk and waited for the call she knew would come. She knew Luka Carolla, alias Johnny Moreno, would call, and she waited, afraid for the women.

CHAPTER 37

SOPHIA WAITED by the telephone. When it finally rang, she wanted to snatch at it, but she let it ring before she picked it up.

'Sophia, is that you?'

'Hello, Teresa.'

'Are you all right? Did everything go OK? Sophia?'

'Yes, where are you?'

Teresa told her about the house, how excited they all were, and that Johnny had already driven off to collect her.

'Pirelli stayed for hours.'

'Is everything all right?' Teresa asked again. Sophia's voice sounded so strange and distant. 'Sophia, are you there?'

'Yes . . . I'll explain everything when I see you. Now can I speak to Mama for a moment?'

Graziella came on the line and began to describe the house, but Sophia interrupted her. 'Mama, listen to me. You once had a gardener, a young boy with reddish hair, he used to work for you. Can you recall his name?'

'What?'

'A gardener, Mama, he had red hair . . .'

'Oh, *si*, Juan! He is Adina's nephew. Now he has a

taxi firm in Palermo, you know the Excelsior Hotel? Papa bought him his first car . . . Juan Bellomo.'

'*Grazie*, Mama, give me Adina's telephone number in Mondello.'

Graziella didn't have it, but she instructed Sophia to look in one of her dresser drawers in the bedroom. She would find a notebook there.

Sophia searched the drawers and found the photographs, the ones that used to adorn the piano at the Villa Rivera. She looked at each one in turn; her little boys, her wedding to Constantino, another of Teresa and Alfredo holding Rosa's hand when she was a toddler. There was a torn one of Frederico, in evening dress, laughing into the camera. Sophia gave a slight, twisted smile, wondering if Graziella had torn poor Moyra from the photo because she had never approved of her.

Next she found an old photo, brown with age, of Roberto Luciano as a young man. The black eyes stared, unsmiling, from a handsome, arrogant face so different from the photo of about the same age of him and his wife on their wedding day. Last was the familiar face of Michael. She could not help but touch it, fleetingly, with the tips of her fingers before she put them all aside and at last found the little worn book.

Adina answered the phone and wept as soon as she heard Sophia's voice. She thought Graziella was sick, but grew quiet when Sophia assured her that she was fine, though they needed help. Very slowly, Sophia outlined the favour she wanted, the debt that could be repaid to Don Roberto's widow. She simply required Juan Bellomo to fix his account books to show himself as the driver of the Lucianos' Rolls-Royce. She also wanted him to go to Milan and familiarize himself with the route from her apartment to Nino Fabio's warehouse. She was not satisfied until Adina had repeated the instructions three times. Then Sophia told her that she must prepare herself for possible questions from the *carabinieri*, that Juan must not deviate from the story as told by Sophia. It was imperative, it could affect Graziella's life.

Sophia then placed a call to Pirelli's hotel, knowing that he would not be there. She left a message for him to the effect that Graziella's recollection was that the driver was called Juan Bellomo, nicknamed Johnny, and supplied his address.

Sophia began to remove all the personal papers from Teresa's study, taking anything that seemed to be of importance and packing them into her briefcase. She then went to each room, searching drawers and bedside tables, removing everything she thought necessary. She did not want to take too much, it was imperative she did not make Johnny – Luka – suspicious, but she had to make sure she took everything important so they would never have to return to the apartment again.

Sophia's one brief taste of what her future could hold, her hoped-for freedom, was over. She knew now she would never be free of the Lucianos; like a curse they clung to her, only now she no longer felt it like a weight dragging her down, it seemed to be giving her strength, as if she were standing outside herself, watching, gently steadying any fear.

Pirelli opened a new packet of cigarettes. Gigante, sitting next to him on a bar stool, gave him a sidelong glance. In front of them stood a row of empty glasses.

'Maybe we should grab a sandwich? What do you think?'

Pirelli gave him a sour look and gulped his whisky down without bothering to reply.

'What's the next move, Joe? What's next?'

Pirelli hunched over the bar. 'I dunno.'

Gigante stared into his drink. 'You know, the only time I saw any kind of reaction from her was when you said the name Johnny Moreno. She seemed to kind of tense up, but I couldn't see her face. But, say it was him at Fabio's place, I mean, if he had somehow wormed his way into driving for her or whatever, do you think even after everything you told her she would have admitted it?'

Pirelli sniffed and hunched even further over the bar. 'You got any kids?'

'No.'

'Well, I got one, a boy, and if he had been shot and my wife was told who had done it, even if she'd robbed a fucking bank with him, you think she wouldn't react? You think she wouldn't do something, say something?'

'Maybe she would, your wife would, but then she's not a Luciano.'

'Jesus Christ, what the hell difference does that make? She's a woman, a mother. You should have seen her when I first met her, she wanted the killer then, even

900

accused me of not trying to find him because she was a Luciano . . . Well, now she knows all there is to know. If she wanted him caught before, stands to reason she wants him even worse now. If she'd recognized him, do you think she wouldn't have said? Wouldn't have reacted? Your witness was wrong . . .'

He ordered another round of drinks. Gigante shook his head, refusing the refill. 'You still gonna see what you can get from the Barzini tip-off?'

With a nod, Pirelli knocked his drink back in one. He gritted his teeth. 'Yeah, while I'm here I'll do whatever I can. You gonna hang around to see the old lady? Do you need to now?'

Gigante shrugged. 'Nah, it's not worth it, I can get the next flight back. With the expenses that cheap bastard handed out I can't afford to stay. Besides, I reckon you'd like the excuse to go back and see the beautiful Sophia, huh?'

'What?'

'Come on, she's something else. You still expect me to believe your meeting was accidental? A quiet supper and you didn't even try to make her? I would have, if I was in your shoes. Christ, what a pair of legs . . .'

Pirelli interrupted by waving his hand to the bartender for another shot. He snapped, 'You've got it wrong, you don't make women like Sophia Luciano.'

'Maybe, but I don't blame you for trying.'

Pirelli glared and turned back towards the bartender. Gigante had always suspected that there was something between Pirelli and Sophia; but now, having met her, he very much doubted that Pirelli would have stood a chance. He grabbed a handful of peanuts, rocking on his stool.

'"A schoolteacher, a whore and a virgin . . ."' Gigante screwed up his eyes, trying to remember '. . . "*Bella Mafia*" . . . Nino Fabio coined that description, or was it "A beauty, a schoolteacher and a whore"? Which one d'you reckon is your Sophia?'

Pirelli knocked back his refill in one and tossed some dollars on the bar to cover the tab. He picked up his coat. 'Don't push it, Gigante, or you'll get that bowl of peanuts rammed down your throat. Call the hotel, see if there's any messages, and I'll grab a cab.'

It was freezing, the snow pelting down. Cab after cab swished past, and Pirelli, frustrated, turned his fur collar up around his ears. Their lights were all off but none of them had passengers. He was actually standing within yards of the entrance to the Luciano apartment, on the same side of the street, but he couldn't bring himself to look in its direction.

Heading down the street, no more than a hundred yards away and hemmed in by the traffic, Luka Carolla inched Teresa Luciano's Buick impatiently forward. The cars were bumper to bumper, furious drivers leaned on their horns. The heavy snow made the windscreen wipers work overtime and increased the congestion by the minute.

Luka was within moments of the apartment block when a taxi turned out of a side street, its hire sign lit up. Pirelli stepped into the road to hail it as Gigante, holding a newspaper over his head, ran from the bar.

'Hey, Joe, she's already called the hotel.'

Half-way into the taxi, Pirelli stopped and turned to Gigante.

'What?'

'Sophia Luciano, she left a message.'

Pirelli's heart stopped. 'For me?'

'No, it's the name and address of the chauffeur.'

Two cars behind in the traffic, Luka Carolla had his hand on the horn, urging the cab to move on. He swore at the delay.

Pirelli climbed into the cab and slammed the door shut. Gigante banged on the window. 'Hey, what about me?'

Pirelli yelled, 'I gotta see the District Attorney.'

The taxi moved on, almost causing an accident with the car behind, which was trying to overtake. The cab driver yelled abuse while Gigante shouted to Pirelli, 'I thought you'd already seen him?'

Pirelli opened the window and stuck his head out. 'I lied! I was making passionate love to Sophia Luciano! See you back at the hotel.'

Gigante, his newspaper disintegrating on his head, gave him the finger. 'Lying bastard,' he muttered, getting his feet soaked as a Buick passed him.

The Buick, driven by Luka Carolla, took a left turn into the underground car park beside Teresa Luciano's apartment block, passing Gigante by inches.

If Pirelli had looked out of the back of the cab, he would have seen him. It was as close as he ever came to finding Luka Carolla.

Pirelli's joke to Gigante would, he knew, end all the

speculation, the nudges and winks. He took out his handkerchief to wipe his face dry.

'You have a good Christmas?' The cab driver's voice was distorted behind the protective barrier. He adjusted his mirror. 'Gonna be freezing tonight.'

Pirelli nodded, but made no reply, he didn't want to get drawn into a conversation. He knew he would never forget her but it was over, a strange feeling, as if part of him was being compressed back into shape. As soon as he returned to Milan he would take the holiday that was owed him and he would make it up to Liza. Just thinking of his family gave him a sense of security, a sense of how much he had almost lost.

Sophia had always lived with her own secrets, weaving lies so that her past could never catch up with her. It was therefore not difficult to lie to Luka, in fact, it was much easier than she had anticipated, because she no longer felt any guilt. The more lies she wove around her interview with Pirelli the more she saw Johnny, or Luka, relax. The snow continued to fall, seeming to wrap her in a cocoon, a private world she alone controlled, and she knew, as she talked, that Luka suspected nothing.

The snow was thicker than ever as Sophia and Luka drove up to The Groves. She looked back to the gates to see them ease shut electronically.

Luka deposited her at the front porch and drove around the back to park. She hardly had time to shake the snow from her coat before Graziella threw open the door. She clasped Sophia to her, drawing her into the impressive hallway.

Rosa hurried down the wide, sweeping staircase, wrapped in a bath towel. 'There's an indoor swimming pool, we've been swimming,' she said delightedly.

Moyra, her hair dripping, peeked over the banisters. 'We swam in the nuddy too, it's wonderful! Wait until you see upstairs, Sophia, this is a palace . . .'

Sophia was pulled this way and that, and all the while Luka hung back slightly, blushing and smiling with pleasure. Sophia said all the right words.

Graziella had written out a long shopping list and Luka began trying to fathom it all out, laughing with her, his arm casually around her shoulders. They all felt as if a great weight had been lifted from them, and nothing in Sophia's manner gave even a hint of what was to come.

Immediately Luka had driven off to do the shopping, Sophia called to Teresa and caught Rosa on her way back to the swimming pool.

'Go and get Mama, and Moyra. I want to talk to all of you, and hurry – we don't have much time.'

They converged on the hallway from various parts of the house, Moyra still drying her hair. Sophia stood at the door of the drawing room and gestured frantically for them to come inside. She then shut the doors as if to keep them all in the room. Teresa knew something was wrong.

'Is this about Pirelli, Sophia?'

'Yes, and you'd better sit down, all of you, because I

don't know how to say what I have to say that'll make it any easier.'

Moyra, always slightly in awe of Sophia's stunning looks, was now even more so. Sophia's face was shining, and her presence filled the room.

Her husky voice held them all. 'You must keep calm, accept what I say and don't interrupt. We don't have much time alone, and we have to work out exactly what we are going to do and how we are going to do it.'

They waited expectantly as she paused a moment, then plunged straight in.

'Johnny Moreno is not who he says he is. He is Paul Carolla's adopted son. His real name is Luka. He is Luka Carolla.'

Luka loaded two more bags of shopping into the Buick. He could hardly close the trunk – there was enough food and wine to keep them going for months. He checked the list in case he might have missed anything, then, satisfied that he had not, he drove to a petrol station. He had been out nearly two hours.

Sophia stood with her arms folded, her fingers gripping her upper arms so tightly she could feel the nails cutting into the flesh. The atmosphere was tense now, she was surrounded by frightened, panic-stricken faces.

She continued, 'He must not have any idea that we know. Mama will begin cooking, and we will prepare dinner as if nothing had happened. Keep him occupied, keep him out of the way. Teresa and I will make sure every exit from the house is locked, there must be no

906

way out, no escape. As soon as we know he can't move out of the house, we eat. We all sit down together as planned. He may not seem dangerous, but remember, Pirelli said he must be exceptionally strong to cut his victims so viciously . . . If you waver, if at any time you feel afraid, you, Moyra, remember Frederico, Rosa your Emilio, Teresa, Alfredo, and you, Mama, think of Papa, my babies, Constantino . . . All of you keep remembering what he has done, and know we will, as we have prayed, at last get justice. And we all want it, we do all want this, don't we?'

Her face was like a beautiful mask as she looked from one woman to the next. Rosa wiped away her tears with the back of her hand, afraid to meet Sophia's penetrating gaze.

'Rosa? Rosa?'

Rosa swallowed and half-rose from her seat as Sophia loomed over her. 'Do you want to leave? Rosa, if you want to leave you had better say so?'

'No . . . *No* . . .'

'Fine, then dry your eyes. Moyra, are you all right?'

Moyra's left leg seemed to have a life of its own, it wouldn't stop shaking. 'I'm OK, and I guess if we can all stick together it'll make it easier, just, don't you think? I mean, what if we're wrong?'

'Then he can prove it, we'll give him that chance. Now go and get dressed, you too, Rosa. You were all expecting to dine in your best, so dress – and act – as if nothing has been said.'

Graziella remained sitting, her hands on her knees, her eyes closed as if in prayer.

Teresa whispered shakily, 'Maybe you shouldn't have told Mama, what do you think?'

But Sophia shook her head. 'We need her, she'll have to slip the stuff into his dinner. She always serves.'

Graziella spoke and, unlike Teresa, there was not even a tremor to her voice. 'I pray God you are not wrong, and I thank God if you are right. I can die in peace.'

Sophia knelt by Graziella, held her hands. 'Mama, he'll have the chance to answer all our questions. It's not until we are sure, and we will be sure when we do it, not until then.'

Teresa was afraid, she knew it. For all her bravado, everything seemed to pale against Sophia's cold, calculating demeanour. Teresa looked to her now, needing to be told what to do.

Sophia was still bending close to Graziella. 'I'll bring you the pills, Mama. Maybe if we crush them into powder . . . You always have a handkerchief up your sleeve, you can empty it like so . . .'

As if playing a game, Sophia slipped a lace-trimmed handkerchief from Graziella's sleeve. But it wasn't a charade, it was for real. She demonstrated how Graziella could empty the powder into Luka's dinner.

Teresa asked, 'Sophia, how are we going to do it?'

The beautiful, mask-like face turned in Teresa's direction, and the dark, slanting eyes were mesmeric. 'He is guilty, Teresa, I know it. In some way I have always had this feeling about him but I never knew what it was, why he made me feel the way he did. He has to die slowly, painfully.'

'Which one of us will do it?'

'No one, all of us, we all do it . . .'

They heard the tooting of the car horn and Teresa crossed to the window. Her whole body was shaking as she stuttered, 'He's here, it's him . . . He's driven straight around to the back of the house.'

The tyre tracks could still be seen, although the snow was still falling. Rosa waited, trembling, in the stables. Luka passed her three times, unloading the groceries. She heard the lid of the trunk slam down, then he passed her a fourth time, whistling. She peered over the stable door in time to see him going into the kitchen.

She hurried down the long gravel drive to the big iron gates, pulled them shut and slipped the padlock and chain around them. Then she ran back, took the keys from the ignition where Luka had left them and went into the kitchen, her heart pounding. She quickly removed her coat and shook the snow from her hair.

Graziella had already covered the kitchen table with the provisions she had taken out of the brown grocery bags. As Rosa slipped the car keys into a kitchen drawer, Graziella asked her to put a pan of water on the stove to boil for the rice. She was then kept busy chopping mushrooms, onions and tomatoes.

The knife was sharp as a razor, and the pattering of Graziella's feet on the tiled floor as she bustled about seemed unreal . . . The old lady was behaving as if nothing untoward had happened, or been said, or was about to take place. She was simply cooking dinner, their first dinner in their new home. The tears streamed down Rosa's face and suddenly she felt her grandmother's soft hand on her neck.

'Onions always make such tears . . . You know, if you place a bowl of hot water at your side you won't cry, did you know that, my little one?'

Rosa nodded and wiped her cheeks. Graziella put a steaming bowl of water beside her and her soft voice calmed Rosa. 'Remember that night, all dressed in your wedding gown that Sophia had made especially . . . It was so beautiful, and you were so happy . . . Remember, Rosa, remember.'

Graziella's eyes held her granddaughter's, and it was not until Rosa nodded, biting her lip to stop herself crying, that Graziella turned back to her cooking. Rosa made herself remember as her knife chopped in quick, deliberate movements.

Moyra was wearing the black dress Sophia had given her for their dinner party in Rome. She came out of her bedroom just as Sophia was passing.

'I think that's a good idea, Moyra.'

Sophia turned as Teresa came towards them. 'Moyra's wearing her black dress, remember, from the night at the Sans Souci? Did you bring yours, Teresa?'

He seemed to appear from nowhere, his blond head resting on his forearms as he leaned on the banister rail. Teresa and Moyra watched as Sophia went to stand close to him.

'Johnny, don't you think Moyra looks lovely?'

Unable to face him, Teresa went straight back into her room, but she could still hear his voice. 'You look beautiful, Moyra, turn around and let me see . . . What a dress, is this one of Nino Fabio's creations, Sophia?'

'Yes . . .'

Luka laughed, giving Sophia an intimate look and started up the stairs. She could see how tight and muscular he was, lithe and fit, but there was nothing sexual in her appraisal, just the echo of Pirelli's words. How strong he must be, Nino Fabio's wound had been so deep it had cut through the muscles of his back . . . He turned and ran on up the stairs, thankful that she could not see the effect she had on him. His body seemed to be on fire for her.

Teresa's dress was still creased from the case and she tried to smooth it with nervous hands.

Rosa's voice wavered as she tried to make conversation. 'Why don't you play the piano, Mama, it's a Steinway? Go and play the piano, I'll change . . . Mama?'

Teresa looked upwards, but Luka had disappeared. 'I'll wait with you, Rosa.'

Rosa whispered, 'No, go downstairs, Moyra's all by herself.'

Obediently, Teresa entered the drawing room. 'Shall I play the piano?'

Moyra turned like a startled rabbit. 'What?'

Graziella could hear the piano in the kitchen, but she did not recognize the tune. She stood with her head slightly cocked to one side . . . She could remember Roberto's voice, laughing as he said there was never any time for him to have his bath as the bathroom was always full. She could remember the children's voices as they played on the landing, but she didn't want to remember their dead faces, their arms wrapped around each other – not yet, not until she had to. She moved to Sophia's side as if for comfort.

Sophia was squashing tablets, a mixture of Valium and Mogadon, with the garlic crusher. 'Where's your hand-kerchief, Mama?'

Graziella took the clean lace square from her pocket and handed it to Sophia. The piano stopped abruptly, then they heard a scream . . . Sophia ran from the kitchen, snatching up the knife Rosa had been using.

Luka, wearing a strange frock coat and an old top hat, was swinging a cane and laughing. Moyra turned, white-faced, as Sophia entered.

'He gave us such a shock! Didn't he, Teresa?'

Teresa was still sitting at the piano, trying to cover her nervousness by leafing through old sheet music. Luka laughed.

'I crept up behind them, I was going to break into song . . . Oh, putting on your old top hat, da-da, da-tra-ta . . . I couldn't remember the words.'

Sophia hid the knife behind her. Fixing a smile on her face she asked Luka where on earth he had got the clothes from. Luka displayed his strange costume and said they must have belonged to the previous owner, they were in an old trunk in his room.

Sophia backed to the sofa and slipped the knife between the cushions. 'Why don't you play something, Teresa? Maybe Johnny would dance for us?'

Sophia stared hard at Teresa, who fumbled frantically through the sheets of music. 'I can't play by ear, I have to have music . . .'

Luka did a quick imitation of Charlie Chaplin, shrugging his shoulders and twirling the cane, scuttling around the room with his feet splayed out. 'I won't dance, don't ask me, I can't dance, don't ask me . . .' He seemed in very high spirits, fooling around, and Teresa couldn't stand it. She slammed down the lid of the Steinway.

'I'll go and help Mama, I'm not in the mood.'

Luka tossed his hat and cane on to the sofa and looked at Sophia.

'Aren't you going to change, too, Sophia?'

'Yes, as soon as I have a moment.'

There was an awkward pause as Moyra hurried from the room. Sophia was angry at her obviousness and relieved when Rosa came in, carrying a tray of champagne.

'Where is everyone?' she asked, the glasses rattling as she put the tray down. She offered a glass to Sophia, her hand shaking visibly.

'Helping Graziella, in the kitchen.' A look passed between them as Sophia took her glass, her dark eyes urging Rosa to offer Luka a glass.

He refused, picked up his hat and cane and said he wouldn't be a moment, there was something he had forgotten. As he left the room, he gave Sophia a strange, unfathomable stare.

Sophia barged into the kitchen and spoke loudly in case Luka should be listening. 'Is everything all right in here, Mama?'

Graziella nodded as she put some serving dishes in the warming oven. Moyra whispered that she was sorry, but her nerve had failed her. It was because he had surprised them. Sophia snapped under her breath that Moyra had better pull herself together because there might be a few more surprises before the night was over.

*

913

Luka knew something was going on. He sat on his bed and gripped the sides of it with his hands. It was Sophia, she was different ... Did she in actual fact know something, had Pirelli said something to her, more than she admitted? He realized he was talking aloud to himself in his desperate attempt to think what would turn her against him, now, after all he had done for her. Could it be that she knew how Nino Fabio had died, was that it? Would she tell on him? If they knew he had killed Nino Fabio would they turn against him, would they not like him any more?

He didn't hear her, not until she had called him for the third time.

The door-handle was beginning to turn and his eyes were transfixed in a wide stare ...

'Didn't you hear me calling you?'

Sophia could see the sweat on his forehead as if he had been doing some kind of strenuous exercise, and beneath his armpits his shirt was sweat-stained.

'Are you all right?'

He backed away, just a single, small step.

Sophia turned and he could see that the back of her dress was open. 'Would you fix my zip?'

He edged towards her and she felt how cold his hands were as he eased the zip upwards.

'You look very beautiful.'

She turned to face him. 'Thank you ... Don't you think you should change? Dinner's almost ready, every-one else is downstairs, waiting.'

He seemed so unsure, and she moved closer. He made as if to take a step away from her, but she caught his hand. 'What is it? Don't you feel well, don't you want to eat?'

His hand was wet with sweat. His fingers tightened on her hand. Suddenly, he blurted, 'You are changed, something has happened . . . You, you're different.'

'Me? It's just your imagination.'

Sophia closed the dining room door behind her. 'He knows something is wrong, and that's your fault,' she nodded to Moyra and Teresa. 'He's very strange, and his room stinks. He's sweating like an animal.'

Teresa put her fingers to her lips to silence Sophia; she had heard something. Sophia picked up fast and pulled her chair out, saying loudly, 'Well, Mama, this looks wonderful. Can I help you?'

Behind them the door creaked and Luka, having changed his shirt, came into the room.

'Now, Johnny, you sit at the head of the table there, in the carving chair, as you are the man of the house.' Graziella smiled at him as she carried the warm soup plates from the hatch. With a large silver ladle she began to serve the minestrone she had made.

When the soup was served, Graziella folded her hands in prayer . . . 'For what we are about to receive, we thank the Good Lord. Amen.'

Sophia raised her glass and smiled. 'To Johnny, for providing us with this wonderful house – for this dinner, too.'

They toasted him, and he slowly seemed to relax. He sipped his wine, like a young boy allowed to dine with the grown-ups, sneaking little glances and smiles. Somehow they managed to talk about everyday things as the bread was passed around the table, then more wine was opened.

The fresh pasta with the steaming seafood sauce liberally poured over it was delicious, and they all congratulated Graziella on her culinary expertise. But none of them, it seemed, could eat more than a few mouthfuls, although the clatter of the cutlery and the continuous refilling of wine glasses at least gave the appearance of a jovial, if tense, dinner party.

Suddenly Teresa leaned directly across to Graziella. 'Mama, you have dropped your handkerchief.'

Sophia bent to retrieve it, shaking it slightly, and as she sat back up to the table, she saw Luka wiping his plate clean with some bread.

CHAPTER 38

THE MAIN course finished, Graziella had cleared the table and brought fresh fruit on a silver platter, and several cheeses. She was just passing the thick cheesecake with fresh raspberries through the hatch when Sophia asked her to sit with them, they could wait for coffee.

By the time Graziella had walked round into the dining room, she could see that Luka was drowsy. He was sitting well back in the carving chair, his face flushed, and he didn't seem to notice that Graziella had locked the double doors behind her as she returned to her seat, and placed the key in front of Sophia.

The room fell silent, and the women looked at each other furtively. Then Sophia picked up a knife. 'Would you like fruit and cheese, or some of Mama's homemade cheesecake? It's got raspberries, and Mama's special crispy biscuit base . . . Luka? Luka?'

Their faces were staring at him through a distorting mirror, elongated noses and wide cheekbones, their eyes and mouths flapping at him. He felt so strange, so relaxed, as if he were floating. He giggled, and it didn't even register that Sophia had called him Luka.

No one moved, no one made any attempt to continue

917

talking. They fell silent, watching him, waiting for him to sleep. It seemed like an interminable time before his head rolled forward.

Sophia quickly took the leather belts, all they had been able to muster between them, and tied his right leg to the chair. As Rosa did his left leg, Moyra pulled at his right arm. His left arm hung limply at his side and he muttered, trying feebly to free himself. But the next moment he was trapped, with both arms and both legs shackled to the chair.

Sophia examined the buckles. 'Make sure he can't get them undone. He's strong, make sure they're tight.'

They eased the chair a fraction away from the table and tied a Hermès scarf around his eyes. By this time his head was slumped on his chest. To ensure that he was completely trapped, Rosa wrapped yet another belt around his shoulders.

After clearing the dishes, they removed the tablecloth, dimmed the huge chandelier to candlelight level, closed the door and the hatch, and left him.

Rosa brought coffee and passed it around the silent group. They had succeeded in phase one; now only time would tell if, when it came down to it, they would be capable of moving into the next phase and making Johnny, or Luka, talk.

Teresa rubbed her arms, feeling a chill, and Rosa lit the fire. The fake logs and coals gave a warmth to the room immediately it was lit.

'Do you think there is any doubt at all, Sophia?'

Sophia shook her head, then stared into the flames as she told them she had known from the moment Pirelli began to describe him. 'I am *so* sure, I brought along all the papers we left at your apartment, Teresa, everything any of us will need. Clothes can be left there. We need never go back, and if this place is ours, we can live here, although I think we should check out just how much of it we own. Perhaps it's leased, we cannot trust a word he ever said to us.'

'No, it's not leased,' said Teresa. She walked from the room and into the hall, and could not resist looking into the darkened dining room, seeing the shrouded figure still bound to the chair. She returned with the deeds and handed them to Sophia.

Sophia asked Moyra to collect her briefcase from her room and she obeyed instantly, as if it were an order. Like Teresa, she took a nervous look into the dining room. She could hear his heavy breathing and his head, wrapped in the Hermès scarf, was still lolling forwards.

Graziella was staring into the fire. She sighed. 'You know this must be a lesson to us all, how easily we have been used. Papa never allowed anyone outside the family to stay in the villa. You remember, Sophia, how angry he was that time . . .'

Teresa was on guard immediately. 'There were reasons, Mama, reasons we don't want to go into now.'

Graziella seemed not to hear her but she had. 'I had my reasons for liking him so much, for not being more suspicious, perhaps different from yours.' She smiled sadly. 'He always reminded me of Michael, sometimes he had a look of Michael.'

Teresa snapped, 'Mama, we don't want to hear about Michael now, OK? If it wasn't for him none of us would be in this situation.'

Sophia, who was checking the deeds of the house, said

sharply, 'Teresa, why don't you go and see if he's awake? This is not the time to argue amongst ourselves.'

Graziella went on, 'I am not criticizing you, Teresa, I am stating a fact. All of us learn from this, we must learn to protect ourselves, never allow anyone to get so close . . .'

Teresa's voice rose. 'We all agreed to let him stay at the villa, it wasn't just me. It wasn't just my decision, you can't put the blame on . . .'

Again Sophia interrupted, suggesting that Teresa check on Luka, but Graziella had hit a raw nerve. Teresa was red-faced with anger.

'Tell her, Sophia, we all agreed.'

Sophia's voice was cold, but soft. 'Not quite, Teresa, but what is done is done.'

'OK, if you want to blame me, blame me.'

Sophia controlled her temper. 'No one is blaming you, Teresa. We are all at fault. As Mama said, we should be more careful in future.'

Close to tears, Teresa left the room, flinging a last remark over her shoulder, 'We have a future then, do we?'

They all looked fearfully at Sophia, who could tell their nerves were on edge, could feel the tension building up in the room. She held up a small red book.

'What's this?'

Rosa looked at it. 'We took it from Barzini's desk, I don't know what it is.' She flicked through it. 'It's full of numbers, and at the back there's a list of names.'

Moyra joined her and they examined it together. Sophia had no interest beyond trying to keep them occupied, stop the tension from breaking out. She went to Graziella and handed her the deeds of the house.

'Check these over, Mama,' she said, then bent close and whispered in Sicilian, 'Leave Teresa alone . . .'

Graziella whispered back, 'But you know what I am saying is true, huh? You know it.'

'Because he's blond and blue-eyed? He's nothing to do with Michael, Mama, and this is not the time to start thinking about Michael.'

Graziella shook her head. 'No, I didn't mean that, I meant about taking more care. He was being cared for in the room above where your babies slept. He could have murdered us all in our beds . . .'

'But he didn't, Mama. We are all here, we are all safe, together.'

But Graziella would not leave it alone. 'We just accepted him, but you know, I can't believe what you say is true. I go over and over it, but it can't be true. All you know is what some detective told you. Don Roberto never put any trust in the police . . .'

'We are going to find out the truth, Mama. That is what this is all about.'

Returning to her chair, Sophia began going through all the folders and documents. Her head was aching but she would not take anything – no more pills, nothing more to drink. She knew she had to remain calm, they were all on the edge.

This was plain to see when Teresa walked back in the room; they all turned to her as if afraid.

'He's still out cold,' she said to Sophia, who gestured for her to come to her side.

It was the thick folder of documents that puzzled Sophia. 'These were supposed to be handed over to Barzini, are these the originals?'

Teresa flushed. 'Yes.'

'But I thought Barzini had them?'

Teresa was shaking as she told them what had taken place at the meeting with Barzini and why she had not discussed it with them. She also told them of Luka's part in contacting Salerno.

Sophia looked hard at Teresa. 'In future you do nothing without consulting all of us. We were paid for the Luciano holdings, the $15 million, yes? So then, why didn't you hand these over to Barzini?'

'I was going to. You see, I felt it was important to make contact with Barzini's partners, make sure they knew we weren't trying to cheat them. But at the same time . . . I'm still not sure if this would be beneficial or not, but we own a New York waterfront pier, not included in the deal, and two warehouses right on the dock. I would like to continue working, with that property as a base. There are vast opportunities . . .' She stopped suddenly, as if everything she was saying had no place, no meaning. Especially now, tonight.

Sophia stared into the flames of the fake fire. 'You start running, Teresa, and your legs will be slashed off. We walk this one, very slowly. Maybe you're right, it is a good basis for a business, and the money split five ways doesn't in the end amount to a fortune, but . . . If we were to start up, we would have to settle something with Barzini.'

Teresa hesitated, then quietly, a little guiltily, explained that Barzini was dead. She described how he had been killed the day she met with him and it was obvious why he had not taken the documents.

Sophia rose slowly to her feet and gripped Teresa's arm. 'And you never told us? Are you mad?'

'I was only doing what I thought best.'

'For whom, Teresa? We are what is left of a family . . . Never, never try to exclude me, Mama, any of us, again.' She released Teresa's arm, leaving a red impression of her slender fingers. Then she continued calmly, 'Well, as it happens it probably could not have worked out better. The other reason Commissario Pirelli was in New York was to meet with Barzini. He had had some information, a tip-off, whatever they call it, that linked Barzini to the murder of our men. Barzini could have been the one who hired Carolla and they are more than likely connected. If they discover what we have done, we could be in trouble.'

'But it was an accident, he ran straight into the road.'

Sophia nodded. 'I heard you the first time. Maybe we can use it to our advantage.'

Moyra and Rosa sat as if at a tennis match, looking from one to the other. Were they arguing? If so, it was very subdued.

Graziella, sitting in a low chair close to the fire, appeared to be sleeping. She opened her eyes and her quiet voice made Sophia turn and bend low to hear what she was saying

'They are like wasps in a nest, kill one and the others will swarm around in retaliation. I used to place a jar of honey on the step, part-filled with water. A lot would die because they wanted the honey. But the heart of them was in the nest, not until the nest was set on fire were they gone . . . Shouldn't someone check on Johnny?'

Teresa hurried from the room without being asked. Sophia looked with renewed interest at Graziella. Graziella talked about Barzini; his fortunate death, she

923

murmured, must be used, but she warned Sophia to take care with Paul Salerno and his willingness to co-operate. 'We have the honey, Sophia, but never forget the nest.'

Rosa and Moyra were not even considered part of the other women's conversation. More for something to do, Moyra picked up the little notebook while Rosa cleared the coffee cups and carried them into the kitchen.

Teresa helped Rosa stack the dishes. Rosa asked, 'What were you and Sophia talking about?'

'The deal with Barzini.'

'I thought you were arguing.'

'No, just clearing up a few things.'

'She's changed, she's different.'

Teresa dried her hands. 'I think, under the circumstances, we are all going to change.'

'Mama, if we find out, you know, if we get him to talk, what's going to happen?'

'You'd better ask Sophia. I've made so many mistakes, Rosa, I should have listened to her in the very beginning. We should have gone to the police as she wanted, handed him over to Pirelli when he came to the villa. But we didn't, Rosa, and it was me who persuaded everyone to keep him safe. It was my decision to get him to work for us, and no matter how I look at it I am to blame for all this.'

Even now Teresa could not tell her daughter of the part she and Moyra had played in Rocco's murder. She had known then that he had killed, but had somehow accepted it as a necessary evil. But the guilt was now manifesting itself and it weakened her, made her realize how foolishly she had acted. Her shame made her vulnerable, and she tried, hesitantly, to explain this to Rosa.

'Everything I did was for me, for you. I felt we were owed, and it's true, I didn't care about the others. Sophia is right, I have made so many mistakes.'

Teresa's face crumpled and she wept openly, holding out her arms pleadingly to Rosa, needing her daughter. They held each other tightly, Rosa trying gently to soothe her mother, whispering that it was all right, no one blamed her.

Luka stirred. His brain would not function and he could barely lift his head. He moaned softly, then slipped back into his drugged sleep. They both heard him.

Rosa whispered, 'We're going to kill him, Mama, for what he's done. I didn't believe we could, but now I do . . . I want to.'

Sophia had come to the kitchen door. Neither had heard her approach. They spun around as she spoke.

'That's right, Rosa. Now, come into the drawing room, Moyra is sure the notebook we took from Barzini is important.'

Moyra was saying, 'Sure, I know I'm right, Mama, we used to make up all kinds of codes working the tables. I mean, see the numbers at the end of the line, that's gotta be a date . . . Then you go to the front to find out the month, and the figures between are the amounts paid in . . . You got no corresponding numbers for, say, this page and this page, because that's a month . . . OK, flick back and here you go, corresponding number. So on the fourth – figure four, that's April, last number eight, so April eighth, you got $5,000,862 . . . This is casino dough, what else brings in cash like that? And on such a regular basis?'

Teresa shook her head, thumbing through the note-book. 'I dunno, it could be some kind of code for keeping records. If Barzini handled the payout to us, then maybe he's used it to pay off others. Want to look at it, Sophia?'

Sophia turned to the last page, to the list of names, and joined Graziella. 'Mama, these names in Barzini's book, have you ever heard of any of them?'

Graziella held it at arm's length to read. 'I gotta get some glasses . . . Ah! you remember, I told you Mario Domino was in Papa's study, all his papers gone? You remember, Sophia? Three men, and two of them are listed: E. Lorenzi and J. Carboni. These men were in Papa's study . . .'

They all heard the awful sound, half-cry half-howl, like that of a crazed dog.

Sophia was out first, running across the hall to the dimly lit dining room. Mingling with the screams was the frantic banging of the chair as Luka tried to free himself, his body twisting and jerking the chair almost off the floor, he was so strong. He was crashing the heavy chair against the table, his head thrashing from side to side, and it looked as if at any moment the chair would fall over backwards.

Luka was in the midst of a nightmare, his bound limbs making it more real than ever before, his terror cutting through his throbbing, hazy, drugged mind.

Sophia walked calmly into the kitchen and filled a large pan with cold water, then dumped it on the hatch. 'Throw this over him, he's hysterical.'

The cold water made him gasp, and it did quieten him. He stopped moving and sat with his head down, his chest heaving as he panted like a dog.

All dressed in black, they sat around the table facing the dripping, bound Luka. They were not sure how to begin, confronted by his pitiful figure. In the end they looked to Sophia to guide them. She opened the large manila envelope and placed on the table in front of Luka the photographs of her children, of Constantino, Alfredo, Frederico . . . She added the sepia photo of Don Roberto Luciano. Then she returned to her seat. The pictures were not for Luka, but for the women, a reminder.

No one spoke, they were still waiting for Sophia. Finally, she said, 'We want to know the truth, we have to know, and we do not care how long this takes, how many days, how many nights. We will wait for you to tell us what we need to know.'

Unable to see her through the scarf, he turned his head as if to hear better. It was *her* voice, it was Sophia . . . He moaned her name pitifully, asking her why she was doing this to him . . .

'Sophia is not alone. We are all here, all of us.'

That was Graziella, or was it Teresa? His chest began to heave again and, panic-stricken, he started to wail. Graziella whispered to Rosa and she slipped out of the room. Another pot of ice-cold water was pushed through the hatch, and Teresa threw it over him. It hit him with such force that it jerked his head back. As before, his howling stopped.

'Why don't you tell us who you are, because we know you are not Johnny Moreno. Who are you?'

He went still, seemed to relax, and gave a shuddering sigh. The scarf, soaked, clung to his face like a second skin. *That was Moyra*, he thought, *she is on my left*. 'Moyra?' he asked.

Moyra looked at Sophia and bit her lip, then cupped her hand over her mouth and whispered, 'What if he won't tell us anything, what do we do?'

927

Sophia was staring at him, her face rigid. 'We wait Moyra, we wait until he tells us all we want to know. Maybe he doesn't think we are really serious . . .'

His head jerked, trying to hear what was going on. He heard the sound of chairs scraping, and began to think it was actually a nightmare, that he would wake up. It was just one of his nightmares like the ones he'd had when he was a little boy. He tried to move his arms, but they were trapped, then his legs . . . He was completely trapped.

Luka's head twisted as if he had picked up a sound, and he rubbed harder against the back of the chair, trying to loosen the blindfold. But again the nightmare crept over him, the suffocating, dark, airless cupboard, his face pressed against the door, his small body hunched as he tried to find the tiny crack of light, the small aperture that he could see through, breathe through. In that chink of light he had seen the men brought into the room, seen them pay over their money, then would come the sickness in his stomach, knowing that the door would open and he would be dragged out . . . He cried for an hour, and they waited. When asked a question, he seemed not to hear. His own terrified, childish screams obliterated everything, raging in his mind, screams that had eventually only been defeated by his own imagination. His only escape all those years ago had been via his mind; subjected to nightmare perversions, his mind had sheared away the pain. No matter what was done to his tiny body it could not hurt him. He had hardly felt the whippings; the scars crisscrossing his back were simply a reminder, the excruciating lacerations had hurt him only momentarily. The past had remained a blur of torture, brought to focus only by the sound of fairground music, a key turning, the key that had locked him in the cupboard. But the sounds that connected him to his nightmares were growing louder now, they jangled in his mind and began to penetrate his safety barrier. It was breaking apart and now, in front of the women, he was experiencing the pain he had hidden inside him for so long. Unknown to the women, he fought a war, raging in his head, fought to find the sanctuary that made his pain bearable. The darkness inside him, that Father Angelo had always felt, had tried so hard to open, was moving out of his control.

Giorgio Carolla had been the one living person who had understood, who knew Luka's sufferings intuitively because he himself had suffered. The two boys had needed each other, been bound, entwined with one another. The death of Giorgio had taken from Luka the first and only love that he had known.

The women now surrounding him, waiting, listening, preparing to judge him, had all unknowingly locked him into his nightmare. His screams, the twisting of his body, his blubbering, infantile voice shrieked on and on . . .

Graziella was the first to rise, unable to stand another moment. Her body strained as if she wanted to go to him, comfort him, and Sophia gripped her arm tightly.

Moyra had covered her face and was now whispering, 'Oh, God, oh, my God, what's the matter with him . . .?'

He couldn't hear her. The straps binding his arms and legs were the ropes they had used to tie him down . . . He whimpered, and a small, plaintive voice began to speak; not like an adult mimicking a child; it actually sounded like a young boy, the words half-formed.

'It hurt me . . . Hurt me . . . No, hurt . . . no, no hurt me, please no, good boy . . . No . . .'

Only Graziella remained in the dining room, still sitting exactly opposite Luka. Sophia gestured for the others to move away, she didn't want Luka to hear them.

Moyra began to cry. 'What have we done? Is it the drugs? What have we done to him?'

Sophia was pale, obviously affected herself but refusing to show it. In the drawing room she poured brandies, handing a glass to Moyra. 'What if it's an act, Teresa?'

'What if it isn't? We don't know.'

Sophia snapped, 'We know he's lied to us, we know everything that Pirelli told me. We know he is a killer, we knew that back at the villa. And we protected him, so don't look at me as if I have done something wrong. All of you, what are you staring at me for? As if I'm guilty of some crime? The only crime I want to know about, I care about, is the murder of my children, my husband, because whoever killed them didn't just end their lives, they took mine too.'

Teresa interrupted, shouting, 'We all lost, Sophia! We all want to know, we all want justice! But not this way . . .'

They heard Graziella's voice, talking so softly they could not decipher her words, but she was talking to him. Sophia, carrying a glass of brandy, went back to the dining room. She paused in the doorway, her hand raised in warning to the others, and they moved silently to look over her shoulder.

Graziella was sitting next to Luka, and she was holding

his hand. Seeing Sophia and the others at the door she raised her free hand in a signal to them to remain silent. One by one they crept further into the room.

Not until they were still did Graziella continue, and if Luka had heard them, he gave no sign. He still cowered back in the chair, but his left hand, even though bound, clung tightly to Graziella's. She stroked it, patted it, seemed to be soothing him.

Graziella spoke so quietly that they all had to strain to hear her voice. She was asking his name, over and over, asking him who he was.

'It's all right, you can tell me. No one is going to hurt you. Tell me, you can tell me.'

It was the child's voice, frightened, and he clung desperately to her hand as he said, 'My name is Luka, but you must not tell him, he mustn't know I've told you.'

'Who mustn't I tell? Who mustn't know who you are?'

Moyra could not understand as they were speaking in Sicilian, and she leaned towards Rosa to ask what was going on. Immediately Luka tensed, his blindfolded head jerked and he cowered back again. Sophia gripped Moyra's arm tightly, warning her to keep silent, and Graziella had to soothe him all over again. It was ten minutes before she could get so much as a whispered word from him. She asked him over and over who he was afraid of, and now she stroked his head, standing close to him, bending down to hear as he whispered his own name, weeping.

'Luka, Luka . . .'

Graziella gave a small look to Sophia, not understanding. He had said he was afraid of Luka, and yet he also said he *was* Luka.

'Are there two Lukas?' she asked gently.

'Yes,' he whispered. 'There are two of us.'

Graziella seemed to have gained his confidence and he gradually appeared less afraid. He continued to cling to her hand, and, after some more words of encouragement, he agreed to tell her what Luka had done.

He related a long, rambling story about stealing a chicken leg, nothing that made sense to the waiting women. The tension of watching him was exhausting. The sweat glistened on Graziella's face, her body was stiff from standing in such an awkward position and her hand ached from his unrelenting grasp, but she never left his side.

'Was Luka a bad boy when he was older?'

'Yes.'

Not one of them dared move as the strange, high-pitched voice described how Lenny Cavataio had died. Only Graziella knew who Cavataio was, the man Don Roberto Luciano had replaced as a witness. Graziella patted Luka's hand, interrupting his description of knifing Cavataio.

'Was Luka given orders? Did someone tell him to do these bad things?'

Eerily, the voice suddenly switched to English, deepening in tone but still furtive, afraid of being overheard. He spoke rapidly, 'He is a professional, do you understand? No one can catch him, no one knows who he is ... Riding a bicycle, little boy on a bicycle. He felt no pain, no hurt. The innocent must feel no pain, must be quick, done quickly.'

Sophia sat back in her chair and closed her eyes as

Luka continued to describe how the child had been offered an ice-cream cornet, a raspberry-flavoured ice cream ... She knew he was talking about the Paluso child. She also knew that Pirelli had been right, right about so many things, but she was sure he could never have visualized what was taking place in that dark room. Facing them all was the man Pirelli had tried to trace for so many months, the dangerous psychopath, the mass murderer, the cold calculating killer. And here was a pitiful, cowering boy, talking in the high-pitched voice of a child no older than her eldest son had been. She could feel no hatred, could not even contemplate revenge, and justice was a meaningless word.

Luka Carolla was insane, and as the full extent of his insanity was unravelled the women had no anger left, felt no satisfaction in having him before them, trapped like an animal. Their faces registered their feelings; instead of hatred there was a certain amount of compassion for the boy bound to the chair. Sophia glanced covertly at each of them. She could feel their wretchedness.

The click of her gold cigarette lighter broke the silence. She inhaled deeply and let the smoke drift from her mouth. They could all smell the heavy Turkish tobacco and like a dog Luka lifted his head, sniffing ... His body stiffened.

Sophia spoke loudly, 'So now we know you killed the Paluso child, do you hear me, Luka?'

Luka's grip on Graziella's hand tightened, hurting her, and she had to wrench herself away. She looked angrily at Sophia. 'Why did you do that?'

'Maybe, Mama, we need to speak to his other self, tell the child Luka to go to hell. He's acting, he's playing with us.'

Graziella eased herself away from him and turned to look at the scattered photographs on the table. She remembered the faces of her grandsons, she did not need the reminder. She reached out and drew all the pictures into her arms. There was no rage inside her, neither was there peace. There was no peace for any of them. If she were to take a gun and blow Luka's brains out, what would that achieve? Graziella didn't want to hear any more, she did not think she could bear any more. Slowly, holding the photographs to her chest, she moved towards the door. Teresa, seeing her sway slightly, got up to assist her from the room.

Rosa pushed back her chair and faced Sophia but did not touch her. Instead she put out her hand to Moyra, who took it. They left the room quietly, together.

Sophia remained sitting, smoking, each breath laboured, scorching her lungs. Then she drew the ashtray close, letting it scratch the table as she stubbed out the cigarette. She studied her perfectly manicured nails resting on the edge of the table, wanting to gouge the shining surface in which her own face was mirrored.

Luka's head lifted and he turned sideways, listening intently. Every tiny move she watched; was he play acting? Could he really put on such an act?

'Sophia? Sophia?'

She waited, but he said no more. Eventually, she replied in a whisper, 'You murdered my sons, they were innocents. Why? Why did you kill my babies, Luka?'

His head twisted and she saw the way his hands curled, making wringing motions as if trying to free himself. He remembered them, lying together, that was how he had first seen them from outside the window. He had felt like weeping, he had held Giorgio Carolla in

934

his arms the night before they operated on him, they had lied to him, told him he would be better, but he had never seen his friend again.

'Who gave the order, Luka? Who told you to murder my children?'

His hands still twisted and turned and he made a guttural sound. She moved silently beside the table until she was close enough to smell his sweat. He cowered back in the chair.

'Nothing can make amends for what you have done, but you will die without a prayer unless you answer me. Your soul will remain in hell, burn there . . .'

He murmured something unintelligible through the wet scarf that clung to his face like a mask. After a while Sophia gave up and walked out. Luka listened for the door to close, but all he heard was her footsteps. Was he alone? Beneath the scarf his lips stretched into a smile; no threats of hell, nothing could touch him, he was untouchable, a professional . . . He must remain in control, only that way could he save himself. The one he had trusted, believed he had loved, had in the end betrayed him. And so it had been throughout his life.

Moyra, sitting on the stairs, saw Sophia walk from the room. She was going to say something, but as she opened her mouth she saw Sophia pause beneath the chandelier in the hall. For a moment she tilted her head back, closing her eyes, and she was so still, so unnaturally still, that Moyra could say nothing. The moment came and went, and Sophia crossed the hall to the coat-rack. She threw a coat around her shoulders and went out, closing the door quietly. The cold draught made Moyra shiver.

935

Suddenly Moyra was afraid. What had Sophia done? She crept towards the open doorway and switched on the lights.

He was still sitting there, still trying to free himself. Moyra felt drawn into the room. She remembered Luka telling her that story about the forget-me-nots.

'Johnny? It's Moyra. Are you all right now?'

She needed to know for herself, had he been involved in Frederico's death? So far nothing she had heard made sense and Sophia seemed only to care about her children.

She untied the damp blindfold and he blinked, trying to adjust to the light. She stared into his face, then gasped and stepped back, almost falling. He terrified her; he was smiling, such an angelic smile, but his eyes were crazy.

His voice was wheedling, plaintive. 'Help me, Moyra, help me.'

Rosa said from the doorway, 'What are you doing, Moyra?'

'Nothin', I just wanted to ask him for myself, I wasn't doin' anything.'

Rosa gestured for her to leave. She wouldn't look at him and he called her name, softly repeating, 'Help me, Rosa, please . . .'

'Look at his eyes,' whispered Moyra. 'Look at his eyes.'

Rosa inched forward and he pleaded with her, 'Untie me, Rosa, please . . .' She pushed Moyra ahead of her out of the room but as she closed the door, she could not resist one look at him.

'Rosa, Rosa . . .' He said it softly, as if making love to her.

She straightened and for a moment he had a faint

hope. Her pretty young face was confused and he tried smiling to encourage her forward. Then she left and closed the door.

Rosa hurried across the hall to the drawing room. He called her name again, just once; 'Rosa!' Then he was silent.

Rosa sat with her mother. 'I went in to see him. Did you hear him calling my name?'

'Yes, yes, I heard.'

'I liked Johnny so much, Mama.'

All Teresa could do was hold her daughter's hand, not in sympathy but understanding, because she too had liked Johnny. But he had become another person.

Sophia joined them, closing the door purposefully, and looked to Graziella's chair by the fire. 'Where's Mama?'

'She wanted to be alone, she's in her room.'

Sophia nodded, then drew the curtain back from the window, rested her head against the ice-cold pane and stood there with her back to them.

After a long silence she said softly, 'We can bury his body in the garden. I've marked out a place, beneath a tree, where the ground is not so hard. There are spades in the garage. We must be careful to remove the top layer, the grass, and replace it after . . .' She turned to face them. 'Do you understand what I am saying?'

Teresa was shaking and her voice wavered. 'Are you going to . . . who's going to do it?'

Sophia's face was like a mask. 'I will kill him, I'll do it alone. But we will bury him together.'

CHAPTER 39

OYRA'S AND Rosa's footprints were clear along the snow covered path. They headed across the lawn, following Sophia's prints, made earlier that night. They came to a tree and saw the area marked out for the grave by the heel of Sophia's shoe.

They began to dig the grave, working hard, in unison. They did not speak as they carefully laid the frozen sods of turf to one side and dug into the hard, dark soil.

Sophia had changed into a cotton gown and had collected an armful of fresh towels and a white sheet. She opened Graziella's door a little and slipped into the dark room.

'Are you all right, Mama?'

Graziella held her hand out and Sophia stood close to the bed, but her mother-in-law let her hand fall on to the covers when she saw that Sophia had changed her clothes. There was something frightening about the white-gowned figure.

'Can I get you something, Mama, to help you sleep?'

Graziella shook her head and said softly, 'Did he talk to you?'

'No, Mama, I think he is in a world of his own, maybe hell, who knows? He certainly put us there.'

'Don't say that . . .' The pale blue eyes searched the dark, hooded ones. She knew what Sophia was about to do and reached for her hand. She held it tightly and lifted it to her lips, kissing the soft skin. 'Stop his heart for me, for him. The boy is so sick. I saw some poison on the top shelf of one of the kitchen cupboards . . . Do you need me?'

'No, Mama.'

'I'll pray for you, for us all.'

'Yes, Mama.'

Barefoot, Sophia went down the stairs and listened at the door. She went into the drawing room and felt between the cushions, brought out the knife. She knew she must not hesitate, must not think about what she was doing, she had to get it over with. She opened the dining room doors.

Luka sat with his head resting back on the chair. His eyes were closed, but the fact that his blindfold had been removed unnerved her. She had not wanted to see his face.

Soundlessly she moved across the room. She let the sheet drop to the floor and placed the towels around the legs of the chair. The third button of his shirt, almost central, was where she would knife him, but the strap Rosa had tied around his shoulders had worked down, it was covering his heart.

She put the knife on the table. Still he didn't move. She began to unbuckle the belt. She had to take it off, leave his chest bare.

Suddenly he turned, opened his eyes. 'Sophia? I knew you would help me, I knew you would be the one.' There was no trace of the child in his voice, he was Luka. She pulled the belt away, found it wet with his sweat. She went back to the table and picked up the knife.

He smiled. He thought she was going to cut through his straps, but as she came close he knew. His blue eyes raged, but he would not allow himself to panic. He had to deny the natural instinct to survive, just as he had as a child. Hide, hide, he told himself, she is going to hurt you, she is going to cause you pain . . . Hide . . . His eyes searched her face. Did she know? he wondered. Know that she could not hurt him?

He seemed to offer his chest to be cut. The knife was poised, held in both her hands. The tiny gold heart on the thin gold chain was like a glowing target. As if she had cut herself she gasped, involuntarily, and her eyes widened . . . She blinked, and instead of going closer she stepped back.

Luka tilted his head to one side. Confused, he watched her put the knife down on the table. She turned to face him, staring at him with almost the same confused expression as his own. She came closer, closer, lifted her right hand . . . He could see she was trembling so much her fingers shimmered, and she was not looking at him, but at the gold locket around his neck.

Suddenly she snatched at the heart. He pulled back and she jerked the chain harder, harder, until it snapped. She held it a moment in her clenched hand as if afraid to open her fingers. Then she moved away from him into the shadow of the room. Her thumb rubbed at the heart but her eyes never left his face. She could feel the tell-tale teeth marks and knew without looking that it was her heart, it was Michael's heart, it was her baby's heart.

'Where did you get this? *Where did you get this?*'

With the heart still clenched in her fist she hit him directly in the face. The chain cut his lip.

'It's mine,' he said.

'No, no, you stole this, you stole this.' She turned, shocked, as the door was rapped sharply. Teresa's frightened whisper asked if she was all right.

'Leave me alone, *don't come in . . .*'

Her breath rasped and she felt as if someone were strangling her. She pressed her face against the heavy wooden doors until she heard the footsteps going away across the marble hall.

To Luka it seemed like an age before she turned to face him again. He watched, becoming afraid, as she slowly circled the table. It was not until she was at the opposite end that he saw her open her hand and look again at the heart.

Sophia could hear Graziella saying how much he reminded her of Michael. She saw him standing at the top of the stairs in the cheap boarding house, saw him with the light circling his head like a halo. He had frightened her because he appeared so ghostly, but was it because he looked like Michael? Could this insane boy be her son? Michael's son?

He couldn't take his eyes off her, nothing she did made sense. It obviously had something to do with his locket. She came closer and he could see the small beads of sweat on her brow, on her upper lip, the sheen of her cheeks made her face shimmer. He looked into her eyes, preparing himself, but it wasn't the same. There wasn't that look on her face, the one he always remembered, the look in their eyes just before they hurt him.

'Please, tell me, where did you get this?'

'It's mine.'

He could see the outline of her body through the thin cotton gown. She was naked underneath; strange, but it was all he could think of, she is naked. There was something in her voice, was it fear? What was she afraid of?

'Where did you find this, please tell me?'

'It's mine.'

She moved closer to the table. 'It is very important, you must tell me. Please . . .'

It was beyond him to understand what was going on, why she was asking him these questions. She was begging him to tell her something he could not. She reached out and touched his face, then withdrew her hand. He was so scared of her he pressed his body back against the chair.

Sophia scrutinized his face as if seeing it for the first time. She suddenly spun round, her eyes darting about the room, looking for the envelope, the one she had brought the picture in. Seeing it fallen on the floor she ran towards it. He followed her every move, saw her snatch up the envelope, open it and withdraw something. It was the one picture she had not placed on the table, the picture of Michael Luciano.

Luka watched with distorted fascination. Why was she behaving so strangely? He saw her take the photograph out inch by inch, then turn her back to hide what she was doing. A soft moan escaped her. He didn't have to tell her, because she knew Luka was their child.

Standing directly in front of him she looked into blue

eyes that, at this moment, registered only mute confusion and fear. Slowly, she began to swing the locket backwards and forwards, backwards and forwards . . .

Even though he didn't want them to, his eyes could not resist following the heart from one side to the other . . . Then he looked into Sophia's darkness. The locket rocked to and fro and then the chain was still, the heart twisting.

'Tell me the names of those who wanted the Luciano family destroyed, and in return . . . In return I will give you the name of your father.'

He gave her nothing but an angelic smile of disbelief. She moved closer. 'I swear on the Holy Virgin that I am telling the truth. I know, Luka, I know.'

His whole body was poised in an unreal stillness. He did not believe her; his pale eyes were accusing, unwavering . . . He could not be tricked. He had no father, no mother. He had been born of the Devil; that was why he had to be punished, why they had locked him away. He did not believe her.

'You ran away, didn't you? From the Holy Sisters? They looked for you at the fairground. Luka, were you there?'

Only his eyes registered the torment of confusion, one moment accusing, the next fearful. How did she know about the fairground?

And his refusal to answer made Sophia doubt. Could she be wrong? She leaned closer. 'Did you go to a fairground? Were you in Catania, Luka? Do you remember?'

He looked upwards, his eyes rolled back in his head.

'Tell me who ordered the deaths of my children. Give me that, at least . . . Luka?'

Silence. His eyelids fluttered, he blinked rapidly, then he stared at her, through her, an unnerving, steady gaze. He seemed to be mocking her, forcing her to be the one to look away, and it made her angry – at last, angry again.

He is not my son, she told herself. *Thank God. He is not my child.* Somehow he had found the heart, stolen it. He was a thief, a killer, and she was wasting time.

'It was the slide, the big, high slide. You came down head-first, on a little rough mat . . . I wanted another turn on the slide.'

Her breath caught in her throat. Dear God, was he lying to her? Why had she mentioned the fairground? He was clever, he always lied, he had to be lying.

She held out the gold heart in the palm of her hand. 'Where did you get this?'

'I don't know,' he said, matter-of-factly.

'Did you steal it from another child? Find it? Why do you have it?'

'Because it belongs to me. I like to swing it in front of my eyes – it eases me to sleep.' He seemed to be playing a game; he showed no fear of her. Instead, he asked slyly, his head tilted to one side, 'How do you know about the fairground?'

'I'll tell you, Luka, if you'll give me the names, tell me who ordered the deaths of the Lucianos.'

He smiled. 'OK!'

Outside the room, Teresa, still wearing her overcoat, rested her head against the door, trying to hear what was happening. She whispered to Rosa that Luka was talking.

'What is he saying?'

Teresa put her hand up to silence her, then she straightened. 'I can't hear.'

Rosa sat by her side. 'It's stopped snowing.'

Teresa looked at her, not understanding.

'It means the grave will show clearly.'

Sophia leaned on the table, about to write on the back of Michael's photograph. Luka, still bound to the chair by his arms and legs, strained forward.

'Barzini.'

'You are giving me a dead man's name, Luka. I know Barzini is dead.'

The strain of interacting with Luka, knowing what she knew, was beginning to break her. She was about to cave in when he said quietly, 'Barzini carried the message to Sicily, that is why his was the first offer to buy out the Lucianos. He was nothing; Paul Salerno is more important, but three, maybe four families were involved. It was imperative that no man as high up in the Organization as Don Roberto should stand as a witness.'

'Just give me the names, Luka!'

'OK, OK. I can give you the names I heard. I was not important enough to be told anything except to be at a certain place at a certain time. I know what I know because I was Paul Carolla's son.'

'Adopted son, Luka.'

Luka snapped out three names, names that meant nothing to Sophia, and she wrote them down on the back of the photograph. She waited for the fourth, pen poised ... She turned to him, and he sat back in the chair, looking directly at her.

'Now it is your turn.'

Slowly, she turned the photograph over, looked down into Michael Luciano's face. She had abandoned Luka, searched for him, and in her mind had given him up again. Now they waited for her to kill him, but how could she? She believed that he had spoken the truth, that he had played no part in the murder of the Luciano men. Luka was the rightful heir to the Luciano family; could she take that away from him? Could she do it? He was Michael's son, he was her son.

'Luka, you admitted you killed the jail cleaner's child; the same gun killed Carlo and Nunzio . . .'

He snapped at her, 'No! I have answered your questions, now it is your turn.'

She turned, refusing to give him the photograph. 'Tell me, Luka – the two children.'

His eyes blazed with impotent fury. Trapped helplessly, he rocked backwards and forwards, shaking the chair. 'Yes! Yes! Yes!'

'You admit it?'

'Yes! Now, keep to the bargain, unless you lied to me. Did you lie to me? Oh, no, you know about the fairground.' He clenched his teeth. 'Who told you?'

'You killed them?'

'Fuck you! *Yes, yes, yes!*'

She turned the photo of Michael Luciano over, leaving it directly in front of him on the table. He laughed, leaning forward to see it.

He shook his head in disgust, his eyes narrowed. 'You lied to me; I spit on this kid.'

'You spit on your father, Luka. He was Michael Luciano. The photograph was taken just before he died. He was twenty-two years old.'

His lips curled and he hissed, spitting like a cat at the

photograph, then looked at her as if for some reaction, smirking. She could see the Luka that could kill innocent children, the man who could mutilate and violate his victims with such ferocity; he was possessed of a madness that turned his eyes to glittering stones. He was shackled by his legs and arms, yet she had the terrifying feeling that he could, if he desired, break loose.

His voice was mocking. 'You lie to me, but you're good. I don't hate you for it, Sophia, I love you. You always were cleverer than the others, I knew it, I always knew it. And I know you'll be the one to cut me loose.' He laughed as she turned towards the knife.

'I know what you want from me. I'll tell Graziella that's what you want. I can see into your mind, I know you want me to say I am Michael Luciano's son. OK, I'd do anything for you. They mean nothing to me. You will have everything I promised you, remember . . .?'

Her fingers tightened around the wooden handle of the knife, her body shielding her actions. Nothing could stop what she had to do. Her voice was no more than a whisper.

'I didn't lie to you, Luka.'

She had to force herself to turn back to him. Perhaps it was a second, perhaps longer, but it was time enough for Luka to look on the face of his father. Whether the ramifications of what he had done penetrated his mind, she could not hesitate long enough to find out. She had to do it now, now, while she could still hear that hideous, sneering voice . . .

If he knew when he looked up that she, Sophia, was his mother, he had no time to accept it, but he accepted the fact that he was about to die. He tried to remain impassive, the professional killer, but the audacious sneer on his face became a trembling, heartbreaking, beautiful smile . . .

The blade went straight between his ribs into his heart. She needed all her weight, all her strength, to push it further. She forced his body against the back of the chair until she was leaning over him, her knee pressed against his thigh. He made a soft gurgling sound in his throat.

She pushed herself away from him. The knife slid from his body without her having to pull, and the clean, deep wound began to bleed freely. The knife slipped from her hand and fell to the floor.

He still sat upright because of the straps, but his head had rolled slightly to one side. A thin trickle of blood ran from his mouth, down his neck. She felt for his pulse; it still flickered. Then she cupped his face in her hands and kissed his still-warm lips. She could taste his blood in her mouth, could feel his soft hair, his skull between her hands . . . Slowly the pulse stopped, and it was over.

Sophia slipped the heart into her pocket. His blood drenched the towels, stained her gown. She picked up the sheet to cover him, keeping her face averted because she was unable to look at him . . . Now blood streamed from his open lips and began to colour the towels beneath his chair. She tucked them closer, afraid the blood would seep into the carpet, then draped the sheet over him.

Sophia unlocked the door and called for Teresa. Rosa came in with her. They said not a word, but untied the straps from around Luka's wrists while Rosa, on her knees, used the knife that had killed him to cut the leg straps. The sheet was still draped over him, hiding his face, but a dark, seeping bloodstain had drenched it. Moyra came in, carrying a grey blanket, which she laid on the floor, ready to wrap his body in.

Once he was free of the straps Teresa turned to Sophia. 'We'll need all of us to lift him out of the chair.'

Rosa pulled the sheet tighter round his head and shoulders, then gripped him under the armpits. Moyra and Teresa took his trunk and legs, staggering as it was a difficult manoeuvre. They carried him to the blanket and Teresa searched his pockets, but they were empty.

Sophia quickly wrapped him in the blanket, then used the belts that hadn't been cut to secure it around his neck and ankles. Between them they carried him through the kitchen and out into the garden.

The grave had been dug beneath an oak tree, its sprawling, gnarled roots clawing across the earth towards the six-foot-deep hole at one side of the snow-covered lawn. The body was dropped into the grave and all of them shovelled the earth over him, Moyra pushing it with her hands. The grave seemed to dominate the vast area of snow-covered lawn, their footprints, everything, pointing to it. Their breath streamed out in front of them, it was freezing cold, but they didn't seem to feel the chill. Sophia was still barefoot, still wearing just the bloodstained cotton shift.

The grave filled, all four stamped on the top to compress the earth. That was when Teresa saw Sophia's bare feet.

'Get inside, Sophia, we'll finish here.'

Sophia ran towards the house as they began to fit the frozen turves back into place. Teresa surveyed their work.

'Quickly, shovel snow across the top.'

Rosa continued stamping. 'That won't be necessary, Mama. Look at the sky . . .'

It was grey, and almost as Rosa spoke the snow started again, small flakes at first, but by the time they had returned to the house it was as if it had been ordained, falling thickly and covering their footprints, hiding the tell-tale signs of the grave.

Graziella slowly drew her curtains back. Through a small gap she had watched them digging the grave, watched them carry the shrouded body, watched them bury him, and not until she was sure they were finished did she open the curtains wide to watch the snow falling. She remained watching until there was no trace left of the freshly dug earth or the grave.

The women returned to the house, each intent on doing the work allocated to her. Teresa carried all Luka's clothes and personal belongings from his room; there were very few. She stuffed the pockets with paper soaked in turpentine and tied them into newspaper parcels with string. Moyra washed down the banisters, Luka's bedroom and the bathroom he had used, putting his toothbrush and comb in a plastic bag. Sophia put the bag into the garbage crusher and turned it on. Outside, Teresa set light to the clothes.

Sophia still wore her blood-soaked nightdress. From the kitchen door Teresa said, 'Take it off, I'll burn it . . . Sophia?'

Teresa had to repeat herself. Sophia's feet were blue

with cold. Slowly, she lifted the gown, remembering the heart in the pocket and taking it out.

'The gown, Sophia, give it to me, I have to burn it.' She looked for something to wrap around Sophia but there was nothing to hand. She took her own coat off and accepted the blood-soaked nightdress from Sophia. 'Get some clothes on, run a warm bath . . . Is that everything?'

Sophia nodded, but just stood there. There was something so pitiful about her nakedness that Teresa went to her and tried to put her coat around her, but Sophia pushed her away.

'Don't touch me, please, don't touch me.'

'Well, get something round you, there's nothing more for you to do.'

Sophia walked up the stairs and into her bedroom. She locked the door after her and half-stumbled across the room towards the bathroom. She wanted to scream, but was terrified that someone would hear her, someone would find out. She almost fell into the white-tiled shower, hitting her shoulder on the wall, but she turned on the water, held her face up to wash away the bloodstains on her body, her hands . . . and still she clasped the little gold heart.

The icy water made her gasp, but she made no attempt to turn on the hot water. The stream of freezing water hurt her, she felt as if someone were slapping her face, her body. She put the heart in her mouth and bit into it; her belly heaved, pressing down, the pain ripping her apart as it had done at her son's birth.

She wanted to feel that she was being punished, wanted someone to know what she had done, wanted to

951

scream aloud her betrayal, her guilt, her murder. But there was no relief, just a terrible feeling of rage against herself. She hit out at the tiles until her fists bled, banged her head against them, yet she would not allow herself to make one sound. This was her punishment, her silence; no one must ever know what she had done. Nothing anyone ever did to her, nothing she could ever do to anyone, would ever alleviate her guilt. She had committed the utmost crime, she had given birth, rejected her own blood and, in the end, slaughtered it. She and no one else had destroyed the family. What she had discarded for her own greed had become a monster, but the secret would remain as silent as Luka's grave. She would protect all that was left with the ferocity and, if need be, the violence, she now knew herself capable of.

The day after Luka's murder, the women, apart from Sophia, went to bed. Having been up all night they slept through the day, exhausted but safe in the knowledge that there was nothing left of him but the hidden grave. It was as if he had never existed.

Sophia had taken the documents and carefully, for the first time, familiarized herself with the family business. Lastly, she looked again at Michel Barzini's notebook. She checked the figures against the missing sums of money, the multiple accounts, the fortune that had mysteriously vanished into thin air. It was too much of a coincidence that, time and time again, the amounts listed by Barzini with strange markings beside them, matched those of the stolen money. The code, possibly known only to Barzini, she couldn't break, but the few initials beside the figures could be the first letters of the banks' names . . . She knew she had neither the experience nor the knowledge of banking systems to decipher it all, but perhaps in time, with Teresa's help, she could.

More important was the list of names printed down the back page. Graziella had recalled two of them, but Luka had named three. They were members of different families, all in diverse businesses, but if they had all joined forces, agreed on the Luciano assassinations and, at the same time, reaped vast financial rewards . . . She was too tired to think further.

At six-thirty she went to sleep for a few hours. By the time she had dressed again she could hear the others talking together in the drawing room. They fell silent when she walked in; it fazed her slightly. But then Graziella, with a warm smile, indicated the chair she usually occupied by the fireside, inviting her to sit in it.

With a conspiratorial look to Teresa and Rosa, Graziella held out her hand. 'This is for you, Sophia. We want you to wear it; we give it to you for your bravery. We love you and trust you, and I kiss you, in the hope that you will receive it and wear it.'

She kissed Sophia on both cheeks, then took her hand, placing on her wedding finger Don Roberto's gold, embossed ring.

Graziella asked that they pledge never again to speak of Luka. As if they had taken the sacred vow of *omerta*, they would always be held by what they had done.

They seemed to be waiting for Sophia either to agree or to make some gesture of acceptance. But she remained, head bowed; could they detect her guilt? If so, she must show no sign. She rose to her feet, clasped Graziella and kissed her on both cheeks. Teresa was next, then Moyra and finally Rosa.

Rosa noticed that Sophia wore a small gold heart on a chain, and asked if it had belonged to Luka. Sophia smiled and answered simply that it had belonged to one of her sons.

It was as if Luka continued to help them from the grave. Even before his death rumours had begun to circulate about who exactly was behind the widows. The murders Luka had committed, the decapitation of Barzini's henchman, even Barzini's own coincidental death, were discussed. It was whispered that perhaps not all the Lucianos had died that fateful night in Palermo; no one knew who had ordered the death of Paul Carolla.

Suspicions mounted and the rumour caught on, because if there was one Luciano left alive, the very thing the families had hoped to extinguish with the slaughter of all the men would backfire. Revenge would come, it had to, it was their law. But until the rumours could be proved wrong the families concerned watched and waited for the first move.

Paul Salerno had been waiting for the contact Luka had promised. When at last Sophia made the contact, Salerno agreed to arrange a meeting. He noted the address and immediately checked it out. The Groves, Salerno discovered, had been owned by Paul Carolla and had been handed over to the women by none other than Luka Carolla. There was nothing illegal in the transaction and, when it was discussed further, pressure was brought to discover the whereabouts of Luka. They had wanted him dead before; he knew too much and was a direct link to the deceased Barzini, the man who had carried out their orders, hiring and paying the killers. The hit on Luka Carolla was upped to $100,000.

Salerno was as good as his word. Three weeks after the murder of Luka and five days after the call he received requesting the meeting, Salerno travelled to Long Island in a chauffeur-driven limousine. The three men who accompanied him were high-ranking *consiglieri* of three major families; the families that had been named by Luka as instigating the Luciano assassinations.

Two others were missing, the meeting was not deemed important enough to warrant sending even a representative. The men with Salerno were Tony Castellano, the US representative for the Corleones, Johnny Salvatore, for the Gambino family, and the hugely fat Nuccio Miano, the paymaster for the Chicago-based Avellino family. All of these men and the families that employed them had diverse interests, but all wanted to gain control of the Luciano empire. They were grey-haired, smartly turned out, and nothing in their appearance gave the slightest hint that they were mobsters.

On the way the men discussed, half-heartedly, the meeting that was about to take place. They fell silent when they reached the impressive avenue of The Groves, partly in admiration but also in slight anger that they had somehow let this prize piece of property escape their attention.

The snow was beginning to thaw, and patches of green showed through the white canopy. The sun shone, showing off the house to full effect. The heavy clang of the electronic gates locking behind them made one man turn. The hair on the backs of his hands prickled, but all remained silent. Their eyes took in everything.

Graziella led Teresa, Rosa and Moyra into the room. They were each introduced by Paul Salerno, acting the polite go-between as he had promised. Graziella gestured to Rosa to leave the room, and it was then he realized one of them was missing.

The women seemed to be waiting for something. They stood in a group, quiet, yet without antagonism. It threw the men slightly as they were all seated. They said nothing, however, but lit their Havanas and accepted glasses of good wine.

The men made no mention of the inconvenience the women had caused them; that's all they felt it was at this stage, an inconvenience, and one that must be dealt with amicably. They had, of course, discussed the women's part in the Barzini deal amongst themselves and wished to have it cleared up quickly. They had come prepared to make a settlement; the women, they felt, had been badly treated and must be shown respect. In return the Commission had ordered that a fair price be paid for the Luciano companies, a fair price put up by the five major families who had ordered the Luciano murders. Roberto Luciano had made a grave mistake in standing against them and it must never be allowed to happen again, but they admitted that Paul Carolla's son had been a very unfortunate choice of assassin, and his involvement had caused a great deal of embarrassment. None of them felt remorse; it had simply been a messy affair, and $15 million was a small price to pay for the Luciano companies. They therefore had come today for the purpose

956

of offering further compensation to the Luciano widows for their treatment.

Rosa tapped on Sophia's door, then opened it slightly. 'They are waiting, Sophia.'

She received no answer and Sophia did not move. She was like a statue; the outline of her beautiful face in the shadows made her appear, in her black dress, like a shadow herself. Rosa slipped out of the room, missing the way Sophia lifted her hand and touched the small gold heart, as if feeling for a pulse in her neck.

Rosa closed the double doors into the drawing room and joined her mother. The women were still standing together while the men flashed glances amongst themselves, wondering why they were being kept waiting.

At last they heard the click of high heels across the marble of the hall. The door handles turned slowly and then the doors swung open wide. Sophia paused a moment, framed in the doorway. Her sleek black hair was coiled in a bun at the nape of her neck, her plain black dress was open at the collar. High black shoes and black stockings made her look stark but demure. The only colour, in contrast to her black clothes, was her lipstick, a splash of crimson that made her appear cruel. Then she gave them the sweetest of smiles and walked calmly to the centre of the room.

Graziella quietly introduced each man to Sophia. They all had to rise from their seats, cross the room and kiss Sophia's hand; she made no move towards them. As they kissed her right hand, they could smell her strong perfume and see that she wore Don Roberto Luciano's ring, the ring that had once belonged to Joseph Carolla.

Sophia gestured for her guests to be seated and, without wasting time on conversational pleasantries, she informed them that she had been named as Don Roberto's heir. She was now, and she wished it to be known, the head of the Luciano family and, as such, had every intention of running his companies, apart from those they had already agreed to sell. She was fully aware of her father's Organization connections, and would leave it to the Commission either to ignore her existence or agree to let the women run their businesses without harassment.

'We tried to deal with Michel Barzini. We were treated without respect almost robbed, and therefore we are no longer interested in negotiations. We still retain the legal documentation on these properties but now our price has gone up; we will only agree to sell if certain conditions are adhered to. My father was always against the trade in narcotics and unless we can be assured that his wishes are respected by the new owners we have no desire to sell. The asking price, however, if you are still interested in doing business with us, has now been trebled.'

Sophia found herself interrupted; there must be some mistake. The men were aware of the fact that she had already been paid a considerable amount for the businesses. Teresa noticed how Sophia touched the gold heart before she spoke.

'You must be mistaken. Barzini had an unfortunate accident before the transaction took place and, as by now you must be aware, he had hired men who physically attacked both myself and my family in an attempt to secure the legal titles to our company without paying for them. Perhaps you should look to those working on your

958

behalf for the return of the funds you wrongly believe to be in our hands.'

Again Sophia touched the gold heart as her eyes focused on each man in turn, resting finally on Paul Salerno. Her gaze was unfathomable and he found it chilling; she was so still, yet he detected terrible anger behind the mask of her face. He, too, had noticed the repeated gesture and recognized it as incredible calmness rather than a show of nerves. Five times he had seen her do it, slowly lifting her hand and placing the index finger on the gold locket at her neck.

Sophia Luciano appeared to be asking for membership of an exclusive club, an establishment that never in its history had allowed a woman to take the oath. She made it clear that she would take the oath if it were required.

'Within days you will receive the full transcripts of Don Roberto Luciano's statements that were prepared for the trial in Palermo. They make interesting reading and show, clearly, that until the end he was a man of honour, a man who could have been trusted but, tragically, was not. We feel it our right to be given compensation; this, I believe, is your law. If we cannot expect this from you, then we will take whatever action is necessary to ensure that Don Roberto Luciano is given the justice he deserves.'

Paul Salerno looked at each man present, then eased forward in his chair. His hands were crossed loosely in front of him and he rested his elbows on the carved arms.

'Signora Luciano, all of us here, as you must be aware, offer you and your family our deep condolences regarding the tragic loss of your family. But we do not have the right to offer you any compensation, even if we wished to do so, because it would be an obvious sign that we were in some way involved, when nothing could be further from the truth. We are simply businessmen, no more, no less. However, we cannot dismiss Michel Barzini's treatment of you, and wish you to know that he acted alone. As such we agree to pay you an extra $20,000 . . .'

Sophia interrupted. '$20,000?' She smiled coldly. 'Your gift is most acceptable, but we need assistance in discovering the identities of those men concerned in arranging our beloveds' murders. Financially, I believe, we should inherit Paul Carolla's estate. As you must be aware, Joseph Carolla named Roberto Luciano as his heir and now that Paul Carolla is also deceased, we . . .'

Paul Salerno interrupted, 'But Carolla has a son.'

Sophia turned to face him. She held his eyes, and he gave way, looking down at his hands.

'Luka Carolla is wanted for the murder of my children, Mr Salerno. Furthermore, he was adopted; Paul Carolla leaves no blood heirs.'

Graziella signalled that she wished to speak to Sophia, and with a small inclination of her head as if to apologize to her guests for the interruption, Sophia went to her side, unintentionally bending away from the men, listening and masking Graziella's whispered words. Salerno took the opportunity to confer with Miano, who was becoming impatient.

The four men waited as Sophia returned to her chair, but remained standing. Salerno coughed. 'Signora, we are aware that this property was owned by Paul Carolla and was recently signed over to Signora Graziella Luciano. When there is a meeting in the near future, we can discuss Paul Carolla's estate, but until that time I am unable to say if any of it can be handed over to you.'

Silvano cleared his throat and adjusted his waistcoat, obviously not approving but refusing this time to say anything. Miano eased his bulk forward. They wanted to leave; it was obvious.

Sophia gave Salerno a dazzling smile, a smile that Graziella would never forget. The sweetness of her soul, like the intangible bloom of youth, was gone. The frozen smile remained firmly in place as Sophia thanked her guests cordially for coming to the meeting, and Graziella turned to see the effect her next words would have.

Sophia played it beautifully. 'The heir to the Luciano estates wants only what is rightfully his. If he is refused, you give the family no option but to look elsewhere ... *Le spine della rosa sono nascoste dal fiore.*'

The other women watched Sophia as she insisted on serving more wine to her guests with her own hands, handing Paul Salerno his glass last. She smiled at him above the rim of her own glass, lifting it as if in a toast. Then she turned her attention to the three other guests, speaking to each man in turn and saying that it was sad that the Lucianos were not given the respect of meeting the two other families interested in negotiating with them. She spoke the two names without any show of emotion.

She ended the meeting as abruptly as she had opened it; courteously, coldly, and without a trace of fear. Her voice had been soft and persuasive, and never at any time less than cordial.

Now, as the three men walked from the room, she rested her hand on Paul Salerno's arm, gave him yet another smile, and this time leaned toward him and kissed him on his astonished lips.

'*Arrivederci*, signor, we thank you.'

The men knew there would never even be so much as a possibility of a woman becoming part of the Organization. It was unquestionable, almost farcical. They laughed together as they discussed the visit but, under the sarcasm, beneath the chauvinistic belief that women should remain at home with the children, beneath it all was the memory of the dismembered body, the dead Barzini, and the fact that the women had already got away with $15 million and still retained the entire Luciano holdings both in America and in Palermo.

They discussed Sophia's request for Paul Carolla's estate and dismissed it out of hand. It was preposterous, but it furthered the rumour that someone was behind them, someone prepared to kill for them. Miano spat in disgust at the thought of men willing to take orders from women. It was beyond their comprehension, a farcical impossibility, that five women would be capable of running a company as diverse and complex as the Luciano holdings, especially with the opposition they could expect, must know they would come across as soon as they began. Five women, one of them just out of school, another a grandmother, and one a well-known little tart from Vegas . . .

The car reached the gates and they opened slowly. They were discussing Teresa Luciano who had, it was well known, been very much a part of her husband's business when he had been alive. It was even known that Don Roberto himself had been angry at her interference.

Last but not least, they discussed Sophia, the one who claimed to be Don Roberto's heir. They smirked at her audacity.

The car passed through the wrought-iron gates which closed automatically and soundlessly behind them, and the hidden video cameras swivelled back into place. Paul Salerno was sitting in the back seat and had noted everything, particularly the security. He could not resist a last look back at the impressive house. He looked up at the top-floor windows and screwed up his eyes; a woman, clothed in black and partially hidden by the security bars, was quite obviously watching them leave. Her outline could have been mistaken for a shadow, but he knew which one of them it would be.

'I think Sophia Luciano's different, a different kind of woman than we're used to, she's . . .'

The men in Salerno's car admitted that she was different; not, they agreed, just in her beauty. Although they didn't like to admit it, she unnerved them. Salerno realized that he was not the only one to have felt it, but he said nothing, listening as they talked. He made an involuntary movement, touching his lips as if he could still feel her kiss, taste the perfume of her dark-red lipstick.

Sophia was, they joked, an unknown commodity, and they laughed. None of them had ever had any dealings with a woman like her, in business or bed. They all agreed with less humour than before that she was *bella . . . bella mafiosa*.

But Salerno didn't laugh. He stared from the window. He had seen, he knew, many beautiful women, and she was most definitely a woman. So what made her so different? The others had got on to the possibility of a

Luciano taking over, wondering which one it could be . . . One man remembered the eldest Luciano boy, Michael, who had been educated at Harvard. They discussed what they remembered of him, while Salerno tried unsuccessfully to blank from his mind the soft sweet whispered, '*Arrivederci*, signor . . .'

The slush spattered on the road and against the gleaming sides of the limo. The cigar smoke made him feel sick and he pressed the button to lower the window, gasping at the freezing air. His mouth felt dry . . . How had she known just which of the families were involved, named them? He went over their meeting almost word for word.

Someone asked him to close the window. He reached for the button; the pain in his gut was like an explosion, blowing his bowels apart. The burning sensation swept through his chest, as if squeezing his heart and constricting his throat, choking him: his limbs thrashed and spittle ran from his lips. His mouth flapped soundlessly, then twisted into a grimace, as if he was desperately trying to say something, warn the other men, but he never uttered another word, never vocalized what he had felt at the meeting. She knew, Sophia Luciano knew, exactly who had ordered the deaths of her family.

Paul Salerno's name was scratched from the list written on the back of the photograph. The image of Michael Luciano, the father of the equally tragic Luka Carolla, was set back in its place of honour: framed behind him were his brothers, beside him his father. Graziella Luciano, widow of Don Roberto Luciano, Teresa, widow of Alfredo Luciano, Moyra, widow of Frederico Luciano and Rosa, the tragic bride-to-be, waited expectantly to hear the outcome of their meeting, waited for the next contact to be made, unaware that Sophia, widow of Constantino Luciano and mother of the little Carlo and Nunzio Luciano, had already made contact. The seeds of the vendetta which had begun with the murder of Michael Luciano and the assassination order to wipe out the entire male line of the Lucianos would continue. *Le spine della rosa sono nascoste dal fiore*: the thorns of the rose are hidden by the bloom.

extracts reading groups
competitions books new
discounts extracts extracts
competitions discounts
books new events reading groups
events books extracts
new extracts discounts
new books reading groups
interviews events new
events extracts extracts books
books discounts
new books events
events new
discounts extracts discounts
www.panmacmillan.com
extracts events reading groups
competitions books extracts new